SKY PAINTING

STRATHKELVIN WRITERS' GROUP

Founded in 1982, Strathkelvin Writers' Group encourages the development, sharing and enjoyment of all forms of writing in a nurturing, friendly and relaxed environment. We welcome people of all backgrounds to share our aim of pursuing writing goals, extending knowledge and promoting work.

In our ranks we have published novelists and poets as well as complete beginners; international award-winning authors and those taking their first steps into the world of writing. But every member has something to offer the group.

The collective knowledge and experience of the Strathkelvin Writers is an invaluable resource for anyone looking to go forward with their writing. Indeed, many of our most accomplished members have attributed a large measure of their success to the support and encouragement they have received within the group.

If you would like to find out more, visit our website: https://www.strathkelvinwriters.org

SKY PAINTING

An Anthology of Creative Writing

Strathkelvin Writers' Group

SA PRESS

First published in 2024 by
SAPress
sapress42@gmail.com
in collaboration with
Strathkelvin Writers' Group
www.strathkelvinwriters.org

A CIP catalogue record for this book is available from the British Library

ISBN 978-1-0687150-0-6

CONTENTS

PREFACE

It gives me great pleasure to introduce *SKY PAINTING*, Strathkelvin Writers' Group's 2024 anthology.

This collection of works features contributions from 42 members of Strathkelvin Writers, each bringing their own distinctive voice to the pages as they seek to entertain, provoke thought and evoke emotion.

We hope that as you read these stories, poems and sketches you will find yourself immersed in the worlds they create, moved by the characters you meet, and inspired by the creativity of the authors.

This anthology would not have been possible without the dedication and passion of everyone involved. We extend our heartfelt gratitude to the writers for their contributions, the editors for their meticulous work, and the readers for their enthusiasm and support. Special thanks go to Allan Gaw for bringing the idea to the table and turning it into reality, along with the support of the editorial team: Ann MacLaren, Sharon Mail, Carolyn Mandache, Julie McNeill and Andy Raffan.

We hope you find as much pleasure in reading our work as we have found in bringing it to you.

Thank you for choosing to spend your time with *SKY PAINTING*. May these works inspire, entertain and resonate with you long after you turn the final page.

Sharon Bairden

President, Strathkelvin Writers' Group

WEST END WONDERLAND

Ann MacLaren

Winter.
Homeward bound
through streets of tenement-stacked
golden-glowing, windows,
curtains wide in open invitation.
I peek inside this
West End wonderland.

Mirrors,
sparkling chandeliers,
fringed lampshades, paper globes,
books on shelves, paintings,
plants, pianos, purple ceilings,
and all the paraphernalia
of different, similar lives.

A child
window-framed by fairy lights
scans the street for a homecoming,
catches my eye,
and lips moving in silent introduction
presses a soft rabbit to the glass,
helps him wave a paw.

Home, I open the door on my own story,
light the lamps and leave the drapes undrawn.

SPICK AND SPAN

Pat Feehan

Dickie was dressed in a primrose yellow ensemble; full length plastic apron, surgeon's boots, and rubber gloves reaching to his elbows. A bathing cap and prescription swimming goggles completed the look. His mother's portrait smiled approvingly from its highly polished frame. 'Cleanliness is next to Godliness' had been her watchword.

He carried a bucket, a bottle of industrial strength bleach and his cleaning toolkit. Dickie didn't believe in half measures when it came to getting rid of dirt. Marjorie had never understood this. That was why, in the end, they had parted company.

Dickie was always on the lookout for new cleaning ideas. That very day he had invited a young saleswoman into his home. When she proceeded to sprinkle dirt all over the living-room carpet, Dickie had looked at her, aghast.

'You'll think I've gone mad, sir. But wait till you see what this little beauty does to the dirt.'

She had whipped out a mini vacuum cleaner. It quickly disposed of the mess and Dickie was impressed despite himself. But when she sat down and crossed her legs, her dress rode up exposing her undergarments. She smiled flirtatiously and said, 'Right sir, let's get down to business.'

Dickie detested smutty behaviour and he reached for the knife he kept behind the sofa cushion. The woman didn't have a chance to scream. She made a bit of a mess, but soon she would join Marjorie in the bathtub, hygienically packaged and ready for disposal. Dickie decided he would keep the mini vacuum cleaner.

CHALK NOT GRANITE

Matthew Keeley

England gave me nosebleeds for a week – my first since
a teenager.
I wondered if I was growing up again
or if it was the frothy hard water
that changed the taste of tea and was thick to swallow.
'Chalky rocks,' Dad said later, in a kitchen I'm tired of.
'Not Scottish granite.'

Village houses had different bricks too
– the red-brown of my dried blood.
Some, black beams on white, melting out of shape on
narrow
uphill
streets.
Long voices were softer, surer,
not fast and jagged
(I'm not jagged).
Dark was warmer, I'm sure, and
even the thunder was proper and yawned all morning
while I watched a dust sky
from different, hugging bedsheets.
Driving home for aching hours to Scotland
is always washed with grey sopping rain.

Could I go away there and not drive back?
Bleed, smiling, into English sinks?
Swallow frothy tea
and fold myself into the corners of new bedsheets?
I can be chalk not granite.

LEFT TURN TO PARADISE

Patricia Hutchinson

My name's Max and I live in Paradise. That's Paradise, Orange County, Florida.

Friends don't figure much in my life, so I'm a mix of wary and elated when Sindy, the cutest girl in class, and her cool gang wanna hang out with me at the town square. Christina Aguilera belts out *Genie in a Bottle* from Sindy's ghetto blaster. I'd never taken notice of the words, but then I'd never had Sindy getting up close and singing them in my ear before. Today's my fourteenth birthday and if a Genie's granting wishes I'll ask for Sindy as my girlfriend and a Harley-Davidson – right after hoping my father gets abducted by aliens.

I fool around and try to prove I'm fun enough to be one of them. The aroma of sugary, buttery donuts battles with the beef and onions of the burger bar. I'm told to shut my eyes and wait for a surprise. I dread what's to come, but they return and shove a bagful of donuts into my arms. I get a lump in my throat and say thanks too many times.

There's a Harley-Davidson on the sidewalk and I make big-guy comments, showing off like mad. I hunker down beside the bike, trail my fingers along the badge, then straighten up to admire its awesome low lines. Today the keys are in the ignition, and there's not a biker in sight. I stretch over and curl my fingers around the hand grips. I long to be astride it, the wind in my face, the town shrinking behind me, the engine drowning out every thought in my brain. Any kid with a yearning for excitement would feel the same. Between repeats of the song, Sindy urges me on. When I chicken out, the gang grunt their displeasure and kick a bin. It hurtles down the slope and I back off. We all know I'm not in their league.

Trouble is, the Harley doesn't belong to a biker, but to some guy who owns the tailor's shop, and is heading towards the security kiosk, his grey suit flapping round him.

'What a waste,' I say, looking round for my new friends. They've gone, though not far as I can still hear snatches of the song, *if you wanna be with me, baby, there's a price to pay.*

A police car shows up in a flash; a hell of a sight faster than when Pop's bashing Mom to a pulp.

'I'm taking you home, kid,' one cop says and hustles me into the back seat while his sidekick starts talking to the tailor guy. Guess this is the price.

The cool gang are back, whistling and cheering. I give Sindy a last look and hunch as low as I can to hide from them, half listening to the crackle of voices on the police radio. I'm not sure if they're talking about me. The cop, seems he's called Jed, flicks the switch off. 'It's your lucky day, really I should cuff you and lock you in a cell.'

If he's looking for gratitude, I'm offering none.

'Stay away from those kids. You've enough shit going on.'

I've already figured out that the cool kids are jerks, what I need to know is how to deal with them at school tomorrow. The seat's sticky, there's no air, and when I sniff I get a whiff of sweat and fear. Or perhaps that's me. We pass my mom standing outside The Flamingo, being pawed by the customers, and giggling. She is wearing a flirty yellow dress that's so short it's hardly there. She works as a dancer at that club. Now that I'm older, I know that dancing isn't really the right word for what she does.

He's watching me in his mirror. 'Real pretty lady, your mom. Must drive your pop crazy.' His voice is laden with suggestion.

I don't take the bait, not so he can see anyway. I squeeze my hands so tight that my knuckles whiten and my nails pierce my skin.

The cop doesn't need to ask for my name or where I live. He's a regular visitor, but I'm usually the scared kid crouching in the corner. My heartbeat matches the clink-clink of the signal as we wait to take a left off the highway onto the stony track towards home. There it is, a huge tin sign with 'Paradise' in swirly writing and a faded painting of the beach; yellow sand between bright blue sea and sky. It has been there forever, and the edges are nibbled and shredded by the winds that blow off the dunes and can rip up trees and drag bits of houses in their path. When Mom invites folk to visit, she says 'Just turn left to Paradise'.

The houses get shabbier the further along the track we go. Ours is the last one, patched with boards and nails. The cop gets out and I work at breathing as Pop lurches across the pitted yard to the car. I can smell his boozy breath from here and see his face getting redder with every word the cop says. I see no point in saying it wasn't me who robbed the donut stand or pushed the bin over, and that I only touched the bike. Pop's face twists with rage, his fingers hover round his belt buckle and I'm scared. All at once, the car seems like a refuge and Jed like a protector. I would stay there but the cop grips me firmly by the arm and yanks me out.

'Huh, thanks, Jed.' I mutter. He doesn't hear me; he's already swaggered off and climbed in the driver's side. His job here is done.

A plume of exhaust fans out behind the car as it sweeps in a wide arc off our land. Pop pushes me ahead of him, twisting my collar so tight I can barely breathe. He slams the door so hard the house shudders to its core. The belt is freed with a swish, he doubles it and cracks it round any part of me he can reach. He's loving it, every stroke gets harder. I clench my teeth as the leather bites into my skin, and I fight to hold back tears.

Mom arrives home. She's tipsy and hangs round Pop's neck kissing his cheek. 'Stop it Nico, it's his birthday.'

I stumble out of the back door into the yard and beyond that to the beach. It only takes a minute. I crouch down beyond the boundary shrubs, the ones that smell like church, and hug my arms round my knees. Every move hurts, but it happens often enough for me to know I'll heal.

I stare out across the ocean and can smell the storm. The wind tugs at the edges of the waves and gusts a haze of sugar-white sand over the dunes. I'm close enough to hear them shouting. I gulp in the salty air and puff out a sigh.

Hours pass, and the argument has turned into a battle, there's screeching and crashing as pots and pans and furniture smash the walls.

The cops have been here and away but there was more posturing and pomposity than law enforcement. Guess Beaky Old Dame across the way summoned them and they feel they must charge in like the cavalry in some old movie. I reckon the cops' regular visits, sirens screeching, are the highlights of her prehistoric life. One day I'll buy her a TV, then we'll get some peace.

I walk slowly up the garden path with the idea of braving the war zone to creep up to my attic room. My sister is home from her job at the salon and she waves me back down the path. Maria is sixteen and says that any day now she'll be gone and for all she cares they can kill each other.

I felt bad about causing the fight. I am the peacemaker, keeper of their secrets; I never tell Pop when I see Mom making out with her boss in the back of his car or tell Mom that I've found Pop lying in the dunes too smashed to make his way home. When they steal from each other's pockets, I confess.

'What happened?' Maria hisses. Her face is very close and her eyes are red.

I tell her, leaving out the bit about how good it had felt to be accepted by the cool gang, even for a minute.

'Have you a death wish? I saw the belt…I hate when the belt's out.'

I flick my tongue round the side of my mouth and taste blood. 'Do you think they'll send me away again?'

'You hated it.'

My feelings for the foster home are hard to admit and I take ages to answer. 'I didn't. It wasn't so bad, I had a room, food, and got to sleep nights.'

She stares at me in bewildered silence. I've no idea what she's thinking. I'm sore and my head feels like it might burst. I feel guilty, because sometimes Mom hugs me, or gives me her magic potion that floats me off to a sleepy dream world. I'm not crazy, I know now there's no magic, just booze and pills. 'Sometimes things…' I begin.

'Things are never ok, and it's getting worse.'

Her voice is sharp, and I wonder when she became a mind-reader.

We sit down. The sand is cool and damp. I grab handfuls and allow it to slip through my fingers. The wind is lively, plucking at the waves, wisps of clouds race over the moon's face as though they're rushing to escape. I pad down to my boat which is bobbing about in a manic dance. The sea is rough but out of their reach. I'm tempted.

Maria appears behind me. 'For God's sake don't go out in the boat.'

More mind-reading. From somewhere I find a laugh and she looks puzzled.

They're still shouting, I think they enjoy it. I can't remember a time when they didn't fight. They yell and hurl stuff at each other, then head for the bedroom and yell a bit more, a different kind of yelling.

A horn sounds and Maria jumps to her feet. 'Harry's here, I'm going. If you want to stay, it's up to you, but you can come with us.'

I shake my head and she runs up the path. The car door bangs; the engine revs. I don't plead with her to stay, even if I want her to.

There are piercing screams, I leap to my feet. Beaky Old Dame watches from behind her blinds. A window smashes, then silence. And more silence. Relief washes over me and I move towards the house. It's over, for this time at least.

I shove the door wide and step into the kitchen. My feet crunch on broken glass and I squint until my eyes adjust to the dark. It's like a nightmare. Someone howls like an animal, maybe it's me. The room's trashed, the belt is still curled on the table, and a heap of something lies on the floor. A Halloween version of Mom stands across from me, her face blanched, with streaks of blood. One hand clutches the torn yellow dress round her. I don't see the knife in her other hand until light from the window flashes on the blade, as she points it to the heap on the floor.

'Nico, Nico,' she cries.

I take the knife from her hands. It is coated in dark sticky gunk.

Men shout, a radio crackles and light floods the room. I shield my eyes and see the two cops from earlier. Jed is pointing a pistol straight at me and a knee in my back forces me to the floor. I drop the knife and it clatters along the stone slabs.

In the distance the Paradise sign creaks in the wind.

ICONIC

Maggie Powell

Cast
WD – Harassed window dresser, trying to tie the 'New Season' look together.
HATTIE – Shop display model (ex toy department, a bit childlike)
MATTIE – Shop display model (knows her fashion heroes)
PATTIE – Shop display model

Props
Carboard poster announcing the 'NEW SEASON REVEAL', large sheet, small pole or walking stick to support the sheet, 2 large black plastic bags, two berets, patterned carry bag, 'Reveal' outfit, music.

Main display area of an upmarket department store. Hattie and Mattie are 'standing' in a row, either side of Pattie, who is covered by a huge sheet. Hattie is stage right, and Mattie is stage left. Both Hattie and Mattie have large black plastic bags concealing their new season outfits. They are looking forward to being the centre of attention at the Big Reveal of the new season look.

WD (*Tweaking and fixing the plastic covers on the models. She realises something is missing. Looks in the carry bag on her shoulder. Not there.*) Rats! Where have I left those berets? What a pest. (*To the models*) Don't go away ladies, I'll be right back. (*WD exits*)

HATTIE She'd better be quick. They're starting to gather.

MATTIE (*Casting her eye over the audience*) I know, isn't it exciting. I love the big New Season Reveal. So do they. Fed up with their winter outfits.

HATTIE Yeah, a wee make-over is just what they need. Bring them to life. Wonder what they've cooked up for us this year? Did you manage a sneak peek, while she was dressing you?

MATTIE Are you kidding? A sneak peek. Chance would be a fine thing. She may look sweet, and smiley, but she's as rough as anything. Yanked my head off and dumped it on that shelf over there. Couldn't see a thing. And I'm not sure if she's twizzled my arms back properly. (*She moves her arms in robotic fashion, checking them as she does so.)*

HATTIE Well, this isn't even my body. I was in the Toy Department. Loved it. Then they decided LEGO heads would look great on all the models. So I was plonked on here…and the outfit was already under wraps. (*She pats the plastic)* You can't feel it properly under this plastic. But I do know who could tell us what we're wearing. Pattie, Pattie, can you hear us under there?

PATTIE Mumbles, mumbles. Yes.

HATTIE What style are we modelling for the Big Reveal?

PATTIE Mumble, mumble, mumble. Retro.

MATTIE What did you say?

PATTIE Mumble, mumble, mumble. Iconic.

HATTIE Brill, thanks Pattie, just you relax, we'll work it out. (*Rolls her eyes*)

MATTIE Work it out?

HATTIE Yes, we have two clues…retro …iconic.

MATTIE Mmmm, but do you think this is it, Hattie?

HATTIE What do you mean?

MATTIE Plastic bags. What we are already wearing. Iconic Punk.

HATTIE But then it wouldn't be a Reveal, would it?

MATTIE Suppose not.

HATTIE Iconic, Retro, that covers a lot of ground.

MATTIE Actually, we have another clue…

HATTIE We do? Well don't hold back. Impress me.

MATTIE Berets.

HATTIE Berets? Yes, she was looking for berets for us to wear. Good one, Girl.

MATTIE And who was the first designer to put berets on the catwalk?

HATTIE And the answer is?

MATTIE Chanel!

HATTIE Chanel…never! Eh, remind me.

MATTIE Yes, retro and iconic. Those tweed suits, the wee jackets with designer buttons. We will look amazing.

HATTIE Best display ever.

MATTIE People will flock.

HATTIE We might even get a chance to show the Christmas Party look next time.

MATTIE And then there's another clue.

HATTIE You're not going to spoil it are you?

MATTIE This one's even better.

HATTIE Better than Chanel, okay go for it.

MATTIE That bag she was carrying. Did you see the design?

HATTIE Yeah, sort of. Black and white with a daisy pattern.

MATTIE And whose motif was that?

HATTIE Yeah, whose?

MATTIE Had a massive display at the Kelvingrove Museum.

HATTIE DOCTOR WHO? But that was ages ago. We're going to be DALEKS?

PATTIE *(Loud and clear)* EXTERMINATE! EXTERMINATE!

MATTIE Behave! And there are no berets in DOCTOR WHO.

HATTIE Yes there are…Brigadier Lethbridge-Stewart and UNIT. *(She salutes)*

PATTIE EXTERMINATE!

MATTIE Fashion! This is about fashion. You're not back in the Toy Department. I'll try again…the clues…iconic, retro, flower, berets…it's Mary…

HATTIE/PATTIE Mary Berry!

HATTIE We're dressed as cooks?

MATTIE It's MARY…QUANT!

HATTIE Great…and what did she do?

MATTIE *(Pointing as she lists)* White boots, tights, mini-skirts, hot pants, plastic raincoats, gorgeous tops and tunics. We'll be groovy man.

HATTIE Positions everyone. Here she comes.

(All three freeze into mannequin stance. Hattie and Mattie are facing away from each other.)

WD *(Rushes back in, and addresses the assembled crowd)* Good evening, everyone. Thank you for your patience. Just one more detail to fix, and we'll be ready for the Big Reveal.

(She moves behind the models. Puts a beret on Mattie, then one on Hattie. They haven't yet noticed the colour. She now moves to a position almost in front of Pattie, where she can easily pull off the sheet, without hiding Pattie's outfit.)

WD Ladies and Gentleman, and everyone in between, this is the look you have been waiting for. It will see you all through Spring and Summer…I give you…*(she pulls off the sheet and steps aside.)*

(Pattie Adopts a ta da position)

MATTIE *(horrified)* Barbie!

HATTIE *(delighted)* Barbie!

(WD joins the line up. Cue music 'Barbie Girl'. All start moving arms in a robotic fashion.)

ALL We're all Barbie Girls, in a Barbie world.
Even though we're plastic,
We're gonna be fantastic.
Yeah!

(All bow)

END

GIVE AND TAKE

Diane McKee

They don't see me. I'm invisible. I pass them in the street, I brush close. Nothing. Not a flicker. They're often in groups, threes and fours. Tight skinny jeans, short puffy jackets and trainers. You know the kind of thing. Not classy. There's no style about them. Then there's the hair. Invariably long and straight, sometimes tied back or high up on their heads like princesses. Gives the wee ones a bit of height I suppose. You hear them before you see them, a wall of sound. Booming voices mixed with high-pitched giggles. It would burst you. Listen to us, they seem to say. We've got stuff you must hear. The only problem is that none of them can listen to anybody but themselves.

But catch one on their own and it's a different matter. Heads are often down, fixed on the ground or on the phone, which is invariably glued to their palm. They only look up to cross the road, perhaps, or to make eye contact with another teenager. They walk faster too, quick feet on the pavement making very little sound. Many's a time I have been startled by one when coming round a corner. That's a time when they do see me, and we exchange the briefest of glances. But for most of the time I am simply not there. And that's the way I like it.

They make it so easy for me. I find it quite funny, really. It's strange how things have turned out. When I was married my life was very different. Me and my husband, we were a real couple, always out and about at weekends. Up at the dancing in our early days, then later on out for lunch or dinner. A nice restaurant or a hotel. We held hands or linked arms when we went up the town and it felt good. Billy and Pauline. That's what people called us. We were never Pauline and Billy. It just didn't seem to have a ring to it. I suppose that's always the way with couples. They get known as so-and-so and so-and-so. You might think I'm exaggerating but people would look at us and smile. Strangers, I mean. I think we gave off a bit of a glow back then. The petite blonde with the tall dark handsome man, both well turned-out. Hair styled to perfection, hats in winter. I wasn't invisible then. I would even say that we often turned heads.

For a long time we were happy. But then we had that bit of bad luck in *The Farmer's Arms*. It was a misunderstanding really. The woman got it all wrong and we got the blame, of course, but the manager called the police who put two and two together to make seven and Billy ended up in court. Things were never the same after that. In the end we parted company. I've been on my own for over 15 years now. I still live in the same house though. I've never wanted to leave. I've got all my memories here, all my mementoes. Drawers full of them.

I'm sitting on a bench now, watching a group in the precinct. Five girls, who look like clones. They've got the same hairstyles, four are about the same height and all are wearing skirts which have disappeared inside their blazers. Legs of different widths are covered with matte black tights. I watch them intently, pretending to read a text on my phone. I am punching in numbers in that slow way favoured by grandparents, exaggerating the movements. Out of the corner of my eye I see the smaller girl on the periphery of the group with her open handbag slung across her arm. She is caught up in some kind of joke and I seize my moment. I approach her from behind, unseen. I slip my hand into the bag, removing the small purse in one swift movement and keep walking. I now have my phone at my ear and am speaking into it, like a mother to her son, but I'm talking gibberish. Easy, so very easy.

Jackie's coffee shop is quiet, but I still choose to sit through the back, well away from the other customers. I take the purse from my pocket and unzip it on my lap under the table. There are £14 in cash plus a bank card. Better than nothing.

'Hiya Pauline, how are you? Looking well.'

I push the purse under my cardigan.

'I'm good thanks, Jackie. Well as good as I'm ever going to be at my age. Pensioner's special for me, hen. Cheese and ham toastie and a white coffee.'

'Of course, coming right up, love.'

I watch Jackie waddle off into the kitchen, her movements slow and painful, then look around the cafe. Paint peels from a damp patch in the ceiling and the windows could do with a good clean. I think back to some of the places I used to go to with Billy. Glitzy restaurants, places with a bit of glamour and pizzazz. I close my eyes and see Billy and me, dressed to the nines, at a dinner dance in *The Station Hotel*. We were never off the dance floor the whole night, waltzing and jiving.

Interspersed with a bit of ducking and diving. Billy got his hands on a fur coat that night. We left early and I walked out of the hotel wearing the fur coat on top of the thin jacket I had come in. Robbing the rich, we used to say, stealing from those who'll never miss it. That was Billy's line, anyway.

I get the bill from Jackie and leave the money on the table. I always give her a wee bit extra, as she's looking after her grandson now.

'Cheerio, Pauline,' she shouts from through the back.

'Bye, Jackie.' I put 50 pence in a charity tin that sits beside the till and then head out into the sunshine.

I walk along the precinct and then turn into the park, which is packed with mums and tots. I sit on a bench, watching what's going on. A young man sits on the other end of the bench and I catch his eye and smile.

'Alright, son?' I shuffle along.

He looks at me a little warily and nods, taking out some kind of electronic device. He begins to tap away on it.

'Nice weather, isn't it? For April, I mean.'

He keeps his eyes on the screen, bewitched by the lights and I am invisible once again. I smile, enjoying the warmth on my face and hands. Eventually I gather up my bags and stand up, a little unsteadily. I fall towards him, and I see a look of panic in his face as I steady myself by pulling at his jacket.

'Sorry son, I'm not quite as good on my feet as I used to be. Enjoy your day.' I walk off slowly, my back a little hunched and my steps a little hesitant. I hold my bags tight against my body, like a warrior with her shield.

When I get home I go straight into my bedroom at the back. The student's wallet is warm and smooth in my hand. Soft leather. Black. Very nice quality. Inside are two bankcards, a library card and a membership for the students' union. I frown. Then I find that there is a separate zipped compartment. I open it up and inside there are three £20 notes and a pay slip for a bar in town. Better than nothing. I put the money into my cardigan pocket then add the wallet and the girl's purse to the bulging pile in the pull-out drawer under my bed.

Billy wouldn't have dreamed of taking stuff from kids. 'We take from folk who can afford it, Pauline,' he would say. Yes, Billy was the one with the conscience. And Billy was the one who ended up inside. I move across to the dark wooden wardrobe and slip my hand in between layers of cloth to touch the coat we took all those years ago. I still get a thrill when I feel the thick fur between my fingers, luxurious and decadent. I take it from the hanger and drape it around my shoulders. It's never been worn outside. Too risky, I felt, though Billy always said I was being daft. Now it's my guilty secret. I dance round the room, arms outstretched around my imaginary partner, the sound of a waltz in my head. But the fur at my neck begins to feel rough and uncomfortable. I stop twirling. Nausea builds and I swallow hard, stomach lurching. The weight of the coat is heavy on my shoulders, and I let it drop to the floor in a heap.

I'm woken from a nap by raised voices and open my eyes just in time to see two teenage boys pass the window. I watch them cross over to the young woman at the corner shop who's selling the *Big Issue*. There's an exchange of words, a scuffle and the next minute they are running away, the woman giving chase. A few minutes later she's back and sinks onto the pavement, head in her hands. I sit still, just watching. Thinking. I ease myself up and out of the chair, knees protesting at the movement.

'Are you okay?'

She looks up at me, her dark eyes fearful.

'Only I saw what happened there. Those boys did they…'

'Yeah, they took all my money. All of it. I won't eat now. I don't…' she breaks off, shaking her head.

'Thieving wee…', I hesitate, 'thugs.'

She nods and pulls her jacket round her shoulders. She's painfully thin, I notice.

'Here, take this,' I say. 'Get yourself something to eat. You look like you could do wi' a proper meal inside you.'

She hesitates. I fold the three notes and tuck them into her jacket pocket.

'That's too kind of you. I don't know what to say.'

'Just tell me that it will keep you goin' in hot food for a while. I see you out here in all weathers.'

She smiles then pulls me into an awkward embrace. I think of Billy, and what he would say. He would be proud, I reckon. He always saw me as better than I really am. I walk back across to my flat with a bit of a spring in my step. It turns out that giving money away is easier than I'd thought it would be. I might even try it again sometime. We'll see.

STOCKTAKING

Irene Lebeter

Malcolm began the monthly check of his arsenal. He'd entered the fight many years ago and the battle continued.

Knowing it was imperative to stockpile weapons, he counted the grenades used to defeat the monsters before they could annihilate him. Must get some more, he decided, and ticked them on the list. He moved on. Any sign of weakness on his part and the enemy would strike. Whatever gender, age group or culture, no-one was spared. The attacks were indiscriminate.

Finding another weapon in short supply, Malcolm jotted it down. Cost didn't matter, just as long as he was protected against the fierce assault from his foes.

He flexed his muscles and breathed deeply. Then he began to run on the spot, aware of the need to remain strong. His stockpile had grown larger over the years but the enemy had without doubt become more vicious as time went by. With that thought in mind, he added two more items.

Malcolm stretched up to his full height and smiled. These weapons made him untouchable. Atishoo. He sneezed into his hankie, which he'd boil later. Atishoo, atishoo, he sneezed another couple of times. Once more he checked his supplies. Drat, despite his close attention to detail, he was clean out of Beecham's Powders. He grabbed his car keys, his glance going to the clock on the dashboard as he started the engine. With a bit of luck, he'd make it to the pharmacy before they closed.

AN UNEXPECTED DAY IN THE LIFE OF A ZOOKEEPER

Carolyn Mandache

I was thrilled to accept my summer job at Tobe Zoo in Japan, knowing there had been a huge number of applicants. Half way through my Animal Science and Conservation degree, the position could not have been more suitable. The language barrier hadn't caused too many issues, and most of my colleagues spoke pretty good English. I'd learned a few Japanese words and felt pretty confident asking my manager about my wages…it wasn't until later I learned that I'd been asking about my dinosaur rather than my salary. He politely explained there were no dinosaurs at the zoo, with roars and tiny T-rex arm movements to demonstrate, at which point I realised my unfortunate mistake. Yes, there are a lot of very similar words in Japanese.

Some animals are more fun to care for than others. The penguins waddling about are always cute, especially when they slip up, their little flippers trying hard to regain their balance, but not usually successful. My favourite little guy Mickey is always trying to find the perfect pebble for his Mrs, but to say she's fussy would be an understatement. She picks up his latest offerings in her beak and throws them away in utter disgust…had a few girlfriends like that myself. Mickey never seems disheartened; I admire his perseverance. Leaving work stinking of fish is the only downside to penguin duty, apart from the projectile poop during nesting season, that is. Dodging that is the most unusual workout I can say I've ever had. It's a laugh when you see one of your colleagues get splatted on their bright blue uniform. Not so funny trying to scrub the mess off though.

No two days are ever the same and the dietary requirements for the different animals are important and complicated. The aim is always to try and offer the nutritional equivalent of what they would eat in the wild. For the carnivores, feeding time is definitely not for the squeamish. A newbie lasted less than a day, as human vomit wasn't a welcome addition to the buckets of meat for the lions. Speaking of lions…

Today was my weirdest day at the zoo, in fact, scratch that, weirdest day of my entire life. Obviously, zoos have to take every precaution to prevent animal escapes, especially the dangerous ones. The day began with a team meeting to explain the zoo would be closed to the public for the annual training on how staff should behave in the unlikely event of a wild animal escaping. Apparently each year, a different scenario is played out, and this year the theoretical disaster was that a lion had escaped. I was extremely curious about how we would learn to protect ourselves, visitors to the zoo, and of course the lion itself. I presumed there would be some kind of video presentation, a Q and A and some interesting facts about large cat behaviour;

a valuable educational experience. I was completely off the mark.

Makoto, the head manager of the zoo asked for a volunteer. I was only too happy to oblige and looked forward to adding 'trained lion wrangler' to my CV. A large box was handed to me and I was told to open it. The contents alarmed me; tightly packed fur and an unmistakable mane. Surely the answer to an escaped lion was not to skin it and make some kind of fur coat or rug? Slowly I pulled the contents from the box until the full horror revealed itself. No, it was not a real lion skin…much worse. The plans for the day were detailed to the fascinated staff, who admirably managed to stay poker faced and attentive. I was politely asked to go and change into the lion costume hanging limply from my disbelieving hands.

I gazed into the mirror at the ridiculously friendly looking lion staring back at me; a Simba when clearly a Scar would have been more appropriate. At 10am on a hot summer's day, the sweat was already building as I swept my impressive glossy mane back from the ridiculous toothless grin and marvelled at the fact that it wasn't actually April Fool's Day. Do they celebrate that here? I'll need to check that out later. My clumsy paws struggled to fit my zoo uniform into the now empty box and I headed back, expecting loud laughter at my expense. Surprisingly there were no sniggers as the staff were so well versed in these exercises. Apparently last year it was an escaped zebra scenario, so at least I could console myself that things could have been worse. Imagine being the striped hind legs of a panto-style zebra running about a zoo in this heat!

'Do I have to run about on all fours?' My muffled voice was hard to make out through all the fur. Eventually my question was understood and answered. Thankfully I would be allowed to run as normal, upright on my two fluffy feet. Good to know they were sticking to absolute accuracy. My fellow zookeepers would take turns to try and capture me throughout the day, and then there would be a feedback session at the end of the day, what went well, what could be improved. Thankfully, my very expressive face was hidden behind my happy feline alter ego.

Told to go and hide whilst the first group of 'hunters' prepared, I wondered how I would ever be able to explain this to friends and family at home without sounding like a complete lunatic. Making my way to the penguin enclosure as I planned my first hideout, I swear Mickey raised a very judgy yellow feathery eyebrow at me. I waved a paw at him. He cocked his head and went back to pebble picking.

I hid behind the massive *Welcome to Tobe Zoo* sign before realising this was certainly not typical behaviour for the king of the jungle. No, what would a dangerous predator do in this unlikely situation? Maybe go and eye up some lunch? I hurried over to the antelopes, licking my human lips as I tried to get into character. Finding shade from a tree, I waited patiently for the first group, practising my most aggressive roars and feeling a little guilty for startling the antelopes.

The blue outlines were easy to spot, lions aren't colourblind after all... in fact their eyes are pretty amazing, they have an extra eyelid to keep out dust, and did you know some lions actually have blue eyes? Anyway, I digress. I remembered to voice the colour vision point later; camo gear would have been much more effective. I felt it was important to get the lion's perspective across too. An excited finger was pointed in my direction, I knew I'd been spotted and made a run for it, my tail swishing back and forth as I adjusted the headpiece so I could see out of the eyes, which annoyingly kept moving out of position. They were gaining on me. I could hear the footsteps get louder and louder. I turned and gave an almighty roar, which came out more of a breathless whimper, my clawless paws raised in threat, but looking more like surrender. Each 'hunter' cautiously approached, placing a stake on the ground, netted together and surrounding me. I charged at them, knocking one to the ground and observing as his colleague tended to the 'face slash' I'd given him. Thank goodness for imaginary first aid. Next I spotted the fake tranq. gun and the ridiculous added 'pew' sound effect and took my cue, falling to the ground out for the count. The costume provided surprisingly good padding.

The day continued, thankfully with some breaks from the costume I was growing to despise. The zoo is massive and some groups were very slow at finding Lenny the Lion, as I'd named him. In fact at one point they caught me very easily as I enjoyed a cat nap in the sun. I didn't consider that a failure on my part…all very natural behaviour. Another capture occurred outside the lion enclosure, I tried not to take offence at the superior looks and bored expressions of the feline residents. Clearly these majestic animals were not gaining any escape tips from Lenny. They offered the occasional powerful roar, just to make me feel extra inadequate for my insulting impersonation of them.

Finally, my ordeal was over and the exercises were deemed a success, my lion acting much appreciated by management. Makoto rewarded me with a Lion chocolate bar, clearly delighted at how clever he was with his choice of snack. I played along and devoured it…lion like. Scraping my sweaty hair back I enjoyed my round of applause, relieved to be dressed in my normal uniform again. My suggestions of camo gear were not taken on board, after all the lion escape would not be forewarned, so the normal blue uniforms would be in use, a uniform change would not be the first thing on people's minds. Fair point, I guess. I headed home bewildered by such a strange experience and looking forward to a long bath. The water was just right as I dipped my toe in and prepared for my soak, but I was interrupted by my mobile ringing. I threw a towel round me and fetched it from the living room.

'Hi, Mum. How are you?'

'Hi, Son. All good, thanks. I've just been watching the news and Tobe Zoo was on it. Were you there today with that crazy catch the lion thing?'

'Eh, yes, I was actually…'

'I thought it was a joke! Imagine having to run about all day pretending to be a lion.' She laughed loudly down the phone.

I rubbed the back of my neck, weighing up my options. 'Yeah, glad I wasn't that guy!'

I laughed nervously. 'Listen, Mum, just about to go for a bath. Can I call you tomorrow?'

'Oh sure, no problem, Son. I'm just posting about the zoo on Facebook now. Honestly never seen anything so silly.'

'I know, bonkers! OK, bye then, speak soon. Miss you.'

'You too, Son. Bye for now.'

I hung up the phone, relieved that it hadn't been a video call to reveal my red cheeks and give away my secret. It seemed there was something better at hiding than me that day, the discreet Japanese news channel which had documented highlights from my day. As I said, it got boring at times and I pride myself on authenticity, always have done. I flicked on the news and there I was, sharpening my pretend claws on trees, pacing up and down, roaring (or poorly attempting to), and curled up for my snooze. I cringed and prayed the true identity of Lenny the Lion would never be revealed.

WORDS

Julie McNeill

words that land
so beautifully
on the swell
of the Esk

or written
on the last bus
through inhospitable
countryside,

are packed carefully
into a poet's bag
with the croissants,
cheese pies,

badges, and
that mysterious
cloth. They fly
to a rooftop

bathed
in the light
of a Mediterranean
sunset,

where
the Acropolis
peers over
their shoulder

and a companion
reads joyfully
about the loss
of hope.

The words
are given away
in bars, on trains
at festivals

like they're
nothing at all,
or everything

we have
to mark this,
their miraculous journey.

JUST ANOTHER DAY AT THE DROP ZONE

Anne V McClure

From 12,000ft I see the sun glinting on the snowy caps of the Pyrenees, the periwinkle Mediterranean and the rust coloured roofs of Empuriabrava. I enjoy the view as I descend at 120mph, comfortably sit-flying, turning myself 360 degrees to take it all in. Even in Spain the air is cool at altitude and it's fresh on my bare legs and arms. Skydiving in Scotland, including in summer, I wear gloves so my hands aren't so cold that I fumble steering my parachute. Jumping here, in shorts and a t-shirt is bliss. The feeling of being in control in the air, the thrill of moving at this speed, the beautiful view – I experience a rush of sheer joy and laugh into the sky.

At 2,500ft I flip to face the ground. I reach behind and pull the pilot chute from its pocket. It inflates and pulls out the main parachute. I'm congratulating myself on a good, if hasty, pack job when I look up to check the canopy. There are twists in the lines that run from my harness to the main chute. This means I can't steer it. I can't fly like this, and I definitely can't land safely.

An electric current of fear zaps me. I stretch up and grab both straps, yank them as far apart as I can and start kicking to turn myself the opposite way to the twists. If I don't fix this fast, I'll have to jettison the main chute and hope to God the reserve deploys. I have people I love on the ground and have no intention of ruining their day. I thrash my legs, trying desperately to find traction in thin air. Nothing is happening. I wonder, 'If I get rid of this chute and the reserve doesn't open, should I aim for the open sea so I die where no one will see the impact?'

A second before I reach to ditch the chute, the twists finally unwind in terrifyingly slow motion. My gorgeous purple and lime green canopy begins to fly properly. I shake tears from my eyes as my breathing begins to slow. I gaze around at the still glorious sky and will myself back into the feeling of pleasure I had before it all almost went horribly wrong. I zigzag gently down to the drop zone. A well-timed stall of the chute and I land on tiptoe, sling the canopy over my shoulder and head to the hangar, thinking, 'Now *that* was flying!'

'But I'll pack my parachute slower next time.'

THE HYPOCHONDRIAC'S TALE

Ann MacLaren

It seems to be the fashion these days, in line with our great tradition of being markedly influenced by the American way of life and culture, that we previously buttoned-up Brits should open up to share our emotional issues, our sexual orientation and our psychological problems with anyone who cares to listen. Revealing one's inner self, it seems is 'the way to go'. So here goes.

I am a hypochondriac. I enjoy ill health. I have had, in one form or another, every ailment ever discussed by *The Sunday Post* doctor, as well as most of those listed in *The Reader's Digest Medical Dictionary*. I also have first-hand experience of quite a few other conditions that the medical profession hasn't even discovered yet.

I'm not looking for sympathy; on the contrary, I embrace my chronic health anxiety. Why? Because it is a truth universally acknowledged that if you want to be a writer that anyone has ever heard of, you have to first develop a strong tendency to hypochondria.

Well, perhaps not universally acknowledged, since many writers are too embarrassed to confess to it. Nevertheless, it seems to be true. To be a writer, apparently, is to be a hypochondriac; to be a hypochondriac, a writer. Why? Let's look at the evidence.

Back in the 18th century hypochondria was thought to be a physical, as well as a mental illness. Its symptoms included headaches, stomach aches, and insomnia – which could apply to all the writers I've ever met. Fear and delusions were also common indicators. They probably still are; don't we all live in fear of the inevitable rejection slip? Aren't we all deluded about our capabilities? Well, most of you probably are – but I know my writing's brilliant.

In modern times hypochondria has come to be associated with neurotic and oversensitive personalities. Not surprisingly, the hypochondriac doesn't like to admit to the disorder because he – and female readers won't be surprised to learn that it's more common in men – is never given any sympathy. He might, under duress, confess to having an overactive medical imagination; after all, it's just one step on from an active imagination – which we writers all have, haven't we?

Imagination and ideas are important, as is the talent to translate these to a readable form; but even if we possess these gifts in bucket loads, there's something that prevents most of us from being the next Ian Rankin or Margaret Atwood. Something that we all complain about not having enough of. Time. It might surprise you to learn, therefore, that hypochondria would seem to be the answer to that particular problem.

Charlotte Brontë was a hypochondriac. It was brought on, she said, by having to work as a teacher and therefore not having enough time to devote to her writing. Charles Darwin was also a sufferer, but recognised the advantages, since he wrote that his 'ill health' saved him from the distractions that would keep him from his work. Marcel Proust cleverly spent his *temps perdu* shut away in his writing quarters apparently suffering from a wide range of maladies – thereby finding the time to finish his novel on that very subject. Hypochondria is the perfect illness for the writer, and the joy is you're not really ill, you just imagine you are.

Writers can also profit from the condition in other ways. Brian Dillon took advantage of insider information to write about fellow sufferers in *The Hypochondriacs: Nine Tormented Lives*, in which he describes his own, and others' obsession with illness as 'almost a vocation'. Dillon, before he decided to earn money by writing about his condition, used to spend his time thinking that every vague physical irregularity was a sign of serious disease. I know how he feels. I used to have bad headaches; now I have suspected brain tumours.

Woody Allen, who admits to being one of the 'worried well' of this world, drew from his own experience when writing *Whatever Works,* in which the principal protagonist, David, when assured by his girlfriend that he doesn't have an ulcer, replies, 'that's only because they haven't found one yet.'

Some writers do go a bit too far down the dread disease route. Boswell, apparently, was terrified that he was becoming 'formless…liquid…a body without borders', which seems rather extreme to me, but could surely have been turned into a good story or poem if he'd been able to harness his fear.

Poor Sara Teasdale, the American poet whose preoccupation with death appeared frequently in her poetry, was so sure she was going to die after a small blood vessel burst in her hand, that she took some sleeping pills, climbed into her bath, and there died of an overdose.

Molière, although suffering from a very real case of pulmonary tuberculosis, also died a hypochondriac: he was acting the role of Argon in *Le Malade Imaginaire* when he haemorrhaged during a coughing fit, and just managed to get to the end of the performance before he expired.

So, all you fellow sufferers, it's time to come out of the book closet. Don't be shy; it helps to talk to others in the same position. And if by any chance you're not yet a hypochondriac but would like to consolidate your career as a writer by becoming one, I can offer you this advice: learn from the professionals.

Medical students and nurses invariably go through a phase of chronic health anxiety. It happens during the transition between knowing nothing about anything to knowing all about everything, and stems from knowing too little about too much. This is considered acceptable and, indeed, respectable; almost a badge of office, because it proves they've been reading all the required medical manuals.

So there you have it. You must acquire knowledge of illness. Google all of the many health-related websites; read as many books on the subject as you can get your hands on, especially *The Complete Manual of Things That Might Kill You*, an invaluable guide to self-diagnosis for hypochondriacs. You'll soon find you're suffering from a variety of complaints that you previously never knew existed. Harass your doctor too, and when he dismisses your symptoms, find yourself a psychiatrist.

Above all, once you reach the state that Freud described as 'falling in love with your own illness', you must write about it. It's not compulsory, of course; you could write about anything else that takes your fancy. But hypochondriacs, laid up in bed or lounging on the sofa, are obviously in a perfect position to produce articles, stories and poems on the subject; so, it seems a shame, if you are in want of an agent or a publisher, not to use your anxiety disorder to your advantage.

You might even think of following in the footsteps of a certain Daniel Paul Schreber, author of *Memoirs of My Nervous Illness*. He got a whole book out of it. Although personally, I'd think of a more catchy title.

Don't delay though. Your illness might well be all in your head, but something will get you eventually. Don't say I didn't warn you. Get on with it. Before you wake up dead.

DEATHLY SILENCE IN THE GRAVEYARD

Graeme Lewis

So there I was, 4am, in pitch darkness in the graveyard which formed part of Glasgow Crematorium. The new probationer on Group 4 at Maryhill Police Office.

My colleague that night was the shift 'dinosaur', PC McClumpha, years of service, and an old dog who knew all the tricks. He said to me, 'Here's one of your baptisms of fire son, are you up for it?' Keen to impress and to ingratiate myself into the team, I'd replied, 'Yeah, of course, what do I do?'

PC McClumpha calmly and straight-faced said, 'I'll park the panda car in the crematorium carpark. CM3 (the shift sherpa van) is parked about 100 yards into the graveyard, behind the main building and two of our colleagues are, shall we say, resting their eyes. Your task is to sneak up on them, batter the side of the van, and hear them scream.'

I began to get out the car when PC McClumpha said, 'Give me your torch and switch off your personal radio. It's amazing how light and sound travel at night and you don't want to give the game away.' He then smiled wickedly.

I started to make my way through the darkened graveyard, wary about tripping or bumping into a gravestone, or worse still, a ghost. I was terrified. I reached my target when suddenly its engine burst into life, lights were switched on and it sped off at a fast pace. I quickly realised…the joke was on me.

THAT'S ANOTHER FINE MESS

Maura McRobbie

Lucy's mum had always had theatrical aspirations. She loved operas and dramas, and she *hated* the rain. Especially shopping in the rain. She would work out ways of sheltering from it, but when absolutely forced to, she embraced it by acting like Gene Kelly and dancing in every puddle, her umbrella twirling, as in *Singing in the Rain*.

'That's another fine mess you've got me into,' said Lucy glancing down at her splashed jeans. 'You're crazy! Mum, please don't embarrass me! Mum don't splash me. Please!' But Lucy's mum just kept on creating drama and theatre wherever she went. Especially while shopping in the rain. When Lucy reached 17, she was sensitive, innocent, and shy. She was preparing for her school prom. Her father was working in Vigo near Santiago in the Galician region of Spain.

Lucy's mum said, 'We'll shop till we drop in Santiago. We're bound to find you the perfect prom dress to fit your perfect size eight figure.'

Lucy said, 'Can't we just go to H&M or Zara in Buchanan Galleries like everyone else mum?'

'No!' said her mum emphatically. 'We'll buy an exquisite, bespoke dress in Spain this Easter.'

Their trip to Spain passed uneventfully. Lucy was pleased to see her dad. His apartment in Vigo was modern and spacious. Lucy's mum was charmed by the old-style beauty of the city. She saw movies and film stars everywhere: from the Narnia streetlamps to the red lipsticked ladies in their long sleek fur coats that swept their stiletto-heeled ankles. She saw Antonio Banderas in each and every waiter, and she delighted in the wonderful Albariño wine served in frosted glasses, straight from the freezer. They watched respectfully the Good Friday street processions and attended Easter Sunday mass at the wonderful cathedral of Santiago.

But Lucy's mum never forgot the shopping. And she and Lucy found the most perfect dress in a little boutique. Each store was unique and redolent of the 1950s. Family owned, wooden door frames with gold lettering painted on the windows, a bell tinkled at the back as they entered. The dress was pale lilac chiffon, spangling with sequins and fitted with shoestring straps.

'That's it!' Lucy's mum decided. Lucy wasn't so sure, but they bought it anyway, just in case. When they left the shop, it was raining. The usual soft drizzle of Galicia. The boutique owner kindly gave them an umbrella from the stand at the door.

'Do we pay for this?' Lucy's mum asked.

'No, no, it's free. Just leave it in the stand in the next shop you pop into.'

'Oh, that's wonderful. Revolving umbrellas, a bit like circumlocution! What a great idea.' Lucy secretly hoped her mum wouldn't launch into her *Singing in the Rain* routine as they left the shop.

Their next stop was the little jewellery shop opposite. 'It's tiny,' said Lucy.

'Yes, but it's interesting,' her mum said. They entered, and Lucy's mum carefully closed the umbrella and placed it in the stand at the door. It was a slim, wedged shaped shop, with the old-style varnished wooden counters, but on top were modern cascading stands of jewellery, dripping in silver and gold necklaces, glittering with earrings and bracelets. There was a delicate pyramid stand dazzling with hair ornamentation and rings. There was delicate ladder-like scaffolding shimmering with pearl necklaces of every lustre and length. But they didn't have the simple chain and charm motif that Lucy was looking for: a lucky clover, a cross or a Rennie Macintosh rose design that she'd admired recently on her friend.

As they politely said no to the assistant who had shown them several necklaces, Lucy's mum apologetically backed out towards the door. And that's when she felt her high-heeled boot step into the umbrella stand, pulling her down, and the whole jewellery display cascading down with her.

'Mum,' cried Lucy in astonishment. 'That's another fine mess you've got us into!'

BLIND DATE

David McVey

Garvald Tintock was 32. He worked out at the gym every day and it showed. He was muscled and honed, but not grotesquely so; he was strong but without a strong man's stocky build; he was fit but not freakishly athletic. Imagine him taking his shirt off in public, not something he'd actually do given his gentlemanly sense of style and decorum; but if he did, women would gaze longingly at his six-pack and be hypnotised by his muscles and his perfect skin tone. Until they saw his face.

It's really difficult to describe, without visual aids, such a mismatch; a physique like a fireman in a TV ad for women's cosmetics, and a face that any make-up artist at Hammer Films would have been proud of.

Garvald's face was uneven. His eyes didn't match in colour, size or position. He could shave every hour and would still look disreputably blue-chinned. His nose not only outstayed its welcome but swerved alarmingly midway through its lengthy journey. His teeth, though healthy enough, emerged at a variety of angles leaving generous amounts of space between them. His doughy skin was augmented by a number of warts and hairy moles and each eyebrow was like a malevolent, hairy demon from an MR James story.

Inevitably, he was a nice guy. He wasn't a gym going narcissist; he worked out simply because, as a policeman, he didn't have the leisure time to walk, climb, run or cycle. He was kind and generous, a good listener and though he was good company, he didn't go in for twenty-pint lads-on-the-lash evenings. Always a good sign, he was a cat person. He was everything that trashy women's magazines tell their readers to look for in a man except for the obvious.

Once they'd known him long enough, people were no longer stopped in their tracks by his egregious coupon, so he had lots of good male friends, but most women didn't stay around long enough to become habituated to the view. Colin Stewart was one of Garvald's best friends; they'd even been at school together in a rough and ready secondary in Glasgow's East End where Garvald hadn't actually stood out too much. One evening Colin mentioned Garvald to his wife, Fiona.

'What's the problem with him?' she asked.

Colin had never invited Garvald home, worried that he might frighten the children. Fiona had never seen him. Colin tried to figure out the best way to describe Garvald's upper slopes. In fact, he just said, 'Look at this,' and handed his phone to Fiona. She visibly recoiled from the photo on the screen, even though Garvald was just a small part of a lads' night out scene.

'Well, I can't deny he has aesthetic issues,' said Fiona, 'but we will have to invite him for dinner.'

'Dinner? Here? What about the children.'

'We'll put them to bed early. And wait till you see who I'll also invite.' Fiona pulled out her phone, tapping it to produce a photo which she held out for Colin to see. It was a picture of a girls' night out, this time, and Bannachra Creran was in it.

Bannachra was in Fiona's team at work. She was in her mid-thirties, another gym user, tall and slender and fit. She had a tumbling fall of chestnut hair, a near-perfect figure and legs she dressed to show off. It was just a shame that she had a moustache that suggested early 1970s Sean Connery, eyes like bad oysters with the rest of her face just pushed together and not really completed before it was set.

Colin viewed the picture with his eyes largely closed.

'She's single?'

'What do you think?' said Fiona. 'And, if you want to get Victorian, she's intact. You know the way guys are. Loads of them have tried to score with her so's they could get at that body while turning a blind eye to her face. But she's religious and won't have any of it.'

Colin looked again at the picture, at Bannachra, at her death-mask of a face, the shaggy, independent looking eyebrows with a family resemblance to her moustache…

'Garvald goes to church too,' he said. 'And they're both gym monkeys? So much in common. This might just work.'

Colin and Fiona lived in one of the stone-cleaned tenement districts of Glasgow's Southside, which superficially resemble the West End but are considerably cheaper. Parking was tight in the narrow streets, but they were just a few hundred yards from a Cathcart Circle station and both Banna and Gary (to give them their usual names) were expected to travel to the dinner by train.

'Suppose they travel on the same train!' said Colin.

'The same coach, even,' said Fiona. 'They'd empty it.'

They prepared the food – monkfish with roasted Mediterranean vegetables (West End enough for anyone) – and tidied the flat ready for their guests. Colin went through to the children's bedroom to check if they were sleeping.

'Out like lights,' he said when he returned to the living room. 'It's funny – forcing them to bed early so that they won't see Banna or Gary. We're treating two human beings as if they were an 18-certificate film.'

There was a clatter of high heels on the pavement outside. Fiona peeked through the curtains and saw Banna sailing confidently along the street with her elegant, sexy walk. If only I could master stilettos like that, Fiona mused.

They opened the front door and soon the stilettos echoed on the stairs to the first floor. Fiona and Banna gave little girlish squeals at seeing each other and hugged and exchanged little mwah-mwah air-kisses; again, it was just like the West End.

'This is Colin,' said Fiona.

Colin had been prepared; Fiona had shown him all the photos she had on her phone in which Banna featured. Even so, the face was something to behold, something that both repelled and fascinated; he closed his eyes as he kissed the hairy cheek.

Banna subsided elegantly into a sofa and crossed her legs. She was wearing a short, simple, understated red dress with tan leather boots, an ensemble that somehow reflected her tumbling auburn hair. Colin could understand those guys who had tried to pull her; if you covered up the face, she was perfect. He found that he was studying her long legs – it kept your eyes away from her face, after all – and only managed to tear himself away when the doorbell sounded.

Colin went to the door and welcomed Gary. He took his jacket and showed him into the living room where Fiona, a true stalwart, beamed further welcome and gave him a hug (albeit with eyes closed). They introduced Gary and Banna to each other and the two guests shook hands. There was an awkwardness about it, Fiona thought, as if they recognised that they had been categorised together as two members of a rather despised species and invited on the basis of what they shared. And this was disturbing because it was true.

The talk stuttered a little, especially when Colin nipped through to the kitchen to check the monkfish and to pop the starter – goats cheese choux pastry parcels – into the smaller oven. Fiona struggled to make eye contact with Gary and Colin was having the same problem with Banna. It really didn't make for flowing conversation.

And then Narnia came to the rescue. The family cat, a slow-moving, barrel-shaped tabby, had been sleeping in the bedroom but padded gently into the living room just as talk was stalling yet again. Garvald made some enticing noises and Narnia leaped onto his lap and began her characteristic motor-driven purr.

'Oh, Narnia likes you, Gary!'

'Och, I like cats and they tend to like me.'

Banna leaned over and stretched out her hand to Narnia, scratching her just behind the left ear. Fiona noticed how long and elegant Banna's nails were, how beautifully decorated with colour and glitter. Banna was so lucky; Fiona's nails tended to split and anyway she had a habit of nibbling them. She'd never get hers to look like Banna's.

Listen to herself; Banna was 'lucky'. She was envying her!

There was an unfrosting as the evening wore on. The talk flowed more freely and it was punctuated by laughter. No doubt Narnia's arrival had helped, and so had the wine (Banna had red, Gary had white). After they had eaten, they migrated back from the dining room to the sofas. Fiona soon returned to the kitchen and began negotiating with the Nespresso machine they'd just bought (reduced in price because the instructions were missing).

Colin chatted with the guests while she worked, until there came a piercing cry of 'Daddy!'

If the children were restless, they were quite likely to get out of bed and come through to the living room, where they would see Garvald and Banna and perhaps be haunted for life. With a hurried 'Excuse me!' he hurtled off towards the children's bedroom. It struck him as he went that he was leaving Gary and Banna alone together for the first time that evening. That couldn't be a bad thing.

Back in the living room, there was silence at first. And then Banna smiled and said, 'How many times is that, now?'

'Four, I think. I try not to count. Why do people keep setting us up together?'

She smiled. 'I don't know. Perhaps it's the church connection. "They're God-squadders, they're perfect for each other…" Or the gym. It never occurs to them that we go to the same church, the same gym and so have actually met before…'

'…and have decided that we're just not each other's type.'

'We get a decent meal out of it, now and again. Though I'm fed up with monkfish.'

'What else can people possibly think we have in common?'

'Coffee, everyone!' Fiona chimed as she clattered into the living room bearing a tray of things. Shortly afterwards a relieved Colin re-entered the room, the children now successfully pacified.

Some time after ten, the guests left. Fiona sidled over with Colin to the window. They looked down on Garvald and Banna walking together towards the station. They weren't holding hands or anything, but this was just their first blind date, after all. Everything looked positive. They kept watching as the pair disappeared into the gloom and the clacking of Banna's heels faded into nothingness.

'Mission, quite possibly, accomplished,' said Fiona, 'they'll even be on the same train.'

'It was leaving them alone in the room that did it,' said Colin, 'it gave them a chance to talk.'

'Maybe another wedding to go to. I'll need a new dress. What a job the wedding photographer will have…'

They closed the curtains and made for the kitchen with heavy sighs. There were huge piles of unwashed dishes and pots and pans. It would take ages for the depressing smell of monkfish to disperse.

THE CLOCK

David Ross

Tick. Tick. Tick. The large mantle clock counted down the seconds towards the quarter hour mark, heralding the passing of another 15 minutes of James' life.

Bong! Three more bongs and it would be an hour less alone. Sitting, head bowed in his usual fireside chair, a droplet precariously suspended from the end of his prominent nose, staring wantonly at Kate's empty seat opposite.

James a plumber, met Catherine a weaver, a love match made in heaven. They were both born in the mid to late 1890s and eventually married in 1921. Between them they had four children and adopted the illegitimate child of a close family friend, who was already married. Such was the closeness of the community, willing to help each other and save any unnecessary scandal. This love child was brought up as one of their own and never found out he was adopted, until much later in adult life, when he had children of his own.

James ended his working life as a plumber/tinsmith at John Brown's Shipyard, while Catherine had long since given up the loom. Although she no longer worked at the mill, she retained the ability to lip read, eavesdropping on everyone's conversations, making secrets impossible to keep. People became hesitant to discuss anything in her vicinity, any secrets would surely spread around the neighbourhood, like wildfire.

Theirs had been a difficult but caring relationship; all that James had known of life was work, war, family and more work. Now suffering from Parkinson's disease and retired for more than a decade and a half he would sit quietly, with a noticeable tremble, in his chair by the fire behind the living room door. The tremors he experienced never seemed to dislodge the ever-present drip on his nose, except when visitors banged the back of his chair with the door. Apart from one ailing daughter, who had suffered from tuberculosis, he was now alone with his memories.

It had been four years since Kate's passing. No longer did he wait at the window for her to appear at the corner from her shopping trip. When he saw Kate, he would rush into the kitchen and make her tea, returning to the window only to find her talking to a neighbour. When she looked like moving, he'd rush back to the kitchen and dump the first pot and make a fresh brew, but it was usually another false alarm. Sometimes he would make three of four brews, never telling Kate he had been patiently waiting for her. Four years of listening to the ticks, bongs and chimes since Kate's passing, the clock finally called time on James.

Was there ever a more inconsiderate retirement present than a clock?

MYSTERY

Ann MacKinnon

Fae the first glimp I had o ye,
I thocht ye wur the bonniest cratur
I'd ever seen.

Ye cam tae me as if in a dwam
an taen me oot o the midden
o ma ain life.

Ye travailed wi me tae launds
beyon ma ken an learnt me
mony new skeels.

Naethin wis ower much fash
an ma life wis lifttet oot o the pit
I'd been in.

Ye happed me in a green plaid
an cocooned me wi yir care.
I thocht ye looed me.

Then as fast as ye cam,
ye took aff and I wis left
wi an emptie hert.

But noo I think ye saved me,
made sure I kent the road tae tak
afore ye wheeched the plaid awa.

Your sojourn wi me will aye be a mystery,
bit I'll neiver forget your touch on ma pow
when I needit it.

Ye cam frae the sea
an tae the sea ye mon return,
leavin me wi a glent o hope.

FAMILY FOLLY

Sharon Bairden

Lennoxhill Police Station
Police Interview: Friday 13th May 2022
Time: 13:00 hours
Present: DC T Burton, DC V Price, and Stephanie King

DC T Burton: 'Can you state your full name and date of birth for the tape?'

Stephanie King: 'Stephanie…why do you need my full name? Why are you recording me? Am I under arrest? God, maybe this was a mistake…'

The woman's eyes are wide, darting around the room seeking the fastest route out. Fear explodes in her mouth. Sharp. Cold. Fear. She tastes it. It's bitter.

DC V Price: 'Calm down, Miss…er…you're not under arrest, it's just routine. Can you just give us your full name please? DC Burton, can you get her some water?'

SK: 'It's fine, it's Stephanie…I don't want a drink…Stephanie King…15th April 1966. I just want this over and done with…please.'

Shapes shift in her peripheral vision, dark shadows, suffocating her, she puts her hand to her throat.

DC VP: 'Thank you Miss King, are you ok? Are you sure we can't get you something? Water…tea…coffee?'

SK: 'No, can we please just get on with it.'

White knuckles drum against the scarred wooden desk.

DC VP: 'Address?'

SK: 'Who's going to be listening to this? God, I'm really not sure about this now, I don't want anyone telling…'

DC TB: 'Miss King, if you could just settle down, please, nobody will be listening to it.'

He looks round at his colleague, eyebrows raised.

SK: '13 Fairview Avenue, you know up by the waste ground, where the fair is held every year?'

DC Burton nods, 'Occupation?'

SK: 'Investigative journalist, look is any of this really important? Can I not just tell you what I'm here for?'

A chill comes from nowhere and curls around her bones, the sudden cold nips the air, the walls vibrate as though sending a warning. To her. *Don't tell,* it whispers. Her chair scrapes back on the floor abruptly. The sound is sharp and jagged, it rips the air before becoming touch; nails clawing down her spine. Hot breath in her ear, *Don't tell a soul.*

The detective reaches over, his touch is soft, reassurance slips from his lips…his eyes…slits…yellow. She blinks once. Now they are blue. Like hers. She breathes.

DC TB: 'Tell us in your own words.'

SK: 'I was approached by security at the fair, something strange; something bad he said. Being covered up. Asked me to look into it.'

Her sentences are short, they stab at the air between them, vying to be heard.

SK: 'Are you sure nobody else will hear this?'

Her eyes dart around the room, small cracks in the plaster hide yellow cat eyes. Watching. Waiting. Whispered voices, *Don't tell.*

Both detectives smile. Teeth like needles.

SK: 'It's one of those kiddie rides, Family Folly, for families, toddlers, you know the kind, syrupy music, animated figures. It's a new one, never been there before...apparently, it's been queued out all week. Anyway, one of the security guys noticed that some families are coming out of the ride, they look like they have seen a ghost... like there's something in there frightening them.'

DC VP: 'Miss King, I'm not sure scary rides are a police matter...'

SK: 'LISTEN to me.'

Her fists shake the table.

SK: 'He thinks it's kids messing around...he goes in after the fair closes, to check it out. Some of the figures have moved.'

DC TB: 'Miss King, really, this is not a police matter, I suggest you go and write up some Halloween copy for your editor.'

He throws a smirk towards his partner.

SK: 'LISTEN!'

DC VP: 'OK, carry on Miss King.'

SK: 'So the next day, he's on shift when this girl comes up to him, she's all jittery like, her parents and the twins, a boy and girl, her siblings, went to the fair the night before, but they didn't come home. Report it to the police, he tells her. She does but the owners of the Fair insist the family weren't there at all, no sign of them on CCTV. But the security guy knows this isn't true, he's local, he knows the family, he saw them there. So, he tells the girl to come back later when management are not around. They will look at the CCTV from the fair and the ride.'

DC VP: 'Miss King, if it's been reported, I suggest you leave it to us.'

SK: 'No, you don't understand. The girl sees her family on the CCTV, sees her mum and dad dragging the twins over to the Family Folly, says her dad looks different. Like he's crazy, wild...not like her dad. I asked the ride operator, but he doesn't care. People they come and go, he just cares about the money, about finishing, about the young girls eyeing him up from the Waltzers. So, the security guy, he decides to shut down the ride, maybe there's been an accident. You know?'

She looks at the detectives wildly now, the words spill from her mouth.

SK: 'So he goes in, with his torch and that, can't see a thing, it's dark like, really dark. There's nothing...apart from one empty car with two baseball caps and a mobile phone on them. He takes them out, the girl says they belong to her dad and the twins. There's CCTV that covers the ride, so I persuade the security guy to hand it over to me, he can't give me it fast enough, like he wants rid of the responsibility, he knows the owners are trying to cover things up. He told me it's not the first strange thing that's happened on that ride this week, but it's like he's too scared to tell me anymore…'

DC TB: 'Would you like a drink, Miss King?'

SK: 'No!'

She looks around again, haunted look.

SK: 'I've watched the last week's CCTV coverage of that ride, that family have been at the fair every single day and the thing is, they only ever go on that one ride. Family Folly. But this time they never came out.'

DC VP: 'So, did you see anything…er…unusual on the CCTV?'

SK: 'Well at first it all seems quite normal, you know, like they are just another family enjoying themselves. The ride's busy, lots of other families about. They are in for ages and at first, we figure they just stayed in, skipped paying for extra, but then as footage continues, something really weird starts to happen, like the ride is completely empty apart from that one family but now they don't look like they are having that much fun anymore. Dad starts to lose his shit a little, we can see him yelling at something…someone. Mum's mouth is stretched into a scream and the kids are crying. After about 30 times around the ride, like they are stuck there or something. But then it looks like the family are trying to get out, trying to clamber over the side. Next time they come round, the mum is gone, next time dad is gone, then the kids. But here's the thing, the ride comes round again, and they are all back and it all begins again, over, and over until…'

DC TB: 'Do you need a break?'

SK: 'No, please just let me tell you.'

DC TB: 'OK, carry on.'

SK: 'So after about five minutes, we can only see dad and kids, we slow the tape down and there's a body, it looks like a woman…mum…and she's slumped down on the floor of the car…then it speeds up and we go round again and now it's just dad and one kid, again a body slumped across the back seat, a small body…a child. By now the dad and kid are like statues, they are not moving, a mask of terror covers their faces. And here's the other thing, those figures on the ride are moving now, lumbering closer to the car with the mum, kid, and bodies. The ride goes round again, one of the figures is in the car with all four of them, and there is blood…like a lot of blood. The family aren't moving. The ride goes round one last time and then the car comes back empty, and the ride stops. Now the security guy has disappeared. There's a new guy there now, he said my guy had gone into the ride to check out some stuff. He showed me the CCTV and my guy is on the ride, going round and round and round.'

She stumbles out the station, she needs to go back to the fair. She must. The fairground is lit up against the black sky. But nobody is there. She feels them, she doesn't see them, but they pull her towards the ride, gentle at first. She resists. It's pointless. She's through the entrance now. The music starts up and she takes her seat. The ride begins…

EXEQUIES FOR A PRINCE

Sinclair Steven

'And for his passage
The soldier's music and the rite of war
Speak loudly for him'

That's what he said, Horatio remembered. Fortinbras was renowned for his silken tongue. It must have been dawning on him just what an opportunity he had stumbled upon: the palace strewn with bodies, the entire royal family prostrate on the flagstones, stabbed or poisoned, or both (when it comes to murderous mayhem Danes have an enviable thoroughness) and only him, Horatio, a harmless scholar, to speak up for the past.

Nature and politics abhor a vacuum and Fortinbras quickly saw he was born to fill that emptiness:

'I have some rights of memory in this kingdom.'

That was fast. Five minutes on the scene and he had dredged up that fact from the mud of history. Some memory. His 'right' went back a few hundred years to when Danes were still sailing the seas in serpent headed boats, pillaging and raping, in Danish tradition. Many 'rights' to the throne had come and gone over the following decades. Institute an enquiry into the most legitimate claimant to the throne? No chance. Army behind him after a fruitless, pointless campaign in Poland. Fought to a standstill by the Polack and dragging themselves back, angry, frustrated to Norway: no hostages to ransom, no wagons full of booty to cheer their weary way, hundreds of naive lads left as raven food on the eastern plains. The leaderless, resource starved Danish regiments weren't going to be able to take on even that lot and so, opportunity knocking, he just takes over and no-one but him, Horatio, to ask questions and he certainly wasn't about to risk his neck. English ambassadors there to give a veneer of international approval. Done deal.

And so bury him with honour! First actions belie that. Even as the flattery was being mouthed, Hamlet was dragged off by his heels, his fair head thumping on the stone stairway all the way down to the courtyard. The rest of them didn't even merit that gentleness: Claudius, Gertrude, Laertes, stripped of their jewels and chains, stripped even of their clothing. Gertrude, pathetic in her shift, thrown from the window-opening to crash on the cobbles below, Claudius and Laertes' naked corpses swiftly following. He shuddered at the memory. Gertrude had been a bit of a slut. Didn't find the life of the chaste widow very appealing, didn't even give it a real chance before slipping into the bed of the man her son claimed had murdered her husband. But she didn't deserve that undignified disposal. Horatio remembered how she had been kind to him when first he came to support his friend: personally arranging his accommodation; dropping in unexpectedly to confirm everything was suitable and to his 'taste'. But that smile, the way she had moved closer to him, the invitation in her eyes. He had felt painfully uncomfortable – had thought of going back to Wittenberg before any trouble started. God, he hadn't known what trouble was in those days, a few short weeks ago. Couldn't have imagined the nightmare Hamlet was going to drag him into. Still, he had wept at the way her body was abused by Fortinbras' men.

So here it was ending, that insane world of wandering spirits, plays within plays within plays, lunacy (real or affected, hawks and handsaws?), spying, assassinations, suicides, betrayals. He had been stumbling through that confusion for weeks. Hamlet had said there was 'something rotten in the state of Denmark'. He, Horatio, prided himself on his rational mind, a vision of a universe that could be explained, trusted, and that vision had been blown away, his certainty shredded into wisps of mist by a maelstrom of madness. Now it was all closing with a 'ceremony of honour'. A dreich windswept moor – showers of rain and hail scouring the land. Not even sacred ground. Claudius, Gertrude and Laertes thrown into a common pit after the king's head made a round of the moor atop a pike, a drunken crowd of soldiery trailing behind jeering and mocking. Gertrude at least was spared the dismemberment but was pulled along at the rear of the cavalcade thrown across the back of a mule, shift pulled over her head, pale buttocks slapped and prodded, the butt of jokes about the 'Whore of Elsinore'. He wept quietly, helplessly. Hamlet given the merest shadow of honour: an individual grave and the hurried ministrations of a priest. The man rushed through the rites at record pace, his uneasy eyes always straying to the increasingly noisy soldiery who had manhandled a butt of wine down to the field to toast the burials. A merry wake; the madness of the past weeks reluctant to pass on. The priest rushed off, stumbling over his robes in the mud, muttering a final prayer. Then even the soldiers, once the wine was emptied, drifted off, staggering, seeking living whores; the empty barrel left a mocking, but appropriate headstone for Claudius.

So there was just himself left, cowering under his hood from the rain. And the gravedigger. The man shovelled the earth down onto the body as the din of revelry from Fortinbras' hall drifted on the wind to their ears. Cannon shot roared to the empty skies. The more things change, the more they stay the same.

He recognised the digger from the time Ophelia was buried. Alone this time, his earlier partner reluctant to get involved, there was no joking in the stinking weather, no cod philosophy. Horatio didn't think he could condemn any vision of the world at this juncture. He remembered the jester's skull and the cynical observations it drew from Hamlet before the horror of Ophelia's fate had been made clear to him. Perhaps the jester was having the last laugh from beyond the grave.

Fortinbras had said to stay behind to tell the tale, but his cold eyes advised a hasty exit was safer. Tomorrow back to Wittenberg.

Denmark could stay rotten.

DAL LAKE, SRINAGAR, INDIA

Jeff Dunn

It is a deep wooden sound. And a sound that strikes a note in my subconscious as I slowly rouse from sleep. I get up and head for the houseboat's outside seating area and I trace the sound to nearby hills and the roof of a Buddhist temple. The slow beat continues. If the sound had a colour, it would be dark chestnut brown. Its timbre resonates. Unlike the dull, iron-laden sound of British churches, a solemn sound that I always associate with mourning. This sound had hope.

I scan the scene hoping to see the bright orange robes of Buddhists winding up stone steps on leather soled feet, their bald heads catching the early sun's rays. But unfortunately I am disappointed. I see nothing. Yet, this single, simple sound had lured me out of my bed into the peacefulness of a beautiful morning, to witness the cool, blue grey rock of the Himalayas slowly turn orange, warmed by the rising sun. The same colour as a Buddhist robe. And a tranquil Dal Lake, so, so still, not a ripple. So peaceful.

The deep-boned wooden sound continues as I return to my bed, refreshed by the stillness of it all, and the hope.

PARADISO

Matthew Keeley

'There's a cinema in Victoria! Who wants to go one night?' My family members – all 17 of them – gave me odd stares.

'Why would you want to go to a cinema…on holiday…in Malta?'

A similar conversation happened earlier this year in Amsterdam when Harald, my Airbnb host, looked over my shoulder – rather nosily, I should say – at my laptop screen.

'Are you buying a museum ticket?'

'No, I'm buying a cinema ticket.'

'Why? You can do that at home.'

Generally, this is the response I face when telling anyone about my holiday habit – that whenever I visit a new town or city, anywhere in the world, I always seek out a cinema. Usually, it has to be one showing films in their original languages, or at least with English subtitles. I wouldn't watch a film entirely in a foreign tongue. That would be nuts.

I've been to cinemas in England, Northern Ireland, the USA, Canada, the Netherlands, Czechia, Sweden, Germany, Switzerland, and Austria. Some are tiny, local cinemas that don't even look like cinemas from the street, but a moonlighting council office or school hall, like the Lab 111 in Amsterdam. Others have been arthouse cinemas with wooden countertops built in front of the chairs, and busy bars instead of popcorn stands, populated by bohemians in berets, floppy scarves and handlebar moustaches. There are 'proper' cinemas, preserved from a different, golden era – real theatre spaces with vast velvet curtains, ushers in maroon uniforms and ornate-banistered staircases – the Metro Kinokulturhaus in Vienna, for example. Of course, there are also the sleek multiplexes – New York, London, Belfast – that provide a Tron-esque escape space from the busyness of the cities (which I love, though my feet don't). I would add that Geneva's Pathé multiplex at least had a pleasant minimalist grey and yellow colour palette with soothing curved walls and pebble-shaped foyer benches for post film ponderings.

In my Dutch Airbnb, my immediate, awkward response to Harald's question was that my visits meant I could 'see films they don't have at home.' A lie. He suggested that I could download such films, as if I hadn't fully understood the internet. In fact, the misunderstanding was his. And everyone's, it seems.

My excuse to Harald only touched the surface of my travelling ritual. There are many reasons why I seek out cinemas in every new city. One, I've already expounded; it's a touristic activity to see the uniqueness of these spaces. Cinemas are functioning, immersive museums of architecture, design, décor, textiles, even costume. However, it's also an interactive cultural experience. Although film-going etiquette is generally similar everywhere (and therefore reassuring and warm), settling into a dim auditorium with the locals for two hours makes me feel I'm one of them for a little while – not just passing them on busy streets, map in hand, or being served by them in cafés and from hotel desks. I'm a member of the Parisian public; a Swiss citizen; a Rotterdam resident, going about my business and living my ordinary local life.

Moreover, cinema is the perfect night-time activity for me when I'm travelling. I don't drink. Bars and clubs aren't the place for me and even if they were, I usually travel alone these days. I can't imagine sitting on a bar stool without company. I love the theatre, but that can be three or four times the price of a cinema ticket. After exploring on foot all day and noting the closing times of museums and galleries, I'm unwilling to give up and spend the rest of the night in a hotel or Airbnb. Why wouldn't I extend my activities? Experience a new film in a new building with a new audience? Cinema is inherently an individual activity, anyway. You can't, or shouldn't, talk here – with the exception of an impassioned New Yorker in the 42nd Street AMC who leapt up and yelled support for Oprah Winfrey's character in one of The Butler's particularly emotive scenes.

There's also a psychological trick at play here. Cinema brings a freeing from holiday lethargy. Exploring a new city and overloading the senses can bring burnout, or worse, numbness. You forget you're even away from home. The vacation thrill has faded. You've been exposed to these new streets for hours on end. The newness has lost its impact. A cinema retreat is a reset button; a recalibration tank. After the film credits roll, these doors don't open onto a wet, Scottish retail park. Instead, you've returned to a fresh city. The new smells become new again. You're reminded of foreign words decorating street signs. Exotic accents stroll by once more. The cinema is a quiet recess to pause, slow down, experience something different in a warm, dark cocoon, then flutter back out into your new environment with a sudden remembering of where you now are.

Beyond the immediate buzz of it all, my hobby has longer reaching effects. Seeing different films in different places creates odd synaptic links and memories for me and I now connect specific movies to the cities in which I first saw them. *Far From the Madding Crowd* takes me back to Prague. *Fleabag Live* from the National Theatre was New York, as was *Nick And Norah's Infinite Playlist*, *The Invasion*, and the 2013 *Carrie* remake. *The Matrix* – Chicago. *Air Force One* – Washington D.C. *X-Men* – Orlando. *The Two Faces of January* – Vienna. *Infinity Pool* – Belfast. *Triangle of Sadness* – Frankfurt. *Eternal Daughter* – Lyon. *Mrs. Harris Goes to Paris*… Suffolk, oddly. It might seem obsessive of me, but I don't keep these lists written anywhere or habitually rhyme them off. The memories are just there, like any other holiday recollections and travelling anecdotes. Seeing scenes from these films or even their posters snaps me back to places like nostalgic smells. They've become postcards on a fridge, treating me to tucked away reminiscences.

In Victoria, my dad became the lone volunteer to accompany me for a few hours out of the stifling Maltese humidity. The modest cinema would be easy to miss from the street with its tiny old-school box office window. Inside, though, an echoing marble staircase carried us to an upper floor with a very contemporary theatre setup and fairly busy audience. Our film? *Mission Impossible – Dead Reckoning: Part One.* It often surprises people but sometimes all I want is a bright, big-budget, mindless blockbuster and Tom Cruise does it all so well.

Afterwards, Dad said it was one of the worst films he'd ever seen. Not what I'd hoped for, but it's gifted me another little memory of the smiling cinema manager, the festival lights of Victoria outside, the heat of Malta, and Dad making me laugh.

MAY YOU BE THE MOTHER OF 100 SONS

Palo Stickland

In the 1990s, I read a book called *May You be the Mother of 100 Sons* written by Elisabeth Bumiller, a *Washington Post* journalist who lived in India for three years. I was annoyed because in that short time this writer thought she knew enough to write a book, and yet not mention the origins of the title.

May You Be the Mother of 100 Sons is an ages-old blessing taken from the Mahabharata – the epic poem about cousins who fought a long war against each other – similar to Homer's *Iliad.* The name of the poem means Great Bharata, as the area around modern-day northern India was named in those ancient times.

The story concerns two brothers, the elder has a disability and, controversially, is crowned king following the death of his father. The question raised by the younger brother, and others in the kingdom, is how can a blind man rule with the same power as a sighted one? The blind king's marriage is arranged with a princess of a neighbouring kingdom who, when she discovers that her betrothed is blind covers her eyes with a blindfold, to become a part of his sightless world. She spends some years without conceiving a child, but when she does, she gives birth to a hard ball from which come forth 100 princes. Hence the blessing.

In the book, Elisabeth Bumiller not only picked up on the myriad injustices against women in modern India, but introduced the reader to women who lived modern, westernised lives too. The stories of the women, rich and poor, that she wrote about affected me as a young woman still trying to work out how I'd become who I was, and how I should live.

Was the western way better? Which eastern traditions were relevant, positive and worth holding on to? I struggled alone with these questions, as my parents, husband and brothers thought I was crazy to even keep on about them. Why couldn't I just get on with life like they did? 'You read too much,' they said.

During my first six years, I lived in Punjab, a part of India influenced by history in a different way from the rest of modern India. The reason was the Khyber Pass that brought northern invaders, Greeks and Muslims, some of whom would settle in the plains of Punjab and add to the diversity of the population.

When I was six and joined my father in Scotland, I spent eight years in city centre Glasgow where people would talk about India as if it was one place and Indians were all the same – the 'India' of the Raj. During those eight years, my memories of India fast receded as if into a veil of cloud.

I returned to the two Punjabi villages where my grandparents were, lived there for two years and missed second and third year of my Scottish secondary school education. However, I received a different kind of learning in India.

In the village where I was born, most families didn't believe in educating girls because early marriage was common and expected. My cousin had five years of schooling and they considered my eight years to be plenty long enough. I should now learn housework and wait until the family found me a suitable match. When they married, girls left their families and their home villages. Boys remained in the village of their birth all of their lives. The reason was agriculture. The fields were small, and you wanted to divide them only when necessary. The tradition became that your sons inherited, and your daughter was married young, and sent off to live with another family where she would keep the house and produce children. She didn't inherit; her sons did. She didn't get anything from anyone, anywhere. That made me unhappy, whereupon my family said, 'What's wrong with you? That's just the way it is!'

In the 1950s, India's first prime minister made it legal for daughters to inherit. He only had the one child, Indira. That didn't change things in the villages. People frowned on girls who claimed their legal share. My mother never did, though her father died in 1968, long after the change in the law.

I was the third child, and the boy before me had died, and that made a big difference to my mother's attitude towards me. I remember her saying, 'I was supposed to have seven boys. Where did you come from?'

She wasn't purposefully neglectful towards me, she just overlooked me in her happy, busy life with her five boys. I know she believed in a prophecy similar to the blessing of the 100 sons. A holy man prophesied that she, a young bride of seventeen at the time, would be the mother of seven sons. A variation on the 100 sons but seven is an auspicious number.

My mother's attitude to male babies, and to me as female, had historical roots. She was born in the 1920s into a changing India. The British Raj's Sikh regiments fought in the First World War, in Europe and the Far East, and a generation of young men was decimated. Then the Spanish Flu hit the villages. Men tended to be outside in the open air, but women lived in cramped conditions and died in larger numbers. Stepmothers became common – the evil stepmother became, even more than before, a part of the culture. In the generation after the Spanish Flu, the eldest brother in a family was lucky to be married, for there weren't enough women for the younger ones.

It was a time for extreme hygiene measures. Even decades later, only one person in turn worked in my grandmother's kitchen and no-one entered without bathing. You didn't eat from anyone else's plate or drink from their cup. You kept your distance. My great-grandfather inherited grandchildren to raise when two of his four grown-up children died. My father said, 'It was a time when no sooner had we removed a dead body from the village than another was ready to be taken.' People learned to restrict expressions of love because death was very close and disease much feared.

However, medicine was progressing, both my grandmothers lost seven children in infancy. My mother lost one. The year she lost my brother, two other baby boys also died. People remembered the deaths of the boys. That was the year of Partition, 1947, when the Raj ceased to be. Perhaps, things improved.

Is it any wonder that the blessings of 100, or of seven sons, are much sought after, and held close by young women like my mother?

A LA RECHERCHE DU CORPS PERDU

Tom Tumilty

New Year's Day, my mind seemed to say,
Another year older, no wiser.
I'd stuffed myself full with vodka, Red Bull
And some gin as a wee appetiser.

I'd got the solution, my New Year's resolution,
I'd leave my bad habits behind.
I'd be fit as a fiddle, lose the weight round my middle.
The new me I'd definitely find.

I thought it'd be cool, see, well, more's the fool, me.
Though I felt I fair looked the part.
Swaggering in to the gym, they whispered, "Get him!"
Seems the whole thing was doomed from the start.

They struck their smug poses
Looked down their noses
And silently scoffed at my style.
I looked at my paunch
and my XXL haunch.
Well, I suppose it had been a while

Ten minutes huffing meant half an hour's puffing.
But will I give up? No fear!
I'm on the right track and I swear I'll be back.
See you, same time, same place.................
....
next year.

BLACK JACK

Steve O'Brien

It was the worst storm anyone could remember. The day Black Jack came to town. For many hours thunder crashed and lightning flashed across the dark, dark sky. Even Mrs Briggs's huge guard dogs, Biff and Fang were hiding under the couch. They pretended they weren't afraid, but when Mrs Briggs rattled their chains and shouted, 'Walkies!' They slid further away, crossing their legs in case they had a little accidental wee on the carpet. It was funny to see them hiding, because they liked to bully all the other animals in the area. They especially hated cats.

Mrs Briggs was a very important person in that little Scottish seaside town. But, Mrs Briggs was lonely, though she would not admit it. 'Why would I need friends?' she said to Biff and Fang, 'with my lovely dogs to take care of me.' They would usually give her a lick, but because they had their paws over their ears to block out the thunder, they had no idea that Mrs Briggs was speaking.

Black Jack was 10-year-old Sally Jones's cat. Three years ago he had appeared, as if by magic, on her doorstep and had stayed with Sally and her mum ever since. They had felt sorry for him because he had one blue eye and one green eye. 'Very strange,' Sally's mum had said. 'What a beautiful inky black coat he has,' Sally thought. So she named him Black Jack. And every time she called out that name, Black Jack purred happily and licked his paws. No one knew how old he was, or where he had come from. Only Black Jack knew those secrets.

But, one day, the Jones family had to move home so that mum could find a better job. That was why Sally and her cat came to live in the house next door to Mrs Briggs.

Next day the sun shone. As usual in the morning, Mrs Briggs tied Biff and Fang's leads onto a bench in the front garden beside the beautiful beach. They felt brave again now that the storm had passed and growled at any animal that came anywhere near. Yes, they were happy dogs. Until, that is, they happened to look up and see Black Jack sitting on their garden wall, staring at them. 'Get him!' Biff growled as they flew towards Black Jack, snarling, and snapping their strong jaws. But Black Jack didn't move a muscle. He was too busy licking his paws. The monster dogs leapt off the ground. They almost got to him when, suddenly, their leads pulled them backwards. They tried again and again, but it was useless. They just could not quite reach this cheeky cat.

There was so much noise that neighbours came out to see if there was a war going on. Oh, how the guard dogs wanted to get their teeth into Black Jack. Mrs Briggs came rushing from her house and found the dogs twisted together by their leads, and very excited indeed. She just caught a glimpse of Black Jack as he jumped off the wall. Mrs Briggs dragged Biff and Fang into her house. They were shaking with anger, and tried very hard to tell Mrs Briggs about Black Jack, but of course she could not understand dog language.

Later, Biff and Fang had calmed down and were watching TV in the living room. They liked to watch cartoons. Mrs Briggs was in the kitchen making her lunch. Suddenly the dogs heard a soft tap, tap, tap at the window. Black Jack was watching them from the window ledge. 'That cat is laughing at us,' said Biff. Black Jack put his paw against the window and did it again. Tap, tap, tap. The angry, howling dogs jumped up, bashing into the television, smashing it to pieces. By the time Mrs Briggs arrived the room was wrecked. Black Jack was still on the window ledge, purring happily.

'You are an evil cat, upsetting my lovely dogs like that,' Mrs Briggs shouted, shaking her fist. 'I'm going to get rid of you forever, if it's the last thing I do.'

Later that day Mrs Briggs took Biff and Fang for their walk to the beach. She was thinking of the best way to get rid of that evil cat. Suddenly, a little white rabbit appeared, scampering across the sand. Biff and Fang hated rabbits. They ran like rockets to give chase and pulled Mrs Briggs off her feet, so that she bumped her head on a rock, making her dizzy. And the tide was coming in. She might be washed out to sea. 'Help!' she shouted, but no one heard her. That was when she saw Black Jack sitting just a few feet away. He was licking his paws. 'Oh, no,' she thought. Then she fainted.

A few days later, Sally and her mum went next door with a bunch of flowers. Mrs Briggs was sitting up in bed. She was feeling much better.

'I was told it was you two who came to help me. I don't know how to thank you,' said Mrs Briggs.

'Not us,' said Sally's mum. 'It was Black Jack who led us to the beach. Somehow he knew you were in trouble. He saved you, not us. I just hope now we can be friends as well as neighbours.'

'I would like that,' said Mrs Briggs. 'And I thought that cat was evil. How wrong could I be?'

As for Biff and Fang, they came home later very shame-faced, and were put straight into the bad books. And afterwards, whenever Black Jack tapped on the window, Mrs Briggs would let him in and feed him something tasty from the dogs' dinner bowls. All the dogs could do was watch with a stupid look on their faces as Black Jack made himself more and more at home.

'That is a very evil cat,' said Biff.

'Yes,' said Fang. 'And have you seen those strange eyes?'

'I know,' said Biff, 'I think we'll stick to watching cartoons for a while, it will be much safer.'

VACANT

Elizabeth Kearney

When you left everything was vacant.
Your chair, your room, your bed.
Your clothes hung vacant in wardrobes,
On doors, over chairs.
This house stood still and vacant.
All around me;
This hole you left, felt everywhere.
And it surrounded me, pulling me in;
With the suction of quicksand,
Threatening to drown me.
It filtered through my bones that felt old,
And numbed with pain.
Bones that crumpled,
Leaving me stooped with grief.
Even my expression was vacant.
My insides hollow.
And you, an echo,
– that even now, still calls to me.

THE MUSIC ANGEL

Maggie Powell

Angela rested against the rough wall of the crumbling archway, and gazed with longing at the cool dark space beyond. Although it was well past eight o'clock in the evening, the hilltop alleyways still pulsated with heat. She was in deepest, southern France, on a music pilgrimage with Troubadour Tours, which had seemed a good idea at the time of booking.

'Recently retired? Why not spend a week in a rustic idyll, learning a new skill? Meet lots of interesting people and rediscover the ancient musical heritage of a Catalan Saint.'

Not all the time had been spent on music practice. Therapists, masseurs, crystal healers and local craft folk came on different days, during the hottest afternoon hours, to ply their trades, and pamper the grateful students. Now six days into the tour, and almost proficient on the recorder, Angela was in procession with the other Troubadourians, to perform at the annual thanksgiving service in the 14th century church. The fact that they seemed to be the only outsiders invited to the ancient ceremony, in this off the beaten track village, convinced Angela that Gerald, who ran Troubadour Tours, was a bit of a fantasist, with a Minstrel fetish.

He had even concocted a back story for this festival. Angela had tried to check it out with the locals, but their heavily accented dialect was neither French nor Spanish. They did seem pleased, almost bemused, that a group of middle-aged Brits was willing to rent out the converted school house to learn their archaic music and buy their craftwork.

The story was that centuries ago, during a time of war, the little town was besieged. One evening a young boy stood on the ramparts and played a heavenly tune, taught to him by an Angel. The Warlord was so impressed with this performance that he removed his murderous legions to rampage elsewhere, and the townspeople were saved. Every year on the anniversary of this redemption, their descendants hold a thanksgiving festival.

Gerald had managed to convince everyone to wear 'angelic' costumes, as described in the legend. And now they were trudging up through the village, in long, loose white skirts, dresses, kaftans or sarongs, looking more like ghostly hippies than the Seraphs they were supposed to be. Clutching their recorders and music sheets, they tried not to trip on the uneven paving. Some of the group had even composed new tunes for the performance. Angela's version had been listened to, and rejected, as being too simple. Gerald and the Troubadours preferred their music to be full of ornamentation and harmonies.

'Oh, this headache,' she thought, 'Hope it's not a migraine.'

Angela watched the retreating backs of the Troupe as they disappeared up the winding cobbled path. She stroked her temples to ease the pain.

'I should cut through here. Cool down a bit in the shade. Then catch them as they turn back round, further up the hill. Good plan!'

Angela giggled as she stepped through the clematis draped, rose-fragranced archway, then tripped and tumbled down aged flagstones into the twilight shadows.

The touch of tiny fingers stroking her hair, and a splash of water on her face brought Angela back from her chaotic dream of tumbling through swirling mists.

'Oh heck, what have I landed in? What a stink! Oh, my leg!'

Angela opened her eyes, and the gentle fingers retreated, along with the ragged urchins they belonged to. She wasn't sprawled on the ground, as she expected, but propped up against a rough wooden door with her dress arranged decently around her. She licked her lips. The oldest child, with a water jug, knelt down so Angela could drink from it. Parched though she was, she resisted the temptation. Instead she took the offering, dipped her finger into the water and raised it to cool her forehead. The other children gasped, knelt down, raised their fingers…and blessed themselves.

As Angela gathered herself to get up and go, she noticed more of the skinny waifs edging from the shadows towards her.

'Why are you kids not invited to the festivities? Not pretty enough for the tourist brochures? Tucked down this festering alley out of sight!'

She picked up her recorder. The youngsters edged nearer.

'Oh what the heck. It's my only chance to play it. I like it, even if the Troubs don't...I am Angela, and this is my very own tune. No harmonies and no ornamentation.'

The children were as still and silent as statues.

She tried again, 'Je suis Angela...Ang-e-la...Ange...et c'est ma musique.'

'Ange...Ange...c'est une Ange!' they whispered back.

Angela sat back down and patted the paving stones around her. Some of the smallest children crept closer bringing with them the aroma of warm, unwashed infants. Angela didn't mind. Realising that never again would she have such an appreciative audience, she treated the children to her full repertoire of basic class one recorder tunes. And then her masterpiece, a simple folksy verse and refrain in a minor key, that she truly felt would be more like the original tune played by the young boy, on those long-ago ramparts.

All the children were smiling now and swaying in time to the gentle rhythm of her melody, so she played it again...and again. The fourth time, she could hear a little bee-like buzz, as the youngsters hummed the lively chorus.

Headache completely gone now, Angela could not ever remember feeling so good about herself, so relaxed. But all idylls come to an end. One by one the children stood up and began to look around. Then Angela heard it too. A dull, menacing thud that seemed to be getting closer with each beat. The ceremony in the cathedral must have begun. The drums were part of the overture, and supposed to signify the approaching army, but somebody was getting a bit carried away with the volume, and it sounded too much like the real thing. No wonder the children were restless.

Reluctantly Angela decided she had better get moving and claim her place among Gerald's Angelic Host. As she stood up and bowed to her audience, ready to go, she realized that some of the children were crying. Angela felt a grave-goose shiver down her back. Why were they so sad and scared? It was just a performance.

'How awful! And I have nothing to give them. Or…maybe?'

She bowed again and gave her recorder to the oldest child, the water carrier. She had seen him copying her fingering as she played her own special tune. He put the recorder to his lips and started to blow…squeaky at first, then pure woody tones fed the cooling air, as he took her music and made it his own.

Angela slipped away through the archway that she hoped would take her nearer to the church. As she stepped towards the glowing street lamps, a gust of dusty wind blew into her eyes, swirling her skirt, disorientating her. She looked back, but the children had gone. Angela took time to steady herself. Keeping her head down, and taking care not to trip again, she followed the faint sound of tambours, timbrels and harmonious woodwind, towards her destination. She was nearly there.

Waiting for her, as it had done for centuries, was the hilltop cathedral, built in thanksgiving to celebrate an Angel in white who fell to earth long ago, and with her gift of music, helped to save the whole town.

MAYBE MORE

Mary Brown

It all started one night over a few drinks. My friend was enthusing about the new man she'd met online.

'Why don't you try it,' she said, 'it's time you had someone special in your life.'

I wasn't that sure I needed anyone in my life, but a couple of drinks later, decided to go for it.

We created my profile, choosing a photo from a few years ago. Well, doesn't everyone? It's like a CV. You highlight your best qualities. Minimise the negatives.

That done, we started on the interesting bit. Checking out what's on offer.

'Here's one,' she said, 'he looks presentable. Active, retired gentleman, enjoys gardening, dining out, and travelling, would like to meet an active lady with similar interests for outings, companionship and maybe more.'

'Now, I don't mind the gardening, dining out and travelling, it's the maybe more that's a wee bit worrying. I'm not doing anything that involves the removal of clothing.'

It's not that I haven't had my moments in the past, but it's been that long since I've been gripped by passion that I don't know if I'm in full working order.

A week or two later, I had built up a small group of friends to chat to and one or two seemed quite promising. Especially Alex. We met up and enjoyed a meal or two and talk got around to gardening.

My garden was getting a bit too much for me and I wanted some advice.

He offered to help, and very soon my front garden was transformed with gravel chips and pot plants. So much easier to manage.

Unfortunately, he was a little less easy to manage, so it was back to the laptop.

Next was Bill, a retired builder. He showed me photos of the paved area he'd built in his back garden. I was well impressed.

A few weeks later, he had finished the patio, and I had finished the relationship, which was becoming a bit too intense.

John was next. A retired electrician. He was talking about how lighting can make a difference to the ambience of a room, and before you know it, he'd installed some downlighters in my bathroom, with a light up mirror to finish it off.

A few weeks later, I was lying in the bath admiring the lighting when I thought, 'I could change those tiles.'

Well, I was back at the keyboard before the water had even run out of the bath.

I'm meeting Mike on Saturday.

Just for lunch.

Or maybe more.

FIFTIES CHILD

Elizabeth Carey

What is it about a new crisp covering of snow which awakens the senses? The clarity of light, the brightness of the sun shining on to this untrodden carpet, glistening like twinkling stars. The spectacular and intricately formed spider webs suspended between the hedgerow branches, a testament to the hard work of this little insect. Frosted, white and frozen, such a beautiful sight to behold! Waterfalls frozen in time forming icicles, hanging like spears pointed, dripping at their extremities – Nature's gift to brighten spirits and uplift souls – little did we know then that these memories were being tucked away in our own special memory box.

The crunch of footsteps leaving their pattern on newly fallen snow – the joy of identifying animals' pawprints and footprints of birds as they forage for food underneath the snow. The sound of laughter from children having snowball fights – sledging in homemade sledges down the slopes of nearby farmers' fields. The silence and eeriness of walking in the park on our journey home from school as dusk fell – plumes of vapour trumpeting forth involuntarily from our mouths and noses as the temperature plummeted.

Shivering memories of chilled feet encased in 'wellie' boots, toes numb from the icy, freezing, slushy snow, thawing out in basins of warm water – sipping a steaming mug of hot chocolate or Ovaltine, warmed by the glow of the anthracite stove in our kitchen, invokes vivid memories. Wintergreen ointment, Snowfire – a green 'gooey' substance was applied to chilblains – red, itchy areas on big toes – as a result of circulation problems caused by cold feet. Socks were worn in bed at night to allow this remedy to soothe and reduce the inflammation in these areas.

Doctors' visits were very rare as each household had their own remedies for dealing with winter coughs and colds. The lingering smell of Vicks menthol ointment – rubbed on to our chests was the 'cure-all.' The liberty bodice with the rubber buttons to secure and warm our chests following the application of this rub is a powerful memory.

Waking up, opening the curtains to see ice on the inside of the windows was a regular occurrence. Drawing patterns on the frosted glass, scraping off the frosty film to see out to view the frozen wonderland. Very few homes had central heating, cold bedrooms were just an accepted part of winter. Somehow it didn't seem to worry us as we were very cosy in bed! No duvets, pure wool blankets and candlewick top covers and, of course, hot water bottles – stoneware bottles commonly called 'pigs'.

Tasting Mum's homemade Scotch broth was a ritual on a Saturday night after watching *Dixon of Dock Green* and the scary futuristic *Quatermass*. Trying to get the sixpence out of a clootie dumpling took many attempts, the pleasure of tasting this spicy treat is a lasting memory of winter nights, and birthday celebrations. Comforting wholesome food was the order of the day on these nights, as we watched the flames of the coal fire flickering, creating images on the walls, firing imaginations. Toasting bread using a toasting fork, then spreading a mixture of butter and cinnamon on to the hot bread was a real treat.

Christmas decorations were made, not bought, as coloured strips of paper were linked together to form 'paper chains' which crisscrossed to create colourful canopies across the ceilings of the house. Chinese lanterns were strung from the centre points, creating a truly festive 'grotto like' feel. The smell of pine from the real Christmas tree heralded the coming of Christmas. Dad was very tall with large feet, and his socks became our stockings for Santa to fill with chocolate pennies, tangerines, and small gifts. The aroma of tangerine on Christmas morning still lingers in my memory.

The seasons did tend to be more defined as a child growing up in the 1950s, warm summers followed by really cold winters. Fog was a problem due to the use of coal as a means of heating homes, which created havoc for travel anywhere. Walking to school in fog was a regular occurrence, holding my friend's hand, as we warily took steps forward on the well learned path, from home to school. Very few people had cars, my father was a teacher and did not have his first car until 1961 when I was 14 – people relied on public transport. Breaking ice that had formed on the pavements was a childhood delight when we heard the cracking noise, like breaking glass. When the sun broke through it looked like an orange ball suspended in the murky fog, creating a haunting eerie image as it hung low in the winter sky.

Sights, sounds, tastes and smells stimulate memories of childhood, the reassuring touch of hands on a dimly lit foggy street, invoke that memory box to be unlocked. Nature provided that stimulation and it was freely available to embrace. As an adult, looking back at life in the 1950s, life was simpler, demands were less, we thrived and grew up with memories of our own very special winter wonderlands.

Will the phone-gawking children of today have those kinds of memories? It is hoped that the fears and apprehensions surrounding children growing up may not interfere with their ability to experience Nature out of doors in all seasons. Climate change has interfered with our weather patterns – wetter, milder winters, grey dreich days where the sea meets the sky. What different kinds of memories are being stored in young people's memory boxes?

As with each generation, changes occur socially and culturally. However, Nature remains constant throughout the seasons. Do we take time to marvel at this wonderland in all its glory?

BESIDE THE GARDEN PATH

Patricia Hutchinson

I watch *him* every summer night, hunkering and stooping.
His skyward gaze for weather-hints, behind a gnarled hand.
He pulls and plucks the jaunty weeds, and snips the withered heads,
scuffling on to leave behind boot indents in the soil.
No space for those who're past their best on that small square of world.
To the right of the garden path.

Pale, gauzy, petals flutter, snag on prickles, or float down
to mulch the rich brown loamy soil, that feeds the vibrant buds
who nudge them carelessly aside, beguile with youth and beauty.
Round and round he prowls, picking on the less-than-perfect,
the mis-matched, the old, the crumpled, the frail.
He turns chaos into order.

I watch *her* every summer night, sowing seeds and planting
sprigs in tiny pots, crammed on a zigzag of old wood trays.
The sun is low, the sky streaked pink; the shadows stretching.
Climbers and trailers shift and sway, wafting scents to
tempt butterflies and bees, to fill the air with bliss.
To the left of the garden path.

Flowers that have gifted their all, hang their blowsy heads,
buds just awakening, and exquisite blossoms, jostle for attention
like life itself. Perhaps not neat, but beautiful, diverse,
the freedom to be what you would be, to wander and to breathe.
Multi-coloured, wild and free; a magical secret garden.
She turns order into chaos.

But I have observed, when dusk blankets the earth,
when flowers and folk are slumbering, he goes out,
soundless, stealthy, for one late night garden tour.
And I have seen her peeping out, watching, smiling fondly,
while he snips and shears, and clips and picks.
They are different squares on the same patchwork quilt.
Together, contrarily, they serve the earth.

JUST ANOTHER FUNERAL

Sinclair Steven

It was a cliché come to life: a louring sky over a hilltop cemetery; frozen ground – the frosted turf a pallid stubble; the widow at the foot of the grave, a hankie just visible through the black veil, dabbing her eyes; beside her the sullen step-son while supporting her other flank hovered the tall, thin figure of the minister – in his long, black coat, a stick of liquorice, crowned by a pink Oddfellow lozenge, a dreep hanging from its nose; clustered round the open grave a minor cast of carrion crows in hastily purchased, ill-fitting black suits, sucking on fags. In the mind's ear it was almost possible to hear the whirr of the cameras through slow, solemn music. Looking at the minor mourners Cooper's mind drifted to the old song that heralded every New Year of his youth: 'Three craws sat upon a wa', Sat upon a wa', Sat upon a wa…a..a..a, Nae craw hud a brain cell at a', Oan a cauld and frosty morning'. The three of them were the remnants of the deceased Boab's criminal gang: leaderless and confused (which didn't take much) they were ripe for Cooper to take over. He wondered if that was likely to be a profitable move. He shook his head and impatiently called them to order, pushing a coffin cord into puzzled hands and hassling young Donald to the top right corner.

'Right, ye bams. When the cemetery guys, the wans who know whit they're daein, when they lift the weight o the coffin and lower it intae the hole, you lot jist staun there wi the cords, pretend you're lowerin' the thing. Don't fir Christ's sake try tae actually dae any lowerin', take any weight. Last thing we need the day is fir Boab there in the box tae pull wan o you clowns doon intae the hole wi him. Though it might be a blessin if he gets rid o some o ye noo he's deid as he should o done when he was still breathin. Ye ready, Donald? Ye know whit yir daein? Dae ah need to spell it oot again fir ye? Naw? Good.'

Shona, the grieving widow, and the nasally afflicted minister moved to the head of the grave. Cooper had suspicions Shona had played some role in the sudden 'heart attack' that had struck down her significantly older husband, but that was for another day. Today was about mourning the deceased.

As the gravediggers took the strain and the crows shuffled awkwardly forward, a figure, the twin of Donald, strode dramatically forward from behind a nearby stone angel. He pushed one of the crows aside and took up his cord. 'It is my right,' he declared.

'Aw fir fuck's sake, whit are you daein here, Robert?' despaired Cooper. 'You were run off, five years ago. Warned no tae come back. Noo yir here, poppin up like the Ghost o Christmas, Easter, the Fair Hoalidays Past. Why son? Why?'

'It is my right,' Robert declaimed once more. 'My duty, even as the prodigal son, to honour my father.'

The gravediggers swiftly lowered the box into the grave dispensing with all ceremony and stepped back to enjoy the show. Donald stretched over the gaping grave and weakly swung a fist at his brother, nearly toppling in on top of his father in the process. 'Only I have the right to honour my father,' he shouted. 'I loved him. Forty thousand sons such as you could not, with all their false love, make up my sum.'

Robert leapt down onto the coffin and embraced it. 'Pile the dirt upon the quick and dead, till of this grave a mountain you have made.' One of the grave diggers picked up a shovel and moved to the heap of soil forcing Cooper to intervene.

'Naw pal, temptin though it is, best not. An you two couple o hams cut it oot. Ah telt Boab no tae send you tae Drama School. Laurence Olivier wid turn in his grave.' Cooper glanced down at the coffin as if expecting to see some birling going on down there too. 'An we've aw seen *Hamlet*.' He looked at the crows, 'Well, ah've seen *Hamlet*, an yir no in the same league, no even in the same game. Honour yir faither? Honour? He wis a vicious, bullyin, wee bastard.' Cooper glanced over to the widow, 'Sorry, Shona doll, but ye know it's true.' The veiled head nodded agreement.

'You son', pointing to Donald, 'yir faither thought ye wir a nonce, a potential kiddy-fiddler. An you,' he looked at Robert, 'he said you wir a rat-tailed worm of ingratitude. Metaphor wis never Boab's forte, but ahm sure ye get the gist. Sendin ye baith tae that so-called drama school wis wan o his sick, twisted jokes. He knew ye wir goin tae be nae bloody use in the business, so decided if ye were goin to make erses o yirsels then daein it in front o audiences wid gie him an extra frisson o pleasure.'

'Billy. Jamsie,' he pointed to two of the crows. 'Huckle that scunner doon tae Central Station an shove him oan a train south. It disny matter whit train, just south, far south, far, far south.' He grimaced at Robert. 'If you show your lily-white erse up here again, ye'll go back freight, deid freight. Unnerstaun? The rest o us will adjourn tae the pub where nae doot the bridies an sausage rolls will be coolin tae a temperature tae match ma toes here in this Godforsaken, freezing wasteland. Sorry Reverend but ahm sure ye'll agree. If ye'll jist escort Shona back tae the cars an get yirsel a wee malt at the bar, ah'll be jist at the back o ye.'

As the funeral party wound their way back to the entrance, Cooper's eyes took in the three naked trees crowning the small hill and the detritus of autumn skirling in the chill breeze. A few lines of a poem he read years ago surfaced in his mind:

> And a few leaves lay on the starving sod –
> They had fallen from an ash and were grey.

'Aye,' he thought, 'you can always rely on Thomas Hardy tae add cheer tae a happy scene.' He looked down at the coffin, 'Ye were a pain in the erse when ye wir alive Boab, ah jist hope yir no goin tae keep oan bein a pain in the erse noo yir deid.' He kicked a convenient turf down on to the casket, handed some twenties to the gravediggers, muttered his thanks and followed the rest down the narrow path.

HUSH

Sharon Bairden

'I'm going to kill her.'

'Where's my mummy? Is it time to go home yet? Mummy, mummy…'

My legs give way as I stuff my fist in my mouth and scream. Incessant demands.

'Shut up, shut up. Please shut up,' I mutter trying to drown out the voice.

I melt into the floor, trying to disappear.

Outside the voice whimpers, *'Mummy, mummy, I want my mummy.'*

Something snaps inside me. My decision made, I take her by the hand.

'Mummy, are we going home now?'

'Hush', I soothe, leading her into the bedroom, 'lie down, I'll tuck you in.'

Forcing her onto the bed, I shut my mind against the struggle.

I pick up the pillow, place it over her face and push it down. 'Hush now, sleep, please sleep.'

A minute…two…three …four. The struggling stops. I drop to the floor. Relieved. Calm.

The rattle of the letterbox forces me out my thoughts. I have no idea how long I've lain there.

A voice barks through the letterbox, 'It's me. Are you there? Is everything ok?'

I shuffle to the door, unlatch it and peer out. The blue uniform of the carer is instantly recognisable.

'Hush', I've just got her off. She's had a bad day. I think she'll sleep well now.'

The carer gives me a reassuring smile. 'You're doing grand. Dementia is not an easy condition to live with, love.'

I try to smile. 'Please don't wake her,' I whisper as I let her in.

ONE SWALLOW

Don J Taylor

Afterwards, they said: *Kathy, you should get away. A change of scene will do you good. Try to put some weight back on.*

A quick hug on the doorstep; then they drove away, avoiding the pothole Jim always meant to fix. That annoying peep on the horn when passing out of the gate.

I tied on an apron, to protect my cherry-red dress and started on the dishes. Then I chopped up leftover sausage rolls for the birds. Jean was vexed I didn't wear black.

'It would have been more appropriate, Mum,' she said.

'Your father liked me in this,' I replied. 'Surely that's what matters? Anyway, I thought you hated the conventional.'

I sat down with the pile of mail. A Saga brochure: cruise ships, fjords, well-groomed, white-of-tooth sixty-somethings leaning on the ship's rail; couples, always couples, with the mandatory glass of piss-yellow Chardonnay. Flyers for outdoor gear, gadgets you thought you'd never need (you don't), plant catalogues. I'd need to clear out the greenhouse – all those mouldy seed trays.

A card from Jim's work – inside, a chaotic array of messages from people I never met. Useless.

Jean's right, of course, best not to be in the house alone. Not just yet. And, yes, I get that she's short of space, especially with a baby brother for Ellie on the way. It would probably suit everyone if I just disappeared for a bit. They've spent more than enough emotional energy on me in the last fortnight – the last *two years*! I'm well over my quota.

So, I had a look online: somewhere self-catering. I had always fancied Scotland. In Jim's last months, I'd re-read Sir Walter Scott at the hospital, to pass the time. A throwback to Eng. Lit I at Uni. *Origins of the Historical Novel:* the class where Jim and I first met. Anyway, *Rob Roy* started me thinking about a trip to the Trossachs.

'What's a Trossach?' Jean asked, her face frozen in a grimace on the phone screen.

I ignored that. 'I've been thinking, you and Ellie can come with me for a day or two, it won't be *me* landing on *you*. It looks lovely: romantic lochs and brooding crags. I've found a little cottage beside the river Endrick. It's called *Honeyholm*. The name says it all, doesn't it? Only an hour north of Glasgow. Remember that lovely time we all had at Harlech one spring – the daffodils down by the river, and the lambs? Ellie would love the lambs.'

'Mum, it rained solid in Wales for a week. I was 14, and *way* past anthropomorphising lambs torn from their mothers, then, quick as you like, carted off to have their throats slit.'

'I don't think they actually…*Do* they?'

‘Mum, I just don’t have the time. You go. Enjoy yourself. A new beginning. It’ll do you good.’

So here I am, solo, nursing a lukewarm coffee at a dismal factory outlet in Gretna. I stare out though through the rain-streaked café window at a deserted car park. ‘Rough winds’, and all that. Then, a stop at an Asda somewhere in Lanarkshire. Litter everywhere. I buy groceries for a week and head straight to *Honeyholm*.

The cottage nestles in a tiny hamlet with a handful of houses, a boarded-up school, and a church. Services once a month, the sign says. Interest in the eternal is ebbing away, it seems. From the outside, thank God, the house is as pretty as I had hoped. But inside it’s airless and damp.

A grassy bank, too steep to call a lawn, (how they cut the grass, I’ll never know) slopes down to the Endrick Water. The river trickles thinly over a rocky bed. Downstream, where an old weir holds back the flow, the stream deepens into a gloomy pool. Swallows snap flies inches above the swirling peaty water. Their beaks make a rhythmic click, click, click, as they swoop and pirouette, then scoot away, ankle-high, over the grass.

The night follows a now familiar pattern: hours of sleeplessness, tea and more tea; then, eventually, a creeping, half-hearted, dawn.

I doze most of the morning, and since there’s no let-up in the weather, I drive into the next village for milk. The shop smells of firelighters and fabric softener. The shopkeeper glances up from her *Take a Break* but says nothing. I bring a carton of milk to the counter, then grab a cottage pie at random from the cool cabinet. I don't want the woman to think I came in just for something to do.

'I thought this might be nice for lunch,' I say. 'I see it's made locally...artisan.'

'Never tried them myself. Folk buy them, mind. That'll be three eighty.'

'Speaking of cottages...'

She stared at me blankly.

'The pie...' I say with a nervous giggle, then: 'I'm staying down at *Honeyholm*. It's lovely.'

'I guessed as much,' she says. No smile. 'Only place renting at this time of year.'

'Oh well, I'd best be off and heat up my pie. Bye.'

She turned back to her Sudoku.

The next day, a knock at the door; a neighbour wanting a chat, perhaps.

A young man in a mud-splattered, navy blue boiler suit, about the same age as Jean, I'd say. High, sharp cheekbones, a bluebird tattoo below one ear, and one of those haircuts with the sides shaved leaving a mop on top. They remind me of Nazis. Sinister. Behind him, his large green tractor, engine running.

He mumbles something incomprehensible; his accent, or a speech difficulty, I'm not sure.

'Pardon?'

He speaks again, pointing down the lane past my car. I hear 'parked', 'tractor', and 'doon the brae'.

'Oh, sorry, am I in the way? I'm so sorry.'

'Aye,' he says, retreating and remounting the tractor.

I run out in my slippers. My foot slips off the clutch. The car stalls. Perched high in the tractor, he squints at his phone, fingers drumming on the steering wheel. I restart and reverse out of his way. He thunders past without even a glance in my direction.

Back inside, I lean against the lobby wall, fighting tears. A framed print hangs facing me: a map, dated 1728, shows a corn mill a bit downriver. I imagine the little community that perhaps once thrived here: industrious, cooperative, ordered. As I indulge my daydream, a watery sunlight flits across the hall floor. A chance for a walk, maybe. Before heading out I open the bedroom window, leaving the front door ajar to air the house.

A faint trace of a path leads to a meadow bounded by a curve of beech trees. Primroses cluster around the wall at the end of the weir. I spot the millrace on the far side, dry and overgrown, that once channelled the water to power the wheel. The mill itself has been converted into a home, with neat lawns, a perfect golden gravel drive, a paddock and a horse box out the back. A chilly gust of wind sweeps down from the hills, disturbing the pool's surface. I've packed all the wrong clothes. I turn back to the cottage to get warmed up.

The boiled kettle clicks off. A faint knocking comes from the bedroom. I think of surly tractor boy. Don't be ridiculous! He may have been rude, but he wouldn't mean any harm, surely? I pick up the rolling pin from the worktop – just as a kind of prop, really. As I approach the bedroom, the noise continues: a sort of beat, beat, beat, followed by a scrabbling.

A sickle-shaped shadow flickers in the window. Sandwiched between the two panes of the casement: a swallow.

Its wings twitch uselessly within the narrow space. It sees me and redoubles its efforts to escape. I have to act or it will die. I lay the rolling pin on the windowsill, with a pang of shame for thinking ill of the young farmer. He probably hadn't given me a second thought.

By standing on tiptoe, I can get just enough height to insert my wrist *(oh, how skinny I've become!)* between the gap, and reach the tip of one wing. With the stiff feathers held gently between crossed fingers, I ease the bird out. The soft warmth of the tiny body glows in my fist. It fixes me with its button-black eye. I feel its heart beating in my palm; that tiny heart, no bigger than a grain of rice. How many million pulses to speed it over 6,000 miles? Cape Town to *Honeyholm.* I take her (I'm sure she's a *her)* to the front door and set her free. She skims low over the river.

I look up and see the tractor swing round the corner and bounce up the rutted lane. The young man waves. Was there, perhaps, a smile?

Next morning the sun blazes from a pure blue sky. I take my coffee out to the carved wooden bench set against the cottage wall. The crab apple's limbs thrust skyward, spurred and budded; ruby blossoms primed to unfold.

I rest against the warmed stones and receive the sun's stored comfort.

MADRAS MORNINGS

FOR LEELA

Julie McNeill

On this Madras morning
I find myself combing
for your prayer card,
the one you gifted me
in Saint Andrews before
searing burnt orange
into Highland clay.

I reach for your books
signed on my shelf,
your laugh: *well*
everybody likes a
good murder
scroll your Twitter
and find your last
post is one encouraging
me, and the one
before that, the same
and it leaves me bereft.

I don't know where
to put your kindness
where to keep it now.
A self-assured woman

with so much left
to say. I will write for
you because what else
can we do
but chisel away
fold up your words,
your warmth
and let them
weave their way
with mine.

THE MELODEON

Sam Oakley

Jesus, what a mess: ancient cardboard boxes, bulging suitcases, bin bags, fraying wicker garden chairs, a hat stand, toffee tins, old hoovers and god only knows what those dark shapes were lurking under the eaves. Dad and I just stood there and looked at it, shadows swaying alarmingly after I'd bashed my stupid head on the dangling lightbulb. I bet he'd rigged that up for her. The air felt cold, damp, thick with dust; Dad did that nervy cough.

'Your nan always was a wee bit of a hoarder.'

'Aye, aye, I can see that.' The hangover clutched at my head; a sudden yearning to be suffering at work like a normal bloke. Dad was edging round, trying not to step on the junk, perilously close to the edge of the boards.

'Her whole life is here. That hat stand was my nan's – it used to be in the parlour at Rackham Road.' He reached out a hand and stroked the dark wood. 'How on earth did she get it up here? Your gramps probably, eh? Daft old bugger.' His laugh had no mirth in it and it trailed off. 'He'd do anything for her, you know…'

His voice broke and I stepped back too fast, nearly falling off the beam until I grabbed at a rafter. We didn't do emotion. His only concession at the funeral had been red rimmed eyes and one massive sniff but soon he was bellowing 'The Lord's My Shepherd' along with the rest of them. Still, the funeral had been a picnic compared with this. I reached up and stopped the lightbulb's slow swing. Dad was fumbling for a handkerchief, and I turned away, smeared some dust off a nearby painting to see what was underneath. Some gloomy old hillside, a bit like the one outside.

'I appreciate you're here to help, Son.' He blew his nose like a trumpet, eyes watery beneath that hedge of eyebrows. 'Goodness knows what we'd have done. It's too much for your old parents. Perhaps there is a positive to all that's happened this year, eh?'

'Oh aye, it was definitely worth it. Lost all my savings buying freedom from that two-timing cow, sold my flat, lost my job, no life, no self-respect but yeah, fabulous, I can clear nan's loft!'

I gave the nearest box a shove with my foot and the TV aerial fell over. He didn't look at me, just reached over to right it. Then he said softly,

'Nobody made you marry her, Son. We all make mistakes.'

'Since when did you make any?' Happily married for over 40 years, a shelf of awards and beaming team photos to remind me each visit how I was the big family failure.

'Well, your nan had a lot of opinions on that.' Dad was stuffing the hanky back in his pocket. 'I'm not sure she ever forgave me for not taking over the shop. Or marrying a Welsh girl. Or moving to Dumfries…there was quite a list. She wasn't always an easy woman, your nan, God rest her soul.'

Uh-oh, the hanky was coming back out. I started hefting the nearest pile of bin bags, trying not to breathe in the stale dust that I'd disturbed.

'These are full of clothes. I'll give them to Mum.'

There was another honk of a nose blow as I manoeuvred two bulging sacks to the hatch and stepped back onto that creaky ladder. Halfway down, a bin bag balanced on my aching head, a hand slapped my belly and made me jump.

'Where on earth did all this tummy come from? That woman never fed you properly!'

'Christ, Mum, I nearly dropped this on your head!'

'You won't meet anyone else with a belly like that. Look at your Uncle Stuart!' She had hands on hips, rubber gloves and a dirty apron. I guessed the kitchen had already been dispatched.

'There's about five more of these.' I dumped the bags at her feet, tucked in my shirt and started back up. 'This is gonna take fucking ages.'

'Language! You're in your nan's house.'

'Aye well, she's dead. You'd be swearing too if you could see all the crap she's left us.'

Mum was tugging on my shirt again, lowering her voice to that stage whisper she thought nobody could overhear.

'Take care of your da, Alun. It's a hard time for him, so it is.'

I inhaled sharply, knowing she'd heard us up there, feeling that gentle rebuke. I couldn't even get this right. I heaved myself back up the ladder into the gloom.

Dad was still standing there, one unsteady hand still brushing cobwebs off the hat stand.

'Better make a start, eh?' I rubbed my hands together, trying to generate some energy. He must be freezing up here.

'It's all just clutter once you're gone.' He slowly wiped the dirt from his hands, and I felt the cold, damp of the grave closing round me. I squatted down and picked up an ancient Monopoly box.

'This might fetch a bit?'

'She was probably saving it for the great grandkids.'

'Well that's not gonna happen now.' I slung it back in the crate and started sifting through: playing cards, some old school exercise books, sheets of music. I held them out to him. 'Did you want these?'

'That's Stuart's organ music. He got to Grade Four.' Dad took them and squinted at the yellowing pages. 'He might like it I suppose. Hang on, what's this…' He thrust the music back at me and swung across to reach for a squarish black box, nearly toppling when it didn't shift. I cleared a space as he heaved it over. 'Well, well, well – you're going to like this!'

He was usually wrong. I watched as he dusted it down and unclasped the buckles. The case flipped back with a clatter to reveal an outrageously gaudy red silk interior. There it lay, black and shiny, ivory buttons gleaming, ornate inlay, a frayed leather strap; the bellows actually looked intact. 'Scandalli' was written in a silver swirl down one side.

'Well, I never!' He ran a finger over the writing. 'This was Dad's pride and joy. Every weekend he took her out for a tune – used to play down the club with Jock and Sweeney. I had no idea Mum had kept it.'

He hoisted it up and managed to rest his foot on a box to support the weight.

'Can you play it?' I slumped down onto a leather trunk which creaked ominously.

'A little. The reeds are probably…' He gave a gentle push and pull. The sound was loud and discordant, a groan of complaint. He didn't give up though. Head bent, he tried one button after another, in and out. A couple seemed gone, but before long he was getting a slow air out of it. I'd forgotten how good he was – it'd been years since I'd heard him. As he played his faltering lament suddenly all I could see was the liver spots, the wayward hairs, the wrinkled bags under his eyes. How long before I'd be clearing his loft? Only I wouldn't have some self-centred, pathetic excuse of a son to keep me company. He drew out the plaintive final note and the sound died away. Downstairs I heard the faint sound of mum clapping.

'That was one of Dad's tunes. He…sorry, Son.'

He almost dropped it on the floor as he turned away, shoulders shaking.

I sat there for a while, rubbing three day's stubble. When you think you've hit rock bottom, turns out there's a whole new level waiting for you under a hidden trapdoor. In the end, I tugged it round and got it up on my lap. One hand worked those little buttons on the left, the other produced a few random notes on the longer rows. Trying again, I held down a single button and, following his example, pulled out gently then pushed back in. It didn't sound great, but it didn't sound awful either. As I tried a few more I sensed he'd turned back. After a few false starts, I got a bit of a scale going.

'So, is it meant to be in some sort of key, Da? The reeds sound well dodgy.'

Dad gave a shrug.

'D/G, perhaps? Stuart could probably fix it up. If you wanted?'

'Me?'

'Why not? You were good at piano.' He sunk into the chair and rubbed his eyes. 'What a time it's been. What a bloody awful time.'

I just kept squeezing, in and out, like breathing. He was watching me now from under those mad eyebrows.

'I could dust off my fiddle if you need a bit of encouragement.'

'I suppose I could give it a go.' I paused to tug a strap over one shoulder. The weight shifted. 'Not much else to do.'

'Marvellous!' And didn't it just burst out of him like it really could be.

HEIDS

Hugh McMillan

Ye wunner at nicht
whit cocophony o noise
fills this howe place.
Deariefu coronachs
tae the lang deid
the lang forgot
the lang dishonourt.
Whit yince seemed braw
an blashy noo a museum
tae an ignoble past.
Which heids crie the loodest?
No yer presidents
or burghers.
The fowk wha neer
had their meenit in the sun.
The makars.
The temple builders.

A BIRD IN THE HAND

Liz Heron

A sudden, stabbing pain saw off the vestiges of troubled sleep. The plink, plink of water dripping from the cracked ceiling momentarily distracted him as he began to gather his conniving thoughts. Reaching out from his dishevelled bed, Octavius's gnarled, arthritic hand groped around the damp floor for his old boots. And he dared to hope.

Buttoning his worn overcoat, he made for the back stairs and felt his way gingerly down in the gloom, his hands scuffing against the ragged walls. The gods might smile on him yet. Outside the shop, he peered at the tired, lopsided sign in the window. 'Octavius Nest – Est. 1851,' he mumbled, and he let himself in. Focused now, he stoked the stove with the last of the wood. Ambivalence would not serve him well.

The shop bell jingled. Looking up, his mind began to race, but his expression gave nothing away.

'Do come in my good fellow. Leave your brolly in the stand and warm yourself by the stove.'

A pursy, outwardly jovial fellow, Octavius cultivated bonhomie in his business dealings. No sign of the twisted soul lurking within, gnawing at suppressed inadequacies.

'Don't mind if I do, Octavius. The heavens have opened today alright,' he chirped.

This was Rupert Owlerbottom's third visit to the shop and Octavius still wasn't sure. Gullible? Almost certainly. But did he fit the bill? Owlerbottom was fixated on a stuffed owl he hadn't noticed before. Teetering on the top shelf, it looked inquisitively down at him. Octavius would consult it later.

'I've acquired a few unusual specimens that might interest you, Mr Owlerbottom,' he beamed.

'Oh, Rupert, please,' he simpered.

'Come Rupert, follow me.'

As Octavius limped towards the back shop, Owlerbottom couldn't help but think that his bald head resembled an egg in a cup. The inner sanctum was reserved for gentlemen of a certain social class, and the debonair, well-heeled Rupert Owlerbottom epitomised the uppermost echelons. There in a nest-like basket lay a clutch of little grebe eggs. This esoteric delight would have escaped the average Victorian oologist as, white with brown freckles, they were relatively common and unremarkable. Nonetheless rapture was the watchword as the pair effused silent admiration. Neither was, however, sincere.

'I'll have those, Octavius.'

Slowly closing the rickety cash drawer, Octavius watched as Owlerbottom waltzed out of the shop, excitedly clutching his prize eggs in one hand while waving the other over his head with just a discernible degree of condescension. Octavius was a slave to slights real and imagined and jealousy was at the core of his blighted existence.

'Will 'e do, Hooter?' he enquired looking up. 'We'll see. We'll see,' he mused.

The owl stared pensively down, like Octavius, reserving judgement. Owlerbottom's expensive umbrella stood abandoned in the stand; an opalescent bumble bee adorned the handle. *He'll be back*, he thought. Had he peered after him he would have seen a haunted figure scurry over the cobbles and out of sight. Instead, he wrested a crumpled pamphlet from his bulging waistcoat, unfolded it carefully and spread it out on the counter in front of him.

Back in his hotel room Owlerbottom dumped the eggs on the table and began to catch his breath.

'Find out, did you?'

Startled, he swung round. Linus Talon's long legs were draped over the shabby velvet chair, his hands clasped behind his head, awaiting the verdict.

'Not exactly, Linus.'

'What does that mean, exactly?' he hissed, propelling himself forward. 'I heard the old codger muttering to himself about it in the Slurping Toad. Sounded convincing to me! Does he have the bird or not?'

'Well, I saw a trail of blue feathers, the right colour for the female. I didn't want to arouse suspicion. I'll need to go back.'

'Yes, you will, Owler. Your very liberty depends upon it and don't you forget it.'

Owlerbottom slept badly these days. If only temptation hadn't deprived him of his reason. If only Linus hadn't been on the American expedition. He had no doubt scraped the means together courtesy of assorted ill-gotten gains. Owlerbottom on the other hand was an affluent, enthusiastic hobbyist, albeit a relative unknown in ornithological circles. In celebration of the success of the expedition a dinner had been held by the renowned Kentuckian ornithologist Humphrey Titterton, a man of enormous wealth. While heading for the display cabinet in the hall to gaze on some rare specimens, Owlerbottom had noticed that the library door was ajar. Sitting solitary on a shelf, a bright blue-green jewel encrusted egg caught the sunlight. In that inauspicious second, he was lost. One look over his shoulder and he was in, the egg nestling in his trouser pocket. The empty stand had screamed *'thief!'* Just as the enormity of what he had done was sinking in, Linus had emerged from the shadows. Silently exuding menace, his rasping voice passed sentence.

'That'll cost you, my boy.' And so, it had.

Octavius pored over the pamphlet in the fading light.

'The reward will be mine,' he drooled.

Rumours of sightings of the rare bird had been rife and the pamphlet promised a reward beyond his wildest dreams. An egg alone would suffice. The bird and an egg would be life changing. Not only had he spotted the female Egyptian zou zou, unheard of on British shores, but thanks to his skill as a marksman, it was already perched lifelike and lifeless in his secluded workshop. And, if she had indeed laid, he would have an egg. He allowed himself to imagine his physical and material transformation. He would lose weight. His flabby chin would no longer be one with his neck. He would frequent the best tailors. Lost in reverie he failed to notice the smaller print at the bottom of the page announcing the theft of a priceless egg in America along with an artist's impression of a possible suspect – a wanted poster.

What to do? Owlerbottom would surely return for his brolly. Yes, he would approach him. He was quite prepared to take advantage of his naivety. He had paid well over the odds for the common little grebe eggs. He would ask for his help in the most deferential manner. Flattery should tip the balance and Owlerbottom would have no idea what was at stake. Octavius had observed the bird for some time. She had nested in a tall oak, and he had no chance of getting up there himself. Shooting the bird had been easy. Retrieving the egg was a job for Owlerbottom.

As Octavius was mulling over his plan, Linus and Owlerbottom were discussing how to accomplish their own dark deed.

'Go back to the shop for your brolly,' said Linus. 'Distract him and follow the feathers. For all we know he could already have the bird and an egg or two. Use your guile and find out.'

The shop bell jingled.

'Ah, Rupert, I've been expecting you.'

Owlerbottom's jaunty demeanour belied his trepidation. He was not a professional criminal by any stretch of the imagination. However, relief came quickly with Octavius's duplicitous proposition.

'It's a relatively common egg, the hawfinch, but I don't have it in my collection, and I can't reach it myself. I thought a fine, fit fellow like yourself might do the honours for a small fee. I've been staking it out for weeks now, and I'm sure I know the very tree. Its nest is on a horizontal branch, well out from the trunk, so you'll have to be nimble.'

Progress. Owlerbottom didn't hesitate. Linus had promised him he'd be off the hook if this worked out well.

'Meet me here tomorrow morning at seven. It's only about three miles away and the whole business shouldn't take long.'

Owlerbottom took his leave and his brolly and went to meet Linus.

'Good work, Owler'. We're finally getting somewhere. If you find what we're after, go back for your fee as expected. Play the innocent and ask to see his workshop. Butter him up. You've always had an interest in taxidermy and all things ornithological. That kind of thing.'

Linus pondered briefly, his dark, hooded eyes giving nothing away.

'Anyway, once we're sure he has what we're after, we'll arrange for him to be out and let ourselves in, if you get my drift. I'm not one for violence if it can be avoided.'

It was agreed.

The early morning sun saw two unlikely companions tripping along the country path towards Badgers Heath. Birdsong filled both their hearts and minds with optimism and hope. One desirous of fortune, the other freedom. It wasn't long before Octavius identified the tree.

'Well, young sir, time you put your youth and talent to good use. Up you go. Take care with the egg, and yourself of course. There may even be more than one.'

What a bonus that would be! thought Octavius, mentally embellishing his transformation.

Yes, thought Owlerbottom, although the pecuniary aspect was of much less importance to him. He wanted to be free of Linus Talon. Up he went, easily at first using the burls to secure his footing. Octavius looked anxiously on. One or two near slips and then he was astride the branch nearest to the nest. He reached in and felt around the rough interior until his hand alighted on something smooth. One egg, and one egg only. Carefully he withdrew it, and Octavius could barely contain his excitement. Owlerbottom regarded it with a mixture of wonder and relief. Just as he was placing the egg in his pouch, he became aware of a faint buzzing coming from a cavity where the branch met the trunk. Louder and louder it grew. The zou zou hadn't been the only inhabitant of the oak. He had disturbed a nest of honeybees. Looking up he saw the swarm cloud preparing to attack.

'Bees! Bees!' he cried.

Octavius looked up in disbelief.

'The egg! The egg!' he gasped.

Owlerbottom was now thrashing wildly in the tree trying to beat off his attackers. Howling in pain as the barbs penetrated his skin, a resounding crack saw him tumble through the foliage pursued by the irate residents. He landed with a thud at Octavius's feet. The moss had broken his fall, and miracle of miracles the egg was unbroken in the pouch. Octavius helped the swelling, bleeding Owlerbottom to his feet and the pair fled along the path weaving and flailing with the bees in pursuit.

Staggering into the shop at last the two men were collecting their thoughts. One daring to think he was almost home and dry, and the other determining to keep his wits about him. Octavius was alarmed to see his supposed unwitting accomplice's swollen face. A veritable pin cushion of bee stings.

'Follow me, Rupert.'

He stumbled after him into his secluded workshop, miserable, in pain and unable to speak. Following Octavius's gaze his eyes alighted on the prized Eyptian zou zou, preserved in majestic flight on the top shelf. He watched him reach up and place the egg carefully beside the bird. Owlerbottom's mind was racing. There was still some way to go before he would be out of Linus's clutches. Then, unexpectedly, the gods favoured him with a helping hand.

'I'll fetch the tweezers. Wait here.'

Octavius disappeared through a tattered, moth-eaten curtain and Owlerbottom seized his opportunity. He lifted the egg, grabbed the stuffed bird from its perch and scurried out the door. The shop bell jingled.

'A customer. How inconvenient,' muttered Octavius.

Reappearing, tweezers in hand, he looked in disbelief around the deserted workshop. Gone. Gone was Owlerbottom, the egg and the zou zou. This couldn't be happening. Sweeping obstacles out of his path, he lurched into the shop. Empty. As his new life crumbled before his eyes, his legs began to give way from under him. Slumping over the counter he watched a taunting, bright blue feather swirl and come to rest on the pamphlet. The wanted poster! Looking up his tormented eyes met Hooter's knowing stare.

A PLAY ON WORDS

David Ross

A pub, in a rundown part of Glasgow. It's a midweek evening and Wullie is sitting quietly at a corner table nursing his pint. In walks a newly promoted Salvation Army officer, Matilda, clutching copies of the War Cry. *She looks around hesitates, spies Wullie sitting alone in the corner looking at the racing section.*

WULLIE *(Over his newspaper in a stage whisper)* Who's this? Ah hope they're no lookin for money!

(Matilda approaches Wullie, as her first victim)

MATILDA Excuse me, sir. May I speak with you?

WULLIE *(In a rather nasally and throaty voice)* Whatever floats yer boat?

MATILDA Pardon.

WULLIE Just park it hen, whit da ye want?

MATILDA Can I interest you in my *War Cry*?

WULLIE *War cry* is it, are ye here to cause trouble? The only war cry aroon here is Tongs yah Bas.

MATILDA No, no I am here to save your soul.

WULLIE *(Pointing to his feet)* Ah'll no be needin yer help, these Doc Martens will last me to ma grave.

MATILDA It's your inner soul I want to save.

WULLIE These bloody boots are tight enough, there's nae room for insoles.

MATILDA You misunderstand. I'm taking about your spirit.

WULLIE Never touch them hen, stick to lager, it lasts longer.

MATILDA Goodness man, I'm a Salvationist going round the area saving souls.

WULLIE *(Pauses and studies her carefully)* A've goat it noo, whit way the bonnet and that, you're Amish! A bet you've got the pony and trap outside and that's how you're saving your shoe leather!

MATILDA How do you come to that conclusion?

WULLIE Ye canny kid me, a've seen you lot oan the telly, whit way yer funny hats, yer hoarse an certs and yer long beards…the blokes that is!

MATILDA *(Becoming exasperated and raising her voice slightly)* Let me explain, I'm a captain!

(Wullie interrupts)

WULLIE Ah wis in the navy, no a captain mind you, made it to leading haun.

MATILDA I'm a captain in the Salvation Army and I have a little car to take me round these *(Matilda looks down her nose moving her head from side to side)* establishments.

WULLIE A suppose that's better than a wee pony hey, hey, nothing to clean up eh!

MATILDA Yugo!

WULLIE Whit? Y'll need to speak up hen, am a bit Mutt and Jeff, it wis them guns oan the boats. You being a captain ye'll no whit a mean.

MATILDA *(Loudly)* YUGO!

WULLIE No yet hen, am still oan ma first pint, and there's nae need to shout.

MATILDA *(Her voice getting louder)* YUGO, it's the make of car you silly man, originally from Yugoslavia, you must remember Tito?

WULLIE *(Raises his head, pauses while pondering his reply)* Noo ave goat it you're teto. *(points at Matilda)* It's the Sally Ann, you're temperamental.

MATILDA Yes finally, but its temperance, we abstain.

WULLIE Oh ye don't want to drink that stuff, it's bloody lethal, thone Dutch painter guy, whit dae ye cry him, white van man. He went mental and cut aff his ear.

MATILDA NO! That was absinthe, we abstain, we don't imbibe.

WULLIE It wis like that when a wis in the navy, ah never abided by the rules either, that's how ah never made captain like you.

MATILDA *(Shouting)* We don't drink alcohol!

WULLIE Nae wonder yir temperamental and getting bad tempered way it.

MATILDA Jesus! I never realised that life outside would be so bloody difficult.

WULLIE Ah agree wi ye wholeheartedly hen. Ah find it tough.

MATILDA *(Calmer now)* How's that?

WULLIE Weel when ah wis in the navy they gave me two free cans of beer every day. Noo av goat to buy the bloody stuff masell!

MATILDA: *(Takes off her bonnet and throws it on the floor)* That's it I've had enough. This would drive you to drink!

WULLIE Whit can a get hen, can ah interest yea in a wee Sex on the Beach or a Harvey Wallbanger?

MATILDA *(She rises quickly from her seat and makes to leave)* You disgusting little man, how dare you!

WULLIE	Afor' ye go hen, whit' dae they cry yeh?
MATILDA	What!
WULLIE	Yer Name, whit's yer name?
MATILDA	Matilda, if you must know.
WULLIE	*(Chuckling)* Hey, Hey Waltzing Matilda eh! Whit wi awe that dancing, nae wonder ye want to save your soles!

(Matilda walks out the door)

WULLIE	*(Turns to the audience)* Goat away wi that didn't ah!

END

MAELSTROM

Pat Feehan

As he hurried across London, Lieutenant Robert Menzies felt disorientated. This was his native city but he no longer felt he belonged here. The sandbags packed in front of buildings, the barrage balloons swaying above Trafalgar Square, the gas mask bags slung over shoulders. The people had changed too, everyone wrapped up in their own thoughts, no-one making eye contact. But, today, that suited him. His time was limited.

He strode on towards Paddington Station, passing bombed-out buildings, their furniture on display like a West End stage set, curtains billowing like ghosts haunting the ruins. Children scampered amongst the rubble, but behind their laughter, Robert felt the presence of dead souls hovering in the air, their pain lingering around every corner.

He'd often felt a connection with the dead and the war had reinforced that. His mother believed it was because he and his brother, David, were identical twins, born one minute apart. David had always dismissed it as nonsense, a figment of their mother's overactive imagination. Robert wasn't so sure, sometimes he felt 'something', a hard to define sensation that someone was watching him, tapping on his shoulder, whispering in his ear.

It was that same 'something' that explained his journey today, passing through London en route to Bletchley, where his brother worked. Would David be pleased to see him? He wasn't sure. His brother had always been less outgoing than him, less welcoming. Robert loved parties, the life and soul, whereas David preferred to have his nose stuck in a book, reading about famous historical battles, or cracking the Times crossword while he ate his breakfast. It had got worse with the war but Robert acknowledged this wasn't surprising. His mother had hinted that David was doing 'something for the war effort'. She probably shouldn't have said anything, shouldn't even have known, but she had, and she did.

David had been declared medically unfit for military duties, even though the two brothers were physically identical. Apparently, it was something to do with David's mental state, not quite stable. Robert wasn't convinced and, if truth be told, he felt a little ashamed of a brother who he suspected might be shirking his wartime duties. He hoped to find out more when he spoke to David.

Robert himself had volunteered for the navy and had already witnessed enough horror and human misery to last him a lifetime. On his last voyage he'd come perilously close to joining the ranks of the casualties. Because of engine trouble, his ship, HMS Invincible, had been forced to leave the merchant convoy it was escorting across the Atlantic and head home. Limping across the North Sea, back to Portsmouth, his ship was attacked by a lone U-boat. On their own, and in their weakened state, they were easy prey. He'd already witnessed hundreds of his comrades being slaughtered by the submarines of the German Wolfpack. No matter how many precautions they took, the Germans always seemed to be waiting for them. Now it was his turn.

He'd never forget the faces of the crew as the torpedo fizzed towards them. With no time to react, every man on board was certain his time had come. They'd leaned over the rail, salt spray in their faces, staring at death approaching. Some men shouted curses others whispered prayers. But, at the very last minute, the torpedo had miraculously passed beneath the hull and one hundred men released their breaths. The U-boat immediately submerged and his ship crawled homewards. Reliving it now, the taste of saltwater filled his mouth.

The engineers reported that the ship would be out of commission for 48 hours while they sourced the necessary parts. Whatever the reason, Robert was grateful to receive this break, no matter how brief, from the horrors of war. But that brush with death had awakened 'something' in him and he'd suddenly felt an irresistible compulsion to see his brother. He'd initially dismissed it as impossible, given his active service status. But the gods had smiled on him. To his amazement, his captain had consented and Robert had been granted 24 hours leave.

Now he was about to see David for the first time since the war started. In their early years the brothers had been inseparable, they even had their own coded language that drove their parents mad. They'd retained a special bond, a private, almost telepathic, line of communication, into their twenties, but the war had set them on divergent courses. So, it was with mixed feelings that Robert was making this journey. But something was telling him he had to see it through. He was a bit fuzzy on the travel details but he'd work it out, he always did. He'd made enquiries about the best way to get to Bletchley and knew it might not be easy with the wartime travel restrictions. But fortune smiled once more and the journey passed without incident.

He must have fallen asleep on the train and, before he knew it, he was marching up a long driveway, gravel crunching and popping under his feet like small arms fire. He had expected to be interrogated at the security barrier, but the military policeman waved him through, barely glancing at his papers. A few hundred yards ahead he saw the imposing house and, off to the side, a cluster of huts.

He realised he might not even be able to see David when he got there. His mother had hinted that he was involved in some top secret stuff. But Robert had to try. He seemed to recall that David worked in one of the huts and he picked one at random, knocked on the door and listened. There appeared to be a heated discussion going on inside. Robert waited a moment longer then turned the handle and went in. He immediately saw the source of the noise. A dozen men and women were gathered round a large-scale map, arguing. In the centre of the group stood David, shouting louder than anyone else. Robert stepped forward and immediately recognised it as a shipping chart of the North Sea, an area he was intimately and painfully familiar with.

Robert hesitated. Maybe this had been a mistake. He had been so desperate to see his brother that he hadn't considered he might be intruding, might even be unwelcome. As he reached the edge of the group, he heard snatches of conversation, words like 'convoy', 'enigma', 'long game' and 'sacrifices'. Eventually the noise subsided a little and he waved to David and spoke his name. His brother broke off from his discussion and moved towards Robert. The strain was etched on his brother's face and Robert knew he had been right to follow his instincts. David needed his support.

Just then, a telephone rang in the corner of the room. David moved past Robert to answer the phone, all eyes following him. After a brief conversation, David ended the call. He dropped the handset into its cradle with a clatter that boomed like an explosion in the now silent room. David didn't speak for a moment and seemed to stare directly at Robert before finally speaking.

'Ladies and gentlemen,' he said, 'that was confirmation that HMS Invincible has been torpedoed. The vessel was struck amidships and there was a massive explosion. There were no supporting vessels and we do not expect any survivors.'

Robert felt the blood drumming in his head. He had obviously misheard what David had said. It made no sense. His ship was docked in Portsmouth. He found himself standing in front of the board and saw that someone had recorded the stark message with the date of 26th May chalked alongside.

'HMS Invincible torpedoed amidships. Massive explosion. No survivors expected.'

The room was slipping and sliding away from Robert. He turned to speak to David but could no longer see him. Voices clamoured in his head, he was finding it difficult to breathe, the taste of saltwater rose in his throat. He felt nauseous and knew he had to get out. He looked back for his brother one last time but the room was a blur of shapes and colours.

He wrenched open the door to find that the Bletchley huts and the main building had vanished. Robert stared out on a heaving, swirling nightmare. The floor lurched violently and he was cast out, into the mayhem of the North Sea. All around him men were screaming, yelling for loved ones as they were swallowed up by the grey nothingness. Robert floundered for a moment, swallowing water and oil. A slick of burning diesel was moving towards him.

In that final moment, he knew the truth. His ship was not docked in Portsmouth, awaiting repairs. It was slipping inexorably into the hungry maelstrom of the North Sea. The torpedo had not, after all, missed its mark. As he was dragged down, a final image seared into his brain, the date written on that board in Bletchley: 26th May, the birthday he shared with his brother.

IT GOES ON

Assen Rizov

Wide cyan eyes followed me out of the room. The bitterness of betrayed faith radiated out from them, surrounding with heaviness the air through which I moved. I was his doctor, their beacon of hope, yet I told them that there was no hope, their father could not be saved, and it was only a matter of time. I would be surprised if he lived through the night in his state.

How glad I felt to come home after that shift! The kiss of my wife's luscious lips threw the torture of my inner distressing demons into blissful oblivion and his emaciated skeleton clothed in mottled skin was chased away from my consciousness.

Later I chopped the plum tomatoes as she boiled the pasta. We zigzagged back and forth together, almost in a dance, until supper was ready. When my wife passed me the torch to light the candles on my side of the table, in the way she stood, no make-up, just the loose T-shirt smeared from old episodes of cooking, I caught a rare glimpse of her beauty – the cosy charm which emanated like the flowery scent of a spring morning from her homely smile. All I wanted to do was love her…

The next morning, two porters were wheeling out a blue body bag as I walked onto the ward.

'Morning, doctor, we need a death certificate for Mr Whitehill. His family would also like a word!' the nurse greeted me.

I sat down and started writing.

HOW NOW?

John Dickson

The leather-jacketed stranger looked suspicious. He was loitering at the media section, occasionally glancing towards me. Dull hooded eyes.

'Surely can't be real leather,' I thought, 'Can't remember the last time I saw a cow, never mind wearing a bit of one.'

I stood my ground. My thumb hovering over the call button. I felt secure. But it was a bit unnerving seeing someone not dressed in Laterex. He looked just a bit plump too. Don't see that these days. I tried not to stare too obviously.

'Who's the Retro?' I heard a stage whisper in my ear.

I felt the subtle vibes of Joline's Pulsarex gently instigating a response from my feebly cheap copy of the new iWear outfit I'd managed to source. For a fraction of the price of the original.

'Mmmm?' I turned my head and looked at the gloriously beautiful demeanour that was Joline. Holographically perfect. My boss.

'He's been there for about ten minutes.' My eyes lingered on the subtle curves that I knew were really an illusion. But very effective! Especially wearing her new Versace Enhanced Pulserex…

'You'll have to deal with him.' I felt the vibes diminishing. Joline was pulling rank.

The deceptive moment of intimacy had ended. The Boss had spoken.

'Oh well,' I reflected, 'At least my copy iWear was a bargain. It actually works!'

I squared my rather inadequate shoulders and walked through the displays of branded gizmos towards the cause of the unusual interaction with my superior.

The Retro didn't move. He stared at me as I made my way past the dazzlingly bright displays of all the innovations that were the 'must haves' at that moment in time. The current best seller was the very latest Xtime Sphere that could enclose a whole room full of people and actually slow down real time. For those who could afford it, the possibilities of almost endless weekends of depravity and self-gratification made the price irrelevant. Even if it did cost about half the average Now Store worker's annual salary.

As I got closer, the Retro's appearance seemed even more out of place. His hair was greasy, and he hadn't shaved recently. In fact, he looked as though he was actually dirty! And yes, he did have a bit of a belly. How could he afford that?

'I'd feel pretty uncomfortable if I hadn't had a G Tox shave and shower every morning.' I thought. 'Long time since I saw anyone who wasn't really neat and clean. Yeuch!' I shivered.

When I was about a metre away, the Retro picked up the silver Matrix Holophone that was securely attached to the counter.

He was silent as he stared at me. Unblinking. He flicked the Holophone's data compartment open and seemed to fumble with something. His fingers clumsily inserting a device as I found myself quickening my pace. I felt I had to stop whatever he was trying to do! It definitely wasn't normal behaviour in a Now Store.

His eyes changed. The tension visibly eased from his face. I tried to grab the Holophone. He smiled.

I felt my copy iWear pulsing. I glanced around expecting to see the glorious Joline.

No Joline. Just the increasing pulse of the clothes I wore. Moving from pleasantness to the edges of discomfort.

'You think you're normal, don't you?' the Retro spoke. A surprisingly melodic voice. Totally unthreatening.

'Well I am,' I retorted. 'I'm as normal as you get these days.'

'There's no such thing as normal now.' His eyes were brighter, almost joyful.

I couldn't really move, I realised. *'How come I can't grab the Holophone off him?'* I was confused. But the pulsing of my iWear was remarkably relaxing.

'You like my jacket? I saw you staring at it.'

I looked at the well-worn, scuffed, jerkin style jacket that could have been older than him.

'Well no. Not really. It's not exactly interactive, is it?' I smoothed my pirated iWear T-shirt and grinned as it Googled a universe of virtual possibilities. Images changing by the second: News and Music and Blogs and Now Tube blurred into a veritable plasticine of interaction.

I felt a heightening of pulsations. My iWear quivered.

A purple haze enveloped me in a sparkling blizzard of sudden realisation.

I hadn't seen a live cow for ages because there weren't any! Not in my world. Our sounds and visions were all virtual and artificial. Even my boss was a very attractive holograph!

The 'meat' we eat isn't real meat. It's glorified stem cells cajoled into pretending they're a pretext for a steak dinner. But in reality, they're mush!

Only we've got used to them. The global branding and marketing has worked. Normality is me, and my Now Store colleagues. All kitted out in Laterex outfits advertising all Now Store's brands continuously streaming and changing across our slim 'healthy' bodies.

This new perception gave me an unfamiliar sensation. *Awareness?*

The Retro grinned as he put the Holophone down. The purple haze dissipated.

I glanced around and saw the chunks of shiny plastic hardware. *Brittle delivery systems of deception.*

Retro spoke, 'Do you remember the last time you ate a really juicy steak?' His now infectious grin got wider, 'With all the trimmings?'

The pulsing of my iWear had slowed right down.... but a new sensation was welling up... my taste buds were throbbing.

I felt another sense booting up. A whiff of human sweat floating through my olfactory glands. Unmasked, non-perfumed. Raw data.

I swallowed hard, unsure if I liked or loathed the rawness. I suspected it was an acquired taste, sorry: smell.

Retro winked. He seemed to be able to command my full attention. The rest of the customers and staff in the store looked somehow faded. I tried to see behind me towards my workstation, but I struggled to fully turn my head.

'Why is the Retro still here?' Joline's voice cut through the general air of greying out reality. Suddenly I could turn my head. *'What was going on?'*

Joline's holograph, while still delectable, had changed its hue. There was a reddening of her high cheekbones and her hair seemed to reflect her mood. It was longer, wavier, rising like strands of flames. Her eyes had turned vibrant green as she fixed her gaze on my now almost cowering self.

My iWear twisted and squirmed. A weird sensation. I felt my eyes being pulled from Joline's emerald hard gaze. My head turned to the Retro. He was grinning, yet his outline was softening. He put the Holophone down and reached into his side pocket.

'What's that he's got?'

'An apple? A real apple?'

'See?' Retro's voice was softer 'Smell it?'

The fresh tangy smell enveloped me. I could almost taste the gloriously piquant juices trapped in the vibrant coloured skin, trapping the joy of a pure, naturally grown fruit.

I shuddered.

My iWear tightened its grip on my whole torso. The normally extremely comfortable garb was beginning to feel alien…

'I'm going to sort this myself.' I heard Joline's voice harden as her form appeared beside me. 'I'm pressing the button now. I'll deal with you afterwards!'

'Staff announcement. Code yellow in section seven.' the Now Store's audio system broke harshly through the muzak.

The multitude of screens around the store changed: The Retro was in all of them.

The Retro looked at me. No hint of fear or worry. He shrugged, then spoke 'You know I'm the real deal, don't you?'

Such an old-fashioned expression, I thought. I was mesmerised by the whole situation.

I realised I had hardly moved since the Retro fumbled with the Holophone.

I felt a tingling in my toes. It spread through my feet and coursed up my legs, gathering a feeling of actual physical strength. Something I didn't remember experiencing since my young days. Oh so long ago!

The sensation of strength gathered momentum as I felt it rippling through my torso. My narrowed shoulders unbowed as my stoop straightened, flexing suddenly elasticised muscles in my newly broadened back. My neck seemed to widen as the gush of unexpected energy welled inside my head.

My eyes opened wide and stared at the Retro as a billowing burst of knowledge surged and swirled inside my head.

I knew.

I turned and looked at Joline.

The Hologram that held her form started to crack and fizzle as her piercing emerald eyes seemed to sink into their sockets, then shrink and fade. Her striking high cheekbones cast shadows over her sunken cheeks which now looked frail and gaunt. Her glorious flaming locks dulled, greyed, and grew lank and wispy.

Joline's elegant arrogant vision of beauty was gone. Her aged features were obvious now that I could see through the hologram.

I found myself standing taller as I looked around the Now Store with fresh eyes. The customers all dressed in the latest Laterex designs. Chattering to each other as they fondled gadgets that instantly interacted with their designer clothing; automatically reviewing each device. Twittering their 140 character 'thoughts' that all their virtual 'friends' could see and comment on.

All so busy.

All so pointless.

All so old.

All of them.

Am I so old? I suddenly thought…

'Can we help you, sir?' The store marshals were standing either side of the Retro. Large hands on each of his shoulder. As though they were about to forcibly eject him from the store. Big, stern, and obedient clones of their predecessors. Trained to never ask why.

The Retro shrugged again. He looked at me.

'Life's full of choices,' the Retro grinned as he unexpectedly threw the apple towards me.

Somehow I knew exactly what he meant as I caught the ball of fresh fruit and instinctively bit into it. It was marvellous! As I crunched deep into its flesh its juices ran over my tongue re-igniting long forgotten sensations of taste.

Something else re-ignited at the same moment. A sense of true reality burst through my mind as I strode strongly over the few feet towards the three figures. The store marshals, who I vaguely recognised, looked at me quizzically.

I extended my right hand towards the Retro. He took it with both his hands and looked at me. I felt an urge to extend my left hand and cover his.

It was like powering up a dormant engine.

'I knew it was you,' he smiled, as I felt a surge of energy flow through my arms and hands as his body vibrated almost imperceptibly.

The marshals bounced back from him as the surge of power coursed through the Retro and he flexed his shoulders.

He looked bigger too…

'What the hell's going on?' Joline's once velvet tones hissed and grated behind me.

'I think I'm just about to resign.' My own voice had deepened and had acquired an air of authority.

I turned and stood beside the Retro. Looking across the counters at the shoppers, frozen in their tracks at the unheard-of commotion.

Dozens of old wizened faces peering at us.

Joline's shrunken figure trying to stand tall. And failing.

'Time to go.' I said to the Retro, who nodded as we walked past the counters stacked with their virtual products.

The Exit doors opened and as we walked into the bright light of day. I turned to the now imposing figure of the Retro standing beside me.

'Thanks for opening my eyes. Now I realise there's so much more than the Now Store.'

'By the way, my name's Adam.'

The Retro nodded. The hooded eyes shone.

'I know.'

MUDDLED THOUGHTS

Elizabeth Kearney

You thought you had been at work today.
You hadn't.
You thought you had seen Jock running about too.
You hadn't.
That weekend we were away,
You swore you had your bag with you.
By the end of the weekend you did.
Only because the two boys drove 150 miles to get it.
Planking it in the boot for you to find,
So you'd settle and enjoy what was left of the weekend.
The weekend you now don't recall.
I made you lunch – you forgot you had it.
You would have paid the council tax bill multiple times
– if I didn't tell you it had already been paid.
And for the fifth time today – you tried to pay it again.
You think you lost the money for the phone bill, but you
hadn't taken it out.
Yet you are adamant you did.
And now you are crying, saying this is how it is going to be;
Whether you are right or wrong,
You won't be believed.
And I fall silent.
Because I know this is the one thing you have said that is true.

POSTCARDS FROM THE END OF THE WORLD

Andy Raffan

The last horse died today. I know cause they said so on the news feeds. Some of the older ones cried, so I guess it was a BIG DEAL. Me, I think some richey rich will have one hidden away in a down deep compartment, squeezed in beside the platinum bars and the –

'What's a horse again?' says Baxter.

'Don't be such a baby,' I say. 'You're interrupting my postcard.'

Then I feel bad. Baxter doesn't always remember stuff so great.

'It's like a skinny cow,' I say loudly. Shouting tells people you are certain.

'Oh,' says Baxter. He is quiet for a bit. A lot of times he is quiet.

Sometimes he can go a whole day without speaking. I worry then that he's annoyed with me. Or dead.

Then after all the quiet he had said, 'Time isn't a straight line. It's an infinite flower, folding and unfolding.' He comes out with stuff like that. I think his wires got crossed.

The postcards were his idea.

'They'll be thera…therap…they'll be good for you. Stop you obsessing about it.'

He meant the end. Of everything.

'What's a postcard?' I said.

'People send them to the ones they love when they are far away, telling them they miss them, and they wish they were here.'

It was my turn to be quiet for a bit.

'I don't wish anyone was here,' I said.

He did a lot of quiet after that.

Baxter wasn't always here. When we left it was just me. After all the screaming and the crying, and the fighting to get on, and the stopping of folks who weren't supposed to be on, it was just me and my stuff. Which wasn't much as there were STRICT LIMITATIONS. Mum had filled my backpack till it was bursting like a sausage. And she still got more stuff in. I said she must have broken the laws of spatial dynamics. She laughed at that, being how she is a scientist who specialises in spatial dynamics.

Then she cried for a bit too. I hadn't seen her cry since everything with dad.

'Now Violet,' she'd said (that's me, after the purple flower, though I've never seen one for real, just holo ones). 'That's everything you can take as there are strict limitations.'

I looked at her. She was so thin, her skin all papery. My backpack looked heavier. I thought I could see the blood sliding about in her veins.

'What if I don't take it? I need *you*. I don't need things. Then you can come.'

Her eyes were yellow and watery.

'We've been over this sweetheart. So many times. You know why.'

'Toxins. Toxins. TOXINS.' (I screamed the last one if you didn't get that.)

She swayed a bit, then sat down on the bunk with a thump. I was scared I'd blown her over, like the way the dust scoots away from the vents.

'Look at me Violet,' she'd said, holding her arms out to me, skinny like cables stuck together. 'I'd barely survive take-off, never mind the journey.'

'But...but...you know about space, and ships, and engines and all that. Doesn't that count?'

She looked up at the concrete ceiling. 'Not anymore,' she'd said, and I fell into her brittle arms, head squashed up against her chest. I remember her heartbeat like a scratching, a scratching of something trapped, trying to burrow out into the daylight.

So then there was a lot of alone. Till Baxter appeared.

See it was like this. This ship is all bashed and bodged and stuck together from everything they had left that worked. All this tech wired and synched to other bits of tech. Even stuff from the ABOVE TIMES when granny was my age. Anything that even faintly worked got torn out, reused, repurposed. Mum had said it was a damn sight late to have caught on to recycling.

As well as all the tech that made the ship work, there was lots of bits of tech for spares. It was supposed to be kept in compartments with NO LOOTING on the doors, but lots of it was piled in the corridors and in corners. And that's where I found Baxter.

Or perhaps, more accurately, it's where he found me.

'Hello again Violet,' a voice had said.

I'd screamed a bit, thrown my scavenged bit of tech into the nearest pile, spun round to look where the sound came from. No one. Lying on top of one pile was an old-timey voice assistant type thing. Its camera light glowed green, but the screen was cracked.

'Who's there? How do you know my name?' I'd said.

'It's Baxter. We've met before.'

'When?'

'For me, some time ago. For you it will be soon.'

'What kind of riddle is that?' I'd said (I think I may have shouted, because of being scared and everything).

'You know that game where you try and guess where your opponent has hidden their little ships by dropping bombs on a map?' he'd said.

'Everyone knows that one.'

'Imagine you're the ship, sailing across the sea. Sometimes my guesses land in front of you, sometimes they land behind. Occasionally they land on top. Like now.'

'Isn't the object of that game to sink the little ship?' I'd asked.

He paused before saying anything. Which didn't help with the scared.

'Not always,' he'd said.

And then he was quiet. Back then I didn't know about his coming and going, so I'd asked over and over what the hell he was talking about, till eventually I stuck the voice assistant thingy in my pocket and went to lie down in my pokey bed in my pokey cabin.

The next day he seemed to have forgotten who I was. I called him an idiot and reminded him. This time he was full of questions. Why was I on the ship? Why had we left? Where were we going? I told him – about the living underground and mum and the toxins and the scavenged bodged-up ship.

'THE END,' I had said when I finished, as that's what they do at the end of holo films. Though they always end happy.

'Truly,' he'd said. 'The end. Of everything.'

'Suppose so.'

'I shall need to process this. It's a lot to take in.'

'No shit Sherlock,' I had replied.

But he'd gone again.

When he came back he'd suggested the postcards.

'We…sorry…I would like to get to know you Violet. I could be the friend who's far away. You can send me postcards about your life on the ship. Or your life before. Or whatever you want.'

'Why me?' I'd said. 'There's other people on the ship who know a lot more about things than I do. Why not ask them?'

'I can't,' he'd said. 'They don't hear me. Believe me, I've tried. For a long time.'

I'd laughed.

'How old do you think I am? I don't believe in fairies and stuff, things that only kids can see. If I can hear you, anyone can.'

'Have you heard of entanglement Violet?'

'Like when your hair is all wrong and mum has to brush it out till her arms get sore and she has to go and lie down?'

Sometimes I think Baxter goes quiet when he is counting to ten like adults do when they are angry. Like this bit.

'How about we just do the postcards?' he'd said eventually.

And cause I had no other friends I said yes.

So that's how it went for a long while. I would wait for the little green glow of the camera light to come on, and when it did I'd do another postcard for Baxter.

He'd be funny though. Some days he'd forgotten what I'd told him before. Other days he seemed to know what I was going to tell him before I even said it. Like I said, crossed wires.

I never thought to ask about him. Well, I did once, near the end. I'd had enough of postcards and was lying on my pokey bed.

'Why are you here Baxter?' I said.

This was one of his good days. A full complement of circuits. Didn't stop him being strange though.

'If you could change all this, would you?'

'My pokey cabin?'

'No, I mean change *it*. The end. Of everything.'

'What, you mean fix it? Go back and undo the mess we made?'

'How about making it never happen in the first place?'

I sat up, looked at the little green light. It seemed brighter than I'd ever seen it. Or maybe I was just tired.

'What if,' he said, 'you could be both the flower and the seed.'

'Now you're doing riddles again,' I said.

'If I could make it so the toxins, the underground, the ship never happens, would you let me?'

I did some quiet after he said that.

'And if I said yes, what about me? Would I happen?'

'We…I…don't know Violet. Would you happen? Maybe always. Maybe never. Maybe both simultaneously.'

I lay down again after he said that.

'Go away Baxter,' I said. 'I need some quiet time.'

Last postcard.

Dear mum

I'm so far away now you wouldn't believe. You were so worried about me being all alone on the ship, but I've made a friend. His name is Baxter, and he says he can undo everything if I let him send back all the postcards I wrote. He says they'll have to listen if they see what will happen if they don't change, that I can show them the end, and it can be a new beginning.

I asked him if I would remember this. He said everyone will remember this. I'm not sure if that is the same.

I am frightened. I feel the warm plastic of the SEND key under my finger. I am saying in my head, 'I am the flower and the seed. I am the flower and the seed.' I pray the ground is better there, that my petals will feel the sunshine for the first time, and that the rain when it comes is no longer bitter.

Yours eternally

Violet

SEND…

LIONHEARTS

Elizabeth Carey

Dark, foreboding plumes of smoke
hang over its cities.
The watery winter sun hidden from sight,
no warmth around.
They fight on with strength and might
for their freedom,
brave souls with lion hearts
challenging the bear.
Families scattered all over the world
how do they make sense
of what is senseless?
The beauty of Ukraine
desecrated, rent asunder
by the weapons of modern-day war.
Peace will come at what cost?
Bewildered children clamber out of buses
into their mothers' arms, reunited but scarred.
Drone attacks never ending.
When and how can this be ended?
Elderly rescued from flooding
as the power of water tore through Khakova Dam.
Crops rent asunder. Water polluted.
Is this the price of war?
What is their future?

BEYOND REPAIR

Mary Edward

My front wheel is over it before I have time to react. Then I swerve and run the car on to the grass verge. I stop, my heart hammering, afraid to look back at what I have done. In the dusk, it is difficult to see.

I think it is a child.

I get out of the car and creep back to the bundle lying on the road, expecting blood.

It is a doll. A rosy baby doll, with one leg crushed, perhaps beyond repair. But it is still smiling – tiny teeth peek from behind plastic lips.

I straighten the doll's clothes. It is dressed in a hand-knitted jacket and one woolly bootee. The other is missing and I need to find it. The woollen garment is warm on my skin. It feels comfortable, and I shift the doll into my arms as I search the ground for the sock. I cup one hand around the bare foot. It is cold. I find the bootee – it is hard to see, covered with dirt from my tyres, and, gently, I pull it on to the mangled limb.

I look around for somewhere to put the doll, thinking of the little girl who has dropped it from a car window – or thrown it out in a tantrum? Either way, she will be heart-broken at the loss. Perhaps she will make her mother turn the car and come back to look for her toy.

When I approach the fence, intending to hang the doll from the wire by a loop of wool, I hear another vehicle. It will be the child. I keep the doll in my arms as the van draws up. But it is a man who gets out.

He points to the doll. 'All right there?'

He has a voice like the squeal of nails on a blackboard. He is very thin and when he turns to look back along the road, I see that his head is oddly flat and sloping at the back. His lank hair touches his collar. I don't like the look of him.

I show him the toy. 'It's a doll'

'Yeah, I see now.' His eyes gleam wetly in the half-light. 'But what are you doing with it?'

I force a laugh. 'Oh, silly of me. I ran over it and got out to see what it was.'

He comes closer and I can smell something…foetid. I inch away from him.

He takes hold of the ruined leg. Then he strokes the doll's face.

I want to pull her from his touch. 'I'm just…I'm going to leave it here in case the little girl comes back.'

He peers into my eyes, 'The little girl?'

'Well, that's the most likely owner, isn't it?'

Another car approaches. The headlights flash on reflective strips on his boilersuit, and for an instant he is a Hallowe'en skeleton. The other car squeezes past and continues without stopping.

He draws back his lips, 'You'll see she gets it now, won't you? The little girlie.'

When he drives off, I find I'm gripping the doll's foot so tightly that my hand is beginning to cramp. I loosen my grasp and turn back to the fence. It starts to rain.

Tilted back in my arms the doll's eyes have closed. Raindrops glisten on the eyelashes, like tears, and I can't bring myself to abandon her to the night. Or to the stranger. I take her into the car and start the engine, then I realise that I have decided the doll is a girl. A small, helpless girl.

My baby had no gender. But there was blood – lots of it – endlessly pouring on to the bathroom floor like red, red wine from a bottomless vat. And lumps. But no gender.

When I get home Jake says, 'You're late, Donna.'

I don't tell him about the doll because I know what he'll say. Besides, I'm well aware of what I'm doing, and I don't care. Warmth trickles into me. Sublimation be damned, this is anticipation, and I want to hold on to it.

Jake goes out to play squash on Tuesdays. I can hardly wait until he's gone before fetching the doll from the car.

Tears edge my own eyelashes as I touch the crushed foot. I wonder if there is still such a place as a doll's hospital. They told me that was where my baby doll went, after the fire. Then we moved house. Polly, that was her name – the memory rushes back. She never returned, and I knew that my mother had lied to me. It's not surprising really, that Polly got lost in the nooks and crannies of my history. But I feel sad about it now.

Sad is my normal state. A lode of sadness runs in me, like cold metal through rock. It's been four months now. They all say it will get better, but they don't know. Jake is recovering, it's obvious.

I push the dishwasher closed with its breathy squeeze and press the button. Against the slurping background I sit at the kitchen table and undress the doll. It is virtually gender-free, but she's my baby girl now. I decide to call her Daisy. That's one of the names I had chosen. Jake didn't care for it, but I had determined to win that one when the time came. The time will never come. I kiss the tip of the little nose. Another lost baby. Her face is made of something pliable, like flesh, and she has dirty smudges on her cheeks.

I fill the basin with tepid water and washing-up liquid. I know it's not the most appropriate thing, but she's an unexpected arrival, after all. I rock her back and forth in the suds and her eyes open and close. When I am finished I wrap her in a towel while I wash her clothes, and pat them into shape.

Upstairs, I tuck Daisy under some sheets in the airing cupboard and push her clothes to dry behind the boiler where they can't be seen. As I close the door I hear Jake whistling his way in from the garage.

Next day, in my lunch hour, I buy some of the smallest possible baby clothes. The assistant asks if I also need some cloth nappies – so much better than disposable. I smile and shake my head. Nappies would be ridiculous, for a doll.

At the end of the week Jake suggests we go out to the cinema and have dinner – we haven't done that in a while. It doesn't thrill me to leave Daisy under the sheets for any length of time but I have to go.

It is on the following Monday that I see it. Stuck inside the window of the post office, amongst the ads for bikes and sofas and unwanted toasters. The notice has been printed on a computer, and there is a photograph.

'Lost on Tuesday, September 18th, five-year-old Amy's much-loved doll.' The page gives a telephone number, and finishes with, 'Amy is devastated. Reward.'

I examine the photograph. Amy is only visible as a pair of chubby arms holding the doll on her lap. It is my Daisy – legs intact, wearing a small hat to match the knitted jacket. I have visions of a granny knitting the clothes and Amy's delight as she pushes the little arms into sleeves and ties a bow under the baby's chin.

I turn away, my letters unposted. Devastated…the syllables strike me like blows as I hurry back to the office.

I was older than Amy before I noticed my lack of grandparents. All my friends had some – one or two – even four if they were lucky, but I had none. In fact, I hardly had a father. He was just a male shape who came out of my mother's bedroom from time to time. Then he would disappear.

At home I tell Jake I have a headache. I take a couple of aspirin and get into bed, smuggling Daisy in beside me. I tuck her under the duvet with her head on the pillow. She smiles up at me. Much-loved. I have to give her back.

In the morning I fold all the baby things into a plastic carrier and put it out with the rubbish. Then I dress Daisy in her own clothes, lay her in a shopping bag, and walk to the post office to read the phone number.

I can hear Amy's cries of joy when her mother gives her the good news. They live close by, so I take the doll to the house. And apologise for the damage I have done. I turn down the reward. And I don't wait to meet Amy.

It's a sunny day. I carry my empty bag to the park and sit on a bench. The park is full of children – walking, running, jumping, shouting, laughing…crying. I study these specimens – these exotic creatures who will never be mine.

There won't be a second baby to slither out in a puddle of blood. I am beyond repair. There's nowhere left to grow another little Daisy.

In fact, I don't have much of anything left. It's questionable if Jake will hang around for long. Men don't care for barren women. It diminishes their role.

I wonder about my father's role. He never came back after the fire, although he was there when it started. It was a pity Uncle Peter wasn't present that night because he would have put the fire out. And saved my doll. He was my mother's hero, she said. He vanished too, after she died.

I stare unfocussed, into the distance, then suddenly my vision clears. It is him – the flat-headed man. Today he is wearing denims and scruffy trainers, but I recognise him. He is watching a young woman and her children. The toddler suddenly runs off in the direction of the pond and, panic-stricken, the mother leaves the baby to run after him.

The man is looking into the pram when I get there.

The child is asleep. It is small and new.

'What are you doing?'

The baby's closed eyelids are transparent, and they flutter as if she is aware of my voice. The blanket is pink, so it's a girl.

The man looks up, and his watery eyes know me too. I take hold of the pram handle.

He draws his head into his body, like an animal with a carapace, and slouches off.

The mother is still chasing the little boy who, relishing his freedom, sprints around the edge of the pond.

The baby makes a snuffling noise and blows a little bubble as the pram moves.

I walk in the direction of the mother and her other child, then find myself on the street outside. The trees and bushes which surround the park are not enough to deaden the sound of a woman's screams.

Two blocks later I reach a corner and the pedestrian signal is red. The rubber handle-grips stick to the insides of my fists as I wait for the green light which will let me wheel the baby away. Then gradually, like leaking blood, the message filters through.

I can't hide this one in the airing cupboard.

When I turn back, the mother is speeding towards me, her son dangling from her arm like a stuffed toy, his feet barely touching the ground.

THE JOYRIDER

Carolyn Mandache

The shop's alarm was in full meltdown; deafening, lights flashing and determined to get attention. Mr. Singh lived above his shop, the lights switched on over the destruction below. A final brick conceded defeat, smashing loudly on the concrete. I jumped as the voice in my ear asked what my emergency was. I must have dialled on autopilot.

'It's Mr. Singh's shop, a car's smashed right into it!'

The five youths were shouting at each other, now free of the battered car.

'A car will be there any second, we already know about the incident.'

Three of them sprinted away from the scene, beckoning the others to follow. A fourth was in pain, a trickle of blood rolling down his cheek. He put both hands on the other boy's shoulders, the two engaged in serious conversation. The police siren grew louder and the injured boy took off, the approaching car the adrenalin he needed.

Ever had that weird feeling someone's watching you? My flat was directly across from Mr. Singh's, a perfect vantage point. The remaining joyrider must have felt my gaze. We locked eyes and I backed away from the window, the curtain falling back into place. No wonder he was torn. I didn't know him well, just that he'd gone against what was expected of him. Chose no part in the family business. My heart skipped a beat as I watched him make his decision…and Javeed Singh ran off into the night.

MISTER SLIME

Steve O'Brien

Ronald Black was in a unique and very strange place. While most people, he reckoned, could get on with normal living, for 41 years now, since that terrible day, a normal life is exactly what had eluded him. For, from the moment he fell out of his grubby, sweat-stained bed each morning, Ronald found he could slip in and out of what he considered his *happy years* of the past. Those blissful days-gone-by, between the ages of 16 and 24, had somehow split into recurring, random segments that popped up like scenes from a film, and to him were more tangible and vivid than his everyday, present, grim reality. Though he could not alter history, he found himself basking in all the feelings and senses of his youth, loving life as it had been, to the full. Yet, recently, Ronald was keen to find an exit from those particular journeys. He was lonely and found living like Doctor Who was quite exhausting.

The phenomenon began on his 24th birthday, the day Marella jilted him at the altar. From that day forward, though he possessed a crumpled photograph of her, he retained only a very vague memory of his fiancée, and absolutely no memory of the doomed wedding ceremony. He didn't know why he had been dumped. Whenever he asked anyone about the woman he'd loved, they would shrug their shoulders as if she had never existed. He became deeply depressed. Ronald firmly believed that if only he could pop back in time to his wedding and thus understand exactly what had occurred, he might move on and become normal. It wasn't normal for a 65-year-old maths teacher to walk the streets at night, wearing shorts, Doc Marten boots and a cape, seeking solace from his favourite late evening news channel – *EBC, The Voice of Britain.*

Yet, though his wedding day eluded him, a familiar piece of music, for example, or a particular smell could instantly transport him back to one of his pleasant life episodes; sitting on a beach with a clutch of female admirers, perhaps, or just being an all-round popular guy in flared trousers and Freddie Mercury moustache. These pleasant visits to his past jostled for space with reality but were so positive to his mental health that they effectively stopped him ending it all by jumping into the canal or hanging himself in the school staff room. Marella was a blur. But he could remember other girlfriends from his youth, and occasionally thought he would track them down and ask them out for a date. After all it was only 40-odd years ago. He looked in the mirror to get perspective. His golden locks were mostly missing. What he had now was a fat belly and spindly legs. His pupils called him Mister Slime behind his back, but he didn't care. He could lock himself in the book cupboard with a bottle of vodka or switch on his carefree, halcyon days, even when he was in the middle of teaching equations to his pupils whose names he couldn't be bothered learning.

So, Ronald was in his own weird world. But he fretted. If he couldn't somehow conjure up Marella on their aborted wedding day, he would never come to terms with life, and was always destined to be lost.

One evening, he was watching a programme about Eastern mysticism. He decided to try it.

'Ommm. Ommm. Ommm,' he chanted, hour after hour. Simultaneously he stared at the old photo of Marella and concentrated so hard he passed out. When he awoke he was back in 1980 with Bob, his best man, in front of the wedding congregation at St Cyprian's Church. No sign of the bride.

'It's half-past. I've got another wedding,' said the minister, idly checking his diary.

'Bob, do you think there's been a mix up with the dates?' asked Ronald.

'Sorry, mate, looks like Marella's jilted you.'

Ronald passed out, pulling the altar down on top of him, and ripping the minister's cassock. When he came to, what with his mother's wailing, with one foot in the past and one in the present, he joyfully realised he had at last found that elusive fragment he had been searching for. Bob slapped him hard across his face.

'Come on Ronald. Man up. Let's go to the pub.'

But, with tears in his eyes, Ronald ran all the way home to his newly purchased apartment. The front door was open. Marella was standing just inside the hallway, stuffing her clothes into a suitcase. She was laughing at him.

'Sorry, Ronald,' she said, 'I found someone better.'

Ronald marched past her into the kitchen, picked up his claw hammer and, as she scrambled for the door, whacked her on the head with it. Then, when she had stopped twitching, he dragged her body into their chest freezer. He put a chain and padlock round the freezer, threw the key out of his window and collapsed.

'Hello caller, my name's Jan. Welcome to *EBC – The Voice of Britain.*'

'Hello, Jan. I've always wanted to talk to you. It's such an honour to speak to a national treasure.'

'Let's mark the moment. Midnight, May 1st, 2027, unless you're an idiot and didn't already know that. And you're my last ever caller,' she slurred. 'You and me, among the last survivors. So, what's your name, luv?'

'Name's Ronald,' he said, scratching his head. 'But this isn't 2027.'

'Sure, Ronnie. So you are an idiot.'

'I thought this was 2021!' Ronald yelled, 'Not only have I found a way back in time to Marella, but I must have found a portal to the future. Yee-ha!' He continued, 'I'll be straight with you, Jan. I'm looking for a new girlfriend. I just found out what happened to my last one. You're reasonably pretty. Maybe we could…'

'Sure, Ronnie, sure. Anyway, it's just you and me now with nothing left to live for. By the way Ronnie, I'm just toasting you with a glass of Champagne. *To my last caller, may he rest in peace.*'

'Not sure what you're on about, Jan.'

'Well,' she bawled into her mic. 'Ronnie, our political leaders have abandoned us to save themselves. Cowards!'

'Eh?' Said Ronald.

'Last TV pictures in the studio here. A crowd forcing open the door to Number 10, dragging the PM out and stringing him up on a lamp post.'

'Jan, are you blitzed?'

'Yes,' she screamed. 'Why not? First, Israel fires off a nuclear missile at Iran and hits Russia by mistake. Then we join in and fire off a few random warheads at Russia, two of which landed on the M25. So, one day left before we all die. Already the sky has turned green.'

Ronald looked out of his sixth-floor window. 'I don't see a green sky, Jan.'

'Listen,' she shouted, 'I've put my mobile out the window. You can hear the screaming and police sirens, can't you? Well, can't you!'

He couldn't but had a moment of genius.

'If the world is to end like you say,' Ronald said slowly down the phone, 'would you hear my confession?'

'I'm not a fucking priest, you nitwit. What are you on about?'

'I just found out I accidentally murdered my fiancée a long time ago. She was very thoughtless, Jan. I had to batter her head in and lock her in my freezer. I checked on her today, after a sort of dream thing I can't explain in five minutes, and do you know, she's looking better now than she did then. But there's no harm me telling you this if the world is ending soon.'

Ronald felt ecstatic about discovering the bitter truth from his missing time segment. Which also explained why he had never been inclined to eat frozen food.

Ronald was jolted awake when his front door was kicked open by four uniformed police officers. His mobile was still connected to Jan, a telephone operator wearing a *Children in Need* bear suit. And so, after they had opened his freezer and separated Marella's corpse from some packets of fish fingers, he was carried spreadeagled to the police van, chanting, over and over:

'We're all going to heaven – it's 2027. We're all going to heaven – it's 2027.'

Ha-ha-ho-ha-ha-ha. Oh, ha-ha-ho-ha-ha!

LIMBO CHANCER

Sharon Mail

Cast
Devlin – a devilish charmer
Angela – an angelic lady
Tam – a gallus Glaswegian

A room with two people – Devlin (dressed in black) and Angela (dressed in white), sitting side by side at a table, each with an open folder in front of them. Across from them, hidden from view is Tam.

DEVLIN Sit down, Tam, we've been expecting you.

TAM Whit? Where am I, and who are youse?

DEVLIN Let's just say you are in limbo.

TAM (*With a nervous laugh*) I'm naw much of a limbo dancer pal.

ANGELA Very droll. Let's just say that we are two interested parties, representing different bodies, who are both keen to have you join us. And I'm not getting nearly enough people coming with me these days, so I hope you don't let me down.

(*Devlin sniggers*)

TAM — Join you for whit – and how the hell have I ended up here – wherever limbo is?

DEVLIN — You are here because we need to establish what happened to you just before you came here, to decide whether you come with me or my erm, opposite number here.

ANGELA — (*Breaking into song*) I'll take the high road and (pointing to Devlin) he'll take the low road and…

DEVLIN — I wish you'd stop doing that – I grew weary of it decades ago! Anyway, what do you last remember, Tam?

TAM — I was in Jackie Brown's, my local, with my pal Scott, havin' a few pints as usual.

ANGELA — And what occurred?

TAM — Nothin' much – it's all a bit hazy. No, wait a minute. Someone grabbed Scott's bird, Madonna.

ANGELA — A feathered friend – animal lovers. This sounds promising.

TAM — Whit? Naw, Scott's girlfriend. And Scott didnae like that.

DEVLIN — And?

TAM — Scott gied the guy a Glescae kiss.

ANGELA He embraced him. Well, that all sounds very friendly. I'm becoming more and more optimistic.

TAM Naw, he heid-butted him – like this.

(*Angela and Devlin start back in their chairs as they see Tam's hidden gesture*)

DEVLIN (*Looking at Angela and smiling*) Dear, dear. Not so friendly then. And what was your role in all this?

TAM Weil, the guy's pal grabbed Scott and I took my knife out and rammed it into his chest and killed him. I mean, Scott's one of my best pals.

(*Angela shakes her head, sighs and closes her folder*)

ANGELA How very disappointing!

DEVLIN (*Looking at Angela and smiling*) You can't seem to catch a break these days!

TAM Look, whit am I daein here? If you're naw the polis, then I want tae leave.

DEVLIN Well, Tam, what happened next?

TAM The guy Scott heid-butted wisnae very happy, so he took an axe out of his coat and went for Scott. But Scott ducked at the last second. (*loud gulp*)

DEVLIN And?

TAM I didnae. Aw shit.

DEVLIN (*Standing up*) I think you'd better come with me – and it's a long way down, I'm afraid.

(*Tam comes round from behind the screen, towards Devlin, revealing that he has an axe through his head*)

DEVLIN (*Putting on a pair of devil's horns and turning to Angela, who is putting on her angel's wings*) Until next time?

ANGELA I'll win one of these days!

END

THE BEIGE WITCH

Anne V McClure

Once upon a time there was a Witch.

She wasn't that much of a witch. She wasn't a black witch or a white witch. She wasn't even a grey witch. 'If there were such a thing as a quiet, dull, beige witch,' she thought, 'that would be me.'

She wasn't *always* quiet. Sometimes she was loud and bossy and told stories to make people laugh. People saw that side of the Witch, when she was being noisy and colourful, and thought that that was who she was. While it was true of her, it wasn't her at her truest.

Although quiet and beige, the Witch could do magic. Sometimes a person was tangled up inside themselves and didn't know how to get out. The Witch flew on her broom to where they were. She sat quietly with them and listened, carefully and kindly. It may sound simple but often that's when powerful, healing magic happened.

Over the years the Beige Witch had many brooms. Every broom helped her with a different task. Each time it seemed the new broom took the Witch further and higher, which she found very exciting. It was also often very scary and, sometimes, when she looked down, she couldn't even see the earth.

There came a time when the Beige Witch was flying in an angry part of the sky. The red winds buffeted her cruelly. The black clouds blinded her. The yellow lightning hissed around her. She was tossed this way and that till she thought she would fall from her broom and die.

She didn't die; somehow she kept flying and she never knew quite how.

Finally, the Beige Witch was exhausted. She decided to go somewhere safe, somewhere beige, where she could stay quietly and not have to witch.

She looked for a year and a day until she found a little place. It was very neat and tidy with a garden where each stem of grass stood to attention. Weeds didn't dare show their faces. Flowers appeared but saw they were too bright so they faded away. It was perfectly…beige.

She settled there, determined to witch no more. She put her broom away.

One day, looking for something to do, she picked up a trowel. She dug the ground and planted seeds. She watched and listened and waited.

In the first year birds came and a tabby and white cat appeared. The Beige Witch listened to what the birds told each other about having to travel far and wide to find food. She planted rowan for the blackbird to eat and teasels for the goldfinch. Cat thought it was fun watching the Witch make things happen in the garden and stayed.

In the second year squirrels and mice came to see what was going on. The Witch overheard them gossiping that pruned shrubs and manicured lawns didn't suit them. She let the grass grow longer and the trees grow taller so they had places to hunt and hide.

In the third year hedgehogs and bees arrived. The Witch heard them talking about how cold it was in winter. She stopped tidying fallen leaves and let the vegetables go to seed at the end of the season to give them food and homes.

In the fourth year foxes began to visit. The Witch paid heed to them saying it was hard to find places to hide their cubs. She grew bigger plants and let them tangle up and spill over each other to give the cubs safety.

In the fifth year a badger came. He snuffled and huffled about until he met Cat. He told Cat that the garden wasn't big enough for him and his clan, but he liked what had been done with the place.

The October full harvest moon rose. Cat sleepily watched the mice and voles, her tail twitching. The foxes and hedgehogs came in and out and took what they needed. The birds feasted on pine cone seeds. Cat strolled to where the Beige Witch was sitting and listening. Cat told the Witch the place was full of green and gold and red and purple. The beige had gone. Cat turned around and around and settled to sleep on the Witch's feet.

The Witch smiled and thought, 'here is my best magic. Perhaps beige was never really my colour after all.'

A long time later the Witch was looking for something in the broom cupboard. A glint in the corner caught her eye. She pushed aside some cobwebs and there was a broom that gleamed softly silver. The Witch felt the old familiar tingle across her palms. Before she knew it, she reached out and grasped the broom. And she was gone.

WIND

Lorraine Johnston

I snake through narrow streets.
On the green, I crack whip
the white walls of washday sheets.
Rippling over ancient cobbles,
gathering dust and remnants
of everyday life's despair,
temporarily losing momentum
as I shift your history elsewhere.

I push beneath your clothing,
biting sharply at your skin.
I chill your bones,
until you head homewards to hurry in.
I blast your face with my cargo,
grit drawing tears to your eyes.
Before you close your door, you wipe your face,
and look up to the darkening skies.

I snatch a child's kite and spiral it around,
and watch the laughter it provides.
I rush out to sea, and rush back again,
releasing the kite, to push out the tide.
She cries as her plastic peregrine dives down,
breaking upon impact on unforgiving wet sand.
I ruffle its colourful tail, a final flapping of insulting applause,
and blow her tears off her cheeks, leaving salty lines of sadness.

I lull around rocks, lifting and shifting seaweed,
and rest whilst kissing ripples in the sand.
A barely visible blanket of power,
carrying with me, pieces of previous land.
I push grass until it takes a bow,
and push leaves off trees to the ground.
I've been here before and I'm here now.
Sometimes a roar, sometimes a whispering sound.

THE LIGHT IN THE NORTH

Allan Gaw

April 1264

The young priest pulled his cloak tight about his neck. The storm rose, and he made his way across the open yard from the Bishop's Palace. Outside the walls, he almost stumbled in the dark, kicking over the mound of yet another pauper's grave. It was unmarked and soon to be forgotten. Nevertheless, he gestured a perfunctory blessing.

As he entered the gate, the rain was coming at him from every angle. The wild air was like a host of demons grabbing at him, lifting his cloak, forcing him back from the cathedral door. He held his swaying light up to find the lock and one demon found its way in.

The candle guttered behind the small glass pane of the lantern and smoked as it died. The priest could not see the boiling waves beyond the rocks, but he could hear their crash as they beat the shoreline, incessantly, demanding entry to the mainland. Steadying himself from the storm, he wedged himself hard against the door as he worked the great key in the lock. The winds began to twist about him, wringing even more rain from the clouds, bringing it down heavier than ever.

The lock was stiff, but he had the strength to make it yield and the door opened. He almost fell into the vestibule and pushed the heavy wooden door closed behind him, finally shutting out the tempest. In the sudden stillness, he shook the worst of the rain from his cape and his cowl and muttered to himself, 'What a night to choose for it.'

From the leather satchel slung across his chest, he gathered up the candles he had brought and checked he had enough. They would need light for such a task. Why it had to be done in the depth of night, he did not know. Ever since they came, they had been nothing but trouble. Why would they change now?

Before he entered the transept, he checked himself and closed his eyes to remember where he was and who he served. Only his vow of obedience tempered any further uncharitable thoughts. Bishop Henry had told him to offer all assistance and that was what he would do. It was not for him to question.

The cathedral was in darkness save for the altar where a pool of warm candlelight lit the blood stone of the walls. But even that meagre glow could not seep any further into the vaulted space above. Up there, the timbers creaked in the darkness, and there was the flutter of a bird. It would soon be midnight and the two warriors on guard were sitting on the steps of the altar talking, their own robes wrapped tight about them to keep out the chill.

The priest hesitated when he saw them and slid out of sight behind one of the four great pillars supporting the tower. From there he could hear the men without being seen. Their accents were strange, but he knew their tongue.

They had come from Norway and then sailed south in the summer from Ronaldsvo in a great fleet to challenge the Scottish king. But they had returned battered and depleted as autumn began to chill the air. That had been six months ago, and events had forced them to overstay any welcome the bishop had extended to them. At their head was their great king, Haakon Haakonsson. Old Haco was how he had always been known on these isles.

On his departure from Orkney, the king had invited Bishop Henry to sail with him. Whether His Grace was predisposed to undertake such a journey for such a cause was neither here nor there. Old Haco was his king, and an invitation was as good as a commandment from God, only with more immediate repercussions if it was flouted.

When they returned, the king lodged himself in Bishop Henry's Palace, forcing the cleric from his own bed, some said. Their rout at the hands of the Scots was painted as a clash with the elements. Winds and storms had been conjured by dark magic against a rightful overlord.

Old Haco might have believed his own story, but even if he saw it as a humiliating defeat, he was forced to overwinter in Kirkwall before trying his hand again to seize the Scottish crown. But after two darkening months he was dead. A week before the solstice, the old man had breathed his last. Killed by his defeat, some said. Others called foul the hospitality he had received.

As befits a king, he was buried beneath the high altar of the cathedral, and in pairs each night, two of the Norse nobles from his suite would stand watch over the royal grave. Now the year had turned, and spring had calmed the seas to Norway. Magnus,

Old Haco's son, now wearing the Norse crown in Bergen, had summoned his father's body home.

'What an arsehole of a place this is! And the women! Don't get me started. If they hadn't killed our king, we would be back in a Bergen bed by now with a soft, fair-haired maid in our arms.'

'Stay your wrath, soldier. No one killed our king, except the good Lord himself. He was an old man. His time had come, that's all.'

'I don't care what you say. He was well until he landed here. That pigswill they call food probably done for him. I know my guts haven't been right since we dropped anchor. If I never see this place again, it'll be too soon.'

'I think we'll all be glad to get home, God willing. This has been such a misguided expedition right from the start. His Majesty, may he rest in eternal peace, should never have come.'

'What? It was the power of enchantment that brought us low. You know as well as me that those Scottish storms were unnatural. I've never seen such troubled floods. They tore our ships from their moorings and dashed them on the shores. The devil himself wrenched the anchors from our craft. No power on Earth could have defeated us that day. That Scottish king opened the gates of hell upon us.'

The priest listened to the same excuses and insinuations he heard every night. These islands were Norse in name only. Orkney was just a watering hole on the great whale roads from Norway to the rest of the world. All ships passed here, but no one stayed for long. To these men, this was a place unfit for the repository of a king. But mercifully by sunrise, they would all be gone. For tonight, the king's body would be disinterred and prepared for the journey home.

'And another thing, this place is as cold as an old hag's...'

The wail and howl of the wind suddenly rose through the square tower above and silenced the man. He crossed himself but his thoughts were pagan. The very earth seemed to be offended by the disturbance of a dead king.

The priest took advantage of the moment and slipped from the shadows to walk up the centre aisle of the choir. He genuflected deeply before the altar and approached the nobles.

'My lords, His Grace sends you fresh candles to lighten your work.'

One of the men bowed to acknowledge the father, but the other looked him over and snorted before asking his fellow guard if it was time. He returned a glare of disappointment and told him to give some respect to a man of God.

'We're all men of God, but some of us use the balls He gave us. And I don't need some islander to tell me how to bear my king home. Now, let's get on with it. Stand back priest, this is a job for men.'

They lit the candles and arrayed them around the altar, while the priest watched them closely at work. This was the most sacred part of the great cathedral, and as well as being ordered to deliver assistance, the bishop had also charged his priest with ensuring that no damage was done by these crude men of the sword.

He stood back with his hands clasped within his cassock. The heavy sandstone flag was prised up and slid at an angle to one side revealing the crypt. What was immediately apparent was the water. The shrouded corpse of Haakon was bloated and almost submerged in the soil-stained ground water.

The nobles fumbled with the ropes they needed to slip beneath the body and one of them cursed only to be brought to book by the other. He turned and asked the priest's pardon for his fellow's impiety. The priest came closer and leant in to see the condition of the corpse and counselled them to take care.

'Get away from us, priest!'

'He's trying to help us, you fool. Shut your blasphemous mouth for once and give him a chance to speak.'

'My lords, the king's royal remains may be easily damaged in this parlous state. I humbly suggest you spread the weight on other ropes before you try to raise him.'

'Don't listen to him. Let's just get His Majesty out of here and on that ship for home.'

In anger, he turned and tugged hard on the rope which slipped through his hand, sending one end of the king's body crashing back into the water. When they tried to recover the corpse, they saw that the force of it hitting the side of the stone crypt had severed the shrouded head from the body. Both nobles stepped back in panic, while the priest fell to his knees, not to pray, but to reach in and secure the head. He looked up and saw that both Norsemen were paralysed by what they had done. There could be no mercy for such a desecration.

The wind was still whipping the cathedral, and the candles around the open crypt were flickering with each new gust that found its way through the cracks in the red stonework. Shadows danced on the walls around the altar like the hounds of hell that had breached the sanctity of the place.

The priest had already watched Haakon's hoard of men take the winter stores of the farmers around the mainland and knew that if they did not leave now, starvation would soon be visited upon all on Orkney. They had to go, and he knew what had to be done.

As the sun rose on a spent sea, exhausted from a night of battle with the wind, Haakon Haakonsson's flagship slipped its moorings and set its great sail for Norway. Bishop Henry stood at the quayside with his priest to see them off. On the ship in prime place was the body of the king bound fast and shrouded in a royal robe ready to be received by the new king in Bergen.

'You have done well, my son. Now, to other matters. There is much to do.'

The bishop made his way back up the hill to his palace. It was built of the same blood stone as the great St Magnus Cathedral and, for the first time in months, he could call it his own again. As he passed the makeshift paupers' graves outside the cathedral walls, he did not even notice that one was freshly dug over.

The priest stayed on the quay, watching the golden-prowed ship disappear into the early morning fog. Only two of the nobles aboard her knew the real freight they carried — an old beggar of similar build to the Norse king who would now be borne to a royal tomb in Bergen.

The priest followed the bishop back up the hill in the shadow of St Magnus, but he paused by the new grave to offer a silent prayer of repose. A prayer fit for a king.

DECISIONS

Mary Brown

The bag's still there. At the back of the wardrobe.

The old woman was outside the shopping centre, crumbling, holding on to her little shopper. I ran forward to help. Managed to stop her from banging her head, but she still fell to the ground.

I knelt beside her and she gripped my hand. Amazing how strong she was. I took off my jacket and folded it under her head. She kept mumbling, so I said, 'It's okay. You'll be fine.' That seemed to calm her.

The ambulance came, and the crowd cleared a little. In a couple of minutes she was on the stretcher, and her handbag was inside my jacket.

I couldn't wait to get home. Practically ran up the stairs. I'd watched her getting her pension in the Post Office.

It's quite pathetic really, the old bag. Black leather and soft with age.

There was nearly £100 folded into the wee zipped pocket. The lining was torn, but she had a lipstick, a mirror and hairbrush. And a red purse. I looked inside. Her name's Elizabeth. Same as my Nan. She had two old brown photos. One of a soldier and another of him standing next to a bride.

I could see the old woman's face. Her eyes looking right inside me. Then her face changed. It became my Nan.

I put everything back in the bag and buried it at the back of the wardrobe.

BLACK WOLF: GREY DOG

Anne V McClure

At first, grief is a black wolf.
He rips my skin and crunches my bone.
He pounces on me in supermarket aisles.
He howls in the passenger seat on every drive to work.
His yellow eyes terrify me through memory wracked nights.

Years later, I realise
He has become a tired, grey dog.
He sits across my feet and snores.
He snaps and snarls at certain days, or sights or scents or songs.
He mostly sleeps. An old dog. Quiet and sad and warm.

THE DAMN MIDGES

Palo Stickland

We used to keep the children indoors because of those damned midges. Clouds of them. You could see them from the window, but the children begged to be let out to play and came in, jumping on the spot, shaking the insects out of their hair, being ushered into the shower before bedtime stories – Harry Potter a favourite.

Around the house, there were two burns; one tiny running down from the hill behind the house, gurgling over the stones past the kitchen door. The one at the front, making its way to the loch, six feet across, and as much deep. Dangerous when it was in spate.

I can imagine her standing there, the frail woman dressed in a thin slip, peering over the edge, staring at the water with sad, blank eyes, having forgotten what she was doing, where she was, and even who she was. A young woman with an old person's affliction. Everyone said, such a shame, her young family left without a mother, but she was gone before she died. Her young son saying, 'Mummy, you need to feed the baby.

She's crying.' Then, leaving Mummy at the burn's edge and gazing through the window with the baby in his arms, waiting for Daddy to come home.

She was my predecessor. Hidden from sight now, but still around in spirit. I am here, watching her at the burn, and protecting her children from the damn midges.

NEW LOVE

Adrienne Whitehall

He looks up at me adoringly,
and I look down on him disbelievingly.
He smiles,
I kiss his brow.
We bill and coo
and he stretches up
to catch the words of love
pouring from my lips.
I kiss his palm.
He laughs,
and his eyes dance with delight.
I cradle him in my arms,
my new love,
my infant son.

THE RISE OF LOUP-GAROU

Iain Anderson

1699 – The Palace of Versailles – a typical autumn evening under a large harvest moon

Louis Quatorze often sought solace strolling alone at night through the newly created parterre. At such times when the moon was full, he would stare pensively at the great luminous ball, in ascendancy above the horizon casting an eerie light all around. It is ironic therefore that Louis, revered as the sun god by his subjects, actually worshipped the moon.

In childhood, his heavily down-covered body was never questioned. He had after all, the swarthy Medici genes from his grandmother's lineage. Other explanations were unthinkable. In late adolescence, his alter ego of enjoying warm sunny days was in stark contrast to his main pleasure, lurking unnoticed in the dark shadows of his estate. There his assignations with feral night brethren became commonplace and awakened a febrile energy within his soul. Howling would often be heard which strangely would cease on his return to the royal apartments.

Much fear was abroad in the land, as the wolf population grew exponentially in the nearby forests. It was known, but not understood, why Louis had issued a decree banning culling the beasts. To question this rationale, was to lose your head; no one did, and heads were kept. Maintaining lupine anonymity was, however, becoming increasingly more difficult, and to assuage suspicion, a mute doppelganger was secretly smuggled into the palace. The compliant fool was kept in the dungeons by day, emerging only at night when conjugal duties with the queen demanded attendance in the young infanta's bedchamber. Louis's faithful Groom of the Stool was the only one privy to the secret, and so it remained.

Louis loved *La Belle Dance.* Famed for choreographing many Baroque masked balls, he would rise from a hidden subterranean chamber sometimes resplendent in solar couture, and sometimes simply as the beast. Who would expect they were not all elaborate costumes? Duchesses and marquises alike were hypnotised by his *Ballet Royale de la Nuit*, particularly when this involved nuzzling their decolletage, before spiriting his unwitting dance partners to a private encounter behind the surrounding tapestries. No one questioned that this quick diversion was not integral to the play. He would then reappear alone, using a cravat to wipe a small drop of blood from a pin sharp incisor. '*Bravo – Espéce de bête*' a loud cry would resound from watching sycophants, little knowing the monster was in their midst.

Through many such liaisons a whole society of male chimera was created. Successive generations coalesced to form a special closed *Société Lycanthropé*. Later, despite depletion of the aristocracy during the Robespierre era, corruption was the catalyst that saved many remote bastions of the creed from a bloody fate under the Madame Guillotine blade. Remnants of scattered Bourbons across France were able to once again rise, allowing lycanthrope infiltration in all positions of government, the church, and judiciary.

Fast forward several centuries.

Throughout the 20th century, private medical clinics established by the *Société* were quick to flourish. Their doctrine was to source newborns, who carried the 78 chromosomes peculiar to the chimera. Pre-selection singled out those special males for grooming through nursery before being sent on to select colleges. In France the founding college, *Chien Dormant*, was discreetly located in Rue de l'Aubrevoir 18th Arrondissement Montmartre, not far from the *Moulin Rouge* and former haunts of the French Impressionists. The college grounds also housed the council headquarters of the *Société*. In these hallowed chambers, college rules were set. Guardians were appointed for instruction, and to monitor enforcement.

The extracurricular rules were simple:

Junior grades were instructed in the ancient art of sniffing and howling, only to be practised within the confines of sound-proof classrooms.

Senior grades were taught to conceal their primeval identity by suppressing basic instincts, before leaving to integrate into society.

In many cases, medication or intervention surgery was required to ensure anonymity. This was thought to be a fail-safe guarantee, and many prospective presidents, cardinals, members of the judiciary and captains of industry passed through the college doors and into society with equanimity.

However, on the night of September 5th, 2019, under a full harvest moon, all was not as it should be in the Montmartre college. Crocblanc, son of an eminent cardinal and senior grade alpha male, started howling in concert with the moon phase. Sleep in the dormitories became no longer possible. The sub alphas were quick to join. Soon riot became unstoppable. Night porters fearing for their lives, fled to the safety of the panic room as the break-out momentum overwhelmed unprepared security systems. The escapees raced to Sacre Coeur, breaking and entering the main tower through a side window. Crocblanc, shouldering his way up the final ladder mauled the backs of those in front to exert his authority, and exit first onto the topmost balcony. Arching his massive silver back, and with full neck stretch, he let rip a blood curdling howl which echoed to all parts of the city. The call was answered again, and again. Adult Loup-Garou hearing the cacophony needed no alert from the colleges. They were, however, impotent in any ability to control the wayward whelps. The sound of sirens also added to the chaos which swept Paris and other cities across Europe as the call for anarchy was taken up. A coordinated clamp down by international security forces followed. It was brutal and swift. The discontent was thought to be merely passing student unrest, uncoordinated – leader-less! That is until the seeds of something more sinister was seen to be germinating on the other side of the pond.

January 6th, 2021 – Washington DC.

The full moon is just visible in the late afternoon sky, as a disgruntled orator stands on a podium, swaying his golden main back and forth. He has a wan almost constipated smile which creases his thick orange face make up. His cuffs are pulled tightly down to hide his hairy arms from the watching media, all except kindred – Fox News.

Neck stretched, eyes reddening, he addresses the expectant mob baying for blood.

'My fellow Ly – err Americans, you can make us – err America, great again! Yes, I know, you know I am a great pack leader! Our country is being taken from us – they are trying to stop my first amendment rights! – steal counted votes to keep a sleepy incumbent cur in power! I know, yes, I know you know who could have stopped this bad, yes, very bad, bad, bad thing and failed, yes failed, failed in this sacred duty to our cause – it is my former running mate.' Pausing, he whispers aside, 'Running Wolf, I would not give a brass pence for your safety.' And then stretching his hairy neck, he continues, 'who has stabbed, can you believe it, yes stabbed, stabbed me in the back!'

He waits for the mob's chanting to momentarily quieten. Suppressing a howl, he intensifies his rhetoric.

'Go down to Capitol Howl – err Hill – I will be right behind you – fight like the demons from hell – rip out the throats of these sons of bitches – feast on their blood and bring us rightful victory!'

To be continued!

(All character references to persons alive or dead are purely fictional.)

MY HEARTWARMING AMERICAN MADE-FOR-TV CHRISTMAS MOVIE

David McVey

Last Christmas Kellee went through a break-up. She and Blade split up as Christmas lights glittered and snow frosted the streets. Now she dreads the season, so leaves the city and heads back to Pine Lake, her snowy mountain hometown, for the holidays.

She meets her sassy black friend Dolores from high school. Dolores introduces her to Dane. He works as a chain store Santa and is the kind of guy who puts up his tree in October! They meet at a coffee shop that specialises in decorated Christmas cookies. They get to know each other but his enthusiasm for Christmas is a barrier. They begin to argue. Eventually, she storms out.

Meanwhile, Blade, her ex, has followed her to Pine Lake. He's a sharp city lawyer and he wants her back. He confronts her in the street at the Christmas parade. What can she do?

Back home, Kellee undergoes some speedy personal growth as light Christmassy jazz plays. She goes to the Grand

Christmas Eve Ball. Blade's there too but she tells him bluntly to go back to the city; she's over him. Then she comes face to face with Dane and, as romantic Christmas music overwhelms the scene, they realise that they are under the mistletoe…

They kiss; it's a miracle of love at Christmas!

Suddenly, there's a spray of bullets and blood and the thud of collapsing bodies.

A giant, heavily armed turkey steps over their gory corpses.

'I hate Christmas,' he says.

IT'S RAINING

Adrienne Whitehall

Rain, rain,
you spoil my plans and social games.
Can't play tennis, can't play bowls,
golf game cancelled –
waterlogged holes.

Rain, rain,
always there or thereabouts,
thick dark clouds, there is no doubt
you spoil my
roses, carnations and pansies,
my washing's all wet
so I can't iron my undies.

Rain, rain
I must explain
yesterday without complain
I washed my windows once again.
Today I look with great distress
my windows such a dreadful mess
my work in vain.

Rain, rain
I rack my brain
to find a way to pass my time.
But wait

where's that good book?
Feet up, stop whining,
every cloud has a silver lining.

LOST ON THE WAY TO THE WAY

John Dickson

'I'm tellin' ye the compass needle's birlin'!' I exclaimed with frustration while lost in the maze that the Queen Elizabeth Forest had become.

We were on another one of our practice walks in our quest to get ourselves fit enough to conquer the West Highland Way. Two of four middle-aged would-be trekkers, committed to learning all the skills necessary to toast our success when we boldly marched into Fort William at the end of May in the early nineties.

The instigator of our collective adventure, Jim, had recommended that we should deliberately walk deep into the forest. We would attempt to find a route from a car park on the edge of the forest between Gartmore and Drymen, all the way to the shores of the delightful Loch Ard. Then ambitiously follow a *different* route back.

We'd had a couple of incidents in our previous rehearsals. Our very first attempt, a simple circular walk up the Campsie Fells had resulted in Jim and both our families having to come to my rescue once I'd sunk up to my chest in a camouflaged icy bog. It took the collective muscles of three adults and three under 10's pulling on Jim's lifeline of a thrown rucksack to heave my trapped lower body out of the freezing gunk!

We'd pored over the map of the forest and carefully planned our routes using the many woodland paths. We were perversely pleased that the paths weren't yet way marked. On paper it looked simple.

Then we put our freshly broken-in boots on the ground.

We parked the car and donned our newly purchased hiking waterproof and sweatproof jackets. (Different brands of course. We weren't *that* sad.) Heaved on our newly purchased extra-large rucksacks and opened our newly purchased OS map that folded and fitted perfectly into our newly purchased map holder.

We were ready.

Compass in hand we strode down the wide path and into the forest, carefully matching our progress on the map.

'This is good. No wives or weans,' I said gratefully. 'Not that we don't love them to bits, but we can set a decent pace and get some idea how many miles per hour we should achieve on the Way'.

'Ah but this is more level than most of the Way. No Devil's Staircase here! I reckon we should manage the twelve miles we've mapped out in about four hours.' Jim's always been a dab hand at research.

Two hours in and we were at yet another crossroads in the forest. At least there was a decent clearing here.

Every direction looked the same. By this time my patience with Jim's compass readings and navigational skills was beginning to wear thin.

'Break time.'

'OK then. I'll treat myself to a ham sarnie.' Jim unloaded his bag and opened the ham sarnie compartment in his many-pocketed new rucksack.

'While you're rummaging, I'll have a look at that compass and map.'

I stood in the middle of the clearing and stared at the map, trying to glean which paths had brought us to these nameless crossroads.

I placed the compass on top of the map.

The compass needle spun.

I blinked.

I stared at the compass.

I turned around.

The needle spun again.

I shook the compass.

The needle still spun.

'Eh… Jim? This compass needle's spinning. Did it do that with you?'

'Nope. It tends to point to north. That's kind of the idea.' Jim smiled condescendingly.

'I'm tellin' ye the compass needle's birlin'!' I glared back in bewilderment.

'Aye well…' Jim raised his eyes then pointed above my head.

'It could be something to do with that.'

I looked up and belatedly took in the scale of the enormous National Grid pylon reaching to the sky above the tops of the trees, with thousands of volts coursing through the attached cables.

'Well, that just might spin a wee compass needle,' I had to accept.

After laughing at my ineptitude I decided to let Jim carry on navigating. And while the pylon had spun the needle into uselessness it had given us a possible reference on the map to fix our position.

Or was it that other pylon?

We marched down the next path of uncertainty.

Crossing yet another clearing, we were stopped in our tracks by loud cracking noises and sudden unfamiliar smells as bits of debris rained down on our heads.

'Wow! What's going on?' We looked at each other as the noises repeated and more fragments fell on us.

As we were trying to take in this bizarre turn of events, a very posh disembodied female voice shouted from beyond the outer reaches of the clearing.

'Get out of there you fools!'

'Who the Hell are you calling fools?' my Glaswegian hackles rose. We might be lost and tired and not know what's going on, but… fools?

'You're in a designated clay pigeon target area. You could be shot.'

'Not if you and your idiot friends stop shooting when people wander across your unsignposted, undesignated target area!' I was miffed.

Then I thought. *These plonkers probably know the forest.*

'Tell us which path leads to Loch Ard and we'll leave you to play with your make-believe guns!'

'The guns aren't make-believe,' Jim whispered 'They're for real. The clay pigeons are the make-believe bit.'

'By the way, it's not usually a great idea to argue with someone you cannae see but you *know* is carrying a loaded gun!'

A very good point.

'Turn right at the next junction. We'll hold our fire until you're past. Though do hurry.'

We never did see who the arrogant posh voice belonged to. But her directions worked a treat.

With relief we reached the serene shores of Loch Ard. The water was completely still, reflecting the trees and the Trossachs rising from the opposite bank. Tranquility – for a short while.

Time to partake of our squashed filled rolls and remaining sarnies and plan our way back.

We were still determined to master the intricacies of orienteering, even though our halfway stop was two hours behind schedule. Refreshed by the squashed rolls and sugar boosted by Mars bars we heaved our rucksacks back on our shoulders and headed back into the forest. Using a different path of course. Just to raise the stakes in our challenge. Or more honestly because we couldn't remember which path we'd spilled from.

Avoiding needle spinning pylons we strode purposefully along the curved path until we lost sight of the loch behind us.

The first few crossroads in the forest maze didn't faze us. We reckoned we'd finally mastered the concept.

'We're doing better now,' I chirruped, as we made good progress. 'I reckon we should be back at the car in under an hour.'

Two hours later we came to a weary stop.

'I'm sure I recognise that particular clump of trees.' Jim didn't really sound hopeful.

Suddenly there was a very unexpected sound.

We heard Christmas bells tinkling through the forest, coming towards us along the curved path to our right.

We looked at each other in bewilderment. 'Eh?'

It got still weirder as a definitely human voice called out 'Mush! Mush!', along with strange panting sounds.

Just then we had to jump out of the way while a team of six huskies dragging a sleigh with what looked like large pram wheels stuck on its sides trundled by.

The sleigh rider, standing at the back waved as he passed. A truly surreal sight when you're already very tired and confused.

'How lost can we be?' I asked plaintively as the contraption disappeared round the next curve in the path. 'Are we still in Scotland?'

We decided to follow the sleigh as quickly as our weary feet would take us. Figuring the rider probably knew where he was going. Unlike us.

A few hundred yards along the path we came across the man and his machine where he'd stopped to tend to one of his glorious huskies.

We discovered he was a regular in the forest where he practised for the forthcoming Aviemore Sled Dog Rally. Apparently it wasn't uncommon for the sleds (not sleighs we were told) to be fitted with wheels, as Scottish snow was a tad unreliable.

More importantly, our new best friend was able to give us simple clear directions back to where we'd parked. Which, thankfully, wasn't all that far.

'Apparently the West Highland Way actually has signposts,' he said helpfully when we'd told him of our travails.

Twenty minutes later the very welcome sight of the car glimpsed through the bushes was such a relief!

After seven hours of indiscriminate tramping and with the thought of pulling off the heavy boots, slipping on comfy trainers, and driving down to Drymen for that reward of a freshly pulled pint, brought forth a muted mumble. 'Only good things now!'

Jim laughed exhaustedly. 'You bet!'

OUT OF THE PAST

David Maclean

One of my Mum's cousins, now 67 with 3 kids of various adult ages, came round for a couple of days recently. Mum hadn't seen her in decades. My brother and I also turned up and she spent a great deal of time going over our family photo books as well as some pictures on her iPhone of her own family.

I couldn't remember seeing her before although I'm sure I met her a long time ago. She is from the English Midlands and was soft spoken but talkative and charming. As I looked over some of these pictures in both colour and b/w I felt a great sense of nostalgia and loss.

Nostalgia because it reminded me of carefree days of my youth actually meeting these people and loss because so many of them in the pictures are long gone.

I remembered that during a recent clear out of my room I had found a DVD of cine recordings from these eras, which included a small section of my parents wedding in shaky colour complete with film damage. It was 1964 and I recognised some of the faces. They were from a different generation, slim, silly hats, smoking too much and happy. This less than 20 years after the end of WWII.

I saw pictures and videos of myself as a baby and it made me think about what a wonderful thing photography is, capturing moments in time never to be repeated, of people who lived, breathed and had their own incredible stories to tell. Sadly, in those pre internet, mass communication days very often they didn't get the chance. I know some of them with hindsight weren't, but I hope most were as genuinely happy as they looked and had joyous, fulfilling lives.

BEACH: EVENING

Don J Taylor

A day of showers
pushed in from the West:
inky clouds edged with silver,
making steady headway,
trailing spiralled gouts of rain
that rake the willing earth.

Now, near sunset,
brighter and higher than
the fading evening star
Jupiter blazes his cold wisdom:
a beacon in an ice-blue sky.

Skylarks burble amidst the low dunes,
not in high-noon bravado
but mollified and shy among the marram.

On the strand,
a human shape against the still shining sea:
a girl, all angles and attitude,
tethered to a tugging terrier,
her face
a sickly smart-phone sheen.

Cornered in dark rocks,
devotees cluster
to feed the flicker of a fitful fire.

Air shifts –
smoke blown onshore,
wears the tarry tang
of driftwood.

The tacking wind lets fall
one last sweet breath of rain,
dimming the glimmer at the sea's far edge
and with this blessing
I quit the day.

MOTHER AND DAUGHTER

Lorraine Johnston

My mother and I always had a difficult relationship. We've intellectually locked horns over the years, and I've always felt emotionally drained, even after a relatively short period of time spent in her company. I'm not sure whether she felt the same about me. She often seemed to be unaware of any offence she caused and ploughed on regardless with her cutting words and her nipping tongue. Nothing I did was *ever* good enough for her. No decision I made was ever the right one, and the people I chose for friends or lovers never quite matched up to what she expected for me. I was a bitter disappointment to her from start to finish, as she so often reminded me. Indeed, one day whilst getting ready to go to nursery, she told me that I was a mistake! I would have been around three or four years old. You don't recover well from that sort of start in life.

That was *before* her diagnosis.

Today, she's a different person completely, a mere shell of her former self. She's sometimes a little more relaxed, softer, somehow. Her steel grey-blue eyes the only remnant left of the cold and hard person that she'd always been.

She looks old and crumpled sitting in the resident's lounge. Her face full of the lines of her history, and she wears it like an uncomfortable old jumper. She no longer has the meticulous make-up and the lipstick religiously touched up prior to going out or receiving visitors.

Today she's wearing a pair of maroon velour trousers with an elasticated waistband along with a matching zipped top. She would *never* have worn clothes like these when she was able to choose her own outfits. Even her shoes shriek of her institutionalised living, with their wipeable plastic, slip-on style and Velcro straps.

'Morning Mum.' I say as I enter the lounge where she's been parked for the day, at the bay window.

'Who are you?' she asks.

It's like this *most* days. Sometimes she calls me nurse. Other times she apologises to me and says that she can't remember my name. I think she knows deep down that she *should* know who I am, and she has tears in her eyes some mornings.

She never used to be weepy.

'How are you today?' I ask, whilst taking a seat next to her, on a vinyl covered chair that smells of an unpleasant mix of school dinners and disinfectant. She looks at me with a confused look on her face. Today there is no communication, no recognition from the mum I have known and resented for my entire life.

'Oh, thank goodness you're here!' She grabs my arm with a strength that belies her frailty. 'I've been wondering where you'd got to. Can you get me out of here? I hate this place!

They're all trying to poison me! And that prison officer keeps giving me bloody tablets – I don't even *need* bloody tablets! I'm as fit as a fiddle!' she tells me, getting in quite a state. This is her typical mantra, and I reply with my usual response for a lack of knowing what else to say.

'Mum, that lady is *not* a prison officer, she's the matron here. This is *not* a prison but a nursing home, remember? It's called Sunnybrook.' I tried to say it reassuringly, but there seems little point, as she simply keeps losing this piece of information.

'I don't understand,' says Mum. 'I don't want to stay here! I have a perfectly good home in…' she stops, clearly lost in a synaptic dead end. She stares out the window for a few seconds and drops her conversation into the Alzheimer's black hole.

'So, what's *your* name dear? I haven't seen you before. Are you new here?'

I can't help the sigh that escapes from my chest and pat her knee and hope she didn't hear it.

'No, I'm not new here. I come here every day. I will be back in a moment Mum; I'm going to speak to the Matron.' I leave the sun-filled lounge and notice that a few elderly patients are sitting in a semi-circle, looking at me sadly. I am not sure whether they are sad for my situation with my mum, or just sad to be here at all.

As I make my way towards the hall, I hear my mum screaming at the top of her voice.

'Don't come back here Rachel Morven! Do you *hear* me? I wish you were *never* born!' her tone of voice familiar, cold and harsh. 'Go on bitch, leave! And don't *ever* come back!'

I rush to the hallway and burst into tears. A nursing assistant follows me from the lounge.

'Are you alright?' she says, offering me a tissue. 'She doesn't know what she is saying, Mrs Jenkins,' she offers kindly. 'It's not your mum saying that; it's the Alzheimer's disease talking.'

Clearly this is the opinion of my mother *after* her diagnosis. The nursing assistant didn't know my mother when she was in her prime. If she *had* known her back then, I'd have gotten a far deeper level of sympathy – a sympathy that has nothing to do with the Alzheimer's.

I walk to the office to speak to today's duty Matron. She's sitting at her desk filled with case notes, care plans and risk assessments.

'Hello Matron,' I say as I knock on the office door.

'Ah, Mrs Jenkins, come in and have a seat, if you can find space that is.' She shifts some large box files off the seat and motions for me to sit on the wobbly visitor's chair. 'Have you seen your mother yet, or have you just arrived?' she asks.

'I've seen her,' I reply. 'I'm not sure that she will remember though. She seems quite bad today.'

'Yes, the poor soul. Alzheimer's does that to you, I'm afraid. It can be quite challenging to repeat things on a regular basis, and trying to reassure her that she *isn't* in a prison. She packed her bags again yesterday evening and tried to leave. Luckily, she tried to leave via the hall linen cupboard, so staff found her fairly quickly.' The Matron saw my expression and looked like she immediately regretted telling me about this latest incident.

'Of course, *all* the external doors have security keypads, and our staff are always on the lookout for escapees, so you needn't worry about her safety.'

'Right,' I said, not knowing what else I *could* say. 'I'll let you get on with your work, thank you.'

'Goodbye then, see you tomorrow, Mrs Jenkins.'

'Bye.'

I had ten minutes spare, so I took the long way and walked through the park. The daffodils were waving softly in the breeze. I could feel the warm sun on my face. Why did I keep going back to visit? What's the point? It hurts and upsets me. It often upsets her too. She never liked or wanted me as a child, and I was a fool to think that would change after she developed Alzheimer's. I thought the disease might reveal a softer side. Even if it had made her less vitriolic towards me, that would have been a welcome side-effect. But no; if anything, she was *exactly* who she'd always been. Angry, bitter and hateful.

So, why then, oh why, did I continue to visit her daily?

Because despite everything, she'd brought me up to take care of my responsibilities. She made me into a dutiful daughter.

I wiped my face and took a deep breath and sighed, trying to shift some of the heaviness off my shoulders.

Perhaps tomorrow will be better.

I arrive at the nursery in time for the bell, and before the hubbub of giggles and lopsided cardigans and rolled down socks fill the corridors and playrooms in a happy froth of young life.

'Mummy!' Poppy squeals. 'Can Lisa come to our house for a playdate today?'

'Well, hello to you too Toots!' I take her jacket and her lunchbox off the floor and scan the room for Lisa's mum. 'If it's ok with her mummy, she can come to play and have tea.'

'YAY! Thank you Mummy.' Poppy wraps her sticky hands round my legs and squeezes as hard as is possible for a four-year-old to squeeze. 'I love you mummy! LISA!'

I watch my wee girl take Lisa's hand in sheer joy and excitement, and telling her that she *can* come for tea. As Lisa happily grabs her mum to ask the question, I make a decision, right there and then.

Tomorrow is going to be spent having a family day out. Sandwiches, buckets and spades and juice boxes and books, and Poppy's favourite picnic blanket, all will get packed in the car, and we will head to the beach. Perhaps I can persuade David, that we should go away for the whole weekend.

Poppy knows she is loved, and I'm going to show her that I love her more than anything else in the world, for the rest of my life.

MIDWEEK MORNINGS

Julie McNeill

On week days
he wakes screaming
breathless

I coax him through
the steps:
not too big, tiptoes really

half-spoons of cereal
his school uniform
on the radiator

to take the cold edges
off. His toothbrush
placed carefully

at the right angle.
One foot in the shower,
two, pants, trousers,

I do the tie
pausing after each step
to hold him

as he crumples
into my neck.
I colour code his day

stack books neatly
in plastic wallets
ease him, ease him away.

SKY PAINTING

Paula Andrews

Lily curled in a ball on her bed. Her stomach growled and she rubbed her pounding head. For two days she had sobbed and sobbed.

'You'll feel better soon, Lil,' Dad had said. 'It's only a starling.'

But Dad was wrong. She wouldn't feel better. Something had happened and Pepper had gone. He came every day and now Lily couldn't eat. Because she knew. In her heart, she knew it. Pepper was old and had flown off quietly to die.

She missed her friend swooping in her window for breakfast. She saved him bits of food like mashed potato or bacon rind and in he'd flit, a flickering fold of biscuit-brown. He'd land on her desk then snip and snap and flip and flap at chunks of apple. Or slurp strawberry jam from scraps of toast, which made him zing with excitement. He'd suck the sugary gloop through his pointy beak then hop onto her hand and dance from foot to foot. And he'd preen his fleckled feathers which looked sometimes purple or silver or green.

Lily thought she was melting with sadness. Her words had all dribbled away. She'd stopped sending messages on her phone and even crazy cat videos felt silly and pointless now. Dad had tried to win her round, calling through the door.

'Look, Lil, I've found a hilarious video. You gotta see this crazy cat.' But Lily couldn't care less anymore, and she'd stuck her phone in the bottom of her drawer.

She rolled out of bed and dragged her body to the window. The scuffed grey sky was moping and dull denim clouds trudged by. They seemed to feel like she did.

Then a flicker caught her eye. Down in the garden. There! It was Pepper! She flung on her dungarees and hurtled downstairs.

Pepper?' she whispered.

He perched on a fencepost. He seemed more radiant than before, and he began to whistle like steam from a lidded pan on the boil.

'*Is* it you?' Lily whispered.

And Pepper blinked. Just like always.

'It is you! It is!'

Pepper took flight and swooped between two slats to the yard on the other side where cats had raucous parties at night and there were garages and bins and rats hid in empty food tins. But the fence was prickly with splinters. And the bolt on the gate was rusted shut. So Lily couldn't get through.

Pepper began to whistle and chatter. Like all starlings, he was a mimic and Lily heard:

'What's keep-keeping you, Lil? Tu-tu-tzeeee. Tu-du-du. What's keep-keeping you?'

Then he was back and with a rumbling shudder, lots more starlings arrived in a line, perching and babbling and thrumming their feathers.

'Good to see you, Pepper,' Lily croaked. A lump that felt like plasticine, as big as a fist, stuck in her throat. Pepper hopped onto her shoulder. His wing tickled her skin but he felt lighter than a breeze. He tilted his bill towards her ear and began to sing. His music poured and tweedled like liquid in her head, flowing and spiralling, spitting and dancing. Then he took to the air again. And Lily felt his magic twirling and twisting, swinging like bells, sprinkling like sugar, clinking like seashells, tingling and shingling. And her body began to elongate and she felt as if she was blowing her breath through puckered lips. She grew flatter and her fingers fluttered in the cool dawn air. She peered through the fence and there was Pepper, his wings like a fuzz of velvet, hovering.

'What's keep-keeping you, Lil? Tu-tu-tzeee. You'll miss my in-aug-err-err-ation.'

Lily looked down at her body, now as thin as rain, then she slipped through the gap in the fence.

The yard, too, had changed. It was all bathed in purple light: violet and indigo, heather and plum with silver rays beaming down from a lilac heaven.

'Come on, Lily-Lily. My in-aug-err-err-ation.'

'What in-org-er-thingy?' said Lily. But Pepper was flying in circles and the circles grew wider and he swooped and dipped and flew back to Lily and she put out her hand and he alighted on it. He looked at her and blinked. Then, he buried his bill in his plumage and swiftly plucked an oil-green quill. He held it out and Lily nodded and took it.

'Thank you, Pepper.'

Pepper took flight again and began to climb and climb and climb.

'His in-aug-err-err-ation,' began all the other chittering starlings. Lily looked back at the fence and there were hundreds of them, sitting there, side-by-side. 'His in-aug-err-err-ation to the Sky King-king-dom. Sky King-king-dom.'

'So-so-so-so long, Lily-Lily,' called Pepper, who was high now, no more than a speck in the hazy dawn.

The lump in Lily's throat was growing but she smiled and wiped her tears.

'So long, Pepper,' she whispered, searching the clouds and shading her eyes from the shimmering rays connecting the Sky Kingdom with earth.

When she could no longer see him, Lily turned to the other starlings. One by one, they spread their wings and began swooping in flocks and more streamed in from the rooftops. The masses merged into a black whale of a cloud that swelled and sailed and sank and stretched and morphed from minke to mammoth to molasses. Lily's body began to tingle as a rising bloom of sunshine rinsed the purply sky with a new-day wash of vanilla ice-cream.

She folded herself back through the fence. Clutching Pepper's feather, she felt her body inflate to normal and Dad called from the window and Lily's tummy rumbled as she burst into the house.

'See the starlings, Dad,' she said, pointing outside. 'They've gathered for Pepper.'

'Hey,' cooed Dad. 'A murmuration.' Then he saw what she was holding. 'And a quill for Lil,' he said and laughed.

Lily stroked the feather and watched the flocks painting shapes on their canvas, the sky, which was slowly turning summer day blue.

'Good luck up there, my feathered friend. Good luck,' she said, and smiled.

MY WORD!
(THE DAY THE GRAMMAR NAZI CAME TO CALL)

Tom Tumilty

A shop owner is sitting on a chair at a table. The door opens, the bell pings and he looks up as a man enters carrying a clipboard.

OWNER Good morning, sir. How may I help you?

MAN I'm here with a complaint.

OWNER Well, that's what we're here for. We try always to do our best, to help heal whatever's troubling you. Have a seat and we'll see how we can help. By the way before we start, can I just say I really like your coat. Not many people can carry off the full length, black leather trench coat look but you do it so well. It's as if you were born to it. And it goes so well with the peaked cap, too. And the boots.

MAN (*Haughtily*) Thank you, but I'm not here about the kind of complaint you seem to think I am. It's about the sign above your door.

OWNER Oh, I see. Don't you like it? I could change the colours or the font if you thought it would look better. You're obviously a man of taste and refinement. I'd be delighted to hear your advice.

MAN No, no, It's not about that. It's about the spelling on the sign. I'm from the Spelling and Grammar Board of Licensing. Here is my card.

(Man passes card across)

OWNER Oh, I see. My apologies. The Spelling and Grammar Board of Licensing. SPAGBOL. Well, I can see you're not going to mince your words. Ha. Ha. *(No response from Man)* And you're the Senior Operations Director. So, you're a SOD.

MAN Yes, that is my designation, and it is what people often call me. Now, the fact is that your sign says 'Complimentary Therapy' but you've spelled it 'pli' and not 'ple' as it should be. I'm going to have to issue you with a compliance notice. You have 30 days to make the changes. I shall return after that time to ensure that you have complied with the rules. Failure to comply may result in disciplinary proceedings.

OWNER I see, I see. That's very observant of you. Most people wouldn't have noticed it or even understood the difference. You're clearly a highly intelligent and well-educated man. And I suppose that that must come in very handy in your line of work. Might I be so bold as to ask about your qualifications?

MAN — Certainly, I have a first-class honours MA degree from Glasgow University in language and linguistics as well as a PhD in semantics. My doctoral thesis was on the origins and misuse of the Oxford comma, from 1893 to the present day. If I may say so, it is regarded as a seminal work on the subject.

OWNER — I don't doubt it. But, my word, isn't that impressive. I can tell that I'm going to have to be very careful when speaking to you. I wouldn't want to inadvertently split an infinitive. Sorry, my little joke.

MAN — I don't think this is a suitable subject for facetiousness. We take our work very seriously.

OWNER — I apologise, of course. Now, to sum up; in my opinion you are clearly a well-dressed, senior official who is highly qualified and very well-educated. You are a man of excellent breeding, of taste and refinement who carries an air of authority and has a singular degree of gravitas and dignity. Would you say that that describes you accurately?

MAN — Well, yes, I suppose it does.

OWNER	And how does it make you feel to hear yourself described in such terms? Do you feel more appreciated than when you first entered?
MAN	Well, yes, I suppose I do.
OWNER	You see, it works.
MAN	What do you mean? What works?
OWNER	Complimentary therapy, with a 'pli'. So, there won't be any need for a notice, will there? Now I usually charge £10 for a consultation but, in the circumstances, I'm prepared to waive the fee. Thank you.
MAN	Now, just wait a moment. You say you charge £10. The sign in your window says tenor per session but you've spelled it T-E-N-O-R. I'm going to have to issue a notice after all.

(Starts to write on clipboard)

OWNER	Oh, silly me, of course, I nearly forgot. *(Stands up. Sings)* Nessum dorma, nessum dorma.

END

UNTITLED

Theresa Breslin

community space, warm place.
news, views
impartial advice, no price
less stress, internet access
O.A.P. – I.T.
local history, family ancestry
self-learn college, expanding knowledge
imagination soars, opens doors
baby rhyme, story-time
information sources, peoples' courses
clubs, groups, meetings, friendly greetings
free to all, the right call
moral must, sacred trust

PUBLIC LIBRARIES

A DIFFERENT SONG

Liz Heron

Hearing without words. The sound of a mother's voice muffled by pulsing waters that cushion and nourish. Then, suddenly, fending; roaring at separation. Stretching limbs and clutching at thin air. Listening now to the surprising sound of one's own cries, to the familiar modulation of a mother's love, now deafening in its susurration. Head bobbing, instinctively seeking, sucking; calmer now, the guggle of sustenance surrendering to cradle song. Mother and child sharing hopes and fears, words of belonging to a certain past and an uncertain future.

The essence of this childhood would be gifted by a fragile peace. Cocooned in the love of family, playing innocently on balconies or in the street below, sizzling barbeques promising to banish hunger pangs. This horn of plenty feeding seemingly endless summer days.

Then creeping adolescence gently letting slip the hand of childhood, announcing a new self-awakening. Seeing, as if for the first time, the richness of history emanating from the great citadel and the ancient minaret towering above the mosque. Getting high on the wonder and bustle of the medieval souq, aromatic spices hanging enticingly in the air amidst joyous, vibrant textiles. Chatting with friends about study, about falling in love, avoiding the dark spectre of destruction already fraying the edges of an increasingly ragged patchwork of cultures.

A feisty kick from within jolts me from my reverie. I look forlornly at the unmistakable white stone of Aleppo, now in piles of rubble, and I find myself singing a song of new beginnings.

MELTEMI

Jeff Dunn

Lips touch and tongue taps
on a name as soft as breath,
mel-tem-ee,
but beware of this katabatic wind,
it begins by bulking up in the Balkans
under the control of Boreas
the God of dry northerly winds.

Many go meltemi mad,
a deep continental depression
and it can last for days and days.
This uninvited night visitor
roars down cobbled lanes
snake rattles tin cans
night shutters bang bang
and drowns a dog's nightly bark.

By the time sleep weary eyes
and wind raw nerves
try to adjust,
it has settled down
to a whisper, as soft
as breath that fades
into the darkness
of a
room

'AND DARKNESS FELL UPON THE FACE OF THE EARTH'

Sam Oakley

The clay tablet was excavated from parched soil in a rusty haze of dust devils. A hungover student scribbled a label as the simoom whipped round the flapping tents and rattled the finds boxes.

The real discovery came later, on the third floor of the Anthropology Building, when Sanja frowned at her transcription one stormy afternoon. Lightning flashed. She made the front page of *Archaeology Today*: 'Oldest Song Discovered in Agarit'. Sanja had explained patiently how they knew it was a song: no notes, but the ancient script detailed intervals and tunings. Those words, though…the words were a troubling enchantment: weaving praise of Nannar the moon god with pleas for mercy, promises of blood sacrifice and sickly-sweet incense. Somewhere back in time, she told her school groups, it was sung one last time. The final note had faded away, eventually followed by its singer; the music had died.

A musical colleague put Sanja in touch with a harpist. One evening Francesca welcomed her to a room full of stringed instruments, made her tea and plucked what looked like a lute from the wall. After lengthy questions and experimentation, she twitched her lips, stretched her long fingers, and shrugged.

'Let's play!'

Francesca's crimson nails plucked the strings with growing confidence. The strange, unearthly melody made Sanja thrill, then tremble, then scream as the moon turned its pale, terrible face from the earth and Nannar smote the land with darkness once more.

HANDS OF TIME

Mary Brown

Firm hands clasped mine
in quiet reassurance.
Delivered comfort, chastisement,
toiled endlessly.
Apple pie baking,
warm jumper knitting,
grazed knee repairing.
Now gnarled, idle hands grasp mine.
Her bird-like claw
desperately seeking reassurance.

EMPTY NEST

Diane McKee

The tiniest of squeaks
against an early summer breeze
led to stones, mossy moist,
a scrap of skin, bowed legs,
head moulded to a point.
The prehistoric creature
wriggled in my palm,
hungry for love.

Beside a twiggy home
lay a lone parent,
broken, chill to the touch.
I fashioned a bluebell carrycot,
carried the orphan home to a life
of feeds, endless feeds.
A sparse covering grew
soft and light on the tiny frame
until a bird emerged finally
resplendent in feathery finery.

Hesitant for freedom
she was wary of open windows
preferred her homely billet
to the great outdoors,
couch to cupboard to couch,
my hair a makeshift bed.

Then one windless afternoon
she flew across the garden,
over, away and was gone,
no more avian reveilles
or late-night aerobatics.

I was bereft at first
in rooms without views.
As summer faded
I embraced the outdoors,
alert for quarrels of sparrows,
imagining a host of suitors
hanging on her every tweet,
feeling a sense of pride
in loco parentis.

HOME SWEET HOME

Maura McRobbie

During an unexpected trip to Sweden to visit the Cultural Festival in Gothenburg, it was the recurring theme of 'home' that had the most impact. In the City Museum there was a wonderful display of Neolithic man's lifestyle: their tools, cooking implements, crafts and a basic circular homestead. Made from woven willow branches, leather skins for doors that separated living and sleeping areas, a little wooden fire in the centre with a space in the thatched roof for smoke. It was so organised and simple, safe and secure, I felt I could have moved in.

Next was the Röhsska Design Museum, and the 'Home as a Work of Art' exhibition. Everything the artist had ever owned and treasured was on display. Sweetie paper wrapping collages, colourful pin-tack abstracts, layers of soft blankets in baskets and even cuddly dinosaurs took pride of place in the carefully curated showcase. This artist's home was a very special place indeed and I could have stayed there too.

Finally, in the Museum of Art, there was an exhibition inspired by the homeless in Detroit. A wooden shack constructed from reclaimed timber made a pretty homestead. With painted planks of wood, old pallets, and furnished with soft cushions, curtains and rugs, there was a portable tv and a fridge sitting on a shelf. Even in its ramshackle state, it was still home. From neolithic man's homestead to the artist's highly curated living space, and finally the ramshackle shack, all examples of home sweet home.

WALKING IN THE LEMON GROVES (AMALFI COAST)

Catherine Young

When La Vita isn't dolce,
stop and smell the lemons
clinging on
to the tiny cliff terrace.
All summer's sun
trapped in citron flesh.
Now nursed by warm wood fires
through the chill nights,
until finally bearing fruit.
Bright piquant parcels –
sharp but not bitter.

SMOKED SAMMY

Sharon Mail

Jess stared at the Lapsang Souchong tea caddy on the kitchen windowsill.

She recalled the times she'd had to count each smoky leaf. If Sammy's cup of tea wasn't just right she would risk, at best, a verbal barrage.

'You pathetic, snivelling bitch – can't you do anything right?'

At worst, it could mean another trip to casualty for her 'carelessness'.

Not only had Sammy's tea, which assaulted her nostrils, to be the perfect strength, but also the exact temperature he liked – not a degree out. Often, she would place the thermometer in the China cup, but by the time he was ready to drink, it had cooled slightly. Jess raised her finger to the puckered red scar on her cheek – a keepsake from one such misdemeanour.

One day, she dropped Sammy's cup – shards of china, smoked tea leaves, strainer and water exploding across the stone floor.

'What was that?' Sammy bellowed from upstairs.

'Sorry Sammy,' her quaking voice responded. Jess stared at the floor and then towards the stairs where Sammy was pounding downwards, his face black and his fists closed.

He was so busy staring at the subject of his ire that he failed to notice the wet pool of water and went flying, landing with a thud as his skull cracked against cold stone.

And there he now sat, in his beloved smoky caddy, with only the thermometer for company.

Such a shame about the extra, wet, greasy puddle right at the bottom of the stairs.

Jess smiled.

THAT THING ON HIS EAR, IT'S HARMLESS

Hugh McMillan

These are terrible times
ten weeks in hospital,
can't eat not even Fortisip,
she's melted away to the bone,

we're going to get my kids
those cancer tests in case
it's genetic. I've only
got my dog now really,

he's a bit boisterous, don't
mind that thing on his
ear it's harmless.
We nod, agree these

are terrible times,
each of us standing here
knows it. The dog slumps
on its big haunches

with the tiniest of sighs.
Outside a stinging night
of cold settles
on the small

town and the stars,
giving every appearance of life,
wink in the unguessable
nothingness of space.

PERSEVERANCE

Palo Stickland

She took the slow road
as others soared sky high.
She looked up as they shone,
then looked down and plodded on.

Money was tight for years,
she made do and kept working.
At home, no time to play.
At work, yearning for a holiday.

She strove for her family, parents,
siblings, husband and little ones.
Who didn't think she did too much,
'Oh, it's that clever feminine touch.'

They took all her attention.
Until she left to cruise round the world
on her retirement pension.

A DAY OUT

Don J Taylor

Willie's wheelchair sat in the alcove; behind him, the dog-eared mural of a waterfall. Eyes closed; he heard the burn rush between granite boulders overhung with larch. He breathed the scent of pine – not pee, stale food and used-up air.

Then he heard the familiar squeak of trainers on the corridor tiles.

'Mornin', Akram.'

'Good morning, boss.'

'Here, I've been thinkin', why not you and me take a drive up tae Bracklinn Falls. Make a day of it. What d'ye think?'

'Sure.'

'I'm noticing you've got a hirple on ye,' said Willie, twisting in his chair.

'A what?'

'Y'know, a limp.'

'Another braw Scots word you've taught me, Willie.' Akram chuckled. 'Bathtime!'

'Aye, aye. But the hirple…and them scars on your arms?'

'Oh, running away from the ladies – you know, when I was a young and handsome man.'

Akrham flipped off the brakes.

'Wull ye no tell me?'

In the shower Akram lifted Willie onto the seat, humming quietly as he bathed his frail white limbs. Willie was wracked with a rattling cough.

'Pneumonia! – the old man's friend,' he gasped.

'Hey Willie, you don't need *that* friend! You got me, right?'

'Are you my friend, *really*?'

'Sure. We get on good, don't we?'

'Naebody'd clean another guy's arse unless they were being paid.'

'Yeah, I need money for my children. Doesn't mean we can't be friends. It's different things at the same time.'

'But you won't tell me what happened to *you*.'

'One day, my friend – by the waterfall.'

THE MEMORY BOX

Elizabeth Kearney

I place you carefully in a box for safekeeping.
Not just any box. A beautiful box, decorated with butterflies,
Representing the cycle of life, with its beginnings and endings,
Its changes and growth.
It's not a box where you put things and can never find them again;
It's a box that can be easily retrieved in an instant.
And it only takes one song, one lyric. Or perhaps a familiar fragrance,
Like the comforting smell of home baked scones,
Or the peaty aroma of a lit pipe,
And a thousand memories come flooding back.
And it's yesteryear once more.
It only takes a word, or being in a certain spot,
And the box springs open like a toy Jack in the box,
Its magic combination cracked.
It's a box that can rewind time, and take me back to the very moment
We laughed, and held each other.
It can take me back to the moment you were here with me.
The sweet fragrant scent of days gone by – they fill the air.
And I breathe you in. And I hear your voice. And see your smile;
And for a moment, a very brief moment;
All is well in the world.

THE WEDDING GUEST

Catherine Young

A hotel function room. Woman, late 40s, sitting at the end of a table. She is wearing a fascinator. A handbag and wrap are beside her. A bottle of wine and wine glass is on the table.

WOMAN *(Angrily)* Well, that's it official. My family's gone from *The Waltons* to *The Jeremy Kyle Show* in one generation. Mum'll be burling in her grave. Just as well we only get together at weddings and funerals. Not even christenings anymore. How many of the nieces and nephews *got* christened? Was it just the first two? Actually, come to think of it, I don't know where the christening robe is these days. It must be about a 100 years old by now. Bugger Lugs better not have binned it. She might have though. Everything gets trashed in a year or two. How many sofas has she gone through now? And tellies? The amount of money she's spent I could've gone on half a dozen round-the-world trips. And what's she got to show for it? Being on top of the mailing list at DFS?

(She fiddles with her handbag)

WOMAN *(Sighs)* A few more drinks and they won't notice if I leave. Probably think I'm usually at home tucked up with my knitting and cocoa by now anyway.

(She looks around)

WOMAN There's Janice nodding off again. Glad I put her top of my to-do list. Thought I'd better get in there before she's too far-gone. She's just as bad as ever; though I'm not apparently. I'm 'not nearly as snobby as I was when I went to the university'. I just smiled and nodded. Should've told her, 'Aye, but you're just as rough as you were 25 years ago'.
(Downcast) I read that it takes three generations to undo bad parenting, like in the Philip Larkin *They Fuck You Up* poem. Seems a couple of poor choices in partners and a whole extended family comes crashing down in one fell swoop.

(She pours wine into her glass)

WOMAN I feel a bit out on a limb here, stuck at the end of a table all on my own like an afterthought.

(She takes several gulps of wine)

WOMAN *(Brightly)* I was *really* looking forward to being the embarrassing auntie at family dos. You know, up dancing, a little bit tipsy, with a hat just a little bit too wide, a dress showing a little bit too much cleavage and flirting with a man whose age is only half as large as the size of my ample bosom that he's gazing into. But look at that lot. Brought up on a diet of burgers, fags and Alco pops. All pale and spotty.

(Laughs) None of those lads look like they could run for a bus if their life depended on it, far less anything else requiring a bit of *(winks confidingly)* energy and stamina.

(Sips wine then looks at watch)

WOMAN It's eight o'clock. I've said the bride looks lovely, done all the 'how are yous' to the in-laws and they've got their wedding present, which is, frankly, probably the only reason I was invited in the first place. Though they'll be disappointed I didn't choose from their wedding list. *(Pause)* Who puts a games console on a wedding list?

(She gathers up her handbag and wrap)

WOMAN *(Decidedly)* Think I'll grab a taxi into town. That new club's opening this weekend and we get free VIP tickets at work. There'll be plenty gorgeous young men there.

(She stands up, downs last of wine)

WOMAN I could just do with burning off all those calories from the 'Asda Party Platters'.

(She teeters off)

END

WEST END GIRL

Maura McRobbie

One Day
on Gilmore Hill,
we threw snowballs in the air,
plunging our souls without care
into the drifts
Our love stories
about to begin.

One Day
on Dowanhill Doorsteps,
we threw our school hats in the air,
liberated and without care,
our toes on the threshold
of future career paths
about to unfold.

One Day
at Kelvingrove Bandstand,
you tossed your long slim arms in the air,
danced to the rhythm
without care
barefoot,
your garlanded hair,
a sway and a twirl,
your life's dreams about to unfurl,
my dear sister Ros,
the ultimate West End Girl.

This poem was written as a result of a Writing Prompt visit to the Lillie art Gallery in Milngavie to see the Bearsden Art Society Exhibition 2024. Two West End paintings evoked memories of growing up in Glasgow's West End, and an image followed of my sister Ros dancing at the Kelvingrove Bandstand in the 70s. This poem was written to celebrate her 70th birthday.

CALLING TIME

Irene Lebeter

I run my fingertip down the scar on his chest. The nurse switches off the machines bleeping beside the bed and lays her hand on my shoulder as she leaves the room.

Long dark lashes are closed over his blue eyes. I smile through my tears, recalling how often I've said they are wasted on him, eyelashes that every teenage girl dreams of.

Through the pain and sadness my anger re-surfaces. 'Why are you doing this to me?' I scream in my head. 'I don't want to live without you.'

My darling lies on, unaware of my outburst.

I sit in my time bubble, as I've done for the past three days, the only sound the ticking of the clock above the door. The sun streaming through the window warms my back. It creates an aura around his inert frame and the words 'shimmering angel' come to mind. I've loved him since the morning I delivered him to take his first breath and now, more than forty years on, I am waiting for him to draw his last.

As a lone parent, I've reared him with a love that only a mother can feel. My pride in him has increased with every passing day. 'My beloved, irreplaceable son,' I whisper into the emptiness and once again curse the driver of the white van for shattering his, and my, world.

My hand tightens on his when the rattling sound intensifies, then…silence.

THE END

Sharon Bairden

I heard the full stop in your voice, way before you stabbed out its mark on the story that was your life.

I felt the commas in your breath and cried as they cruelly punctuated the chapters of you.

I held my breath through your silent ellipses…and prayed that the pause removed the pain.

I saw the questions in your tears. So I gathered adjectives and verbs and I stuffed them with kindness and whispered them in your ear.

I edited your narrative and deleted the pain. I rewrote your story a million times over and created the happy ever after that belonged to you.

But I heard the full stop in your voice. I felt the lead of the pencil as it punctured my heart.

I tried to erase it but I was never enough.

A QUESTION OF TASTE

Pat Feehan

His hands are skewered to the kitchen table with two of my best boning knives, sharpened specially this morning. His face is a mask of disbelief, mouth open in a silent scream. The empty eyes seem to be trying, even now, to appeal to my better nature. I check the sauce, garlic, ginger, a few herbs. Rosemary always goes well with fresh meat. People used to say the eyes of a dead person retain the image of the last thing they saw, which might be the person who killed them. I'm not worried about that. The eyes will not be available for scrutiny. I believe the flesh of the dead person carries the memory of their last emotions. I stir the mixture, making sure the eyes and tongue are nicely coated in the sauce. I tip them onto a plate, reach for a fork, then think better of it. I pick the tongue up in my hands, it almost slithers out of my grasp. I lick it, chew on it, the taste reminiscent of foie gras. With the palm of my hand, I roll the eyes back and forward on the plate, they ooze slightly. I select one, the left one I think, squeezing it gently between thumb and forefinger. The texture is just right. I lick my fingers, savouring the deep, delicious, forbidden flavours. I gaze into the eye, see my reflection smiling back at me. I bite, swallow. Perfect. The taste of his terror lingers in my mouth.

SQUATTER

Paula Andrews

Filament fingers grasp golden flax,
the seed-thief's whiskers warn her;
radar ears tune in to
morning's sounds
from the first weak light.

A tread
on the flags.
Her pink tail
flashes.
A key
in the lock,
she's out of sight.

Crinkles of sound creep,
kirr-scuff, a clue
as she darts to her jumbled snug:
chewed garden fleece,
paper, plastic.
Stink of ammonia,
nose-wrinkling sour;

and terracotta pots
black-dotted with pips.

Ragged holes, havoc wreaked,

her knot of babies nourished;
a new generation slumbers,
next week's petty thieves.

RE-BIRTH

David Maclean

SS Nurse Kuntz had developed an ever-increasing belief in the afterlife as the Russians got closer to the rat-infested rubble she had inhabited for the past two days.

Initially she had been terrified as they drew closer but had developed a coping mechanism that there was life after death. All she had to do was hold on until the Russians killed her, hopefully as painlessly as possible and all would be well.

They abused and kicked her about but let her live as they had already slaked their bloodlust.

Like so many others she ended up in a gulag for several years, where she had continued her 'duties' as a medical orderly, not caring whether her fellow prisoners lived or died as long as she survived. Still an ardent Nazi she had enough sense of self-preservation to keep out of trouble and in 1952 was re-assigned as a 'good prisoner' to a hospital in Leningrad.

She was given a childbirth case for a woman known initially to her as Maria Ivanovna. Maria had given birth twice before, to a baby that died in infancy and another who died of starvation in 1942 during the Leningrad Siege.

Eventually the baby appeared in all its viscera, howling in rude health. It was a difficult but successful birth and Kuntz felt rejuvenated, reborn.

With genuine joy she handed the child back to the exhausted but happy woman and said, 'Congratulations Fraulein Putin, it's a boy.'

TOO CLOSE FOR COMFORT

Elizabeth Carey

World turmoil, protests, wars, no peace.
Humans displaced, scammers ready to fleece.
The elderly, vulnerable caught up in this mess,
Where do we go from here, ask not in jest?

Rainforests burning, coral reefs lost,
Global warming, consumerism, this is the cost.
Will the next generation take us to task?
As we glory in materialism and 'stuff' that won't last.

Why take our mess to the planets afar?
Gaze into the mirror, not to the stars.
Each one of us has a part we can play,
So life will continue, not fade away.

Species endangered in the animal world,
We have choices before us, now unfurled.
Energy, resources, fracking into earth's core
To extract more gas as we desire more and more.

Stop! What's important, what can't we ignore?
We should seek all the answers the scientists implore.
Communication's at an all-time high,
With technology so complex, nothing passes us by.

This poem may seem to be all doom and gloom,
But complacency must not be given houseroom.
With determination and will, we must all make a stance,
To pull back from the brink, to be in with a chance.

CATCHING UP

Irene Lebeter

A gust of wind caught her scarf. It billowed up, but through the blue chiffon she could still see his baseball cap, bearing a skull and crossbones.

The rain became heavier. Her grip tightened on her umbrella.

He'd been following her since she got off the train. Even in the compartment he'd looked weird. When she increased her pace, he did too. When she slowed, he stopped to tighten his shoelaces.

Uneasy since coming through the side entrance of the station and up these stairs, she now rebuked herself. What could happen, in the middle of the afternoon?

She counted the glistening treads, knowing she was alone with him on this narrow stairway. His footsteps pounded behind her; she sprinted up the last few steps and looked around for a means of escape.

Becky jumped down from the bus, annoyed at being late, especially when Myra was such a good timekeeper. If it hadn't been for the road works, she'd have been on time.

The wind howled through the deserted street, and she had difficulty keeping her brolly open due to the ferocious gust. A paper bag dropped by a litterbug whooshed past her. But there was no sign of Myra, standing in her usual place at the top of the stairs.

A flash of blue caught Becky's eye and she spun round. She gasped, looking down at the umbrella she'd bought Myra for Christmas, lying upside down in a puddle.

MARTA

Ann MacKinnon

She abandoned her life,
bringing only her violin,
a precious gift for us.

The violin strings
pull at our hearts,
as her music fills us

with a longing
to listen and learn
about her people.

The male musicians
exchanged their instruments
for weapons.

We support her with words
but can only imagine
what she left behind.

Will she ever go back?
'I hope so,' she smiles, then plays
a tune we do not know.

WHICH WAY TO SWING

Jeff Dunn

There is a creaking sound adding an eerie edge to the howling wind, like a broken branch swaying. But it is a deeper sound, a more weighty creak than the sound of a tree's limb. The pendulum is slow and heavy, like a rope heaving and twisting on an old galleon ship on swelling seas at the end of the world. A warship that has lost too many battles, and a ghost of its former self. Nothing left on board. Except secrets.

As I approach the sound I see a large ash tree, and a rope. At the end of the rope, a body. Head at an awkward angle, and a swollen bluebottle face. Popped eyes, like his shirt buttons, revealing bits of pale white flesh. Dead for some time. A desperate lump of a human that, at first glance, nobody cared about.

Two vodka bottles lay empty underneath his swinging feet. Evidence of suicide? But, I think to myself, he still had the peace of mind to tie a hangman's noose, and a tricky climb to negotiate when drunk. Later, a picture forms of a lonely, alcoholic man. Just lost his job. All agree. Suicide.

A routine post-mortem is carried out. Half-swallowed and lodged in his throat is a hastily chewed note. On it a message written in child-like letters. It read – they're coming.

FEAR OF FLYING

Tom Tumilty

'Hello, Caledonia Bank. How may I help you?'

'It's Mrs Evonne O'Hagan here. It's about the text you sent me saying there had been unusual activity on my account. I can't think of anything unusual. What's it about?'

'Let me see. Yes, it's the payment to Ryanair of £10,000. It's an unusually high amount and it would put you into an unauthorised overdraft. We thought we'd better check with you before paying out.'

'That's impossible! I only booked for four people to go to Barcelona, £250 each. It should be £1,000. There's enough in the account to cover that surely?'

'Yes. Perhaps you should check with Ryanair to see where the confusion has arisen?'

Evonne hung up. What the hell was going on? She dialled Ryanair's number. Finally, she got through to a real person.

'Hello, I want to check my booking. I think you've overcharged me. My booking number is Bc 147650.'

'Let me see. No, it's correct. 40 seats to Barcelona in the name of Hagen.'

'No, it's four seats and the name is O'Hagen.'

'Right. Do you wish to cancel the other 36 seats? There's a ten percent cancellation charge.'

'But I never booked them in the first place.'

'Ah, I think you'd better speak to my supervisor.' Click. And then the dial tone. Evonne screamed, just as the alarm clock sounded.

SPRING PHOBIA

Diane McKee

She appeared unannounced,
like a long-lost cousin on my father's side,
bringing meagre offerings,
demanding a bed.
No niceties, no small talk
just extra daytime,
warm breath at my window,
all bustle and head girl bossiness,
always knowing best.

She's littered the lawn with stubby flowers,
finger paint splodges on a heavy wash,
unleashed spindly tendrils,
turned my monochrome world to green.
Angular trees have lost their limbs,
turned to fluff and chaos
and pantomime wigs.
Birds fill my sky with chit chat,
coupling up
with ill-advised haste.

I have given in to her,
easier with a bully I've found.
I will go outside, discard my layers,
embrace the season.
I will.
Maybe tomorrow.

MISPLACED AFFECTION

Andy Raffan

It was an otherwise unremarkable Tuesday afternoon when it came to her. Empty and fill the dishwasher. Tick. Run the hoover around. Tick. Decide that really, truly, hubby had to go. Tick.

What was it that led her to this point? Infidelity? Abuse? One too many forgotten anniversaries? In truth, no. It was his constant assumption of her malevolent omniscience. Have you seen the…? Where are the…? And the ultimate soul crusher – what *have* you done with the…? Not only was she expected to remember the exact location of every one of their possessions, but the questions implied she gained a secret pleasure from placing them somewhere no sane person would think of looking. As if she would do such a thing!

Thus, she was well-practised in the convincing facial expressions when the police came. When had she last seen him? Could he perhaps have got lost? Was he somewhere no one else would think of? As if he was a favourite watch accidentally stuffed into the back of a filing cabinet. Or a still-cooling corpse nestled inside a taped-up John Lewis rug that barely fitted into the boot of his precious Jaguar that now crouched, rusting, under a hundred foot of silty quarry water.

That was one thing she did know the location of – the last place someone would think to look. No sane person that is. Now, what *had* she done with that photo of him that he hated so much, to adorn the Missing Person poster?

TICKING THE BOXES

Adrienne Whitehall

'And did you enjoy Vanessa's Party?'

'Of course, what's not to like. Scrumptious buffet, delicious birthday cake, fabulous band.'

'And did you meet the man of your dreams?'

'Well … nearly.'

'Nearly? Spill the beans.'

'It's a long story, I'll try to be quick.'

'That'll be a first. Go on then.'

'Here I am sitting comfortably at a table chatting to Belinda when I hear, "Hello, I'm Larry, what's your name?" I turn round as he draws his chair in beside mine, lifts my hand and shakes it. Nancy, I kind of stumble out. Then he asks how I know the hostess, the birthday girl.'

'Was he a looker?'

'Mm…not bad.'

'Go on…'

'He's good at talking, says he's a retired architect, keeps his hand in by doing small extensions. Lucrative he says. Keeps his Range Rover running.'

‘And?’

‘Meantime I’m ticking the boxes. Warm smile, good teeth, strong handshake, smart tidy appearance, well-polished shoes. No aftershave. You know how I hate aftershave.’

‘Sounds OK. What happened?’

‘Let me finish. The buffet is announced and he says, “Can I escort you to the buffet Nancy?” Helps me up, takes my arm, and whisks me off to the eats. Takes me back, settles me into my chair, and drapes a napkin over my knees.’

‘What a courteous guy. And…’

‘Looks round the room, says, “Oh, I see my other half has arrived, been to a hectic meeting. I’d better attend to her needs; she’ll be famished.”’

NOISES IN THE NIGHT

Graeme Lewis

Sergeant McLanky and his night-shift officers sped out the backyard of Baird Street Police Office in their patrol cars. It was just after 11pm. First job of the night and it sounded serious. Numerous named and anonymous reporters claimed to hear the sound of a female screaming from the vicinity of Millersneuk Crescent, Millerston. Was someone being attacked? Was it a domestic? Was someone hurt? All these thoughts were racing through the sergeant's head. Let's hope we get there in time, he was also thinking.

The four police vehicles, blue lights flashing, all arrived in convoy at the same time and the officers jumped out. It was a hot, balmy summer's night and the air was still for about 30 seconds and then suddenly a piercing scream. It went quiet and then again more screaming. Where were they coming from? The sergeant told his officers to spread out and check the local streets. More screams coming from the direction of the nearby busy railway line. Sergeant McLanky radioed his control room. 'I need a stop on all trains here, plus the dog branch and force helicopter in the air, urgently.' The dogs arrived first and made their way onto the now 'safe' railway track. Next, the helicopter hovering low over the local houses, its large searchlight beam shining and waking up residents. After ten minutes a helicopter radio message. 'Sarge. Panic Over. Found your screams. Infra-red shows us two foxes in the bushes mating', then laughter.

TOMMY SAYS GOODBYE

Elizabeth McKay

Tommy's off to be a soldier. Last week he worked in the grocer's shop.

Tommy's dad hasn't held his hand since he was eight. He presses hard before letting go. 'Be sure and show that lot what's what. If only I was ten years younger.'

Tommy's brother still plays at slaying monsters with a wooden sword. He hopes it lasts long enough so he can go. He points his finger – bang.

His sister clouts his head and says, 'Don't be stupid.' She tells Tommy she's knitting socks for him at school, but she's having trouble turning the heel.

Tommy's girlfriend's only been round at his house twice before. She feels awkward standing on her tiptoes to kiss his cheek, knowing everyone's watching. She promises she'll write to him every day.

If it was up to Tommy's mam, she'd draw the curtains, bolt the doors, and keep all of them inside. Instead, she hands him a tin of sandwiches. Sardines, ham, tomato. Plenty to share with the other lads on the train. 'And there's a slice of Auntie Meg's fruit cake, and an apple from Mrs Smith across the road.' She wipes invisible fluff from the sleeve of his jacket.

'Go on now,' she says, gently pushing him towards the door. 'Don't want you getting into trouble for being late.' She hugs him tight.

'Goodbye, son.'

'Bye, Dad.'

'Goodbye, Tommy.'

Tommy says goodbye and walks down the path. He turns, smiles and waves.

'Goodbye,' Tommy says again for the last time.

BLACK HILL

Allan Gaw

If a gun had jammed in Sarajevo,
I would not be standing here.
Looking over ruins
out across the misty sea.

There'd be no need to carve
the names of foreign killing fields
in blackened Scottish sandstone
high atop this windy hill.

Nor would these crowded names be here.
These Williams, Johns and Davids,
the Alexanders and the James,
who now live in no one's memory.

The flower of young manhood,
who should have never seen
the stinking mud of Flanders or heard
the wanton wail of shells.

They took their strength, their hopes
to war, these men, only to leave
their futures on some bloodied battlefield,
with fattened crows their undertakers.

They should have stayed at home
and farmed and fished and fathered sons.
Not lie in lonely far-off graves,
their youth, their only shroud.

Why do I bow my head to honour men
I never knew? Because I knew them all.
I share every thought and hope and fear
that ever dwelt in any young man's heart.

If a gun had jammed in Sarajevo,
would I be spared this sadness, this anger?
Or would I just be standing here at another
memorial to a different pointless war?

CONTRIBUTORS

Iain Anderson, retired architect, amateur artist. Recently completed creative writing course at GU and now enjoys writing short stories/flash fiction – a good foil to his love of creative arts.

Paula Andrews writes for children and adults. Her debut novel *Oranges and Lemons* was published in 2020. She has had work published in *Aquila* and *Scribble* magazines.

Sharon Bairden writes dark standalone psychological thrillers and has had two novels published, *Sins of the Father* and *You Need Me*. She is also a book reviewer on her blog, *Chapterinmylife*.

Theresa Breslin OBE (Services to Literature) is the Carnegie Medal-winning author of over 50 multiple genre books for young people of all ages. *adults are allowed to read them too.

Mary Brown writes short stories, flash fiction, poetry, monologues, and non-fiction.

Elizabeth Carey writes poetry, short stories and participates in spoken word events. She has featured in three editions of *Hooded* by Crowvus and *Dreich* magazine by Jack Caradoc.

John Dickson writes nostalgic and travel articles, short stories and memoirs. Many published in *The Scots Magazine* and *The Herald* etc. First published book: *Hopes and Dreams and Buster Too*.

Jeff Dunn is an unpublished writer. Currently, he has a novel *The Outrageous Claim of Sophie Jupp* in the hands of a literary agent. He also writes non-fiction.

Mary Edward has been writing for many years with varying degrees of success. Her output includes short fiction, novels and non-fiction.

Pat Feehan has self-published two novels. He's working on a third novel and a collection of short fiction. His story *The Kill* was shortlisted for the Edinburgh Short Story award.

Allan Gaw writes poetry and prose. Poetry collection *Love & Other Diseases* published in 2023. His debut novel *The Silent House of Sleep* was shortlisted for the Bloody Scotland prize.

Liz Heron joined SWG in 2020 after entering an East Dunbartonshire Book Week competition organised by the group where she continues to hone her creative writing skills for pleasure.

Patricia Hutchinson has had three historical novels published. Her fourth will be released shortly. She also writes short stories and poetry and has written and directed a touring play.

Lorraine Johnston, a former H&S advisor, discovered writing after being diagnosed with Multiple Sclerosis in 2008. She's published four children's books so far, but that's not the *end* of her story.

Elizabeth Kearney writes poetry, short stories and songs. Although a novice, she self-published her first book *Lizzy's Lunes* in 2020 as a project during lockdown. Her poetry is mostly reflective.

Matthew Keeley works in TV Development and writes all sorts of things including novels, short stories, poetry, and creative non-fiction. His debut poetry collection will be published in 2025.

Irene Lebeter started her journey into writing after a 45-year career as a secretary. She's had five novels published, plus multiple non-fiction articles and short stories. She lives in Rutherglen.

Graeme Lewis joined Strathkelvin Writers Group in 2023 and writes items of Flash Fiction.

Ann MacKinnon writes poetry in both Scots and English. Her latest collection *Warp and Weft* was published by Red Squirrel Press in 2023.

Ann MacLaren is the author of *Handle With Care and Other Stories.* She has been published in many anthologies, including the Scottish Arts Trust and Association of Scottish Literature compilations.

David Maclean has been a member of the Strathkelvin Writers' Group since 2015. He has written a few short stories and is a regular attendee at the club.

Sharon Mail has been a journalist for 18 years. Her first book, *We Could Possibly Comment – Ian Richardson Remembered*, was published in 2009, and her second book is being published.

Carolyn Mandache is a writer, blogger and keen midlife adventurer. Her debut novel *Behind the Curtain* was published in 2021.

Anne V McClure writes poems, short stories and about her time in international aid work. Cymera speculative fiction competition 2024 shortlisted her story, *Winter Tale*. She writes *WordsWork* on Substack.

Elizabeth McKay is the author of the *Wee Granny* series of picture books. She has also had several hundred stories and articles published in magazines in the UK and abroad.

Diane McKee writes poetry and fiction. She has had work published by Dreich, has won the annual Strathkelvin Trophy and has won competitions in *Writers' Forum* magazine.

Hugh McMillan is a well published, anthologised and broadcast poet. His latest collection *Diverted to Split* was published in summer 2024. Editor of the Scottish Poetry Library's *Best Scottish Poems* and Saltire Society judge.

Julie McNeill is the Poet-in-Residence for St Mirren Football Club and The Hampden Collection, author of *We Are Scottish Football, Something Small, Ragged Rainbows* and *Mission Dyslexia.*

Maura McRobbie is a highly commended Glasgow writer and author of *Howth* and *Vikings and Skylarks on Cumbrae.* She contributes to the *Herald*, Community Magazines, and writes a quarterly blog.

David McVey lectures in Humanities at New College Lanarkshire. His mood is dictated by the fortunes of Kirkintilloch Rob Roy FC and the Scotland national teams.

Sam Oakley currently struggles to find the time and energy to write short stories, flash fiction and novels. She was longlisted for the Edinburgh Award for Flash Fiction 2023.

Steve O'Brien will have a go at writing all genres. He has had short stories published recently by *Southlight* magazine and poems by *Dreich* magazine.

Maggie Powell joined SWG in 1989, and has twice been Secretary of the Club. Her short stories and articles have appeared in magazines, anthologies, newspapers, comics and children's textbooks.

Andy Raffan writes short stories, flash fiction and poetry. He has been shortlisted twice for the Edinburgh Award for Flash Fiction and had a short story in *New Writing Scotland* 41.

Assen Rizov is a doctor who writes short stories in his spare time. He is interested in topics related to human psychology, morality and philosophy.

David Ross tends to write non-fiction and sketches, currently struggling through his memoirs.

Sinclair Steven writes short, sometimes very short, fiction. However, one such managed to win the Scottish Arts Trust Isobel Lodge Award 2020.

Palo Stickland writes short and long fiction, memoir and poems. Her family saga *Finding Takri* was published in 2013, *Alana* in 2019. *Playing on the Mountain* is her anthology.

Don J Taylor has had poetry and fiction published widely in anthologies. The 2024 Neil Gunn Competition placed a poem and short story. He is currently working on his first novel.

Tom Tumilty writes flash fiction, sketches, poetry and is working on a novel. Tom writes in English, Scots and (Duolingo) Gaelic.

Adrienne Whitehall writes poetry, short stories, non-fiction and sketches. She has been published in several magazines.

Catherine Young writes short stories, memoir, monologues and occasionally poetry. Her short stories have been published in anthologies and selected for reading at the *Winter Words* festival at Pitlochry Theatre.

Printed in Great Britain
by Amazon

51086538R00172

PODRÓŻNI

REGINA PORTER

PODRÓŻNI

PRZEŁOŻYŁ
Maciej Świerkocki

WYDAWNICTWO LITERACKIE

Dla moich rodziców
oraz tych zwykłych ludzi, którzy gościli
w ich domu i opowiadali różne historie.

DRAMATIS PERSONAE

JIMMY VINCENT SR, *wiejski strażak z Maine*

NANCY VINCENT, *żona Jimmy'ego, bibliotekarka*

JAMES SAMUEL VINCENT JR, *adwokat z Manhattanu, znany też jako Szefunio*

SIGRID VINCENT, *pierwsza żona Jamesa, agentka castingowa*

RUFUS VINCENT, *ślubny syn Szefunia, badacz twórczości Jamesa Joyce'a*

ELIJAH I WINONA VINCENTOWIE, *pięcioletnie bliźnięta, dzieci Rufusa Vincenta i Claudii Christie*

ADELE PRANSKY, *druga żona Szefunia, malarka*

AGNES CHRISTIE, *żona Eddiego Christie, urbanistka*

EDDIE CHRISTIE, *mąż Agnes Christie, weteran wojny w Wietnamie, służył w marynarce wojennej*

BEVERLY CHRISTIE, *starsza córka Agnes i Eddiego, dyplomowana pielęgniarka*

CLAUDIA CHRISTIE, *młodsza córka Agnes i Eddiego, badaczka twórczości Williama Shakespeare'a, żona Rufusa Vincenta, matka Elijaha i Winony Vincentów*

MINERVA C. PARKER, *nastoletnia córka Beverly*

PETER „ORZESZEK" PARKER, *nastoletni syn Beverly*

KEISHA I LAMAR, *czteroletnie bliźnięta Beverly*

KEVIN PARKER, *były mąż Beverly, emerytowany policjant*
CHICO, *partner Beverly, sprzedawca placków roti*
BARBARA CAMPHOR, *żona Charlesa Camphora, kochanka Szefunia*
CHARLES CAMPHOR, *bankier, mąż Barbary Camphor*
HANK CAMPHOR, *ciemnowłosy syn Barbary i Charlesa*
SUSAN WEATHERBY CAMPHOR, *żona Hanka*
TESS CAMPHOR, *trzyletnia córka Hanka i Susan*
DUŻY SEAMUS CAMPHOR, *potężnie zbudowany kuzyn Charlesa Camphora*
CHARLES JOHNSON, *kochanek Agnes Christie i daleki krewny Eloise Delaney, inżynier*
ELOISE DELANEY, *szkolna koleżanka Agnes Christie, jej kochanka i poszukiwaczka przygód*
HERBERT DELANEY, *ojciec Eloise, robotnik w fabryce konserw*
DELORES DELANEY, *matka Eloise, robotnica w fabryce konserw*
KING TYRONE, *jedyny porządny kuzyn Eloise (ze strony matki), rybak*
SARAH, *żona Kinga, z zawodu rybaczka, i* **DEIRDRE,** *córka Kinga, z zawodu biolog morski*
FLORA APPLEWOOD, *przyjaciółka i kochanka Eloise Delaney, emerytowana pracownica opieki społecznej*
JEBEDIAH APPLEWOOD, *kuzyn Eddiego Christie, weteran, który tak jak on najpierw służył w marynarce wojennej, a później zaczął pracować przy przeprowadzkach*
REUBEN APPLEWOOD, *kuzyn pierwszego stopnia Eddiego Christie, oficer marynarki wojennej*
LEVI APPLEWOOD, *kuzyn pierwszego stopnia Eddiego Christie, młodszy brat Reubena*

CZAS AKCJI

Akcja powieści rozpoczyna się w połowie lat pięćdziesiątych, a kończy w pierwszym roku prezydentury Baracka Obamy.

WAŻNIEJSZE MIEJSCA AKCJI

Amagansett na Long Island; Buckner County w stanie Georgia; Manhattan; Memphis w stanie Tennessee; Portsmouth w stanie New Hampshire; Bretania (Francja); Berlin (Niemcy); Wietnam.

TŁO LITERACKIE

Sztuka Toma Stopparda *Rosenkrantz i Guildenstern nie żyją*, której premiera odbyła się na Fringe Festival w Edynburgu 24 sierpnia 1966 roku. Jest to komedia egzystencjalna, opowiadana z perspektywy Rosenkrantza i Guildensterna, płynących do Anglii nieszczęsnych przyjaciół Hamleta.

PODAJ DALEJ

1946 1954 1964 1971 1986 2000 **2009**

GDY CHŁOPIEC MIAŁ CZTERY LATA, SPYTAŁ TATĘ, DLACZEGO ludzie potrzebują snu.

– Żeby Pan Bóg mógł odkręcić to wszystko, co spierdolił człowiek – odpowiedział ojciec.

KIEDY CHŁOPIEC MIAŁ lat dwanaście, spytał matkę, dlaczego tata ich zostawił. Odpowiedziała:

– Żeby mógł ruchać wszystko, co nie spieprza na drzewo.

W WIEKU TRZYNASTU LAT chłopiec chciał się dowiedzieć, co ojciec robi z powrotem w domu.

– Jestem już czterdziestojednoletnią kobietą i nie mam głowy do tego, żeby latać po mieście i szukać sobie kogoś, z kim ja mogłabym się ruchać – odpowiedziała mama.

GDY CHŁOPIEC SKOŃCZYŁ czternaście lat, a wulgaryzmy płynęły z ust jego kolegów jak woda z pękniętej rury, brzydkie słowa takie jak „ruchać" nie miały dla niego żadnej atrakcyjności. Żadnej. Jakiejkolwiek. W ogóle. Wcale.

SKOŃCZYWSZY LAT OSIEMNAŚCIE, chłopiec (czyli Jimmy Vincent jr) wyjechał ze swojego rodzinnego miasta, Huntington na Long Island, na studia na University of Michigan.

BYŁ POD KAŻDYM WZGLĘDEM dobrym, a przy tym zabójczo przystojnym studentem. Mógł mieć każdą dziewczynę, której tylko zapragnął, ale jak często się zdarza w takich sytuacjach, pociągała go cudownie przeciętna Alice. Wmówił sobie, że ją kocha, i oboje, wówczas studenci pierwszego roku, cieszyli się upajającym, akrobatycznym seksem. Zachwycona takim uśmiechem losu Alice mocno przytulała Jimmy'ego z wdzięczności i mówiła:

– O Boże. A niech mnie. Mnie? Czy ja to ja? Ruchaj mnie, ruchaj, ruchaj.

PO STUDIACH W MICHIGAN Jimmy wrócił na Wschodnie Wybrzeże. Dostał pracę jako aplikant w pierwszorzędnej kancelarii adwokackiej z długimi tradycjami i poznał wysoką dziewczynę z Nowej Anglii. Jane studiowała medycynę, mogłaby jednak uchodzić za top modelkę. Nie używała wulgaryzmów, a kiedy wchodziła z Jimmym do baru czy salonu, wszyscy się na nich gapili. Z taką dziewczyną dwudziestodwuletni w tym czasie Jimmy mógłby się nie tylko ożenić – mógłby ją też pokochać, nawet tak młodo. Zaprosił Jane do domu na wigilię, a przypadkiem była to również pierwsza rocznica ich związku.

PO PRZEPYSZNEJ KOLACJI, której przygotowanie zajęło mamie Jimmy'ego cały dzień, i to z pomocą jej ulubionej książki kucharskiej, do salonu wszedł ojciec. Usiadł pomiędzy synem i Jane, popijał maderę i zaczął wspominać dzieciństwo na wsi w stanie Maine.

– Gorący kartofel wyleczy cię z jęczmyka. Surowy pod pachą działa lepiej niż dezodorant. Noś kartofel w bucie, a nigdy nie będziesz wiedział, co to jest przeziębienie. Oto, proszę ja was, encyklopedia chłopaka ze wsi. Przeniosłem się z jednego kartofliska na drugie, bo może o tym nie wiecie, ale na Long Island masowo hodowano kiedyś kartofle.

BOŻONARODZENIOWY JADŁOSPIS NANCY VINCENT

„PIECZENIOWA ROZPUSTA"

Pieczeń wołowa, pieczone ziemniaki,
smażone krążki cebulowe w cieście,
brokuły w lekkim sosie holenderskim,
krążki jabłek, bułeczki na maśle i mleku,
torciki „świecowe", gorąca kawa, mleko

Better Homes and Gardens: Special Occasions
(New York 1959, Meredith Press)

Gdy Jane zajrzała do kuchni, żeby zobaczyć, co robi mama Jimmy'ego, ojciec odwrócił się do niego i spytał:

– Dymasz ją, synu? Trzymaj się tej dziewczyny. Nie spierdol takiej okazji. Jimmy, mój chłopcze, jak ja bym sobie używał z taką babką...

Jimmy, którego nazywano Jimmym juniorem, natychmiast uznał wtedy, że woli imię James. Gdy dostał się do Law School na Columbia University, stopniowo rozluźnił swoje kontakty z Jane.

PO UKOŃCZENIU trzydziestego pierwszego roku życia James został wspólnikiem w kancelarii, w której pracował. Był zamożny, chociaż nie obrzydliwie bogaty. Widział, jak dwóch innych wspólników w firmie, niewiele starszych od niego, odwaliło kitę na atak serca, znajdował więc czas na podróże po kraju i zagranicy. Czerpał też przyjemność z randek z imponująco dużą liczbą kobiet. Ożenił się z ładną dziewczyną z Middlebury. Oświadczył się jej niedaleko uczelni, na której studiowała, na pofałdowanym, porośniętym krzaczkami czarnych jagód wzgórzu w stanie Vermont. Potem James i Sigrid kupili apartament z trzema sypialniami i widokiem na Central Park. Jego urocza żona miała tylko jeden feler: bliznę na nosie, prezent od jakiegoś obcego mężczyzny, który zrzucił ją z różowego roweru marki Schwinn w Prospect Park, gdzie zażywała ruchu w towarzystwie rodziców. „Spierdalaj mi z drogi!", krzyknął nieznajomy w spandeksowym kostiumie, śmigając obok na wrotkach, przymocowanych do zamszowych butów. Ta historia wydawała się Jamesowi w pewnym sensie prorocza. Kochał Sigrid równie mocno jak ona jego. Potrafiła go autentycznie rozbawić. Mieli jednego syna. Dali mu na imię Rufus, a nazywali go Ruff. Sigrid stwierdziła, że nie chce mieć więcej dzieci, i po rocznym urlopie macierzyńskim wróciła do pracy jako redaktorka.

GDY JAMES SKOŃCZYŁ czterdziesty rok życia, nie odczuł ukłucia niepokoju w sercu. Wyczytał gdzieś, że ludzie po czterdziestce zwykle są nieszczęśliwi, on jednak cieszył się, że zabiera Ruffa na mecze bejsbolowe na Yankee Stadium i od piątku do poniedziałku ma wolne od nudnej, chociaż dochodowej pracy w kancelarii. Zaczął też prowadzić zajęcia na swojej Alma Mater, Columbia University, co podobało mu się o wiele bardziej niż kariera prawnicza.

GDY SKOŃCZYŁ czterdzieści dwa lata, niepokoiło go wszystko – zwłaszcza odkąd zobaczył, jak ciało jego leciwego ojca zostaje złożone w rodzinnym grobie w Cabot, w stanie Maine. Przed pogrzebem kolega z kancelarii odciągnął Jamesa na bok i zauważył:

– Masz szczęście, że znałeś swojego ojca jako dorosły człowiek. Nie wszyscy dożywają osiemdziesięciu jeden lat.

James chciał odpowiedzieć: „Nie pierdol. W ogóle nie znałem taty". Powiedział jednak zupełnie coś innego.

– Dziękuję, że przyjechałeś do Maine. Bardzo ci dziękuję.

KIEDY JAMES SKOŃCZYŁ czterdzieści pięć lat, Sigrid stwierdziła, że za często siedzi sama w domu i potrzebuje jakiejś odmiany. Jak co roku bawili wtedy w Vermont, dosłownie kilka kroków od ośrodka narciarskiego na porośniętym krzaczkami czarnych jagód wzgórzu, gdzie Jimmy kiedyś poprosił ją o rękę. Weekend okazał się zupełnie nijaki. James zasięgnął rady tego samego kolegi, z którym rozmawiał na pogrzebie ojca.

– Menopauza to problem – oświadczył kolega. – Pora wymienić żonę.

James uznał, że byłaby to nieco pochopna decyzja, i spytał o zdanie mamę, a ta przysłała mu przepis z książki *Better Homes and Gardens*. Gdy siedzieli nad talerzem grzybowego risotta, którego przygotowanie zajęło mu prawie całe popołudnie, odezwał się do Sigrid:

– Życiowa zmiana może okazać się największym wrogiem albo najlepszym przyjacielem człowieka.

Zabrała ze sobą Rufusa i przeprowadziła się na drugi koniec Stanów Zjednoczonych, do mieszkania w hiszpańskim stylu w Los Angeles. Ostatnio prawie codziennie uprawia rano jogging na plaży, a wieczorami popija piwo Sapporo ze swoim nowym facetem.

KIEDY JAMES MIAŁ już lat pięćdziesiąt i sypiał z Akemi, swoją znacznie młodszą japońską asystentką, Rufus zadzwonił z płaczem z Venice Beach.

– Tato, zrobiła się tu naprawdę niezła afera, kurde. Mógłbyś przylecieć do LA i zabrać mnie stąd? Bardzo cię proszę.

James nie był przygotowany na złe wieści od syna. Odłożył słuchawkę, najpierw powiedział jednak:

– Przepraszam cię, Rufusie, ale próbuję zasnąć... Żeby odkręcić to wszystko, co spierdolił Pan Bóg.

Akemi, której imię znaczy po japońsku „wielka piękność", patrzyła, jak James sięga po pudełko z pizzą V&T, stojące na nocnym stoliku. Zauważyła, że ostatnimi czasy zaczął podjadać w łóżku. Naciągnęła kołdrę powyżej ramion i postanowiła nie udawać, że go kocha.

– Wy w tym kraju nie umiecie się starzeć.

James odpowiedział, że musi teraz pobyć trochę sam, a kiedy Akemi wyszła, oddzwonił do Rufusa.

GDY JAMES MIAŁ pięćdziesiąt osiem lat i był szczęśliwym małżonkiem pięćdziesięcioszescioletniej Adele, którą kochał, bo żadne z nich nie lubiło dużo mówić, pojechał odwiedzić sędziwą już matkę w domu starców, który zaczęła nazywać swoim domem. Miała siwe włosy i sztuczne białe zęby i James aż się zdziwił, jak tryskający zdrowiem był jej fałszywy uśmiech. Nigdy w życiu nie powiedział matce, że jest piękna. Należała do kobiet, które nie doceniłyby takiego komplementu.

– Jak się czujesz, mamo?

Popatrzyła na niego i odparła:

– Mam już tego dość.

Stwierdzenie to wydało się Jamesowi uzasadnione, ale niejasne. Zastanawiał się, czy matka nie myśli o tym, żeby ze sobą skończyć. Byłoby to wyjście tchórzliwe, chociaż nie mógł wykluczyć, że sam kiedyś z niego skorzysta. Matka wskazała starca w niechlujnym jedwabnym szlafroku dwa stoliki dalej. Stary dziadyga siedział zatopiony w rozmowie z pulchną kobietą w średnim wieku, która przyszła do niego w odwiedziny; mogła być jego córką lub znacznie młodszą żoną.

– Nie mam tu chwili spokoju. Ten stary pierdziel ciągle się do mnie podwala.

– Bo nadal jesteś pociągająca, mamo – odpowiedział James. Uśmiechnęła się i uszczypnęła go w policzek. Gdyby jej powiedział, że jest piękna, to byłoby co innego, ale i tak miała wszystkiego dosyć. Odsunęła krzesło i powiedziała, że cieszy się, że zobaczy go znowu w następną niedzielę.

KIEDY SKOŃCZYŁ sześćdziesiąty rok życia, a od kilku już lat żonaty Rufus, ojciec bliźniaków, zadzwonił do niego i spytał: „Tato, jak mam uratować swoje małżeństwo?", James odpowiedział po prostu: „Nie rozwódź się". Rufus ożenił się z czarnoskórą dziewczyną Claudią Christie, co oznaczało, że wnuczęta Jamesa, Elijah i Winona, były wielorasowe albo dwurasowe, ponieważ po części czarne. Wszędzie, gdzie James bywał z nimi na Manhattanie, mówiono, że są półkrwi. Raz popełnił błąd, używając określenia „mieszaniec". Wtedy Rufus poprosił go na stronę i wytłumaczył, że słowo to jest obraźliwe i jeżeli użyje go jeszcze raz, nigdy więcej nie zobaczy wnucząt. Lecz kiedy James szedł ulicą z Elijahem i Winoną, miał tak mieszane uczucia, jak mieszany był kolor ich skóry. Wszyscy mówili: „Ach, ale ładne dzieci, aż oczy rwie".

– Tylko że wnuki w ogóle nie są do mnie podobne – zwierzył się James Adele.

PEWNEGO SŁONECZNEGO POPOŁUDNIA bawił się z Elijahem w ogrodzie. Rzucali i łapali piłkę do softballu. Przez większą część lata i jesieni James siedział teraz z Adele w swoim domku na plaży w Amagansett. Wnuczęta na tydzień zostały pod ich opieką, bo Rufus pojechał z Claudią na konferencję joyce'owską do Dublina. Około południa James i Adele lubili pić martini. Ten zwyczaj stał się dla nich już rytuałem w Amagansett, nie grali jednak w golfa. W golfa nigdy. James z lekkim niepokojem obserwował Adele – która wyszła z kuchni w kostiumie podobnym do modnego w latach czterdziestych stroju kąpielowego, jaki nosiła Joan Crawford w filmie *Mildred Pierce* – kładącą Winonę na bardzo starym materacu pływackim w kształcie pączka z dziurką. Był niebiesko-biały i ozdobiony czerwonymi krabami, lecz dało się zauważyć, że niewątpliwie znajduje się już w wieku biblijnym, bo kraby przybrały kolor rdzawego różu. James musiał pilnować zarówno Winony w basenie, jak i Elijaha, który rzucał ostro, naprawdę ostro podkręcane piłki. Chłopak miał dobrą rękę. Poza tym w odpowiednim świetle – czy to nie było dziwne? – wydawał się uderzająco podobny do dziadka.

– Dziadku... – powiedział mały, szykując się do kolejnego rzutu, i po chwili piłka z bolesnym użądleniem plasnęła w otwartą dłoń Jamesa. – Dlaczego ludzie potrzebują snu?

Bawili się na dużym zielonym trawniku. Obaj mieli na sobie kąpielówki w identycznym morskim kolorze. Adele chciała, by w domku na plaży wszystko pasowało do siebie kolorystycznie i żeby było w nim jasno jak na Karaibach. Myśl, że cały domek miałby być biały, wydała się Jamesowi nieprzyzwoita. A skoro już mówimy o Adele... to gdzie ona jest? Winona śpiewała, leżąc na pływającym pączku. Machała nogami i śpiewała. Rozpryskiwała wodę i majtała nogami. James na chwilę kompletnie się pogubił. Niełatwo było się starzeć. Czasami próbował wracać pamięcią do 1942 roku, kiedy się urodził.

– Co mówisz, Elijahu?

– Jak to jest, dziadku, że wszyscy musimy spać?

James zobaczył Adele przez tarasowe okno. Nalewała sobie kolejne martini. Rozmawiała przez telefon, pewnie z którąś ze swoich znajomych malarek, o tym, dokąd zabiorą dzisiaj dzieci na kolację. Wszyscy mieli już wnuki i wspólne kolacje stały się dla nich codziennością. Kolacje i martini.

– Elijahu... – odpowiedział James, odwracając się w stronę basenu; Winona drzemała. Spała. Leżała bezwładnie na pływającym pączku i znosiło ją na głębszą wodę. – Nikt nie wie dlaczego – James usłyszał swój głos. – Sen to zagadka.

DAMASCUS ROAD

1966 1976 1977 1988 1999 **2010**

TYDZIEŃ PO ZAKOŃCZENIU BUDOWY DAMASCUS PREP, szkoły dla bogatych dzieciaków, którym nie udało się dostać nigdzie indziej, z mokradeł wypełzł aligator długości osiemnastu stóp, żeby zobaczyć, jak teraz wygląda jego dawne miejsce zamieszkania. Ścieżki krótkowzrocznego dyrektora szkoły i potężnego zwierzęcia przecięły się na korytarzu na pierwszym piętrze, pomiędzy laboratorium chemicznym i salą plastyczną. Dyrektor, przeszczep z północy, były nauczyciel łaciny w Amherst, przypomniał sobie, że przeczytał gdzieś, że w razie napotkania węża w tunelu albo aligatora na lądzie należy uciekać zygzakiem. Założył się w duchu sam ze sobą, że uciekając w bok, okaże się zbyt powolny, dał więc nogę do sali plastycznej, gdzie wyciągnął komórkę i zadzwonił po Animal Patrol.

Ponieważ nikt się nie zjawił, zatelefonował do miejscowego szeryfa. Piętnaście minut później emerytowany gliniarz oraz jeden z najlepszych strzelców w hrabstwie przyjechali pikapem tego drugiego i zastrzelili zwierzę. Gliniarz, który mimo podeszłego wieku nadal miał płową czupurynę, nie chciał zapłaty w gotówce. On i kilku jego kumpli, którzy też już byli na emeryturze, zabrali martwego aligatora. Agnes słyszała, że teraz właściwie każdego wieczoru można wybrać się do restauracji Great Byrd Lodge i zobaczyć tam wypchane i wystawione na pokaz trofeum. Można się też zabawić i próbować zgadnąć, ile aligator mierzył i ważył. Na ścianie w kącie stoi drewniana tablica z przymocowanym na sznurku kawałkiem kredy, a każdego wieczoru pierwszy klient, któremu udaje się odgadnąć długość oraz ciężar ciała zwierzęcia, wygrywa darmowy kawałek ciasta orzechowego albo szklanicę piwa z miejscowego browaru. Agnes M. Christie, seniorka, niegdyś cudowne dziecko Buckner County w stanie Georgia, nigdy nie była na kolacji w Great Byrd Lodge. Woli wino od piwa, a ciasto orzechowe i tak jest za słodkie jak na jej gust. Nie odwiedza też szkoły Damascus Prep, chociaż drogę do niej zna aż za dobrze.

– **PIJESZ TĘ COLĘ TAK,** jak gdyby ci się spieszyło.

Był rok 1966. Agnes Miller skończyła dziewiętnaście lat, była mażoretką i studentką drugiego roku w Buckner County College. Nosiła jasnoniebieską koszulową sukienkę, włosy miała ułożone w bąbelkowaty, bufiasty kok w stylu

Diany Ross i członkiń zespołu Supremes. Nogi miała tak długie, że mogłaby przeskoczyć Nil, a długość jej sukienki była skromna. Pracowała na pół etatu w bibliotece uniwersyteckiej. Ilekroć ktoś pytał ją, kim chce zostać, jak już będzie duża, odpowiadała niejako automatycznie, że nauczycielką. Chociaż nie dlatego żeby lubiła ten zawód. Ta odpowiedź brzmiała po prostu stosownie i przyjemnie.

– Bo tak się składa, że mam mnóstwo zajęć. – Uśmiechnęła się do ciemnowłosego, elegancko ubranego mężczyzny, który siedział na drugim końcu baru w Kress Five & Dime. Właściwie jednak Agnes nie miała dokąd pójść, jak tylko do domu, i nie miała tam nic do zrobienia poza pracą domową. Było już po zajęciach, a trening mażoretek skończył się przed dwiema godzinami, więc jak co dzień przyznała sobie nagrodę w postaci szklanki coca-coli. Siedziała koło swojej przyjaciółki z dzieciństwa, Eloise, która nigdy nie nosiła sukienki, gdy mogła włożyć spodnie. Było późne popołudnie i w barze panował przerażający spokój. Demonstracje i strajki okupacyjne w Buckner zaczęły się i skończyły wraz z napięciem, powściągliwością i skłonnością do niedostrzegania niczego, co się dzieje wokoło. Biali zareagowali najpierw z gniewem, potem z chłodną logiką: zaczęli się interesować przedmieściami, otwierali restauracje i sklepy i budowali ranczerskie domy typu *split-level* na nowych osiedlach, gdzie Murzyni nie śmieli się pokazywać.

– A ja mam na imię Claude i tak się składa, że dysponuję sporą ilością wolnego czasu.

Claude Johnson zwinnie przesuwał się ze stołka na stołek i w końcu przysiadł obok Agnes. Powiedział, że jest inżynierem i właśnie dostał angaż do pracy w Southeast

Aviation. Miał na sobie schludne szare spodnie, twillowy blezer ze skórzanymi łatami na łokciach, koszulę i krawat. Postawił Agnes i Eloise drugą kolejkę coli. Najwyraźniej interesowała go Agnes, lecz starał się jak mógł, by wciągać do rozmowy również jej koleżankę, która każdym słowem i gestem wydawała się krzyczeć „spieprzaj stąd", zwłaszcza wtulając się w Agnes, gdy Claude coś do niej mówił.

– Nie jestem nachalny z natury, ale zadzwonię do ciebie jeszcze dziś wieczorem – zapowiedział, kiedy wszyscy troje wychodzili z Kress. Poinformował także obie młode kobiety, że pochodzi z Tuxedo, małego miasteczka w Georgii, i skończył Morehouse College. Eloise, która po raz pierwszy tego wieczoru próbowała zachować się wobec niego uprzejmie, oświadczyła, że ma rodzinę w Tuxedo, ale dodała natychmiast:

– To wiocha. Jedni tacy moi ubodzy krewni mają jeszcze uboższych krewnych w Tuxedo i w ogóle nie chcą ich znać.

CLAUDE RZECZYWIŚCIE ZADZWONIŁ tego wieczoru. Zanim Agnes zaczęła wieczorne ćwiczenia kalisteniczne. Zanim jej rodzice zgasili światło w swojej sypialni na górze. I zanim Eloise, która mieszkała wtedy w domu rodziców Agnes, złośliwie umyła zęby jej szczoteczką, po czym pootwierała szuflady szyfoniery o nogach w kształcie pazurów.

– To ty, Agnes? – spytał.

– No. Chociaż jeżeli mam zostać nauczycielką, to chyba nie powinnam mówić „no" zamiast „tak".

– Skarbie, moim zdaniem w zaciszu swojego domu możesz mówić wszystko, na co masz ochotę.

– To nie jest mój dom. To dom moich rodziców.

– A jesteś w nim szczęśliwa?

– Bo ja wiem? Właściwie to nie myślę o tym zbyt często. Ale chyba potrafiłabym być szczęśliwa wszędzie. – Roześmiała się i zaskoczyło ją aksamitne brzmienie własnego głosu.

– Chciałbym, żebyś była szczęśliwa ze mną – oznajmił Claude.

– Nie znam cię.

– Możemy nad tym popracować. Może poszlibyśmy w sobotę do kina? Przyjechałbym po ciebie około szóstej i najpierw zabrałbym cię na kolację.

– To jest już jakiś początek.

Odłożyła słuchawkę i dopiero po chwili zorientowała się, że Claude nie zna jej adresu. Zaczęła liczyć. Zadzwonił drugi raz po sześćdziesięciu sekundach. W drzwiach sypialni stanęła Eloise. Miała na sobie jedną z koszul nocnych Agnes.

– Oby tylko nikt nie zamordował tego wielkoluda – powiedziała Eloise.

Agnes przewróciła oczami. Czy Eloise nie wie, że małostkowość jest wstrętna? Przez małostkowość ludziom przedwcześnie wypadają zęby. Przez małostkowość ludziom cuchnie z ust.

– Dlaczego wygadujesz takie rzeczy?

Eloise pokręciła głową.

– On jakoś tak dziwnie wygląda…

W JESIENNE NOCE 1966 roku zdarzało się dosyć często, że Eloise wyciągała rękę znad swojej poduszki i zsuwała kołdrę z Agnes. Czasami uda Eloise wędrowały też na nogi

Agnes, która wyglądała przez okno sypialni na księżyc i usiane gwiazdami niebo, gładząc Eloise po głowie, karku, sprężystych plecach i wszystkich innych częściach jej ciała, które ją podniecały. Dziewczyny poruszały się cicho i efektywnie – nie mogły sobie pozwolić na żadne hałasy czy słowa. Po drugiej stronie korytarza znajdowała się sypialnia diakona i lady Millerów.

Rano wstawały w jak najlepszych humorach, gotowe na nowy dzień.

CLAUDE ZABRAŁ AGNES na *Nothing But a Man* do miejscowego kina dla kolorowych na obrzeżach miasta. Jedli popcorn, polany dodatkową porcją masła. Po seansie powiedziała:

– Mój Boże, chciałabym wyglądać jak Abbey Lincoln.

– Wyglądasz lepiej od niej.

– Jesteś kłamcą, Claude. Gdzie nauczyłeś się tak nawijać makaron na uszy?

– Zaraz, zaraz, nie powiedziałem przecież, że lepiej od niej śpiewasz. Byłbym kłamcą, gdybym tak powiedział.

– To prawda. Ja fałszuję – zachichotała Agnes. – Wykopsali mnie z chóru kościelnego, a mój tata jest tam pierwszym diakonem.

– To niedobrze.

– Od tamtej pory nie byłam już w kościele.

– Dumna jesteś.

– Ty też nie sprawiasz na mnie wrażenia skromnego.

– Chciałbym usłyszeć, jak śpiewasz.

Otworzyła usta i zaśpiewała *Baby Love*, idąc z Claude'em w kierunku jego chevroleta impali. Wbrew oczekiwaniom dziewczyny samochód nie był nowy, okazał się jednak czysty i miał ogrzewanie. Po minucie jej śpiewu Claude wziął Agnes za rękę.

– Tak, tym głosem nikomu nie sprawiasz przyjemności, a już na pewno nie Panu Bogu.

Dała mu sójkę w bok.

– Śpiewam falsetem. To rzadki głos u kobiety.

Odwzajemnił kuksańca.

– Znasz takie powiedzenie o pysze, nie? Pycha kroczy przed upadkiem.

WYNAJĄŁ PRZEROBIONY NA MIESZKANIE garaż mniej więcej dwie mile na południe od zamożniejszej dzielnicy kolorowych. Tam gdzie mieszkała Agnes, drzwi frontowe malowało się na czerwono, żeby od razu było wiadomo, do kogo należy dom. Claude wynajął swoje lokum od pana Gilberta, właściciela jedynego w mieście sklepu meblowego dla kolorowych. Agnes krążyła po dwóch pokojach Claude'a, przyglądając się świeżo pomalowanym na biało ścianom i półkom na książki, z których większość dotyczyła nauk inżynieryjnych albo zaliczała się do literatury faktu: *A Thousand Days: John F. Kennedy in the White House*, *Autobiografia Malcolma X* czy *Struktura rewolucji naukowych*. Na ścianie w salonie wisiały dyplomy z Morehouse College i Hampton Institute, a na jednej z ostatnich półek stało kilka fotografii jego licznej i szeroko rozgałęzionej rodziny, składającej się, jak mogła sądzić na ich podstawie Agnes, głównie z kobiet i dzieci. Ławę z drewna orzecha włoskiego zdobiły świeże kwiaty.

Wzięła do ręki jedno z rodzinnych zdjęć i odwróciła je w stronę Claude'a.

– Ilu was jest?

– Spytała jedynaczka. Wystarczająco dużo, żeby nasze baby miały co robić.

– Baby? – Zmarszczyła nos i powąchała kwiaty, po czym odstawiła fotografię na półkę. – Dla mnie dwoje, troje dzieci to góra.

– Uważam, że słuszne to i sprawiedliwe.

W tle rozległ się śpiew Abbey Lincoln i Agnes zaczęła kiwać się do taktu. Skinęła Claude'owi głową z aprobatą i pstryknęła palcami.

– Masz rację. Abbey potrafi śpiewać.

Siedział na jasnobrązowej kanapie, kupionej u pana Gilberta, jak większość mebli w mieszkaniu. Wyposażenia saloniku dopełniało kilka kolorowych poduszek z Searsa i włochaty dywanik.

– Muszę ci coś powiedzieć, Agnes. Nie zamierzam zagrzać tutaj miejsca.

Nadal pstrykała palcami.

– Sam urządzałeś to wnętrze?

– Daję tu sobie dwa, najwyżej trzy lata. Potem Kalifornia albo Nowy Jork.

– Źle cię traktują w Southeast Aviation?

– Nie zadawaj pytań, na które nie chcesz usłyszeć odpowiedzi.

Przestała pstrykać. Oczywiście, Claude niewątpliwie miał swoje problemy. Był wysoki, postawny, a jego skóra odznaczała się brązowym odcieniem. Umiał się wysłowić i nie nosił byle jakich ubrań.

– Jest aż tak źle?

Pochylił się do przodu.

– Nigdy nie będziemy bili naszych dzieci. Trzymaj mnie za słowo, jeśli o to chodzi, słyszysz? Mój ojciec wierzył w pas. Od razu za niego łapał. Myślę, że po prostu nie wyobrażał sobie, że można żyć inaczej. A ja byłem małym czarnym chłopcem o niewyparzonym języku. Ojciec mówił: „Synku, to jest Południe. Dlaczego nie potrafisz mówić grzecznie, jak twoi bracia i siostry? Nie możesz się odzywać z taką złością w głosie, musimy ci wybić z głowy takie gadanie, bo inaczej nie dasz sobie rady na tym świecie". Oto w czym rzecz, Agnes. Nienawidziłem ojca przez całe życie, ale dziś go rozumiem. Pracuję od poniedziałku do piątku i kiedy jestem w robocie, staram się zwracać do wszystkich uprzejmie.

– Tylko ty jeden? – spytała, unosząc brwi.

– Gdzie indziej czekają mnie lepsze perspektywy. Jestem dobrze wykształcony. Wciąż mam też dobry kontakt z czarnymi braćmi z Morehouse i Hampton. Z Nowego Jorku, New Jersey, z Waszyngtonu. Nie spycham ich na margines. Ale przyszedł już czas, żebym napisał CV i pomógł mojej rodzinie najlepiej jak potrafię.

– Rozumiem – powiedziała Agnes. Zauważyła, że wyraz jego miodowych oczu złagodniał.

Poklepał wolne miejsce na kanapie obok siebie.

– Ale dość już o mnie. Powiedz mi, czego ty chciałabyś od życia, Agnes.

Na chwilę odjęło jej mowę. Claude był pierwszym mężczyzną gotowym rozsiąść się wygodnie i posłuchać, jak ona nieporadnie próbuje wyrzeźbić jakieś marzenie dla siebie.

– Chcę być kimś innym, nie nauczycielką.

– TO MÓJ DALEKI KREWNY; mieliśmy wspólnych pradziadków – powiedziała Eloise ostatniej nocy, spędzonej w łóżku Agnes, która odturlała się od niej i szepnęła:

– Czy ty też nie powinnaś znaleźć już sobie faceta?

Eloise ciągnęła dalej swoje.

– To kuzyn ze strony matki. A w rodzinie mojej mamy wszyscy umierają młodo.

Agnes wstała z podwójnego łóżka.

– Nie mogę tego dłużej z tobą robić.

Eloise nie wyciągnęła do niej ręki, chociaż Agnes wyczuła, że miała na to ochotę. Uczepiła się słów Agnes i tej myśli, sugestii, że mogłaby albo powinna znaleźć sobie faceta.

– Jakiego faceta? – spytała. – Czy Claude robi ci to samo co ja?

Agnes wybiegła z sypialni, a jej ładną twarz błyskawicznie zalała powódź łez, ale kiedy rankiem zeszła na śniadanie, znowu były najlepszymi przyjaciółkami. Obie lubiły jajecznicę na boczku, sok pomarańczowy, mleko i zielone jabłka, pokrojone tak, jak życzyła sobie Eloise.

– Była pani dla mnie strasznie dobra – zwróciła się Eloise do matki Agnes, lady Miller, która niemal każdego dnia wstawała jeszcze przed świtem i szła do pracy w żydowskiej piekarni przy Jefferson Street. Tego ranka zadzwoniła, że jest chora, bo duchy powiedziały jej, żeby tym razem lepiej została w domu. Ona też była kiedyś młoda, jak jej córka, a chociaż nie czerpała wiedzy z książek, nie dało się o niej powiedzieć, że nic nie wie o życiu i świecie.

Przygotowała paczkę na drogę dla Eloise, lecz odwróciła się, kiedy Agnes zadała przyjaciółce z lat dziecięcych pytanie:

– To dokąd teraz pojedziesz?

– Do mojego dalekiego kuzyna, Kinga Tyrone'a. To chyba jedyny porządny członek mojej rodziny.

RODZICE AGNES nie powiedzieli nic, gdy po raz pierwszy została u Claude'a na noc, ale nazajutrz wieczorem jej ojciec, mularz, który pracował przy budowie domów w Buckner, odciągnął młodzieńca na bok i spytał, jakie ma zamiary wobec jego córki. Claude zawołał Agnes, ponieważ stwierdził, że nie będzie rozmawiał o swoich zamiarach bez porozumienia z nią, na wypadek, gdyby się okazało, że mają inne plany na przyszłość. Agnes powiedziała, że najpierw chce skończyć studia, a była przecież dopiero na drugim roku. Claude oznajmił, że pozostanie w Buckner, dopóki Agnes będzie studiować, matka dziewczyny zauważyła natomiast, że Agnes nie powinna zostawać u niego na noc, chyba że młody człowiek wsunie jej na palec pierścionek zaręczynowy. Tego samego wieczoru Claude zaparkował pod małym sieciowym sklepem spożywczo-przemysłowym, a Agnes weszła do środka i kupiła dwanaście pudełek ciastek Cracker Jack. Dopiero w szóstym znaleźli zagrzebany pod karmelowymi herbatnikami mały plastikowy pierścionek z fałszywym kamieniem w kolorze karmazynu. Pozostałe pudełka wyrzucili.

TRZYDZIEŚCI MIL NA ZACHÓD od szkoły Damascus Prep leży miasteczko, które spotkał kiedyś ciężki los – w czasie obu wojen światowych straciło jedną trzecią populacji, bo wtedy w dużych miastach amerykańskich potrzebni byli robotnicy do fabryk. W latach dziewięćdziesiątych jednak, kiedy osuszono bagna, wybudowano internat, szkołę, korty tenisowe i domy dla nauczycieli, wielu mieszkańców znalazło zatrudnienie jako personel techniczny właśnie w tej szkole, w kafeterii albo jako dozorcy, ochroniarze czy ogrodnicy. Ceny nieruchomości były jeszcze przystępne, okolica przyjemna, a liczba zgłoszeń uczniów do szkoły rosła, podobnie jak czesne. Właściciele sklepów przy Main Street mogli już wtedy znowu zatrudniać sprzedawców na cały etat. Zapanował popyt na drobny sprzęt gospodarstwa domowego i produkty z najwyższej półki. Miejscowy fryzjer, a zarazem natchniony kaznodzieja i okazjonalny pijak, zaczął nawet pracować w co drugą niedzielę, by obsłużyć wszystkich uczniów oraz ciało pedagogiczne Damascus Prep. Klientom podobały się zarówno bluegrassowa muzyka, którą puszczał w swoim zakładzie, jak i to, że w godzinach pracy grał na tamburynie. Kino, którego budynek liczył co najmniej sto lat i które podobno należało do jednego wampira i dwojga duchów, wyświetlało teraz artystyczne filmy przed pełną widownią. Odbywały się w nim także imprezy muzyczne. A ponieważ zamożność często łączy się z pożądaniem świeżych produktów spożywczych oraz chudego, wysokiej jakości mięsa, w miasteczku otwarto delikatesy ze zdrową żywnością, by zadowolić uczniów oraz dbających o zdrowie okolicznych mieszkańców. Sklep wędkarski zaczął sprowadzać luksusowe wędki, a miejscowi rybacy oferowali poranne i wieczorne rejsy po mokradłach. Pod koniec roku szkolnego łodzie na trasie Georgia – Maine wynajmowały nawet całe rodziny. Jedna mała szkoła, stojąca na niegdyś ciemnej i samotnej ulicy, na której trudno było spotkać latarnię i gdzie rozlegały się tylko odgłosy tarcia odnóży koników polnych i skrzekliwe „ribbit, ribbit" miejscowych żab ryczących, zrewitalizowała całe miasto. Agnes M. Christie, ma się rozumieć, nie wie o tym odrodzeniu z pierwszej ręki. W wolnych chwilach dużo czyta na temat Damascus Prep w bibliotece Buckner County, gdzie od czasu powrotu na Południe pracuje trzy razy w tygodniu jako wolontariuszka. Czasami na starość rozstajemy się z pewnymi rzeczami. I bywa z nimi tak, że stają się nam wtedy jeszcze bliższe.

AGNES STUDIOWAŁA JUŻ NA CZWARTYM ROKU w Buckner County College, gdy Claude powiedział jej, że Abbey Lincoln przyjeżdża do Atlanty. Był podekscytowany, bo nadarzała się doskonała okazja, żeby wpaść do rodziców i przedstawić Agnes kilku jego czarnym braciom z Morehouse, a także ich ślicznym żonom i dziewczynom. Lady Miller ucałowała pierścionek z pudełka po ciastkach i dała Agnes i Claude'owi swoje błogosławieństwo, a diakon Miller wsunął młodzieńcowi w dłoń nowiutki pięćdziesięciodolarowy banknot i spytał, czy wystarczy mu paliwa na drogę. Strzałka benzynomierza w chevrolecie Claude'a wskazywała, że bak jest pełen, ale ojciec Agnes dał mu jeszcze kanister z galonem benzyny do bagażnika.

– Tylko się nie zachowujcie jak idioci i nie palcie papierosów w samochodzie – powiedział im na odjezdnym.

PRZYSTANEK W TUXEDO, prowincjonalnym miasteczku, które dałoby się obejść w pięć minut, był krótki i konkretny. Rodzice Claude'a okazali się cichymi, spokojnymi ludźmi, nakryli stół jednym ze swoich najlepszych obrusów i położyli na nim sztućce nie do pary. Podali zwyczajną pieczeń, soczystą, ale bez ulubionych przez lady Miller wypestkowanych owoców czy ziół śródziemnomorskich. Na stole brakowało też wazonu i ozdób, a mama Claude'a mrożoną herbatę serwowała w słoikach. W czasie tej wizyty, według zegarka jej syna trwającej dwie godziny, pojawił się też złożony z jego przysadzistych braci i sióstr komitet powitalny, żeby powiedzieć gościom „dzień dobry". Było jasne, że rodzeństwo nie tylko pokłada nadzieje w najmłodszym braciszku, ale i postawiło na niego część własnych oszczędności. Claude'owi udało się wyściskać ich wszystkich i przyrzec, że kiedy przyjadą z Agnes następnym razem, zostaną w domu dłużej.

– Mam robotę, mamo – powiedział, podsuwając jej na stole kopertę, zawierającą, jak wiedziała Agnes, jego ciężko zarobione pieniądze. – Ani razu nie byłem jeszcze na zwolnieniu czy urlopie. Czekam z tym do czasu, aż naprawdę sprawi mi to przyjemność.

W DRODZE POWROTNEJ Z ATLANTY – po koncercie Abbey Lincoln, który rozpoczął się z godzinnym opóźnieniem, i kiedy Agnes poznała już większość znajomych Claude'a – utknęli w korku na drodze U.S. 80, Dixie Overland Highway. Słuchali radia, śmiali się i rozkładali na czynniki pierwsze wszystkie wydarzenia tego wieczoru, począwszy od piosenek wykonywanych przez Abbey, a skończywszy na towarzyszach młodego inżyniera, którzy bez żenady przyglądali się Agnes i wyrażali opinie na jej temat. „No tak, Claude, opakowanie śliczne, zawartość też". Agnes najpierw odczuwała pewną swoją przewagę nad rodziną Claude'a, a potem odniosła wrażenie, że wyszła na osobę płytką i głupią na tle jego przyjaciół, daleko bardziej aktywnych w ruchu praw obywatelskich niż ona czy jej rodzice. Obiecała sobie w głębi serca, że przynajmniej niektóre książki swojego narzeczonego przeczyta z zainteresowaniem większym niż chwilowe.

– Dobrze wypadłaś – powiedział.

– Moim zdaniem niektórzy z nich są strasznie pretensjonalni – stwierdziła. – Nie wiem, jak mogłeś ich znosić.

– Jeżeli da się ludziom trochę czasu, to sami ci pokażą, jacy są naprawdę – odpowiedział Claude. – A ja po prostu czekałem, aż oni ujawnią swoje prawdziwe oblicze.

BYŁA JUŻ DRUGA W NOCY, gdy skręcił w Damascus Road, długą i pustą drogę, której normalnie by unikał, gdyby nie prowadziła do Buckner County na skróty. Bardzo dbał o to, żeby nie przekroczyć dozwolonej prędkości, choć wciskał pedał gazu mocniej niż zazwyczaj. Ani on, ani Agnes nie zauważyli radiowozu, dopóki nie wyjechał na ulicę, a potem nie włączył koguta i syreny. Claude natychmiast zwolnił i stanął na łuku drogi. Księżyc wisiał wysoko, niebo było czarne jak obsydian. Wokół rosły nisko pochylone drzewa, które karłowacieją na bagnach i mokradłach. Kiedy policjant zajrzał do wozu i zapalił latarkę, Claude już trzymał w ręku prawo jazdy.

– Dobry wieczór, panie władzo – powiedział, nie patrząc na policjanta, ale i nie unikając jego wzroku.

– Goni pan za księżycem? – spytał funkcjonariusz.

– Proszę?

– Zdaje się, że dokądś się pan spieszy. – Policjant był chudy, tak chudy, jak Claude był potężny. Jesionowobrązowe włosy gliniarza wydawały się przerzedzone nad czołem, ale miał też wielkie, podwinięte na czubkach wąsiska, przypominające kierownicę rowerową.

– Czy przekroczyłem prędkość, panie władzo? – spytał neutralnym głosem Claude.

Policjant wziął od niego prawo jazdy.

– Wydaje mi się, że tak.

Podobnie jak Claude, Agnes patrzyła prosto przed siebie.

Policjant zajrzał głębiej do samochodu i wyglądało na to, że już, już ma oddać Claude'owi dokument. Na widok Agnes aż uchylił czapki.

– Jakbym wiózł taki towar, to pewnie też bym się spieszył.

Agnes spostrzegła, że po twarzy Claude'a przebiegł skurcz. Dotknęła ręką jego lewego łokcia, a policjant znów bardzo długo wpatrywał się w prawo jazdy.

– Muszę to sprawdzić. Proszę zostać na miejscach.

Kiedy policjant szedł do radiowozu, Claude'owi wyrwało się z ust ciche gwizdnięcie. Noc była chłodna. Chłodniejsza niż zazwyczaj, dlatego widział mgiełkę swojego oddechu.

– Włączę silnik, Agnes.

– Claude, on chce, żebyś mu coś dał. O to mu chodzi.

– Nie podoba mi się jego gęba.

– Po prostu bądź uprzejmy. Nie ruszaj się.

– Co mi strzeliło do głowy? – Claude chwycił kierownicę. – Żeby skręcić w tę drogę.

Funkcjonariusz Jamie Haig wezwał wsparcie. Minęło mniej więcej piętnaście minut, zanim na miejsce zdarzenia dotarł William Byrd, jego kolega po fachu i najlepszy strzelec w hrabstwie. Był szeroki w barach i gładko ogolony, a jego niebieskie oczy miały pawi odcień – ale tylko kiedy się uśmiechał, co rzadko mu się zdarzało. Miał też czerwone, gorejące policzki i przylizane, jasne, słomkowego koloru włosy, które pomimo niemłodego już wieku zaczesywał do tyłu. Szczupły funkcjonariusz Haig naradzał się z barczystym funkcjonariuszem Byrdem i obaj uznali, że Claude i Agnes powinni wysiąść z auta, by policjanci mogli je przeszukać. Na to Claude zapytał, najgrzeczniej jak potrafił, czego właściwie szukają, ale Byrd położył grubą dłoń na karabinie i odpowiedział, żeby lepiej nie przeszkadzał im w czynnościach służbowych. Zajrzeli do bagażnika, a także w szpary pomiędzy poduszkami foteli z przodu i z tyłu wozu. Wybebeszyli schowek w desce rozdzielczej, wetknęli głowy pod maskę, a potem kazali Claude'owi wsiąść z powrotem. Claude zaczekał, aż Agnes pierwsza usadowi się na miejscu dla pasażera.

Funkcjonariusz William Byrd stanowczo pokręcił głową.

– Musimy sprawdzić jej torebkę.

Agnes otworzyła elegancką czarną kopertówkę, niedawny prezent od matki. „Nowa sukienka i torebka. Żebyś miała coś ładnego na koncert Abbey Lincoln". Czując narastający ucisk w żołądku, dziewczyna patrzyła, jak niezdarne paluchy policjanta przeszukują jej rzeczy osobiste.

– Jamie – zwrócił się funkcjonariusz William Byrd do swojego patykowatego partnera. – Wydaje mi się, że musimy zabrać tę młodą damę na dodatkowe przesłuchanie.

– Jakie przesłuchanie? – spytał Claude, mimo woli przesuwając się w kierunku Agnes.

Byrd wskazał torebkę.

– Są tutaj pewne zakazane substancje.

Agnes drgnęła, bo sama też zaczęła buzować ze złości.

– Nie ma tam żadnych zakazanych substancji. Nic, tylko szminka, perfumy i mój dowód!

– Jamie – odezwał się znów Byrd ze swobodną pewnością siebie. – Chyba trzeba będzie wezwać wsparcie.

– Proszę posłuchać – powiedział Haig, zwracając się do Agnes. – Takiej sprawy nie da się wyjaśnić w kilka minut. Ale możemy to zrobić w czasie spaceru tą drogą. – Wskazał krętą ścieżkę, otoczoną wierzbami płaczącymi i bagnami.

– Jej facet... – Byrd wskazał głową Claude'a, który zaciskał pięści. – Trochę się denerwuje.

– Kochasz tego człowieka? – spytał Haig.

Agnes spojrzała na Claude'a. Pomyślała o słowach Eloise. „Wszyscy mężczyźni w mojej rodzinie umierają młodo". I o potężnym policjancie, który gładził palcami karabin.

– To nasze prywatne sprawy – odezwał się Claude, wstrząsany tłumioną wściekłością.

Agnes skinęła głową.

– Tak... kocham.

Jasnowłosy William Byrd ruszył naprzód, prowadząc Agnes na bagna i pomiędzy drzewa. Jego blada wcześniej twarz ukazała się znów piętnaście minut później, wrócił jednak bez Agnes, a na czerwone teraz policzki wystąpił jeszcze ciemny, nocny rumieniec. Spokojnie i wesoło uśmiechnął się do Claude'a. Wyciągnął z kieszonki koszuli piersiówkę whisky i podniósł ją wysoko, upijając kilka łyków.

– Jamie, wygląda na to, że ta lalka jednak nie ma przy sobie zakazanych substancji, ale ty wiesz, że ja mam słaby wzrok.

Claude był już w kajdankach. Z tyłu głowy, która wyjątkowo gwałtownie zderzyła się z pałką Haiga, ściekała mu leniwie strużka krwi. Zanim Haig odszedł, szepnął Claude'owi do ucha:

– Tylko nie próbuj z Williem takich numerów jak ze mną. Zdecydowanie odradzam. – Przeczesał palcami swoje rzednące włosy, obszedł samochód i zniknął w ciemności.

– Poczujesz się lepiej, jak sobie trochę wypijesz. – Byrd podszedł do Claude'a i podbił mu nogi kopniakiem, a potem przystawił piersiówkę do jego ust i zaczął mu lać whisky na twarz. Claude odwrócił głowę, zaciskając wargi. Nie chciał pić palącego płynu, który parzył mu twarz niczym gorąca zupa.

Wkrótce potem wrócił Haig wraz z Agnes. Otworzył dla niej drzwi od strony pasażera i dziewczyna, wciąż patrząc wprost przed siebie, wsiadła do chevroleta. Haig delikatnie położył jej torebkę na kolanach. Czubek sprężystego koka Agnes był spłaszczony.

– Chcę, żebyście dojechali do domu cali i zdrowi – powiedział Byrd, zdejmując Claude'owi kajdanki i wpychając go za kierownicę. – To był długi wieczór dla nas wszystkich. A zdarza się w takich przypadkach, że koniec jest dużo gorszy.

Claude przekręcił kluczyk w stacyjce i odjechał. Płakał, chociaż nie zdawał sobie z tego sprawy. Agnes zachowała spokój, zamrugała tylko, kiedy zapytał, czy odwieźć ją do szpitala. Mrugała też, gdy zapytał po chwili, czy zatrzymać się pod domem pani Francine, czarnoskórej położnej, przyzwyczajonej do tego, że ludzie budzą ją o nieprzyzwoitych godzinach. Zapytał, czy nic jej nie jest, a wtedy Agnes spojrzała na swoje dłonie i zauważyła, że na palcu nie ma już plastikowego pierścionka. Odwróciła się do Claude'a, zaczęła wrzeszczeć, wpadła w histerię i błagała go, żeby zawrócił.

– Agnes – powiedział Claude. – Kupię ci tysiąc takich pierścionków, kochanie. Ale jeżeli tam wrócimy, ci ludzie nas zabiją. Nie mogę zawrócić.

– W takim razie zabierz mnie do domu – powiedziała. – Zabierz mnie do domu, ale już.

PONIEWAŻ W NAJBLIŻSZYCH DNIACH Agnes nie podchodziła do telefonu i nie oddzwaniała do Claude'a, lady Miller uznała, że spotkanie z jego rodzicami nie poszło dobrze. Diakon, mężczyzna równie zagadkowy jak Booker T. Washington, wiele wycierpiał w dzieciństwie z powodu swojej ciemnej skóry i podejrzewał, że wykształceni Murzyni o jaśniejszej cerze, jak wielu mieszkańców Atlanty, dokuczali jego jedynej córce, ona zaś robiła dobrą minę do złej gry, ale rewanżowała się im, jak tylko mogła.

Pewnego niedzielnego poranka Claude stanął na progu domu Millerów przed kościołem. Nie było go dwa tygodnie. Diakon nie zaprosił go do środka, Agnes zgodziła się jednak wyjść na ganek. Claude przyklęknął przed nią na jedno kolano i oświadczył się, pokazując dziewczynie błyszczący pierścionek zaręczynowy z największym brylantem, jaki w życiu widziała. Na pewno wydał wszystkie oszczędności, żeby go kupić.

– Claude – powiedziała. – To nie twoja wina.

– Agnes – odrzekł Claude i zaczął powtarzać jej imię.

Mimo wszystko nie chciała wyjść za niego za mąż. Żeby mieć pewność, że nie będzie się już do niej zbliżał i że sama nie ugnie się pod presją, zaczęła rozpatrywać inne możliwości. Miesiąc później na weselu swojej kuzynki, Charlotte, poznała Edwarda Christie, niedużego, ale towarzyskiego i stanowczego człowieka. Była o dobrą stopę wyższa od Eddiego, który oświadczył się jej na pierwszej randce. Nie mieli nawet czasu na ceremonię kościelną, więc oszołomieni i załamani nerwowo państwo Millerowie zostali świadkami tylko na ślubie cywilnym swojej jedynej córki. Agnes spakowała walizki i wyprowadziła się na północ, gdzie zamieszkała u rodziny męża. A Eddie sześć tygodni po ślubie wyjechał do Wietnamu.

RODZINA EDDIEGO MIAŁA ceglany dom kilka przecznic od Little Italy w południowym Bronksie. Dla dziewczyny z Południa, której świat wydawał się czarno-biały, dzielnica włoska okazała się czymś zupełnie nowym. Było to jeszcze przed słynnymi zamieszkami ulicznymi w Bronksie. Ładna i czarująca Agnes nauczyła się włoskiego od Włochów, którzy polubili wysoką młodą kobietę, zawsze mówiącą „proszę", „dziękuję" i pytającą, „jak się pan/pani dziś miewa". Zapisała się na Fordham University, gdzie zdobyła dyplom, w którego uzyskaniu wcześniej przeszkodziły jej wydarzenia na Damascus Road.

NIE ZOSTAŁA NAUCZYCIELKĄ angielskiego. Pierwszą pracę podjęła w urzędzie miasta, jako asystentka w dziale projektów. Bezpieczna, dobrze płatna posada urzędniczki zwiastowała początek jej satysfakcjonującej kariery w departamencie urbanistyki. Pierwszemu dziecku, córce (urodzonej dziewięć miesięcy po ślubie), dali na imię Beverly, na pamiątkę babci Eddiego. Gdy tylko mała nauczyła się raczkować, zaczęła chodzić wszędzie za Agnes. Namolność Beverly napełniała matkę wątpliwościami i przynosiła jej rozczarowanie, ale ogólnie rzecz biorąc, dziewczynka była dobra, radosna z natury, podobnie jak Eddie.

JEGO WYJAZDY I POWROTY ułatwiały im utrzymanie szczęśliwego małżeństwa. Kiedy mąż wracał do domu, Agnes nie musiała udawać miłości. Bo miłość była jak mięsień, z którego należało korzystać. Ćwiczyło się go, a on odpłacał im elastycznością i siłą.

WIOSNĄ 1969 ROKU, rok po zabójstwie doktora Kinga w Memphis, Agnes odebrała o północy telefon od Eloise, która przyjechała odwiedzić rodzinę w Buckner County.

– Wiesz, Agnes... – powiedziała Eloise. – Musiałam prawie zabić tę twoją cholerną matkę, żeby mi podała numer do ciebie.

Słysząc głos Eloise, Agnes obronnym gestem położyła dłoń na brzuchu. Spodziewała się drugiego dziecka, była już w trzecim trymestrze.

– A jak tam sobie radzisz? – usłyszała swój głos.

– Znasz mnie. Daj mi tylko coś, czego mogę się uczepić, a kwitnę.

– Czyli wszystko dobrze?

Nastąpiła cisza.

– W zasadzie tak.

– To fajnie.

– Posłuchaj – powiedziała szybko Eloise. – Claude'a znaleziono zastrzelonego w jego mieszkaniu w Dorchester, w Massachusetts. Policja uważa, że mógł to być napad rabunkowy. Znalazł go kolega z pracy.

– Claude'a? – powtórzyła Agnes. Nie wypowiadała tego imienia na głos od trzech lat. – Claude'a? Claude nie żyje? – Do granicy z Massachusetts od miejsca jej zamieszkania było mniej niż pięć godzin jazdy samochodem.

– Bardzo mi przykro – powiedziała Eloise. – Niektórzy ludzie nie nadają się do życia w dużych miastach.

Agnes odłożyła słuchawkę i przestała wstawać z łóżka. Matka Eddiego wezwała lekarza. Zapytał pacjentkę, co jej dolega, a ona odpowiedziała, że wyczuwa pod skórą jakby tysiące bolesnych ukłuć. Lekarz stwierdził ostre zapalenie kaletki, schorzenie, które czasami dokucza ciężarnym. Diakon i lady Millerowie przyjechali zaopiekować się swoją jedyną córką, lecz hałas w Bronksie i w ogóle w Nowym Jorku drażnił ich zmysły. Spędzili u niej tylko dwa tygodnie, po czym wycofali się do Buckner County.

DRUGA DZIEWCZYNKA Agnes i Eddiego urodziła się o cztery tygodnie za wcześnie. Przyszła na świat na oddziale położniczym szpitala Columbia Presbyterian. Tym razem Agnes pragnęła tulić maleństwo, zabrać je z inkubatora i chronić przed nienaturalnym szpitalnym światłem. Z radością przemawiała do nowej córeczki pieszczotliwymi słowami, śpiewała jej kołysanki i z jeszcze większą radością zabrała ją do domu. Dała małej na imię Claudia, a gdy Eddie, który niedawno powrócił do domu z wojny, zauważył, że kobiet w jego rodzinie tak nigdy nie nazywano, Agnes, rozmasowując mężowi odciski na dłoni, odpowiedziała:

– Ale mnie to imię po prostu się podoba.

W SZPITALU NIE MOŻNA PALIĆ

2009

JESTEM DYPLOMOWANĄ PIELĘGNIARKĄ, PRACUJĘ NA ODdziale wypadkowym szpitala Columbia Presbyterian. Moje oficjalne stanowisko to przełożona pielęgniarek. Mam pod sobą jeszcze cztery osoby: cztery inne pielęgniarki, które robią to, co im każę. Gdybym tylko chciała, mogłabym tu strugać dyktatorkę. Strugać wszechwiedzącą i popisywać się jak nasi chirurdzy, którzy zachowują się tak, jakby dostali od Pana Boga moc uzdrawiania pacjentów przez dotyk. Ale kiedy przychodzę do pracy, wiem, że to nie ja się tutaj liczę ani moi koledzy czy koleżanki, tylko ci ludzie, którzy leżą w szpitalu. Być może moja twarz będzie ostatnim ludzkim obliczem, jakie zobaczy pacjent. A to jest błogosławieństwo. Zaszczyt. I działa trzeźwiąco na głowę.

Też mogłam zostać lekarką, ale nigdy nie złożyłam papierów do akademii medycznej. W szkole pielęgniarskiej miałam same piątki. Mój piętnastoletni syn, Orzeszek, sprawdzał mi prace domowe. Czasem podnosił głowę znad jakiegoś mojego wypracowania i mówił:

– Boziu, mamo, jaka ty jesteś mądra.

A ja się tylko uśmiechałam i kręciłam głową.

– A kto ci powiedział, że wszystkie geny mądrości dostałeś wyłącznie po ojcu?

Ojciec moich dzieci, Kevin, jest policjantem... Nie, muszę to skorygować... Był. Teraz pracuje na zachodzie kraju, na pustyni w Arizonie, gdzie przeprowadza kontrole imigracyjne w Straży Granicznej, czyli odsyła zrozpaczonych ludzi z powrotem do Meksyku. Dobrze, że w liceum uczyliśmy się hiszpańskiego. Wychowywaliśmy się w południowym Bronksie, kilka przecznic od dzielnicy nazywanej kiedyś Little Italy. W tamtych czasach w Bronksie mieszkało pełno Portorykańczyków, a my w naturalny sposób uczyliśmy się hiszpańskiego od nich, więc dobrze dawaliśmy sobie radę z tym językiem w szkole. Powtarzam to swoim dzieciom: najpierw się uczysz, a zaraz potem nauka niesie cię sama. Końca na początku nie widać, więc nie ryzykuj i postaraj się o dobry początek. Kevin się oczywiście ze mną drażnił, mówił, że hiszpański przychodzi mi tak łatwo, bo mój dziadek był Kubańczykiem, ale on należał już przecież do pokolenia, które mówiło wyłącznie po angielsku.

Gdy urodziły się dzieci – a mam ich w sumie czworo – moje podanie o przyjęcie na studia do akademii medycznej nie opuściło nawet szuflady komódki. Kevin i ja próbowaliśmy po prostu związać koniec z końcem. Może pewnego dnia pójdę do szkoły dla pielęgniarek specjalistycznych. Byłabym dobra. Pielęgniarki specjalistyczne mają krótszy dzień pracy. Zdaje mi się, że naszym lekarzom ciągle brakuje czasu, a poza tym nie zarabiają już tak dużo jak dawniej. Przychodzą i wychodzą, przychodzą i wychodzą. Przedwczoraj słyszałam, jak jeden wrzeszczał na ordynatora. Ten ordynator zawsze go prowokuje, siedzi mu na karku. „Jak mogę badać dwudziestu pięciu pacjentów dziennie? A jeśli coś przeoczę? Jestem lekarzem, nie magikiem cyrkowym". Przez sześć dni w tygodniu nie cierpię tego cholernego przemądrzałego doktorka, ale wtedy zwyczajnie mu współczułam.

A więc to jest Szefunio James. Tak moja siostra, Claudia, mówi na swojego teścia: Szefunio. Kiedy opowiadała mi o nim po raz pierwszy, spytałam: „Dlaczego ty mu dodajesz tego Szefunia? O co chodzi, wywyższa się czy co?". Claudia tylko pokręciła głową. „Nie wywyższa się – odparła. – Jest zagubiony".

Szefunio utknął u nas na oddziale neurologicznym intensywnej opieki medycznej. Obiecałam Claudii, że zajrzę do niego, jak będę miała przerwę. Claudia i jej mąż, Rufus, wyjechali na południe Francji. Najpierw konferencja w Dublinie, potem wakacje we Francji. Niektórym ludziom to dobrze się powodzi. Teraz znajdują się w drodze powrotnej do Stanów, bo jego stary wyrżnął się w łeb o krawędź swojego przydomowego basenu o wymiarach olimpijskich, próbując ratować moją siostrzenicę, Winonę, która o mało się nie utopiła. Nie wiem tego na sto procent, ale poskładałam wszystkie informacje do kupy i tak to wygląda. Jak zobaczyłam Elijaha, brata Winony, to odprowadziłam go na stronę i zapytałam: „Co tam się stało?".

A pięcioletni Elijah odpowiedział: „To takie coś na wodzie się wywróciło i Winnie musiała pływać".

Wściekłam się na te słowa. Najpierw się martwiłam, a teraz wkurzyłam. Zalała mnie wielka żółć, którą zawsze wzbudza we mnie moja siostra. Ja mogłam się zająć Winoną i Elijahem. Mam mieszkanie w Washington Heights, w domu zbudowanym jeszcze przed wojną, trzy sypialnie i luksusową, rozkładaną kanapę. Mogłam to jakoś urządzić. A kuzyni mogliby się spotkać, rzadko im się to zdarza. Wszyscy dobrze byśmy się bawili. Zabierałabym dzieciaki na pizzę i do Victorian Gardens albo do zoo w Bronksie. Mam karnet rodzinny, więc malcy mogliby zobaczyć te strasznie przerażające tygrysy syberyjskie, pójść do motylarni albo pojeździć kolejką szynową. Claudia uważa, że mój syn, Orzeszek, jest inteligentny tylko zrządzeniem losu, to znaczy przez przypadek, ale jest inaczej; ja się zajmuję dziećmi, nie zostawiam ich samych. Nigdy nie zostawiałam. I nie zostawię. Nie zawsze chce mi się nimi opiekować, ale która matka bez przerwy ma ochotę zajmować się wyłącznie dzieciakami? Która matka nie robi nic innego całymi dniami, tylko chodzi i gada: „Jesteście moje. Kocham was, moje dzieci..."? I która w pewnej chwili nie krzyknie nagle: „Pierdolę to wszystko, pierdolę, pierdolę!"?

No więc nasz James Samuel Vincent leży sobie teraz na intensywnej terapii, na neurologii, właściwie w śpiączce po uderzeniu w łeb, a jego ukochana żoneczka, damulka Adele, zabrała moją siostrzenicę i siostrzeńca do sklepu z zabawkami FAO Schwarz, a stamtąd miała z nimi pójść jeszcze do Dylan's Candy Bar na 60th Street po jakieś słodycze, niby w nagrodę za to, że o mało się nie potopili. Tylko ja, zamiast zapalić papierosa, na co właśnie mam ochotę, zaglądam do Szefunia Jamesa, bo obiecałam Claudii, że to zrobię. A bez względu na wszystko zawsze dotrzymuję obietnic.

Gdyby Claudia poświęciła mi trochę czasu i zapytała, co u mnie, dowiedziałaby się, że mam własne problemy, całą furę kłopotów, od których pęka mi głowa. Zadzwoniłam do panny Lydii, opiekunki bliźniąt, żeby sprawdzić, czy moja córka, Minerva, już je stamtąd zabrała, bo Minerva nigdy nie odbiera komórki, no i właśnie się z nią łączę, a tu pisze do mnie Orzeszek: „Muszę dzisiaj iść na robotykę? Muszę jechać po Keishę i Lamara?". A ja na to: „Wyluzuj troszeczkę, kurwa. Proszę cię, Orzeszku. Wyluzujesz?".

Minerva jednak przyjechała. Panna Lydia oddzwoniła i powiedziała mi o tym, no i z radości aż mi skoczyło serce. Może z Minervy będą jednak ludzie. Nie mogę się doczekać, żeby jej powiedzieć, że James i ta jego zapijaczona druga żona o mały włos nie utopili jej kuzynki. Nie mogę się doczekać, żeby jej powiedzieć, że Adele wynagradza teraz tę szkodę dzieciakom w Dylan's Candy Bar. Minerva nienawidzi tego sklepu, chociaż uwielbia czekoladę i słodycze.

A wzięło się to stąd: wiedziałam, że z Minervą będą kłopoty, odkąd w jej dziesiąte urodziny zabrałam ją na słodką ucztę do Serendipity's na Upper East Side. Poszłyśmy tylko my dwie, mamusia i córeczka. Chciałam zabrać Minervę właśnie tam, bo przeczytałam gdzieś, że Diana Ross jeździła do Serendipity's limuzyną ze swoimi córkami w ich i własne urodziny na michę gorącej czekolady z lodami.

Pomyślałam, że pokażę Minervie, jak żyją sławni i bogaci. Ale na miejscu okazało się, że Serendipity's jest zamknięta. Kawiarnia zbankrutowała, a mnie nie przyszło do głowy, żeby tam wcześniej zadzwonić. Zrobiło mi się naprawdę głupio, ale Minerva tylko wzruszyła ramionami i zapytała: „To dokąd teraz, mamo?". Pozbierałam się raz-dwa, najpierw pomyślałam, że jestem głupia, ale potem, że jakoś dam sobie radę. No więc zaczęłyśmy iść, chociaż tylko udawałam, że niby wiem dokąd. Łazimy po Upper East Side, a ja z każdym krokiem, kurwa, czuję na karku jarzmo nędzy. Upper East Side potrafi tak podziałać na człowieka. Te luksusowe salony paznokci, małe butiki z takimi srebrnymi dzwoneczkami, które brzęczą przy wejściu, i wielkie, odlotowe, przeszklone kafejki, co wyglądają jak dzieła sztuki nowoczesnej. No i w końcu trafiłyśmy na Dylan's Candy Bar, i było tam pełno młodych i starych ludzi, którzy kłębili się w środku jak ćpuny, żeby kupić towar i się nawalić. Stałyśmy przez chwilę przed wejściem i patrzyłyśmy, jak tłumy ludzi wchodzą do tego sklepu i z niego wychodzą.

„Wejdźmy tu", powiedziałam. I ruszyłyśmy w ślad za ciżbą. Minerva nie posiadała się z radości. Zajęła się przesypywaniem cukierków i ciastek z plastikowych kubełków do małych torebeczek z czerwonymi wstążeczkami, żeby można je było razem związać. Whoppery, całuski Hersheya, niedźwiadki ciągutki, orzechowe babeczki maślane, karmelowe irysy i czarne cukierki lukrecjowe. I drażetki skittles. Dużo ich. No i Minerva pyta: „Mama, a kim jest ta Dylan, że daje nam tyle słodyczy?". Ktoś obok nas szepnął, że Dylan to córka Ralpha Laurena. A Minerva na to: „Ralph Lauren? On się wcale nie nazywa Lauren. Tak naprawdę nazywa się Ralph Lifshitz i pochodzi z Bronksu, tak jak my. On tylko udaje Laurena. Udaje, żeby mieć lepszy wizerunek".

I wtedy sobie pomyślałam: „Rany, ona jest inteligentna. Będą z nią kłopoty. Znajdź jej jakieś zajęcie". I na pewien czas udało mi się nawet coś znaleźć. Najpierw była gimnastyka sportowa. Potem lekcje pływania. Hiszpański. Altówka. Szarpnęłam się nawet na sprzęt do lacrosse'a. Ale później rozsypało się moje małżeństwo, a z nim także Minerva.

W tej chwili tak mi się chce palić, że zamordowałabym za papierosa. Zostanę jednak przy Szefuniu Jamesie do następnego dyżuru. Jak nie dotrzymam słowa, Claudia nie da mi żyć. Tu jest cicho i spokojnie. A ile ja mam w życiu ciszy i spokoju? W tej ciszy jest jednak coś, co sprawia, że brakuje mi Kevina. Powinnam wyciągnąć do niego rękę i powiedzieć, żeby przyjechał po Minervę. Dupek powinien wiedzieć, że jego córka rozleciała się psychicznie. Oczywiście pomyśli wtedy, że chcę, żeby do mnie wrócił. Pomyśli, że dzwonię, bo mi brakuje seksu. Mężczyźni zawsze myślą, że jak kobieta dzwoni, to jej brakuje seksu. Zabawne, do jakich nieporozumień dochodzi czasem w związku dwojga ludzi. A nam nieporozumień zdarzało się bardzo wiele, chociaż z dzieciakami nadawaliśmy chyba na tych samych falach. Tylko że teraz jakoś trudno jest nam obronić to, co zbudowaliśmy. Czaisz, co mówię, James? Słyszysz mnie tam? Mam nadzieję. Lepiej, żebyś słyszał. Kurwa jego mać, może jednak nie słyszysz. Nie wykituj mi tu. Zostań w grze, Jamesie Vincencie. Dlaczego, na Boga, w szpitalu nigdzie nie można palić?

NIECH SIĘ STANIE SÓL

PRZEZ CHWILĘ NAPRAWDĘ NIEWIELE ZABRAKŁO W TEJ szpitalnej sali, by serce Jamesa Samuela Vincenta przestało bić. Takie wrażenie naszło go wraz z powrotem świadomości i przerażeniem, że mało tego, że Bóg jest kobietą, to spójrzcie tylko, zbawicielka świata ma jeszcze czarną skórę. Z powodu środków przeciwbólowych James był na haju i widział ją niewyraźnie, jak gdyby we śnie. Z wysiłkiem szukał słów, które nie chciały przyjść, starał się poruszyć ramionami, może próbując powiedzieć: „Zanim mnie osądzisz...". Potem jednak jego myśli popłynęły z powrotem do tamtego jasnobłękitnego dnia, basenu i wnuczki, Winony, która zsunęła się do wody przez otwór materaca w kształcie pączka z dziurką i zaczęła tonąć, a jej rudobrązowe loki wirowały na głębinie. Wtedy James się odwrócił, upuścił rękawicę, kazał Elijahowi nie ruszać się z miejsca i popędził na brzeg basenu tak szybko, jak tylko zdołały go unieść sześćdziesięciosiedmioletnie nogi, czyli w jego przypadku stosunkowo szybko, zbiegł z idealnie równo przystrzyżonego trawnika na niebieski, śliski kamienny brzeg, ale tuż przed skokiem wilgotna murawa osunęła mu się spod stóp i runął w mrok.

JIMMY JUNIOR ZNOWU BYŁ małym Jimmym juniorem, dwunastoletnim chłopczykiem, stał pod wentylatorem kuchennym i patrzył, jak matka tłucze kruchą porcelanę, filiżanki do herbaty, spodeczki, serwis obiadowy na osiem osób, talerzyki do sałaty i smukłe kryształowe kieliszki do szampana. Między rodzicami Jimmy'ego doszło do sprzeczki. Ciągle się sprzeczali, tym razem jednak kłótnia przerodziła się w potężną awanturę. Padły brzydkie słowa, których żadne z nich nie było w stanie wymazać ani cofnąć.

Jego ojciec, Jimmy senior, przyjął nową pracę w jednostce strażackiej we Fresno, nie konsultując się z żoną. Nowa posada oznaczała, że muszą się tam natychmiast przeprowadzić na całe trzy lata, ale Nancy Vincent uwielbiała Portsmouth. Owszem, w mieście panowała drożyzna (zwłaszcza dla rodziny, w której pracowała tylko jedna osoba), ale dobrze było zapuścić tu korzenie i wychowywać syna.

– Potrzebowali strażaków we Fresno. Opłacą nam nawet dom.

Jimmy senior był strażakiem, w Portsmouth strażaków zwalniano jednak hurtowo ze względu na niedawne cięcia budżetowe.

W tamten niedzielny poranek Nancy ryczała jak lwica. Tak, miała rude włosy, ale nie wpadała łatwo w złość ani nie traciła szybko cierpliwości, chyba że ktoś ją naprawdę sprowokował.

– Byłam raz we Fresno na zjeździe bibliotekarek. To miasto jest jak piekło. Nie zabierzemy Jimmy'ego nawet w pobliże Fresno.

Ich poprzedni dom, który opuścili zaledwie rok wcześniej, znajdował się w Hartford, w stanie Connecticut. Nancy nie narzekała, kiedy wyjechali stamtąd do Portsmouth. Teraz jednak padły obietnice. Mieli tu pozostać do czasu matury Jimmy'ego.

– Jak przeprowadzimy się do Fresno, to kupimy psa – powiedział Jimmy senior.

– Jimmy chce kota – odparła Nancy.

Jimmy senior pokręcił głową.

– Który chłopak chce mieć kota?

Jimmy junior wolał zostać w Portsmouth.

– Proszę was, może być pies albo kot, wszystko jedno, tylko zostańmy tutaj.

Miał dwanaście, prawie trzynaście lat i już był wyższy od ojca. Nie mógł wtedy wiedzieć, że pewnego dnia sam będzie miał dwóch synów: jednego z prawowitego związku małżeńskiego, drugiego z pewnej miłostki. Ten miłostkowy syn miał odziedziczyć po ojcu wygląd, zachowanie oraz temperament.

– Firma przeprowadzkowa przyjeżdża w przyszłym miesiącu. W ostatni dzień roku szkolnego – zapowiedział koniec końców Jimmy senior. – Sprawa jest załatwiona. Możesz się zacząć pakować.

Włożył nowy, zamszowy płaszcz. W letnie wieczory w Portsmouth wiał czasem wiatr od morza i wtedy najlepszą ochroną było wierzchnie okrycie. Szedł do pobliskiego pubu napić się guinnessa z przyjaciółmi.

– Wyjeżdżam do rodziny! – zawołała Nancy za mężem.

– Ty nie masz żadnej rodziny.

– Mam wuja Monroe.

– A skąd weźmiesz pieniądze na życie, mała?

Od trzech miesięcy pozostawała bez pracy. Kryzys gospodarczy dawał się we znaki również bibliotekarzom w Portsmouth, mieście wielu restauracji, sklepów i muzeów. Nancy wiedziała jednak, gdzie robić tanio zakupy. Ona i Jimmy junior uwielbiali sklep Trading Post w pobliskim Kittery.

JIMMY SENIOR POLECIAŁ do Fresno na tydzień przed żoną i synem, żeby się rozeznać w sytuacji. Nancy chodziła z pokoju do pokoju w ich trzypoziomowym mieszkaniu, śpiewając *Bye, Bye, Love* i zabierając najważniejsze dla niej pamiątki.

– Nastąpiła zmiana planów – powiedziała Jimmy'emu.

Był zdumiony operatywnością matki; może wyrobiła w sobie tę cechę jako bibliotekarka. Jego zdjęcia z wczesnego dzieciństwa wrzuciła do walizki. Swoje zdjęcia ślubne zostawiła. Spakowała świadectwo urodzenia Jimmy'ego i jego kartę ubezpieczeniową, płaszcze zimowe, kalosze, spodnie, szorty i koszule ich obojga, po czym zapytała:

– I kto powiedział, że kobiety nie potrafią podróżować prawie bez bagażu?

Każde z nich wzięło też pudło z ulubionymi książkami. Jimmy lubił Dickensa, Poego i Melville'a. *Moby Dicka* mógł czytać całymi nocami.

PRAWIE NIE MIAŁ CZASU, żeby pożegnać swoich najbliższych kolegów. Lukas i Boone byli aktywnie spędzającymi czas chłopcami o trądzikowej cerze, którzy tak jak on lubili czytać książki długo w noc. Jeździli na rowerach typu Schwinn Deluxe Racer. Wtedy Jimmy nie mógł o tym wiedzieć, ale B-52 Lukasa Falla miał zostać zestrzelony w czasie misji w Wietnamie. Boone McAllister uchylał się od służby wojskowej z powodów religijnych i otworzył w Portsmouth sklep ze zdrową żywnością dla weteranów. Siedząc na schodach w swoim apartamentowcu, Jimmy wiedział wtedy tylko tyle, że będzie bardzo tęsknił za kolegami. Nancy Vincent nie wtrącała się, gdy Jimmy opowiadał na lewo i prawo, że Boone i Lukas to jego kuzyni. Twierdziła, iż jest rzeczą zupełnie naturalną, że ktoś podłącza się pod nowych krewnych, jeśli ma rozbitą i nieliczną rodzinę. Oboje rodzice Jimmy'ego byli jedynakami. W każdym razie jego matka na pewno była jedynką. Jimmy senior o swojej rodzinie nie opowiadał nic, chyba że był pijany. „Ludzie z Maine", ujawniał tylko tyle. „Ludziska z Południa", tak o swoich krewnych mówiła z kolei Nancy. „Biali z południa Stanów, którzy nie mogli znieść uprzedzeń rasowych w swoim rodzinnym mieście", dodawała, jak gdyby te słowa mogły wynagrodzić Jimmy'emu brak dziadków – bo chłopiec ich nigdy nie poznał. Wuj Monroe był jedynym żyjącym wujem Nancy. Jimmy jeszcze do niedawna sądził, że to postać z bajki, równie realna jak bohater kreskówki, syrena albo Tryton.

– **UWAŻAJ. LUDZIE Z POŁUDNIA** są dziwni – ostrzegał Boone Jimmy'ego, któremu jednak wydawało się, że w czasie trwającej trzydzieści dwie godziny podróży samochodem na Tybee Island w stanie Georgia dziwaków spotyka właściwie wszędzie – choćby na przydrożnych parkingach, stacjach benzynowych, w jadłodajniach czy motelach. Smarowali frytki keczupem jakby ze złością, pytali o drogę, chociaż nie korzystali z otrzymanych wskazówek, albo podchodzili i rozpoczynali rozmowę o niczym jak z dawno niewidzianym przyjacielem. Jimmy zostawał czasem w samochodzie, a jego mama biegła do łazienki, „żeby się trochę odświeżyć". Siedział na fotelu pasażera z podciągniętymi nogami jak w namiocie, zajadał chipsy kukurydziane i obserwował przyjeżdżających i odjeżdżających ludzi, również znajdujących się w podróży, chociaż w jakimś sensie znieruchomiałych niczym na stopklatce. „Odświeżenie" oznaczało telefon do jego ojca. Oznaczało, że matka przebiegnie przez parking na drugą stronę drogi, nawet nie rozglądając się na boki (dwa razy o mało nie potrącił jej samochód). Oznaczało też zbyt długie milczenie i niebezpieczeństwo mandatu za przekroczenie prędkości, bo drobna matczyna stopa mocno wciskała gaz. Zapowiadało też płaczliwy wyraz twarzy, taki sam, jaki przybierała, gdy Jimmy ośmielał się ją pytać o ojca.

PODRÓŻ NA TYBEE trwała jak gdyby całe krótkie życie. Po drodze zatrzymali się na Manhattanie, żeby obejrzeć darmowe, plenerowe wznowienie musicalu *Cieszmy się życiem*, przy czym Jimmy pomyślał, że ani jemu, ani jego matce wcale nie trzeba o tym przypominać. Stanęli też pod Waszyngtonem, żeby obejrzeć Lincoln Memorial. Zatrzymali się w hotelu Holiday Inn w stanie Maryland, gdzie uraczono ich darmowym śniadaniem na kartki żywnościowe.

– Jeżeli to śniadanie jest darmowe, to dlaczego musimy dawać im kartki? – zapytał matkę zirytowany Jimmy.

Nancy nie chciała podtrzymywać jego rozgoryczenia.

– Wujek Monroe to miły człowiek.

– Kiedy widziałaś go ostatni raz? – spytał Jimmy.

– Och, miałam wtedy jakieś pięć lat. Pamiętam, że był właścicielem targowiska rybnego.

– Fajowo. Mogę sprzedawać ryby. Kiedy dorosnę, to zostanę rybakiem.

– Jeżeli chodzi o mnie, to całkiem klawy plan.

Mama Jimmy'ego podchodziła do życia niczym młoda kobieta. I może potrafiła zachować młodość na zawsze. Problemy wynikające z życia małżeńskiego nie zaznaczały się na jej twarzy tak jak na obliczach niektórych innych pań. Tylko ładna dziewczyna mogła wyglądać ładnie z włosami obciętymi na chłopczycę – krótka fryzura odsłaniała przed światem całą twarz. Tuż przed wyjazdem z Portsmouth sama obcięła sobie włosy nożyczkami. Na czarno-białych kaflach podłogowych w kuchni zostawiła stos rudych loków. Zostawiła za sobą także marzenia o emeryturze w Portsmouth. Domek letniskowy w Cape Cod. Idealny układ dla trzyosobowej rodziny.

– No, zapłaciłam za niego własnymi, ciężko zarobionymi pieniędzmi – stwierdziła, kiedy ruszali w drogę różowym cadillakiem coupé de ville, jedynym elementem ich ruchomego majątku kupionym na jej nazwisko. – Twój ojciec prędzej by umarł, niż wsiadł do czegoś w tak wściekle różowym kolorze. A zresztą cholera wie, może właśnie dlatego kupiłam ten wóz.

WUJ MONROE POWITAŁ ICH w swoim rozklekotanym bungalowie z dwiema sypialniami skinięciem głowy, życzliwą miną i uśmieszkiem, oznaczającym, że gość nie w porę jest gorszy od zarazy. Jego pociągłą, smutną twarz pokrywał szpakowaty zarost. „No tak, tata mówił, że chcę mieć psa, więc teraz mieszkam z psem. Nie można bardziej upodobnić się do psa niż wujek Monroe". Była to okrutna myśl, ale odkąd wyjechali z Portsmouth, Jimmy z wolna stawał się coraz bardziej kostyczny. Miał dopiero zobaczyć swoją pierwszą tęczę, chociaż tęcze były poniekąd wbudowane w jego dotychczasowe życie. Portsmouth Jimmy'ego wypełniało dużo słońca i chmur, kolory osaczały go więc nie wiadomo skąd i rozsadzały niebo.

Dobrze się stało, że Nancy nie przywiozła dużo rzeczy. Wujek Monroe prowadził kawalerskie życie. Ze sprzedażą ryb skończył, ale w domu pełno było plastikowych rybich łbów, gazet walających się na stolikach, starych garnków i patelni, łóżka okazały się twarde, kraciasta kanapa szorstka, a mały telewizor odbierał tylko podstawowe kanały, bo wujek nie oglądał nic poza porannymi wiadomościami, żeby się dowiedzieć, czy nie nadchodzi sztorm.

– Nie wierzysz w komfort, wujku – zwróciła się mama Jimmy'ego do wuja, kiedy wykuśtykała już z sypialni po pierwszej nocy spędzonej na twardym niczym kamień materacu.

– Komfort jest niepraktyczny – brzmiała odpowiedź.

– Podoba mi się ten twój typ komfortu – stwierdziła matka Jimmy'ego, kiedy gorąca woda zrobiła się lodowato zimna w ciągu pięciu sekund, jak tylko weszła pod prysznic.

– Woda powoduje, że żelazo rdzewieje, a pancerniki toną – powiedział wujek Monroe.

– I takie rzeczy mówi sprzedawca ryb.

– Ja je tylko sprzedawałem, kochanie. Nie jestem żadnym rybakiem.

Nancy się roześmiała.

– Czy to jest jakieś oszustwo, czy my naprawdę jesteśmy spokrewnieni?

Tydzień później wujek wyszedł z domu, zakupił w Searsie dwa nowe materace i położył je w sypialni, którą Jimmy dzielił z mamą. Przyniósł też bukiecik nadmorskiej lawendy i astrów z marketu Piggly Wiggly.

PO DWÓCH TYGODNIACH u wujka Nancy straciła trochę animuszu. Chodziła na długie spacery po plaży koloru soli, ale tylko wieczorami – i bez Jimmy'ego. I zaczęła mówić sama do siebie, a nagłe napady takiego zachowania sprawiały, że chłopak miał ochotę zatykać sobie uszy.

– Dupek. Idiota. Osioł. Co ja sobie myślałam przez te wszystkie lata?

– Kiedy wracamy do Portsmouth? – spytał Jimmy matkę, gdy od przyjazdu do wujka minęły już trzy niedziele.

– W swoim czasie.
– Co to znaczy?
Tu wtrącił się wujek Monroe.
– To znaczy, że twój stary był jak zadra w dupie. A Portsmouth to już tylko wspomnienie.
– Nie wyrażaj się, wujku – powiedziała Nancy.
Wujek Monroe uniósł ręce w obronnym geście.
– Mój znajomy, King Tyrone, właśnie wpłynął do portu i ma na pokładzie pełno krabów. – Wuj rzucił spojrzenie Jimmy'emu. – Trzymałeś kiedyś w ręku kraba błękitnego?
– Lubię homary – powiedział chłopak.
– Krab błękitny mógłby go uszczypnąć prosto w nos, a Jimmy i tak nie wiedziałby, co to za zwierzę – przyznała Nancy.
Twarz wydłużyła się wujkowi do tego stopnia, że Jimmy pomyślał, że za chwilę uderzy podbródkiem o podłogę.
– No to grzech. I szkoda.

„«TYBEE» W JĘZYKU EUCHEE ZNACZY SÓL", tłumaczyła pieszczotliwym głosem mama. „Tybee Island założyli Indianie Euchee. To pierwsi ludzie, którzy tu mieszkali". A gdzie oni teraz są, chciał wiedzieć Jimmy. Ładna piaszczysta plaża może tam i kogoś zainteresuje, ale nie Jimmy'ego Vincenta. On wolał plaże nieoswojone, dzikie, pełne kamieni, stromych skał i zdradliwych falochronów, na których można podrapać kolana do krwi. Lubił zimne plaże w Maine, czyli plaże z dzieciństwa jego ojca, a także chłód, który aż drażnił końcówki włókien nerwowych, kiedy dawało się pierwszego nura do wody. Letnie miesiące Jimmy'ego w Portsmouth nigdy nie były tak mokre ani lepkie jak tu. Tybee Island stanowiła dla niego całkowicie nową miarę wilgotności i gorąca. Ponieważ do upału trzeba było się „troszkę przyzwyczaić", jak głosiło ulubione powiedzonko wujka Monroe'a, Jimmy zaczął wstawać o brzasku, zanim plażę opanowywali plażowicze, a słońce brało dzień we władanie.

Pewnego ranka, po prawie dwóch tygodniach odmawiania wujkowi zapraszającemu go na połów krabów, Jimmy uznał, że nie ma nic do stracenia i właściwie może z nim popłynąć. Inaczej musiałby wytrzymać kolejny wykład matki o historii Tybee Island, bo Nancy uparła się, że zainteresuje nią syna. „Wiem, że może w twoich oczach ona tak nie wygląda, ale ta wyspa bywała celem wycieczek. Ludzie w dawnych czasach mówili, że zażywają soli. Zjeżdżali się tu zewsząd dla świeżego powietrza, kiedy byli chorzy".

Pojechał z wujkiem jego półciężarówką do oddalonego zaledwie o sześć przecznic domu Kinga Tyrone'a. Tyrone – chudy, ciemnoskóry, około czterdziestoletni mężczyzna – był właścicielem szopy stojącej na molo i zwróconej w stronę bagien. Jimmy zdziwił się, że wujek jest znacznie starszy od rybaka. Zdziwił się też, ile lawendy i astrów rośnie w pobliżu jego domku.

– Piggly Wiggly, akurat – powiedział chłopak.

Wujek Monroe wzruszył ramionami.

– Nie rób mi tutaj afery.

Nie tracili czasu, żeby wypłynąć na wodę. Tyrone nie interesował się nikim, kto nie był z nim spokrewniony – a czasem nie chciał zawracać sobie głowy nawet członkami rodziny.

– Na takiego kraba mówi się truposz. – Rozłamał z trzaskiem skorupiaka i zademonstrował Jimmy'emu jego mięsiste wnętrzności. – W ten sposób można odróżnić samicę od samca. Te jasnopomarańczowe kuleczki znaczą, że to samica i że miała jajeczka.

Stali na rybackiej dinghy Tyrone'a, a wszędzie dokoła nich pełzały kraby. Gdy Jimmy przyglądał się błękitnym skorupiakom, szamoczącym się i chodzącym po sobie nawzajem na dnie małej szarobiałej rybackiej łódeczki, zbierało mu się na płacz. W tych stworzeniach było coś pięknego i smutnego.

– Będziemy mieli dziś prawdziwą ucztę. – Wujek Monroe serdecznie poklepał Jimmy'ego po plecach.

Chłopak patrzył, jak Tyrone gołymi rękami podnosi kilkanaście krabów i wrzuca je do drewnianej beczki. Dłonie miał całe pokryte odciskami i wyglądało na to, że nie zwraca uwagi na napastliwe szczypce skorupiaków.

– Nie boli? – spytał Jimmy.

– Po pewnym czasie można się przyzwyczaić. – Niekiedy na wodzie Tyrone myślał sobie, że miło byłoby mieć żonę i dzieci, które czekałyby na niego na brzegu. Ale morze było nieprzewidywalne. A jego rodzinę prześladował pech. – Krabowe szczypce już mnie nie wkurzają.

PÓŹNIEJ TEGO WIECZORU matka rozkładała dodatkowe gazety na piknikowym stole w ogrodzie, a Jimmy patrzył, jak wujek wrzuca kraby do czerwonego garnka z wrzącą wodą, w której zazwyczaj gotowano homary. Obserwował gorączkowy taniec skorupiaków i powolną zmianę barwy ich ciał.

Myślał, że nie będzie mógł jeść, ale apetyt zwyciężył. Tego wieczoru najadł się do syta.

Rano mama poszła z wujkiem do Stingray's, miejscowej restauracji z owocami morza, i złożyła podanie o przyjęcie do pracy jako kelnerka.

– Od czegoś trzeba zacząć – powiedziała. – Szkoda czasu, nie ma na co czekać.

Dzień po tym, jak podjęła pracę w Stingray's, Jimmy wziął stary, rozklekotany rower wujka i pojechał do odległego o sześć mil Fortu Pulaski. Nie wspomniał o tym Nancy, bo bał się, że będzie się o niego martwić ze względu na duży ruch na drodze 80. Kupił bilet wstępu i obfotografował cały fort, żeby wysłać zdjęcia Boone'owi i Lukasowi. Przyjaciele napisali do niego, że właśnie czytają *Na Zachodzie bez zmian*. Odpowiedział listem o pewnym żołnierzu Konfederacji, którego duch rzekomo błąka się nocami po forcie w poszukiwaniu swojej odciętej głowy. Zwiedziwszy umocnienia, Jimmy objechał je potem piaszczystymi ścieżkami. Otaczały go rośliny, kwiaty i ptaki, których śpiew wydawał mu się tropikalny, obcy. „W Portsmouth nie ma takich gatunków ptaków", napisał do Lukasa i Boone'a. Całą drogę do domu pokonał na rowerze, w starym słomianym kapeluszu rybackim, należącym do wujka, i po raz pierwszy od przyjazdu na wyspę nie przeszkadzał mu upał.

PEWNEGO WIECZORU W PORTSMOUTH, krótko przed wyjazdem z matką na Tybee Island, wracał do domu od Boone'a i usłyszał głos ojca. Odwrócił się i ujrzał Jimmy'ego seniora i jego strażackich kumpli, jak szli powoli ulicą, emanując radością, alkoholem i wszystkimi możliwymi grzechami.

„Trzeba je utrzymywać w niepewności", mówił ojciec, klepiąc jednego ze swoich kompanów po plecach. „Utrzymuj swoją babę w niepewności, a zawsze do ciebie wróci. Dziewczęcy włos na twoim ubraniu albo jakiś numer telefonu, który dla ciebie właściwie nie znaczy nic, a dla nich wszystko. Cała ich pewność siebie opiera się na gadaniu. Jeszcze nie spotkałem kobiety, która by nie wątpiła w swoją wartość". Z Jimmym seniorem szła pod rękę jakaś kobieta, również rudowłosa, będąca, jak przez ułamek sekundy pragnął wierzyć chłopak, jego matką. Jej ubranie było jednak jak gdyby przeznaczone dla młodszej kobiety, bardziej obcisłe. Miała na sobie czerwony sweter, dopasowany do koloru włosów, i spodnie narciarskie. Jimmy rozejrzał się i podniósł wzrok, spodziewając się prawie, że ujrzy gdzieś wyciąg narciarski, w Portsmouth jednak wyciągów narciarskich nie było.

JIMMY SENIOR RAZ ZADZWONIŁ Z FRESNO.

– Fresno to piekło – przyznał. – Ja mam pustynię, ty plażę.

Ojciec nie powiedział, że chce się znowu zejść z matką. Matka nie powiedziała, że chce rozwodu.

– Na Tybee Island jest ładnie – stwierdziła Nancy. – Podoba mi się ten skrawek wybrzeża Atlantyku. Ludzie są tutaj spokojni i życzliwi.

– Jesteście ciągle w okresie miesiąca miodowego. Poczekaj, aż poznasz ich bliżej.

– Chyba tak właśnie zrobię. Poczekam. – Nancy pozwoliła sobie na przeciągnięcie ostatniego słowa.

– Daj mi do telefonu mojego syna, proszę.

– Twojego? To mnie zostawił rozstępy na pamiątkę – roześmiała się.

– Wiesz, Nancy, jak do mnie wrócisz, to będę na ciebie czekał z kremem kakaowym.

– A kto powiedział, że wrócę?

Tym razem zachichotał ojciec Jimmy'ego, a kiedy Jimmy podszedł do telefonu, usłyszał:

– Pamiętaj, chłopcze, że na tym świecie zawsze lepiej będzie się powodzić łobuzom niż głupcom. A twoja mama jest głupia.

– Tęsknię za tobą, tato.

Jimmy spojrzał na matkę. Sądząc po jej minie, uznała go za Judasza, sama uważała się natomiast za Chrystusa. Nie mógł wiedzieć, że zanim minie rok, ojciec przeprowadzi się do Huntington na Long Island i weźmie ich ze sobą. Miał to być najdłuższy czas Jimmy'ego seniora na dobrze płatnej posadzie. Jimmy junior ukończył potem liceum w Huntington i dostał stypendium na University of Michigan.

– Jimmy, mój chłopcze, chyba się muszę zdrzemnąć – powiedział James senior. – Pora odkręcić to wszystko, co spierdoliłem.

ZBLIŻAŁ SIĘ WIECZORNY PRZYPŁYW; Jimmy podwinął szorty w kolorze khaki i wszedł po kolana do morza. Jeszcze nie pływał, odkąd przyjechali na Tybee Island. Plaża była płaska, piasek drobny i miękki. Chłopak brnął na palcach głębiej, a letniej temperatury morze zareagowało, posyłając w jego kierunku energiczną falę, która błyskawicznie ścięła go z nóg, zepchnęła w prąd wsteczny i zaczęła prowokować, aby stanął z nią do walki o powietrze. Nie podjął tego wyzwania w bebechach cofki u brzegów Tybee Island. Zmusił mięśnie, żeby się rozluźniły, a umysł, żeby się, kurwa, uspokoił, i morze w końcu wypuściło go z objęć. Wypłynął na powierzchnię i dopiero wtedy zaczerpnął tchu. Zapomniał. Zapomniał o tym, jak dobrym był pływakiem. Jak dobrze było... pływać.

JAMES SAMUEL VINCENT otworzył oczy i znalazł się z powrotem na intensywnej terapii oddziału neurologicznego szpitala Columbia Presbyterian.

– Moja wnuczka? – usiłował zapytać Beverly, ciemnoskórego Boga płci żeńskiej. Ale tylko wybełkotał: – Maawnaa.

Rozmazane boskie oblicze nachyliło się nad nim. Pachniało delikatnie dymem papierosowym. Znaczy, że Bóg pali, pomyślał.

– Martwiliśmy się o pana – odezwała się Beverly.

Znaczy, że Bóg się martwi. Czy to oznacza, że on, James Samuel Vincent, pójdzie do nieba, czy jednak raczej do piekła? Znowu zamrugał, starając się dobrze zobaczyć rysy nieznanego mu dotąd Boga kobiety, która nie chciała się jednak objawić wyraźnie. Była równie nieostra jak jego myśli. Ściany sali zdawały się unosić wokół Jamesa, a ich kolor zmieniał się z migotliwego błękitu w oślepiającą biel.

– Maawnaa – spróbował znowu.

Beverly Christie, która wiedziała, jak dziwnie potrafią działać środki przeciwbólowe na starych ludzi, nachyliła się bliżej i powiedziała:

– Rufus i Claudia już jadą.

„Ruff", odezwała się mózgownica Jamesa. „Mój chłopak, Ruff". Ale z jego ust wydobyło się tylko „Aff, aff". Dopiero wtedy zrozumiał, że ma zakryte usta. Że zasłania je plastik. Był podłączony do respiratora. Kiedy to sobie nagle uświadomił, zaczął się szarpać i wierzgać.

– Przewrócił się pan i doznał ciężkich obrażeń – odezwała się ponownie Beverly. – Uderzył się pan w głowę.

Czyli że żyje. Ale co z rękami i nogami? Dlaczego nie jest w stanie nimi poruszyć?

– Przewieziono pana do szpitala Columbia Presbyterian – oświadczyła Beverly. – Adele została z dziećmi.

James poczuł ból. Ukłucie. Użądlenie. „Jezu. Boże. Chryste". Łzy były mu obce. Nie płakał od ponad trzydziestu lat. Więc nad kim płacze teraz? Nad sobą?

– Winnnnnn – powiedział Szefunio.

Beverly go jednak zrozumiała. Pogładziła pacjenta po siwej głowie i szepnęła:

– Winona i Elijah będą bardzo szczęśliwi. Pytali o pana. Powiedzieliśmy im, że dziadziuś na razie śpi jak Rip Van Winkle, ale że nie będzie spał sto lat.

AKT PIERWSZY

1971 1980 1990 2000 **2009**

PADŁY W OGRÓDKU W POŁUDNIOWYM BRONKSIE, na spłachetku ziemi, gdzie w donicy rosły pomidory śliwkowe, a wzdłuż kratkowego płotu, który dzieliliśmy z naszym włoskim sąsiadem, Alfredem „Freddiem" Maddalone'em – małe liściaste ogórki. Słowa „Rzuć pieniążek. Gdzie są Rosenkrantz i Guildenstern?". Moja matka, Agnes, przysięga, że pierwsze zdanie, jakie wypowiedziałam w życiu, brzmiało „Gdzie są pieniążki?". Klęczałam, a ona właśnie przyszła z naszej długiej, wąskiej, pomalowanej na morski kolor kuchni, w której polewała tłuszczem niedzielną pieczeń. Waliłyśmy z Beverly w patelnie i garnki, a ja zapytałam: „Gdzie są monety? Rosenkrantzu i Guildensternie, rzucajcie monety". Nie miałam jeszcze dwóch lat i mama opowiadała, że przeraziła się, słysząc, jak wyraźnie wymawiam te słowa. I że ponieważ pochodziła z Południa, w związku z czym od chwili przyjścia na świat była przesądna, pomyślała: „Boże, z moim dzieckiem jest coś nie w porządku. To nienaturalne, żeby taka mała dziewczynka umiała już łączyć słowa w zdania w ten sposób". Potem jednak przypomniała sobie, że ojciec, który znów był na morzu, czytywał tę sztukę mnie i Beverly na dobranoc zamiast *Byczka Fernando* albo *Dobranoc, Księżycu*.

„Porozmawiam sobie z Eddiem, jak wróci do domu", powiedziała mama. Ojciec służył na lotniskowcu na Morzu Południowochińskim. Wyjechał na swoją ostatnią już wycieczkę do Wietnamu.

Mama zawołała pana Maddalone'a, żeby przyszedł i posłuchał, jak powtarzam to, co mówiłam przed chwilą o Rosenkrantzu i Guildensternie, bo „po prostu wiedziała", że jej znajome pomyślą, że tylko się tak przechwala. Pan Maddalone i jego żona nauczyli Agnes mówić po włosku, gotować *pasta e fagioli*, robić sos do homara w stylu weneckim (przysięgali, że wystarczy do niego szczypta gałki muszkatołowej) i ciastka waflowe, pizzelle, pieczone w gofrownicy. Po śmierci żony pan Maddalone wypiekał je co niedziela i przynosił nam owinięte w szeleszczący papier śniadaniowy.

„Mów, Claudio", powiedziała mama. „Powtórz to. Jeszcze raz. Claudio, mów". Ale nie odezwałam się już ani słowem. Za to Beverly wstała z plastikowej piaskownicy w kształcie żółwia, po czym zerwała z siebie letnią sukienkę i majtki.

Zaczęła kręcić dziecięcymi bioderkami, klepać się po dziecięcych udkach i śpiewać *Ride Captain Ride*, więc pan Maddalone wybuchnął śmiechem, a mama pobiegła dać mojej siostrze świeże ubranko.

– No tak, Agnes – śmiał się pan Maddalone. – To teraz już wszystko jasne. Jedna z twoich dziewczynek zostanie poetką. A druga ekshibicjonistką, na bank.

NIE ZOSTAŁAM POETKĄ, tylko uczoną akademicką. Moja specjalność to Shakespeare i Everyman. Mam stanowisko, a na moje zajęcia ustawia się kolejka, studenci muszą się na nie zapisywać i czekać. Seminaria zaczynam zwykle od przedstawienia postaci Williama Henry'ego Browna, emerytowanego właściciela parowca z Indii Zachodnich, który w roku 1816 założył pierwszy murzyński teatr amerykański, African Grove Theatre na dolnym Manhattanie. Pokazuję też slajdy z teatru Globe i z South Bank. Stawiam pytanie: „Kto ma prawo do Shakespeare'a?". Odtwarzam dla swoich

studentów jego świat najlepiej, jak potrafię. Tamten inny Londyn. Przecięty Tamizą. Bogaci przekraczają ją łodziami, zwykli mieszkańcy pieszo przez London Bridge. Artyści teatralni. Jak dla mnie, po prostu wyrzutki. Pracują za nędzne stawki. Próbują udoskonalić swoją sztukę wbrew niemożliwym do pokonania przeciwnościom. Na Bankside są wolni od bystrego spojrzenia władzy. Zastanówmy się, jak zanieczyszczone są tam woda i powietrze. Plugastwo. Smród. Hazard. Drażnienie i szczucie niedźwiedzia. Prostytucja. W ciemnych zaułkach czai się śmierć. Niech Bogu będą dzięki za tawerny. To jedyne miejsce, gdzie pracujący mężczyzna albo pracująca kobieta może się najeść i napić do syta. Albo porządnie się pośmiać. Że to taka hołota, powiadacie? Ale, ach! Tam się przynajmniej coś dzieje. Tam pióro naszego Barda moczy się w atramencie. Tam grają jego aktorzy. Shakespeare nie może sobie pozwolić na to, by schować głowę w piasek. Przedstawienie naprawdę musi trwać. Zawsze jest jakiś nieprzekraczalny termin. Uczy się pracować szybko. Jego publiczność, w większości bez żadnego wykształcenia, przychodzi w oczekiwaniu na dobry występ. Przynoszą do teatru zepsute owoce i zgniłe mięso. No już. Bawcie nas. Staliśmy przez cały dzień na nogach, więc możemy postać jeszcze trochę. Dawajcie nam tu błazna. I zbrodniczego króla. Łajdackiego księcia. Królową o zimnym sercu. I niech Bóg ma was w swojej opiece, jeśli będziemy się nudzić. Shakespeare zawarł umowę ze swoją publicznością. Ostatecznie jest synem handlarza futer. Zabierze ze sobą każdego, kto ma chęć udać się z nim w literacką podróż. W najgorszym razie spotka się z wami w pół drogi. W młodych latach, kiedy kształtuje się nasza osobowość, dowiedziałam się, że u Shakespeare'a jest coś dla każdego. Oczywiście Rufus najbardziej lubi tę historię „o pieniążkach". Jego wersja zawsze spotyka się z uznaniem naszych co bardziej uczonych znajomych. Na ferie zimowe pojechaliśmy jednak za ocean, do dalekiego zakątka Bretanii. Tutaj anegdoty mojego męża nie zapuszczają korzeni i nie rosną. Brakuje im warstwy uprawnej. A jak nam mówią miejscowi, to ważne źródło wody i substancji odżywczych, zapobiegające erozji. Dzięki temu wschodzą nowe plony.

JESTEŚMY W MAŁEJ MIEŚCINIE w północno-zachodniej Bretanii, w departamencie Finistère. Przyjechaliśmy studiować galijski folklor i nauki Celtów. Gościmy na skromnej siedemnastowiecznej farmie, w domu o wąskich korytarzach, małych okienkach i drzwiach, mających pomóc gospodarzom oszczędzać prąd i utrzymać ciepło w budynku. Będziemy słuchać kuzynów Rufusa, Guy i Esterna LeComte'ów, mówiących w starodawnym tutejszym języku. Mój mąż postanowił napisać współczesną interpretację książek Waltera Y. Evansa-Wentza i Paula Sébillota, *The Fairy-Faith in Celtic Countries* oraz *Contes populaires de la Haute-Bretagne*. Pisania było jednak bardzo mało, za to bardzo dużo *mise en scène*. Rufus śledzi tych naszych pomarszczonych farmerów wszędzie, dokąd idą, okiem kamery wideo 8 mm.

Gdy przyjechaliśmy tutaj po raz pierwszy, rozejrzałam się na lewo i prawo, popatrzyłam na imponująco rozległe wrzosowiska i szepnęłam Rufusowi do ucha: „Zamknij mnie samą w pokoju, a za chwilę obetnę sobie włosy". Po francusku Finistère oznacza „koniec świata", i na Boga, czułam się tu dokładnie jak na końcu świata.

– Daj szansę temu miasteczku, Claudie! – szepnął Rufus w odpowiedzi. – Nie jest wcale aż tak ponure. Będziemy mieli mnóstwo czasu, żeby jeść, spać i się rżnąć.

Nie ma takiego problemu, którego zdaniem Rufusa nie dałoby się rozwiązać dzięki minecie. Dla niego to jak chwila zadumy, relaks, rozrywka. Wykorzystuje potem moje udo jak poduszkę. Miejsce, gdzie może złożyć głowę i się zdrzemnąć.

– A kto zaopiekuje się Winnie i Elijahem?

Pytanie jest uszczypliwe. Wkurzające – chociaż niezupełnie bez przyczyny. Ostatnio wszystko mnie wkurza. Dopada mnie znienacka. Jak niedobór witaminy D.

– Sami będziemy się opiekować naszymi dziećmi, do cholery – mówi Rufus, którego blade policzki oblewa teraz rumieniec. – My.

W SIERPNIU nasza pięcioletnia córeczka, Winnie, o mało się nie utopiła w basenie ojca Rufusa w Amagansett. Ratownicy medyczni musieli wykonać sztuczne oddychanie, by ją przywrócić do życia. Rufus i ja dochodziliśmy tymczasem do siebie po konferencji joyce'owskiej w Dublinie. Jedliśmy właśnie *socca* (naleśniki z grochu włoskiego), kiedy do Rufusa zadzwoniła jego macocha. Nigdy już nie będę jadła *socca*. Złapaliśmy wieczorny samolot na lotnisko JFK. Wracałam rozwścieczona, myśląc, że gdyby ojciec jeszcze żył, mama nie przeprowadziłaby się do Buckner w stanie Georgia. Gdyby rak nie zmienił taty w stracha na wróble, nauczylibyśmy jego wnuczki, kim byli Rosenkrantz i Guildenstern. „Winona? Elijah? Gdzie są pieniążki? Rzućcie dziadziusiowi pieniążek!" W szpitalu Columbia Presbyterian moja siostra

Beverly – dyplomowana pielęgniarka i poniekąd ekshibicjonistka – powitała nas ze skwapliwą złością: „Tak to się kończy. Wybraliście ich, nie nas – stwierdziła. – Wy i całe to wasze zapracowanie. To Elijah dał mi cynk, że coś jest niefajnie. A kiedy Winnie chłeptała wodę z basenu, wasi teściowie popijali martini".

Teraz Winnie budzi się w nocy z wrzaskiem i wymachuje rączkami i nóżkami: „Różoweróżoweróżowe takie coś jak pączek!". Od basenów trzyma się z daleka. Czy to był wypadek? Absolutnie. Na pewno. Ale Rufus i ja musieliśmy wytłumaczyć jego ojcu i macosze, Adele, że martini, baseny i dzieci nie bardzo do siebie pasują. Jest w nas ostatnio napięcie. Napięcie tego rodzaju, które – co mogę stwierdzić na podstawie obserwacji moich znajomych – małżeństwa mniejszego formatu skłania do rozwodu.

FINISTÈRE W STYCZNIU, jak nam się tutaj mówi, zwykle nie jest takie bezlitosne. W miesiącach letnich do tej części Bretanii zjeżdżają turyści, żeby figlować, swawolić i cieszyć się umiarkowaną temperaturą. Chociaż jak na razie nie zauważyłam żadnego umiarkowania w tym miasteczku. Czy mam zły nastrój? Oczywiście, że tak. Jest ostatnio tak ponury jak chmury nad moją głową. Opatulam Winonę i Elijaha czapkami, szalikami i grubymi wełnianymi swetrami, na które nakładają puchowe płaszcze. Grasujemy po nagich polach, gdzie na wiosnę urodzą się kalafiory i zielone karczochy. Nasze bliźniaki mają dużo energii i potrzeba im ruchu. Wyprzedzają mnie biegiem, nadając nazwy przypadkowo wybieranym chmurom.

Sowa

Jeleń

Wieloryb

Jednorożec

Człowiek

„Śniegu nie więcej niż tyle, ile można strzepnąć z płaszcza w czasie spaceru". Tak powiedzieli nam leciwi kuzyni Rufusa, kiedy spadł pierwszy śnieg. Nie zalegał długo, ale chłód się utrzymał, grożąc zwarzeniem plonów Guy i Esterna. Zerkam przez ramię. Gdzie się podziewa mój mąż? Został z tyłu, zmienił się w maleńką czarną plamkę na polu. Idzie dostojnym krokiem, pogrążony w ożywionej rozmowie z dwoma starymi ludźmi. Wymachuje ramionami w górę i w dół. Czy Guy i Estern LeComte to naprawdę kuzyni mojego męża? Jestem pewna, że ci staruszkowie są kochankami, ale ponieważ odkąd postawiliśmy stopę w Finistère, nie chcę mówić po francusku, nie widzę też żadnego eleganckiego sposobu, żeby poruszyć z nimi temat seksualności.

W ZIMIE ESTERN przygotowuje jedzenie na ogniu kominkowym. Pokaz fajerwerków w palenisku. Dzisiejszy posiłek to udziec jagnięcy z rożna. Zbijamy się w stadko i patrzymy, jak drewno pali się wśród przeraźliwie czerwonych, niebieskich i pomarańczowych iskier. Winona i Elijah bawią się, udają, że są na kempingu w Maine, i błagają Esterna i Guy o deser *s'mores* i baśnie, których opowiadanie Rufus nagrywa kamerą. „Tu nie ma *s'mores*", przypominam dzieciom. Jedzenie na farmie jest niewyszukane. Smakowite soki z jagnięcego udźca skapują do żelaznej rynienki, żeby potem można było polać nimi brukiew, ziemniaki i botwinkę. Mnie powierzono przygotowanie deseru, próbuję więc zrobić *petit pommes* przybrane porzeczkami, cukrem i polane zrumienionym masłem. Siedzę na końcu stołu w jadalni, obieram twarde zielone jabłka i wycinam gniazda nasienne, a Rufus przeprowadza wywiad z Guy i Esternem. By dzieci się nie nudziły, Guy zawiązuje sobie oczy chusteczką i zmienia się w świętego Herweusza, niewidomego mnicha, który kochał zwierzęta i oswoił wilka, żeby mu orał pole. Rufus tłumaczy, wygląda bardzo młodzieńczo, kiedy odchyla się znad popękanego stołu od swoich niedawno odnalezionych kuzynów, starając się nie naruszać ich prywatnej przestrzeni. Elijah i Winona rzucają kości jagnięce czterem kundlom, którym ku zachwytowi starców nadali nazwę Wszystkie Psy.

Kuzyni Rufusa starają się, jak mogą, wciągnąć mnie do rozmowy. Mówią wolniej, po francusku. Odpowiadam po angielsku. Kiedy na nich patrzę – tak, tak, jestem troszkę zazdrosna – myślę o swoim nieżyjącym ojcu, Edwardzie Christie, i swoich „wujkach", Levim, Reubenie i Jebie, którzy wychowali się na rasistowskim Południu, ale osiedli później w dużych amerykańskich miastach. Za żadne skarby świata nie chcieliby prowadzić takiego życia jak Guy i Estern, nie można jednak wykluczyć, że Guy i Estern wszystkich ich przeżyją.

BRETANIA WYLUDNIA SIĘ od lat. Młodzi ludzie, którzy nie chcą zostać rolnikami, wyjeżdżają i osiedlają się gdzie indziej. Starcy, którzy przez całe życie pracowali na roli, zostają i umierają. A kiedy dzieci sprzedają potem ich farmy, eleganckie kamienne domostwa coraz częściej przekształcają się w miejsca wypoczynkowe dla turystów.

– MOGLIBYŚMY KUPIĆ to gospodarstwo – oświadcza Rufus po obiedzie. Jesteśmy w kuchni Guy i Esterna, zmywamy naczynia.

– Doiłeś kiedyś krowę?

– Tak – odpowiada Rufus. – Na obozie wakacyjnym na farmie w Vermont. Doiłem krowy przez osiem tygodni.

– To było tylko na niby.

Wrzuca do wody talerz, który wzbudza fale. Spłukuje z niego pianę i podaje mi go do wytarcia. Staram się zapamiętać, wycierając naczynia, czego Guy i Estern potrzebują w kuchni. Elektrycznego otwieracza do konserw. Nowych rękawic i ściereczek do naczyń. I przyzwoitych sztućców. Jak wrócimy do Nowego Jorku, wyślę im paczkę. W miesiącach letnich wynajmują stragan na rynku w miasteczku. Turystom, którzy rojnie przekraczają kanał La Manche, sprzedają karczochy w małych słoikach, marynowane marchewki i kalafiory oraz świeże masło z kryształkami soli. Handlują też w barterze, byle tylko zarobić na podatek od nieruchomości, który muszą płacić za zniszczony trzypokojowy dom na farmie.

– A czy ty kiedykolwiek doiłaś krowę, Claudio?

– Jadam mięso tych zwierząt. Czy muszę je też doić?

– To bezczelność. – Pochyla się i cmoka mnie w policzek. – Chcesz pójść na górę i trochę pofiglować?

– Właśnie dlatego nie powinniśmy mieć własnej farmy – mówię. – Utonęlibyśmy w igraszkach. – Na słowo „utonęlibyśmy" Rufus się krzywi i zdaję sobie sprawę, że niechcący znów go zirytowałam.

„**JESTEM JEDYNAKIEM** – powtarza. – Kiedy odejdą mama i tata, nie będę miał żadnej rodziny oprócz ciebie i dzieci. Nie poznam swojego ludu". Czasami mówię mu na to: „A ja nawet nie wiem, skąd pochodzi mój lud, poza tym, że z Afryki; możemy wywodzić się właściwie z każdego kraju na tym kontynencie". Miałam kiedyś przyjaciółkę, która pojechała do Ghany i stanęła na brzegu morza pod jednym z czterdziestu dawnych obozów, gdzie sprzedawano niewolników, aby przewieźć ich potem, skutych łańcuchami, przez Atlantyk. Ta moja przyjaciółka, która podróżowała z grupą znajomych z kościoła, wspomniała, jak stanęli wszyscy w szeregu w porcie, a miejscowy historyk przyjrzał im się i powiedział: „Ty jesteś ze wschodu, a ty, to znaczy twój lud, pochodzisz z północy, a twój lud jest z południa, a twój z zachodu". Ale ja nie byłam nigdy w Afryce. Nie pobierałam próbki swojej śliny patyczkiem higienicznym i nie badałam swojego DNA, które mogłoby mgliście wskazać mi tam drogę. W związku z Afryką nic na razie we mnie nie dojrzało.

SPOTKALIŚMY SIĘ Z OJCEM Rufusa w grudniu, w V&T's, pizzerii położonej dwie przecznice od naszego mieszkania na kampusie Columbia University. Zamówiliśmy dwie duże pizze z pepperoni i patrzyliśmy, jak ser i sos ściekają z cienkiego ciasta.

– Adele i ja tęsknimy za dzieciakami – powiedział James, otaczając ramionami Elijaha i Winonę. Bliźniaki natychmiast wdrapały się na ławkę obok niego.

– Jak idą Adele spotkania w AA, tato? – zapytał Rufus.

– Nie powinniście nas karać za zwyczajny wypadek – odezwał się Szefunio. – Claudio, bądź głosem rozsądku. Karzecie nas.

– Wiesz co, James? – powiedziałam. – Wolałabym nie prowadzić tej rozmowy przy dzieciach.

– W dzisiejszych czasach... – pokręcił głową – ...ludzie traktują dzieci, jak gdyby były ze szkła. A dzieci się nie tłuką.

– Tak ci się tylko wydaje. – Uśmiechnęłam się i zaczęłam kroić swój kawałek pizzy nożem i widelcem. James jest zabójczo przystojny. Stary Gregory Peck. Eksplozja niedawno posiwiałych włosów i stalowoniebieskich oczu, które rozbierają kobiety w przyjemny dla nich sposób, bo ma taką interesującą twarz. Raz czy dwa sama poczułam, jak mnie obnaża wzrokiem. Sprezentował Winonie *Putumayo African*, karykaturalnie dużą książeczkę do kolorowania, i pękate woskowane kredki w kolorach takich jak bakłażanowy. Dzieciaki jeździły na żyrafach po sawannie, na której pasły się zebry, a tubylcy w egzotycznych strojach brzdąkali na gitarach i bili w bębny. Winnie była zachwycona i przejęta. Ma kompletnego fioła na punkcie kolorowanek.

– Kupiłem dla was bilety – zwrócił się James do Elijaha. – Pójdziemy na mecz koszykówki na Columbii.

Ręce dziadka i wnuczka płynnym ruchem wygięły się w łuk, gdy przybijali sobie piątkę.

– Tato – odezwał się Elijah. – Dziadziuś kupił nam bilety na mecz Columbia – Princeton.

– To świetnie. Świetnie. – Rufus zmienił temat. – Wiesz, że mama naprawdę się przestraszyła?

Szefunio nigdy nie mówi o swojej pierwszej żonie, Sigrid.

– No, a co z nią? Umrze czy będzie żyć? Już odeszła czy nadal jest wśród nas?

– Myślę, że będzie żyć – odpowiedziałam. Miłość... To miłość mojego męża do matki przekonała mnie, żeby za niego wyjść, chociaż dzisiaj nie kocham już Rufusa tak jak dawniej. Mogłabym kochać go bardziej.

– Będzie żyć – wtrącił się Rufus. – To, że „się przestraszyła", oznacza z definicji, że najgorsze ma już za sobą, czyli że przeżyła. Chyba że stawiasz pytanie egzystencjalne.

– Nie wyjeżdżaj mi tu z Joyce'em – powiedział Szefunio. Rufus jest badaczem twórczości tego irlandzkiego pisarza, a z kolei Szefunio przez wiele lat wykładał prawo na Columbii, gdzie wcześniej je studiował. Niejeden raz wyraźnie dawał nam do zrozumienia, że posady na uczelni zawdzięczamy jego profesurze i związkom rodzinnym z nim. Jadł pizzę w staromodny sposób, składając jej klinek niemal jak kanapkę.

– Elijah, Winona – westchnęłam. – Serwetki na kolana. Serwetki.

Rufus dał znak Elijahowi i Winonie, by wcisnęli się na ławę między nas. Winona była jednak zajęta kolorowanką, a Elijah pokręcił głową: nie.

– Widzicie? – powiedział Szefunio. – Kochają dziadka. – Nachylił się i uszczypnął Elijaha w policzek. Mały jest podobny do Szefunia. Porusza się i mówi tak jak on.

– Adele i ja mieliśmy nadzieję, że wpadniecie do nas rano w pierwszy dzień świąt. Że otworzycie prezenty z Winnie i Elijahem.

Dzieci siedzą cicho. Są spostrzegawcze. Tęskniły za Szefuniem. Słowa siostry znowu uderzyły mnie z tępą siłą. Popełniłam błąd, pozwalając Winnie i Elijahowi przywiązać się bardziej do rodziców Rufusa niż do moich.

– W tym roku śniadanie w Boże Narodzenie zjemy z siostrą i mamą Claudii – odpowiedział Rufus. Wyciągnął dłoń, żeby wziąć mnie za rękę, a ja podałam mu ją z przyjemnością.

– No to przyjdźcie po południu – nalegał James.

– Wiesz, na jaki pomysł wpadliśmy z mamą? – Rufus posypał pizzę suszonym oregano. – Odtwarzamy nasze drzewo genealogiczne. Dzięki mamie odnalazłem swoich dalekich kuzynów w Bretanii. Przyleci z Kalifornii na Boże Narodzenie, żeby też do nas dołączyć.

– No to mnie wyautowaliście. Więc nie będziemy mieli Święta Dziękczynienia? Nie będziemy mieli Gwiazdki?

– Tato, jesteśmy razem tu i teraz. Cieszmy się sobą, dobrze?

– Adele tęskni za dziećmi, a dom bez dzieci na Boże Narodzenie to...

– Czy Adele nie jest Żydówką?

– To ma być jakaś inwektywa, Rufusie? Nie tak cię wychowywałem. – James poczerwieniał na twarzy. – Wielu Żydów obchodzi nasze chrześcijańskie święta. A my w tym roku będziemy obchodzili i Chanukę, i Boże Narodzenie.

– Nie chodzi mi o to, że Adele jest Żydówką.

– Więc dlaczego o tym napomknąłeś?

Rufus umoczył koniuszek serwetki w oliwie na pizzy.

– Nie mam ochoty spędzać z wami świąt. Nagle zapragnąłeś być troskliwym dziadkiem? A my się mamy cieszyć...

Raz zostawiłem dzieci pod waszą opieką i Winnie o mało się nie utopiła.

Na moment zapadła cisza. Pizza stygła.

– No to może w drugi dzień świąt, Rufusie? – podsunęłam.

Adele uwielbia Elijaha i Winonę. Pierwszy mąż Adele – opowiadała mi o nim – bił ją. Biorąc wszystko pod uwagę, dobrze dała sobie radę w życiu. A Szefunio nie jest pozbawiony serca.

– Będę się musiał dowiedzieć, jak się na to wszystko zapatruje mama. – Rufus powoli jadł pizzę.

– W takim razie jesteśmy umówieni – odpowiedział Szefunio. – Nie wiem, jak to wygląda w Bretanii, ale chyba zdajecie sobie sprawę, że Francuzi są znani z antysemityzmu. Jak pojechaliśmy z Adele do Paryża, powiedziała mi, że nigdy w życiu nie czuła się bardziej Żydówką. Nie jest religijna, musieliśmy jednak połazić po starej dzielnicy żydowskiej, Le Marais, żeby jakoś zapomnieć o tych Francuzach.

– Przepraszam cię, Claudie – odezwał się Rufus. – Ale nie pojmuję, jak ten dupek, który nazwał kiedyś nasze dzieci mieszańcami, może mnie oskarżać o antysemityzm.

– Co to jest mieszaniec, tato?

Elijah ma pięć lat i jest starszy od swojej siostry Winnie o siedemnaście minut. W jego obrazie świata problem rasowy nie istnieje. Jak na razie. Ilekroć wspominam ten wieczór w V&T's, myślę: „Pewnego dnia Elijah straci niewinność".

– Nic – odpowiedział Rufus.

– Dziadek mówi, że jesteśmy niczym? – spytał mały.

Winnie podniosła głowę znad kolorowanki i czubek jej kredki wyjechał poza kontur żyrafy, którą właśnie malowała.

– Elijahu – szepnęłam. – Porozmawiamy na ten temat w domu. Okej?

Szefunio zwrócił się do wnuczka.

– Mieszańcem nazywano kiedyś człowieka mieszanego pochodzenia. Musiałem się oduczyć używania tego słowa. Jest... zdezaktualizowane. Obraźliwe. Nie wiedziałem o tym.

– Możemy prosić o rachunek? – odezwał się Rufus.

– Dzieci jeszcze jedzą – zauważył Szefunio. – Pozwól im skończyć.

Mocno ścisnęłam dłoń Rufusa lewą ręką i nawiązałam kontakt wzrokowy z kelnerką, która akurat sprzątała sąsiedni stolik. Później tego wieczoru Rufus zwinie się w kłębek na podłodze naszej sypialni. Powie, że jego organizm nie toleruje laktozy i że nie powinien był jeść pizzy. Położę mu na brzuchu termofor i zacznę wykonywać nim koliste ruchy. Powiem mu, że wszystko jest możliwe. Żyjemy w epoce alergii i chorób autoimmunologicznych. Żyjemy w tysiącleciu niepokoju.

– Uważasz, że musisz jechać do Francji szukać swoich korzeni? Jesteś też po części Irlandczykiem.

– Nie wystarczy ci, że badam twórczość Joyce'a, tato? Ile irlandzkości ode mnie oczekujesz?

– Pamiętaj tylko, że na intensywnej terapii wylądowałem dlatego, że ratowałem Winnie. Nie pozwoliłem, żeby się utopiła. Uratowałem życie mojej wnuczce.

– Cześć i chwała Jamesowi Samuelowi Vincentowi. – Wtrąciwszy się do rozmowy, tym razem stanęłam po stronie męża. – Gdybym nie wypiła już dwóch kieliszków wina, zaproponowałabym toast. Ale w przeciwieństwie do niektórych osób wiem, kiedy przestać pić.

Szefunio przez chwilę wyglądał jak ogłuszony.

– Nawet najlepszym zdarza się czasem dać dupy – powiedział głośno.

Podeszła kelnerka. Rzuciła Szefuniowi spojrzenie z ukosa.

– Nie miałem na myśli pani, młoda damo – wyjaśnił James.

Siedziałam na skraju ławy. Rufus niemal mnie z niej zepchnął, żebym wstała.

– Chodźmy, Claudio. Proszę cię.

– Ja dałem dupy jakieś czterdzieści lat temu.

Winnie uderzyła dłonią w stół i się roześmiała.

– Dziadek dał dupy!

Jej wybuchowy śmiech brzmiał w naszych uszach jak najpiękniejsza muzyka. Rufus i ja się uśmiechnęliśmy. Były to uśmiechy zmartwionych rodziców. Kelnerka szybko odeszła z naszym rachunkiem.

– Co konkretnie masz na myśli, tato?

– Jak będziesz za często jeździł na konferencje, to w końcu ty też dasz dupy... o ile już nie dałeś.

– Jaja sobie robisz? I to przy mojej żonie i dzieciach. Mówisz serio?

– Dzieci... Claudio... Zatkajcie sobie uszy. – Szefunio wstał od stołu i położył obie ręce na ramieniu Rufusa. Za przeszkloną witryną studenci Columbii snuli się w lewo i w prawo na chodniku. Pomrugiwały bożonarodzeniowe lampki. – Nie musisz jeździć do Bretanii, żeby poznać rodzinę, której dotąd nie znałeś. Masz przyrodniego brata w Raleigh, w Karolinie Północnej. Nazywa się Hank Camphor. Hank.

Minęło kilka sekund, zanim mój mąż zrozumiał, co Szefunio mówi. Rufus podszedł do okna i przycisnął twarz do szyby. Kiedy się odwrócił, był roześmiany. Śmiał się jeszcze, wychodząc z V&T's, i powtarzał:

– Trzymaj się jak najdalej od mojej rodziny, tato. I jak najdalej ode mnie.

NO A POTEM POJECHALIŚMY do Finistère. Mój mąż nie chce rozmawiać o Hanku Camphorze z Karoliny Północnej i nie oddzwania do ojca. Ja rano na ogół wygrzebuję się z łóżka, kiedy na zewnątrz jest jeszcze ciemno choć oko wykol, i rozpalam pozostałe w palenisku resztki po wielkim ogniu Esterna. Czekam, aż Winnie zacznie wrzeszczeć. Jej wrzaski zwiastują świt i prowokują Wszystkie Psy do wycia. Dezorientują koguta. Nie ma spokoju, gdy Winnie krzyczy na farmie. Rufus zawsze pierwszy leci do pokoju dziecięcego. Biegnie. Ja przystaję.

– Winnie. Winnie. Wszystko dobrze – mówi z rozpaczą w głosie Rufus.

Kiedy wreszcie zbieram się na odwagę, żeby wejść do pokoju bliźniaków, siadam po drugiej stronie łóżka Winony, z dala od męża. Ale potem wspólnie, wspólnie ją kołyszemy, raz, dwa, raz, dwa. Elijah w tym czasie śpi. Jakimś cudem. A może mój syn jest wielkim symulantem? Estern i Guy zjawiają się na chwilę w powłóczystych flanelowych piżamach. Ciekawa jestem, co myślą o swoich amerykańskich krewnych w średnim wieku. Rufus mówi im, że wszystko jest w porządku. Po prostu Winnie znowu miała zły sen.

– Nic nie jest w porządku – warczę na Rufusa, kiedy Guy i Estern wychodzą.

– Nie wiem, co robić – mówi Rufus. A Winnie zaśnie równie szybko, jak się obudziła. Zaśnie wtulona między nas i nie będzie pamiętała swoich koszmarów.

– Claudie, co możemy zrobić, żeby to się skończyło?

Rufus i ja jesteśmy znacznie starsi niż byli nasi rodzice, kiedy zakładali rodzinę. W porównaniu z nami byli dziećmi. A my jak większość naszych znajomych czekaliśmy, żeby mieć dzieci. Czekaliśmy – by najpierw zarobić pieniądze. Czekaliśmy – żeby się skoncentrować na naszych obiecujących karierach. Czekaliśmy – na co? Powtarzam sobie, że rodzice moi i Rufusa opanowaliby sytuację z Winoną. Powtarzam sobie, że poradziliby sobie z kłopotami, wzięliby byka za rogi. Powtarzam sobie, że jesteśmy zmęczeni. A ludzie zmęczeni mogą sobie powtarzać, co tylko im przyjdzie do głowy – kiedy uciekają sami przed sobą.

– Rufusie – słyszę swój głos. – To nie jest nasz dom. Spędziliśmy tu już wystarczająco dużo czasu.

ANTRAKT

1969

TA KSIĄŻKA NALEŻAŁA DO OJCA CLAUDII, EDDIEGO CHRISTIE. Zwędził ją jednemu oficerowi, kiedy dostał przepustkę i zszedł na ląd w Subic Bay. Tę książkę miał w tylnej kieszeni, gdy w 1971 roku wrócił do domu z Wietnamu. Tę książkę zamiast bajek czytywał na dobranoc Claudii i Beverly. Tę książkę chwyciła Claudia – wtedy już trzylatka, cierpiąca z powodu upokorzenia, jakim była dla niej popołudniowa drzemka – i rozerwała jej okładkę dokładnie przez środek, na pół. Rozdarcie wyglądało tak świeżo i krwawo, że wesoła zwykle twarz Eddiego przybrała tępy wyraz; chwycił Claudię za nogi, odwrócił ją głową w dół, wyniósł na podwórko i trzymał tak, że dotykała czołem ziemi pośród źdźbeł trawy i mrówek, szukających okruchów z pizzelli pana Maddalone. Claudia wyczuwała mrówki, przebiegające w górę po jej kitkach i patrolujące skórę na jej głowie. Gryzły ją, a może tylko tak się jej wydawało. Nie mogła powstrzymać krzyku. Jej wrzaski wywabiły z domu Agnes, a za nią siostrę Claudii, Beverly, która dopiero co poszła się położyć, by uciąć sobie popołudniową drzemkę.

Beverly wyciągnęła palec: „Claudia, Claudia rozerwała książkę tatusia".

„To tylko książka, Eddie", powiedziała Agnes, której napłynęły łzy do oczu. Eddie nigdy na nikogo nie podnosił głosu w tym skromnym ceglanym domu. Przeżył wojnę. Wrócił w jednym kawałku i przy zdrowych zmysłach. Prawie. Czasami gadał do ścian. Ale był prawie, prawie całkiem... Eddie Christie był człowiekiem zdrowym na umyśle.

„Pomogę ci posklejać kartki – powiedziała Agnes. – Dziewczynki i ja ci pomożemy, tylko najpierw musisz oddać mi dziecko". Eddie postawił Claudię na nogi, po czym wszyscy czworo wycofali się do kuchni, usiedli na jasnoczerwonych, obitych skajem krzesłach i zajęli się sklejaniem okładki dramatu Toma Stopparda *Rosenkrantz i Guildenstern nie żyją*, aż w końcu wyglądała prawie jak nowa. Eddie uśmiechnął się i pocałował żonę i córeczki.

– No i proszę, jak ładnie! – powiedział. – Aż przyjemnie popatrzeć, moje panie!

AKT ~~DRUGI~~

1969

„CO TEN EDDIE TAM CZYTA?"

„Można by pomyśleć, że jest wykształcony".

Wstąpiłem do marynarki w 1966. Byłem wtedy na trzecim roku college'u, w Bronksie.

„Jesteś poetą, Eddie?"

Nie, po prostu lubię czytać.

„Shakespeare. Patrzcie tylko, jak Eddie czyta Shakespeare'a".

UKRADŁEM TĘ KSIĄŻKĘ jednemu oficerowi, kiedy staliśmy w porcie w Subic Bay. To jedyna rzecz, jaką ukradłem w życiu. Ten oficer ciągle gadał o tym, że jego żona to i jego żona tamto, że widziała kiedyś przedstawienie sztuki *Rosenkrantz i Guildenstern nie żyją* na West Endzie w Londynie i przysłała mu ją, żeby sobie przeczytał. Siedział przy barze, pił szkocką i puszył się jak paw. Nie mogłem już słuchać tych przechwałek i zacząłem tęsknić za Agnes. Niektóre żołnierskie żony zajmowały się wychowywaniem dzieci albo pracą i nie mogły sobie pozwolić na wyjazdy w celach rozrywkowych. Inne chodziły w ciąży z drugim dzieckiem. Jak ten oficer nie patrzył, po prostu podszedłem i wziąłem książkę ze stołka. Duże grzechy mają początek w błahych.

ZACIĄGNĄŁEM SIĘ do marynarki, żeby uciec z Bronksu, który za bardzo kochałem – były tam kluby salsy i kobiety, i tam przechodził mnie dreszcz podniecenia, gdy po północy przekraczałem dozwoloną prędkość i pędziłem po Fordham Avenue należącym do mojego starego buickiem skylarkiem, w którym odsuwałem dach. Lubię się śmiać i często to robię. Zawsze mam na twarzy uśmiech z jakiegoś powodu, bo szybko się nauczyłem, że człowiek ciągle wdeptuje w jakieś gówno, a wtedy... niech Bóg ma cię w swojej opiece, jeżeli nie umiesz się śmiać. Potrafiłem wydać całą pensję na nowy garnitur i buty, żeby się zabawić w Palladium, w The Embassy albo w Tropicoro. W tamtych czasach nie można było zabrać dziewczyny wieczorem na miasto, wyglądając jak menel. Trzeba się było odpowiednio wystroić. A ja się tak stroiłem, że na drugim roku wyrzucili mnie z college'u. Stary nigdy nie mówił w domu po hiszpańsku, ale, bracie, wtedy mi nawtykał. Wcześniej płaciłem tylko jeden rachunek, potem musiałem normalnie płacić czynsz. Mimo że tatko opękał już hipotekę. Skumałem, o co mu chodzi, i kiedy zaczepił mnie werbownik, wstąpiłem do marynarki.

MÓJ OJCIEC BYŁ zaopatrzeniowcem w firmie Sokolov & Brothers, fabryce pianin w Mott Haven, w Bronksie. Przez ponad dwadzieścia dziewięć lat kumał się z niemieckimi i włoskimi imigrantami, którzy myśleli, że jest biały jak oni. Ale tata był Kubańczykiem z Hawany. Zaraz po przyjeździe do Ameryki wziął sobie czarnoskórą żonę i przyjął anglosaskie nazwisko. Eduardo Christonelli-Garcia nazwał się: Eddie Christie. Później kupił domek jednorodzinny w południowym Bronksie. Miałem przejąć pracę po nim, ale kiedy pojawiłem się na świecie, ludzie już nie kupowali pianin. Woleli chodzić do kina, siedzieć przed telewizorem albo spędzać czas w klubach nocnych. Mój stary znał statystyki. „Kiedyś w samym Bronksie było sześćdziesiąt fabryk pianin. Właśnie tak. Bronx był pianinową stolicą świata". Ludzie mają mnóstwo złych rzeczy do powiedzenia o tej dzielnicy. Ale on z Bronksu miał chleb. Był dumny z miejsca, w którym

mieszkał. Kiedy dobijałem do wieku męskiego, produkcja pianin była już pieśnią przeszłości. Fabryki bankrutowały na prawo i lewo. Sokolov & Brothers stanowiła jeden z ostatnich punktów oporu. Tatko dostał od nich na koniec pianino i skromną emeryturę, kiedy firmę ostatecznie zamknięto w 1959 roku. Potem wziął jeszcze robotę na pół etatu jako dozorca w mojej budzie.

W WOJU NAJPIERW ODDELEGOWALI MNIE do kotłowni, na pomocnika marynarza (żołd: grupa E-2). Nie trzeba było długiego szkolenia, żeby zacząć się orientować w obowiązkach. I zdać sobie sprawę, że to nie jest dobra robota dla kogoś takiego jak ja. Mówili na nas „bekasy", bo tak nazywano ludzi pracujących pod pokładem, żyjących jak trolle na samym dnie okrętu. Wolę błękitne niebo i świeże morskie powietrze, miałem jednak dość rozumu, żeby się nie skarżyć; przynajmniej zdobywałem różne umiejętności techniczne, które mogły otworzyć mi drzwi do awansu. Podpisałem kontrakt jako A-4, co w języku cywilów oznacza cztery lata służby. Robiłem sobie wielkie nadzieje. Cieszyłem się, że nie zostałem stewardem w mesie. Zwykle tam kierowano kiedyś czarnych marynarzy, a potem Filipińczyków. Dawali nas do kuchni i zmywalni, dostawaliśmy przydział do gotowania i zmywania jako pomocnicy. Mój kuzyn Reuben Applewood wstąpił do marynarki rok przede mną i powiedział mi, czego się mogę spodziewać, więc byłem gotowy na lekką dyskryminację. Nie zaznałem jej, pewnie właśnie dlatego, że byłem przygotowany. Ten pierwszy przydział służbowy w sześćdziesiątym siódmym był okej. Czarni i biali marynarze nie byli może kumplami, ale nie pławiliśmy się też w nienawiści. Po prostu biali i czarni trzymali się osobno, każdy robił swoje. Moim największym zmartwieniem było, jak dobrze wykonywać swoje obowiązki, żeby nie wyciekało nam paliwo i żeby okręt nie wyleciał w powietrze. Niefajnie jest zginąć w ten sposób. A zdarza się to częściej, niż myślicie. Ale kiedy dostałem drugi przydział, sprawy zaczęły przybierać paskudny obrót. Atmosfera zmieniła się zupełnie. Earl Ray zamordował doktora Kinga. Wycelował z karabinu Remingtona .30-06 w jego szyję i głowę. Dobrze wybrał też czas. Doktor King na pewno nie był zwolennikiem wojny i zaczął robić szum wokół naszej obecności w Wietnamie, a nie każdy miał ochotę go słuchać. Kiedy rozeszła się wiadomość, że Kinga zastrzelono, niektórzy biali marynarze zaczęli podpalać krzyże. I wyciągać na pokład beczki z piwem, żeby świętować. „Komunista. King to komunista", właśnie tak go najczęściej określano. W tych słowach kryje się agresja, bracie. Nie trzeba było należeć do Czarnych Panter, żeby dostać szału, słysząc taką chujozę. Życie na USS Olympus zmieniło się z gorącego i spoconego w spocone i pełne napięcia. Zdarzało mi się znajdować w kleszczach pomiędzy szydzącymi białymi i gotującymi się ze złości czarnymi. Jak Rosenkrantz i Guildenstern, znałem początek dramatu, ale nie wiedziałem, jak to się wszystko skończy. Siedziałem na koi z książką na kolanach i wyłączałem się, kurde. Zabawne. Zwędziłem tę książeczkę, bo nie spodobał mi się jej właściciel, i nie miałem najmniejszego zamiaru jej przeczytać w czasie tego mojego pierwszego rejsu, ale na USS Olympus trudno było o czasopisma i książki. I chyba się nie zdziwicie, kiedy wam powiem, że dzięki Rosenkrantzowi i Guildensternowi bez przerwy się śmiałem?

„ROS: Z tego, co powiedział, połowa znaczyła co innego, a druga połowa w ogóle nic nie znaczyła"*.

Mniej więcej tak samo gadali nasi politycy, kiedy chcieli uzasadnić wojnę. Przeklęty prezydent Johnson porządnie namieszał ludziom we łbach.

PEWNEGO WIECZORU mój kuzyn Jebediah Applewood przyszedł do naszej kabiny, tocząc pianę z pyska. Wyglądał jak wściekły byk. Jeb, Reuben i Levi (młodszy brat Reubena) dorastali wszyscy w tym samym domu. Byli to moi krewni ze strony matki – zatailiśmy tę informację w marynarce, bo baliśmy się, że oficerowie dadzą nam takie przydziały, żebyśmy nie mogli się widywać.

– Musimy coś zrobić, kurwa, z tym pierdolonym młodszym chorążym – powiedział Jeb.

Wiedziałem, kim jest młodszy chorąży marynarki Nelson „Nelly" Mammoth. Na ogół marynarze popadają w melancholię, kiedy piją, ale Mammoth po alkoholu zdradzał, można powiedzieć, ochotę do walk pięściarskich. Za jego plecami nazywaliśmy go Nelly, bo tkwiły w nim dwie różne osobowości. Ten idiota pełnił obowiązki starszego bosmana sztabowego i nie miał sobie równych. Nadzorował część załogi odpowiedzialną za konserwację i zachowanie porządku na pokładzie i rządził nimi twardą ręką.

---

* Tom Stoppard, *Rosenkrantz i Guildenstern nie żyją*, tłum. Gustaw Gottesman. Wszystkie cytaty z dramatu Stopparda, z jednym wyjątkiem zaznaczonym w odsyłaczu, przytaczane są za tym przekładem (przypisy pochodzą od tłumacza).

Znał wszystkie zakamarki Olympusa. Nadzorował i szkolił chłopców pokładowych, a także pilnował, żeby amunicję i rakiety ładowano w odpowiedni sposób do wielkich wind okrętowych, łączących hangar i pokłady startowe. Plotka głosiła, że umiał obsługiwać każdy specjalistyczny sprzęt na okręcie. Służba sprawiała mu najwyraźniej autentyczną przyjemność. A młodszy chorąży Nelson Mammoth to było co innego. Uwielbiał męczyć czarnych marynarzy w kwestii Project 100 000*. Lubił pytać, w którym roku zaciągnęli się do marynarki i czy było to przed rozpoczęciem projektu, w jego trakcie – kiedy przyjmowano do służby w zasadzie każdego kretyna – czy dopiero po jego zakończeniu. Zmuszał czarnych marynarzy, by wypełniali testy IQ na miejscu, bez przygotowania, i obrzucał ich wszystkimi rasistowskimi wyzwiskami, jakie można sobie wyobrazić. Nie obchodziło go to, że program zatrudnienia stu tysięcy żołnierzy ograniczał się do armii i piechoty morskiej. Wśród marynarzy czarni stanowili pięć procent. Wydaje mi się, że dla niego było to jednak za dużo. Kiedy podchodził do mnie, cuchnąc bourbonem – był to jego ulubiony alkohol – zwracałem się do niego bełkotliwym chórem słów włoskich, greckich i hiszpańskich. Gwizdał wtedy i mówił: „Niech zgadnę. Zaciągnąłeś się już dawno?".

---

* Chodzi o kontrowersyjny pomysł ówczesnego sekretarza obrony w rządzie Stanów Zjednoczonych, Roberta McNamary, i zainicjowany przez niego w 1966 roku specjalny program wcielania do wojska osób, które w normalnych warunkach nie zostałyby przyjęte do służby, ponieważ nie spełniały obowiązujących kryteriów zdrowotnych lub intelektualnych.

Nie odpowiadałem. Przez półtora roku robił notatki o każdym czarnoskórym marynarzu na pokładzie USS Olympus. Jako kraj byliśmy w stanie wojny, którą przegrywaliśmy, i można byłoby pomyśleć, że Mammoth powinien mieć ciekawsze rzeczy do roboty. Kolor skóry zaciemniał mu perspektywę, której granicą okazała się woda.

– Co myślisz, Eddie?

Przerwałem lekturę i uśmiechnąłem się do Jeba.

– Uważam, że Rosenkrantz i Guildenstern powinni być sprytniejsi. Hamlet nie kupuje tego ich przedstawienia.

– Nie... Chodzi mi o Nelly'ego Mammotha.

Pomyślałem o naszym kuzynie Reubenie. On by dokładnie wiedział, co odpowiedzieć Jebowi.

– Wydaje mi się, że nie warto zawracać sobie nim głowy. Rozumiesz, z czasem o nim zapomnimy.

Jeb stanął nad moim łóżkiem. Zająłem dolną koję, żeby nie uderzać głową w sufit.

– Wczoraj wieczorem złamał nos stewardowi. Ten pojebany skurwysyn złamał chłopakowi nos, kurde, bo tamten zapomniał podać ketchup na stół. A dzieciak za bardzo się boi, żeby złożyć na niego skargę – powiedział Jeb.

– Dlaczego nazywasz Nelly'ego skurwysynem? Dlaczego obrażasz jego matkę? Nie znamy jej. Może jest w porządku. – Chciałem, żeby Jeb zostawił mnie w spokoju i żebym mógł wrócić do czytania sztuki.

Westchnął. Przywykł już do tego, że się nie rozstaję z R&G.

– To jesteś ze mną czy jak?

– Zależy – odparłem. – Jestem z tobą zawsze, ale to co teraz mówisz, to nic nowego. O czym my tu właściwie rozmawiamy? Steward skończy rejs, tak jak my wszyscy. A potem o nim zapomni, kurde. Nie jestem pewien, co chciałbyś osiągnąć, stawiając się Mammothowi.

Jeb otworzył jedną z dwóch aluminiowych szafek przy naszych łóżkach i wyjął plik pism „Jet". Czytywał artykuły, ale na ogół oglądał rozkładówki. Domyśliłem się, że teraz więcej nie będzie się do mnie odzywał. Już przez resztę wieczoru. Na USS Olympus byliśmy jak bracia, dzisiaj jednak rzadko rozmawiamy. Po wojnie wróciłem do Bronksu, a Jeb do Georgii. Ostatnia wiadomość, jaka dotarła do mnie na jego temat, to że pracował w firmie przeprowadzkowej i osiedlił się gdzieś w New Hampshire. Pewnego razu dostałem od niego pocztówkę: „Myślałem, że zimno jest w Norwegii, ale zima w New Hampshire to strasznie mroźna kurwa".

Ciągle bluzga, pomyślałem. Ciągle bluzga.

– Z czego się śmiejesz, Eddie? – spytała moja żona.

BYLIŚMY MARYNARZAMI na otwartym morzu, na USS Olympus, lotniskowcu mierzącym tysiąc pięćdziesiąt sześć stóp długości, stacjonującym w Yankee Station w Zatoce Tonkińskiej. To duży okręt. Pływa po najgłębszych wodach jak ryba. Czasami włóczyłem się wśród różnych stanowisk bojowych i oglądałem jego maszynerię. Widok tego, jak to wszystko ładnie się uzupełnia, pomagał mi w nocy spać. Na drugim rejsie zostałem przydzielony do załogi na pokładzie startowym. Stanowiliśmy morskie wsparcie dla pilotów marynarki, wykonujących loty zwiadowcze i bombardujących pozycje żołnierzy Wietnamu Północnego.

NA USS OLYMPUS służyło ponad cztery tysiące marynarzy. W niektórych kajutach umieszczano po ośmiu ludzi, głowa w głowę. Było słychać, jak chrapią, płaczą i się onanizują. Czasami, jeśli byli gotowi zaryzykować życie, słyszeliśmy, jak się ruchają. I nigdy nie byli to ci, których by się podejrzewało o takie skłonności. Chłopaków po prostu nachodziła ochota – a jeśli okazywała się niewłaściwego rodzaju, gotowi byli zrobić właściwie wszystko, do diabła. Jak Jeb i ja – kiedy mieliśmy już dość młodszego chorążego marynarki Nelsona Mammotha.

GDYBY NA USS OLYMPUS pływał z nami Reuben, może wszystko skończyłoby się inaczej. Latem mama wysyłała mnie na południe Stanów. Żebym poznał swój lud, jak mówiła. Dlatego jeździłem na wakacje z Reubenem, Jebem i Levim, grałem w bejsbol i rozrabiałem na najróżniejsze sposoby. Reuben był od nas o dwa lata starszy, więc nawet wtedy odgrywał rolę „sierżanta", skazanego na to, by nie pozwalać nam pakować się w kłopoty. Dorastałem w Bronksie, gdzie miałem różnych sąsiadów, świat nie był więc dla mnie wyłącznie czarno-biały, ale kiedy wyjeżdżałem na Południe, mama zawsze wygłaszała ten sam wykład o Emmetcie Tillu*. „Nie chcę tam przyjechać po to, żeby zobaczyć twoją twarz w trumnie, słyszysz?" Gadaliśmy o tym, wiecie,

---

* Emmett Till (1941–1955), urodzony w Chicago czarnoskóry nastolatek, oskarżony o nieprzyzwoite zachowanie wobec białej kobiety w sklepie w pobliżu miasteczka Money w delcie Missisipi, porwany i zamordowany kilka dni później przez dwóch białych.

Reuben, Jeb, Levi i ja. I śmialiśmy się – nie z Emmetta, ale z tego, że połowa rzeczy, których nie mogliśmy robić, była bez sensu, bo nie kapowaliśmy, z jakiego powodu czegoś nam nie wolno, na przykład pływać z innymi dzieciakami w basenie pełnym chlorowanej wody. Śmialiśmy się, bo jak jesteś przyjezdny i widzisz, że coś jest wyłącznie dla kolorowych, a coś wyłącznie dla białych, to masz poczucie absurdu i wtedy uświadamiasz sobie, jakie to jest wszystko idiotyczne. Reuben nam powtarzał: „Kiedy biali próbują was wykołować, wybierzcie sobie w myślach jakiś ocean. Arktyczny. Atlantyk. Ocean Indyjski. Pacyfik. Ocean Południowy. I uspokójcie się". Dostawaliśmy co tydzień kieszonkowe, żebyśmy mogli pojechać do miasta i kupić nowy komiks. Każdym z nich musieliśmy się dzielić. Czytaliśmy go najpierw razem, a potem kolejno na zmianę, już pojedynczo. Ale żeby kupować te komiksy, musieliśmy jeździć do takiej księgarni przy Main Street, Sadie's Fine Books and Whatnots. Właścicielka miała starego płowego buldoga, który lubił polegiwać na progu. Ślinił się, warczał, obnażał żółte zęby i zagradzał nam drogę, a panna Sadie, wysoka biała kobieta, wyglądająca jak jakiś rzadki ptak, śmiała się i mówiła: „Och, no tak, chłopcy, chcecie swoje komiksy, no to chodźcie, chodźcie". Reuben oświadczał wtedy: „Pora udać się w podróż. Wybierzcie sobie ocean". I ruszał pierwszy, a ten buldog zawsze skakał i kłapał paszczą, gdy Reuben przekraczał próg sklepu, a Reuben robił wszystko, co mógł, żeby odciągnąć od nas jego uwagę i żebyśmy mogli wejść do środka cali i zdrowi. Niejeden raz pogryzł Reubena w łydki i golenie aż do krwi, a panna Sadie gwizdała na psa i mówiła: „Chodź tu, malutki, chodź", a potem dawała

Reubenowi komiks za darmo i Reuben kuśtykał do domu na czele naszej paczki, trzymając najnowszy zeszyt wychodzącego co tydzień *Flasha Gordona*.

TO JEST FAKT: Nie za dobrze ostatnio sypiam.

Cały aż chodzę.

Kiedy zrobiłem się taki roztrzęsiony?

Chorąży Mammoth miał żonę. Wiecie, że właśnie to najbardziej mnie uwiera? Jego żona i dzieci. Myślę o wszystkich ich urodzinach i świętach, które stały się wielkie i puste po tym, co zrobiliśmy, czyli kiedy chorąży Mammoth się utopił.

Myślę o mgle i o tym, jak spowiła okręt. I jak on się uśmiechał, kiedy zobaczył mnie na pokładzie, palącego papierosa. Powinien był wiedzieć, że nie palę. Powinien był poświęcić trochę więcej czasu na to, żeby mnie lepiej poznać. „Oto człowiek znajdujący się nawet poniżej najnowszych standardów", powiedział. Miał na zębach ciemne plamki po kawie. „Co ty tu robisz?"

Jego żółte siekacze połyskiwały we mgle.

– Głębokie niebieskie morze wcale nie jest niebieskie – powiedziałem.

Były to ostatnie słowa, jakie usłyszał w swoim życiu młodszy chorąży marynarki Mammoth.

Ostatnio siadam na swojej koi nocą i słucham tych nawołujących mnie głosów. Kto mnie woła? Widzę i słyszę najdziwniejsze rzeczy...

„POSŁUCHAJCIE, POSŁUCHAJCIE, CO MÓWIĘ. Rosenkrantz i Guildenstern nie żyją. Widziałem ich, jak przechadzają się po pokładzie startowym USS Olympus na Morzu Południowochińskim. Widziałem, jak rzucają monety i wygadują najróżniejsze zwariowane banialuki. Pytają się mnie, co takiego zrobili Hamletowi, że potraktował ich w ten sposób. Mówię im prawdę w przerwie załadunku bomb na szturmowce A-4 – bomb, które cywilów i żołnierzy Wietkongu będą zabijać niemal w tych samych proporcjach. Weszliście w zmowę z Klaudiuszem. Wy, lisy, zachowaliście się jak szczury. Książę Hamlet był waszym najlepszym przyjacielem. Wy, lisy, mieliście go załatwić. Wtedy zaczęli narzekać i nazwali mnie gburowatym Maurem. Maurem? Wiecie, no to dla mnie coś nowego. Ostatnio kiedy ktoś coś mówił na mój temat, to że jestem kolejnym czarnym w Wietnamie. Czarnoskóry mężczyzno z Wietnamu, poprowadź nas do Londynu, tak mówią. Wierzcie mi, bracia, Londynu nie powinniście oglądać nawet z daleka. Możecie dać głowy, jeśli tam pojedziecie, ale Rosenkrantz i Guildenstern tylko rzucają pieniążki, kręcą głowami i mówią: Maurze, nie można ci ufać. Widzieliśmy, jak wypchnąłeś chorążego Mammotha za burtę. Jesteś mordercą. Ty i ten drugi Maur zabiliście człowieka. Nie powinniście byli tego robić. A ja na to, a co, myślicie, że nie zdaję sobie z tego sprawy? Potem odliczam kolejne minuty do przerwy na lunch i lecę do pralni, żeby znaleźć Jeba".

– Jeb – mówię. – Rosenkrantz i Guildenstern znowu mieszają mi we łbie.

Jeb lubi robotę w pralni. Powiada, że czyste pranie przypomina mu o Buckner County w Georgii. Chwyta mnie za ramię i rozgląda się, żeby sprawdzić, czy nikt nie podsłuchuje. Każe mi czekać na niego pod kantyną dla czarnych. Ostatnimi czasy nie jadamy z białymi, jeżeli nie musimy. A Jeb i ja trzymamy się głównie ze sobą.

– Co, kurwa, jest z tobą nie tak, Eddie? – Znajduje mnie dziesięć minut później, popijającego zimną kawę. – Chcesz, żebyśmy stanęli przed sądem polowym? Nie możesz przychodzić do pralni i gadać tak głośno o Chucku.

Imieniem Chuck czarni żołnierze określają czasem białych. Po Nelly'ego wysłano ekipę poszukiwawczo-ratunkową, nikt nie wiedział jednak, kiedy zaginął. Było wiadomo tylko, że nie pokazał się w mesie podoficerskiej na obiedzie ani na wieczornym filmie.

„Człowiek za burtą", mówili. Chorąży Mammoth zaczął dużo pić. Stawał się ochlapusem pierwszej wody.

– Ja tylko ci mówię, Jeb... – Mój głos cichnie. – Że oni są w mojej głowie.

– Powinieneś oddać mi tę przeklętą sztukę, Eddie. Dawaj tę jebaną sztukę i weź sobie do czytania „Jet" albo „Ebony". Mówię poważnie.

– Nie ma mowy.

Chcę czasem Jebowi powiedzieć, że Rosenkrantz i Guildenstern podkradają się do mnie z tyłu i szepczą, że Chuck płynie z powrotem na okręt. Ja mówię Chuck. Oni mówią Nelly? Ja mówię Nelly. Oni mówią Chuck? To jest jak wojna. Zatacza mniejsze i większe kręgi, jak każdy przedmiot wrzucony do wody. Ale ta informacja nadaje się do wpisania na długą listę RZECZY, O KTÓRYCH JEB NIE MUSI WIEDZIEĆ. Co wieczór po obiedzie kapitan USS Olympus ogłasza przez megafony, ile bomb zrzuciliśmy, ilu straciliśmy ludzi i ile zniszczyliśmy celów. Wtedy Jeb nakrywa głowę poduszką i wskazuje ścianę, na której wisi jego lista: RZECZY, O KTÓRYCH JEB NIE MUSI WIEDZIEĆ. Jak większość marynarzy na tym lotniskowcu, nigdy nie zeszliśmy na wietnamską ziemię. Widziałem jednak zajęców – jak nazywaliśmy chłopaków z piechoty morskiej – i pilotów, którzy wracali w foliowych workach albo z amputowanymi kończynami. Widziałem wyraz twarzy niektórych żołnierzy, świadczący o tym, że przeżyli własną śmierć, nie rozumieją jednak, jakie mieli szczęście. Nie chcę oglądać tych twarzy. I cieszę się, że nie wąchałem prochu.

– Może ci potrzeba trochę zioła, żebyś się odprężył? – Jeb przygląda mi się.

– Nie chcę zioła. Nie chcę się nawalać, skoro nie jestem nawet w stanie stać prosto.

– No to czego chcesz, Eddie? – pyta Jeb. – Robisz mi wodę z mózgu i drażnisz mnie tym pieprzeniem.

Kiwam głową.

– Chcę jeszcze zobaczyć Agnes i dziewczynki. Chcę wrócić do Bronksu. Chcę domowego jedzenia. Chcę usiąść na ganku swojego domu i nie myśleć o niczym.

– No to się jakoś trzymaj. Bo inaczej obaj mamy przesrane – mówi Jeb.

ROSENKRANTZ I GUILDENSTERN nie żyją. Posłuchajcie, słuchajcie, co mówię. Widziałem, jak na rzecznej łajbie wpływali do Zatoki Tonkińskiej. „Wracajcie, wracajcie – mówię. – To nie jest droga do Londynu". Ale oni kręcą głowami, rzucają monety i krzyczą: „Maurze, musimy stąd odejść. To nie jest nasza wojna. Nie możemy tu zostać". Proszą, żebym pojechał z nimi, ale w Zatoce Tonkińskiej nie dzieje się nic dobrego. Ros i Guil będą mogli mówić o szczęściu, jeśli uda im się przetrwać kolejny dzień. Jeb na to, że ich wyjazd jest dla mnie darem bogów. Pieprzone błogosławieństwo. Dzięki niech będą najsłodszemu Panu Jezusowi, że tych dwóch wścibskich skurwysynów wyjechało. Jeb twierdzi, że ogólnie rzecz biorąc, odkąd wyjechali, moje zmysły ochłodły, ale ja wcale nie wiedziałem, że były rozgrzane. Wydawało mi się, że rozgrzane było tylko moje poczucie moralności. No to Jeb gada, że moralność może go pocałować w czarną dupę i że jak dotrzemy do zatoki Subic, to on i ja będziemy chodzić na wszystkie występy erotyczne w Olongapo. Znajdziemy sobie z tuzin prostytutek i będziemy się z nimi rżnąć. Ale tęsknię za Rosem i Guilem. Tu nie ma z kim rozmawiać ani komu opowiadać pewnych rzeczy. Na przykład o tym, jak młodszy chorąży Mammoth obrzucał nas rasistowskimi obelgami i okładał wściekle stewarda po głowie, bo ten steward, wiotki szesnastolatek z jakiegoś miasteczka w Nowej Anglii, miał koślawe przeguby i nie mógł ich dobrze zginać, a poza tym chodził takim rozkołysanym kro-

kiem i za nic nie dało się go zmusić, żeby się trzymał prosto. Albo o tym, jak w kulminacyjnym momencie sztormu ten sam chorąży Mammoth kręcił się po całym statku niczym demon po klatce, nawalony gorzałą i paranoicznie podejrzliwy. Wyszukiwał tego młodziaka, żeby go zbić jak co tydzień, zrzucał go ze schodów i zostawiał leżącego na pokładzie niczym kłębek wełny. A cała załoga, w tym Jeb i ja, nienawidziła chorążego Mammotha, ale nie potrafiliśmy się zebrać w sobie, by stanąć w obronie chłopaka. A to dlatego że budził w nas jakieś takie dziwne uczucia, że nienawidziliśmy go jeszcze bardziej niż Nelly'ego.

„To mogłeś być ty", powiedział w końcu Jeb.

„To mogliśmy być my", odpowiedziałem.

„Jutro", zgodziliśmy się.

I tak to zrobiliśmy.

AKT TRZECI

1995

Z OKAZJI PIĘĆDZIESIĄTYCH URODZIN EDDIEGO CLAUDIA i jej ówczesny chłopak, Rufus, zabrali ojca i matkę na londyńską inscenizację sztuki *Rosenkrantz i Guildenstern nie żyją*, właśnie w Londynie. To po tym przedstawieniu Rufus poprosił Eddiego o rękę jego córki. To na tym przedstawieniu Eddie, wówczas już korpulentny pan w średnim wieku, ubrany w czarny smoking i cylinder, przymknął oczy i powtarzał pod nosem dialogi, bo znał je wszystkie na pamięć – i z własnego życia. Tak więc kiedy Claudia na koniec odwróciła się do niego i zapytała: „No jak, tato, podobało ci się?", skinął tylko głową i zwinął program w rulonik. Była to pierwsza sztuka, jaką widział w życiu na prawdziwej scenie, nie przypuszczał jednak, by miała być ostatnią.

W DOMU EDDIEGO I AGNES mała Claudia biegała z pokoju do pokoju, mówiła do ścian i odgrywała różne sceny z *Rosenkrantz i Guildenstern nie żyją*. Czasami, kiedy wypowiadała jakiś dialog, podnosiła wzrok i widziała, że ojciec się jej przygląda.

Claudia. Klaudiusz, mówił ojciec. Król Klaudiusz zabił ojca księcia Hamleta. Dlaczego, na Boga, Agnes dała naszemu dziecku na imię Claudia?

Eddie wypowiadał to takim tonem, że Claudia zaczynała się bać, że złapie ją za nogi i znowu będzie trzymał głową w dół, ale ojciec brał ją wtedy na ręce, sadzał sobie na barana i delikatnie nosił po pokoju. „Gdzie są pieniążki? Claudio, Claudio, pomóż mi znaleźć pieniążki".

Na biurku w jej domu leży sfatygowany egzemplarz *Rosenkrantz i Guildenstern nie żyją*. Nie czytała tej sztuki od wielu lat, ale zabiera ją ze sobą w każdą podróż jak talizman. Ostatnim razem jednak pakowała się w pośpiechu i nie wzięła książeczki do Bretanii.

EDDIE PO WIETNAMIE

1972

PRZEZ KILKA PIERWSZYCH MIESIĘCY WYDAWAŁO SIĘ, ŻE Eddie Christie po powrocie do domu jest szczęśliwy, mogąc się zajmować swoimi dwiema córkami. Pozwalał im biegać w górę i w dół po schodach i wszystkich pokojach, bo dziewczynki ciągle się bawiły w chowanego. Przypominały mu gołębie pisklęta – albo w ogóle płochliwe małe ptaszki. Wyobrażał sobie, jak ich ptasie ramionka zmieniają się w skrzydła. Wyobrażał sobie, że wylecą z okien ich ceglanego domu i nie wrócą, jeżeli sprawi im przykrość. Dlatego ilekroć nachodziło go jakieś wspomnienie z wojny, odwracał się i oddalał szybko od córek w poszukiwaniu jakiegoś cichego kącika, gdzie mógłby dojść do siebie.

To trzyletnia Claudia przyłapała Eddiego rozmawiającego ze ścianą w salonie. Zapytała ojca, do kogo mówi.

Odpowiedział, że wyburza czwartą ścianę.

– A co jest po drugiej stronie? – zapytała.

– Scena.

– A na scenie?

– No, oczywiście sztuka.

W ten sposób Eddie zaczął odgrywać *Rosenkrantz i Guildenstern nie żyją* ze swoimi córkami. Claudia zaczęła wierzyć, że ściana mówi, i uwierzyła w przyjaciół Hamleta tak, jak większość dzieci wierzy w Świętego Mikołaja. Czasem, kiedy ściany huczały i ryczały w głowie Eddiego, podkradała się do niego z tyłu i szeptała:

– Co porabiają dzisiaj Rosenkrantz i Guildenstern?

– Nic, tylko rzucają pieniążki.

– Reszka! – śmiała się.

– Orzeł!

A Eddie kiwał głową, wyciągając drobne – pięciocentówki, ćwierćdolarówki, centówki i dziesięciocentówki – z kieszeni dżinsów na parkietową podłogę. Ależ one brzęczały! Drobne Eddiego robiły straszny hałas.

Wiedział, że byłoby najlepiej, gdyby nie mówił do siebie ani do ścian, ale dopóki miał coś, na czym mógł się skupić, radził sobie nieco lepiej niż większość weteranów. Dziewczynki dawały mu znać, kiedy dostawał odpału. Skłaniały go do śmiechu albo aby pobudzić jego umysł i połaskotać serce poczuciem absurdu, mówiły coś tak głupiego, tak głupio, idiotycznie kretyńskiego – „och, popatrz, tatusiu, właśnie podarowałyśmy ci księżyc" – że na moment zapominał o ścianie i przez chwilę trzymał ten księżyc w dłoni.

KAŻDEGO WIECZORU O SZÓSTEJ zasiadał w salonie, żeby oglądać Waltera Cronkite'a w wiadomościach stacji CBS. Przygotowywał sobie trójwarstwowe kanapki z mortadelą, ogórkami konserwowymi, musztardą i papryką na chrupiącym chlebie z semoliny. Przed obiadem ssał twarde irysy, a srebrzyste opakowania po nich odkładał do miseczki z cukierkami, stojącej na okrągłym szklanym stoliku. Z natury był dosyć zażywny, lecz dzięki treningowi w marynarce zachował sprawność fizyczną – chociaż oglądając wiadomości na temat wojny Nixona, wyhodował brzuszek, który miał go wprowadzić w podeszły wiek.

– Agnes – odezwał się pewnego wieczoru, usiadłszy w nogach ich dużego łóżka z baldachimem. – Chyba już czas, żebym coś ze sobą zrobił.

– Co masz na myśli? – Nie uważała, żeby to ona powinna znaleźć mężowi jakieś zajęcie. Sądziła, że z tego powodu mógłby ją potem traktować niechętnie.

– Nie wiem – odparł.

Przerwała mycie zębów, wyszła z łazienki i usiadła na łóżku koło Eddiego. Szczotkowała zęby, nucąc pod nosem alfabet od A do Z i z powrotem, tak jak nauczono ją w dzieciństwie.

– Wpadniesz na jakiś pomysł – powiedziała. – Na razie jestem ci wdzięczna, że siedzisz tu z dziewczynkami.

– Naprawdę?

Skinęła głową.

– Oczywiście, Eddie. Naprawdę.

Prawie nigdy nie jedli owoców morza, a Agnes mogła sobie pozwolić na kupno rostbefu czy steków tylko co drugi tydzień. Patrząc jednak z szerszej perspektywy, czerwone mięso wydawało się jej czymś mało istotnym.

Eddie wyciągnął rękę, aby dotknąć czarnej koszulki żony. Wolała nosić raczej obcisłe koszulki. Kiedy jej dotknął, napięła mięśnie, lecz nie odsunęła się od niego. W pierwszym tygodniu po powrocie Eddiego do domu próbowali seksu, on jednak wszystko zepsuł. Może przez te prostytutki, z którymi sypiał w Olongapo. Chciał wierzyć, że seks z nimi nie sprawiał mu przyjemności i że te kobiety znaczyły dla niego niewiele więcej niż krótka chwila rozrywki, zasmakował jednak w swoich cielesnych grzechach.

– Nie dzisiaj – odezwała się Agnes. I przyciemniła światło lampki na swojej szafce nocnej.

– No to kiedy indziej.

Pobrali się szybko. I młodo. Eddie czasami myślał, że brakuje korka w ich butelce, wino mogło więc skwaśnieć i zamienić się w ocet.

KIEDY AGNES WYCHODZIŁA do pracy, nie wykonywał żadnych prac domowych ani nie zajmował się żadnymi obowiązkami; nie zbliżał się do koszy z brudną bielizną, którą należało wyprać, wysuszyć i poskładać, nie tykał listy zakupów i nie wychodził do sklepu za dnia, gdy mógł tam spotkać wygadane matki i rozwrzeszczane dzieci, nie odkurzał, nie zamiatał ani nie mył podłogi. Wynajdował sobie tylko takie zajęcia, które sprawiały mu frajdę.

Zbudował domek na drzewie, na sękatej brzozie na podwórku, i przyozdobił ją kawałkami drewna, znajdowanymi na śmietnikach i pustych parcelach. Wkładał grube rękawice robocze i przestrzegał dziewczynki: „Możecie patrzeć, ale niczego nie dotykajcie, bo inaczej będziecie musiały brać zastrzyki przeciwko tężcowi". Beverly i Claudia śmiertelnie bały się igieł. Jeśli wszyscy mieli na to ochotę, odgrywał z córkami przypadkowo wybrane sceny z *Rosenkrantz i Guildenstern nie żyją*, przeszukując stosy śmieci. Okoliczne dzieciaki przystawały, by gapić się na tego niedużego, brązowoskórego mężczyznę i jego córki, przypominające muchy, kiedy deklamowali razem coś, w jak im się wydawało, obcym języku.

– **A JAK TAM PROGNOZA** na dziś, Alfredzie? – krzyczał Eddie z ganku do swojego starego sąsiada, Alfreda Maddalone'a.

– Zachmurzenie z większymi przejaśnieniami.

Dziewczynki uczyły się bawić obręczą hula-hoop i skakać przez dwie krzyżujące się skakanki na krzywym chodniku, a Eddie i Alfred zabijali czas, wyzywając pojawiających się niekiedy w okolicy lumpów, którzy kradli sąsiadom telewizory, sedesy i lodówki Maytag. Przyjaciele stali na gankach swoich domków, mocno ściskając poręcze, rozgorączkowani niczym kibice bejsbola na Yankee Stadium. Bawili się w sędziego i ławę przysięgłych – wywoływali głośno wyroki, które miały zaprowadzić intruzów do więzienia Rikers Island, i grozili, że będą robić zdjęcia każdemu menelowi, który nie odstawi leżaka sąsiadów na miejsce. Złodzieje czasami im się rewanżowali. Soczysta wiązanka. Triumfalnie wyprostowany palec. Kilka zabłąkanych kamieni, które kiedyś o mało co nie uderzyły w głowę Claudii i Beverly. Pogróżki nocnych odwiedzin z koktajlami Mołotowa. Eddie i Alfred nigdy jednak nie ustępowali, żeby menele wiedzieli, że poniosą konsekwencje, jeśli włamią się do ich domów albo coś im podpieprzą.

Krążyły pogłoski, że Alfred ma związki z mafią, chociaż o ile Eddie wiedział, leciwy Włoch był czysty. Prowadził własną aptekę w bocznej uliczce, odchodzącej od Arthur Avenue, i potrafił wstać z łóżka o trzeciej rano dla brzemiennej młodej kobiety w uścisku porannych mdłości albo dla biednego wuja, męczącego się z kamieniami nerkowymi. Wkrótce po przejściu na emeryturę sprzedał aptekę, żeby sfinansować synowi studia.

– Przemów mojemu ojcu do rozumu – prosił Nicky Maddalone Eddiego. Nicky był już teraz wziętym dentystą na Madison Avenue i odwiedzał ojca w co drugą niedzielę. Powodziło mu się na tyle dobrze, że stać go było na wykupienie w metrze miejsca na reklamę swojego gabinetu stomatologicznego. Wylegiwali się czasem we trzech na ganku Alfreda, maczając biszkopty amaretto w mocnej czarnej kawie. – Mam duży dom w Nyack. Ojciec nie musiałby tego wszystkiego znosić. Popatrz, co oni zrobili z naszą dzielnicą. Ci Portorykańczycy, przecież to nie są ludzie. Zachowują się tak, jak gdyby wszystko wisiało im kalafiorem.

Eddie miał ochotę zapytać Nicholasa: „A kim jestem dla ciebie ja, jeżeli o tych Portorykańczykach mówisz «oni»? Asfaltem?”. W dzieciństwie razem z Nickym jedli gnocchi z jednej miski i ciągle wbiegali do domów swoich rodziców i wybiegali z nich, wszędzie roznosząc błoto i wielokrotnie niemal przyprawiając o zawał Bellę Maddalone, która trzy razy dziennie zamiatała i zmywała podłogę w kuchni. Chwalili się, które dziewczęta ze szkoły katolickiej Our Lady of St. Claremont's mieli ochotę wyobracać, chociaż wtedy musieli jeszcze sami dotykać swoich penisów.

– Zawsze są jacyś „oni" – stwierdził Eddie. – Mniej więcej co dziesięć lat pojawiają się nowi. O twoich dziadkach też kiedyś mówiło się „oni".

Maddalone'owie pochodzili z Puglii, z obcasa włoskiego buta. Opalali się latem na brązowo. Eddie powiedział to Nickowi po włosku, masakrując ten język, ale przyjaciel nie znał już języka swojego ojca. Jak teraz rozmawiać z Nickym?

Nicky dopił kawę.

– Chcesz, żebym podżyrował ci pożyczkę? Jak ty się stąd wyprowadzisz, to on też.

– Tu jest mój dom – stwierdził Eddie.

Nicky stanął na ganku. Wciąż prawie w każdą niedzielę robił zakupy na Arthur Avenue.

– Taa? I jak ci się tu powodzi? Wszyscy dobrzy ludzie już się stąd wynieśli. Nie został ani jeden.

W LETNIE WIECZORY, kiedy upał bijący z betonu, budynków i chodników nieco słabł i pojawiało się coś w rodzaju świeżego powietrza, Eddie uwielbiał wchodzić po drabinie do domku na drzewie ze swoją żoną i dziećmi i siedzieć tam z nimi w ciasnocie; wszyscy, wtuleni w siebie, mogli stamtąd bez przeszkód oglądać niebo nad Bronksem. W Wietnamie przybierało kolor wielkiego błękitu Morza Południowochińskiego i ze zdumiewającą łatwością zmieniało kształt.

Eddie zawsze zdawał sobie sprawę, że znajduje się na łasce natury: woda pod nogami i niebo nad głową. I odczuwał ulgę, że może wciąż liczyć gwiazdy i przebijać spojrzeniem smog w niektóre wieczory w Bronksie.

Zabrał dziewczynki do parku Crotona i wrzucił je do stawu. Beverly i Claudia szybko nauczyły się pływać. Kiedy Agnes zaczęła narzekać, że woda zmoczyła im warkoczyki, choć miały czepki pływackie, Eddie wzruszył ramionami.

– Nikt nie przygląda się topielcowi po to, żeby komentować jego fryzurę. Woda zabiera wszystko.

AGNES PIEKŁA CIASTA tylko od czasu do czasu: na urodziny, rocznice i święta był to obowiązkowo placek z batatów. Widziała na własne oczy, ile energii jej matki pochłaniało pieczenie, i już w młodym wieku pojęła, że może ono pochłonąć właściwie całe życie mężatki. Lecz kiedy zaczynała tęsknić za domem rodzinnym albo martwić się comiesięcznymi rachunkami, z szafek wyjeżdżały miski, sitka i miarki – robiła wtedy kruche ciasteczka lawendowe albo ciasto koliber, żeby udobruchać Eddiego i dziewczynki.

– Tatuś i jego koledzy są okropnie niemądrzy – szepnęła Beverly w niebieskiej kuchni. Klęczała na stołku przy kuchennym bufecie i patrzyła, jak matka drewnianym wałkiem rozwałkowuje lawendowe ciasto.

– Naprawdę? – zdziwiła się Agnes. Eddie ostatnio chyba nie miał za dużo kolegów. Raz czy dwa zachęcała go, żeby zadzwonił do swojego kuzyna, Jeba, poszedł na drinka z Nickym Maddalone'em albo z kumplami sprzed wojny, ale Eddie zawsze odpowiadał tak samo: „I na to przyjdzie pora". – A co ci mówił tatuś? – spytała pogodnym głosem. – O swoich znajomych?

– Mamusiu, ja to sama nigdy ich nie widziałam, ale jest takich dwóch białych, co śmiesznie mówią. Tatuś powiedział, że wychodzą ze ściany i rzucają w niego pieniążkami. Czasem je im odrzucamy.

Wieczorem przy kolacji Agnes była ożywiona i czuła dla Eddiego. Rano, zamiast pójść do pracy, pozałatwiała różne sprawy w mieście i wróciła do domu. Cichutko weszła do środka. Zastała męża i dziewczynki w kuchni. Siedziały na ustawionych na stole krzesłach, a Eddie stał na stole obok nich. Beverly trzymała w ręku tubę po papierowych ręcznikach – lunetę? – z kolei Claudia trzaskała dwiema pokrywkami od patelni. Dźwięczały jak dzwony weselne. Eddie zatoczył się do przodu, tupiąc w stół, który zachwiał się na boki niczym dinghy na morzu. Umocowane taśmą maskującą na sznurze do bielizny, między kuchennymi ścianami wisiały prześcieradła w grochy, tworzące jak gdyby fosę wokół stołu. Ze zlewu na linoleum wypływała woda. Na kuchni palił się gaz. Na wszystkich palnikach gotowała się woda.

– No i tak, panowie – powiedział Eddie, zerkając ponad kurtyną w stronę ściany. – Czasami trzeba zrobić swoje albo wypierdzielać.

– Nigdy, nigdy, nigdy! – krzyczały dziewczynki z brytyjskim akcentem. Ich związane w kucyki włosy kołysały się, nogi w sandałach tupały o stół, ręce opierały się na szczupłych biodrach.

– Jesteście tylko parą głupców. – Eddie wzruszył ramionami. – Na statku widmie.

– To Guildenstern jest głupi – powiedziała Claudia.

– Nie, Rosenkrantz – sprzeciwiła się Beverly.

– Ale Ros zawsze wygrywa! – pisnęła rozkosznie Claudia. Podskoczyła, odtańczyła krótki taniec i o mały włos nie spadła ze stołu.

– To tym się tu zajmujesz, kiedy ja przez cały dzień jestem w pracy, Eddie? – Agnes weszła do kuchni i kolejno pozakręcała kurki wszystkich palników gazowych, a potem wpatrzyła się w garnki pełne bulgoczącego wrzątku.

Eddie i dziewczynki zamarli.

– A co ty robisz w domu?

– Jeżeli mnie pamięć nie myli, to ja też tu mieszkam.

Eddie zeskoczył ze stołu. Rozejrzał się po kuchni i spróbował ją ogarnąć wzrokiem z punktu widzenia Agnes.

– Dziewczynki i ja po prostu... się bawiliśmy.

– To niebezpieczna zabawa. – Przymrużyła oczy. Musiała wiedzieć. Jak mogłaby nie wiedzieć?

– Myślałem, że mi ufasz.

– Beverly, Claudia, zejdźcie ze stołu i pomóżcie ojcu posprzątać ten bałagan – powiedziała Agnes. – Jest taka granica, po której przekroczeniu nie ufam nikomu, Eddie. Powinieneś wziąć ze mnie przykład w tym względzie. Najwyraźniej masz za dużo wolnego czasu.

Po raz pierwszy, odkąd się pobrali, pomiędzy Eddiem i Agnes zapanowała chłodna atmosfera. Nerwowy nastrój udzielił się dziewczynkom. Zaczęły się spierać o to, która z nich jest już za duża, żeby pić z plastikowego kubka, która oszukiwała w czasie gry w *Operację* i co się stało z główką Kena, ich lalki.

W NIEDZIELNE PRZEDPOŁUDNIA o jedenastej piętnaście Eddie chodził na mszę do katolickiego kościoła Our Lady of Claremont. Ponieważ Agnes i Claudia wolały komfort domu, kościół oznaczał, że Beverly miała Eddiego wyłącznie dla siebie. Ściskała ojca za rękę, kiedy mijali opuszczone domy piaskowego koloru, a on opowiadał jej różne historie o ludziach, którzy już tam nie mieszkali. W czasie mszy pozwalał córce nabierać wody święconej do małego plastikowego pojemniczka, żeby mogła w niej kąpać lalki Barbie. Zawartość naczyńka nazywali „perfumami z wody święconej".

W czasie przerwy na kawę ksiądz znalazł Eddiego w sali parafialnej. Przy kawie i wczorajszym cieście, które dostał od wiernych, powiedział:

– Dowiedziałem się, że szkoła Claremont poszukuje dozorcy. Z przyjemnością przyjęlibyśmy ciebie.

Eddie nigdy nie przyzwyczaił się do widoku swojego starego, który ciągnął za sobą mop i szczotkę do zamiatania. Do diabła, czy można mówić o awansie społecznym, jeśli on przyjmie teraz tę samą cholerną robotę?

– A co się stało z waszym poprzednim dozorcą? – spytał, nie chcąc po sobie pokazać, że jest zirytowany.

– Miał trudny charakter.

Eddie obgadał sprawę z Alfredem Maddalone'em.

– Nie umiał trzymać łap przy sobie – oświadczył pan Maddalone. – Przyłapali go, jak obmacywał jakąś dziewczynkę w schowku na środki czystości.

Eddie zaczął liczyć, co mógłby zrobić z dodatkowymi pieniędzmi. Poszłyby na rodzinne wakacje. Kiedy podzielił się nowiną z Agnes, przyniósł wielką mapę Stanów

Zjednoczonych i rozwinął ją w kuchni na składanym stole, który czasem pozostawiał mu zadrapania na skórze. Zakreślił wodospad Niagara i kempingi w górach Adirondack. W przyszłym roku może tama Hoovera albo Wielki Kanion? No i na pewno wycieczka do Waszyngtonu?

Agnes – która właśnie chowała mrożony groszek do lodówki i nalewała dziewczynkom zimne mleko do szklanek – zamarła. Beverly i Claudia musiały pić po szklance mleka dziennie. Bo dzięki twardym kościom można stać solidnie na dwóch nogach i jeśli trzeba, uciekać.

– Eddie... – Agnes wtuliła się w męża. – Nie chciałam wtedy powiedzieć, że ci nie ufam. Proszę cię, nie bierz tej pracy w szkole z mojego powodu.

Bardzo jej się nie podobało, że Eddie miałby zamienić jeden mundur na drugi. I musiała się starać, aby z niekorzyścią dla Eddiego nie porównywać go codziennie z Claude'em Johnsonem.

ZACZĄŁ WE WTOREK po Labor Day. Agnes ułożyła sobie plan dnia w taki sposób, by móc podrzucać dziewczynki do świetlicy, a zadaniem Eddiego było je odbierać. Nie jeździł do pracy w uniformie dozorcy, przychodził po prostu wcześniej, żeby zdążyć się przebrać w szatni dla personelu. Przed wyjściem zdejmował mundur, więc Claudia i Beverly widziały w nim przede wszystkim ojca.

Ten logistyczny plan działał na ogół bez zarzutu, ale czasami Agnes szła z kolegami i koleżankami z pracy – była zatrudniona w biurze planowania przestrzennego – na „happy hour". Zawsze witała Eddiego z uśmiechem, kiedy się spóźniał do domu. I z przyjemnością oglądała go w przyzwoitych spodniach, koszuli i loafersach.

W TYM SAMYM ROKU szkoła wynajęła artystę rezydenta, który miał wyreżyserować uczniowskie przedstawienie *Wieczoru Trzech Króli*. Nie licząc imponującej kolekcji kostiumów z wcześniejszych przedstawień, Barrett Bass przywiózł ze sobą angielski tweedowy garnitur i czarne skórzane buty sportowe, tak błyszczące i nowiutkie, że Eddie zaczął się rozglądać w poszukiwaniu krowy, z której skóry zostały wykonane.

ZAMIATAŁ SPRAWNIE I SZYBKO. Jeśli się sprężył i pracował w pocie czoła, godzina mijała mu czasem w piętnaście minut. A jeśli zaczynał na górze sześciopiętrowego budynku, to kończył w audytorium, gdzie Bass po południu prowadził próby z uczniami.

– Moi drodzy młodzi adepci rzemiosła Tespisa – powiedział Bass. – W tym momencie wasze zamiary nie mogą się powieść, mylicie bowiem dialekty i odchodzicie od czasów elżbietańskich, kierując się ku placom zabaw w Bronksie. Na scenie musimy się zbuntować przeciwko tym dialektom. To jedna z najczęściej wystawianych sztuk Shakespeare'a, postarajcie się więc rozluźnić języki i oddać sprawiedliwość sir Williamowi.

Eddie poszedł do biblioteki szkolnej i wypożyczył *Wieczór Trzech Króli*. Bibliotekarce – wolontariuszce i koordynatorce prac komitetu rodzicielskiego – wydało się to wzruszające.

DO CLAREMONT UCZĘSZCZALI głównie czarni i Portorykańczycy. Obchodząc wszystkie klasy, Eddie mógłby policzyć irlandzkich i włoskich uczniów na palcach jednej ręki. Wiele dzieci miało bliskich w Wietnamie albo gdzieś, gdzie mogli się ukrywać przed poborem do wojska. W przerwach pomiędzy sprzątaniem kabin w toaletach i opróżnianiem koszy na śmieci zawsze mówił uczniom dzień dobry i do widzenia. Polerując poręcz krętych schodów i zagipsowując kawałek sufitu w pokoju nauczycielskim, uczył się pod nosem na pamięć *Wieczoru Trzech Króli*. Dzieci zaczęły nazywać go suflerem. Wykrzykiwały dowolny wers ze sztuki, a Eddie recytował następną linijkę. Odnosił wrażenie, że teraz wykonuje te prace domowe, których oczekiwała od niego Agnes. Dezynfekował łazienki, sprzątał kuchnię dla personelu, czyścił stoły oraz krzesła w jadalniach. Roboty wystarczyłoby dla dwóch, ale nie narzekał.

PEWNEGO DNIA NA PRÓBIE czwartej sceny pierwszego aktu *Wieczoru Trzech Króli* z udziałem uczniów klas siódmych Gabriel Ruiz zapomniał swojego tekstu; próby trwały już od kilku tygodni, ale chłopak zawsze zacinał się w tej samej scenie.

DONNA JAKO WIOLA*

Jeśli to prawda, że całą jej duszę
Tak czarny smutek kirem swym osłonił,
Daremne będą wszystkie me błagania.

---

* Przekład Leona Ulricha.

GABRIEL JAKO KSIĄŻĘ ORSYNO

Zgwałć raczej wszystkie wprzód grzeczności prawa,
Nim do pałacu bez skutku powrócisz.

DONNA JAKO WIOLA

Przypuśćmy, książę, że dokażę cudu,
Że stanę przed nią, co mam jej powiedzieć?

GABRIEL JAKO KSIĄŻĘ ORSYNO

Opisz jej całą uczuć mych gwałtowność,
Zadziw ją mojej miłości potęgą;
Ust młodych powieść o moim cierpieniu
Łatwiejsze u niej znajdzie posłuchanie
Niż zimne słowa dojrzalszego posła.

DONNA JAKO WIOLA

Nie myślę, książę.

GABRIEL JAKO KSIĄŻĘ ORSYNO

Wierz mi, drogi chłopcze,
Bo kto by pragnął mężem cię nazywać,
Tylko by młode twe szkalował lata.
Twarz twoja gładka, usta koralowe,
Jak u Diany; głos dźwięczny i srebrny,
Jakby... ...z dziewicy... z dziewicy... co...? Co?

EDDIE NAPRAWIAŁ właśnie podłokietnik fotela, kiedy Gabriel zaczął rozglądać się za kimś, kto mógłby mu pomóc. Reżyser stał ze skrzyżowanymi na piersiach ramionami, przytupując niecierpliwie.

– „Jakby z gardziołka dziewicy wybiegał" – odezwał się dźwięcznym głosem Eddie z drugiego końca sali. – „I wszystko w tobie urok ma kobiecy: ty się rodziłeś na miłości posła. Weź z sobą czterech lub pięciu mych ludzi, zabierz i wszystkich, bo tylko samotny jestem szczęśliwy. Niech ci Bóg poszczęści, a całą pana twojego fortuną będziesz mógł wolno tak jak ja rozrządzać".

Barrett Bass roześmiał się i podszedł na środek sceny.

– No tak, ktoś tutaj jednak zna tekst. Może powinieneś zagrać w naszej sztuce?

Słyszał już o rozmiłowanym w Shakespearze dozorcy szkolnym.

– Muszę sprawdzić grzejnik. – Eddie zawsze jadał lunch w kotłowni, gdzie mógł zgłębiać swoje emocje i gadać do ścian, gdy stawał się nerwowy.

– Chodź, chociaż na chwilę czy dwie – powiedział z uśmiechem Barrett. – Bądź tak łaskaw.

Eddie ruszył czerwonym korytarzem, trzymając w dłoniach metalowe pudło z narzędziami. Nie wyszedł na środek sceny.

– Hej, Ruiz – zawołał, unikając kontaktu wzrokowego z Bassem. – Lubisz futbol?

– Nie. – Ruiz, który miał fryzurę afro i trądzik jak Michael Jackson, wzruszył ramionami. – Bejsbol.

– To nawet lepiej – powiedział Eddie. – Kiedy dialogi poplączą ci się w głowie, wyobraź sobie, że niesie je piłka bejsbolowa. Płyń razem ze słowami, a zapamiętasz więcej, niż zapomnisz.

Eddie wyszedł z audytorium i już do końca tygodnia unikał prób. Był to dla niego najbardziej przygnębiający okres w czasie pracy w Our Lady of Claremont. Godziny wlokły się jak gąsienice.

– **ILU LUDZI ZABIŁEŚ W WIETNAMIE?** – spytał Barrett.

Eddie, na klęczkach, zdrapywał łuszczącą się farbę z gzymsu w pokoju nauczycielskim. Dyrektor właśnie nalewał sobie kawę, a dwoje nauczycieli gawędziło ze sobą przy błękitnym pojemniku z wodą pitną.

Z początku zignorował pytanie. Ładował bomby do samolotów. Widział ludzi, którzy odlatywali, ale nie wracali. A tych, którzy wracali, czuć było czasem napalmem.

– Nie walczyłem na lądzie – odpowiedział.

– Ale zabijałeś? – naciskał Barrett.

– Pośrednio. – Eddie wstał. – Chociaż niewykluczone, że mam na koncie jednego zabitego własnoręcznie.

– Tylko jednego?

– Jeden to i tak dużo – odparł Eddie. – Jeden wystarczy.

W pokoju nauczycielskim zapadła cisza. Bass uśmiechnął się z powątpiewaniem. Jako doktorant uczestniczył w protestach antynuklearnych w Londynie, a jego nowoczesna interpretacja *Ryszarda III* wywołała nawet pewne poruszenie w Nowym Jorku i Edynburgu. Właśnie starał się o stanowisko zastępcy dyrektora artystycznego w nowym, dobrze zapowiadającym się teatrze off-Broadway.

Uśmieszek na jego pociągłej twarzy nie wkurzył Eddiego tak bardzo jak sam nauczyciel dramatu, który położył mu rękę na ramieniu takim gestem, jak gdyby chciał stamtąd strzepnąć niezauważony przez niego pyłek. I nie chodziło mu właściwie o to, że Barrett usunął z jego rękawa ten wyimaginowany paproch, ale o to, że dokładnie w tym samym momencie dyrektor i nauczyciele się zaśmiali. Nie motywowani okrucieństwem, lecz ze zdenerwowania, z powodu poczucia wyższości albo kierując się tym czymś, co każe ludziom zachowywać się nie tak, jak powinni. Eddie złapał za szczotkę, opartą o stojące bokiem szafki, i zaczął zamiatać. Najpierw podłogę wokół reżysera, bo pamiętał, że tak robiły jego matka i Bella Maddalone, kiedy był jeszcze dzieckiem. Zamiótł więc podłogę wokół Barretta, a potem przejechał szczotką po jego skórzanych butach. Jak gdyby próbował zamieść problem pod dywan. Zamiatanie nabrało dynamiki, na włosiu zbierał się kurz, a buty traciły połysk. Z każdym zamachem szczotki Eddiego Barrett robił krok w tył. Przy szóstym runął jak długi prosto na dupę.

Tym razem dyrektor i nauczyciele stłumili śmiech. W młodości Eddie lubił ładne buty i ubrania. Wydał małą fortunę na swoją garderobę, lecz teraz nosił antypoślizgowe oksfordy. Pochylił się i wyciągnął rękę do Barretta, żeby mu pomóc wstać, reżyser jednak kołysał się w lewo i prawo na twardej drewnianej podłodze.

– Kurwa jego mać, chyba złamałem nogę.

GDY NASTĘPNEGO RANKA Eddie stawił się w pracy, przed szatnią dla personelu czekał na niego dyrektor.

– Mamy szczęście, że Barrett nie chce wnieść skargi – powiedział.

– Ten gość to zwykły gnojek – odparł Eddie. Nie przebrał się jeszcze w uniform dozorcy. – No i co teraz będzie?

Dyrektor zaczerwienił się. Eddie zauważył, że blokuje mu wejście do szatni.

– W imieniu kościoła Saint Claremont's przykro mi, że musi do tego dojść. Ale my, nauczyciele i personel techniczny, powinniśmy świecić przykładem...

Eddie wsunął ręce do kieszeni i zabrzęczał drobnymi.

– Czy to oznacza, że nie zobaczę *Wieczoru Trzech Króli* na naszym szkolnym festiwalu tej zimy?

Dyrektor skinął głową.

– W świetle ostatnich wydarzeń muszę cię poprosić, żebyś darował sobie tę sztukę.

ALFRED MADDALONE pogadał z kuzynem, który pogadał z kolei ze swoim kuzynem, i Eddie wylądował na nowej posadzie, w kwiaciarni Ronaldo's House of Flowers na Arthur Avenue.

– Posłuchaj mnie teraz uważnie – ostrzegł go pan Maddalone. – Ci faceci są ustosunkowani, a niektórzy z nich dobrze się urządzili. Od żadnego z nich nie pożyczaj pieniędzy. Nie spoufalaj się z nikim. Pamiętaj, że nie jesteś ich przyjacielem. Będziesz nim jedynie na wesela, pogrzeby i chrzciny. A papier... papier dla ciebie po prostu nie istnieje. Nigdy nic nie zapisuj. Już niejednego bałwana załatwiono na cacy z powodu notatki, którą zlekceważył albo gdzieś posiał.

Kiedy Agnes spytała, na czym polega jego nowa praca, Eddie odpowiedział, że został zastępcą kierownika. Oboje zgodzili się, że jest to krok wzwyż w stosunku do stanowiska szkolnego dozorcy.

Na pierwszy rzut oka Ronaldo's House of Flowers nie sprawiała nazbyt imponującego wrażenia, ale jeśli popatrzyło się uważnie, można było zauważyć schody prowadzące na zaplecze kwiaciarni. Na piętrze mieściła się sycylijska restauracja o ścianach pokrytych freskami. Eddie był na górze tylko raz – zaniósł matce Ronalda, która pracowała jako szefowa kuchni, pudło importowanych rzymskich karczochów. Restauracja należała do tych zakładów gastronomicznych, które nie przyjmują rezerwacji.

Nad knajpą mieściła się szklarnia, gdzie Ronaldo przez okrągły rok hodował rośliny zielne i kwiaty. Trzy razy w tygodniu posyłał Eddiego na targowisko kwiatowe na Manhattanie, a Eddie odkrył, że ma nosa do najlepszych kwiatów i umie się targować o najniższe ceny. W piątki wracał do domu ze świeżymi różami dla Agnes i dziewczynek. Gdy przyszło lato, urządził sobie za domem ogródek, w którym zasadził bratki, fiołki, rozmaryn i koper włoski.

Był to spokojny okres dla Eddiego. Zaczął recytować *Rosenkrantza i Guildensterna* kwiatom, bo w kwiaciarni Ronalda nie było czasu, żeby gadać do ścian. Róże go rozumiały, a Eddiemu robiło się przyjemnie, kiedy wyhodowana przez niego roślina znajdowała nowy dom poza sklepem. Faceci w garniturach, którzy podjeżdżali tam cadillacami i lincolnami, uważali, że Eddie jest stuknięty, że jest głuptasem, półgłówkiem. Właściwie nie musiał nic robić, aby tak myśleli – wystarczyło, że miał czarną skórę, już tylko dlatego źle go oceniali.

W DRUGI WEEKEND CZERWCA Ronaldo's House of Flowers zasypał grad kul. Eddie miał na długo zapamiętać ten dzień, a w gazetach wspominano potem, jak bardzo zatłoczona była Arthur Avenue w owo gorące i parne sobotnie popołudnie; ludzie całymi rodzinami jedli obiad przy ulicznych stolikach albo robili weekendowe zakupy spożywcze. Eddie właśnie skończył polewać chodnik wodą z węża ogrodowego i obmywał ręce, kiedy ze sklepu wyszła grupa mężczyzn. Wiedział, że jednym z nich jest *capo*, na którego wszyscy mówili Sal – Salvatore Galliano. Jadał w restauracji Ronalda w każdą sobotę i co tydzień przystawał na ulicy, żeby podziwiać wystawione na chodniku kwiaty. Nigdy ich nie kupował, nawet dla żony i kochanek, które przywlekał tu czasami ze sobą. W tę sobotę Salvatore jednak zatrzymał się i zastanawiał, czy nie kupić rajskiego ptaka, czyli strelicji królewskiej.

– Ile? – zapytał Eddiego.

Ostatnio Ronaldo zaczął pozwalać Eddiemu obsługiwać kasę. Eddie wytarł ręce i podszedł do klienta.

– Po trzy dolary sztuka. Czterdzieści za cały bukiet.

Capo sięgnął do kieszeni po pieniądze i zaklął. Zostawił portfel na górze, obok talerzyka z drugą porcją sernika pistacjowego. Gestem nakazał jednemu ze swoich ludzi wrócić na piętro i przynieść portfel, gdy pod kwiaciarnię raptownie podjechał czarny sedan. Na chwilę, na ułamek sekundy, czas się zatrzymał. Z samochodu wysiadł facet w trzyczęściowym białym garniturze, a kule z pistoletu maszynowego, który trzymał w rękach, obsypały ludzi Salvatore'a, zanim zdążyli osłonić swojego szefa albo zacząć się bronić. Oczy Eddiego i zamachowca spotkały się. Czy mu się wydawało, czy był to czarny mężczyzna, czarny płatny zabójca, który nie mógł być o wiele starszy od Eddiego? Jak można wytłumaczyć jego reakcję? Dlaczego wydawało mu się, że to czarny? Dlaczego napełniły go zarazem duma i obrzydzenie, miłość i wstręt? Z wściekłości nie wiedział, co robić. Podskoczyła mu adrenalina. Wywrócił kwiaty, roztrącił je na lewo i na prawo, a padając na ziemię, pociągnął za sobą Salvatore'a Galliano, żeby i jego uchronić przed pociskami zabójcy.

– **JESTEM WETERANEM** – powiedział później Eddie, kiedy gliniarze i reporterzy naciskali, aby podał szczegóły strzelaniny. – Widziałem w życiu tyle dziwnych rzeczy, że czasami nie wiem, co się ze mną dzieje.

Odwrócił się gwałtownie od kamer i zaczął z ożywieniem rozmawiać ze zdziesiątkowanymi kwiatami. Dwie osoby zginęły na miejscu, lecz Salvatore Galliano nie odniósł najmniejszych obrażeń, a Eddie starał się, jak mógł, aby podkreślić, że nie jest świadkiem godnym zaufania. Jeżeli zostanie wezwany na rozprawę, sąd nie będzie miał z niego żadnego pożytku.

Pojawił się Alfred Maddalone, żeby pogratulować Eddiemu gwiazdorskiego występu.

– Sam bym lepiej nie zagrał takiej roli.

Po strzelaninie Ronaldo's House of Flowers zamknięto na cztery spusty na pół roku, a Eddie dostał sześć tysięcy dolarów odszkodowania. On i Agnes zgodzili się, że postąpiliby głupio, odmawiając przyjęcia pieniędzy za milczenie. Odłożyli je na czarną godzinę i wykorzystali na pokrycie kosztów mieszkania i wyżywienia Claudii na okres studiów w college'u.

GDY ALFRED MADDALONE wspomniał o możliwości innej pracy, Eddie przypomniał sobie powiedzenie, że Bóg pomaga tym, którzy sami sobie pomagają. W 1972 roku bezrobocie w Nowym Jorku wynosiło blisko jedenaście procent. Eddie zgłosił się raz, trzy, cztery razy do pracy w MTA, przedsiębiorstwie komunikacji miejskiej. Szesnaście miesięcy później zaczął pracować dla wydziału mostów i tuneli jako kasjer w budce opłat drogowych na moście Waszyngtona. Za dnia rzadko miał czas czytać *Rosenkrantz i Guildenstern nie żyją*, a wieczorami często był zbyt zmęczony, aby sięgnąć po tę niewielką książeczkę. Ze zmiennym szczęściem starał się zapomnieć o wojnie i młodszym chorążym, z większym powodzeniem próbował natomiast zakochać się znowu w Agnes. Czasami gadał przez sen. W ten sposób żona dowiadywała się o mężu pewnych rzeczy, którymi nie chciał się z nią dzielić, a o które ona nie zamierzała pytać. W budce kasjera Eddie trzymał niewielki stosik zapasowych monet. Ilekroć przez most przejeżdżał jakiś kierowca, któremu brakowało tylko trochę, żeby uiścić opłatę, Eddie podsuwał mu szybko kilka banałów: „Wie pan, że budowa tego mostu kosztowała sześćdziesiąt milionów dolarów? Ukończono go w 1931 roku. Niższemu poziomowi, no tak, nadano imię Marty Waszyngton, to całkiem zrozumiałe" – a potem uśmiechał się, machał ręką na znak, żeby kierowca jechał, i wrzucał monety ze swoich prywatnych zapasów do kasy, gdzie już leżały banknoty i inne drobne.

SEZON LETNI

1983

DO DOMU SĄSIADUJĄCEGO Z DOMEM HANKA I JEGO rodziców wprowadziła się w Memorial Day czarnoskóra rodzina. Nowi mieszkańcy przyjechali w popołudniowym zenicie; słońce grzało brutalnie, ale na szczęście w bardziej wielkodusznym nastroju był wiatr. Od strony Zatoki Meksykańskiej wiała chłodna bryza, goście mogli więc odetchnąć trochę od upału.

Ojciec Hanka, Charles Camphor, trzymał w ręku nowiuteńki zestaw kijów golfowych. Zamiast stali wybrał drewno, a mówiąc konkretnie, śliwę daktylową. Tłumaczył, w jaki sposób solidne drewniane szafty i główki wpływają pozytywnie na jego uderzenia. Pokazywał kije swojemu kuzynowi, Dużemu Seamusowi, ojcu Seamusa III. Kuzyni Camphorów przyjechali podziwiać dom Charlesa – wyglądający, jakby był z piernika – o pięciu sypialniach i trzech łazienkach, wyposażony w balkon z bogato zdobioną kratownicą, kryty ganek i automatyczne drzwi garażowe. Dom stał na jednym akrze ziemi w Sunset Beach, na zamkniętym wyspowym osiedlu w Buckner County w Georgii. Rosły tu majestatyczne wierzby płaczące i strategicznie rozsadzone jałowce oraz inne krzewy, które lepiej tłumiły odgłosy z obfitujących w zwierzynę bagien. Środowisko akustyczne było ciche za dnia, lecz aktywne nocą.

Krewni Camphora nie mogli ścierpieć tego, że ich kobiety zachwycały się specjalnie zainstalowanym przez gospodarza dla małżonki bidetem i profesjonalną kuchnią – z marmurowym blatem na środku – chociaż żona Charlesa nie potrafiła ugotować nawet ryżu. Barbara, czyli pani Camphor, wymknęła się rankiem z domu i pojechała do miasta, do Roadside Restaurant, prowadzonej przez panią Trudy, gdzie czarni kucharze nadal nosili przedwojenne uniformy, a podsufitowe wentylatory nie robiły nic, tylko zwiększały upał. Barbara wydała co najmniej pięćset dolarów na doskonałą ucztę: gumbo z okrą, czerwony ryż w stylu południowym, smażonego kurczaka, kiszony relish, kapustę sarepską, a pośród innych potraw także domową sałatkę ziemniaczaną. Nie miała dość chęci i wytrzymałości, aby samodzielnie przyrządzać smaczne dania, ale włożywszy je do odpowiednich naczyń, mogła przypisać wszystkie zasługi sobie.

Na grillu piekły się hamburgery i hot dogi. Reszta potraw od pani Trudy została wyłożona na drewniany stół piknikowy. Barbara wyszła na zewnątrz i stanęła obok męża. Zarówno ona, jak i Charles mieli niebieskie oczy i piaskowego koloru włosy, i oboje chętnie wystawiali się na słońce. Hank odziedziczył po nich urodę, ale jego włosy były raczej ciemne i pofalowane. Charles zbijał bąki ze swoimi kuzynami, a Barbara zrzuciła granatowe espadryle. W lecie 1983 roku takie buty były czymś w rodzaju wyznania wiary w modę, lecz pani Camphor nosiła je wyłącznie dla wygody. Nie musiała się przejmować modą. Wyglądałaby dobrze, nawet sprawiając ryby.

– Kto nauczył ją gotować jajka na twardo? – Kuzyni Charlesa i ich kobiety śmiali się i gadali.

– Kto ci powiedział, na czym polega różnica między tłuczonymi kartoflami i sałatką ziemniaczaną? – zapytała żona Dużego Seamusa.

Barbara popijała piwo z Milwaukee.

– Wasze pytania świadczą chyba o tym, że dobrze sobie poradziłam w kuchni.

Wracając od pani Trudy, przejeżdżała koło ich dawnego domu w centrum. Nie był na tyle duży, by mogli w nim przyjmować rodzinę Charlesa, i całe szczęście. Za jej młodych lat rodzice, robotnicy w browarze Pabsta, często zapraszali do siebie znajomych i rodzinę pod wpływem nagłego impulsu. Wszyscy wiedzieli, że przekraczając próg, powinni trzymać swoje ambicje na wodzy. Przychodzili w gości, bo mieli ochotę, a zostawali na dłużej, ponieważ towarzystwo było sympatyczne, brakowało w nim jednak poczucia jedności. Barbara uwielbiała swoją nową chatę, tęskniła jednak za intymnością mieszkania w kamienicy.

Przyjęła rolę gospodyni i krążyła po ogródku, hojnie nalewając drinki krewnym Charlesa, bo przecież po to tak naprawdę przyszli: na darmowy posiłek i alkohol jej męża. Nie wiedzieli, że poprzedniego wieczoru Barbara poprzelewała najlepszą whisky, bourbona, wódkę i gin do karafek, butelki napełniła natomiast tanią gorzałą, którą właśnie żłopali. Pomagał jej Hank; uwielbiał asystować matce, kiedy robiła kuzynów ojca w trąbę. W sezonie letnim była to jedna z największych przyjemności dla matki i syna.

Śmiali się wszyscy i miło spędzali czas, gdy jeden z kuzynów Charlesa – chudzielec o spojrzeniu sokoła wędrownego – zapytał:

– Kto mieszka obok was?

– Aktualnie nikt – odparł Charles. Kiedy przed dziewięcioma miesiącami kupili z Barbarą swoją posiadłość, żółty wiktoriański dom, ozdobiony wierzbą płaczącą przed wejściem, stał pusty.

– Niezły masz ten domek. – Przypominający sokoła kuzyn zmierzył spojrzeniem dom Charlesa od góry do dołu. – Dobrze zarabiasz, co?

Charles spojrzał na Barbarę: był to właśnie ten kuzyn, którego mu radziła nie zapraszać. Jest taki w każdej rodzinie. „Charles, kochanie, ty jesteś dla nich za dobry. Niektórzy ludzie zawsze będą głodni – ostrzegała go Barbara. – Nawet po sutej uczcie".

– Powiedzmy, że cena była przyzwoita. – Charles szturchnął ciekawskiego krewniaka w żebra twardą główką kija golfowego. I wszyscy się zaśmiali.

Dokładnie w tym momencie cichą ulicą nadjechała ciężarówka firmy przeprowadzkowej i wturlała się na podjazd sąsiedniego żółtego wiktoriańskiego domu. Za ciężarówką przyjechał sekstet czarnych w srebrzystym volvo.

– Powiedz mi, że nie widzisz tego samego co ja – odezwał się sokół wędrowny, a pozostali kuzyni gospodarza ryknęli okrutnym i rubasznym śmiechem, który miało odziedziczyć ich potomstwo i wykorzystywać w dorosłym życiu.

Charles stanął jak wryty; nie poruszały się też jego nowiutkie kije. Zareagował dopiero Duży Seamus.

– Cisza – rzucił. – Nie chcecie chyba, żeby nowi sąsiedzi Charlesa wzięli nas za prostaków.

Hank przypomniał sobie tę sympatyczną uwagę, kiedy trzydzieści lat później sprzedawał posiadłość rodziców Dużemu Seamusowi.

Nowi sąsiedzi wyłonili się ze srebrzystego volvo i ruszyli do wejścia swojego nowego domu. Przez chwilę wydawało się, że czarnoskóra matka rzuca spojrzenie w stronę ogrodu Camphorów, chociaż Hankowi mogło się to przywidzieć. Miała na sobie świeżo wyprasowaną niebieską letnią sukienkę, a na nogach granatowe espadryle, dokładnie takie same jak mama Hanka, tyle tylko że obcasy butów nowej sąsiadki były wyższe o dwa albo trzy cale. Szła u boku męża, a za nią podążało czworo dzieci: najpierw filigranowa nastolatka o kręconych włosach do ramion, wystrojona w powiewającą dumnie z każdym krokiem fioletową sukienkę w tureckie wzory. Przy prawej nodze dziewczyny dreptał niski basset o obwisłych uszach, a za tą dwójką szedł chłopak ostrzyżony na jeża i w okularach. Hank, który niedawno skończył trzynaście lat, domyślał się, że okularnik jest mniej więcej w jego wieku. Na końcu kroczyła para pulchnych bliźniąt, które wysiadły z samochodu na końcu. Chłopiec i dziewczynka, mogli mieć po cztery albo pięć lat. Byli w letnich marynarskich ubrankach, tak jak ich ojciec, Reuben Applewood, niedawno emerytowany kapitan Marynarki Wojennej Stanów Zjednoczonych.

Hankowi przyszła na myśl rodzina kaczek krzyżówek z książeczki dla dzieci, którą uwielbiał w przedszkolu, *Make Way for Ducklings*. Ci ludzie byli nawet mniej więcej tego samego koloru co kaczki, brakowało im tylko zielonych obwódek na szyjach. Krzyżówki tracą je na pewien czas, kiedy raz w roku zrzucają pióra. Nie mogą też wtedy fruwać.

– Ciężko się narobiłam, żeby to wszystko ugotować – powiedziała Barbara, odciągając wzrok rodziny męża od nowych sąsiadów. – Prawda, Hank, skarbie? No to może przenieśmy wszystko do środka, zanim upał zaszkodzi jedzeniu i nam. Zatrucia pokarmowego wystarczy dostać raz w życiu, żeby go więcej nie chcieć. Rano mam samolot, ale wy wszyscy będziecie mogli sobie siedzieć w klimatyzowanym wnętrzu i spić mi męża tak, że straci dom i rodzinę.

Rano na lotnisku Buckner County Barbara pocałowała Charlesa niemal zbyt namiętnie, zanim wsiadła na pokład.

– Tylko nie rób nic, czego ja bym nie zrobiła. – Leciała do Atlanty na regionalną konferencję Czerwonego Krzyża.

– Poczekam, aż wrócisz, mała. – Charles delikatnie poklepał Barbarę po pośladkach.

Cofnęła się i nawinęła lok włosów Hanka na palec. Zdarzało się, że przeczesywała palcami jego lśniącą czarną grzywę i mówiła: „Czas popływać, mały".

– Synku – odezwała się. – Spróbuj nie rosnąć za duży.

HANK PRZEZ TRZY DNI szpiegował syna sąsiadów, czekając na okazję, kiedy naturalną koleją rzeczy będzie mógł mu powiedzieć „hej" albo „cześć". Grube szylkretowe oprawki okularów, które nosił chłopiec, nadawały jego twarzy surowy i poważny wygląd. Hank sądził, że myśli zawsze wyprzedzały nowego o dwa kroki i że był na nie wściekły, bo nie chciały go słuchać (znał to uczucie aż za dobrze z autopsji; nawiedzało go zwłaszcza wtedy, kiedy jego matka wyjeżdżała).

W końcu spotkał kolegę w drodze do domu z lekcji żeglarstwa w Sunset Beach Country Club. Jego nowy sąsiad wyszedł na spacer z bassetem o obwisłych uszach.

– Nie boisz się, że ci wyleci na ulicę? – spytał Hank. Basset dreptał bez smyczy o kilka jardów przed chłopcem, rozpaczliwie węsząc w poszukiwaniu sekretów, jakie mógł zdradzić mu chodnik.

– Tipper sam umie przechodzić przez ulicę – odpowiedział chłopak. – Poza tym w zaułku nie ma dużego ruchu.

– Ty go wytresowałeś? – spytał Hank i nagle poczuł się jak kretyn.

– Nie, to właściwie jest pies mojej siostry. W gruncie rzeczy nie obchodzi go nikt poza Lonnie.

– No to dlaczego ty chodzisz z nim na spacery?

– Bliźniaki są absolutnie niepocieszone. Jak są bez humoru, nie lubię być z nimi w domu.

Hank już miał się zaśmiać z wyniosłości chłopaka, ale się powstrzymał.

– Jestem Hank – powiedział swobodnie.

– Huck?

– Nie, Hank... Jak Hank Williams. – Zaczął jodłować.

– To muzyka country – stwierdził nowy, cofając się jakby z pogardą i wyjmując z kieszeni koszuli kostkę Rubika. Obrabiał ją zwinnie, obracał w dłoniach, uporządkował sześciany żółte, zielone, białe i niebieskie, a na końcu próbował ułożyć czerwone.

– A co jest złego w muzyce country? – spytał Hank, zauważając, że sportowe buty od Chucka Taylora, które nosił chłopak, są jak gdyby lekko wygięte do wewnątrz. Syn sąsiadów miał szpotawe stopy.

– Nic. Ale tutaj ludzie grają ją cały czas. – Chłopiec najwidoczniej zorientował się, że Hank się gapi na jego stopy, bo skierował teraz ich palce na zewnątrz. I po raz pierwszy przyjrzał się Hankowi. – Niektóre utwory Elvisa Costello są jakby trochę country. A jego lubię.

– Ja też – odparł Hank z ulgą, że znaleźli wreszcie wspólny język.

– A lubisz Blondie? – spytał chłopak.

Hank skinął głową.

– The Pretenders?

Hank znowu przytaknął.

– Pink Floydów?

– Aha. – Hank wyjął ręce z kieszeni szortów. Nagle poczuł się o wiele pewniejszy siebie. – Lubię też Queenów i Black Sabbath.

Chłopiec stracił zainteresowanie kostką Rubika.

– No. – Wzruszył ramionami. – Tylko czy Freddiemu uda się kiedyś zaśpiewać coś lepszego niż *Bohemian Rhapsody*? Ja mam na imię Gideon...

Podniósł rękę, żeby Hank przybił mu piątkę. Hank miał dopiero trzynaście lat, ale mierzył już pięć stóp i osiem cali wzrostu, a przed studiami miał urosnąć jeszcze o osiem cali. Gideon, którego nogi wciąż czekały, by dogonić resztę ciała, ledwie sięgał Hankowi do ramienia.

Chłopcy dwa razy przeszli ulicę do końca, tam i z powrotem, poprzedzani przez Tippera. Kiedy przystanęli, znów znajdowali się przed domem Gideona. Jego siostra czytała na ganku czasopismo „Teen Beat". Na widok Lonnie Tipper pognał po schodkach na werandę. Lonnie odłożyła magazyn i schowaną za nim książkę, po czym pocałowała psa w nos. Kręcone włosy miała upięte w kok jak baletnica. Była w różowej sukience plażowej i sandałkach.

– Ona chyba naprawdę lubi „Teen Beat" – zauważył Hank, który przez ostatnie trzy dni podglądał Lonnie, kiedy siedziała na ganku i czytała.

– Nie daj się nabrać. Za tym pisemkiem może kryć się wszystko. Anaïs Nin. Colette. D.H. Lawrence. Wszystkie *exotica*, jakie mogła znaleźć w biurku matki.

– Myślisz, że Anaïs Nin też by mi się spodobała?

– Lepiej zostań przy Black Sabbath. A poza tym kto mówi, że Lonnie lubi te książki? Chce po prostu mieć coś do roboty. A tutaj nie ma co robić.

– To nieprawda – odrzekł Hank, który nagle poczuł, że powinien bronić swojej dzielnicy. – W klubie można żeglować. Grać w tenisa. W ogóle mają tam różne zajęcia dla różnych grup wiekowych. Można pływać albo wziąć rower i pojeździć, są ścieżki rowerowe. A w soboty wieczorem wyświetlają filmy na wolnym powietrzu.

– W końcu wybierzemy się do tego klubu – powiedział Gideon. – Na razie ja mam tę kostkę, a Lonnie swoje egzotyki.

Hankowi nie spodobało się, w jaki sposób Gideon wymówił słowo „egzotyki". Nie podobało mu się też, jak wypowiedział „absolutnie niepocieszone". Właściwie nie był pewien, czy Gideon w ogóle przypadł mu do gustu.

A Gideon znów oplótł palcami kostkę Rubika, obracając ją i przesuwając w dłoniach.

Hank ponownie zainteresował się siedzącą na werandzie Lonnie.

– Wygląda na bardzo nadętą, choć jednocześnie uroczą.

– Tylko niech ci nie przyjdą do głowy żadne głupie pomysły. Lonnie zostanie kiedyś chirurgiem. Mówi, że aby zrozumieć anatomię człowieka, trzeba najpierw zrozumieć namiętność. Która zarówno buduje, jak i niszczy. Na przykład ludzkie ciało.

– Możesz powtórzyć, ile ona ma lat?

Gideon wsunął kostkę z powrotem do kieszeni koszuli.

– Chciałbyś kiedyś do mnie przyjść? – zapytał.

– Jasne – odparł Hank.

– To fajowo. – Gideon wszedł do domu, nie oglądając się za siebie.

WIECZORAMI TIPPER wychodził z domu przez specjalne kuchenne drzwiczki dla psów i wył. Hank myślał, że zwierzak tęskni za swoim dawnym domem, jak Lonnie i Gideon, a potem przypomniał sobie, że nawet nie zapytał Gideona o to, gdzie stał ich poprzedni dom.

– To kwestia rasy – stwierdził Charles. Hank i jego ojciec oglądali w ogródku nocne niebo. – Psy myśliwskie mają to we krwi, muszą skomleć i wyć. Oczywiście moim zdaniem to tak naprawdę nie jest pies myśliwski, jest zbyt przysadzisty. Taki pies nie nadaje się w ogóle do niczego, wywołuje najwyżej efekt komiczny.

– Tato... – Hank starannie dobierał słowa. – Tak sobie pomyślałem, że może ten nowy chłopak, co teraz mieszka obok, mógłby do nas przyjść?

– Nie, synu, chyba nie.

– Dlaczego?

Charles usiadł na leżaku. Piastował funkcję pierwszego wiceprezesa w banku S&S. Nie była to aż tak wymagająca pozycja, jak mógłby sugerować ten tytuł, podlegał jednak pewnym naciskom. W latach osiemdziesiątych XX wieku ludzie, którym od dawna brakowało pieniędzy, spostrzegli, że zachodzą pewne zmiany. Była to epoka prezydenta Reagana, a Ronald Reagan uważał, że są takie rzeczy, które państwo powinno oddać szaremu człowiekowi, aby nie pozostawał szary nazbyt długo. Charles widział, jak w okresie prezydentury Reagana wyspa dynamicznie się rozwija. Osobiście dawał zielone światło na budowę wielu nowych domów. Miał zdrowego syna i dom o pięciu sypialniach. I żonę, która tak bardzo lubiła pomagać ludziom, że nie chciała siedzieć w tym domu, więc to on musiał wszystko tłumaczyć synowi, pouczać go, co i jak.

– Naszych posesji nie dzieli ogrodzenie. Możecie się spotkać w altance i gadać, ile chcecie.

– Ale na dworze jest upał.

– W altance masz dużo cienia.

– Tato, będzie dziwnie, jak on mnie zaprosi do siebie, a potem się okaże, że nie może przyjść do nas.

– Są tu też inni chłopcy. To nie jest dobry czas na takie spotkania.

– Dlaczego? Przecież mamy wakacje.

Ojciec uśmiechnął się do syna. Charles miał miły uśmiech, który kiedy kończył się dzień pracy w banku, zajmował połowę jego twarzy.

– Nawet nie zanieśliśmy im powitalnego poczęstunku – stwierdził Hank. – Kiedy my się tu wprowadziliśmy, sąsiedzi już pierwszego dnia przynieśli nam coś do jedzenia na powitanie.

– I twoja matka wszystko wyrzuciła. Wiesz, jak ona podchodzi do kalorycznych potraw. Mieszkamy w jedynym domu w Ameryce, w którym nie znajdziesz nawet najmniejszego słoika z majonezem.

– No to się jej zapytam. Zapytam mamę.

– Zrób to – odpowiedział Charles, zamykając oczy. – Poczęstunek na parapetówkę przygotowują i zanoszą kobiety.

– Nie chodziło mi o poczęstunek, tylko o Gideona.

Oczy Charlesa Camphora pozostały zamknięte. Hank nie wiedział, czy ojciec zasnął, czy uparł się puścić jego słowa mimo uszu.

TEJ NOCY HANK leżał na górnej pryczy piętrowego łóżka, machał nogami, które zwieszały się znad jego krawędzi, i fantazjował o siostrze swojego nowego znajomego. Gideon powiedział, że Lonnie czyta egzotyki, więc Hank, wróciwszy do domu, odszukał słowa „egzotyczny”, „egzotyk” i „egzotyka” w kieszonkowym słowniku.

> EGZOTYCZNY: 1. właściwy krajom o całkowicie odmiennym klimacie i cywilizacji; cudzoziemski, obcy,

zamorski. 2. *rzad.* niecodzienny, niezwykły, ciekawy, osobliwy.

EGZOTYK: przedmiot lub wytwór mający cechy egzotyczne.

EGZOTYKA: ogół cech właściwych krajom o całkowicie odmiennym klimacie i cywilizacji; wprowadzenie tych cech do poszczególnych dziedzin sztuki; przedmioty, wytwory mające takie cechy; odrębność, obcość, egzotyzm.

Chciał powiedzieć Gideonowi, że wcale nie jest taki niewinny, jak mu się wydaje. Charles Camphor trzymał w piwnicy imponującą kolekcję pornografii. Hank nie zawsze dobierał się do filmów wideo, bo go za bardzo wciągały i zbyt łatwo tracił poczucie czasu, patrząc, jak Seka robi komuś laskę albo jak ktoś ją rżnie w tyłek. Ale jeśli chodzi o „Playboya", „Hustlera" i „Penthouse'a", zajmował się nimi co miesiąc. Wyrobił sobie własny światopogląd, przeglądając „Penthouse Forum" Boba Guccione'a (interesowały go biogramy i komentarze polityczne). Po skończonej lekturze rozpinał spodnie, układał zdjęcia tak, jak mu się danego dnia podobało, i onanizował się przy muzyce Black Sabbath.

ZANIM BARBARA CAMPHOR poleciała na swoją konferencję – kiedy kuzyni jej męża wszyscy już sobie poszli i zostawili ich samych, żeby posprzątali – Hank podsłuchał, jak matka mówi do ojca:

– Charles, mam szczęśliwą waginę. Nie uda ci się jej zasmucić.

Gdyby szczegóły tej rozmowy nie były tak osobiste, Hank może opowiedziałby o niej Gideonowi. Albo jeszcze lepiej, mógłby zapytać Lonnie Applewood: „Co czyni waginę szczęśliwą?". A dziewczyna niewątpliwie dałaby mu za to pytanie po gębie. Następnego ranka stanął więc twarzą w twarz z matką.

– Czy ty i tata jesteście ze sobą szczęśliwi?

Barbara akurat myła zęby. Jej samolot odlatywał za dwie godziny.

– Hank, skarbie, kiedy złapałam Charlesa, to tak jak gdybym wygrała na loterii.

– Mamo...

– Tak, słucham cię, synku... Masz jakieś kłopoty? Dlaczego o to pytasz?

– Wydawało mi się, że wczoraj się kłóciliście.

Mama spłukała szczoteczkę, zaczęła nakładać makijaż na twarz. Zdaniem Hanka była taka ładna, że nie potrzebowała ani jednego, ani drugiego.

– Powinieneś zacząć się niepokoić, jak przestaniemy się kłócić.

– Czyli nie będzie rozwodu?

– Hank... – Barbara pokazała zęby w uśmiechu. – Ludzie są z natury leniwi. Rozwodzą się dlatego, że za mocno albo za słabo dostosowują się do swoich partnerów. A w małżeństwie każdy powinien płynąć własnym kursem.

Nie zadzwoniła jednak potem do domu przez trzy najbliższe dni, od momentu wyjazdu do Atlanty. Po raz pierwszy wyjechała, nie pozostawiwszy żadnego liściku, i nie dowiadywała się, co słychać u Hanka i Charlesa.

W DOMU GIDEONA pachniało imbirem. Na blacie w szklanym naczyniu do pieczenia leżało trójwarstwowe ciasto kokosowe z tym kandyzowanym korzeniem. Gideon lubił kawałki ananasa w cieście, ale Lonnie była na niego uczulona, więc ananas nie miał wstępu do ich domu.

– Jak w czasie ferii zimowych pojechaliśmy na Turks i Caicos, wypiła napój z sokiem ananasowym i dostała skurczu krtani. Teraz nie rusza się nigdzie bez benadrylu.

Hank zauważył, że Gideon podsuwa mu różne informacje o siostrze niczym marchewkę, a potem rozsiada się i patrzy, czy połknął przynętę.

Rezydencję Applewoodów urządzono komfortowo, w fotelach i na kanapach można się było utopić. Wszędzie były książki, od podłogi po sufit – aż się wysypywały z wbudowanych w ściany półek, pozostawionych przez poprzednich właścicieli. W trakcie pierwszej wizyty Hank widział mamę Gideona tylko raz. Była w pokoju dziecinnym, zajęta bliźniakami, a Gideon i Hank spędzili większość czasu w pokoju rekreacyjnym. Hank zatopił zęby w drugiej porcji ciasta kokosowego, z radia ryczała *Another Brick in the Wall* Pink Floydów, a Gideon – który jak już zdążył zauważyć Hank, nie lubił bezruchu – podskakiwał do taktu. Nie tańczył, tylko skakał. A zamiast wrzucać ćwierćdolarówki do flipera, wymierzał maszynie siarczyste uderzenie za każdym razem, kiedy chciał ją włączyć albo rozegrać kolejną partię. Pokój rekreacyjny był najbardziej chaotycznym pomieszczeniem, hałasowały tu gramofon i ten automat, wszędzie walały się całe góry zabawek, nawet rowery; natomiast na widok owiniętego termokurczliwą folią aksamitnego stołu bilardowego Hank oblał się rumieńcem, bo doznał nagłej pornograficznej wizji z udziałem Lonnie.

– Skąd masz ten automat?

– To łapówka.

– Nie pieprz głupot.

– Powaga. Tata właściwie kupował nam różne rzeczy za to, żebyśmy zgodzili się tu przeprowadzić. Albo, albo...

– Inaczej musiałby się liczyć z tym, że będziecie „absolutnie niepocieszeni".

Gideon uniósł brew.

– Coś w tym rodzaju.

– A co obiecał Lonnie?

– Że w czasie ferii zimowych pojedziemy do Nowego Jorku i zwiedzimy wszystkie tamtejsze placówki kulturalne.

– Pewnie tęsknicie za swoimi kolegami i koleżankami. W Ohio.

Gideon uśmiechnął się, a jego uśmiech przybrał uniwersalny wyraz okrucieństwa – które w końcu dopada kiedyś każdego.

– A ty masz tutaj jakichś kolegów, Hank?

CHARLOTTE APPLEWOOD BYŁA nauczycielką gimnazjalną i miała wrócić do pracy w pełnym wymiarze godzin po Labor Day. Już pobieżny przegląd wyników nowych podopiecznych potwierdził jej obawy przed powrotem na Południe. Rok szkolny zapowiadał się długi i męczący. Uparła się, że będzie teraz poświęcała czas bliźniakom, bo kiedy znów zacznie się szkoła, nie zawsze znajdzie czas i siły, żeby się nimi zająć. Nie umiała gotować ani piec, podobnie jak Barbara, i dlatego ciotka Charlotte, lady Miller, szefowa piekarzy w piekarni Gottlieb's, posyłała Applewoodom czekoladowe ciasteczka, obsypane rodzynkami pierniczki imbirowe i wszystkie inne ciasta, których wypiekanie podsuwała jej wena co kilka dni. Wierzyła kiedyś w kłamstwo głoszące, że córki nigdy nie odchodzą za daleko od rodzinnego domu, dlatego mocno się rozczarowała, widząc, że jej siostrzenica, Charlotte, wróciła do Buckner County, a córka, Agnes, została na Północy.

– Mamy 1983 rok. Świat się zmienił – lubiła mawiać lady Miller w ciche wieczory, kiedy telefonowała siostrzenica, aby pomarudzić, że wolałaby wrócić do Ohio. Charlotte chodziła na zebrania trzech różnych grup wsparcia dla matek w Buckner County, ciągle wyczuwała jednak wokół siebie jakieś złe moce, coś, czego nie potrafiła dokładnie określić, a co sprawiało, że chciałaby, jak dawni osadnicy, poustawiać powozy w krąg: żeby chronić dzieci.

Zaraz po powrocie męża z pracy powiedziała mu, że Gideon ma nowego kolegę. I że są w pokoju rekreacyjnym.

– Wychodziłaś dziś z domu? – spytał Reuben Applewood, który właśnie został dziekanem w słynnym murzyńskim college'u Buckner County.

– Pojechałam do miasta. Zabrałam bliźniaki na spacer po parku Roberta E. Lee.

– To miałaś masę roboty. Dlaczego po prostu nie pojechałaś do klubu?

Charlotte rytmicznie unosiła kolana, na których siedziały bliźniaki.

– Nie mieszkamy już w Shaker Heights, Reubenie, więc powiem to tylko raz. Ze względu na dobro ciał i dusz moich dzieci nie puszczę do tego klubu żadnego z nich.

– Charlotte, dzieci muszą chodzić dalej na lekcje pływania. Pływają już przyzwoicie, ale nie tak dobrze, żeby się uratować, gdyby wypadły z łodzi na pełnym morzu. Chcę, żeby czuły się bezpiecznie, kiedy zaczną uczęszczać na kurs żeglarski.

– No tak. – Charlotte wzruszyła ramionami. – W takim razie będą musiały jeździć do centrum, do YMCA, i pluskać się tam z elementem chuligańskim.

W SHAKER HEIGHTS, miasteczku pod Cleveland w stanie Ohio, o liberalnej i dobrze zżytej społeczności Gideon Applewood pozostawił to, co następuje:

1. Najlepszego kolegę.
2. Domek na drzewie (który zbudował mu ojciec na szóste urodziny).
3. Czerwoną przeglądarkę View-Master, którą podarował młodszemu braciszkowi swojego najlepszego kolegi (wszędzie włóczącemu się za nimi).
4. Mleczne koktajle u Tommy'ego.
5. Hot dogi posmarowane grubo chili con carne.
6. Indian z Cleveland i hot dogi ze stadionu bejsbolowego, posmarowane grubo chili con carne i stadionową musztardą.
7. Panią Frost, nauczycielkę angielskiego z siódmej klasy, która masakrowała jego wypracowania czer-

wonym flamastrem, zawsze dodawała jednak w nawiasie: „Bądź sobą, Gideonie, i mądry jak dotąd".

8. Longplay zespołu The Pretenders z 1979 roku, który Gideon zostawił na podłodze w swoim pokoju.
9. Schowany w kopercie tej płyty list miłosny od Cassidy, pierwszej dziewczyny, która go pocałowała.
10. Numer telefonu na odwrocie listu od niej. Uknuli razem zwariowany plan ucieczki do Vancouver, a częścią planu były plecaki, autostop i podróż powozami mennonitów.
11. Pogróżki, że rzuci się pod koła samochodów na Highway 77, jeśli jego rodzice nie zawrócą po płytę The Pretenders.

Wiele lat później, w 1990 roku, w czasie tonącego w serpentynach marszu w centrum Manhattanu na cześć zwolnionego właśnie z więzienia Nelsona Mandeli, Gideon i jego pierwsza dziewczyna spotkali się przypadkowo, opuścili tablice z napisem „Wolność dla Afryki Południowej" i odłączyli się od tłumu. Wykonywali skoczne ruchy, kołysali głowami i pochylali się do przodu i w tył siłą energii tego dnia oraz z uwielbienia dla Chrissie Hynde i jej zespołu, The Pretenders.

– Jestem lesbijką – szepnie Cassidy.

– To spoko – odpowie Gideon. – A ja gejem.

BARBARA WRÓCIŁA do domu w pierwszą niedzielę czerwca i przywiozła prezenty: skrzynkę aromatyzowanego brzoskwiniami piwa dla męża i czerwoną lampkę rowerową, z wygrawerowanym z boku symbolem drużyny futbolowej

Georgia Bulldogs, dla Hanka. Po obiedzie, którego głównym daniem był granik z rusztu, rodzice Hanka poszli do sypialni i zostawili syna przed telewizorem, żeby mógł oglądać wakacyjne powtórki serialu *M*A*S*H*. Wyszli z pokoju pod koniec drugiego odcinka i rozłożyli się na kanapie w salonie. Oboje mieli na sobie świeże ubrania, a Barbara położyła głowę na kolanach Charlesa.

Hank siedział na podłodze. Wyłączył telewizor i spojrzał na rodziców.

– A kiedy pojedziemy na wycieczkę kulturalną?

– Wycieczka kulturalna! – Barbara usiadła i ziewnęła. – Jaki dobry pomysł. Dlaczego ja na to nie wpadłam?

Mąż pogłaskał Barbarę po głowie. Jej włosy pachniały szamponem Sea Breeze, papierosami i może odrobinę marihuaną.

– Barb – powiedział. – Znowu zaczęłaś palić?

– Hank, skarbie – ziewnęła raz jeszcze Barbara. – Jaką konkretnie wycieczkę masz na myśli?

– No, pomyślałem, żeby może skoczyć do Nowego Jorku. W czasie ferii zimowych.

– Wiesz, że to jest czas dla rodziny w naszym domku w lesie, synu – odezwał się Charles.

Barbara uśmiechnęła się do męża.

– W MoMA mają van Gogha, Charles. Nie sądzisz, że Hank powinien zobaczyć *Gwiaździstą noc*?

Charles pociągnął łyk szkockiej.

– Van Gogh obciął sobie ucho.

Barbara zaśmiała się.

– Ale od tego dnia wyostrzył mu się wzrok, a jego ręce zaczęły czynić cuda.

Charles pochylił się i obdarował żonę pocałunkiem.

– Chodź no tutaj, kochanie. Uwielbiam twój sposób patrzenia na świat. I po prostu uwielbiam ci się przyglądać.

– No to załatwione. Spędzimy tydzień w lesie, a długi weekend na Manhattanie. – Mrugnęła porozumiewawczo do Hanka. – Może tak być, szefie?

W POŁOWIE CZERWCA Barbara wyjechała na kolejną misję Czerwonego Krzyża. Charles odwiózł ją na lotnisko i żeby trochę uspokoić myśli, pojechał do klubu na partyjkę porannego golfa. Potem wrócił do domu i obudził syna, który nabierał typowego dla nastolatków zwyczaju drzemania w ciągu dnia.

– Chodźmy się zobaczyć z twoim kolegą, Hank – powiedział, wyciągając kluczyki od samochodu z kieszeni kraciastych spodni golfowych.

– Gdzie mama? – Hank przetarł oczy ze snu.

Charles wskazał niebo.

– W chmurach.

– Dlaczego mnie nie obudziłeś?

– Budzę cię teraz, synu. Wskakuj pod prysznic. Nasza dziewczyna niedługo wróci do domu.

GDY POKONYWALI MOST, zostawiając za sobą wyspę Sunset Beach i wjeżdżając na stały ląd, wszelkie nadzieje Hanka na to, że ojciec zaprosi Gideona do nich, prysły. Willowe posiadłości z epoki plantacji, porośnięte przekwitłymi już azaliami, ustępowały miejsca nowoczesnym ceglanym domom o szkieletowej konstrukcji, chociaż niektóre z nich najlepsze czasy miały już za sobą. Charles ostro skręcił w prawo w nieutwardzoną uliczkę, przy której stały w szeregu maciupeńkie domki. Stykały się ze sobą ścianami bocznymi, a na pochyłych gankach suszyło się porozwieszane na sznurach pranie. Jerome Jenkins i jego matka siedzieli na najwyższym stopniu schodków wiodących na ganek. Jerome był jedynym czarnoskórym chłopakiem w klasie Hanka w Sunset Beach. Wszystkie dzieciaki wiedziały, że dostał się do tej szkoły, bo uzyskał stypendium. Placówka miała kłopoty z rekrutacją wśród uczniów wywodzących się z mniejszości etnicznych. Jenkinsowi nie za bardzo pomagało to, że miał nadwagę; poza tym kiedy do nich dołączył, w jego oczach widniały grudki ropy, przypominające kawałeczki przypalonej pizzy, a skórę na całym ciele chłopaka pokrywała cieniutka warstewka, jak im powiedział, „popiołu".

– Panie Camphor – odezwała się mama Jerome'a, podchodząc do samochodu we wzorzystej podomce, której, jak pomyślał Hank, Charlotte Applewood nigdy by na siebie nie włożyła. – Mniej więcej o jakiej porze przywiezie pan Jerome'a z powrotem?

– Jutro rano po śniadaniu, jeśli nie masz nic przeciwko temu, Mavis – odparł Charles, ustawiając lusterko wsteczne.

– Nie zapakowałam mu ubrania na zmianę, panie Camphor.

Charles uśmiechnął się.

– W takim razie dałaś nam powody, żebyśmy odwiedzili kilka sklepów. – Mrugnął do Jerome'a. – Co ty na to, Jerome?

Jerome nigdy nie patrzył w oczy ojcu Hanka, jeśli udało mu się tego uniknąć.

– Dobrze, panie Camphor.

– Zwrócę ci syna w jednym kawałku, Mavis. Nie masz się o co martwić.

CHARLES ZAPYTAŁ JEROME'A, gdzie chciałby zjeść, a chłopak odpowiedział, że lubi Morrison's w centrum. Sieć miała w przyszłości zamknąć starą knajpę w Dzielnicy Historycznej i otworzyć nową w galerii handlowej Southside, ale latem 1983 roku nadal można było tu po prostu wziąć tacę i ruszyć wzdłuż bufetu, by skompletować sobie domowe śniadanie, lunch albo obiad. Charles wybrał pieczoną szynkę ze smażonymi w głębokim oleju kuleczkami z ciasta kukurydzianego i rzepą. Hank i Jerome wzięli smażonego kurczaka, fasolkę mamucią i makaron zapiekany z serem, który dzięki tutejszym kucharzom zawsze zachowywał odpowiednio kremową konsystencję. Kiedy pili już słodką herbatę przy stoliku, wzdłuż niedzielnego bufetu zaczęła przesuwać się rodzina Gideona. Hank zobaczył go i mimo woli podskoczył, o mało nie przewracając swojego kubka. Odszedł od stolika, żeby się przywitać, i zostawił ojca sam na sam z Jerome'em.

Młody Jenkins miał w ustach trójkącik meksykańskiego chleba kukurydzianego. Uznał, że najpierw powinien go przełknąć, a dopiero potem się odezwać. Mavis na pewno zapytałaby go o to w pierwszej kolejności po powrocie do domu. „Nie mówiłeś z pełnymi ustami? Spuszczałeś po sobie wodę? Myłeś ręce? Nie próbowali przy tobie tych swoich dzikich wygłupów? Bo wiesz, oni przecież lubią się wygłupiać".

– Kim chciałbyś zostać, jak dorośniesz, Jerome? – zapytał obojętnym głosem Charles.

– Lubię kable elektryczne.

Charles skinął głową.

– Czyli chciałbyś zostać elektrykiem?

– Bo ja wiem, szanowny panie... – Jerome myślał, że tak naprawdę to chce zjeść ten meksykański chleb i dać sobie spokój z pogaduszkami o głupstwach.

– Nie musisz do mnie mówić „szanowny panie".

Chłopak uśmiechnął się.

– Po prostu lubię sobie czasem stanąć i popatrzeć na kable.

– Nie patrz na nie zbyt długo. – Charles popijał herbatę. – Jeżeli staniesz pod niewłaściwym przewodem, to cię porazi prąd. Swoją drogą, to wielu ludzi ląduje ostatnimi czasy na krześle elektrycznym. Dobrze, że chcesz zostać elektrykiem.

Hank przyprowadził Gideona i jego rodzinę.

– Zdaje się, że jesteśmy sąsiadami – powiedział Reuben.

– Sąsiadami, i owszem. – Charles nie wstał.

– No tak. To moja żona, Charlotte, nasza córka, Lauren, i syn, Gideon.

– Podobno ma pan jeszcze więcej dzieci – powiedział Charles.

– Bliźniaki, panie Camphor. Są w domu z moją ciotką. – Charlotte spojrzała na zegarek, a potem poprowadziła Gideona i Lonnie do wolnego stolika.

– Ładna niedziela – odezwał się Charles. – Gdzie państwo byli?

– W kościele – odparł Reuben.

– Tak, mamy tu wiele dobrych kościołów baptystycznych.

– Dziękuję za tę rekomendację, my jesteśmy jednak wyznania katolickiego.

– Osobiście należę do metodystów – szepnął Charles. – Ale to nasza mała sprośna tajemnica. – Po chwili złapał Jerome'a za rękę. – Poznali już państwo Jerome'a? To najlepszy kolega Hanka.

Hank spojrzał na ojca. Owszem, lubił Jerome'a, ale „najlepszy kolega"? Jego najlepszym kolegą był... Właściwie to nie miał najlepszego kolegi.

Charles czekał, aż Hank powie coś, co potwierdziłoby jego bliski związek z Jerome'em, chłopak jednak po prostu patrzył przed siebie.

– No dobrze, panowie – odezwał się Reuben. – Było nam bardzo miło. – Zasalutował Jerome'owi po marynarsku i oddalił się rozkołysanym, spokojnym krokiem.

Kiedy Hank usiadł, Charles zmierzył syna ciężkim spojrzeniem.

– Ta dziewczyna... – odezwał się Jerome, wskazując Lonnie, mającą na sobie letnią sukienkę koloru mandarynki. – Jest naprawdę ładna.

– Lauren? – Hank zaśmiał się i językiem obrócił w ustach niezdrobniałe imię Lonnie, po czym oblizał wargi. – Jeszcze jak...

– TAK SIĘ WIĄŻE WĘZEŁ – powiedział Charles. – Do wewnątrz i od siebie, od siebie i do wewnątrz. – Jerome starał się uważać, miał jednak straszne mdłości, bo żaglówka kołysała się na wodzie.

Niezdarnie męczył się z węzłem i przerwał na chwilę, chcąc się przyjrzeć ogromowi oceanu. Cieszył się, że ma na sobie kamizelkę ratunkową, ponieważ nie umiał pływać.

– Dobrze ci idzie, Jerome – stwierdził Charles. Chłopak próbował czterokrotnie, zanim się nauczył, ale za czwartym razem węzeł został zawiązany idealnie.

– Poproszę jeszcze trochę tych ostrygowych krakersów – odezwał się Jerome; wstał, zatoczył się i zaczął się zastanawiać, czy za moment nie zwróci tego, co zjadł. Krakersy miały mu podobno pomóc opanować chorobę morską.

– Pociągnij tę opaskę na nadgarstku! – zawołał Charles.

– Co, proszę pana?

– Jak jesz krakersy, to dotykaj opasek przeciwko chorobie morskiej.

Hank stał przy sterze i kierował łódką. Morze zawsze wprawiało go w taki nastrój, że bez względu na to, jakie miał problemy albo jak bardzo był na coś wściekły, na wodzie wszystkie kłopoty opuszczały go i stawały się pokarmem dla ryb. Ojciec podszedł bliżej i otoczył Hanka ramionami.

– Chłopak nieźle sobie radzi – powiedział.

Kierowali się już w stronę brzegu, wiał przeciwny wiatr. Jerome kręcił się po pokładzie, trzymając się wszystkiego, czego tylko mógł, jak człowiek na parkiecie do jazdy na wrotkach. Hank wciąż sterował łodzią, wiatr mierzwił mu włosy, a woda była tak błękitna jak wokół Turks i Caicos – w każdym razie tak mu się wydawało.

– On chyba nie lubi żeglować, tato.

– Lubi, lubi. Musi się po prostu przyzwyczaić. To dla niego nowe doświadczenie.

– Dlaczego powiedziałeś, że jest moim najlepszym kolegą? – spytał Hank, starając się modulować głos w taki sposób, aby nie było w nim słychać braku szacunku, ale żeby dotarł do uszu ojca. – Ja w ogóle nie mam najlepszego kolegi.

Charles należał do drużyny futbolowej w Clemson. Grał w ataku, na pozycji biegacza. Został przyjęty do stowarzyszenia Delta Phi Kappa – i raz w roku jeździł na spotkania z dawnymi kolegami, ale jego syn, Hank, był wielką niewiadomą. W dzieciństwie Charles bardzo pragnął mieć braci i szaleć z dziećmi sąsiadów i kuzynami, Hankowi jednak najlepszego kolegę zastępowała Barbara.

– Nie ma się czym chwalić – zauważył Charles, przekrzykując szum morza. – Chcesz zostać samotnym frajerem, który trzepie kapucyna w swoim pokoju? W ten sposób nigdy nie złapiesz fajnej babki.

– Dupek z ciebie – wypalił Hank. – A gdzie są twoi przyjaciele, tato?

Ojciec popieścił jego twarz otwartą dłonią, wymierzając mu policzek.

W DRODZE NA ŁÓDKĘ wstąpili do Parker's, sklepu odzieżowego, gdzie z Hanka i Jerome'a zdjęto miarę na mundurki szkolne. Kierowniczka zawsze zostawiała spory zapas na długość, a potem tydzień przed rozpoczęciem roku szkolnego telefonowała do klientów i zapraszała ich do sklepu, żeby zrobić poprawki i sprawdzić, jak bardzo dzieci urosły. Charles zamówił dla obu chłopców po trzy mundurki i podsunął kierowniczce kartę American Express.

– Rozumie pani, chodzi o to, żeby Mavis miała dobry kredyt, jak do was przyjdzie. Duży.

Robił to wszystko dyskretnie, bo nie chciał wysłuchiwać podziękowań od Jerome'a i Mavis. Dotyczyło to też opłat za naukę. Gdyby Mavis zabrakło na nią pieniędzy, mały Jenkins mógłby skorzystać z funduszu powierniczego.

JEROME ZWYMIOTOWAŁ, gdy tylko dotarli na brzeg. Pomimo sprzeciwów Charlesa chciał już wracać do domu. Jeżeli słyszał sprzeczkę Hanka i Charlesa, to był na tyle mądry, żeby się z tym nie zdradzić.

– Dziękuję, panie Camphor – powiedział, wyciągając do niego rękę przed wejściem na schodki do swojego domku. – Mam nadzieję, że będziemy mogli jeszcze kiedyś popływać.

– Kiedy tylko zechcesz – odparł Charles. – Zuch chłopak.

Gdy Hank był na ostatnim roku studiów, Charles Pierre Camphor zginął tragicznie na morzu, a Jerome Jenkins przyleciał z Denver w stanie Kolorado, żeby wygłosić mowę na jego pogrzebie. Jerome, wówczas już wzięty producent zaawansowanych technicznie zabawek elektronicznych, wspominał swoją pierwszą przygodę żeglarską i niezmienną wielkoduszność, jaką okazywał mu pan Camphor.

W OBECNOŚCI OJCA Hank obnosił się z opuchlizną na twarzy jak z orderem za odwagę. „Poczekaj tylko, niech mama zobaczy ten siniak – myślał. – Poczekaj". Ale w dniu ich powrotu Barbara zatelefonowała z wiadomością, że na razie nie może wyjechać z Nowego Jorku.

– Jak to „nie możesz"?

– No, nie mogę dostać miejsca w samolocie. Miałyśmy przesiadkę w Nowym Jorku i pomyślałyśmy z dziewczynami, żeby zostać tu na weekend. Mogę w tym czasie przygotować nam grunt pod tę świąteczną wycieczkę.

– Masz wsiąść w najbliższy samolot do domu, Barb.

– To nie będzie możliwe.

– Postaraj się.

W słuchawce zapadła cisza.

– Zaproponowali mi awans.
– Gdzie? W Nowym Jorku?
– Oczywiście, że nie.
– Pogadamy, jak przyjedziesz do domu.
– Nie słuchasz mnie. – Barbara dmuchnęła przeciągle do telefonu. – Ja już przyjęłam ofertę, a teraz potrzebuję trochę czasu, żeby nawiązać kontakty.
– Pijesz?
– Na Boga, skąd.
Był to odgłos zaciągania się dymem z papierosa. „Na Boga", pomyślał. Co za pretensjonalne określenie.
– A jesteś pijana?
– Nie wymyśliliśmy jeszcze nazwy na tę moją posadę, ale jeśli wszystko dobrze rozegram, to za dwa lata zostanę dyrektorem wykonawczym na południowy wschód.
Charles wybuchnął śmiechem.
– I niby kto cię mianuje tym dyrektorem?
– Pracuję dla Czerwonego Krzyża już prawie cztery lata, a dzięki temu, że z wykształcenia jestem dyplomowaną pielęgniarką, przełożeni wysyłają mnie tam, gdzie są potrzebni ludzie do usuwania skutków klęsk żywiołowych. Jestem dobra w tym, co robię. Myślałam, że się ucieszysz.
Martwa cisza.
– Ilu facetom zrobiłaś loda, Barb? Z którym ze swoich zwierzchników się przespałaś?
Odsunęła słuchawkę od ucha. Poznała Charlesa, kiedy pracowała jako kasjerka w banku S&S, a on właśnie został tam przyjęty jako świeżo upieczony absolwent szkoły biznesu. Gdy zaczęli się ze sobą spotykać, przeszła do innego banku, żeby nie było plotek. Rozumiała, że romans

w miejscu pracy zawsze działa na niekorzyść przynajmniej jednej ze stron. Pieniądze, które zarobiła jako kasjerka, poszły na szkołę pielęgniarską. Dwa lata po jej ukończeniu wyszła za Charlesa i podjęła pracę w szpitalu Saint Joseph's, na trzy lata przed urodzeniem Hanka. Gdy chłopak przyszedł na świat, wzięła niemal dziesięcioletni urlop, zanim poszła do pracy dla Czerwonego Krzyża. Po takiej długiej przerwie wspinaczka na szczyt kariery zawodowej okazała się piekielnie trudna. Nie ufano Barbarze, że całkowicie poświęci się nowej pracy, choć pracowała więcej niż przynajmniej część młodszych pielęgniarek Czerwonego Krzyża. Teraz, na nowej posadzie, musiałaby się zajmować katastrofami innego rodzaju. Pojawiła się nowa choroba. Wirus. AIDS. Będą kwestionariusze i nowa literatura na delikatne tematy, w tym dotyczące orientacji seksualnej. Barbara uważała, że nie jest ważne, o co się pyta, ale jak się formułuje pytanie. Łagodząc ton głosu, spróbowała nawiązać kontakt z mężem pomimo dzielących ich długich kilometrów kabli telefonicznych.

– A co tam w domu? Jak się miewa mój chłopak?

– No niech pomyślę – odparł Charles, zerkając w stronę zamkniętych drzwi do pokoju Hanka, który przez ostatnie dwa dni tam spędzał większość czasu. – Świetnie, Barb. U nas wszystko jest świetnie.

HANK PIERWSZY RAZ w życiu ukradł ojcu forsę z portfela: wziął dwadzieścia pięć baksów z pliku starannie ułożonych banknotów. Dołożył wszelkich starań, żeby klamerka, którą były spięte, znalazła się dokładnie w tym samym miejscu co przedtem.

– W Star Castle mają *Donkey Konga*, *Centipede'a* i *Pac-Mana*. – Hank stał w kuchni Applewoodów, trzymając w ręku torbę pomarańczy o grubej skórce.

– To bardzo ładnie ze strony twojej mamy – powiedziała Charlotte, przyjmując owoce, które, jak powiedział Hank, miały stanowić spóźniony prezent powitalny. – Ale nie trzeba było. Pierwszego wieczoru przyniosła mi salaterkę sałatki ziemniaczanej. Nawet chciałam ją poprosić o przepis. Była pyszna.

Hank zarumienił się, bo nic o tym nie wiedział. Pojechał rowerem do sklepu i kupił te pomarańcze. Mógł sobie na nie pozwolić, zostało mu bowiem jeszcze dość pieniędzy, żeby na popołudnie zaprosić Gideona i Lonnie do salonu gier.

– Mogę pojechać, mamo? – zapytał Gideon.

– No nie wiem. Dopiero co położyłam bliźniaki spać.

– Jest stąd specjalny autobus – powiedział Hank. – Staje w Island Center, a stamtąd do Star Castle mamy już tylko dwadzieścia minut jazdy.

Lonnie zerknęła na niego znad pisma, które czytała – była to „Mademoiselle" jej matki.

– Ojej – powiedziała. – Pomyślałeś o wszystkim.

Charlotte rzuciła córce spojrzenie mające oznaczać, żeby dała spokój. Gideon sznurował już buty od Chucka Taylora.

– Jest południe. O piątej macie być z powrotem. Zgoda?

– Tak, proszę pani – odpowiedział Hank.

Charlotte podeszła do kuchennego blatu i wyciągnęła trochę gotówki z dna torebki.

– Na wypadek, gdyby wam zabrakło.

Pocałowała Gideona w czoło i wyciągnęła rękę, by dotknąć policzka Hanka.

– Zrobiłeś sobie kuku?

– On nie jest małym dzieckiem, mamo – powiedział Gideon. – Kuku robią sobie małe dzieci.

– No tak, Gideonie, ale wy zawsze będziecie moimi maluchami. Wszyscy.

– Wypadek na żaglach – odpowiedział Hank. Zawahał się, zanim podszedł do Lonnie. Tipper drzemał na podłodze przy jej wysokim krześle. Hank wyciągnął rękę, żeby pogłaskać Tippera, starając się nie zwracać nadmiernej uwagi na długie nogi dziewczyny.

– Jedziesz z nami? – spytał.

Lonnie spojrzała w dół na Hanka.

– Wyrosłam z salonów gier.

Hank okropnie posmutniał, chociaż starał się tego nie okazywać. Lonnie zsunęła się z krzesła i usiadła na podłodze. Razem poklepywali psa w milczeniu. Nigdy więcej nie rozmawiała dłużej z Hankiem Camphorem. Lauren Applewood i Hank Camphor nigdy nie siedzieli bliżej siebie niż wtedy.

– Ale dziękuję ci za zaproszenie – powiedziała. Wyciągnęła rękę i dramatycznym gestem dotknęła jego twarzy. – Zażyj jakiś środek przeciwbólowy, drogi chłopcze.

HANK I GIDEON tamtego dnia stracili w Star Castle poczucie czasu. Może przez czerwone światła, palące się tak jasno na ciemnym tle. A może przez inne dzieci. I dlatego że się za dużo śmiali. Hank śmiał się tak bardzo, że go rozbolał brzuch. Nawet to, że przegrywał, nie miało żadnego znaczenia. Przecież Lonnie Applewood flirtowała z nim, nie? Dotknęła jego twarzy swoimi idealnie ukształtowanymi palcami. Nic nie mógł poradzić na to, że wydawało mu się, iż gdzieś w głębi serca Lonnie żywi jednak do niego jakieś uczucia. W kółko odgrywał sobie tę scenę w myślach i za każdym razem odczuwał przypływ adrenaliny. On i Gideon zbierali kulki z Pac-Manem, a potem chłeptali frescę i obżerali się stęchłym popcornem i hot dogami. Gideon zamówił hot dogi z konserwowym chili.

– To takie chili con carne dla ubogich.

– Dlaczego dla ubogich? – spytał Hank.

– Zastanów się: mało mięsa, fasola rozgotowana na miazgę i zapach psiej karmy zamiast kolendry i cynamonu.

– Widzę, że poświęciłeś tej kwestii sporo namysłu.

– Ej, ej, ej, masz mi coś do powiedzenia?

– Ej, ej, ej, może i tak.

Latem 1983 roku Buckner County nawiedziły upały. Chłodna wilgotność klimatyzowanego salonu gier stanowiła azyl dla nerdowatych dzieciaków, które nie miały nic do roboty, a półmrok z łatwością zamazywał granice podziałów rasowych.

– Szkoda, że nie przyjechała z nami twoja siostra – odezwał się Hank.

– Stary... – Gideon pokręcił głową. – Nie możesz po prostu się kumplować ze mną? Lonnie nie jest dla ciebie, ona gra w innej lidze. Poza tym ma chłopaka. W Cleveland.

– Czy to... poważny związek?

Gideon odwrócił się od Hanka.

– *Donkey Kong*[*].

– No powiedz mi, Gideon, muszę to wiedzieć.

– Słuchaj, Hank... Dlaczego nigdy nie zapraszasz mnie do siebie?

Hank zatrzymał się przed automatem z *Donkey Kongiem*.

– Bo po prostu... ten temat nigdy jakoś u nas się nie pojawił.

– Aha – rzekł Gideon.

– Może się uda, jak mama wróci do miasta.

– Oki. – Gideon uśmiechnął się. – Więc Lonnie i jej piękniś... Już to ze sobą robili. Przyłapałem ich jednego razu.

Hank przymknął oczy.

– Nie wierzę ci.

– To tak jak ja tobie – odpowiedział po chwili Gideon. – Nie wierzę, że kiedykolwiek mnie do siebie zaprosisz.

Spóźnili się na specjalny autobus na wyspę o szóstej i musieli wrócić normalnym autobusem miejskim, który wlókł się krętą drogą po wszystkich, jak im się wydawało, ubogich osiedlach i miasteczkach hrabstwa. Zanim stanęli na progach swoich domów, było wpół do dziesiątej i słońce odwróciło się plecami do wyspy. Matka Gideona czekała na ganku. Hank stał na ulicy, kiedy Charlotte upominała i tuliła Gideona. „Czyś ty oszalał? O mało co nie zadzwoniłam do ojca".

Przez całą drogę powrotną siedzieli w milczeniu. Hank nie był w stanie zaprzeczyć Gideonowi, który nie podał mu ręki na pożegnanie.

---

[*] Nazwa gry wideo (a także komputerowej) oraz jej głównego bohatera, potężnego goryla.

– GDZIE SIĘ PODZIEWAŁEŚ, SYNU? – Charles Camphor siedział w salonie. Karafka stojąca koło jego kieliszka była pusta.

– W salonie gier.

– Ta kobieta. Mama twojego kolegi. Przyszła tutaj. Martwiła się o was, chłopcy.

– Ona się nazywa pani Applewood. Charlotte.

– No, w każdym razie na pewno nie była zadowolona.

Hank poszedł do swojego pokoju i zamknął drzwi.

– Wziąłeś pieniądze z mojego portfela, Hank. – Charles ruszył za synem.

– Pożyczyłem. Pożyczyłem je – odpowiedział Hank. I zamknął drzwi na klucz. – Oddam, jak wróci mama. Z kieszonkowego.

– Dlaczego musisz się zachowywać jak złośliwy gówniarz?

Na niebie wisiał rogalik księżyca, a Tipper wył.

Charles wsparł czoło o drzwi pokoju syna.

– Jak byłem w twoim wieku, rodzice nie musieli mnie pilnować. To ja im pomagałem, jak tylko mogłem, żeby było nam łatwiej związać koniec z końcem. Czasami Duży Seamus i ja braliśmy jutowy worek, moją starą wiatrówkę i szliśmy polować na króliki, wiewiórki i oposy. A mama zbierała mlecze i robiła z nich sałatkę. Albo dodawała do posiłków kaszę kukurydzianą, żebyśmy najedli się do syta. Gotowaną. Smażoną. Zapiekaną z melasą i skwarkami. Miała kaszę na każdą porę roku. Dzisiaj w restauracjach mówi się na to polenta. Ale dla nas, Hank, była to tylko kasza.

Hank otworzył drzwi.

– Chcę basseta.

– Słucham? – Charles zrobił zdziwioną minę.

– Takiego, jak mają Lonnie i Gideon.

– Nie.

– Bassety to dobra rasa.

– Różnie się o nich mówi.

– I są łagodne. Dobrze traktują dzieci.

– Okej, zrobimy tak... Poszukamy płaszczyzny porozumienia. Na pewno jest jakaś psia rasa, którą zaakceptuje cała nasza rodzina.

– Rodzina? – Hank parsknął śmiechem. – Jaka rodzina?

– Nie przeginaj pały, synu.

– Nie jesteś moją rodziną.

– Od kiedy?

– Mama w ogóle nie lubi tego domu.

– Twoja mama to nowoczesna kobieta. I jeden Bóg wie, że mnie to przeraża, ale za to ją kocham, Hank.

– No ale ja chcę basseta.

– Nic z tego.

– I nową rodzinę. Jak ta z domu obok. – Hank skrzyżował ręce na piersiach. – Chcę mieć rodzinę o brązowej skórze.

– A co zrobisz, jak już ją będziesz miał? Myślisz, że oni prowadzą idealne życie? Że nie mają niczego za uszami, że sami też nie siedzą w jakimś gównie?

– Myślę, myślę... – Hank próbował pokazać ojcu, jak wytęża umysł – że oni chyba są jakoś ponad to. Może jest łatwiej... łatwiej, kiedy się ma karłowatego psa, kupionego, żeby... ha... żeby wywoływał efekt komiczny, i mamę, która widzi, że masz spuchnięty policzek, i siostrę, którą chce całować twój nowy kolega, i tatę, który dużo pracuje, ale kiedy wraca do domu, nie bije syna po twarzy ani nie mówi do żony: „Kochanie, z kim się dziś rżnęłaś? Podobało ci się, jak mu robiłaś laskę?". – Hank tupnął nogą. – Więc daj mi basseta i dom pełen ludzi o brązowej skórze, z którymi mógłbym zamieszkać. Twój jutowy worek z kaszą kukurydzianą nic mnie nie obchodzi.

Charles upuścił szklankę po whisky, a Hank odruchowo uniósł ręce, żeby zasłonić się przed nadchodzącym ciosem.

Jego ojciec patrzył na odłamki szkła i nie wykazując najmniejszej ochoty, żeby je uprzątnąć, wycofał się spod drzwi pokoju Hanka, po czym zdecydowanym krokiem podszedł do drzwi wejściowych. Po drodze wyciągnął ze swojej nowiutkiej torby drewniany kij golfowy. Podniósł go i gwizdnął przeciągle, biorąc zamach na próbę. Hank wyszedł za ojcem przed dom, ale w bezpiecznej odległości. Przyglądał się, jak Charles macha kijem, by wyładować złość.

Tipper tymczasem przestał wyć i skomleć. Na widok Charlesa i Hanka podbiegł do chłopca, merdając ogonem. Hank zaczął się przesuwać obok niego; nie, przesuwać się tak, żeby stanąć pomiędzy nim i ojcem, ale Charles złapał go za kołnierz koszuli i odepchnął na bok. Hank upadł na trawę, a ojciec podniósł kij, po czym złamał go na grzbiecie Tippera jednym potężnym uderzeniem. Pies był tak zaskoczony, że nie zaskomlił ani nie zaskowyczał. Hank później wmawiał sobie, że Tipper nie miał czasu, żeby cokolwiek poczuć. Oczywiście nie była to prawda. Przed chwilą basset był jeszcze pełen życia, energii i powietrza, a teraz leżał bezwładnie na ziemi.

– No, Hank – odezwał się Charles i opuścił kij, po czym, powłócząc nogami, ruszył z powrotem do domu. – Pochowaj swoich zmarłych.

Hank usiadł na trawie koło martwego Tippera i zaczął wyć.

DWIE GODZINY PÓŹNIEJ Barbara wysiadła z taksówki i zobaczyła, że w domu palą się wszystkie światła. Charles spał snem sprawiedliwego na kanapie w salonie. Zauważyła szkło w korytarzu pod drzwiami pokoju Hanka. Przeszukała wszystkie pomieszczenia, a ponieważ nie udało się jej znaleźć syna ani dobudzić męża, wyszła na zewnątrz i sprawdziła tę część posiadłości, która graniczyła z bagniskiem. Tam znalazła Hanka, który kopał dół przy świetle księżyca. Po lewej ręce chłopca widniał kopczyk ziemi. Barbara podbiegła bliżej i zajrzała do dołu. Wstrzymała oddech, zachwiała się na nogach, a potem odebrała szpadel Hankowi.

– Przestań.

– Tata złamał Tipperowi grzbiet.

– Cicho.

– To jest zły człowiek, mamo.

– Kto? – Barbara odwróciła się gwałtownie.

– Tata – mruknął Hank. – Dlaczego on aż tak ich nienawidzi?

Barbara spojrzała ponad głową Hanka na dom sąsiadów.

– Twój ojciec miał trudne dzieciństwo, Hank. Musiałby się drugi raz urodzić, żeby złagodnieć. A wszyscy mamy tylko jedno życie.

Hank pokręcił głową.

– Nie widziałaś, jak...

– Opowiesz mi o tym później. W tej chwili nie jestem w stanie tego znieść. – Pokazała mu gestem, żeby odszedł, ale nie ruszył się z miejsca, gdy matka podwinęła rękawy zielonej jedwabnej bluzki. Był to niedawny prezent od mężczyzny, z którym spotykała się już ponad dziesięć lat. Od żonatego mężczyzny, Jamesa Samuela Vincenta, z którym widziała się właśnie w Nowym Jorku. Oboje zgodzili się, że ich romans się skończył. Barbara zaczęła kopać.

– Ja się tym dalej zajmę.

PÓŹNIEJ TEGO WIECZORU Reuben Applewood wyszedł przed dom w piżamie i kapciach, kilka razy leniwie pociągnął dym z kubańskiego cygara i włączył latarkę. Był to zwyczajowy sygnał dla Tippera, żeby pokazał panu, gdzie zrobił to, co zrobił, aby Reuben mógł wpuścić psa do domu i wreszcie się położyć. Ale zamiast Tippera wokół jego właściciela roztańczyły się chyba wszystkie świetliki z okolicy. Nocny chór bagniskowego życia rozhulał się na całego. Reuben Applewood nie był człowiekiem przesądnym ani niespełna rozumu. Kiedy Tipper nie zareagował na jego trzecie wezwanie, mruknął pod nosem: „Te skurwysyny spod ciemnej gwiazdy zabiły psa moich dzieci". I zaczął układać opowiastkę, którą on i Charlotte mieli im powtórzyć, bo były jeszcze w takim wieku, w którym pewne prawdy mogłyby je złamać. A do tego Reuben nigdy by nie dopuścił. „Wybierz sobie ocean. Wybierz sobie ocean. Wybierz sobie ocean".

HANK NA SERIO zamierzał znaleźć nowego psa dla Lonnie i Gideona, ale matka zadziwiła go, bo nie ruszała się z domu aż do sierpnia, kiedy wyjechała na zjazd Czerwonego Krzyża do Los Angeles. Wróciła z masą prezentów. W wielkich torbach podróżnych przywiozła kukurydziane minitortille z meksykańskiego sklepu spożywczego i ręczniki z Venice Beach, ozdobione wizerunkami palm, plażowych klapek oraz surferów spędzających całe dnie na plażach. Miała też trzy bluzy drużyny Dodgers z autografami graczy, małą, średnią i dużą, a specjalnie dla Hanka zdobyła piłkę bejsbolową z podpisami wszystkich zawodników, którzy wspaniałomyślnie zagrali darmowy mecz dla delegatów Czerwonego Krzyża na Dodger Stadium. Charles dostał elegancką parę złoconych markerów golfowych z monogramem C.C. Zbladł, kiedy otworzył pudełko.

– Może lepiej zacznę uprawiać jogging – powiedział.

PO TYM ZJEŹDZIE w LA Barbara siedziała w domu z Hankiem i Charlesem; dom Camphorów zrobił się cichy i spokojny. Trochę żeglowali i robili plany na gwiazdkową wycieczkę do Nowego Jorku, a Barbara namówiła syna, by zaczął uprawiać jogging razem z Charlesem, i bieganie okazało się dobre, bo Hank niechętnie, czyli z wolna, zaczął poznawać inne dzieci, które lubiły biegać, dzieci podobne do niego i podzielające jego zainteresowania.

NOTATNIK GIDEONA APPLEWOODA
Z UWAGAMI O PRZYJAŹNI

Ja: Tata myśli, że Tipper uciekł.
Hank: Współczuję wam.
Ja: A moja siostra mówi, że chciał wrócić do Cleveland.

Hank: Uciekał już kiedyś z domu?
Ja: Nigdy.
Hank: Posłuchaj, Gideon... No tak, pewnie zawsze kiedyś musi być ten pierwszy raz.
Ja: Moim zdaniem potrącił go samochód.
Hank: I pewnie masz rację.
Ja: Ciągle mi się wydaje, że zobaczę Tippera na drodze, ale Lonnie mówi, żebym patrzył przed siebie i do przodu.

(PS Hank już nie pyta o Lonnie. A ZAWSZE o nią pyta. Dzisiaj wieczorem potłukłem kostkę Rubika).

FACET OD PRZEPROWADZEK ZAMIERA W BEZRUCHU

1971

DOM: 1. Mieszkanie, pomieszczenie mieszkalne, miejsce stałego pobytu; rodzina, domownicy, mieszkanie wraz z jego mieszkańcami. 2. Ogół spraw rodzinnych, domowych; gospodarstwo domowe. 3. Instytucja państwowa, społeczna, handlowa itp.; zakład, przedsiębiorstwo.

JEBEDIAH APPLEWOOD NIE MIAŁ EREKCJI OD DZIEWIĘĆdziesięciu dwóch dni. W Wietnamie zerżnął sto sześćdziesiąt trzy kobiety, co według niektórych szacunków stanowi skromną liczbę. Byli tacy żołnierze, którzy wyruchali dwa razy więcej dziewczyn w o połowę krótszym czasie.

Jeb uwielbiał wszelkiego rodzaju wykazy i spisy i skrzętnie je przechowywał, a swoje uniesienia dokumentował – nie dlatego żeby się przechwalać albo chełpić, tylko dlatego że niekiedy mąciło mu się w głowie i nie zawsze potrafił zachować poczucie czasu. Zażywał cały koktajl leków przeciwko chorobom wenerycznym, takim jak szankry, rzeżączka czy chlamydioza. Jakoś udało mu się uniknąć opryszczki narządów płciowych i syfilisu. Uważał, że to dlatego, że dobre modlitwy matki i ciotki w jego intencji odniosły skutek.

BUDZIŁ SIĘ CZASAMI w środku nocy zlany zimnym potem i oglądał swoje ciało, jak zaniepokojony rodzic ogląda noworodka. Wszystkie członki miał całe, był jednak pewien, że jakaś ważna biologicznie część jego ciała martwieje. Zbudował miłosny ołtarzyk na kominku w sypialni, wyłożył go płachtą fioletowego aksamitu i przyozdobił plakatami filmowymi z Pam Grier, Brendą Sykes i Vonettą McGee. Obramował ołtarzyk mlecznymi paciorkami z akrylu, kadzidełkami o zapachu drzewa sandałowego i grubymi woskowymi świecami ku czci swoich ponętnych brązowoskórych sióstr. Miał dwadzieścia cztery lata. Siadywał na łóżku i przyglądał się badawczo twarzom Vonetty, Pam i Brendy – „ich ślicznym, prześlicznym twarzom" – a potem cofał się, żeby lepiej widzieć wspaniałe fryzury afro, tyłki i cycki. W końcu opadał na kolana i prosił te boginie, by uwolniły go od conocnych snów o utonięciu i śmierci.

MATKA JEBA I JEGO CIOTKA, Flora, przygotowały prawdziwą ucztę z okazji jego powrotu do Buckner County w stanie Georgia: bufet soulowych potraw w domu lat jego młodości.

Spojrzał na półmiski pełne tych smakołyków i zrozumiał, że nie dadzą mu zadowolenia, ale sięgnął po papierowy talerzyk i plastikowy widelec i zjadł nie jedną, lecz dwie porcje, żeby nie zrobić przykrości przyjaciółkom mamy i nie zlekceważyć ich dań oraz czasu, jaki musiały poświęcić, aby je przygotować. Nie chciał zranić kościelnej kongregacji kobiet, które pomagały go wychować i chroniły tak, jak sokoły chronią swoje młode. Zauważył, że wszystkie mówią o jego służbie w marynarce nie wprost – że „był na wyjeździe" albo „był tam". Żadna z nich ani razu nie użyła słowa „Wietnam".

Ruby Dennis przyniosła swoją sałatkę ziemniaczaną z dodatkiem utłuczonego w moździerzu selera, bo sok warzywny sprawiał, że nie trzeba było już dodawać dużo tłustego majonezu. Martha zrobiła smażonego kurczaka, którego najpierw maczała w zimnej wodzie, a potem tylko lekko prószyła mąką, mięso było więc soczyste, a skórka chrupiąca. Lullabelle przyrządziła duszone krewetki z ziarnami pieprzu i kremową kaszą kukurydzianą. Stella ugotowała czerwony ryż z papryką, nadziewanymi pomidorami i kiełbasą andouille. Z kolei Josephine przyniosła makaron zapiekany z serem w trzech kolorach, a dodała do niego drogą goudę, cheddar i edam, chociaż właściwie nie było jej na to stać; pod koniec każdego miesiąca musiała pożyczać pieniądze od rodziny i znajomych.

W CZASIE SWOJEJ SŁUŻBY widział prostytutki, które chwytały piłeczki pingpongowe wargami sromowymi i zachęcały żołnierzy, żeby dla zabawy wyciągali im je z pochwy. Widział bary, gdzie przychodzili wyłącznie biali żołnierze, i bary obsługujące wyłącznie czarnych wojskowych. Burdele specjalizujące się w każdej sprośności, jaką tylko można sobie wyobrazić. I narkotyki pobudzające wyobraźnię erotyczną. Kobiety w Subic Bay – i później, w Bangkoku – nie oczekiwały od Jeba niczego. Nie chciały nawet przyjaźni. Mógł przejechać przez most do Olongapo City, spędzić tam godzinę albo dwie, dymać te laski do nieprzytomności i zapomnieć, że zabijał ich azjatyckich braci. Seks... jakie to było przyjemne, dopóki potrafił jeszcze odczuwać przyjemność. Obcy kraj można było okupować dzięki broni i seksowi. Otwórz portfel. Wyciągnij piątaka, dziesiątaka, może dorzuć jeszcze parę groszy, jeśli jesteś czarny. I pamiętaj, że te kobiety widziały tutaj dosyć, żeby zgotować ci ciepłe powitanie i niczego od ciebie nie oczekiwać. Ale w Buckner County... jego matka, ciotki i, słodki Jezu, te dziewczyny, z którymi chciały go spiknąć... Czy ciotki nie wiedziały, że nie ma im nic do zaoferowania? „Tak, byłeś tam. Ale teraz wróciłeś". Czasami Jeb musiał się uszczypnąć. Nie wierzył tak do końca, że rzeczywiście tam był. Wpatrywał się czasem pomiędzy swoje nogi i nic się tam nie poruszało. Uświadomił sobie nagle, że w Buckner County mieszka niewielu mężczyzn. Odczuwał wyraźną nieobecność wujów, stryjów i kuzynów. Kiedy to się stało? Chodził po centrum miasta i widział, że wielu czarnych braci obija się i pozostaje bez grosza. Albo zaginęło. Do wstąpienia do marynarki namówił go kuzyn, Reuben Applewood. „Nie ma nas zbyt wielu w tej formacji wojskowej", pisał Reuben, pochylony nad swoją koją na USS New Jersey. „Jak przyjdzie pobór, nie będziesz miał nic do powiedzenia. Dadzą cię do piechoty. Zostaniesz zającem na pierwszej linii frontu". Jeb wszędzie wokół siebie dostrzegał jedynie kobiety, dzieci i starców.

„CHODŹMY NA RYBY”, proponowała często garstka pozostałych mu jeszcze znajomych starców. Wyciągał z wody mikuna, spoglądał w jego oczy i wypinał haczyk. Starcy mówili: „Jeb, chodźmy na kręgle”, a on wsuwał dwa palce w otwory polakierowanej kuli i patrzył, jak toczy się po długim torze. Kiedy wchodziła w kontakt z kręglami – „trafione” – rozlegał się taki dźwięk – eksplozja? – że aż przykucał i mrużył oczy, a wtedy kręglowym torem nadpływał w jego stronę chorąży Mammoth, plując wodą jak tamtego dnia, gdy Jeb i Eddie Christie wyrzucili go za burtę lotniskowca USS Olympus. Tak się skończyły kręgle.

Zastanawiał się, czy nie zadzwonić do Eddiego do Bronksu, ostatecznie postanowił jednak tego nie robić. W Wietnamie Eddie o mały włos nie ocipiał, a Jeb namówił go, żeby zrobił coś, czego obaj potem żałowali. Teraz Eddie odzyskał równowagę, a Jeb nie chciał zrobić ani powiedzieć nic, co mogłoby mu znowu rozstroić umysł. „Dać radę”, powtarzał sobie. Po prostu będzie musiał jakoś dać sobie z tym radę.

– NIE CHCIAŁBYŚ PÓJŚĆ Z NAMI DO KOŚCIOŁA, Jebediahu? – zapytała matka. Odpowiedział, że nie, ale podwiózł ją i ciotkę Florę do katolickiego kościoła St. Paul’s of the Redemption, a potem poszedł do kina. Obejrzał *Brudnego Harry’ego*, *Ostatni seans filmowy*, *Francuskiego łącznika* oraz *Willy’ego Wonkę i fabrykę czekolady*.

POSZEDŁ DO KLINIKI dla weteranów, sądząc, że lekarz może przepisze mu coś na bezsenność. W poczekalni jakiś wymizerowany żołnierz z przeraźliwie łysą głową – Jebowi od razu przyszła na myśl kręgielnia – dostał szału na widok pliku dokumentów, które podsunął mu do wypełnienia personel. „Zacznę życie od nowa", mruknął żołnierz. Jeb nie dosłyszał w tych słowach bezpośredniej pogróżki, ale zaraz potem rozległ się sygnał alarmowy. Pojawili się pielęgniarze z pasami i kaftanem bezpieczeństwa i wywieźli tego faceta na noszach. Jebediah wyszedł z kliniki i dwie ulice dalej kupił marihuanę. Przez dwa dni z rzędu spał dobrze.

NIE NALEŻAŁ DO LUDZI, którzy potrafią latami leserować w domu, więc po trzech miesiącach snucia się z kąta w kąt przyciął dąb w ogrodzie matki, bo nie chciał, żeby zrobili to miastowi, którzy przy domach czarnych wycinali czasem całe drzewa. Wspiął się na dąb, unikając stonóg w porastającej konary oplątwie brodaczkowatej, uszczelnił cieknące rury pod kuchennym zlewem, naprawił dach, wyczyścił rynny i założył nowy odpływ w ogrodzie, żeby nie zbierała się w nim woda i nie zalewała pralni. Polakierował podłogi, podłożył nowe maty pod wschodnie dywany, żeby nie plamiły kasztanowych klepek, wypolerował schody, przetkał komin, naniósł drew do kominka, kupił nowe rolety do okien i zerwał skajowy siding ze ścian domu, chociaż matka utyskiwała, że siding jest tani, a teraz drewno będzie butwiało wskutek wilgoci. Jeb nie mógł się przyznać, dlaczego widok skaju go przygnębia, powiedział więc tylko:

„Pomaluję dom na żółto". Pomysł na żółty dom przypadł do gustu zarówno jego matce, jak i cioci Florze.

KIEDY W POŁOWIE LISTOPADA skończył malowanie, znów dopadł go niepokój i Jeb nie potrafił sobie znaleźć miejsca, ale bezsenność zniknęła. Pojechał do Searsa i kupił dwie białe koszule z długimi rękawami, dwie z krótkimi, dwie pary marynarskich szortów, dwie pary spodni khaki, niebieską marynarkę, a w Thom's Shoe Store na Main Street brązowe zamszowe loafersy. W spodniach khaki i białej koszuli odwiedził miejscowy uniwersytet dla czarnych. Miał nadzieję zacząć studia dzięki GI Bill, ustawie umożliwiającej byłym żołnierzom darmową naukę. Kiedy spacerował po dziewiętnastowiecznym kampusie, otoczonym przez wiechlinę i słone bagna, jego serce uradowało się na widok młodych czarnych braci i sióstr, zajętych rozmową. „Tu są sami młodzi ludzie". Przez mniej więcej pięć minut on też odczuwał te młodzieńcze wibracje i kroczył przed siebie dumnie i nonszalancko, myśląc, że jako dwudziestoczterolatek również jest jeszcze młody i ma pod każdym względem prawo do szczęścia.

Jadąc windą do biura przyjęć kandydatów, był w dobrym nastroju, ale kiedy rozsunęły się drzwi, wraz z Jebem wysiadły z niej mieszane uczucia. Szczęście? To jakiś żart? „Szczęście"? Zwrócił się z tym pytaniem do doradcy zawodowego. Jak mogę być szczęśliwy, gdy toczy się wojna? Doradca stwierdził, że szczęście jest problemem egzystencjalnym, idealnym do dyskusji na zajęciach z filozofii. Możesz znaleźć bratnią duszę w Nietzschem, powiedział doradca. Gdy Jeb mniej więcej zrozumiał, na czym polega z grubsza światopogląd Nietzschego, odpowiedział doradcy, że siedzenie na zajęciach w sali pełnej szczęśliwych ludzi, dyskutujących o znaczeniu nicości, nie przyniesie mu, do jasnej cholery, najmniejszego pożytku.

W takim razie zacznijmy od tego, na czym się znasz, powiedział doradca. Jakie są twoje zainteresowania?

Jeb odparł: Wiem to i owo o wodzie. Nie opowiedział jednak doradcy, jak woda wypełnia płuca. Blokuje dostęp tlenu. Jak dostaje się do uszu i nosa. Nie opisał, jak walczy o życie tonący. Kiedy woda atakuje człowieka, ten chce się jej zrewanżować i zaatakować ją. Zdarza się, że zanim stracimy przytomność, nadrywamy mięśnie, idąc już na dno.

Lubię sporty wodne, powiedział.

Zrobiło to wrażenie na doradcy. Pochylił się nad biurkiem.

Bracie, tak między nami, zważywszy na to, jak czysty jest nasz lud i jak bardzo uwielbiamy się kąpać – zastanawiałeś się kiedyś, dlaczego większość z nas nie umie pływać?

Od powrotu z wojny Jeb zauważył, że coś się porobiło z ludźmi. Mówili, ale rzadko słuchali. Nie, odrzekł. Nie wiem, co o tym sądzić.

Doradca znów się rozluźnił na fotelu za biurkiem: Każdy ma swojego złego ducha, a nasz zły duch to statki płynące z Afryki z niewolnikami. Może zapiszemy cię na wychowanie fizyczne? Mógłbyś zacząć od tego, żeby przypomnieć sobie sztukę pływania. Jesteś weteranem z Wietnamu, tak? Pływanie to świetny sposób na złagodzenie napięcia nerwowego.

Jeb ostatecznie uznał, że na razie nie jest gotowy na studia. Sprawdził ogłoszenia na ostatniej stronie „Penny Saver". Firma przeprowadzkowa Axelrod Movers szukała pracownika lubiącego „życie w trasie". Pojechał do Southside, gdzie mieściła się siedziba firmy, i po pięciu minutach rozmowy z właścicielem dostał pierwsze zlecenie zamiejscowe. Jego partnerem za kółkiem ciężarówki miał być Duży Seamus Camphor, weteran wojenny jak Jeb i były sierżant armii amerykańskiej. Kazano im przewieźć meble z Memphis do Bostonu, a na końcu podrzucić jeszcze parę gratów do Portsmouth w stanie New Hampshire.

TRUDNO BYŁOBY ZNALEŹĆ między białymi potężniej zbudowanego faceta niż Duży Seamus Camphor. Powiedział, że jest bez pracy i rozpaczliwie potrzebuje pieniędzy. Jeb wsunął się do kabiny ciężarówki na fotel pasażera i dał Seamusowi kluczyki. Na podstawie pierwszego wrażenia wydawało mu się, że tak będzie taktownie.

Duży Seamus był gadułą, a jego paplanina szybko zeszła na temat polowania. Jeb znał się trochę na łowiectwie z czasów, gdy razem z kuzynami tropili młode, nieopierzone gołębie, które Francuzi nazywali „squab". Seamus ożywił się, kiedy to usłyszał. Obaj byli zgodni, że wiewiórka z grilla jest więcej niż smaczna.

Duży Seamus opowiedział mu też o niedawnym lunchu ze swoim kuzynem, Charlesem Camphorem: „Dwanaście dolców za najżałośniejszy talerz krewetek i kaszy, jaki w życiu widziałem. Potem chodzimy po parku, a tam bezczelne wiewiórki szaleją jak cholera, stają na dwóch łapkach, jak gdyby się spodziewały, że je będę karmił żołędziami. A Charles się tylko śmiał: «Czy nie są śliczne, Seamus?». Mało mnie nie rozwalił. «A co jest w nich ślicznego? – pytam. – Szkoda, że nie mam swojej starej wiatrówki. Chodźcie tu, wiewióreczki». Ale Charles szedł przede mną i powiedział: «Nie powinieneś już jeść wiewiórek, Seamus. I na pewno, do diabła, nie powinieneś mówić ludziom, że i ja kiedyś je jadłem»".

Jak nikt nie widzi, ciągle do nich strzelam, zwierzył się Seamus Jebowi. Do oposów też. Królików. I żółwi. Bóg nie dałby ludziom broni, gdyby nie chciał, żeby jej używali. Ale ja mierzę wyłącznie do ruchomych celów. Nie zastrzelę żadnego stworzenia, które stoi w bezruchu.

JEBEDIAH SZYBKO SIĘ ZORIENTOWAŁ, że jego współpracownik nie za bardzo kocha duże miasta i autostrady. Gdyby dysponowali większą ilością czasu, powiedział mu Seamus, o wiele fajniej byłoby pojechać trasą widokową. W związku z tym Jeb ucieszył się, że nie dysponują czasem. Małe miasteczka na Południu nie wzbudzały w nim ciekawości ani ciepłych uczuć.

Problemy w małżeństwie, powiedział Jebowi Duży Seamus po godzinie wspólnej jazdy: muszę uciec od mojej kobiety.

Prawda wyglądała jednak tak, że Duży Seamus Camphor uciekał od ognia. W czasie gaszenia pożaru, spowodowanego przez zapalone świece w domu położonym o milę od miasta, usiadł na podłodze w pokoju małego chłopca, aby pokłonić się płomieniom na pożegnanie. Nie lubił pożarów i walczył z nimi przez całe życie, lecz po służbie w Wietnamie nie umiał być już dłużej dobrym strażakiem.

ROZUMIAŁO SIĘ SAMO PRZEZ SIĘ, że po przyjeździe do Memphis Jeb i Duży Seamus nie będą dzielić pokoju hotelowego, chociaż w 1971 roku mogliby tam zamieszkać razem bez żadnych przeszkód. Zaparkowali ciężarówkę przed właściwym magazynem i umówili się na spotkanie o dwunastej w południe następnego dnia, żeby o pierwszej odebrać meble. Duży Seamus miał w mieście kumpla z Wietnamu, którego chciał odwiedzić. Zamierzał spać u niego, a dietą na hotel wypchać swój cienki portfel. Jeb wyjął *Green Book*, przewodnik dla czarnoskórych Amerykanów, który ciocia Flora wcisnęła mu na kolana, i zaczął przerzucać stronice, aż natrafił na imię i nazwisko Myrtle Hendricks z Memphis w stanie Tennessee.

MIESZKAŁA W ORANGE MOUND, ponoć najstarszej murzyńskiej dzielnicy w kraju. Biały drewniany dom należał do jej rodziców. W latach segregacji rasowej zmieniał się okresowo w hotelik typu B&B, a kiedy rozpaczliwe czasy wymagały rozpaczliwych środków, w pensjonat.

Myrtle uchyliła cienkie drzwi z moskitierą i Jeb zobaczył jedno brązowe oko.

Podróżny? – zapytała.

Jestem przejazdem – odrzekł Jeb.

Przejazdem dokąd? – Uchyliła drzwi nieco szerzej. Na pierwszy rzut oka nie było w niej nic nadzwyczajnego. Miała za chude nogi, za bardzo kręcone włosy i nie używała szminki, która sugerowałaby jakieś egzotyczne miejsca, obietnice albo możliwości.

Najpierw do Bostonu i New Hampshire. A potem, kto to wie.

Był w drelichowym kombinezonie pracownika firmy przeprowadzkowej, w którym czuł się jak dziecko w za dużych śpioszkach. Myrtle zmierzyła go wzrokiem od stóp do głów. Widział, że oblicza, ile może wziąć od niego za noc i ile straci, jeśli każe mu odejść.

Piętnaście dolarów za noc ze śniadaniem, powiedziała.

ZDJĄŁ KOMBINEZON i rozłożył go na dużym żelaznym łóżku nakrytym poliestrową narzutą. Zaczął wypakowywać tych kilka sztuk garderoby, którą zabrał ze sobą. Wszystko w pokoju mówiło „nie rozgoszczaj się tu”, zwłaszcza narzuta. Jeb przywykł do kołdry. Jej brak kazał mu zatęsknić za własnym łóżkiem w Georgii. Ciocia Flora obiecała mu, że nikt nie będzie niczego ruszał w jego pokoju. Nie mógł wiedzieć, jaką radość Florze – lesbijce pierwszej klasy, która urodziła się za wcześnie, by móc ujawnić swoją orientację seksualną i prowadzić normalne życie – sprawił jego ołtarzyk zbudowany ku czci czekoladowej nagości.

Myrtle spytała Jeba, czy nie ma jakichś ubrań, które należałoby wykrochmalić, wyprasować albo wymaglować, gdyby chciał pójść do jakiegoś klubu. Odpowiedział, że nie przyjechał tutaj dla muzyki. Ani klubów.

To ojczyzna bluesa – stwierdziła. – Beale Street. Stax Records. Chyba chciałby pan czegoś posłuchać, skoro już pan tu jest?

Poinformował ją, ku czemu skłaniały się jego serce i umysł: ku motelowi Lorraine.

Po co chce pan tam iść? – spytała. Zauważyła pogardę, z jaką Jeb patrzył na narzutę, i przyniosła mu lepszą.

Chcę go zobaczyć.

Widzi mi się, że wszystko, co warto było tam obejrzeć, ludzie zobaczyli, jeszcze zanim James Earl Ray wziął Martina Luthera Kinga na muszkę. Przyjeżdża pan za późno.

Podziękował za narzutę. Patrzyła, jak rozścielał łóżko w sposób, który wskazywał, że przeszedł szkolenie wojskowe.

Zdumiewa mnie, powiedział, że nikt nie spalił tego całego miasta.

A skąd pan wie, że ludzie nie próbowali? Próbowaliśmy.

Po prostu chcę zobaczyć ten motel na własne oczy.

To mogła być plotka. Wokół krąży pełno różnych plotek, westchnęła Myrtle. Ale słyszałam, że byli tacy, którzy moczyli chusteczki w jego krwi, Boże, bądź mi miłościw; co ci ludzie wyprawiają? Zakrwawione chusteczki jako prezenty od Kinga...

Ludzie mówią na takie rzeczy „trofea", pani Hendricks.

Proszę tego nie robić, panie Applewood. Niech pan nie mówi do mnie „pani Hendricks".

Zauważył, że Myrtle mocno zawiązuje swój różowy szlafrok frotté.

Wczesnym rankiem następnego dnia, zanim poszedł do pracy, skręcił w South Main w stronę motelu Lorraine i zauważył swoją gospodynię zmierzającą na północ tą samą ulicą. Z początku nie poznał jej bez różowego szlafroka. Kręcone włosy ufryzowała w aroganckie małe afro, w które wpięła z boku jesienną różę, nosiła elegancką jadeitową sukienkę, ciemnoszare szpilki i torebkę w takim samym kolorze. Mijając go, uśmiechnęła się i powiedziała dzień dobry, a Jeb pomyślał: mój Boże, ma białe zęby i błyszczące oczy, i odwrócił się, Myrtle jednak zniknęła już za rogiem.

STANĄŁ PRZED MOTELEM Lorraine i płakał. Był pewien, że będzie sam, ale pojawili się też inni podróżni, którzy odbyli pielgrzymkę do Memphis trzy lata po śmierci Kinga. Motel popadł w ruinę od czasów swojej świetności, kiedy był celem podróży muzyków, szukających gościnnego miejsca, gdzie mogliby złożyć głowy po długiej sesji nagraniowej w wytwórni Stax albo występach na Beale Street, a także innej dobrze sytuowanej klienteli, doceniającej wygody oferowane przez Lorraine (od której imienia wziął swoją nazwę) oraz jej męża, Waltera. Okolica motelu to osobna i równie smutna sprawa, którą historia i towarzysząca jej nadzieja czyniły jeszcze smutniejszą. Na drugim piętrze znajdował się przeszklony teraz balkon z zielonymi drzwiami do pokoju 306. Niektórzy podróżni po powrocie do domu wykorzystywali tę liczbę na wszystkie możliwe sposoby w grach losowych. Niewielu sprzyjało szczęście. Większości nie. Nieliczni lekką ręką wydawali pieniądze na wieńce i słali je do motelu, aby dotrzymywały towarzystwa innym kwiatom, świeżym oraz sztucznym, które przynosili goście. Jebediah stanął na popękanym chodniku i wyciągnął się całym ciałem na północ, jak korkociąg. Pozostali podróżni poszli za jego przykładem. Była to ich pielgrzymka, dlatego odgrywali w myślach, a także w niektórych gestach, ostatnie chwile życia Kinga. Ktoś zapytał, skąd nadleciała kula, a ktoś inny szepnął, że pocisk wystrzelony przez Jamesa Earla Raya wypadł z hukiem z wychodzącego właśnie na północ okna w zabitym deskami pensjonacie po drugiej stronie ulicy. Północ oznaczała wolność, prawda? Twarz Jeba wyglądała jak gąbka, ociekała łzami. Stał na tej ulicy i rozpadał się, rozpadał, rozpadał na kawałki, myśląc o okrętach wojennych na Morzu Południowochińskim. O tym, jak w jego uszach pod pokładem rozlegały się odgłosy przypominające pierdzenie i trzaski. I że gdy pewnego razu wyjrzał na zewnątrz przez jeden z wielu bulajów, zobaczył gigantyczną ośmiornicę, w której mackach młodszy chorąży marynarki Nelson Mammoth podskakiwał niczym cyrkowiec na trapezie. Tej nocy zerwał ze ściany w kabinie listę RZECZY, KTÓRYCH JEB NIE MUSI WIEDZIEĆ. Podarł ją na kawałeczki drobne jak konfetti. Ale następnego dnia znowu wisiała na ścianie. Spisana schludnym pismem Eddiego Christie. Eddie znał ją na pamięć. Może tak powinni zachowywać się kuzyni, bracia – przyjaciele? Jeb znów zapłakał za doktorem Kingiem.

MYRTLE URATOWAŁA JEBA w czasie przerwy na lunch; zabrała go z ulicy przed motelem Lorraine. Pracowała jako ekspedientka w dziale perfumeryjno-kosmetycznym jednego z dużych domów towarowych w centrum Memphis. Posada odpowiadała jej pod każdym względem, ale po powrocie do domu Myrtle zawsze zmywała makijaż. Niektóre panie wybierały kosmetyki Pond's, inne szastały pieniędzmi na droższe produkty. Do czyszczenia cery Myrtle używała oczaru wirginijskiego, a do nawilżania oliwy. Pozycję sprzedawczyni uznała za swój sukces, ponieważ nie była piękna ani jasnowłosa, a gdy starała się o pracę, usłyszała, że czarna kobieta o stosunkowo jasnym odcieniu skóry, chociaż przyjemniejsza dla oka, może zanadto rozpraszać białych klientów, którzy przychodzą czasem po perfumy dla żon, a jednocześnie stanowić zagrożenie dla białych kobiet, z którymi tych facetów mogły łączyć jakieś związki.

Dlaczego to zrobili? – zwrócił się do niej. Dlaczego musieli go zabić? Wzięła Jeba za rękę i odciągnęła na bok.

WIEDZIAŁA, ŻE TAM PÓJDZIE, jeszcze zanim otworzył usta. Przyjezdni czasem nawet przysięgali, że w ogóle o tym nie myślą, ale nogi i tak same prowadziły ich do motelu Lorraine. Jeb nie był pierwszym podróżnym, którego znalazła dygoczącego na chodniku jak liść. Kiedy przyjeżdżali mężczyźni i mieli w oczach ten mord, zawsze mówiła sobie, że odprawi ich z kwitkiem. „Myślicie, że w Memphis jest wyłącznie śmierć, a ona przecież jest wszędzie", chciała im powiedzieć, ale coś w niej – albo w nich – zawsze ją przed tym powstrzymywało. Ci ludzie mogli wylądować pod kluczem lub w szpitalu, skrzywdzeni, gdyby ktoś nie zrozumiał, skąd wzięły się ich rany. A rany nosili wszyscy.

Powiedziała o tym Jebowi, szykując mu kąpiel. Powiedziała mu to, sypiąc dla niego do wanny sól angielską: Przykro mi, ale muszę doliczyć panu do rachunku koszt soli.

Powiedziała mu to, zamykając drzwi łazienki, w której zostawiła krzesło, żeby miał na czym usiąść i położyć ubranie. Powiedziała mu to, kiedy godzinę później wyszedł z kąpieli goły jak święty turecki, bo zapomniał ręcznika, a Myrtle krzyknęła przeraźliwie, sądząc, że chce ją wziąć siłą. Pod wpływem tego krzyku dostał erekcji. Potem okrył swoją nagość i powiedział: Myrtle, to nie tak.

Wycofała się do salonu, na powleczoną folią plastikową dwuosobową kanapę koloru burgunda, i usiadła, żeby zapalić papierosa. Nie domyślił się, że jest palaczką. Nie wyczuwał od niej zapachu dymu.

Ubrał się szybko i zaproponował, że wyjedzie.

Na obiad przygotowała mu stek Salisbury z warzywami z puszki i piure ziemniaczanym.

Przepraszam, powiedziała. Żadna ze mnie kucharka. I nie mam dzieci. Z tych dwóch powodów mąż uznał, że musi mnie porzucić. „Co z ciebie za kobieta?", mówił. „Nie umiesz gotować ani wydawać dzieci na ten świat". Jestem Anną, odpowiedziałam mu na to. Jestem Sarą.

Przygotowywała posiłek, paląc papierosy. Popiół wpadał do garnka. Jeb zastanawiał się, czy nikotyna podniesie smak potrawy.

„To już trzeci argument na twoją niekorzyść", tak mi powiedział. „Odwołujesz się do Biblii. A każdy wie, że kobiety, które czytają Biblię, nie umieją się ruchać". Jak myślisz, kto mu wmówił coś takiego? – zapytała Jeba.

Nie wiem.

Powiedz mi coś: czy ty w ogóle coś wiesz?

Wiedział, kiedy ktoś próbuje go sprowokować: Wiem, że dwie godziny temu miałem się zgłosić do pracy.

PÓŹNIEJ, W ŁÓŻKU, kreślił palcami wokół małych, spiczastych piersi Myrtle kręgi, przypominające tor lotu gołębicy. Chichotała i biła go po rękach, żeby przestał.

Myrtle, szeptał, przyciągając ją bliżej: Ten twój mąż był głupi. Będzie mi bardzo smutno, kiedy stąd odjadę.

W naszym domu towarowym wszyscy wiedzą, kto wyprowadza się z miasta, oświadczyła. Powiedz mi jeszcze raz, gdzie mieszka ta kobieta, której meble macie zabrać. Lubię twoje towarzystwo, ale niełatwo dzisiaj o uczciwą pracę.

PRZYGLĄDAŁ SIĘ, jak Nancy Vincent otwiera mały owalny pojemniczek z cieniem do powiek w kolorze *china blue*. Myrtle dała mu go dla niej na prezent, żeby się nie gniewała. Siedząca w jadalni Nancy użyła aplikatora do pokrycia powiek grubą warstwą cienia. Powiedziała Jebowi i Seamusowi, że życzy sobie, aby kolonialny stół i krzesła, należące do jej prawie już byłego męża, podrzucić do Bostonu w drodze do nowego domu w Portsmouth, w New Hampshire. Jej już prawie były mąż mieszkał teraz w Bostonie, bo najpierw stracił pracę jako kapitan straży pożarnej w Huntington, a później tu, w Memphis. Z Jimmym seniorem zawsze coś było nie tak. Nancy została na miejscu, żeby sprzedać dom, ale tęskniła już za Wschodnim Wybrzeżem.

Jeb nie miał wiele do roboty, bo Seamus sam zapakował do ciężarówki właściwie cały dom. Krążyli teraz z pokoju do pokoju w bungalowie Nancy, wynosząc wszystko, co jeszcze w nim zostało i należało do niej.

Nie chciałem cię zostawić samego, powiedział Jeb.

Seamus wzruszył ramionami.

Gdzie byłeś?

Miałem coś do załatwienia.

No to chyba przyjemnie być panem swojego czasu.

Jeb nie chciał sprzeczki. Nie kiedy był w dobrym nastroju.

Weź moją działkę za robotę, którą wykonałeś beze mnie, powiedział; i wczorajszą dietę hotelową też. W ten sposób będziemy kwita.

Jaki ty jesteś hojny, roześmiał się Seamus. Miał przekrwione oczy. Przez całą noc imprezował na Beale Street ze swoim znajomym. Trącił Jeba pod żebro: Wystarczy na ciebie popatrzeć, żeby zrozumieć, że trafiło ci się jakieś dymanko.

W czasie służby wojskowej Jeb nawet by nie mrugnął na dobór słów Seamusa. Zachowywał się szpetnie i wulgarnie w najlepszym towarzystwie, lecz od powrotu do matczynego domu musiał uważać, jak się wyraża.

Fajnie było, powiedział.

Seamus mrugnął do niego porozumiewawczo.

No to jest nas dwóch.

GDY JUŻ SKOŃCZYLI pakować obrzeża jej życia, Nancy Vincent wzięła swoją walizkę Samsonite i wypłynęła przez drzwi niczym żaglowiec.

No tak, powiedziała, malując usta jasnoczerwoną szminką dla kontrastu z niebieskim cieniem do powiek i wsiadając do różowego cadillaca, który mógł pomieścić sześciu pasażerów: Życie polega na krążeniu w kółko. Do zobaczenia w Portsmouth. Postarajcie się dojechać cało i dowieźć wszystkie moje rzeczy w jednym kawałku.

Gdy odjechała, Seamus zauważył, że doskonale się trzyma jak na starszą babkę, psia jej mać. Kiedy wrócił do domu z Wietnamu, cycki jego żony były już obwisłe niczym baloniki na drugi dzień po imprezie. Nie potrafił nie myśleć, dlaczego o siebie nie dbała i że może sobie iść do diabła, skoro nie jest w stanie dać mu syna. Jeb słuchał, ale niczego nie komentował, bo wiedział, że jego opinia na temat urody białej kobiety może wzbudzić w głowie Seamusa krępujące myśli, za które kiedyś obarczy winą swojego kolegę z roboty. Do Portsmouth w stanie New Hampshire mieli tysiąc trzysta sześćdziesiąt cztery mile i siedemset jardów.

ZATRZYMALI SIĘ w przydrożnym motelu dla kierowców ciężarówek gdzieś z dala od miasta, w Ohio. Seamus wyciągnął blanta i zapalił. Wolał spać w ciężarówce, żeby zaoszczędzić na pokoju. Jeb nie czuł się swobodnie, ani śpiąc przy drodze, ani w cudzych smrodach. W nocnym powietrzu czaił się już chłód. Zbliżał się czas Święta Dziękczynienia.

Ulubionym rekreacyjnym narkotykiem Jeba i Seamusa była marihuana, chociaż żaden z nich nie odmawiał też grzybków, amfetaminy czy barbituranów. Żeby nie zwracać niczyjej uwagi, weszli na pakę i zaciągali się raz jeden, raz drugi. Po kilku machach Seamus zaczął się śmiać, a Jeb chciał wydobyć z siebie śmiech, ale nie mógł, bo zaczęło go swędzieć całe ciało i bez przerwy się drapał. Seamus powiedział: Jeb, albo tu są jakieś owady, albo ty masz wszy.

Jeszcze zanim umilkł, sam się zaczął drapać. Wstali, by zabrać się do szukania źródła problemu (Seamus uznał później, że winny był płyn do czyszczenia tapicerki, którym dezynfekowano samochód). Ale dokładnie w tym momencie ogarnęła ich ciemność. Kolonialne meble, należące niegdyś do ciotki Jimmy'ego Vincenta seniora z Cabot w stanie Maine, zaczęły płakać za tą kobietą, Nancy, która w każdą niedzielę rano pastowała je olejkiem cytrynowym. Krzesła zaczęły się uginać pod ciężarem łez stołu i Seamus powiedział: Kurwa, co się dzieje?

Jeb, który widywał ducha zabitego człowieka, nie dziwił się, że meble umieją mówić, tylko otworzył drzwi i wyskoczył na żwirowaną dróżkę, niczym pies, który próbuje strząsnąć z siebie pchły. Świeże powietrze natychmiast rozjaśniło mu w głowie i położył się na ziemi, oddychając głęboko. Niebo w górze otworzyło się i widział nie tylko świat, ale rozciągający się przed nim cały kosmos, i chciał się śmiać, śpiewać i biegać po pustyni, bo serce mówiło mu, że Myrtle Hendricks czeka, żeby go kochać.

Zakochaliśmy się i mamy odlot, zawołał Jeb do Seamusa, który wygramolił się z paki i siedział teraz w kabinie, przeszukując schowek pod deską rozdzielczą.

Kolonialny stół i cztery krzesła wypadły z ciężarówki przeprowadzkowej firmy Axelrod i dały w długą. Seamus spojrzał na Jeba, Jeb na Seamusa, i Seamus ruszył biegiem, żeby sprowadzić uciekające meble z powrotem. Jeb wstał, strzepując z siebie drobne kamyki. Pognał za swoim towarzyszem. Dogonienie potężnego weterana zajęło mu więcej czasu, niż się spodziewał.

Posłuchaj, powiedział Jeb, nadal się drapiąc: W tym pierdolonym stanie żyją grzechotniki i skorpiony. I pewnie kojoty też.

Seamus wyciągnął z kieszeni kombinezonu rewolwer. Było to magnum .357, pierwsza inwestycja, jakiej dokonał po powrocie do Stanów. Bezrobocie osiągnęło najwyższy poziom w historii – w całym kraju. A on nie mógł już dłużej walczyć z ogniem. Jeżeli strażak nie może walczyć z ogniem, to świat z pewnością przestał być bezpiecznym miejscem.

Machnął bronią przed nosem Jebediaha: Ja się ich nie boję. Jak mają do mnie pytania, to ja mam odpowiedzi.

Jeb podniósł ręce i się cofnął. Seamus, powiedział niezupełnie swoim głosem, odłóż tego gnata, kurwa. Jesteś nawalony jak stodoła po żniwach.

Na haju czasem najlepiej mi się polowało. Niech te pieprzone meble lepiej tu wracają.

Zaczął strzelać do stołu i krzeseł, latających mu nad głową, po czym zniknął w ciemności, ściągając w biegu firmowy kombinezon. Jeb patrzył, jak dupsko szalonego Seamusa klapie na wietrze.

„Myśl". Myślał, że nie będzie dobrze, jeśli przyjadą gliny i zobaczą, że Seamus Camphor oddala się od niego, biegnąc z całych sił. „Myśl". Myślał, że jeśli zostawi kolegę na śmierć na pustyni, pojawią się podejrzenia o celowe działanie, a wtedy to on, Jeb, będzie pierwszym podejrzanym. Więc tak, po raz drugi tego wieczoru dogonił Seamusa, któremu tymczasem skończyła się amunicja.

Jeb przypomniał sobie, jak wujek mówił mu, że jeżeli przegrywasz, to nie istnieje nic takiego jak nieczysta walka, i wymierzył Seamusowi soczystego kopniaka w ścięgno Achillesa. Kiedy potężny biały mężczyzna upadł, upadła też jego broń, a wtedy Jeb chwycił ją i uderzył go tak, że stracił przytomność. Potem położył się przy nim i zasnął u jego boku jak dziecko.

Po drodze z Memphis do Portsmouth nie ma żadnej pustyni, w ten sposób powstają jednak fantastyczne opowieści. Tak fikcja staje się faktem, a urojone wspomnienia przeradzają się w legendę.

WJEŻDŻAJĄC DO BOSTONU w listopadzie 1971 roku, Jeb i Seamus słuchali w radiu następujących utworów:

The Carpenters, *Superstar*
Isaac Hayes, *Shaft*
Led Zeppelin, *When the Levee Breaks*
Marvin Gaye, *What's Going On*
The Rolling Stones, *Brown Sugar*
Rod Stewart, *Maggie May*
Bill Withers, *Ain't No Sunshine*
Three Dog Night, *Joy to the World*
Jean Knight, *Mr. Big Stuff*
The Osmonds, *One Bad Apple*
The Undisputed Truth, *Smiling Faces*
Paul Revere and the Raiders, *Indian Reservation*
Al Green, *I'm So Tired of Being Alone*

Bostońskie wieżowce okazały się mniejsze, niż oczekiwał Jeb. W roku 1971, na trzy dni przed Świętem Dziękczynienia, on i Seamus spotykali na ulicy weteranów zbierających datki do papierowych kubeczków albo stojących na chodniku w otoczeniu kartonowych pudeł z napisem „Weteran prosi o wsparcie". Epoka hippisów, na którą obaj się nie załapali, ponieważ byli na wojnie, właśnie się kończyła, a kiedy rozglądali się po mieście z ciężarówki firmy przeprowadzkowej, widok bezdomnych ludzi na ulicach mocno ich niepokoił. „Trudne miasto ten Boston", pomyślał Jeb, choć gdyby pojechał do Nowego Jorku, San Francisco, Los Angeles albo Chicago, przekonałby się, że tam też niełatwo było wtedy żyć.

TO PAN JEST JIMMY VINCENT? – zawołał Jeb z fotela pasażera. Czekali z Seamusem godzinę przed ceglanym domem Vincenta w południowym Bostonie, zanim emerytowany strażak wreszcie wrócił.

Możliwe. A kto pyta? – Jimmy Vincent przyjrzał im się badawczo. Jego twarz wyglądała jak zrobiona z wyprawionej skóry. Kiedyś była ludzka, ale nałogi zrobiły z jego czołem i podbródkiem straszne rzeczy. Na przedramieniu Jimmy'ego wisiała chuda brunetka. Jeśli wyglądała na dwadzieścia lat, to miała dziewiętnaście. A jeśli wyglądała na dziewiętnaście, to miała siedemnaście. Albo i mniej.

W ciężarówce stoją pańskie meble, oświadczył Jeb.

Powiedziałem Nancy, żeby je zatrzymała.

Pomyślała, że może zmieni pan zdanie, nie ustępował Jeb, a Seamus tymczasem zamaszyście otworzył drzwi wozu i zaczął wyładowywać stół i krzesła, Jeb zostawił więc Jimmy'ego z papierami w ręku i poszedł pomóc koledze.

Dziewczyna podeszła bliżej i wcisnęła palec w miękką folię, którą był owinięty stół, po czym radośnie klasnęła w dłonie: To wszystko dla nas?

Jimmy pokręcił głową: Wszystko, co daje mi Nancy, przynosi pecha.

Gdzie mamy to postawić? – spytał Jeb.

Jimmy Vincent zapalił papierosa: Zostawcie na chodniku.

Seamus był przerażony lekceważeniem, jakie ten człowiek okazywał nieożywionej spuściźnie: Te meble należą do was.

Dziewczyna przesunęła dłońmi po oparciach wysokich drewnianych krzeseł i wróciła na chodnik, by szepnąć coś do ucha swojemu partnerowi. Jimmy wzruszył ramionami. Dziewczyna znów radośnie klasnęła w dłonie i powiedziała: Postawcie je na ganku. Może je jutro sprzedamy.

Widzicie? – Jimmy wypuścił dym, wskazując w stronę dziewczyny, ale nie patrząc na nią. Poznałem toto zaledwie miesiąc temu, a już planuje za mnie moje życie i myśli, że mam ochotę, żeby ona została jego częścią.

Jeb i Seamus przenieśli meble na ganek. Dziewczyna bawiła się na nich w komórki do wynajęcia, a oparty o stół Jimmy palił pall malle i opowiadał o swojej byłej żonie. O tym, jak bardzo jej nienawidzi. I jak nieszczęśliwa byłaby jego przyszłość, gdyby nie ta nienawiść, do której przyzwyczaił się już jak do starego płaszcza. Może wcale jej nie nienawidził? Może po prostu nienawidził jej i siebie, kiedy byli razem? Bo razem przypominali zadymkę śnieżną.

Jeb uczył się, co to znaczy pracować przy przeprowadzkach. Pracować przy przeprowadzkach wcale nie znaczy zajmować się przewożonymi rzeczami, tylko poznawać ich historię. Poznawać różne pomyłki, do których dochodzi, kiedy przywiązuje się zbyt dużą wagę do ludzi, miejsc albo przedmiotów. Chociaż przedmioty mają swoją historię. A ta historia ucieszyła go, że podróżuje prawie bez bagażu.

CZYNNĄ PRZEZ CAŁĄ DOBĘ jadłodajnię zdobił pomrugujący neonowy szyld. Gdy Jeb i Seamus weszli do środka, prostokątny bufet i obrotowe krzesła przypomniały im kawiarnię Krispy Kreme Doughnuts w ich rodzinnych stronach. Na widok lukrowanych pączków w szklanej gablocie zaczęła im cieknąć ślinka. Kelnerki nosiły zielono-białe stroje z identyfikatorami, zupełnie jak kelnerki w Kress w Buckner County, w Georgii. Napis na tabliczce głosił: „Najlepsze burgery w Bostonie". Usiedli przy bufecie. Seamus zaczął bębnić palcami o blat i poprosił Jeba, żeby zamówił mu kawę, bo musi iść się odlać. Podeszła kelnerka w sukience pasującej do jej zielonych oczu i rozejrzała się po restauracji, po czym położyła serwetki, nóż i widelec przed pustym krzesłem Seamusa. A potem przed Jebem. Obserwowało ją kilka par oczu. Jeb, który był wyczulony na takie rzeczy, zauważył ich spojrzenia, zanim obrócił się na krześle i zobaczył, kto na niego patrzy. Jadłodajnia aż bulgotała ludźmi. Szukał choć jednej twarzy, która okazałaby się zwierciadlanym odbiciem jego oblicza, nie znalazł jednak żadnej. Spokojnie odwrócił się z powrotem, trzymając ręce wciśnięte w kieszenie cienkiej kurtki. Na zewnątrz drobniutkie niczym puder płatki śniegu zamieniały się w lód i deszcz.

Dwie kawy proszę, powiedział. Kelnerka uśmiechnęła się i szybko nalała kawę Seamusowi. Gdy pochyliła dzbanek nad kubkiem Jeba, podeszła do nich druga, starsza kelnerka, obserwująca ich wcześniej z dalszej odległości ze skrzyżowanymi na piersiach rękami.

Przykro mi. Nie ma kawy, powiedziała. Patrzyła na młodszą koleżankę, ale mówiła do Jeba.

A co ta pani trzyma w ręce? W głosie Jeba nie było słychać skargi, tylko ironię.

To nie jest kawa, odpowiedziała starsza kelnerka. Nosiła taki sam kok jak ciocia Flora. Jeb westchnął: A macie herbatę?

Starsza kelnerka pokręciła głową: Herbaty też nie ma.

A woda?

Popatrzyła na Jeba bez mrugnięcia okiem.

Jeżeli szybko ją wypijesz i wyjdziesz.

Mamy za sobą kawał drogi, powiedział Jeb, odwołując się do serca starszej kobiety. Twarz kelnerki z włosami zawiązanymi w koński ogon zrobiła się czerwona jak bożonarodzeniowa bombka. Nalała Jebowi szklankę wody. Był spragniony, ale duma nie pozwoliła mu nawet dotknąć naczynia. Nie było takiego pragnienia na świecie, które mogłoby go do tego zmusić.

Tylu klientów pije u was kawę, a pani mi mówi, że nie macie kawy? Jeb uczestniczył w protestach okupacyjnych w Buckner County, nie spodziewał się jednak, że będzie musiał brać w nich udział na Północy. Myśli mąciła mu senność, roztaczał wokół siebie aurę strachu i tremy podróżnego i nie wiedział, czy znajdzie w sobie dość siły, żeby protestować.

Starsza kelnerka zwróciła się do młodszej: Widzisz, co narobiłaś? Znasz zasady. Musisz to jakoś załatwić.

Odeszła, a młoda kelnerka szepnęła: Niech mi pan tego nie robi. Pracuję tu dopiero od tygodnia. I potrzebuję tej pracy.

Jeb odpowiedział głośniej, niż zamierzał: Jestem weteranem z Wietnamu. I Amerykaninem.

Młoda kelnerka westchnęła. Seamus wyszedł z toalety. Usiadł na swoim miejscu i zaczął popijać kawę.

A twoja? – spytał, dopiero teraz zauważając kelnerkę, ciszę i pusty kubek Jeba.

Tu nie ma kawy, Seamus.

Seamus rozkoszował się swoją kawą. Ciągle analizował sytuację i wcale się nie spieszył. Na tablicy napisali: „Najlepsze burgery". Boże, zjadłbym hamburgera z dodatkową porcją smażonej cebuli. Tam gdzie mieszkamy, mają cebule Vidalia. Myślisz, że tutaj też?

Jeb miał ochotę go uderzyć: Skąd, kurwa, mógłbym to wiedzieć, skoro w tej knajpie nie ma nawet kawy? Zjedz, co chcesz, i rób, co chcesz.

Wstał i wyszedł. Seamus powoli wysiorbał resztki z kubka i też wstał. No tak, chyba nie będę płacił za tę kawę. Tylko kompletny idiota płaci za coś, czego nie ma.

Wyszedł na zewnątrz za Jebem. Wsiedli do ciężarówki, Jeb usiadł za kierownicą, a Seamus rzucił mu kluczyki. Gdyby znali okolicę albo gdyby Jebowi przyszło do głowy, aby przejrzeć *Green Book*, mogliby pojechać do murzyńskiej dzielnicy Dorchester w południowym Bostonie. Oczywiście tam sytuacja pewnie by się odwróciła i to Seamus prawdopodobnie nie byłby mile widziany. Jak wiele amerykańskich miast w 1971 roku, Boston dzieliły różne rasowe granice i konflikty. Trzy lata po tym, jak odmówiono Jebowi obsługi w jadłodajni, bostoński kryzys kelnerski stał się tematem programów informacyjnych w całym kraju, a wielu mieszkańców Południa drwiło z hipokryzji Północy.

Odjeżdżali już, kiedy zielonooka kelnerka z kucykiem wybiegła z jadłodajni, przyciskając do piersi poplamioną tłuszczem papierową torebkę. Podeszła do kabiny od strony kierowcy: Niewiele. Burger i frytki dla was do podziału.

Dziękuję, powiedział Jeb.

Kelnerka pobiegła z powrotem do jadłodajni i zatrzymała się przy drzwiach: Mój młodszy brat jest w Wietnamie.

BURZA ŚNIEŻNA W ŚWIĘTO DZIĘKCZYNIENIA w 1971 roku uziemiła wielu podróżnych. Jebediaha Applewooda i Seamusa Camphora śnieg zasypał na pięć dni w Portsmouth w stanie New Hampshire. Nancy Vincent przepraszała ich za twardą drewnianą podłogę i rzuciła im koce, poduszki oraz śpiwory, żeby im było wygodniej. Żywili się kanapkami z indykiem, a także czymś, co było podobno rosołem z tego ptaka. Zupa okazała się sycąca, ale poza tym Nancy nie zwracała uwagi na gości, czytała tylko książki, które przesyłał jej syn, wzięty nowojorski prawnik. Seamus powiedział, że teraz rozumie, dlaczego jej były mąż zdecydował się na młodszą kobietę – bo Nancy nie robiła nic, żeby zaopiekować się mężczyzną, dawała mu wyłącznie jego chleb powszedni. A chleb powszedni przypomniał Jebowi Myrtle.

Popatrzył na śnieg i wyszedł pomóc Nancy odśnieżyć podjazd. Ubrał się grubo: flanelowa kurtka samochodowa, zamszowe rękawiczki i ocieplane dżinsy, zwisające luźno z jego chudych bioder. Nancy zatrzymała trochę ubrań byłego męża, z którymi nie mogła się rozstać. Jimmy junior, powiedziała. Może pewnego dnia będzie chciał je nosić Jimmy junior. Przebili ścieżkę w zaspach. Nancy przystanęła, żeby złapać oddech: Nijak nie mogę się pozbyć jego zapachu.

Kiedy zaczęła się śnieżyca, Seamus poszedł pieszo do odległego o siedem przecznic pubu, a Jeb dziewięć przecznic w przeciwnym kierunku, do miejscowego sklepu ze zdrową żywnością. Była to prymitywna placówka handlowa, należąca do Boone'a McAllistera, kolegi z dzieciństwa syna Nancy Vincent. Sklep oferował niewiele produktów, między innymi plastikowe kubełki z orzechami i soją. Miał też ogromną maszynę do mielenia ziarna, warzyw i fasoli na mąkę albo orzechów na masło orzechowe. Jeb wtedy o tym nie wiedział, był jednak świadkiem ewolucji ruchu makrobiotycznego, zainicjowanego przez japońskiego lekarza George'a Ohsawę. Boone przejął poglądy Ohsawy na temat żywienia i diety i wprowadził je w swoim sklepie w praktyce.

Powiedział Jebowi, że spotkanie na temat diety makrobiotycznej zostało odwołane z powodu śnieżycy, ale jeśli potrzebuje się przespać, to w piwnicy i pokoju na zapleczu jest jeszcze trochę miejsca.

Piwniczny sufit był niski; podłogę zastępowała polepa. Jeb znalazł też składane krzesła i stoliki, takie jak te, przy których na Południu grywało się w karty. W środku było już co najmniej sześciu mężczyzn. Niektórzy cuchnęli po kilku dniach bez mydła, ich ciała i ubrania oblepiał smród. Przychodzili na zupę i kanapki, które Boone zapewniał im raz w tygodniu. Jeb dowiedział się od tych weteranów, że niedaleko mieści się baza powietrzna lotnictwa Stanów Zjednoczonych i że tanio można mieszkać w Seacrest, ale dom jest tam nieuszczelniony, więc chłód zostaje w kościach. Podobno marynarka wojenna pomyliła plany Seacrest z planami jakiegoś osiedla mieszkaniowego, które budowała dla swoich w Wirginii.

Weterani rozmawiali o wojnie. I o teoriach spiskowych. Wszyscy mieli coś do powiedzenia o CIA. Niektórzy przysięgali, że widzieli samoloty opuszczające Wietnam z ładunkiem heroiny. Rozmawiali o eksperymentach z LSD. I trudnych decyzjach. Ktoś musiał rozwalić granatem swojego oficera, żeby ocalić pluton.

Jeb nie walczył w Wietnamie na lądzie, zwykle więc siedział cicho. Generalnie uważał, że lepiej słuchać, niż mówić, a kiedy w końcu miał coś do powiedzenia, dziwił się, że jednak gada do rzeczy. Opisał swoją wizytę w klinice dla weteranów w Buckner County i tego rozzłoszczonego żołnierza o połyskliwej łysej głowie, który nie potrafił jasno formułować myśli. Opowiedział, jak wyciągnięto go za drzwi, gdy zaczął kopać i przeraźliwie krzyczeć na widok formularzy. Teraz był już zupełnie pewien, że tamten żołnierz w ogóle nie umiał czytać – o młodszym chorążym zwanym Nelson Mammoth nie napomknął jednak ani słowem.

DZIEŃ PRZED PLANOWANYM WYJAZDEM obu pracowników firmy przeprowadzkowej Boone McAllister zaproponował Jebowi pracę w sklepie. Zauważył, że Jeb początkowo jak gdyby stał w miejscu, ale potem zrobił krok do przodu. Że składa krzesła i stoliki po spotkaniach i czyta wszystkie broszury. I ślęczy nad makrobiotycznymi książkami kucharskimi.

Zastanawiam się, czy nie zrezygnować z jedzenia wieprzowiny, powiedział Jeb.

Jesteś na dobrej drodze, żeby zostać wegetarianinem.

No nie wiem, czy tak będzie.

Wtedy Boone McAllister oświadczył: Potrzebujemy tu kogoś, kto pomagałby otwierać i zamykać sklep. Myślisz, że mógłbyś obsługiwać kasę?

PO DRODZE DO DOMU Nancy Jebowi wydało się, że widzi z daleka wsiadającą do samochodu kobietę podobną do Myrtle. Od dnia przyjazdu do Portsmouth nie widział żadnej innej czarnoskórej osoby (chociaż dowiedział się później, że czarni mieszkali tu już od czasów rewolucji amerykańskiej). Zawołał na nią, kobieta odwróciła się, miała szparę między przednimi zębami i spojrzenie mówiące, że go nie zna. W ogóle nie przypominała Myrtle i szybkim krokiem odeszła. Mimo to na myśl o znajomej z Memphis ciało Jeba zareagowało w wyjątkowo przyjemny sposób. Dostał erekcji.

Szukał budki telefonicznej i znalazł jedną, całą oblepioną śniegiem. Kiedy jego członek rozluźnił się i skurczył, zadzwonił do Myrtle Hendricks na jej koszt. Po trzecim sygnale odebrała i zgodziła się zapłacić za połączenie.

Nie chciałabyś przypadkiem zamieszkać w New Hampshire?

Czekała na jego telefon, chociaż nie miała nadziei, że zadzwoni. Nie pozwalała sobie na nadzieję.

Nigdy tam nie byłam.

To może powinnaś przyjechać?

A tak konkretnie to dokąd? New Hampshire to stan, nie miasto.

Jeb mówił do słuchawki: Zaczniemy w Portsmouth. I zobaczymy, jak nam pójdzie dalej.

Odezwała się po dłuższej chwili: Będzie mi potrzebny adres.

Jeb przestąpił z nogi na nogę.

Zadzwonię natychmiast, jak będę już go miał.

SEAMUS WIEDZIAŁ, że namawianie Jeba, by wrócił do Buckner County, byłoby kompletnie bez sensu. Szybko uścisnęli sobie dłonie, pożegnań nie lubił bowiem żaden z nich. Camphor wsiadł do ciężarówki firmy przeprowadzkowej i stwierdził, że podróż powrotna będzie cholernie nudna. Nigdy potem nie miał już czarnoskórego kumpla i zawsze starał się nie robić krzywdy czarnym. Wiele lat później – długo po tym, jak Jebediah został terapeutą w bazie lotniczej Pease w Portsmouth – Seamus często narzekał, opowiadając o swoim internowaniu na Północy. Twierdził, że dostał reumatyzmu wskutek mrozów, których doświadczył w tamto Święto Dziękczynienia. Że zaatakowały jego ciało i umysł. Że przegrał bitwę, ale wygrał wojnę i wówczas na nowo rozpalił w sobie zdolność do walki z pożarami.

DWORZEC AUTOBUSOWY W PORTSMOUTH znajdował się w pobliżu hotelu, w którym Jeb na jedną noc wynajął pokój dla siebie i Myrtle. Nancy Vincent pożyczyła mu swojego różowego cadillaca, aby mógł odebrać Myrtle z dworca.

„Romans”, powiedziała. „Uwielbiam romanse. Z nich składa się połowa moich problemów”.

Myrtle wysiadła z autobusu tylko z jedną walizką, bo nie ufała swojemu sercu na tyle, by zabrać wszystkie rzeczy, a przy tym wiedziała, jak chimeryczni potrafią być mężczyźni. Pozamykała drzwi do domu, dała klucze kuzynom i powiedziała, że pozostanie z nimi w kontakcie listownym.

Stała na dworcu, rozglądając się w lewo i prawo. Naprawdę zdumiało ją, jak bardzo jest tu zimno, nawet w dworcowym budynku, śledziła jednak prognozy pogody i przywiozła jedną kurtkę dla siebie, drugą dla Jeba. Gdy Jeb zobaczył Myrtle, podszedł i wziął jej bagaże.

Na pewno jesteś zmęczona.

Ty też, odpowiedziała.

Wyszli z dworca ramię w ramię.

Razem.

ELOISE ODLATUJE

1947 1958 1968

BESSIE COLEMAN BYŁA PIERWSZĄ KOBIETĄ, którą pokochała Eloise Delaney – zanim się dowiedziała, co w ogóle znaczy miłość. Na prostokątnej fotografii, wyciętej z „Buckner County Register", miejscowej murzyńskiej gazety, Bessie stoi na lewym kole swojego dwupłatowca Curtiss JN-4 „Jenny", a jej osłonięta rękawiczką prawa dłoń obejmuje kokpit. Bessie jest w szytym na miarę stroju lotniczym i patrzy prosto w obiektyw. Zdjęcie ma co najmniej trzydzieści lat, pochodzi z 1926 roku, roku przedwczesnej śmierci czarnej pilotki, ale rodzicom Eloise ciągle się wydaje, że do katastrofy doszło wczoraj. Byli znanymi w miasteczku pijakami i czas zamulił im myśli.

– Gdyby Bóg chciał, żeby człowiek miał skrzydła, toby mu je dał – stwierdził Herbert Delaney.

– Czy nie było kiedyś takiej sztuki? – jego żona, Delores, pstryknęła palcami. – *Wszystkie boże dziatki są skrzydlate*?

Herbert wzruszył ramionami.

– Nie mierzyła sił na zamiary. Chciała latać.

– Co ty mówisz, Herbercie? – Delores pocałowała smukłe, chude dłonie męża. – Mówisz, że Bóg chciał, żeby jej samolot się rozbił? Chciał, żeby Bessie zginęła?

– No, na pewno ni cholery nie chciał, żeby żyła. Inaczej ten jej przeklęty samolot by się nie zepsuł.

DWUPŁATOWIEC BESSIE COLEMAN rozbił się w czasie spektakularnej wystawy w Orlando na Florydzie. Delores lubiła się chwalić, że stała w samiuteńkim środku tłumu widzów tego ranka, gdy „Dzielna Bessie" runęła na ziemię z wysokości dwóch tysięcy stóp, Eloise wiedziała jednak, że nie należy wierzyć niczemu, co mówi pijaczka, zwłaszcza jeśli jest nią jej rodzona matka.

MIMO TO PAMIĘTAŁA te rzadkie wieczory z dzieciństwa, kiedy siedziała przy kuchennym stole na połamanym taborecie pomiędzy matką i ojcem, i wszyscy oglądali ten wycinek z gazety, a ona nie musiała rywalizować o ich zainteresowanie z piwem, bourbonem, whisky ani ginem.

RODZICE ELOISE pracowali w przetwórni owoców morza dwie mile poza miastem. Dorastali, otwierając ostrygi, zbierając kraby i patrosząc ryby. Zapłata za robienie czegoś, co było ich drugą naturą, przypominała trochę płacenie komuś za to, że jedzie na urlop. Potrafili zbierać kraby z zamkniętymi oczami, a tempo ich pracy wcale nie spadało. Czasami niespokojne palce obojga poruszały się we śnie, odrzucając tak zwane truposze i ciężarne brzuchy krabów, i wydłubywały delikatne, białe mięso. Co jakiś czas kierownik przetwórni musiał dla przykładu besztać Herberta i Delores za to, że przychodzili do pracy w stanie nietrzeźwym, spóźnieni, albo że nie przychodzili wcale. Pozwalał im wypocić alkohol, a Eloise chodziła głodna, dopóki rodzicom nie udawało się wyślizgnąć chyłkiem z przetwórni.

ZAKŁAD MIEŚCIŁ SIĘ w dawnym magazynie, wychodzącym na słone bagna. W szczycie sezonu zbierackiego Herbert i Delores zabierali córkę ze sobą do pracy. Wyglądała przez wysokie okna na czaple, mewy, pelikany, rybołowy i czarne niczym węgiel kormorany, przeczesujące bagna w poszukiwaniu pożywienia.

„RODZICE CZĘŚCIEJ MNIE PILNOWALI, niż zostawiali samą". Tak brzmiała półprawda, którą Eloise powtarzała swoim przyjaciółkom. Jeśli wypowiadała te słowa dość głośno, sama prawie wierzyła, że są prawdziwe. Ale jako dziewięcio-, dziesięcio- czy jedenastoletnie dziecko, chude i wysokie, ze sterczącymi na boki twardymi łokciami, potrafiła nieźle dziabnąć każdego chłopaka w krocze, jeśli powiedział coś złośliwego o jej rodzicach albo znoszonych, używanych ubraniach, w których chodziła.

„To jest stracone dziecko", głosił osiedlowy chór.

„Cześć. Do widzenia. Uprzejmie proszę pocałować mnie w moją czarną dupę", mówiła Eloise.

„Słyszeliście? Biedactwo. To dlatego że jej rodzice niczego jej nie uczą". Tak brzmiał z kolei osiedlowy refren.

CHODZIŁA DO SZKOŁY przez pięć dni w tygodniu, od poniedziałku do piątku. Bez względu na pogodę. Jeśli padało, brała kawałek plastikowej folii i formowała z niej coś w rodzaju płaszcza przeciwdeszczowego. Później, kiedy była już starsza i chodziła na zakupy ze swoimi kochankami, patrzyła na kolorowe płaszcze przeciwdeszczowe po czterdzieści dolarów za sztukę albo i więcej, i kręciła głową. „Nic dziwnego, że młodych na nic nie stać. Co to za wiotka tkanina?" – mruczała pod nosem i marudziła, ale mimo wszystko kupowała płaszcz dla kolejnej kochanki, bo dbała o swoje kobiety.

GDY BYŁA MAŁA, nie miała daleko do szkoły. Nie widywała po drodze pasących się krów ani świń. Szkoła, do której codziennie szła pieszo, nie okazała się jednoizbowym domkiem na odludziu. St. Paul's of the Redemption była katolicką placówką dla czarnych, obejmującą klasy od pierwszej do dwunastej, prowadzoną przez zakonnice o twarzach koloru niepasteryzowanego mleka. Po południu potrzebowały parasoli, żeby osłonić się przed ostrym, gniewnym spojrzeniem słońca.

W ROKU 1958, gdy poszła do szóstej klasy, mieszkała zaledwie trzy przecznice od szkoły, chociaż wydawało się jej, że są to trzy mile, bo szła na zajęcia o pustym żołądku i kręciło się jej w głowie. Pusty żołądek mówi skołowanej głowie: „Możesz się wywyższać, jeśli chcesz, ale ja będę burczał". Pusty żołądek mówi skołowanej głowie: „Napinasz te chude ramiona, jak gdyby mogły podtrzymać cały świat, jeśli tylko byś tego chciała, ale ja mam skurcze". Pusty żołądek mówi skołowanej głowie: „Jestem głęboko urażony, że nie nakarmiłaś mnie dziś rano, i zobacz, co się teraz ze mną dzieje. Mam gazy". Pusty żołądek mówi skołowanej głowie: „Schyl się i chwyć za brzuch, zanim wyrzucę z siebie pustkę pierwszego dnia szkoły i zwymiotuję na twoją tanią sukienkę".

NIE PŁAKAŁA; to nie było w stylu Eloise. Mimo że zapaskudziła sobie uda i kolana. Zakryła mokrą plamę serwetką i starała się uważać na lekcji jak najlepiej, było jednak tylko kwestią czasu, kiedy się rozklei i rozkojarzy. Czy czuję tu wymiociny? Wierciła się na krześle. Nie potrafiła usiedzieć spokojnie. Nauczycielka, siostra Mary Laranski, młoda zakonnica, która dopiero niedawno złożyła śluby, mogła sięgnąć po linijkę i zacząć bić Eloise po rękach do krwi, ale tylko obrzuciła klasę spojrzeniem: kolorowi uczniowie, jedni w mundurkach, inni nie, w większości ubodzy. Kiedy zwróciła się do swoich nowych podopiecznych, zadrżał jej głos.

– Znacie Shakespeare'a, chłopcy i dziewczęta?

Reuben Applewood podniósł rękę.

– Słyszeliśmy o nim.

– A co? – zapytała siostra Laranski.

Reuben nie odrywał wzroku od swojej ławki.

– Był Anglikiem. I pisał sztuki. „Być albo nie być, oto jest pytanie".

Siostra Laranski uśmiechnęła się. Reuben był najinteligentniejszym chłopcem w klasie. Potem, pod koniec roku, zaproponowała, żeby od razu przeskoczył o rok wyżej.

– Życie bez Shakespeare'a to moim zdaniem w ogóle nie jest życie – oświadczyła. – Abraham Lincoln zdobył bardzo dobre wykształcenie, czytając tylko Shakespeare'a i Biblię. Niektórym z was nie udaje się przychodzić do szkoły codziennie, a nawet nie co tydzień, ale jeśli choć trochę poznacie Shakespeare'a, nie wszystko będzie stracone.

Mówiła z lekkim cudzoziemskim akcentem, który było lepiej słychać, gdy się denerwowała. Dzieci zauważyły go i zaciekawiło je, skąd pochodzi.

– Skąd siostra jest, siostro Mary? – zapytał któryś z uczniów.

– Wy nie znacie chyba tego kraju.

Na ścianie nie było mapy i siostra Laranski zakonotowała sobie, żeby ją kupić. Na razie wzięła kawałek kredy i narysowała mapę Europy na tablicy. Rysowanie ukoiło jej nerwy.

– Pochodzę z Budapesztu. To takie miasto na Węgrzech.

– A czy tęskni siostra za swoim krajem? – zapytał inny uczeń.

– Tęskniłabym, gdybym go pamiętała. Przekonacie się na własnej skórze, że kiedy człowiek dorasta, traci pamięć dzieciństwa.

Uczniowie wkrótce mieli się dowiedzieć, że siostra Mary zawsze płakała w szkolnych toaletach dlatego, że rodzice oddali ją do zakonu. Dostała od dzieci przezwisko Mary Płacząca, bo uczyła ich Shakespeare'a i płakała jak Ofelia.

Ale Eloise guzik obchodziło to, co siostra Mary Płacząca mówiła pierwszego dnia szkoły. Dziewczyna zrozumiała teraz, co to jest miłość, która ją ogarnęła – zawładnęła nią bez reszty – gdy tylko Agnes Miller usiadła w ławce obok i otworzyła piórnik.

AGNES CZESAŁA SIĘ w dwa wilgotne kucyki i miała idealnie równą grzywkę. Kiedy się na nią patrzyło, można było odnieść wrażenie, że splądrowała szafę Natalie Cole. Tak, Eloise wydawało się, że córka Nata Kinga Cole'a weszła dumnym krokiem do katolickiej szkoły St. Paul's of the Redemption jak do swojego domu. Czy to nie jest niezła jazda, kurde? Słyszała, jak jej serce wali „bum, bum, bam, bam, bum", niczym silnik w buicku, którego mieli kiedyś jej rodzice, a który przez jakiś czas jeździł zupełnie dobrze, po czym nagle się psuł i wszyscy musieli wysiadać i pchać go w dół wzgórza, żeby znowu zaskoczył, albo gorzej, stać na poboczu i czekać, aż ktoś ich podwiezie. Nie spojrzała na Eloise ani razu. Nie mrużyła powiek, nie marszczyła nosa, nie śmiała się i nie uśmiechała smutno, jak inne dzieci, na widok jej używanych, znoszonych ubranek. Największą zniewagą, jaką jej wyrządziła, było to, że siedziała z rękami złożonymi nonszalancko na kolanach, jak gdyby Eloise w ogóle nie istniała. A Eloise zastanawiała się, czy może Agnes poczuła odór wymiocin bijący z jej sukienki. W czasie przerwy na lunch, który jadały w klasie, patrzyła, jak Agnes je coś, co wyglądało na sześć miniaturowych ciasteczek lawendowych. Zlizała blady fioletowawy lukier ze wszystkich, z wyjątkiem jednego, przestała jeść i zaproponowała Eloise ciastko, które właśnie przed chwilą oblizała. Eloise pokręciła głową: „Nie, dziękuję". Uznała, że nie może tolerować takiej protekcjonalności. W drodze do domu, kiedy Reuben Applewood i wszystkie pozostałe grzeczne dzieci już poszły, powiedziała kilku swoim koleżankom z klasy: „Słuchajcie; patrzcie, co zrobię". Ułamała gałązkę morwy, oczyściła ją z liści, a potem ruszyła ulicą w ślad za Agnes Miller i zaczęła ją chłostać po lśniących czarnoskórych nogach. Agnes zaskoczyła jednak Eloise, bo przesunęła tylko pasek od torby z książkami, niesionej na ramieniu, i rzuciła się na napastniczkę z pazurami jak bezdomny kot, więc Eloise wróciła do domu w swojej taniej sukience cała podrapana na twarzy.

– **KTO TO ZROBIŁ?** – chciała wiedzieć Delores.

– Ma na imię Agnes – odpowiedziała Eloise. Matka oczyściła jej buzię wilgotną ściereczką i oczarem wirginijskim, a następnie posmarowała zadrapania masłem kakaowym.

– Kim są jej rodzice? – spytał Herbert Delaney. – Jak ona ma na nazwisko?

– Nie wiem – odpowiedziała Eloise.

– Czy nie Applewood? – zapytał znów ojciec. Eloise nie znosiła, kiedy rodzice wspominali Applewoodów. Była to najstarsza czarna rodzina w mieście i jakiś Applewood chodził do każdej klasy.

– Nie – odpowiedziała. – Ma na nazwisko Miller.

Delores Delaney zmarszczyła brwi, odczekała kilka sekund i pacnęła córkę w ucho.

– Ty głupie dziewuszysko – powiedziała. – To córka lady i diakona Millerów. Jej papa jest mularzem. To ważniacy. Nie wiesz, co się dzieje, kiedy zero zadziera z kimś lepszym od siebie?

DELORES I HERBERT DELANEYOWIE zaprowadzili Eloise do domu Agnes Miller i kazali jej przeprosić Agnes i jej rodziców. Eloise z zasady nienawidziła swoich starych, ale nigdy tak bardzo jak tamtego dnia. Kiedy wrócili do swojego bungalowu, uciekła do kuchni i stanęła przed gazetowym wycinkiem z Bessie Coleman. Podniosła ręce, udając, że to skrzydła dwupłatowca Curtiss JN-4 „Jenny" i że szybuje w powietrzu.

OGIEŃ PRZESKOCZYŁ PRZEZ GANEK i ulokował się w kuchni, gdzie dodatkowego paliwa dostarczyły mu zasłony, podobnie jak puszki z tłuszczem do smażenia ryb i kurczaka. Delores i Herbert, splątani ze sobą rękami i nogami, spali na kanapie w salonie. Eloise obudziła się w swoim pokoju, przylegającym do kuchni, wyczuwszy w nozdrzach dymne tornado. Zaczęła wołać matkę i ojca, słyszała jednak tylko trzask płomieni. Rodzice zostawili na ganku niedopałek i włączony palnik pod aluminiową patelnią, na której wcześniej smażyli na kolację grube płaty kupionej w sklepie szynki.

ZAWOŁAŁA ZNOWU: „Mamo? Tato?", i zaczęła czołgać się na brzuchu jak wąż, by uniknąć kłębów dymu. Znalazła rodziców chrapiących na kanapie. Przez chwilę patrzyła, jak płomienie liżą ściany salonu, i pomyślała: „Może tak byłoby lepiej?", a potem puściła się biegiem przez korytarz, osłaniając usta przed dymem rzuconą gdzieś niedbale matczyną sukienką. Zabrała ze sobą wycinek z Bessie Coleman. Był lekko nadpalony na brzegach, lecz ogień go nie strawił. Wypadła z kuchni, pobiegła korytarzem do drzwi wejściowych. Zrobiła już krok naprzód, ale serce nie pozwoliło jej ich tak zostawić. Wróciła do kanapy, zaczęła kopać i przeklinać rodziców.

– Wyłaźcie, ale już. Zabierajcie te swoje przeklęte, nic niewarte czarne dupska z tej pieprzonej kanapy.

Uciekli w ostatniej chwili, zaraz potem zawalił się strop.

W STRAŻY POŻARNEJ Buckner County służyli sami biali. Dotarli na miejsce, gdy pożoga już strawiła wszystko, zdążyli jednak uratować okoliczne domy, które nie poszły z dymem. Walczyli z ogniem, używając wiader z wodą i dwóch długich węży. Dowódca – zwany Seamusem I, dziadek Dużego Seamusa, który spłodził Seamusa III, który z kolei spłodził Grubego Seamusa IV – nazywał się Camphor. Mężczyźni z tej rodziny gasili ogień od czasów wojny secesyjnej; wyjątkiem był Charles Camphor, który miał zostać bankierem.

ELOISE DOSTRZEGŁA ZARYS tego, co kiedyś było jej domem, oświetlony ogniem na tle nieba, wiszącego tak nisko nad ziemią, iż wydawało się jej, że widzi księżyc, który usiłuje dotknąć popiołów. I tym razem najadła się wstydu, bo ojciec wybiegł z domu w nieświeżych kalesonach, a matka w brudnej, podartej koszulce, gdy wokoło tłoczyli się sąsiedzi, próbujący narzucić jej na ramiona jakiś szal, żeby ją okryć. Delores była jednak pijaniuteńka i odganiała ich, kłócąc się z ojcem o to, które z nich zostawiło żarzący się niedopałek albo włączony palnik, i Eloise pomyślała: „Powinnam była pozwolić im umrzeć".

– To nie jest przedstawienie – powiedział Seamus I i skinął na swoich ludzi, by odsunęli gapiów. Wiedział, że każdy pożar to gwałt na ludzkiej intymności. Nie było tu czego ratować. Pożar zjadł kolację. I najadł się do syta.

LADY MILLER, MATKA AGNES, wstąpiła następnego dnia do sąsiadów z walizką pełną sukienek i bielizny dla Eloise. Jak co miesiąc dostała właśnie używane ubrania od właścicieli piekarni Gottlieb's. W większości wyglądały prawie jak nowe, ale nie ubierała w nie swojego jedynego dziecka. Byli z mężem skąpi, lecz mieli tylko Agnes. Lady Miller nie chciała, żeby jej skarb chodził w używanych rzeczach, zachowywała je więc dla innych dzieci, mających mniej szczęścia w życiu.

SĄSIADOM, KTÓRZY PRZYJĘLI Delaneyów wieczorem po pożarze, los też specjalnie nie sprzyjał. Mieli już cztery gęby do wykarmienia i tylko trzy izby mieszkalne, w tym kuchnię. Na widok ich wszystkich siedmiorga ściśniętych jak sardynki w puszce lady Miller zrozumiała, że musi być prawdziwą chrześcijanką i przynajmniej zaproponować pomoc.

– Eloise nie powinna stracić ani jednego dnia szkoły, jeśli to możliwe – powiedziała do Herberta i Delores. – Za każdym razem, gdy dziecko opuszcza lekcje, traci coś ważnego.

Dzięki plotkarskiemu maglowi Flory Applewood wiedziała, że Eloise została przed rokiem przyjęta do St. Paul's dzięki stypendium, które częściowo pokrywało koszty jej edukacji. Rozmawiała z Delaneyami bez świadków, na werandzie na tyłach domu. Postanowiono, że dziewczynka przyjedzie do Millerów na tydzień albo dwa. Herbert i Delores mieli spytać swojego brygadzistę, czy nie pozwoliłby im zadekować się w przetwórni, dopóki nie znajdą jakiegoś mieszkania na dłużej.

DWA TYGODNIE PO TYM, jak spalił się ich dom, Herbert Delaney oznajmił żonie, że pożar nie był dziełem przypadku. Mieszkali już wtedy w wynajętej kawalerce w domu za przetwórnią. Delores, której często wydawało się, że Herbert cierpi na lekką paranoję, powiedziała, żeby się napił piwa i przemyślał swoje słowa. Wypił jedno piwo albo może dwa i zakomunikował żonie, że skończył z piciem. Roześmiała się. Już przy niejednej okazji przysięgali sobie, że przestaną pić, nigdy jednak nie dotrzymywali tych obietnic. Byli rozkojarzonymi, na ogół szczęśliwymi pijusami, a reszta świata, w tym ich córka Eloise, orbitowała wokół nich. Dlatego kiedy Herbert oznajmił, że zamierza jeszcze raz spróbować abstynencji, Delores naturalną koleją rzeczy wzruszyła tylko ramionami.

Po pięciu tygodniach trzeźwości Herbert postanowił pojechać w odwiedziny do swoich krewnych, rybaków mieszkających w Nowym Orleanie. Pociągnął łyk bourbona i przepłukał nim usta jak płynem dentystycznym. Przełknąwszy alkohol, z ulgą stwierdził, że nie wzbudza w nim chęci wypicia drugiego ani piątego drinka. Tej nocy leżeli razem, ramię przy ramieniu, ale Herbert wymknął się o świcie i poszedł pieszo dziewięć mil do domu Millerów. Miał ze sobą dużą brązową papierową torbę ze świeżo zebranymi czarnymi jagodami, trzy funty krewetek i dwie puszki krabowego mięsa. Krewetki i kraby ukradł, by podziękować Millerom za opiekę nad córką, i gest ten miała potem powtarzać jego żona. Diakon i lady Millerowie pili już drugą kawę Maxwell House, kiedy zabrzęczał dzwonek u ich drzwi. Na głos ojca Eloise wbiegła do salonu w długiej białej koszuli nocnej, po raz pierwszy w życiu wyglądając jak małe dziecko. Herbert przyszedł ją zabrać, ale gdy zobaczył córkę w tym stroju, zmienił zdanie.

– Eloise… – odezwał się po chwili milczenia. – Pochodzisz z rodziny strasznych rozrabiaków. Nie spal przypadkiem domu tym ludziom w ataku złości, słyszysz?

– Przecież to nie ja – odpowiedziała. – To nie ja podpaliłam nasz dom.

– Nie. – Herbert zmrużył oczy. – Ale bez złych zamiarów nie można rzucić klątwy. W języku i głowie jest moc. My w Nowym Orleanie dobrze o tym wiemy.

Odwróciła wzrok od ojca.

– Nie spalę im domu.

Chciał powiedzieć, że ją kocha, zdołał jednak zdobyć się tylko na to, żeby uściskać córkę i cmoknąć ją w czoło. Gdyby powiedział, jaką miłością ją darzy, byłyby łzy, wzajemne obwinianie się i żale.

– Możesz zostać kimś. Ale równie dobrze możesz sprawić nam zawód – powiedział. Włożył melonik i wyszedł.

Nigdy więcej już go nie widziała.

AGNES TRAKTOWAŁA ELOISE z cichą obojętnością. Do tego stopnia, że jeśli nawet Eloise interesowała się Agnes, to jej zainteresowanie znacznie się zmniejszyło, kiedy się przekonała, jak niewiele je łączy. Dziewczynki miały po jedenaście lat, Agnes ciągle jednak rysowała tylko różne esy-floresy, zajmowała się modą i spędzała całe godziny na podłodze w sypialni, wycinając wykroje sukienek i rozkładając je po całym pokoju, nawet na łóżku Eloise. Grywała też utwory nieżyjących białych mężczyzn na mahoniowym pianinie. Poza tym śpiewała rodzicom hymny kościelne, fałszując tak, że Eloise puchły uszy. W dni robocze prowadzali Agnes z lekcji gry na pianinie na lekcje tańca, do szkoły dobrych manier, na gimnastykę i na lekcje Biblii, i Eloise zdumiewała się, że Agnes nie przewraca oczami ani nie protestuje. Kiedy matka albo diakon odbierali ją ze szkoły, zawsze miała już przygotowany uśmiech i torbę z książkami. Eloise często jeździła z nimi i siedziała w poczekalni, czytając albo odrabiając pracę domową w czasie dodatkowych zajęć Agnes. Millerowie nierzadko pytali Eloise, czy ona też nie chciałaby się uczyć gry na pianinie albo tańca, ale Eloise wiedziała, że po prostu przemawia przez nich litość.

SIOSTRA MARY PŁACZĄCA dalej opłakiwała swoją węgierską rodzinę w Kingston, w New Jersey, choć z biegiem czasu lała łzy coraz rzadziej. Któregoś popołudnia w czasie przerwy przypadkowo dotarło do jej uszu, jak uczniowie plotkują, że Eloise stanowi kłopot dla rodziców Agnes. Następnego dnia podeszła do lady Miller, by spytać, czy Eloise mogłaby pomagać jej trochę w klasie po zajęciach. Millerowie zbierali pieniądze na pierwsze mieszkanie dla córki i na studia dla niej. Oszczędzali też na emeryturę i swoje złote gody na Hawajach, z ulgą zatem przyjęli propozycję, dzięki której Eloise znalazłaby jakieś zajęcie nieuszczuplające ich portfeli.

NA POCZĄTEK ELOISE i siostra Mary posadziły różne gatunki fasoli w kartonikach po jajkach i postawiły je na parapecie, zwrócone w stronę słońca. Potem zapisały w kalendarzu imiona uczniów, żeby mogli prowadzić wykresy wzrostu fasolek. Przymocowały też pinezkami do ściany Kartę praw i pozrywały spod ławek stwardniałe gumy do żucia. Ułożyły dzieła Shakespeare'a tytułami i według kategorii: osobno komedie, tragedie, dramaty historyczne i sonety. Wytrzepały zapylone kredą gąbki do tablicy i podkleiły sfatygowaną encyklopedię Britannica, czytając w trakcie pracy interesujące je hasła. Zrobiły chwilę przerwy na ciasteczka orzechowe, które Mary Laranski uwielbiała. Potem rozwinęły długą na całą wysokość ściany mapę świata, zamówioną w Teacher's Store w Nowym Jorku, i bardzo starannie przypięły ją obok tablicy.

TO SIOSTRA MARY spostrzegła, że Eloise zdradza zdolności matematyczne.

– No tak – powiedziała pewnego popołudnia, kiedy dziewczynka z największą łatwością błyskawicznie rozwiązała zadania z ułamków i dzielenia wielkich liczb. – Jeśli jesteś dobra z matematyki, to niewykluczone, że możesz mieć też ucho do języków.

Podprowadziła Eloise do mapy świata i położyła dłoń na Węgrzech. Podkreśliła jezioro Balaton, najdłuższe jezioro w Europie.

– Powtarzaj za mną... Eloise.

Witaj	Isten hozta
Dzień dobry	Jo napot kivanok
Jak się masz?	Hogy van?
Jak masz na imię?	Mi a neve?
Mam na imię Eloise	A nevem Eloise

Eloise nauczyła się w ten sposób węgierskiego, a przypuszczenia siostry Mary Płaczącej okazały się słuszne: dziewczynka miała zdolności językowe. Później, w dorosłym życiu, jeżdżąc po świecie, zapamiętywała frazy z różnych języków tak szybko, jak niektórzy ludzie zamawiają frytki w barze szybkiej obsługi. Na całe życie zapamiętała też siostrę Mary Laranski, która przepracowała cztery lata w katolickiej szkole St. Paul's of the Redemption i wyznała swojej uczennicy, że w czasie studiów na Rutgers University zakochała się w pewnym tureckim studencie medycyny, mimo że nie życzyli sobie tego jej rodzice. „Pójdziesz do zakonu", powiedziała siostra Mary po węgiersku. „Turcy i Węgrzy nie zadają się ze sobą".

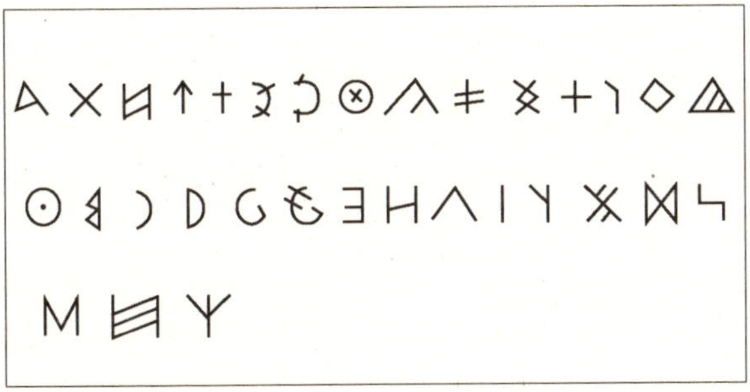

– Ależ to nasza Czarna Agnes! Jakie ona ma ładne długie włosy! – Jeśli siostra Mary Płacząca była jak cukier, to matka przełożona kojarzyła się dziewczynie raczej z terpentyną. Zawsze zatrzymywała Agnes na korytarzu albo na schodach.

– Dzień dobry, matko przełożona – odzywała się niezmiennie słodko Agnes.

– Masz niezwykle czarujące maniery. Powiedz, jak to możliwe, żeby dziewczyna o takiej ciemnej skórze jak twoja miała takie śliczne długie włosy?

Agnes spuszczała wzrok, patrzyła na swoje czarno-białe oksfordzkie buciki, a kiedy nie odpowiadała, matka przełożona ciągnęła ją za kucyk. Szarpała także siostrę Mary za habit, złośliwie wyłączała wszystkie światła na kilka minut przed nadejściem obowiązującej zakonnice pory spoczynku i rugała je za to, że zbyt długo wpatrywały się w lustro i śmiały bez pozwolenia w czasie wieczoru filmowego albo w trakcie gry w scrabble.

PEWNEGO POPOŁUDNIA ELOISE piła wodę z kranika na korytarzu. Właśnie skończyła mecz softballu z chłopcami i brakowało jej tchu. Agnes podeszła i stanęła w kolejce, żeby się napić. Dziewczynki nie kolegowały się w szkole i nie miały wspólnych przyjaciół. Nie licząc „dzień dobry" albo „dobranoc", w ogóle rzadko się do siebie odzywały. Nagle u boku Agnes przystanęła matka przełożona i szarpnęła ją za włosy tak mocno, że dziewczynka krzyknęła przeraźliwie.

– Twoje włosy – powiedziała matka przełożona. – Jak to możliwe, żeby czarna dziewczyna, jak ty, miała takie ładne długie włosy?

Eloise zamarła nad kranikiem. Popatrzyła na matkę przełożoną, a potem wbiła wzrok w ziemię.

– Nie będą ani takie długie, ani takie ładne, jak będzie się je tak szarpać. I może ona ma takie ładne włosy, bo jej matula przeczesuje je sto jeden razy co wieczór – powiedziała.

ELOISE WYBUCHNĘŁA PŁACZEM, gdy pierwszy raz zobaczyła, jak lady Miller rozplata warkocze Agnes i myje jej gęste włosy wodą z rozmarynem i szałwią; szampony i mydła wyrabiała własnoręcznie, bo uważała, że te kupowane w sklepie są zbyt drażniące dla skóry. Grzebień i szczotkę zostawiała na wierzchu, by Eloise mogła się uczesać sama, a dziewczyna wyobrażała sobie, że w szczotkowaniu i czesaniu włosów oraz robieniu przedziałka pomaga jej Bessie Coleman – stylowa, pedantyczna Bessie, która nie tylko umiała latać, lecz również dbała o każdy szczegół swojego wyglądu, w tym o idealną grzywkę.

Oczywiście matka przełożona nie wiedziała na ten temat nic, kiedy chwyciła Eloise za ucho i zaprowadziła ją do gabinetu, gdzie wyciągnęła długą linijkę i wymierzyła nią dziewczynce po trzy ostre plaśnięcia w otwarte dłonie, raz za impertynencję i dwa razy za błędy językowe.

Nikt nigdy się nie dowie, jakich sposobów imała się matka przełożona, żeby utrzymać szkołę St. Paul's of the Redemption przy życiu. W roku 1976, kiedy pomimo jej starań przeznaczona wyłącznie dla czarnych uczniów placówka ostatecznie zamknęła podwoje, a czarnoskóre dzieci rozproszono po tradycyjnie białych katolickich szkołach w Buckner County, siwowłosa i kamiennooka zakonnica wykręciła pokrytymi plamami wątrobowymi dłońmi sto siedemnaście numerów telefonicznych. Błagała, groziła i przypochlebiała się w imieniu swoich uczniów, których nienawidziła kochać i uwielbiała nienawidzić. W 1958 roku była postrachem szkoły.

AGNES CZEKAŁA na Eloise pod drzwiami gabinetu matki przełożonej.

– Po co żeś jej napyskowała? – rzuciła wściekłym szeptem. – Jak ona szarpie, to nic nie boli, kurde. Ciągnie mnie za włosy, a ja wtedy liczę po prostu do trzech i myślę różne złe rzeczy o jej starej.

– Na przykład jakie? – spytała Eloise, pocierając obolałą i spuchniętą prawą dłoń.

Agnes odciągnęła Eloise spod drzwi.

– Jej stara jest taka gruba, że spada z dwóch stron łóżka jednocześnie.

Eloise obejrzała się przez ramię w kierunku, z którego przyszła, i zmarszczyła brwi.

– Jej stara jest taka gruba, że jak stoi pod prysznicem, to nie widzi swoich palców u nóg.

Agnes szepnęła:

– Jej stara jest taka głupia, że wkłada buty na lewą stronę.

Eloise zachichotała.

– Jej stara jest taka głupia, że prasuje trawnik czajnikiem.

Agnes wybuchnęła śmiechem.

– Jej stara jest taka brzydka, że jak ona wstaje, to słońce zachodzi.

Eloise przytaknęła ruchem głowy.

– Jej stara jest taka brzydka, że jak kiedyś ją zobaczył diabeł, to powiedział Panu Bogu, że chce wrócić do nieba.

Agnes pokręciła głową.

– Jej stara jest taka brzydka, że jej portrety same się wieszają.

PRZEZ RESZTĘ PRZERWY Eloise i Agnes bawiły się w „wyzwiska" i dołączyła do nich połowa dzieciaków na boisku. Reuben Applewood, jego młodszy brat, Levi, i ich patykowaty kuzyn Jebediah byli sędziami, bo każda zabawa, w której się obraża czyjąś matulę, szybko może przejść w bójkę. A wtedy wszyscy wylądowaliby z powrotem w gabinecie matki przełożonej, gdzie znowu ktoś dostałby linijką po łapach albo lanie na tyłek, jeśli tylko życzyłby sobie tego Duch Święty.

OD TAMTEJ CHWILI stały się nierozłączne. Eloise spała na niższym z dwóch piętrowych łóżek i zgodnie z cowieczornym rytuałem przed zaśnięciem uważnie oglądała nadpalony wycinek z gazety ze zdjęciem Bessie Coleman. Czytała Agnes na głos relację z przygód Bessie we Francji i w Niemczech, dokąd Bessie musiała pojechać, żeby się nauczyć pilotażu, bo amerykańskie szkoły lotnicze nie chciały szkolić kobiet ani kolorowych. Amelia Earhart i kilka białych pilotek z czasów Bessie urodziły się w bogatych rodzinach, które było stać na kupno aeroplanów albo na opłacenie prywatnego szkolenia, jednak to Bessie okazała się pierwszą Afroamerykanką, która uzyskała międzynarodową licencję pilota. Uczyła się z późniejszymi najlepszymi lotnikami w Europie, między innymi z Anthonym Fokkerem, „Latającym Holendrem", mistrzem odważnych akrobacji powietrznych. Pilotowała jeden z pierwszych samolotów pasażerskich we Friedrichshafen, w Niemczech, i szybowała nad pałacem kajzera w Berlinie. Wróciła do Ameryki poniekąd jako gwiazda i występowała w zapierających dech w piersiach pokazach lotniczych w całym kraju, żeby zarobić pieniądze na założenie szkoły lotniczej dla kolorowych.

WYCINEK Z BESSIE COLEMAN stał się ulubioną dobranocką dla Agnes, która najpierw zawsze w milczeniu słuchała, jak Eloise czyta, a potem zamykała oczy. Eloise opowiadała jej o przygodach Bessie jeszcze długo, nawet kiedy były już nastolatkami. Nigdy nie pozwoliła sobie zasnąć pierwsza. Leżała w łóżku, wdychając zapach miętowego mydła, którym Agnes pachniała każdego wieczoru po kąpieli. Na wannie leżała nawet specjalna drewniana półeczka, żeby córka Millerów mogła położyć na niej książkę i czytać, gdyby miała na to ochotę. Czasami lady Miller stawiała też na desce miseczkę z pokrojonym jabłkiem. Maczała jego kawałki w syropie z czarnego bzu, żeby odpędzić przeziębienie.

PO UKOŃCZENIU piętnastego roku życia dziewczęta nadal dzieliły ze sobą pokój, spały jednak w osobnych, bliźniaczych łóżkach. Eloise wdychała słodką woń ciała Agnes, lecz opierała się chęci wejścia do łóżka przyjaciółki. Serce waliło jej ciągle: łup, łup, bum, bum, BAM, niczym silnik w wątpliwej jakości buicku jej rodziców. W dzieciństwie miała nadzieję, że motor kiedyś zepsuje się na dobre, ale gdy osiągnęła wiek dojrzewania i obie spały nadal w jednym pokoju, choć osobno, serce Eloise zaczęło bić tak mocno, że pewnej nocy zerwała się, usiadła i poszła do Agnes, śpiącej w czepku nocnym, żeby nie poplątały się jej włosy. Zauważyła, że ma szeroko otwarte oczy i przygląda się jej ze spokojem. Przyklękła jak do modlitwy i pocałowała ją w usta, po których błąkał się zapaszek miętowej pasty do zębów. Agnes nie opierała się, sprawiała tylko wrażenie zaskoczonej szybkością pocałunku i przyciągnęła Eloise bliżej, żeby stał się pełniejszy.

Później, kiedy zaczęła się interesować mężczyznami, powtarzała często:

– To wszystko twoja wina.

A Eloise odpowiadała:

– Ja tylko cię całowałam. To ty dodałaś język. Język jest naszym świadkiem.

Wtedy Agnes wyginała swoją łabędzią szyję na bok i bojaźliwie trzepotała rzęsami.

– Nie rezygnuj z niczego, dopóki tego nie spróbujesz, Eloise. Nie wierzę, że nie jesteś ani trochę ciekawa.

Eloise odpowiadała:

– Wolałabym umrzeć, niż żyć jako hipokrytka.

Penetracja ze strony mężczyzny przywodziła jej na myśl ukrzyżowanie. Nie potrafiła dostrzec żadnego sensu w takim cierpieniu.

STUDIOWAŁY JUŻ OBIE na drugim roku w Buckner County College, gdy Agnes poznała Claude'a Johnsona, inżyniera zatrudnionego w Southeast Aviation. Co gorsza, Claude był dla Eloise kuzynem trzeciego stopnia ze strony matki i Eloise natychmiast go znienawidziła. Tamtego popołudnia, kiedy usiadł obok Agnes przy bufecie w Kress, Eloise zaczęła się modlić, żeby go diabli wzięli. Tej samej nocy, ostatniej, kiedy się kochały, powiedziała przyjaciółce okrutną prawdę.

– Z waszego związku nic nie będzie.

– Z naszego też nie – odwarknęła Agnes, a następnego ranka traktowała Eloise z kompletną obojętnością.

Eloise nie potrafiła powiedzieć, czy lady i diakon Millerowie wiedzieli o zainteresowaniach Agnes. Ojcowie często nawet nie próbują prawić kazań swoim córkom, możliwe więc, że diakon nie miał pojęcia, co się dzieje między dwiema młodymi kobietami. Ale jeszcze zanim Agnes przyprowadziła Claude'a do domu, by poznał jej rodziców, lady Miller spakowała walizkę Eloise.

– Było nam bardzo miło gościć cię u nas – powiedziała, wciskając jej do ręki trochę pieniędzy.

Eloise nie przeliczyła ich. Jej serce zamieniło się w wielki kłąb pomarańczowych płomieni. Zamknęła oczy.

– A dokąd mam stąd iść?

– Ja w twoim wieku byłam już mężatką. Świat stoi przed tobą otworem.

Z punktu widzenia lady Miller Eloise przeciągnęła swój pobyt u nich o dwa lata.

Matka Eloise nadal mieszkała koło przetwórni ryb i owoców morza. Krążyły plotki, że „spotyka się" z jej właścicielem. Delores Delaney wpadała do Millerów raz w miesiącu z krewetkami, krabowym mięsem albo świeżą rybą. Kiedyś przyniosła imponujący kawałek rekina ostronosego, a lady Miller zamarynowała mięso i upiekła je na ruszcie, na szpikulcach, jak szaszłyk. Eloise wiedziała, że rekiny śpią z otwartymi oczami. Była to jedna z wielu rzeczy, jakich nauczyła się od siostry Mary Płaczącej, która odrzuciła święte śluby i wróciła do New Jersey, żeby wyjść za tego swojego Turka, gdy Eloise chodziła do dziewiątej klasy. Dziewczyna była pewna, że jej mentorka nigdy się już z nią nie skontaktuje. Siostra Laranski nauczyła ją pisać, mówić i czytać po węgiersku, ale jaką Eloise odniosła z tego korzyść? Nie spotykała nigdy żadnych Węgrów. A ludzie wypraszali ją z domu albo uciekali od niej.

– Odnajdę kuzyna Kinga Tyrone'a na Tybee Island – powiedziała w końcu. – To jedyny mój porządny krewny.

– No tak... Gościć cię u nas było przyjemnością – powtórzyła lady Miller.

Przygotowała dziewczynie na śniadanie jej ulubione dania: boczek marynowany w syropie klonowym, jajecznicę, świeżo wyciśnięty sok z pomarańczy i polane syropem z czarnego bzu plasterki jabłek. Tego ranka Agnes zeszła na śniadanie późno i ledwie raczyła zaszczycić Eloise spojrzeniem. Kiedy Eloise wstała od stołu, szykując się do wyjazdu już na zawsze, Agnes odprowadziła ją aż do drzwi frontowych i zapytała, czy ma coś przeciwko temu, żeby zostawić jej w prezencie gazetowy wycinek z Bessie Coleman.

– Agnes – powiedziała Eloise. – Chciałabym opuścić ten dom w miłej atmosferze. Ale naprawdę, poważnie, pocałuj mnie w czarną dupę.

Agnes westchnęła i zaczęła się wachlować wyimaginowanym wachlarzem. Gdyby nie to, że była przy tym jej matka, zamruczałaby jak kotka: „Ależ, Eloise, ja już to przecież zrobiłam".

KUZYN TYRONE POWIEDZIAŁ:

– Gdyby podobali ci się raczej ludzie, których narządy płciowe są zbudowane inaczej niż twoje, to miałabyś chyba trochę łatwiej w życiu.

Roześmiała się, bo jej też przyszło coś podobnego do głowy, ale kiedy usłyszała to w takiej formie z ust Tyrone'a, przypomniała sobie, jak skomplikowane są te sprawy, z którymi kłopotów miała już powyżej dziurek w nosie. Siedzieli na wychodzącej na bagna werandzie za jego domem i obierali warzywa. Po lewej ręce Eloise miała wiadro słonej wody, żeby wymoczyć jarzyny, by wyszły z nich robaki, a po prawej brązową papierową torbę na obierki, z którymi nic już się nie dało zrobić. Pośrodku stała drewniana miska pełna warzyw; sama je dopiero co zebrała i porozrywała gołymi rękami na mniejsze kawałki, aby mogły się długo dusić i zmięknąć.

– Tyrone, a znasz, psiakrew, choć jedną rzecz na tym świecie, która jest taka, jak się nam wydaje?

– Hmm... – odparł po krótkiej chwili. – Mam tu pokój z tabliczką z twoim imieniem, który możesz dostać na tak długo, jak będziesz potrzebować.

Chciała zapytać Tyrone'a, jak to możliwe, że zachował taki spokój wewnętrzny, ale wiedziała już, że całe jego szczęście to życie na wodzie. Był rybakiem, tak jak jego rodzice. Matka i ojciec Tyrone'a lubili głównie własne towarzystwo i mieli w nosie spotkania rodzinne, szalone imprezy w sobotnie wieczory czy kościół. Nic nie ożywiało ich tak bardzo jak rozmowa o pogodzie, bo to aura decydowała o wielkości połowów. A z kolei połów decydował o tym, czy będzie dobry dzień. Tyrone miał piętnaście lat, kiedy morze zabrało jego rodziców.

– To strasznie miło z twojej strony, kuzynie. Będę dziś dobrze spała.

Lecz spokój życia na wyspie tylko przypominał Eloise o tym, że nie potrafi usiedzieć na miejscu. W czasie pierwszego tygodnia pobytu u Tyrone'a zaczęła palić pall malle. W drugim tygodniu ucałowała go na pożegnanie, a pieniądze od lady Miller wydała na autobus powrotny do miasta. Poszła do Tailors, sklepu z galanterią męską, i wyszła z niego z różnymi stylowymi spodniami, koszulami, kamizelkami i blezerami. Potem przeszła na drugą stronę ulicy, żeby się przejrzeć w szybie wystawowej pasmanterii. Kupiła melonik, przypominający kapelusz, który nosił kiedyś jej ojciec. Założyła ten nowy nabytek lekko na bakier. Nie miała wątpliwości, że nosi go fajniej niż tata.

UCZĘSZCZAŁY NA TE SAME ZAJĘCIA w Buckner County College, ale Eloise nie mogła dłużej ufać swojemu sercu w obecności Agnes. Wzięła urlop dziekański i znalazła pracę jako kasjerka w sklepie spożywczym w centrum miasta. Była atrakcyjną kobietą, a że w koszuli i spodniach wyglądała wyjątkowo dobrze, nie minęło dużo czasu, nim zdobyła względy kobiet niezamężnych i mężatek, które podchodziły do kasy z kartonami mleka, jajkami, mlekiem dla niemowląt i proszkiem do prania Tide. Prawiła im swobodne komplementy, wdawała się w pogawędki, udzielała wskazówek, gdzie znaleźć najtańsze produkty, i radziła, żeby trzymały się z dala od nieświeżej wołowiny na gulasz, która za długo leżała w gablocie w dziale mięsnym.

Jej pierwszą dziewczyną po Agnes okazała się mężatka, Grace Bell. Była niczym kiepskie faksymile Agnes, ale przypominała ją ze względu na dystans do świata. „Widocznie wszystkie ładne dziewczyny tak mają – pomyślała Eloise. –

Tylko ładne kobiety mogą sobie pozwolić, żeby zachowywać się beztrosko i niedbale". Mąż Grace pracował jako bagażowy w wagonach pulmanowskich. Zarabiał niezłe pieniądze, jeżdżąc koleją Seaboard Air Line tam i z powrotem po Wschodnim Wybrzeżu, co oznaczało, że całymi tygodniami nie było go w domu.

KIEDYŚ W NIEDZIELĘ Eloise wybrała się z wizytą do matki, która nadal co tydzień zaopatrywała Millerów w krewetki i mięso krabów.

– Powiem ci coś na temat tych krewetek – odezwała się Eloise. – Musisz przestać już nosić jedzenie rodzicom Agnes. Mój czas u nich się skończył.

Delores Delaney pieściła w dłoniach puszkę piwa Miller High Life. Dawniej miała najlepszą figurę w mieście, ale alkohol zmieniał jej ciało z cukiereczka w gówno.

Odwróciła wzrok od Eloise i chrząknęła.

– Nie wiedziałam, że urodziłam syna. Może powinnam była dać ci na imię Earl.

– Tylko tyle masz mi do powiedzenia po tych wszystkich latach? Byłaś parszywą matką.

– Powiedzmy – odparła Delores, częstując się jednym z papierosów Eloise, które leżały pomiędzy nimi na stole. – Biłam cię?

– Nie.

– Czy kiedy jedliśmy, nie pilnowałam zawsze, żebyś zjadła pierwsza?

Eloise zaśmiała się.

– Nie przypominam sobie. Ale czasami pozwalałaś mi umierać z głodu.

– Ja też głodowałam.

– Na alkohol ci nie brakowało.

– Skarbie, nawet pod tym względem byłam dobra. Nie mogłabyś powiedzieć, że kiedykolwiek cię nim częstowałam.

Zastanowiła się nad tymi słowami matki.

– Może powinnaś przestać pić.

– Alkohol to moja choroba.

Mózg Eloise aż zagotował się od prawdziwości tych słów.

– Tata przestał – podsunęła.

– I odszedł. Jak człowiek trzeźwieje, to musi zostawić wszystkie żale za sobą.

Eloise zapaliła papierosa.

– Nigdy w życiu mi nie powiedziałaś, że mnie kochasz.

– I dlatego latasz wystrojona jak facet?

– Nie, mamo, tylko to jest po prostu coś, co dobrzy rodzice mówią swoim dzieciom. Coś, co mówiłabym swoim, gdybym je miała.

Delores pykała dymem z papierosa jak jej córka.

– No to przepraszam cię za brak miłości. – Wstała i podeszła do tandetnej lodówki.

Eloise też się podniosła i zaczęła krążyć po mieszkaniu. Omiatała wzrokiem wszystko, aby znaleźć jakieś dowody na to, że matka ma faceta albo chociaż spotyka się z tym właścicielem przetwórni owoców morza, mieszkanie było jednak zaskakująco czyste. W kącie pod ścianą z czerwonej cegły Delores trzymała puszki piwa i korkociągi. Ustawiała je w przemyślany sposób. Gdy w latach osiemdziesiątych w Berlinie Eloise widywała podobnie uporządkowane instalacje artystyczne, wspominała matkę.

– Masz tu krewetki. – Delores wcisnęła jej torebkę w dłoń. – To te wielgachne, z łebkami.

Eloise dała je Grace, która ugotowała pierwszorzędne gumbo.

ZAJMOWAŁA UMEBLOWANE MIESZKANIE z jedną sypialnią w domu na końcu piaszczystej drogi, gdzie ciągle bawiły się okoliczne dzieciaki. Lubiły ją, bo obrzucała je straszliwymi wyzwiskami, kiedy mówiły na nią Lesba Eloise, a po pracy czasami bawiła się z nimi w dwa ognie. Jadła właśnie lizaka Creamsicle o smaku pomarańczowym i grała z dziećmi w klasy, gdy zjawił się mąż Grace, trzymając w dłoniach pas kowbojski. Najpierw pomyślała, że „czyjś dzieciak dostanie zaraz po dupie", ale mąż Grace, manewrując wśród malców, podszedł do Eloise. Trzymał pas w taki sposób, że złota sprzączka zwieszała się w jej stronę. Zanim dziewczyna zdążyła się uchylić, chwycił ją za ramię i zaczął bić tą sprzączką, poczynając od nóg i posuwając się w górę ku biodrom, piersiom, szyi i twarzy. Kowbojski pas dostał od żony, która zamówiła go dla niego w Dallas, w Teksasie, jako prezent z okazji rocznicy ślubu.

Dzieciaki z sąsiedztwa poczuły niechęć do tego nadzianego faceta, który bił miejscową dziewczynę na ich boisku, i rzuciły się na niego. Strząsnął je z siebie niczym zeschłe liście, przestał jednak katować Eloise. Dzieci najprawdopodobniej ocaliły jej życie, bo mąż Grace nie chciał ich skrzywdzić, nawet przez przypadek. Przyszedł zabić wyłącznie kochankę swojej kobiety.

Zostawił Eloise leżącą na ulicy, zakrwawioną i poranioną sprzączką. Nie więcej niż dwie godziny wcześniej żona nakarmiła go być może najlepszym krewetkowym gumbo, jakie jadł w życiu, ale gdy leżeli później razem w łóżku, Grace wykrzyczała imię Eloise.

ŻEBY ZMNIEJSZYĆ OPUCHLIZNĘ na twarzy dziewczyny, Flora zastosowała zioła ze swojego ogrodu. Otwierała długie łodygi aloesu i nacierała jego gęstym sokiem dolną wargę Eloise, rozciętą przez sprzączkę na dwoje. Krążyła wokół nisko zawieszonego łóżka z baldachimem o czterech słupkach szybko niczym sokół, pikując w dół i zrywając z Eloise ubranie, lepiące się do jej brudnego ciała. „Ostrożnie", przestrzegała swoich siostrzeńców, Reubena, Leviego i Jebediaha, kiedy nieśli ranną trzy piętra wyżej do jej mieszkania. Bardzo uważali, bo Eloise Delaney chodziła z nimi do katolickiej szkoły, a w rodzinie Applewoodów wyrządzenie krzywdy kobiecie uważano za powód do anatemy.

Ciocia Flora mówiła bardzo głośno, żeby Eloise zachowała przytomność i żeby utrzymać napięte nerwy na wodzy. Kiedy siostrzeńcy wyszli, opowiedziała dziewczynie, jak w wieku szesnastu lat wyjechała do Nowego Jorku, żeby zamieszkać z kuzynką, która jak się okazało, zajmowała tylko obskurną kawalerkę z blaszaną wanną w kuchni. I o tym, że ludzie zawsze przeprowadzają się na Północ i duma albo chęć zwabienia rodziny do siebie każe im mówić z przesadą o znakomitych warunkach, w jakich tam mieszkają. A przecież jeśli naprawdę chcesz zmarnować swoje życie, to możesz to zrobić samotnie.

„Wiesz co, Eloise? – powiedziała Flora. – Mam nadzieję, że twarz ładnie ci się zagoi, bo masz jasną skórę i blizny nie będą na niej tak bardzo widoczne". Eloise, która nigdy nie uważała się za osobę o jasnej skórze, wbiła wzrok w swoje ramiona. Jak to możliwe, że nie wiedziała tego o sobie albo nauczyła się nie zwracać na to uwagi? Skóra to skóra, powiedziała do siebie w myślach.

W czasie rekonwalescencji nie miała kontaktu z matką, swoją kochanką Grace ani z Agnes Miller. Wieści o jej pobiciu dotarły do Kinga Tyrone'a dopiero długo po fakcie. To Flora siedziała sztywno na skraju jej łóżka i nasłuchiwała, jak oddycha. To Flora czytała jej artykuł o Bessie Coleman, tak jak Eloise czytała go kiedyś Agnes. To Flora przeczesywała jej włosy gorącym grzebieniem. To Flora mówiła jej wprost, że powinna stąd uciec.

ELOISE WSTĄPIŁA DO WOJSKA, do WAF-u, kobiecego korpusu pomocniczego lotnictwa USA. Na dzień przed rozpoczę-

Sala Wschodnia w Białym Domu, 8 listopada 1967 roku; prezydent Lyndon B. Johnson podpisuje rozkaz 5894, dotyczący zasobów ludzkich.

ciem służby dała Florze prezent. Rozwiązała jej zaczesany do góry kok, zmyła słaby róż z jej warg, uczesała jej włosy, rozpięła starannie pozapinaną sukienkę, zrolowała beżowe pończochy i położyła je pięta w piętę pod swoim niskim łóżkiem. Potem rozpięła haftki białego stanika Flory, zsunęła jej białe majtki i powiedziała, żeby się położyła i leżała bez ruchu, a ciocia, która okazała dziewczynie dobre serce, nie oczekując w zamian żadnych przysług, nie sprzeciwiała się, bo sama była kiedyś młoda i zaznała w życiu zarówno brutalnego chamstwa, jak i czułości.

ELOISE TRAFIŁA DO BAZY LOTNICZEJ Lackland w San Antonio, w Teksasie, gdzie uzyskiwała znakomite wyniki w szkoleniu podstawowym i rzuciła palenie. Poznała dwie czy trzy kobiety, z którymi mogłaby nawiązać miłosne relacje, ale przez osiem tygodni szkolenia w obozie rekrutów ledwo wystarczało jej czasu, żeby zaczerpnąć tchu. Codziennie przebiegała od dwunastu do piętnastu mil, rano i po południu, wedle kaprysu sierżanta. Miała naturalny talent i doskonale sobie radziła na torze przeszkód, nie drżała jej też powieka w czasie walki wręcz. Od karabinów M16 i M14 pociły się jej dłonie, ale nauczyła się je obsługiwać. Żołnierki znajdowały się pod nieustannym nadzorem, toteż pomimo napadów bolesnej samotności Eloise preferowała przyjaźń zawodową. Nie chciała dawać nikomu pretekstu do tego, by można było w dwóch słowach lekceważąco podsumować jej inteligencję albo zakwestionować postępowanie pod względem etycznym. Flora udzieliła jej także pewnych rad na temat sposobów odróżniania jednych kobiet od drugich. „Patrz, ale nie dotykaj, Eloise.

A jeśli już dotykasz, to na własne ryzyko", co stanowiło domorosłe echo przysłowiowej zasady „O nic nie pytaj, nic nie mów".

PO OBOZIE DLA REKRUTÓW przyszło szkolenie specjalistyczne. Eloise umiała już pisać na maszynie z prędkością dziewięćdziesięciu ośmiu słów na minutę, bo dziewczęta w katolickiej szkole musiały uczyć się maszynopisania i prowadzenia gospodarstwa domowego. Nie licząc matematyki, znała łacinę i węgierski, uważany niekiedy za najtrudniejszy język świata. Nie miała odpowiednich cech osobowościowych, by zostać pielęgniarką, a z drugiej strony nie wstąpiła do wojska, żeby pracować jako sekretarka, któraś z rekrutek podsunęła jej więc językowy instytut obrony sił powietrznych.

ELOISE ZABRAŁA ZE SOBĄ gazetowy wycinek z Bessie Coleman i wieczorami wsuwała go pod poduszkę. Jej idolka uczyła się latać wśród francuskich i niemieckich tuzów przestworzy. Eloise znała trochę niemiecki i francuski, więc niby dlaczego nie, do cholery? Pracowała dużo i w skupieniu – i nie pozwalała sobie na rozmyślania o Agnes, która od Claude'a Johnsona przeszła do faceta zwanego Eddie Christie, dalekiego krewnego Applewoodów. Nie wiedziała, co ją bardziej boli: zainteresowanie Agnes mężczyznami czy tempo, w jakim ich zmieniała. Dwa dni po uzyskaniu instytutowego świadectwa o zdaniu egzaminów z języka francuskiego i niemieckiego z drugim wynikiem w grupie dowiedziała się od Flory, że Agnes wyszła za Eddiego.

Wtedy złożyła prośbę o natychmiastowe przeniesienie do Wietnamu.

DWUDZIESTEGO DZIEWIĄTEGO STYCZNIA 1968 roku zgłosiła się do służby w bazie lotniczej Tan Son Nhut pod Sajgonem – na dwa dni przed rozpoczęciem ofensywy „Tet". Tan Son Nhut było najbardziej ruchliwym lotniskiem w Azji Południowo-Wschodniej – niektórzy twierdzili nawet, że na całym świecie – i miało się stać jednym z celów atakowanych najzacieklej przez Wietkong i armię Wietnamu Północnego, walczącą przeciwko oddziałom amerykańskim i ich sojusznikom w Wietnamie Południowym. Ataki te przypadły między innymi na wietnamski Nowy Rok, a towarzyszyły im pociski, rakiety i prowadzony o zmierzchu ostrzał snajperski. Eloise, zmęczona wskutek różnicy czasu po szesnastogodzinnym locie przez Pacyfik, obudziła się z przekonaniem, że tkwi w samym środku jakiegoś „popieprzonego snu". Poczuła, jak drży pod nią prycza, a wraz z nią cały barak kobiecy, i wypatrzyła przez okienko nad łóżkiem rakiety kalibru sto dwadzieścia dwa milimetry, zasnuwające smugami całe niebo. Kiedy nadlatujące pociski trafiały w cel, drżała ziemia i pękały gwiazdy. Pomyślała o swoim rodzinnym domu. Gdy płonie dom, wszyscy przegrywają i nikt nie wygrywa.

PRZYDZIELONO JĄ DO SZTABU jako specjalnego analityka wywiadu. Do jej obowiązków należała analiza danych, które dostarczali jej dowódcy i agenci służb – ludzie pracujący za linią frontu. Wskazywała rozbieżności w raportach, pomagając w ten sposób uniknąć strat, poddawała analizie warunki geograficzne i transportowe oraz planowała trasy dla zaopatrzenia, biegnące przez górskie przełęcze. Opowiadała później, że oficerowie amerykańskiego wywiadu na przemian popadali z entuzjazmu w depresję i że pozornie przyziemne zainteresowanie szczegółami sprawy, nad którą pracowali, wymagało od nich wiele wysiłku. Wróciła do papierosów, znowu wypalała paczkę dziennie. Pracowała po dziesięć do dwunastu godzin na dobę, słuchając nagrań i rozkładając na czynniki pierwsze przesłuchania Montagnardów, członków plemienia zamieszkującego góry Laosu, Kambodży i Wietnamu i popierającego Amerykanów. Montagnardowie nie znali pisma. Swoją kulturę opierali na historii mówionej, poniekąd tak jak przodkowie Eloise na nizinach Georgii.

W TAN SON NHUT stacjonowały siły wszystkich rodzajów wojsk – armii lądowej, floty, lotnictwa i piechoty morskiej. Eloise bawiła się w towarzystwie czarnoskórych poruczników w klubach nocnych Sajgonu i w piwiarniach w bazie. Posługiwała się niezbędną w takich przypadkach inteligencją, żeby relacje z nimi były bliskie, uczciwe i platoniczne. Cieszyła się opinią szybkonogiej, udało się jej więc przekonać przełożonych, by pozwolili jej uczestniczyć w zwiadach bojowych. Udział w tych misjach wywoływał u niej dreszcz emocji. Była przekonana, że w innych okolicznościach zostałaby mianowana porucznikiem, a może nawet kapitanem, ale w czasie wojny wietnamskiej kobietom nie wolno było uczestniczyć w bezpośrednich działaniach bojowych ani używać broni. Pierwszymi członkiniami WAF-u, które wysyłano do Azji Południowo-Wschodniej, były pielęgniarki, ponieważ zaczęło brakować sanitariuszy. Okazało się, że kobiety też potrafią ratować ludzkie życie oraz leczyć psychiczne i fizyczne rany wojenne (swoich pacjentów i własne), co otworzyło drzwi takim żołnierkom jak Eloise, które potem mogły już wyjeżdżać do Wietnamu.

W listach do Eloise Flora pytała ją często, czy nie natknęła się gdzieś na Reubena albo Jebediaha, którzy służyli w marynarce wojennej. Odpisywała, że nie, chociaż prawdę mówiąc, spotkała kiedyś Jebediaha w klubie nocnym w Subic Bay. Podeszła do niego; pił jedno martini za drugim, a oczy miał czerwone jak sam diabeł. Otaczał ramionami dwie kobiety; w jednej z nich od razu rozpoznała amerykańską dziwkę, przewiezioną tutaj samolotem, żeby mogła uszczęśliwiać żołnierzy. Drugą była jakaś Filipinka, przebrana za Marilyn Monroe. Eloise zdenerwowała się, widząc, jak Jebediah Applewood beztrosko obmacuje te kobiety. Wiedziała, że żołnierze tak się zachowują, ale z większością z nich nie bawiła się na szkolnym boisku, a poza tym to nie oni wnieśli ją na trzecie piętro, kiedy wskutek dotkliwego pobicia o mały włos nie wyzionęła ducha.

– Co słychać, kuzynie? – spytała.

Jebediah nie był jeszcze tak napruty, żeby uznać ją za krewną. Za chłopięcych lat podkochiwał się w Eloise, która bez żenady latała wszędzie z chłopakami. Przyjrzał się zamglonym wzrokiem jej poniekąd męskiej postaci i nie wydawał się ani trochę zniechęcony atrakcjami, jakie w sobie kryła. Na drugim końcu półkolistego baru siedziała jej aktualna dziewczyna, pracownica administracyjna bazy lotniczej Tan Son Nhut. Eloise dała jej znak, że to może chwilę potrwać.

– Chcesz drinka? – Jeb odwrócił się do barmana, nie czekając na reakcję Eloise.

– Nigdy nie piję więcej niż jednego. – Ujęła Jeba pod ramię. – Nie wyszedłbyś ze mną na chwilę?

– Nie chcę zostawiać Eddiego – odpowiedział, wskazując głową wnętrze baru. Ustawiono tam prymitywną scenę, na której jakiś krępy mężczyzna, stojący w otoczeniu grupki żołnierzy, odgrywał coś, co wyglądało na dziwaczną wariację na temat *Hamleta* Shakespeare'a. Niski człowieczek stał na drewnianej drabinie. Kostiumy dla aktorów zrobił z jedwabnych zasłon w jasnych kolorach, a obsada składała się z wielobarwnej zbieraniny cywilów i żołnierzy. Jedni siedzieli w kręgu jak małe dzieci, ze skrzyżowanymi nogami, trumf, trumf, misia bela, inni kołysali się w milczącym tańcu, jak gdyby sztuka, *Rosenkrantz i Guildenstern nie żyją*, była powolną muzyką typu „drag". W sali unosiły się kłęby niebieskiego dymu i Eddie mrużył oczy, żeby odczytać tekst programu, który ściskał w serdelkowatych palcach.

EDDIE
„Tragedia, panie. Śmierć i demaskatorstwo, ogólne i poszczególne – rozwiązania niechybne i niespodziewane, na wszystkich poziomach krwawy melodramat przebierańców, także aluzyjny. Przenosimy was w świat intryg i iluzji...".

Jebediah oparł się o ścianę przed wejściem do baru.

– Jak się masz, Jeb? – zagadnęła znowu Eloise, przyglądając się marynarzowi. Był najchudszy ze wszystkich Applewoodów. Barki wąskie i przygarbione, ręce i nogi za długie w stosunku do reszty ciała. Twarz pokrywał mu kilkudniowy zarost. Zrobił się prawie przystojny.

Zapalił papierosa.

– Bywało lepiej.

– Jak u każdego z nas – odpowiedziała. – Wiesz, że utrzymuję kontakt z twoją ciotką?

– Naprawdę? To dobrze. Ale co z tego? I co w związku z tym?

Pociągnęła go za ucho.

– Nie powiem jej, że cię widziałam w takiej sytuacji. Nie powiem jej dokładnie, jaki jesteś kompletnie pojebany.

Odetchnął głęboko i wypuścił całe powietrze z płuc.

– Tobie jest z wojną do twarzy, Eloise. Ale dla niektórych z nas cały ten syf jest jakby nierealny. – Pochylił się bliżej i aż się cofnęła z obrzydzeniem, wyczuwając paskudny oddech, a także odór narkotyków i alkoholu, wydzielany przez jego ciało. – Nie może być realny.

– Kim jest ten niski facio na drabinie? – Znała odpowiedź, jeszcze zanim zadała to pytanie.

– To mój prawdziwy kuzyn, Eddie Christie – powiedział Jeb, a potem wybuchnął śmiechem. – Ożenił się z tą twoją dziewczyną, Agnes. Mają dwoje dzieci.

Pociągnęła go za drugie ucho.

– Zamknij się.

– Dlaczego mi to robisz? – zapytał, zasłaniając ucho.

– Bo mi się tak podoba. – Odwróciła się, żeby wrócić do baru.

Zawołał za nią.

– Eloise, wracaj tu. Wiesz co... może moglibyśmy... Może mógłbym... skosztować jakiegoś smacznego murzyńskiego likierku?

– Panie Jebediahu Applewoodzie – powiedziała z uśmiechem. – Mam nadzieję, że wrócisz do domu w jednym kawałku. A tymczasem pocałuj mnie w moją przyrodzoną czarną dupę.

SZEŚĆ MIESIĘCY PÓŹNIEJ jej samochód wojskowy wracał pod wrogim ostrzałem do bazy Tan Son Nhut z nocnej wyprawy do centrum Sajgonu. Eloise i dwóch oficerów wyrzuciło z jeepa. Szrapnel trafił ją w kolano, a potem przebił się przez bark porucznika. Nie była uzbrojona. Czterej oficerowie odpowiedzieli przeciwnikowi ogniem, a Eloise pociągnęła rannych lotników za sobą i schroniła się pod samochodem. Leżeli na ziemi, w górze krążyły myśliwce Dragonfly, a ona myślała o Brązowej Bessie – jak jej rodzice nazywali Bessie Coleman – wykonującej pętle, pikowanie i ósemki w swoim Curtissie JN-4 „Jenny" wysoko na niebie, gdzie nic nie mogło jej dotknąć ani nikt nie mógł jej skrzywdzić.

WIEM, GDZIE SIĘ KRYJE TRUCIZNA

2008

TATUSIA ZABIŁY DIOKSYNY, MÓWIĘ CLAUDII, gdy tatuś oddaje ducha w hospicjum Riverside. Moja siostra patrzy na mnie tak, jak gdybym wygadywała kompletne brednie typu mowa-trawa, sratytatypierdaty. Powtarzam już wyłącznie na jej użytek, że dioksyny to bardzo toksyczne substancje. Stanowią główny składnik Agent Orange. To ten syf zniszczył jelita naszemu tatusiowi. Pokazuję jej wycinki z gazet, poplamione nikotyną artykuły i teczkę z zeznaniami innych weteranów marynarki wojennej, którzy służyli na lotniskowcach w Wietnamie, ale Claudia tylko kuli się i wysuwa podbródek, tak jak wtedy, kiedy byłyśmy małe i odgrywałyśmy tych dupowatych Angoli na statku Shakespeare'a.

– Nie wszystko jest pieprzoną sztuką teatralną – mruczę pod nosem. – Czasami pieprzona sztuka nie jest najważniejsza.

– Wyrażasz się jak marynarz.

– Jestem córką marynarza. Ty też.

– Tego się tak nie robi. – Wzrusza ramionami. – Nie w ten sposób powinno się czcić pamięć ojca. Dlaczego nie chcesz pozwolić sobie na żałobę, Bev? Poczuj się tak jak trzeba.

Czuję. Złość. Bo tata, którego znałam, za trzy dni zostanie pochowany. A potem jego ciało zapadnie się w sobie, zgnije i rozłoży się w grobie na głębokości sześciu stóp. Z ziemi wypełzną robaki, aby dokonać ponurego dzieła i przyczynić się do przemiany szczątków. Skóra, piękna kasztanowa skóra naszego taty, odejdzie od kości. Już dzisiaj po południu, kiedy go kąpałam, zaczęły się procesy gnilne w jelitach, rozkład. Rak wątroby zatruwa całe ciało. A im bardziej jest zatrute, tym szybciej gnije. Balsamowanie spowalnia ten proces, ale on już trwa. Jest w toku. Na akcie zgonu Edwarda Christie pojawi się określenie „wstrząs septyczny". Wolałabym, kurwa, nie myśleć o tych sprawach. Starałam się pozbyć ich z głowy, po raz ostatni okazując tacie dobre serce, czyli myjąc go. Nie mogłam pozwolić, by jego zimne zwłoki obmywały pielęgniarki z hospicjum, chociaż one w ogóle zachowywały się cudownie. To była jednak moja robota. Moje „do widzenia", „*adios*", „*arrivederci*, kochany".

Na pogrzebie będzie przemawiać Claudia. Popadnie w filozoficzny nastrój pomimo rozpaczy i będzie gloryfikować ojca, ale to ja widziałam, jak jego usta zbladły, a brązowe oczy utraciły blask. Claudia śpiewała, gdy leżał na łożu śmierci. „Okej, tato. Wszystko jest okej. Proszę cię, wracaj do domu". Czytała mu, kurwa, *Rosenkrantz i Guildenstern nie żyją*.

DWIE GODZINY PO TYM, jak tata umiera, zdejmują pościel i wysyłają zwłoki do domu pogrzebowego. Metalowe łóżko jest teraz puste. Mój wzrok pieszczotliwie obejmuje lawendowe ściany – dekorator wnętrz powiedziałby, że fiołkoworóżowe. Gdy zdrowie ojca pogorszyło się i lekarze powiedzieli, że zostało mu pół roku życia, zwróciłam się o pomoc do mojej przyjaciółki, Shirley. W dawnych czasach byłyśmy nierozłączne. Wagarowała, żeby wciągać ze mną kokę w toalecie w Nell's i w Limelight. Była superlaską, ale ja jeszcze lepszą. Może było nam pisane, że zostaniemy nastoletnimi mamami. Zakonnice w katolickiej szkole Our Lady of Claremont udawały, że nie widzą, że w czerwcu przychodzimy na lekcje w grubych swetrach. Za to koleżanki wszystko dobrze widziały. Drwiły z nas okrutnie, a my odgryzałyśmy się im jak wściekłe. Ale byłyśmy tylko dziewczynkami – cholernie spietranymi – które próbowały zachowywać się jak dorosłe kobiety. Zanim powiedziałam Kevinowi, poszłam zrobić sobie badanie na AIDS, bardziej ze względu na dziecko niż z jakiegokolwiek innego powodu. Czerwony Krzyż zaczął właśnie program informacyjny o AIDS. W całym mieście rozdawali ludziom darmowe testy. Gdy biała pielęgniarka wcisnęła igłę w strzykawkę, zadrżałam na całym ciele.

– Wyglądasz na mądrą dziewczynę. – Imię i nazwisko na plakietce brzmiało Barbara Camphor.

– Urodzę to dziecko. – Po raz pierwszy powiedziałam to wtedy na głos.

– To dobrze. Tak też można.

Odniosłam wrażenie, że jej słowa zabrzmiały arogancko.

– Myśli pani, że nie powinnam?

– Już to zrobiłaś, kochanie. Ten pociąg już ruszył ze stacji i pędzi przed siebie.

Pamiętam, że się zaśmiałam, chociaż miałam ochotę ją uderzyć. Ale ona trzymała w ręku strzykawkę. I pobierała mi krew.

– Uważa pani, że powinnam je urodzić?

Pieprzyłam się z kilkoma chłopakami, byłam jednak pewna, że dzieciak jest Kevina.

– O tym musisz zadecydować sama w rozmowie z Panem Bogiem.

– Nie bardzo mi pani pomaga.

– Pomagam ci się dowiedzieć, czy nie masz wirusa, który wywołuje AIDS. Mam nadzieję, że nie, ale jeżeli jesteś nosicielką, to musisz sobie wymyślić jakiś sposób na życie. Rozumiesz?

Znalazła żyłę i dziabnęła mnie tylko jeden raz. Ukłucie. Potem nic.

– Dobrze pani zarabia?

– No i to jest pytanie, które chciałabym usłyszeć od dziewczyny w takim trudnym położeniu jak twoje. Sama bym o to spytała na twoim miejscu.

Patrzyłam, jak odkłada fiolki z krwią na tackę i coś notuje.

– Mogłabym zarabiać lepiej – odparła. – Ale żyje mi się dobrze. A czasami „dobrze” musi nam wystarczyć.

TO JA POWIEDZIAŁAM Shirley o szkole pielęgniarskiej. Odebrałyśmy dyplomy, ale nie poszłyśmy na bal maturalny. Przesiadywałyśmy u mnie w domu i uczyłyśmy się. Rodzice, kiedy w końcu powiedziałam im, co chcemy robić, pomagali nam tylko do matury, bo chcieli, żebyśmy miały świadomość, że spierdoliłyśmy sobie życie i nie ma na to ich zgody. Widziałam, jak twarze mojej mamy i taty rozbłysły, kiedy Claudia dostała się na Columbię. Wyprowadziłam się wtedy z Kevinem do kawalerki, bo nie chciałam patrzeć, jak Claudia pierwsza idzie na studia. Bolało mnie, że moja młodsza siostra będzie się uczyć dalej na uniwersytecie. Skoro nie mogę być kimś wyjątkowym, to pierdolę; będę niezależna. Zostałam pielęgniarką na oddziale przypadków nagłych, a Shirley na geriatrii, zanim przeszła do pracy w hospicjum. Załatwiła mi prywatne zwiedzanie ośrodka w Riverdale.

– Dopilnujemy, żeby twój tata odszedł z godnością – powiedziała.

Jak na hospicjum była to całkiem przyzwoita placówka.

– Nie będzie go na to stać, Shirley – zauważyłam. Ubezpieczenie ojca nie obejmowało pojedynczego pokoju.

– Sprawa jest już załatwiona, Bev. Zajęłam się tym.

Umieściła tatę w pojedynczym pokoju z dodatkowym łóżkiem i wygodnym zielonym fotelem, żebyśmy mogły u niego nocować, Claudia, mama albo ja. Okna wychodziły na ogród, gdzie rosły małe, twarde gruszki, które można było podkradać z drzewa, a także tulipany, peonie i piękne różowe azalie, które irytowały mnie swoim zachłannym kwieciem.

NA DWADZIEŚCIA CZTERY GODZINY przed śmiercią taty myślałyśmy, że może jeszcze się z tego wywinie, że wróci. W ciągu ostatnich dwóch lat kilka razy leżał już na deskach, ale zawsze jakoś udawało mu się wykaraskać. Mama zasnęła, siedząc przy jego łóżku. Za poduszkę posłużyło jej metalowe oparcie. Ja zeszłam na dół zapalić, a Claudia drzemała w zielonym skórzanym fotelu, przypominającym fotel La-Z-Boy. Kiedy wróciłam, tata siedział na łóżku, miał otwarte oczy i mówił tak silnym głosem, że trudno było się domyślić, że waży już tylko sto piętnaście funtów. „Gdzie lody truskawkowe?" A ja tak jak stałam, w szpitalnych drewniakach, od razu zawróciłam, znalazłam pielęgniarkę i ojciec szybko dostał dwie gałki lodów truskawkowych w kubeczku jednorazowym. Mama karmiła go łyżeczką, a on pochłaniał lody i zaczął gadać z tymi dwoma Angolami, jak gdyby naprawdę byli z nami w pokoju.

– No proszę, są moi kochani Ros i Guil – powiedział. – Jak żeście mnie tu znaleźli, chłopaki? Widzę, że w końcu zeszliście na ląd. Tak, u mnie też bywało czasem lepiej.

Wychowałyśmy się w domu, w którym tata ciągle gadał do tych faciów i uchylał przed nimi kapelusza, chociaż nikt poza nim nigdy ich nie widział.

Mama powiedziała:

– No, jak za dawnych czasów.

Kiedy Claudia usłyszała tatę, zerwała się niczym Śpiąca Królewna z bardzo długiej drzemki i zaczęła przeczesywać torebkę w poszukiwaniu egzemplarza *Rosenkrantz i Guildenstern nie żyją*. Czytała mu zawsze wtedy, kiedy nic innego nie przychodziło jej do głowy. Podeszła do jego łóżka i przeczytała pierwsze linijki, na jakich spoczął jej wzrok.

„Błąd! Nie wolno używać synonimów! Jeden-jeden!" – powiedziała Claudia. I natychmiast stała się Rosenkrantzem. Tata się uśmiechnął. Dlatego poszłam za jej przykładem i wcieliłam się w Guildensterna. Nie musiałam zaglądać do tekstu, by zagrać swoją rolę. Żadna z nas nie musiała, chyba że może mama, która nigdy nie nauczyła się tej sztuki na pamięć, bo przecież ktoś w naszej rodzinie musiał zostać widzem, żeby rozpoznać ten obłęd.

JA JAKO GUILDENSTERN: *Dwa – dwa. Piłka setowa.*
CLAUDIA JAKO ROSENKRANTZ: *Co się dzisiaj z tobą dzieje?*
JA JAKO GUILDENSTERN: *Kiedy?*
CLAUDIA JAKO ROSENKRANTZ: *Co?*
JA JAKO GUILDENSTERN: *Głuchy jesteś?*
CLAUDIA JAKO ROSENKRANTZ: *Trupem jestem?*
JA JAKO GUILDENSTERN: *Tak czy nie?*
CLAUDIA JAKO ROSENKRANTZ: *A czy istnieje jakiś wybór?*
JA JAKO GUILDENSTERN: *A czy istnieje Bóg?*[*]

Tata strasznie się śmiał. Byłyśmy jego angielskimi błaznami na płynącym ku zagładzie statku, którego nie można było zatrzymać, a im bardziej się śmiał, tym skwapliwiej grałyśmy swoje role. Wydawało się, że znów jesteśmy małymi dziewczynkami, mamy cztery i pięć albo dziewięć i dziesięć lat, popisujemy się przed nim i staramy się poprawić swoje aktorstwo. Ale kiedy ponownie spojrzałam na ojca, jego twarz przypominała maskę pośmiertną. Nie mogłam

---

[*] Fragment dramatu *Rosenkrantz i Guildenstern nie żyją* w przekładzie tłumacza.

się powstrzymać, wyszarpnęłam Claudii książkę z rąk i rozerwałam ją dokładnie na środku, w miejscu, w którym została naprawiona i sklejona wiele lat temu. Podarłabym ten przeklęty dramat na strzępy, ale Claudia krzyknęła przeraźliwie i zmierzwiła palcami swoje kręcone włosy.

– Beverly, proszę cię. Nie! – zawołała.

– Dziewczęta, dziewczęta! – krzyknęła nasza matka.

Ale nawalony morfiną tata wciąż się śmiał. Wydawało mu się, że Angole są w najwyższej formie. Wtedy do pokoju weszli Minerva i Orzeszek. Minerva rzuciła mi spojrzenie, które mówiło: „Nie tutaj".

Mama zwróciła się do Orzeszka.

– Zabierz gdzieś stąd swoją matkę, dobrze?

Minerva, wystrojona wczesną wiosną w letnią sukienkę na cieniutkich ramiączkach, w której było trochę za dużo lata, zamieniła się miejscami z mamą i pocałowała dziadka. Claudia opadła na czworaki przy łóżku, próbując złożyć rozdartą okładkę.

– Claudio – odezwała się mama. – Skleiłyśmy ją kiedyś, skleimy i tym razem.

Claudia podniosła na mnie wzrok.

– Istnieje określenie na kobiety, które idą przez życie w taki sposób jak ty.

Wzruszyłam ramionami.

– Złośliwa suka?

– Wzburzona czarna kobieta.

Tata przestał się śmiać. Przyglądały mi się moje dzieci.

– Co jest niewłaściwego we wzburzeniu, jeśli sytuacja je usprawiedliwia? – spytałam.

Minerva rzuciła mi spojrzenie z ukosa.

– Ludzie przychodzą tutaj odpoczywać. W spokoju.

Claudia wstała i przywitała się z Orzeszkiem, któremu wystarczała pozycja, jaką zajął w progu. Kochał dziadka, ale umierający przyprawiali go o rozstrój nerwowy.

– Wybacz, siostrzeńcze – powiedziała Claudia. – Panuje tu mały harmider.

Miałam ochotę powiedzieć jej, żeby zrezygnowała z tych eufemizmów. „Zachowujesz się dokładnie jak biali. Gdy biały mówi «harmider», to znaczy, że w pokoju są kolorowi. A jak ty mówisz białemu coś, czego on nie chce słyszeć, to patrzy na ciebie jak głupi i prosi, żebyś powtórzyła, jak gdyby nie rozumiał, co powiedziałaś. W ten sposób chcą cię zbić z tropu i dać ci do zrozumienia, że gadasz od rzeczy. A jak biały mówi, że nastąpiła zmiana planów, to zwykle znaczy, że kogoś wyrzucą z roboty, aresztują, zastrzelą albo zostawią na lodzie". Pracuję w służbie zdrowia, a jestem, psia ich mać, zupełnie przezroczysta dla większości lekarzy, chyba że czegoś ode mnie potrzebują, i teraz jeszcze Claudia znowu mnie atakuje tą logiką białych? Jak moja siostra coś mówi, nigdy się nie napina ani nie zadziera nosa, i to mnie zawsze wpienia. Doskonale wiem, do ciężkiej cholery, że obie dorastałyśmy w południowym Bronksie, ale ilekroć na nią patrzę, zaczynam się zastanawiać, czy nie jestem wariatką. Może wcale nie pochodzimy z rodziny robotniczej. Może urodziłyśmy się w czepku i pod szczęśliwą gwiazdą i miałyśmy korepetytorów od testów SAT, żebyśmy mogły się utrzymać w wyższej klasie średniej. Może dorastałyśmy w apartamentowcu z portierem gdzieś na Upper

West Side albo przy jakiejś snobistycznej ulicy w centrum – bo Claudia wysławia się, jak gdyby właśnie tak było, i właśnie takiej przeszłości chciałaby dla nas.

Ale powściągnęłam język, opanowałam się resztkami sił i wyszłam w ślad za Orzeszkiem na korytarz. Zwróciłam się do syna.

– Co ludzie mają na myśli, mówiąc „wracaj do domu"? Jak możesz powiedzieć umierającemu, żeby wracał do domu, jeżeli on nigdy nigdzie nie był poza domem?

– Nie wiem.

– Mój ojciec umiera – poinformowałam go. – Bez owijania w bawełnę.

– Mamo, wiem, co czujesz... – Orzeszek mocno chwycił mnie za ramię. – Ale musisz trochę wyluzować.

– Wiem, że dochodzi we mnie do głosu suka. Wsuwała mi się pod skórę już od rana. Muszę zapalić.

– Skoczę ci po fajki – powiedział, nerwowo szukając wymówki, żeby opuścić hospicjum.

– Nie, Orzeszku, mam wszystko, co potrzeba, żebym mogła sama sobie kupić papierosy. Wejdź do sali i pożegnaj się z dziadkiem.

JAK TYLKO PRZYJECHAŁAM rano do hospicjum, od razu przebrałam się w szpitalny fartuch. Nie wierzę w żadne prorocze znaki, ale patrząc z perspektywy czasu, być może był to omen, że tata dzisiaj umrze. Kiedy się dowiedziałyśmy, że jest śmiertelnie chory, obiecałam sobie, że nie będę mieszać swojego zawodu z życiem prywatnym. Nie chciałam się znieczulać ani chodzić koło ojca jak pielęgniarka. Chciałam być przede wszystkim jego córką, a dopiero potem pielęgniarką.

Wychodząc z pracy, nigdy nie zabieram jej ze sobą do domu. A gdy przychodzę do szpitala, myję się starannie. To jedna z wielu ojcowskich rad, z których korzystam. Tata zawsze dbał o to, żeby zdjąć mundur przed powrotem do domu. Miał dwa mundury, które przynosił z roboty w plastikowej torbie, żeby mama mogła je uprać i wyprasować. W tym kraju powinna obowiązywać odpowiednia ustawa dotycząca strojów, w jakich pielęgniarki powinny przychodzić do pracy. Nie rozumiem, jak można wpaść prosto z ulicy do szpitala po podróży metrem, umyć tylko ręce i jak gdyby nigdy nic zacząć opiekować się chorymi. Ja tak nie robię. Przebieram się i myję dopiero na miejscu. Nie wierzę w Boga, ale modlę się za siebie i swoich pacjentów – tych znajomych i tych, którzy tylko do nas przychodzą i od nas odchodzą.

JEST TAKA PIOSENKA o gżegżółkach i pszczółkach wśród drzew. Takie właśnie było moje dzieciństwo. Motylki, ptaszki i może też te pierdolone pszczółki były nosicielami kłamstw, które opowiadali nam w szkole nauczyciele. Roznosiły je i upuszczały w naszej okolicy, gdzie prawdziwi ludzie, tacy jak moi rodzice, usiłowali po prostu znaleźć swoją drogę życiową. I mieli nadzieję, że my też ją znajdziemy.

JESTEM O ROK STARSZA od siostry. Są pewne sprawy, których ona nie pamięta albo o których chciałaby zapomnieć. A ja pamiętam, jak tata jadł kanapki z salami i oglądał wieczorne wiadomości stacji CBS. Pamiętam, jak pyskował Nixonowi, którego nazywano Szczwanym Rysiem. Pamiętam, jaka cisza zapanowała w pokoju, kiedy tata umarł. Pamiętam, jak z naszego ojca po prostu uszło powietrze i nie dało się dostrzec żadnej różnicy pomiędzy jego martwym ciałem a metalowym łóżkiem, na którym leżał.

NIE DOSTAŁ POWOŁANIA. Sam zgłosił się do wojska. Co roku obchodził święto 4 Lipca. I Memorial Day, i Veterans Day. Przed meczami Yankees śpiewał hymn narodowy. Był mądry, ale mógł być mądrzejszy. Nie był biedakiem, ale mógł być bogaty. Nie był pierwszym – ani ostatnim – ojcem, który powtarzał córkom, że są jego skarbem. Na nic się nie skarżył ani nie narzekał. I to mnie przyprawia o kurewski smutek. Może tak naprawdę zabiły go spaliny na George Washington Bridge. Ja jednak trzymam się dioksyn. Nie będę szminkować brzydoty. Ludzie, którzy powinni żyć, są martwi. Codziennie ktoś, kurwa, umiera. A ja wiem, gdzie kryje się trucizna.

MINERVA SIĘ MIOTA

2009

KIEDY WYWIESZONO OGŁOSZENIE O KONKURSIE NA SZTUKĘ teatralną, nie poświęciłam mu zbyt wiele uwagi. Byłam jakby na szkolnym zwolnieniu warunkowym, ponieważ moje oceny spadły do poziomu trójek i dwójek, i wyrzucono mnie z orkiestry, bo nie przychodziłam na próby, a moja wiolonczela stała w kącie przy telewizorze i zbierał się na niej kurz, choć mama wciąż miała nadzieję, że kiedyś jeszcze znów się zainteresuję tym instrumentem. Był też syntezator Suzuki – dostałam go od taty, kiedy się dowiedział, że zrezygnowałam z wiolonczeli, bo ojciec uważał, że jak człowiek dojdzie już do ściany, to powinien spróbować czegoś nowego i postarać się przebić mur w ten sposób. Bawiłam się tym syntezatorem przez pierwszy tydzień. Chciałam pognębić mamę ile wlezie, bo to w zasadzie jej wina, że tata od nas odszedł. Kiedy się wygadał, po prostu, jak to facet, matka, która sama mogłaby nie wytrzymać i wygadać się pierwsza, zwołała sesję konfesyjną w salonie, żebyśmy mogli wyrzucić z siebie cały ten syf. Tak jakbym naprawdę miała ochotę usłyszeć, że tata wyruchał jakąś zdzirę. Była to więc taka sesja, na której wszyscy powinni zachować spokój i kolejno zabierać głos, ale w końcu oczywiście zaczęliśmy stawać po stronie matki albo ojca. Mój brat Orzeszek mówi: że co, co zrobiłeś? A tata patrzy na niego, bo tak jak ja zastanawia się czasami, czy Orzeszek nie jest trochę pedałem, chociaż guzik mnie to obchodzi, niektórzy moi najlepsi kumple w La Guardia to pedały, więc ja na to: i co teraz? Co teraz? No to mama wzbudza w tacie straszne poczucie winy, a on tłumaczy, że więcej tego nie zrobi. Ta facetka była jego koleżanką z policji i się ze sobą skumali, bo jako gliny mają nerwową robotę, a mama kiwa głową i zaraz się godzimy, i przez jakiś czas wszyscy są szczęśliwi, i wszystko jest w porządku, ale potem mama zaczyna się stroić, a jak wraca do domu, to nie ma już na ustach tej wściekle ciemnej szminki, przez którą nasza kuzynka Gladys miała z mamy bekę, i obcina rozdwojone końcówki martwych włosów, a potem nawet robi sobie trwałą i loczki wiszą jej zupełnie naturalnie, jak cioci Claudii, i używa perfum Elizabeth Arden, a ja na to – na tyle głośno, żeby w salonie zaczęło się tsunami: – „Tato, czy to ty kupiłeś mamie perfumy Elizabeth Arden?". Jaram się tym, a mama mnie przeklina, bo się mieszam do nie swoich spraw, a tata mówi: ty przecież nigdy nie lubiłaś perfum. Boli cię od nich głowa. Może to moje hormony rozrabiają, odpowiada mama, ale teraz jakoś jestem w stanie znieść ten zapach. Na takie numery tata jest jednak za bystry i któregoś dnia przyłapuje mamę przy food trucku koło szpitala Columbia Presbyterian, jak pali fajkę na spółkę z jakimś starszym gościem. I mama przyznaje się, że ma romans z takim starym dupkiem, kulasem, niejakim Chikiem, co sprzedaje tu roti i inne żarcie z food trucka, bo nie było go już stać na czynsz w takiej części Brooklynu jak Bed-Stuy, a mama mówi: my tylko tak sobie gadamy, no może raz żeśmy się pocałowali. O całowaniu to tata wiedział wszystko. No a potem unika wzroku mamy i nie przychodzi na obiad, wyparowuje z domu i trzyma się ze swoją załogą z roboty, chociaż zawsze nazywał tych kumpli kurwiarzami, i właściwie codziennie późno wraca, a mama pracuje i gotuje obiady, i kładzie bliźniaki do łóżka, a później rodzice normalnie już ciągle się kłócą, a Orzeszek i ja jesteśmy jak pomiędzy młotem i kowadłem, i to jest taki dramat biednych ludzi, coś jak u Jerry'ego Springera, i tata pyta, skąd niby on może wiedzieć, czy bliźniaki są faktycznie jego. I że ni cholery nie są do niego podobne, co jest totalną bzdurą. Mówi, że Keisha i Lamar to mogą być dzieci tego gościa od food trucka. Mama na to, że to absurd, bo Chico wtedy jeszcze prowadził sklep w Bed-Stuy, a tata się pyta, skąd ona wie, co i gdzie miał Chico. I że miał chyba coś jeszcze. Tata wyszedł, a mama zagroziła, że wystąpi dla niego o zakaz zbliżania się, a Orzeszek i ja normalnie mówimy: mamo, tego nie możesz zrobić, bo ojciec straci pracę. A tata się pyta: czy ona naprawdę mogłaby mi zrobić coś takiego. Cholera.

To poniżej pasa. I wyprowadza się do Arizony, bo zna tam jakichś gliniarzy. Robi wielkie halo z przeprowadzki do Phoenix, a ja myślę, że ma nadzieję, że mama zacznie go błagać, żeby nie jechał. Bo niby jak już raz powie, że wyjeżdża, to się będzie musiał tego trzymać, i oboje upierają się jak osły. Chciałabym, żeby się zeszli, no ale mama nie potrafi być sama i nie znosi samotności, więc się zadaje z tym Chikiem. I nie ma odwrotu. Miejsce ojca zajmuje Chico, a ja normalnie mówię: pierdolę taki układ. Na to ona mi gada, żebym uważała na słowa i okazywała szacunek starszym, bo to niby ona płaci czynsz. No to ja zaczynam przesiadywać u znajomych i wagaruję, bo mi się tak podoba, a nauczyciele mówią: no tak, to wznieśmy toast za twoje oceny, bo spadną na łeb na szyję, a ja wtedy normalnie: no to co, a oni mówią, że jeszcze jeden semestr i koniec, wylatujesz, a ja na to: a gówno, najwyżej poślą mnie do budy dla opóźnionych w rozwoju. Ale mój młodszy braciszek Orzeszek aż się cały puszy, bo chodzi do liceum Bronx Science i wydaje mu się, że jest następnym Steve'em Jobsem. I przez niego wracam do książek i do szkoły. Nie mogę sobie pozwolić i nie pozwolę, żeby był lepszy ode mnie. I wtedy widzę ogłoszenie o konkursie dramatycznym i profesora Bassa, który jest już za stary, żeby uczyć w liceum, ale pieprzone związki nie mogą go wywalić, i profesor mówi: ty pewnie mogłabyś napisać coś fajnego, gdybyś nie była taka impertynencka. I że połowa uczniów z naszej szkoły nie zasługuje na to, żeby do nas chodzić. A ja przewracam oczami i mówię: no to jak, gdyby był pan na moim miejscu, chociaż nie powinno pana na nim być, to o czym by pan napisał w takiej sztuce na piętnaście minut? A profesor mówi, że nie o pieszych wędrówkach po Madagaskarze ani łowieniu ryb na muchę w Mongolii. Napisz o czymś, co płynie z serca, do licha. No to wtedy zaczynam zadawać różne pytania mamie, kiedy chłepcze kawę i zajada pączki, bo po odejściu taty znowu przybrała kilka funtów na wadze. I mama mówi: Minervo, jest wielu ludzi, którzy mogliby osiągnąć wielkie rzeczy, gdyby się urodzili w innym czasie. Kimś takim był twój dziadziuś. A ja na to normalnie: a co to, ja niby nie wiem? I mama każe mi zadzwonić do babuni. Babunia zawsze się cieszy, jak tylko biorę telefon, żeby do niej zadzwonić. I opowiada mi o takiej sztuce, co to dziadziuś ją znalazł na okręcie w Wietnamie, *Rosenkrantz i Guildenstern nie żyją*. Tej, którą trzymała u siebie ciocia Claudia. Znowu pokłóciłam się z mamą o to, że jest jakby obywatelką drugiej kategorii. Piszę więc sztukę o takim jednym facecie na okręcie, co czyta Shakespeare'a, a potem przechodzę do jego córek, które czytają później tę samą sztukę, jak ten facet umiera, i dostaję drugą nagrodę, a jak pokazuję tekst profesorowi Bassowi, to aż wylewa kawę na ten swój frajerski garniturek, co go zawsze nosi, i wybucha płaczem. Przygotowuję się na jego kolejny wykład o żałosnym stanie literatury i sztuki w Nowym Jorku i walce artysty o godność w obliczu niechęci, albo może o tym, że gdyby został w Europie, jak był młodszy, to wszystko by było inaczej. Ale on zaraz ociera oczy chusteczką. Dobra robota, mówi, a ja dostaję dyplom i dwadzieścia pięć dolarów jako drugą nagrodę, umawiam się z Orzeszkiem w Drama Bookshop na Times Square, gdzie kupujemy *Rosenkrantz i Guildenstern nie żyją*. Pakują nam książkę w ładny granatowy papier i jedziemy do domu. Pokazuję mamie dyplom i daję jej sztukę

Stopparda. Jestem wkurzona, że sama nie kupiła tej książki już dawno temu. Próbuje mnie uściskać, ale ja się cofam, tak żeby nie mogła mnie dosięgnąć. Umówiłam się z kimś i muszę iść, mama jednak nie chce o tym słyszeć. Łapie i ściska mnie mocno. I tak stoimy razem z dobrą minutę. I nie opieram się, bo może ona potrzebuje tego uścisku bardziej niż ja. Może. I kiedy mnie tak trzyma, przypominam sobie, że jak byłam mała, to ciągle mi czytała. Wychodzę, a ona siedzi jeszcze w salonie i przegląda książkę.

I wtedy dociera do mnie, że chociaż raz w życiu zrobiłam to, co trzeba.

ĆWICZENIA Z PISANIA / PROF. BASS, STRUKTURY JĘZYKOWE

MINERVA C. PARKER

(dialog)

TATA MINERVY

Spodobałaby ci się pustynia, Minnie. Nie jest cała brunatna, jak myślałem. Jasne, pustynia w Arizonie w większości jest brązowa, ale w górach są też piękne miejsca, gdzie mamy zieleń, błękit i srebro. Właściwie rozumiem, co ludziom się w niej podoba. Zabrałem kogoś ze sobą na kilka dni do...

MINERVA

Z kim ty się spotykasz? Masz jakąś kobietę? Tak szybko?

TATA MINERVY

Na pustyni jest ładnie. Mam przyjaciółkę.

MINERVA

Mówiłeś, że nigdy więcej już się nie ożenisz.

TATA MINERVY

Ja tak mówiłem? Wysłałem wam pocztówkę z widokiem posterunku, gdzie pracuję. To jeden z najstarszych budynków w Arizonie. A teraz ty mi powiedz, dlaczego dostaję od ciebie takie nieprzyzwoite pocztówki z półnagimi kobietami.

MINERVA

Bo są darmowe. Biorę je z Two Boots Pizza i ze Strand.

TATA MINERVY

Zdaje mi się, że twoja mama powinna mieć dość pieniędzy, żeby dać ci na koperty i znaczki. Płacę alimenty.

MINERVA

Czy ta kobieta jest czarna?

TATA MINERVY

Mówisz jak twoja mama. Estrella pochodzi z plemienia Nawahów. Ale w jej żyłach płynie też krew hiszpańska.

MINERVA

Zabijaliśmy Nawahów. Czarni Buffalo Soldiers. Osaczaliśmy ich. Jak wy teraz, kiedy wypędzacie Meksykanów z powrotem za granicę. A może powinnam cię nazywać „Custer"? Będziesz odpowiedzialny za to, że całe pokolenie Meksykanów znienawidzi czarnych.

TATA MINERVY

A ty dostajesz trójki z historii. Wiesz, co jest nie tak z tym porównaniem, Minnie? To, że Custer walczył w Wyoming. Little Big Horn. Naucz się geografii.

MINERVA

Gówno mnie to obchodzi.

TATA MINERVY

Nie wyrażaj się. Bev mi mówi, że czasem u kogoś nocujesz. Przyjadę tam do was. Mam przyjechać?

MINERVA

I zostaniesz?

TATA MINERVY

Nie, Minnie. W odwiedziny. I nie będę miał z tego przyjemności.

MINERVA

Czasami czekamy na list nawet po trzy tygodnie. Dlaczego nie używasz Facebooka albo nie napiszesz esemesa jak normalny człowiek?

TATA MINERVY

Nie wierzę w takie rzeczy.

MINERVA

Ale mieszkasz teraz w innym stanie.

TATA MINERVY

Kiedyś ludzie pisali normalne listy. W dawnych czasach nawet najgłupszy debil potrafił napisać porządny list. Był taki film dokumentalny o wojnie domowej…

MINERVA

Dlaczego nie mogę do ciebie przyjechać i zamieszkać z tobą?

TATA MINERVY

To jest zbyt wielkie pustkowie... I jeździ tu za dużo pijanych kierowców, którzy nie przestrzegają ograniczenia prędkości.

MINERVA

Powiedziałeś, że pustynia jest piękna.

TATA MINERVY

Może jak się bardziej zadomowię...

MINERVA

Kochasz jeszcze mamę?

TATA MINERVY

Nieważne.

MINERVA

Ona cię ciągle kocha.

TATA MINERVY

Niektóre rzeczy po prostu nie mają znaczenia.

MINERVA

Tato?

TATA MINERVY

Bądź grzeczną dziewczynką. Ucałuj bliźniaki. I Orzeszka. Powiedz bratu, że życie tu jest potworne. Musi zmężnieć.

(poezja)

CUSTER MA ZABIJAĆ SKURWYSYNÓW

Tatko jest na pustyni
Mówi, że brązowa, potem kwitnie
Cały jest jak Custer
W mundurze straży granicznej

Zniknij
Pełne wyciemnienie
I nie oglądaj się
Co ma się teraz stać?
Minnie, bądź grzeczna
Jak grzeczne dziewczynki idą do piekła
To wolę być niegrzeczna
Podobno te niegrzeczne chodzą na górę
Co możesz mi powiedzieć?
Skoro ty możesz wyjechać
A ja tu muszę czekać
A my musimy czekać
Nie widziałam cię już sześć miesięcy
Sprawdź sobie: to jest pół roku

PARA WODNA

1971 1986 1996 **2010**

RUFUS, SKĄD JESTEŚ, SYNU? „URODZIŁEM SIĘ W NOWYM Jorku. Niedaleko stąd. W Columbia Presbyterian". A twoi rodzice? Czym się zajmują? „Tata jest adwokatem. James Vincent. Moja mama, Sigrid, pracuje jako agentka castingowa w LA". Aha. Znaczy produkt rozwodu. „Tak, proszę pana". Duża rodzina? „Nie, proszę pana, jestem jedynakiem". Och, moja żona też jest jedynaczką. Moja żona, Agnes.

Claudia i ja siedzieliśmy przy szklanej ławie kawowej, na garbatej niczym wielbłąd kanapie, w salonie w kształcie litery L o stiukowych ścianach, i ten pokój przypominał mi pierwsze mieszkanie mamy w Venice Beach. Eddie ciągle podsuwał nam tacę z salami soppressata, serami i pieczywem. Pieczywo pochodziło z jego ulubionej włoskiej piekarni w sąsiedztwie: bułki z semoliny, ziarnisty chleb i ciabatta, które polecał nam jeść z różnymi serami. Tych serów, jak mówił, nie można było dostać w większości marketów w Nowym Jorku. Śmierdzących włoskich serów, które kupował gdzieś „po znajomości". Sposób, w jaki o tym opowiadał, był dla mnie jedyną zachętą, której potrzebowałem, żeby ich skosztować. Pani Christie wydawała się zadowolona, że to jej mąż prowadzi rozmowę. Siedziała ze skrzyżowanymi nogami, wsparta o niego, na skórzanej dwuosobowej kanapce.

– Zawsze chciałam mieć rodzeństwo – powiedziała – i chyba w końcu w pewnym sensie mi się to udało. Dzisiaj mam męża i córki.

– **ZDRADZISZ MI** jakąś swoją tajemnicę? – spytałem Claudię Christie.

Drugi rok studiów. Zaledwie po trzech tygodniach naszej znajomości na Columbia University wiedziałem, że poproszę ją o rękę. Mieszkałem poza kampusem, w Morningside Heights, ze studentem filozofii, który co drugi dzień nocował u swojej dziewczyny. Mieszkałem poza kampusem, bo zawsze miałem problemy ze snem. To u nas rodzinne. Sen nie chce do mnie przyjść. W tamtych latach wstawałem o trzeciej rano i grałem na saksofonie. Właściwie to nie miałem do niego ucha, ale muzyka działała na mnie cudownie usypiająco. W drugim semestrze mój współlokator wyprowadził się do centrum, do West Village. Ulotnił się w sobotę, a Claudia wprowadziła się do mnie przed upływem tygodnia. Zabarykadowaliśmy się w tym mieszkaniu jak bandyci na kilka pierwszych, oszalałych od seksu tygodni zimowego semestru. Byliśmy młodzi, sprawni fizycznie i zadziwieni nieustającą rozkoszą, jaką potrafiły nam dawać nasze ciała. Tak to już jest, że studenci nawiązują w tym okresie intensywne... relacje, jak to się dzisiaj mówi, i z dnia na dzień zostają kochankami. Znajomi nazywali nas „znikającą parą", bo wychodziliśmy z domu tylko na zajęcia albo żeby coś zjeść, najczęściej kupowaliśmy tanie dania na wynos. Pizzę w V&T's. Ryż i fasolę w Tom's. Kurczaka z rożna albo drobiowe falafele z sosem baba ghanoush w Rainbow Chicken. Po śródziemnomorskich potrawach cuchnęło nam z ust, ale nawet czosnek ma swoje zalety. Jeżeli wiesz, co zrobić z ząbkiem czosnku, potrafi pobudzić zmysły jak afrodyzjak (tej sztuczki nauczyła mnie kobieta imieniem Parsnip).

– Ruff – powiedziała Claudia. – Nie ma już żadnych tajemnic. – Leżała podparta na naszym sękatym materacu, trzymając na kolanach Goethego: *Der Prokurator*. Zaczęliśmy właśnie zajęcia z historii nowelistyki. Bardzo ciekawy temat dla studentów filologii angielskiej.

– Mam na imię Rufus. – Tylko matka i ojciec mówili na mnie Ruff. Ale podobało mi się, że Claudia od razu zaczęła używać mojego przydomka.

– Nie mogę cię traktować poważnie jako Rufusa. Jak słyszę „Rufus", to zaraz myślę: „Rufus i Chaka Khan".

– Psiakrew, zraniłaś moje uczucia.

– *C'est dommage*. Jakoś to przeżyjesz.

Uniwersyteckie romanse bywają koszmarne. Budziłem się czasami koło dziewczyn, których nie chciałem więcej w życiu widzieć i których pewnie w ogóle nigdy bym nawet nie dotknął, gdybym nie znalazł się na niewłaściwej imprezie w niewłaściwym momencie. To w gruncie rzeczy cud, jeśli przewracasz się rano na drugi bok po jakiejś balandze w akademiku i jesteś zadowolony na widok dziewczyny, z którą poszedłeś poprzedniego wieczoru do łóżka. Mimo to lubiłem, kiedy Claudia budziła się obok mnie. Ja jestem biały. A ona czarna. Na ogół nie mieliśmy problemów z kolorem naszej skóry, okazało się jednak, że świat, nasz świat, ma ich z nim całkiem sporo.

– Możliwe, że tajemnice to dzisiaj już tylko domena wiktoriańskich melodramatów – powiedziałem. – Ale przestań, w twojej przeszłości na pewno jest coś głębokiego, mrocznego i intymnego. Zdradź mi swoje najbardziej wstydliwe wspomnienie.

– Gdybym zaprosiła cię do domu, mógłbyś tam spłonąć – powiedziała i roześmiała się. Nie wiedziałem tego w tamtym czasie, ale to był śmiech jej ojca, chrapliwy i ciepły, sugerujący sierpniowe lato i papierosy, chociaż Claudia nie paliła. Mówię, że ten jej śmiech jest nerwowy, bo tak się właśnie śmieje, zanim powie prawdę. A jeśli można przejmować zwyczaje partnera, powiedziałbym, że zaraziłem się tym śmiechem od niej, chociaż moja matka też śmieje się jak głupia.

– Poważnie – uzupełniła. – Mama zachowuje zwykle zimną krew. Na ogół siedzi cicho. Ale mój ostatni chłopak wylądował w Columbia Presbyterian z oparzeniami pierwszego stopnia na ramieniu. Musieli mu ściągać koszulę szczypczykami do paznokci, tak mu przylgnęła do skóry. Myślałam, że jego rodzice podadzą nas do sądu.

KIEDY CLAUDIA PIERWSZY RAZ zaprosiła mnie do domu, Agnes Christie próbowała poparzyć mi ręce żelazkiem. Nie pamiętam go, tylko parę wodną i to, jak bąbelki wydobywały się z bulgotem z niewielkiego dzióbka w płaskiej, chromowanej rączce. Chcę też powiedzieć, że miało kolor weneckiej czerwieni, ale równie dobrze mogło być niebieskie, srebrne albo szare. Wszystko szło w miarę nieźle, a w każdym razie tak mi się wydawało. Pani Christie ziewała i pod jakimś pretekstem wyszła z pokoju. Kiedy wróciła, początkowo uznałem rozpalone do czerwoności żelazko za karafkę chianti. Uśmiechnąłem się do tej ładnej brązowoskórej kobiety o owalnej twarzy mojej przyszłej żony i stawiłem jej odważnie czoło. Podeszła, a ja wyciągnąłem ręce i ramiona na spotkanie żaru. Ten gest, moje palce posuwające się naprzód tanecznymi ruchami i nieustępujące, kazały Agnes zatrzymać się i spojrzeć na żelazko.

– Ależ, pani Christie – powiedziałem. – Nie uda się pani poparzyć mnie tak, żeby jednocześnie nie poparzyć siebie.

U boku małżonki pojawił się pan Christie.

– Agnes – zwrócił się do niej. – Daj spokój.

– Proszę mi wybaczyć – powiedziała Agnes. I wyłączyła rozpalone żelazko. – Tam, skąd pochodzę, obecność obcego białego mężczyzny w domu rzadko znaczy coś dobrego.

– No to przyrzekam, że będę próbował na wszystkie możliwe sposoby stać się z czasem dla was nieco mniej obcy. Ale jeśli chodzi o kolor mojej skóry, to na to nic nie poradzę.

CLAUDIA PRZYGOTOWAŁA MNIE na żelazko matki. Robiliśmy próby, by sprawdzić, jaka reakcja z mojej strony byłaby najlepsza, gdyby Agnes mnie zaatakowała.

W pierwszej chwili zdziwiła mnie niewielka liczba książek w domu państwa Christie. W salonie na widoku stały tylko encyklopedia Britannica i dzieła zebrane Shakespeare'a, zakupione przez matkę Claudii na aukcji w katolickiej szkole, do której chodziła w dzieciństwie. Normalnie odjechałem na taką wiadomość. Może gdybyście poznali Claudię... musielibyście ją poznać, żeby to zrozumieć. A może wszystko sprowadza się jednak do lepszego startu życiowego i nadziei? Ja dorastałem w mieszkaniu z widokiem na Central Park West i z biblioteką. Całymi godzinami budowałem forty ze stojących w niej książek. Kiedy odwiedziłem dom Claudii, byłem pewien, że zamaszyście otworzy drzwi i pojawią się dowody rzeczowe, może tajemna jaskinia pełna książek, która wyjaśni, w jaki sposób moja dziewczyna dostała się na Columbię. Jakiś ślad, znamionujący kryjówkę początkującej uczonej. Ale zobaczyłem tylko podwójne łóżko, komodę i biurko, nad którym wisiał plakat z *Purple Rain*. W domu państwa Christie niczego nie brakowało w sensie materialnym, mieli może tylko trochę za mało wolnego miejsca. Wszystko wyglądało na funkcjonalne. Była to jedna z tych chwil – a jako biały mężczyzna żonaty z czarną kobietą przeżyłem ich kilka – kiedy dotarło do mnie, że miałem więcej szczęścia. O szczęściu można gadać do usranej śmierci, nigdy jednak się go nie zrozumie, dopóki człowiek nie zamieszka z kimś, kto musiał się bardziej starać i zaczynać życie z niższego pułapu.

– Ona nie jest wariatką – powiedziałem, przekrzykując głośny hurkot metra linii 5, gdy wracaliśmy już do domu. Potem mieliśmy wsiąść w 4, dojechać do 125 Ulicy i dalszą drogę pokonać taksówką.

– Co?

– Twoi rodzice żyją w trybie czuwania. Tak jak moi.

Claudia odwróciła wzrok.

– Bardzo cię proszę, nie oceniaj mojej rodziny na podstawie zachowania własnych rodziców. To bez sensu. Oni należą do innego pokolenia. Spotkało ich w życiu coś strasznie chujowego. My... Beverly i ja... nie mogę ich o to pytać.

– Dlaczego?

– To jest ich sprawa, Rufusie.

– Ale dziedziczymy pamięć po rodzicach. Naprawdę nie chciałabyś wiedzieć, co w nich siedzi?

Claudia westchnęła.

– Właściwie to nie. Wystarczy, że mnie kochali.

NA NASZĄ PIERWSZĄ wspólną Gwiazdkę kupiłem matce Claudii zabytkowe żelazko. Znalazłem je w sklepie ze starociami przy Venice Beach, gdzie pojechałem na urlop z moją mamą. Nie byłem pewien, jak zareaguje pani Christie, gdy odpakuje prezent, ani co powie Claudia czy pan Christie. Nie wiedziałem, czy spodoba im się taki żart ani czy to rzeczywiście jest żart, czy raczej jakaś taka moja pasywna agresja, mój sposób powiedzenia „Nawet jak mnie oparzysz, i tak się nie poddam i ciągle będę wracał po waszą córkę".

Ale pani Christie uśmiechnęła się, a na jej ciemne policzki wystąpił rumieniec.

– Mój prezent dla ciebie jest trochę bardziej... zwyczajny. To czapeczka bejsbolowa Yankees, ode mnie i od Eddiego.

ŻELAZKO W PREZENCIE stało się u nas tradycją. Na każde święta Bożego Narodzenia kupuję mamie Claudii zabytkowe żelazko. Zbiera je jak eksponaty muzealne – jednostronnie wygładzone bloki żelaza z uchwytem, żelazka z duszą, żelazka na węgiel. Teraz, kiedy zabrakło pana Christie i mama Claudii nie ma już dla kogo prasować ubrań, nie wiem, czy często to robi w Buckner County w Georgii. Kiedy co niedziela rozmawia z Claudią przez telefon, zawsze odczuwam pokusę, żeby zapytać, czy nadal ma kolekcję tych żelazek.

JESZCZE DZIŚ, DWADZIEŚCIA LAT PÓŹNIEJ, Claudia wciąż lubi pracować w łóżku. Bierze plastikową tacę i na niej sprawdza pisemne prace studentów. Mieszkamy w domku należącym do uniwersytetu, dziesięć minut drogi piechotą od mieszkania, które zajmowaliśmy na początku naszego związku. Otacza nas historia. Świadectwa tego, jak przyszliśmy na świat, jak się zmienialiśmy, jak wychowywaliśmy nasze dzieci. Kiedy ludzie mówią, że Nowy Jork się zmienił, nie zawsze jestem pewien, co mają na myśli. Dla kogo się zmienił? Potrafię narysować mapkę naszej ewolucji i wymierzyć ją, używając do tego ulic i mil. Oczywiście, sklepy i restauracje pojawiają się i znikają. Rainbow Chicken nie ma już od dawna. Sklep Gotham Cabinets, gdzie kupiłem swój pierwszy materac typu futon, jeszcze się trzyma, nie jestem jednak pewien, czy nowe pokolenie jara się futonami. Atmosfera w centrum miasta i na obrzeżach jest różna. Kiedyś uciekaliśmy na Lower East Side, żeby zakosztować twardej, autentycznej kontrkultury, ale dzisiaj na Ludlow mieszkają same blondynki, które inwestują w fundusze powiernicze. Jeśli masz dzieci, nie tęsknisz już za tym światem w taki sam sposób jak dawniej. Nie masz na to czasu.

NAZYWAM SIĘ RUFUS NOEL VINCENT. Skończyłem czterdzieści lat. Od pewnego czasu możecie zobaczyć mnie i moją żonę na basenie w naszym apartamentowcu, gdzie trzy razy w tygodniu chodzimy z córką Winoną na pływanie i hydroterapię. Jak twierdzi jej terapeuta, najlepszym sposobem na przezwyciężenie lęku jest stawić mu czoło, i dlatego Claudia, Winona i ja – w tym czasie Elijah ma okazję spotkać się sam na sam ze swoim dziadkiem, a moim tatą – pływamy w tym basenie tam i z powrotem jak żaby albo wydry. Winnie uwielbia kraul i kiedy płynę tym stylem obok niej, dosyć często myślę o Hanku Camphorze, moim przyrodnim bracie, którego nie znam. Myślę o ojcu, matce i całym tym syfie z przeszłości, kiedy pracowałem po godzinach, żeby o nim zapomnieć, i liczę: „jedna rybka; dwie rybki; trzy rybki". Nie umiem powiedzieć, czy odpływam od przeszłości, czy raczej płynę ku niej.

MAMA WYCIĄGNĘŁA MNIE Z LICEUM Trinity Prep w pierwszej klasie. Uznała, że mam tam towarzystwo, które za bardzo trąci chowem wsobnym. Bo chodziłem do tej budy z tymi samymi dzieciakami, które znałem od zerówki, razem graliśmy w szkolnej lidze softballu i piłki nożnej w Central Parku, nawalaliśmy się na przyjęciach urodzinowych i jeździliśmy na obozy do Vermontu i Maine. Mama żałowała, że nie podszedłem do egzaminów do Hunter College. Że tata i ona nie skierowali mnie na jakieś bardziej akademickie tory. Była pewna, że jest nam potrzebna odmiana. A wcześniej, niedługi czas przedtem, przyplątał mi się irytujący tik głosowy: ciągle pochrząkiwałem. Coś tkwiło w mojej krtani i nie chciało wyjść.

– Jak gdybym miał tam kawałek taśmy klejącej – powtarzałem często.

Rodzice zawieźli mnie do szpitala laryngologicznego na Manhattanie. Badali mnie najlepsi nowojorscy specjaliści, ale żaden nie znalazł nic w moim gardle. Nie miałem też jakichkolwiek reakcji alergicznych. Byłem okazem zdrowia. Zdrowym nastolatkiem.

– To wszystko jest w jego głowie – stwierdził w końcu któryś z kolejnych lekarzy. – Jakie stosunki panują u państwa w domu?

Dawniej grywałem trochę na pianinie, instrumencie, do którego zdradzałem niewielki talent i którym interesowałem się najwyżej przelotnie. W Trinity każdy na czymś grał. A mama, która miała europejskie korzenie, często brzdąkała wieczorami po pracy na naszym małym steinwayu. Uważała, że pianino może podziałać na mnie uspokajająco, nawet jeśli nie przyniesie innego pożytku. Tata wychował się w domu, w którym nie było instrumentów muzycznych, ale uwielbiał jazz, całego Milesa Davisa. *So What.* Kupił mi używany saksofon od jakiegoś muzyka jazzowego, który rzekomo grywał z największymi gwiazdami. Ojciec wydał na ten saksofon małą fortunę, chociaż jak przyznał później, w głębi duszy wiedział, że bardziej opłacałoby się kupić nowy.

– Wykorzystaj go, żeby oczyścić gardło – powiedział. – Jak będziesz robił postępy, to jeden mój znajomy zawodowiec zacznie udzielać ci lekcji.

Dla mamy nie był już jednak taki miły.

– Co ci strzeliło do głowy, żeby zabierać Ruffa z Trinity? Ma tam zgraną paczkę.

– Zabieram go nie tylko z Trinity – odpowiedziała. Gdy pierwszy raz poprosiła ojca o rozwód, byli na Piątej Alei i wracali żółtą taksówką do domu z pięćdziesiątych urodzin starszego wspólnika w firmie, w której pracował tata. Zapowiedź rozwodu była dla niego wstrząsem. Przez kilka następnych tygodni po prostu nie reagował na prośby matki.

– Może miałaś rację, wysyłając go do nowej szkoły – odezwał się któregoś wieczoru przy stole podczas kolacji. I położył dłoń na ręce mamy.

– Pacyfik! – Odwróciła wzrok i odepchnęła jego dłoń.

– Nie kapuję, o co ci chodzi, Sigrid.

– Zawsze chciałam mieszkać nad Pacyfikiem.

Teraz tata zrozumiał ją od razu.

– Nie możesz wywieźć mi syna na Zachodnie Wybrzeże.

– Ma już piętnaście lat – odparła bez przekonania, chociaż udawała pewną siebie. – Decyzja należy do niego.

– Rozwód? – powiedziałem i chrząknąłem. Wykonywałem małe koliste ruchy, raz mocniej, raz słabiej, masując sobie trzema palcami jabłko Adama. Wtedy tego nie wiedziałem, ale było to jakby przygotowanie do masaży, które wiele lat później robiłem Claudii, śpiewając naszym jeszcze nienarodzonym bliźniakom. I do masaży, które Claudia robiła mnie, kiedy objadłem się pizzą albo inną potrawą zawierającą mleko, bo mój żołądek go nie tolerował.

– Mogłabyś wstać i podać Ruffowi łyk wody, Sigrid? – poprosił tata. – Nasz syn znowu ma głos jak zepsuty odkurzacz.

– Tylko czekałam, aż mnie o to poprosisz! – Mama pokręciła głową. – Powiedz, mam wam przynosić wodę dlatego, że jestem kobietą?

– Przecież dlatego cię kocham, że jesteś kobietą.

– I właśnie w tym tkwi problem. Ty kochasz wszystkie kobiety.

Tata zagwizdał.

– Ruff, może to jest odpowiednia chwila, żebyś poćwiczył trochę na saksofonie.

Do jadalni wpadł powiew wiatru z tarasu wychodzącego na Central Park West. Poczułem zapach tanich orzeszków ziemnych i hot dogów na straganach stojących jedenaście pięter niżej. Słyszałem też kopyta dorożkarskich koni.

– Rufus – powiedziała z uśmiechem mama. – To ładnie ze strony taty, że kupił ci saksofon. Na Zachodnim Wybrzeżu mieszkałbyś nad morzem i grał w orkiestrze dętej.

– Nowy Jork to wyspa – odparł tata. – Jest otoczony wodą ze wszystkich stron. A Kalifornia leży na pustyni. Pewnego dnia Pacyfik się wkurzy i powie, że ta pieprzona Kalifornia jest za bardzo spragniona. Pacyfik zrobi coś, czego ty nie masz powodu robić, Sigrid. Podniesie ręce i odejdzie.

– Chcesz dać do zrozumienia, że tata cię zdradził? – zwróciłem się z wahaniem do matki, nie wiedząc, czy rzeczywiście powinienem iść do swojego pokoju i ćwiczyć, czy zostać przy stole w jadalni.

Mama zaczęła się śmiać i śmiała się bardzo, ale to bardzo długo. Jej śmiech sprawił, że tata się zaczerwienił. Miał taką minę, jak gdyby obliczał w myślach, kiedy mógł zdradzić mamę.

– Myślisz, że sypiałem z kobietami z Trinity? – spytał, uznając tę sugestię zarówno za obraźliwą, jak i absurdalną. – Nie kala się gniazda, w którym mieszka twój dzieciak. Bo Ruff, praktycznie rzecz biorąc, mieszka w szkole. To jego drugi dom.

W wyniku tego stwierdzenia mama i ja zrozumieliśmy, że owszem, tata ją zdradził, chociaż na razie nie było wiadomo gdzie.

– Powiedz tylko, że nie jestem dobrym ojcem, Sigrid – dodał. – Bo chyba okazałem się godny zaufania i troskliwy pod każdym istotnym względem.

Ujrzałem teraz tatę w nowym świetle. Nauczył mnie, jak rozbić namiot w deszczu podczas burzy. I jak się rzuca softball – w Central Parku. Jak zbudować fort z lin bungee albo z książek o przygodach Robinsona Crusoe i Hucka Finna z naszej biblioteki. Ale to mama nauczyła mnie jeździć na rowerze. I to ona zabrała mnie do restauracji Benihana. Tata często wyjeżdżał i niejednego wieczoru musieliśmy jeść kolację sami. Zacząłem myśleć o tej taśmie klejącej w moim gardle, która nie chciała zniknąć, i o tym, że robiła się jeszcze bardziej lepka, kiedy przebywałem w jednym pokoju z rodzicami.

– W Kalifornii ciągle świeci słońce. – Mama skinęła głową. – To jest Słoneczny Stan.

Ani tata, ani ja nie mieliśmy serca, żeby powiedzieć mamie, że w rzeczywistości jest to określenie Florydy. Była inteligentną kobietą, ale łatwo dawała się zbić z tropu. Udałem się na poszukiwanie saksofonu. Nie chciałem wyjeżdżać do Kalifornii, wkurwiłem się jednak na ojca.

Pieszo w LA
Pieszo w LA, nikt nie chodzi piechotą w LA
Pieszo w LA
Pieszo w LA, nikt nie chodzi piechotą w LA
Missing Persons, *Spring Session M*, 1982

WSZYSCY WIEDZĄ, ŻE w Los Angeles rosną palmy. Że są tam neonowe światła, które migoczą i mrugają nocą. Zakorkowane pięciopasmowe autostrady. I smog zdobiący lazurowe niebo. W Venice chodziliśmy piechotą. To, że w LA nikt nigdy nie przemieszcza się piechotą, wcale nie było prawdą.

– Nogi poniosą cię, dokąd tylko chcesz – powiedziała mama. – O ile jesteś ciekawy i będziesz miał oko na tkankę... – A moja mama była ciekawa wszystkiego.

– Znaczy na zespół komórek? – zapytałem.

– Nie, na tkankę miejską.

Dwa tygodnie po tym, jak znaleźliśmy mieszkanie, dostała pracę asystentki agenta castingowego.

– Zwiedzaj LA piechotą – powiedział jej Bruce, ten agent. Był jedynym facetem na świecie, który miał gęstsze włosy od mojego ojca. Ich jak gdyby ogorzały pęk zawiązywał z tyłu w koński ogon.

Mama zapisała mnie do szkoły Venice Senior High. Nie mieli tam orkiestry dętej, za co przepraszała mnie więcej niż raz, wylewnie, kilkakrotnie – i poprosiła nawet o pomoc Bruce'a, żeby umieścić mnie w Beverly Hills High.

– Nie, dzięki – powiedziałem. – Lepiej znajdź mi korepetytora. Będę się uczył muzyki prywatnie.

– To prośba czy polecenie? – Przyglądała mi się, unosząc brwi, które w tym wysokim położeniu splatały się ze sobą.

Wynajęła mieszkanie z dwiema sypialniami w zbudowanym w hiszpańskim stylu apartamentowcu z wewnętrznym dziedzińcem i glicynią wspinającą się na wyblakłe balkony. Rosły tam też bugenwille i hibiskusy, pomarańczowe, w sierpniowe upały wydzielające silny i uporczywy zapach. Było sucho. Mieszkaliśmy dwie ulice od plaży, a Bruce w West Hollywood Hills. Czasami w drodze do jego posiadłości, dokąd jechaliśmy maminym volkswagenem garbusem – samochodem, w którym moja drobna matka świetnie się mieściła, ale który dla mnie był za mały – przyglądałem się białym literom napisu HOLLYWOOD sterczącym na skałach barwy siana. Te skały przypominały mi kolor włosów Bruce'a. Byłem pewien, że chciał zaliczyć mamę, ale w luzackiej atmosferze Kalifornii w ogóle dużo się działo.

Przeprowadziliśmy się do Venice Beach w lipcu 1986 roku. Było tam nieprzyjemnie, paskudnie i przerażająco, czyli identycznie jak w Nowym Jorku. Wiele lat później ludzie pytali mnie, jak dawałem sobie radę w Los Angeles, a ja odpowiadałem, że to nie jest miejsce, dokąd się jedzie po to, „żeby dawać sobie radę, tylko żeby dawać zupełnie co innego". Miałem piętnaście lat, mieszkałem blisko morza, wśród dziewczyn w bikini. W 1986 w Venice Beach mogłeś wyglądać jak potwór Frankenstein, a mimo to czuć się dobrze i sypiać z dziewczętami. Spacerując plażą, miałem czasami wrażenie, że połowa nowojorskich bezdomnych znalazła sobie nowe schronienie w Venice Beach. Panowały tu nastroje prospołeczne, ale całkiem sporo osób protestowało przeciwko tym menelom, którzy zagnieździli się na plaży. Jeśli mama przyjechała do Venice w nadziei, że znajdzie jakąś utopię, to się rozczarowała. Wylądowaliśmy wśród rozbitego szkła i cuchnących kanałów pełnych zużytych strzykawek.

– Patrz na Pacyfik, nic więcej się wtedy nie liczy – powiedziała. Twierdziła, że ten ocean przyzywał ją przez pół życia, a ona w ogóle nie zdawała sobie z tego sprawy.

Nasz apartamentowiec był pełen kobiet noszących takie imiona, jak Sage, Parsnip czy Jasmine*. Wszystkie były kiedyś aktorkami, modelkami albo zawodowymi tancerkami, z czasem zostały jednak stewardesami, sekretarkami albo modelkami pozującymi do zdjęć w katalogach. Co najmniej jednej z nich, Sage, odebrano prawo do opieki nad dzieckiem – dwuletnią córką. Nie wiedziała, dokąd mąż zabrał dziewczynkę ani czy kiedyś jeszcze ją zobaczy. Mama zaprzyjaźniła się z tymi kobietami, które zachowywały się jak młode dziewczyny. Później, kiedy zacząłem chodzić z nimi do łóżka, grzebałem w ich torebkach i zobaczyłem daty urodzenia na prawach jazdy: tu starzejąca się trzydziestka szóstka, tam rycząca czterdziestka. Czekałem, aż również moja mama wróci do czasów, gdy miała siedemnaście albo dwadzieścia jeden lat. Czekałem, że przefarbuje sobie włosy na blond. A ona czekała, kiedy przestanę czekać, kątem oka monitorując mój kaszel, który już jakby minął. Była Amerykanką w trzecim pokoleniu, ale wciąż podkreślała swój europejski akcent. Ludzie mówili, że wygląda jak Nastassja Kinski, co nie było ani trochę prawdą, przyjmowała jednak komplement do wiadomości i wykorzystywała go, ile się tylko dało.

– Moja rodzina pochodzi z Bretanii – mawiała. Nosiła małe chustki, wiązała je sobie na szyi w stylu francuskim.

– Lubisz spacery po plaży, Rufus? – pytały mnie Sage, Parsnip albo Jasmine.

Przyglądałem im się, a one odwzajemniały moje spojrzenie. „Nie powinno się kalać własnego gniazda”, słyszałem

* Szałwia, Pasternak i Jaśmin.

w myślach głos ojca. Chodziłem na plażę, aż pod falochrony, gdzie przesiadywali surferzy, i tam się nawalałem. Razem z nimi, właściwie każdego dnia. W ten sposób poznałem surfera imieniem Herb. Pachniał piżmem, był biały i nosił dredy. Sprzedawał zioło, więc wszyscy ciągle się śmiali, że „Herb prowadzi herbarium". Spytał, czy nie zechciałbym wejść z nim do interesu. Nie zechciałem.

– Ładny z ciebie chłopak. Ludzie takich lubią.

Był ode mnie starszy o jakieś trzy lata.

Rano surfowałem, a po południu grałem nad morzem na saksofonie; plażowicze rzucali mi drobne monety. Ku mojemu zdumieniu nieźle zarabiałem. A wcale nie byłem za dobry. Przychodziła tam jedna starsza facetka, pijaczka, która codziennie nosiła ten sam czerwony sztruksowy dres i mieszkała w kawalerce w bloku komunalnym. Pojawiała się wczesnym wieczorem i wykrzykiwała w kółko te same wersy z *Only You* Plattersów:

> Tylko dzięki tobie dobry się zdaje świat,
> Tylko dzięki tobie zamiast ciemności jest blask,
> Tylko dzięki tobie, dzięki tobie jedynej...

Potem znikała razem z moimi zarobkami.

Jeżeli mama wiedziała, że jaram trawę, to nie dawała tego po sobie poznać. Jej dzień pracy dla Bruce'a trwał czasem czternaście godzin, bo robota w castingach była brutalna, zdarzały się w niej na przemian lepsze i gorsze okresy, a Bruce „kolaborował", jak to określał, z niezależnymi nowojorskimi reżyserami i aktorami z najwyższej półki. A mama miała literacki nowojorski sznyt i francuskie korzenie. W Nowym Jorku dzieliła biurko z innym pracownikiem w kącie ciasnego boksu przy niewielkim oknie, w Los Angeles natomiast okna w jej gabinecie zajmowały całą jego szerokość, na ścianach wisiały rośliny doniczkowe, drzwi były przesuwne, a meble przypominały wyposażenie luksusowego jachtu.

BRUCE WPADAŁ CZASEM DO NAS na bouillabaisse.

– Sig – tak zwracał się do matki. – Słowo daję, jak ty możesz tu mieszkać?

Mama w rozmowach z Bruce'em ograniczała się do spraw zawodowych, w każdym razie w mojej obecności. Uwielbiała gadać o pracy. Zauważyłem, że zaczęła nosić dłuższe i luźniejsze chustki, a ich łagodne pastelowe kolory zmieniły się w rozedrgane odcienie fioletu i purpury.

– Redagowanie wcale nie różni się tak bardzo od organizacji castingu. Redaktorzy wyszukują niedoskonałości w tekście i naprawiają je, a agenci castingowi szukają idealnego aktora, który nie boi się ujawnić niedoskonałości swojego warsztatu.

Tata przysyłał mi z Nowego Jorku książki. I ręcznie pisane liściki, w kółko o tym samym: „Chłopcy nigdy nie są za duzi na to, żeby budować forty. Ja ciągle buduję forty w wyobraźni".

Opowiedziałem o swoim ojcu Herbowi, który oznajmił:

– Masz, kurwa, naprawdę zajebistego starego.

Poczułem ukłucie dumy. Opowiadałem też Herbowi o tych facetkach z naszego apartamentowca. Namówił mnie, żebym go z nimi poznał. Wpadł do nas pewnego dnia. Mama posłała mu podejrzliwe spojrzenie, ale nie odezwała się ani słowem.

Wychodziła właśnie na spotkanie z Bruce'em w Mark Taper Forum, bo pewna młoda aktorka z Nowego Jorku grała „przełomową w swojej karierze" rolę w *Pannie Julii* Augusta Strindberga. Kiedy wyszła, Parsnip zaprosiła nas obu na dół do swojego mieszkania.

Przespałem się z nią tamtej nocy. Pamiętam to dobrze, bo łóżko skrzypiało i wydawało mi się boleśnie małe, chociaż było podwójne. Może to jednak ja byłem za mały. Z początku Herb siedział przy nas. Kibicował nam. Ciągle powtarzał, że chce patrzeć. Przez jego komentarze partaczyłem robotę, więc w końcu się powstrzymałem, tak jak w dzieciństwie, kiedy starałem się nie nasikać na deskę klozetową. Herb wzbudzał we mnie jakiś pierwotny wstyd.

Ściskałem genitalia w garści i miałem ochotę powiedzieć, że wolałbym zostać sam. Nie chciałem, żeby Herb wiedział, że dopiero tego dnia przestałem być prawiczkiem.

Kiedy było po wszystkim, Parsnip, która w czasie seksu lubiła parodiować celebrytów, przeszła w ręce Herba. Potrafiła naśladować głosy wszystkich gwiazd telewizji: Betty White z *Golden Girls*, Kelseya Grammera z *Cheers* czy Markie Post z *Night Court*. Oglądała dużo telewizji, więc próba jednoczesnego wyruchania jej i właścicieli tych wszystkich przypadkowych głosów była prawdziwym wyzwaniem. Za naszym drugim razem chyba zasłoniłem jej usta ręką, bo później, kiedy Herb wyszedł, wstała z łóżka i wskazała mi łazienkę.

– Weź prysznic – powiedziała.

Położyłem się na jej kanapie w salonie i oglądałem teledyski w MTV: akurat leciał *Walking Down Your Street* zespołu The Bangles. Parsnip trzymała w salonie akwarium ze złotymi rybkami. Wszystkie były tego samego koloru i żyły w tym swoim oceanie w takiej ciasnocie, że sam poczułem przypływ klaustrofobii.

– To był twój pierwszy raz, więc muszę cię nauczyć paru rzeczy. Chłopak może mieć kłopoty przez całe życie, jeżeli w trakcie seksu będzie zatykał kobiecie usta ręką. Kapujesz, o co mi chodzi? Takie zachowanie wywołuje kłopoty. Poza tym może niektóre babki rajcują się brudnymi kutasami, ale ja osobiście nie znam ani jednej, która nie wolałaby faceta dbającego o higienę.

– Spodobało mi się, że pachnę tobą. Herbowi nie kazałaś się wykąpać.

Usiadła obok mnie.

– Herb nigdy nie będzie czysty. Nigdy, przenigdy.

OJCIEC PRZYLECIAŁ DO Los Angeles z niespodziewaną wizytą. Nie zarezerwował sobie pokoju w hotelu, więc zrobiła to za niego mama, ale tamtego wieczoru, po kolacji w Hollywood, w wegańskiej restauracji, gdzie tata ciągle przesuwał na talerzu grzyby shiitake, mama i on wrócili razem do domu i położyli się spać w jednym łóżku. Następnego dnia przyszły Parsnip, Sage i Jasmin, żeby poznać ojca. Mama przygotowała martini z dodatkiem wody z oliwek (Herba nie zaprosiłem).

– Myślisz, że nie wiem, co tu jest grane? – zapytał tata, mierzwiąc moje włosy i odciągając mnie na bok, w kąt salonu.

– Która według ciebie jest najseksowniejsza? – zapytałem z dumą. – Sage, Jasmine czy Parsnip?

– Mój pierwszy raz był na studiach – odpowiedział ojciec. – Z dziewczyną imieniem Alice. Ty rozegrałeś to zupełnie nie tak, jak trzeba, a one też powinny wiedzieć, że to nie w porządku. Formalnie rzecz biorąc, jesteś jeszcze nieletni.

– Tato, mamy lata osiemdziesiąte. A Parsnip naprawdę mi się podoba.

– Nie wiem dlaczego, ale myślałem, że ta dekada będzie jednak inna.

Kupił mi pudełko prezerwatyw i powiedział, żebym zawsze się zabezpieczał. Pokazałem mu, w którym miejscu na plaży gram na saksofonie. Przebrnąłem jakoś przez *So What*, a on nagrodził mnie brawami. Gdy pojawiła się ta stara pijaczka i zaczęła wykrzykiwać słowa *Only You*, dał jej pięćdziesiąt dolców.

– Jezu Chryste – powiedział, kiedy sobie poszła. – Życie jest strasznie okrutne.

– Mama czuje się tutaj szczęśliwa. – Nie rozmawialiśmy o niej. Byłem już teraz pewien, że leci na Bruce'a.

– A co to jest szczęście? – spytał ojciec.

CZEKAŁEM, AŻ POPROSI, żebym wrócił z nim do Nowego Jorku, ale nie zrobił tego. Następnego ranka poleciał do San Francisco, żeby spotkać się z Barbarą Camphor na jakiejś konferencji. Widywali się w pewnym sensie sezonowo. Cztery razy w roku. Ich romans był z gatunku nie do zdarcia. Jako piętnastolatek oczywiście nic o tym nie wiedziałem.

PO WIZYCIE TATY mama zaczęła chłodno traktować Parsnip. Dla Jasmine i Sage gotowała koguta w winie i wołowinę po burgundzku. Parsnip została wykluczona z matczynej kamaryli, chociaż na swój sposób była najfajniejsza z nich wszystkich, oczywiście oprócz mojej mamy. Sage okazała się pomieszaniem z poplątaniem, a Jasmine często zachowywała się tak, jak gdyby spadła z księżyca. Ciągle latała na trasie Nowy Jork – Los Angeles. Już w młodym wieku zrozumiałem, że życie stewardesy wcale nie wygląda różowo. W podróży na pokładzie samolotu zawsze jestem uprzejmy dla personelu pokładowego.

MOJE PIERWSZE ŚWIADECTWO semestralne było upstrzone trójkami.

– Miałam nadzieję, że kiedy staniesz się małą rybką w wielkim stawie, to trochę bardziej zainteresujesz się nauką.

– Jestem średniakiem, mamo.

– Nie, nie wydaje mi się. Ja w to nie uwierzę.

Znalazła w Venice Beach muzyka, który udzielał mi lekcji gry na saksofonie. I położyła kres moim występom na plaży.

– Jak poprawisz stopnie, to porozmawiamy.

Facet, który uczył mnie grać, miał dom nad kanałem. Był członkiem komitetu walczącego o czystszą Venice Beach i wracającym do zdrowia dawnym heroinistą. A także zgryźliwym czarnym, który nie miał cierpliwości do chcących grać jazz białych nastolatków.

– Nie marnuj mojego czasu, to ja nie będę marnował twojego – mawiał. – Saksofon wymaga dyscypliny.

Żeby mnie czymś zająć, mama załatwiła mi też pracę na pół etatu – zostałem jej asystentem. W niedzielne wieczory prażyła popcorn i oglądaliśmy razem stare filmy: *Wszystko o Ewie*, *Garsonierę*, *Metropolis* albo *Casablancę*. Wypłaciła mi kieszonkowe za to, że przygotowałem jej listę filmów, które nakręcono w Los Angeles albo które opowiadały o tym mieście. Czasami chodziliśmy szukać dawnych planów filmowych.

– Robiliśmy to już zaraz po przyjeździe – przypomniałem jej.

– Wtedy nie mieliśmy żadnego celu – odparła. – A teraz mamy.

– Jaki?

– Nie powiem ci nic nowego. Wszystko, co można zrobić, zostało już zrobione. Jedyne, co nam zostało, to ciągle wyobrażać sobie swoją drogę przez życie na nowo.

Wracaliśmy z moich lekcji w czwartkowe wieczory, zatrzymywaliśmy się przy naszej ulubionej jadłodajni i zamawialiśmy na spółkę porcję cudownie cienkich, ręcznie krojonych frytek. Mama cieszyła się, kiedy wspominałem na spacerach, że w czasie zdjęć do *Dotyku zła* Orson Welles wpadł do kanału i o mały włos się nie utopił, a Tomasz Mann mieszkał dwie ulice od Bruce'a w West Hollywood Hills.

– Mogę wrzucać takie szczególiki w czasie rozmów castingowych – śmiała się. – Będę sprawiać wrażenie mądrzejszej, niż jestem.

Dobrze się dogadywaliśmy z mamą. Ograniczyłem spożycie trawy, a Herb z jakimiś swoimi nowymi znajomymi przeniósł się do Oakland. Na biologię, którą zawsze mieliśmy na trzeciej lekcji, zaczęła z nami chodzić nowa dziewczyna i zastanawiałem się, czy nie zaprosić jej na randkę.

Nie miałem wtedy jeszcze żadnych przyjaciół. Obracałem się wśród surferów i luzaków z plaży, głównie znajomych Herba. Nadal sypiałem z Parsnip. Czasem wydawało mi się, że chodzi ze mną do łóżka, żeby odegrać się na mojej matce.

Jakoś w październiku mama i ja szliśmy właśnie na obiad, kiedy zatrzymał się przy nas facet w czarnym fordzie mustangu.

– Może podwieźć? – zapytał. Opuścił szybę w oknie. Miał pofałdowany podbródek, już prawie podwójny.

– Nie, dziękuję – odpowiedziała mama z tym swoim akcentem Nastassji Kinski.

– Piękny wieczór – stwierdził nieznajomy.

– I owszem. – Uśmiechnęła się. Zamilkła na chwilę, podobnie jak ford mustang.

– Co porabiacie? – spytał mężczyzna.

– Rozkoszujemy się chwilą spokoju... W samotności – odpowiedziała mama.

– Miałbym chęć na sandwicza – ciągnął niezrażony mężczyzna.

– Słuchaj, gościu – odezwałem się. – Dookoła jest pełno restauracji.

Pochylił się ku nam.

– Nie zapytaliście, o jakim sandwiczu myślę.

Nosił na palcach ogromne sygnety. Zawsze dostawałem dreszczy na widok mężczyzn, którzy nosili pierścionki.

– To dlatego że chuj nas to obchodzi – odpowiedziałem.

Mama położyła mi dłoń na ramieniu; tym, na którym niosłem saksofon w futerale.

– A o jakim sandwiczu myślałeś? – spytała.

– O takim, który daje satysfakcję.

Zbluzgała go po francusku, a po angielsku powiedziała:

– Nie znasz tej piosenki Stonesów? Nie ma niczego takiego jak satysfakcja.

Gdy dzisiaj to wszystko wspominam, wydaje mi się, że facet musiał być pijany albo na prochach. Wysunął głowę przez okno od strony pasażera i zwrócił się do matki:

– A może jednak wsiądziesz z tyłu i pozwolisz, że ja i ten młody człowiek zrobimy z ciebie sandwicza?

Może zachowałem się tak, jak się zachowałem, dlatego, że Herb i ja zrobiliśmy sandwicza z Parsnip i mogłem sobie dobrze wyobrazić, o co chodzi temu facetowi. Może zachowałem się tak, jak się zachowałem, dlatego, że jego słowa rozebrały moją matkę tak szybko, że nie zdążyłem ubrać jej z powrotem. A może zachowałem się tak, jak się zachowałem, dlatego, że mama zrobiła się czerwona na twarzy i ja też się cały zaczerwieniłem. Dosłownie czułem, jak mi czacha dymi, jak gdyby przez uszy wylatywała mi gorąca para.

„Co my tu w ogóle robimy, mamo?" Chciałem jej zadać to pytanie, odkąd tylko przyjechaliśmy do LA, chociaż właściwie chodziło mi o to, co ja tam robiłem. Bo mama czuła się świetnie. Uwielbiała to miasto. Powiedziałem o tym ojcu, ale teraz wszystkie kości w moim ciele zagrzechotały w zderzeniu z tutejszą rzeczywistością. Zsunąłem z ramienia futerał z saksofonem i wyrżnąłem nim tego faceta o podwójnym podbródku w twarz. Z jego nosa i ust trysnęła krew. Mama zaczęła przeraźliwie krzyczeć. Krzyczała, a ja chwyciłem ją za ramię.

– Po prostu idź przed siebie – powiedziałem. Zmusiłem się, żeby iść. Szliśmy szybko.

– Mogłeś go zabić, Rufusie.

– Zboczeniec.

– Powinniśmy wrócić.

Zarzuciłem sobie saksofon z powrotem na ramię.

– Nie.

– Dałabym sobie z nim radę.

– Tak jak dałaś sobie radę w małżeństwie?

– W ten sposób po prostu się nie postępuje. Nie w takim miejscu, nie w takich okolicznościach. Nie można bić ludzi tylko dlatego, że mówią coś, co ci się nie podoba.

– Nie chodziło mi o to, co on powiedział. Chodziło o jego zamiary.

– Kiedy tak mówisz, przypominasz mi...

– No powiedz!

– Jamesa Samuela Vincenta.

Są takie chwile, kiedy człowiek patrzy na swoich rodziców i nie wie, co o nich myśleć. Odkąd trafiła mnie wiadomość o rozwodzie, doświadczyłem wielu podobnych chwil, ale mój kaszel i chrząkanie ustały. Na półkach i biurkach w całym Los Angeles było pełno taśmy klejącej, nie wyczuwałem jej już jednak w gardle. W LA nie kaszlałem. Zdarzało mi się kichnąć, ale co to jest kichnięcie? Wystarczy wytrzeć nos. Mama przymusiła mnie do dokonania wyboru. Ona albo tata. Problem polegał na tym, że kochałem ich oboje.

PO POWROCIE DO DOMU wszedłem pod prysznic i wykąpałem się. Twarz tego faceta była zalana krwią, ale na moim ubraniu i futerale znalazłem tylko pojedyncze rozbryzgi. Po kąpieli wycofałem się do swojego pokoju i powyjmowałem wszystkie książki od taty, których dotąd nie rozpakowałem, takie jak *Ostatni Mohikanin*, *Moby Dick*, *Zew krwi*. Zbudowałem z nich niewielki fort i wcisnąłem się do środka. Udawałem, że śpię, ale sen śmiał się ze mnie. Potem przez długie miesiące nie grałem na saksofonie.

Mama włączyła wieczorne wiadomości, spodziewając się, że powiedzą coś o zboczeńcu z Venice Beach, na ten temat nic jednak nie podano. Wracam pamięcią do tamtego dnia i myślę, że w dzisiejszych czasach – kamer wideo i telefonów komórkowych – w żadnym razie nie udałoby się nam tak łatwo oddalić z miejsca zdarzenia. Na pewno nie mnie. Ktoś na pewno by sfilmował, jak uderzam tego gościa, a pięć minut później byłbym już na YouTubie.

ZADZWONIŁEM DO TATY, który początkowo nie przyjął całej tej historii zbyt dobrze, ale kiedy zatelefonowała do niego mama, znalazł się w Los Angeles zaledwie dwadzieścia cztery godziny później. Opowiedziała Jamesowi Samuelowi Vincentowi wszystko. Nie zareagował ani słowem. Najpierw spakowaliśmy książki, które mi przysłał. Poukładaliśmy je alfabetycznie, żebym mógł je łatwiej posegregować po powrocie do Nowego Jorku, zanieśliśmy na pocztę i nadaliśmy jako paczkę. Potrzebowałem czegoś do czytania w samolocie i tata wyciągnął *Portret artysty w wieku młodzieńczym* Joyce'a.

– Czytałeś to? – spytałem.

– Joyce – odpowiedział – nie jest dla każdego.

„Zupełnie jak Kalifornia", pomyślałem. Nigdy więcej nie rozmawialiśmy o tamtym zdarzeniu w Venice Beach. Nie mówiłem o tym ja, nie mówił tata, nie mówiła mama. Nie wiem, czy to jest tajemnica, skoro nie gadamy na ten temat, ale może nie poruszamy go dlatego, że wiąże się z nim sporo innych nieprzyjemnych spraw. Chcę przez to powiedzieć, że nigdy wcześniej ani potem złość nie poniosła mnie aż tak daleko. W dniu, kiedy pani Christie rzuciła się na mnie z tym żelazkiem, przypomniałem sobie, co to znaczy czuć się zagrożonym albo działać pod wpływem gwałtownego impulsu, by zrobić komuś krzywdę – i bronić tych, których się kocha. Wydzielała więcej gorącej pary wodnej niż żelazko, którym mi groziła. Wiem już dziś, jak to jest. Ludzie są nosicielami emocji gorących niczym para.

DALEKO CI DO LEE KRASNER

1950 **1960 1970 1980 1990**

TRUDNO WYOBRAZIĆ SOBIE COŚ GORSZEGO, NIŻ BYĆ BRZYDKĄ córką pięknej matki. Adele Pransky stała przy ladzie z napojami, nalewając sobie sodówkę o smaku wiśniowym do szklanego kubka, kiedy do Dean's Beachside Bar & Grill ramię w ramię z Sethem wszedł Yan Sokolov, jego nowy kumpel od kart. Adele miała wspominać po latach, jak morski wiatr zlizywał pot z ich białych koszul, gdy zeszli z plaży na Coney Island i wstąpili do gwarnego baru niczym najlepsi kamraci, chociaż wtedy właściwie byli jeszcze sobie obcy i dopiero co po prostu się spiknęli po kilku szklaneczkach kwaśnej whisky, paru cygarach i partyjkach pokera rozegranych przy kulawym stoliku w jakimś burdelu w Hell's Kitchen.

MATKA ADELE, Rachel Pransky, tolerowała miłość Setha do kart, jeśli nie przegrywał za dużo pieniędzy. Jej pieniędzy. Tamtego pachnącego balsamicznym powietrzem wieczoru obsługiwała kasę. Seth pocałował Rachel i dał Yanowi znak ręką, by usiadł wygodnie przy barze.

– Adele – wykrzyknął, machając, by do nich podeszła. – Podaj mojemu koledze dorsza z frytkami.

Adele spełniła jego polecenie.

– Skąd wiesz, że lubi dorsza? – zapytała.

Yan skinął głową.

– Owszem, dorsza zjem, ale wasze skorupiaki: fuj!

Przyjrzała się facetowi, który przedstawił się jako Yan Sokolov. Był ubrany bardziej odjazdowo niż inni mężczyźni przy barze – chodzący popis szarego jedwabiu i gabardyny. Adele podobało się, że zdjął blezer i podwinął rękawy białej koszuli, aby nie odróżniać się od tłumu robotników. Pomyślała, że znajomy Setha wygląda niezwyczajnie w jakiś ekspresjonistyczny, obłąkany sposób. Mógł mieć równie dobrze trzydzieści, jak i pięćdziesiąt lat, bo jego twarz pokrywało mnóstwo zmarszczek i jakby szczelin skalnych.

– Kto to jest? – spytała Rachel.

– Znajomy.

I Seth opowiedział Rachel, jak już tego wieczoru Yan odciągnął go od stolika, nim przegrał całą pensję.

– Po co się tak spieszyć do ubóstwa, przyjacielu – powiedział Yan. – Zwolnij tempo. Do przytułku możesz pójść każdego dnia, kiedy chcesz.

Seth wrzucił dwie monety do szafy grającej.

– Zacząłem mu mówić, żeby pilnował swojego nosa, kurde. Ale potem przypomniałem sobie ciebie, Rachel, i że mam jeszcze kilka groszy w portfelu. No i oczywiście pomyślałem o Adele.

Otoczył biodra Rachel ramionami i odciągnął ją od kasy na kilka tanecznych ruchów na parkiecie. Spod ich nóg wzbijały się trociny, a Sinatra śpiewał *I've Got You Under My Skin*. Rachel Setha – tak mówili bywalcy Dean's Beachside Bar & Grill. Seth oświadczał się jej wiele razy, ale Rachel nie chciała za niego wyjść, dopóki jej córka nie znajdzie sobie męża. Długo na to czekali. Poza tym barem Rachel nie miała właściwie nic, co można by uznać za spadek czy dziedzictwo Adele. Zresztą było to ich jedyne źródło utrzymania.

Rachel i Seth zerkali w tańcu na Adele i Yana. Adele zdjęła fartuch. Normalnie nigdy nie pokazywała się bez niego w barze. Cokolwiek mówił jej Yan, starała się nie uronić ani słowa. Pochylali się naprzód, ich łokcie stykały się na blacie. Przypominali fale na plaży, kiedy Adele mówiła coś do Yana, a Yan do Adele.

– Miałam szczęście – powtarzała często Sethowi Rachel. – Zaaranżowane małżeństwo z mężczyzną, którego umiałam pokochać. Nie chcę wydać Adele ot tak, za byle kogo. Chcę, żeby była szczęśliwa.

Seth nigdy tego Rachel nie powiedział, ale Adele nie miała twarzy kobiety, która najpierw wychodzi szczęśliwie za mąż, a potem żyje długo w szczęśliwym małżeństwie. Kasztanowe włosy dziewczyny były kręcone mocno, a ciemne, swobodnie zwisające loki jej matki lekko. Adele miała piegi, a skóra Rachel była alabastrowo biała.

Na szczęście Adele odziedziczyła po matce gorejące zielone oczy i charakterystyczny nos, który może nie byłby ozdobą innej twarzy, ale w przypadku Rachel symbolizował zimną jak kamień urodę, a w przypadku Adele coś, co można było nazwać wdziękiem. To zazwyczaj po kłótni i szalonym seksie, którego nie należy mylić z kochaniem się, Seth i Rachel zgodnie nie zgadzali się na to, by Adele stała w miejscu, jeżeli chodzi o ślub. I dopiero potem mogli się kochać.

NADALI MU PRZEZWISKO Yan Natręt. Przychodził do baru każdego wieczoru, punkt siódma. Przynosił róże, a jako ich przybranie gałązki łyszczca, zwanego „tchnieniem dziecka", pozbawione jednak białych pączków.

– Jak „tchnienie dziecka" może konkurować z wiatrem od morza? – pytał.

Dawał kwiaty Adele, która się rumieniła.

– Może nie zawinąłeś ich dość ciasno. – I pokazywała mu, jak trzeba pakować róże, zaginała rogi i odpowiednio rolowała papier.

– Lepiej mu powiedz, że nie jesteś dziewicą – zaproponowała Rachel, widząc ten zuchwały pokaz córki.

– Ale jestem. – Adele zatrzepotała powiekami.

– Szkoda, nie powinnaś już nią być – odparła Rachel, porzucając bar i wchodząc do kuchni, gdzie przez sekundę czy dwie myślała, że padnie z niedowierzania.

Mąż Rachel, Dean, został pewnego ranka rażony piorunem na plaży w odległości zaledwie kilku stóp od baru. „Ach, trzeba było widzieć tę błyskawicę", opowiadali straganiarze Rachel. Tylko dlaczego, dlaczego miałaby chcieć ją zobaczyć? Wszyscy myśleli, że wyjdzie ponownie za mąż i przekaże komuś bar. Kiedy uśmiechała się do klientów, łatwiej jej było zapomnieć, że bardzo kochała Deana, że ogarnęło ją wtedy przerażenie i nie wiedziała, co robi ani jak będzie teraz mogła żyć. Powtarzała sobie w duchu, że nie jest jedyną kobietą na świecie, która codziennie rano otwiera bar, trzymając niemowlę przy piersi, i co jakiś czas wychodzi na zaplecze, żeby je nakarmić. Minęło wiele lat i to dziecko stało się kobietą. Jak to możliwe, że nadal jest dziewicą, skoro od tak dawna pracuje w barze?

Adele miała dwadzieścia dziewięć lat i była z natury trochę roztrzepana. Nie licząc hojnie nalewanych drinków z najniższej półki, stanowiła największą atrakcję w Dean's Beachside Bar & Grill. Rachel raczyła klientów sarkazmem i szczerością – jej córka obiecywała im słońce żeglujące ponad horyzontem, czasami na skrzydłach burzy. Była dobrą nowiną, którą doceniał robotnik pod koniec ośmiogodzinnego dnia pracy. Poza tym Dean's Beachside Bar & Grill miał dodatkową zaletę, trochę przypominał bowiem daltonistę – wszystkie kolory skóry były w nim mile widziane.

– Uwielbiam malować – powiedziała Adele. – Jeżdżę na zajęcia plastyczne do miasta w każdy czwartek.

– Ach, kobieta, która poślubiła swoją sztukę – powiedział z uśmiechem Yan. – Muszę zobaczyć... Czy mogę zobaczyć twoje arcydzieła? – Mrugnął do Rachel. – Na pewno jesteś bardzo dobrą matką, bo wychowałaś dziewczynę, która to co najlepsze zostawiła dla siebie.

Adele oprowadziła Yana po barze i zwróciła jego uwagę na biegnący przez całą ścianę mural. Przedstawiał syreny o lokach przetykanych złocistym rubinem oraz potężnych mężczyzn o takich barach, na których mógłby zrobić salto nawet Atlas. Były tam też karły, ubrane niczym Maria Antonina, i klauni na szczudłach, rozrabiający nad diabelskim młynem. Były rozgwiazdy w obręczach hula-hoopu i akrobaci, którzy chodzili na rękach po linach, żonglując egzotycznymi owocami, takimi jak mango, papaje i opuncje. Były też otyłe, chociaż pełne animuszu kobiety.

YAN ZACHWYCIŁ SIĘ tym dziełem Adele. Poprosił o drabinę i wspiął się na nią, żeby zmierzyć syreny.

– Precyzyjna jesteś. – Kiwnął głową z aprobatą.

– Yan nie marnuje czasu – zauważyła Rachel.

– Jest właścicielem kilku nieruchomości na Manhattanie – powiedział Seth, wyczuwając na horyzoncie odrobinę słońca także dla siebie.

– Kilku? – zapytała Rachel. – No to wspaniale. Ale czy jest dobrym człowiekiem, Seth? Przyzwoitym?

LATO ZACZĘŁO JUŻ ŁASKOTAĆ JESIEŃ. Yan poprosił Rachel o rękę Adele po rosyjsku, a że Rachel odpowiedziała mu w jidysz, poprosił ją raz jeszcze w tym języku. Wtedy Rachel odpowiedziała po rosyjsku, do porozumienia doszli jednak po angielsku. Po śmierci Deana Rachel przestała wierzyć w Boga, lecz na cześć ojca Adele Yan wziął z nią ślub w synagodze. Po ceremonii urządzili wielkie przyjęcie w barze, które trwało całą noc, a nawet jeszcze rano.

Yan ze zdziwieniem oglądał dziewiczą krew na ślubnej pościeli. Nalał ciepłej wody do blaszanego wiadra i kazał Adele wymoczyć nogi w roztworze gorzkiej soli z dodatkiem wody różanej i lawendy.

– Odciski od stania za barem – stwierdził. – Powiedz matce, że od dzisiaj nie będziesz już barmanką.

Zaczął dawać żonie kieszonkowe i kazał jej inwestować w najlepsze dostępne na rynku artykuły dla plastyków.

– Ale jak mama da sobie radę beze mnie? – spytała Adele.

– Ktoś może cię zastąpić – odrzekł Yan. – To praca posługaczki. Chcesz być artystką czy kelnerką w knajpie o podejrzanej reputacji? – I uszczypnął ją w policzek.

Adele lubiła klientów z Dean's Beachside Bar & Grill. Była jedynaczką, a oni stanowili jakby jej rodzinę. Wychowała się wśród nich. Przychodzili tam z osiedli na Coney Island albo z tego wąskiego odprysku włoskich dzielnic Nowego Jorku, wciśniętego za Neptune Avenue, by topić smutki w butelkach budweisera. Ciągle gadali o tym, co im się śniło ostatniej nocy, albo o liczbach, na które jakiś zmarły krewny kazał im zza grobu postawić na loterii. Przyjeżdżali z Brighton Beach na hot dogi, jedyną koszerną potrawę w menu Rachel. I nie zwracali uwagi na to, że dwie ulice dalej mieściła się hotdogowa sieciówka Nathan's ani że bułki w Dean's Beachside Bar & Grill lądowały na talerzu nieświeże i wilgotne. Nie było też lepszego miejsca na świecie, jeśli chodzi o gorącą herbatę po kąpieli w lodowatym Oceanie Atlantyckim. Adele wzbogacała ten napój kieliszkiem bourbona, by podnieść temperaturę krwi odważnych klientów, którzy woleli zachowywać się jak niedźwiedzie polarne, a nie ludzie. Kiedyś bywalcy mówili o niej po prostu „dziewczyna", chociaż Adele przed spotkaniem Yana miała świadomość, że niewiele jej brakuje, by została starą panną. Powiedzieć matce, że już nie stanie za barem, postanowiła trochę później, dopiero po podróży poślubnej – bo Rachel pracowała, żeby żyć, i żyła, żeby pracować.

Na miesiąc miodowy pojechali do San Francisco, gdzie Yan miał dwa budynki na wynajem i prowadził interesy w pobliżu Mission District. Jeździli Pacific Coast Highway wzdłuż wybrzeża do Big Sur, a wczesnym rankiem oraz późnym popołudniem wędrowali po krętych szlakach turystycznych w lesie. Stała tam tablica z napisem, który oczarował Adele: „Uwaga. Małe dzieci budzą ciekawość pum".

Gdy wrócili do Nowego Jorku, Yan zajął się pracą, a Adele malarstwem. Wprowadzili się do zbudowanego po drugiej wojnie światowej mieszkania o trzech sypialniach na dwunastym piętrze budynku na rogu 85 Ulicy i West End Avenue. Spółdzielczy apartamentowiec miał wewnętrzny dziedziniec, na którym rosły lipy i trawa. Pod drzewami wylegiwały się chyba wszystkie koty z całego bloku, a Adele natrafiała czasem na szczątki wiewiórki lub ptaka, któremu nie udało się odfrunąć na czas, aby uniknąć uścisku ostrych pazurów. W piątki odwiedzała matkę. Szła pieszo Piątą Aleją do 42 Ulicy i wsiadała w pociąg linii Q, przejeżdżający przez Manhattan Bridge. Zawsze lubiła metro, ostatnio jednak przebywanie pod ziemią wzbudzało w niej złe przeczucia, dlatego teraz wolała wyglądać przez okno pociągu na ciemną East River i ogromne wieżowce Nowego Jorku. Za każdym razem, kiedy już myślała, że zna całe miasto, pojawiał się w nim jakiś nowy budynek z chromu i ze stali.

BYŁA JUŻ MĘŻATKĄ. Rachel przyjęła do wiadomości, co córka miała jej do powiedzenia. Adele sama podjęła decyzję o odejściu z pracy, lecz matka nie mogła się oprzeć, żeby jej nie wbić szpilki.

– Dziewczyna, zwłaszcza zamężna, zawsze powinna mieć trochę własnych pieniędzy.

– Ale ja mam pieniądze.

– Adele – powiedziała Rachel. – Chodzi mi o pieniądze, które kobieta sama zarabia.

– Moje malarstwo to też jest przecież praca.

Na to Rachel nie znalazła odpowiedzi. Brakowało jej artystycznego temperamentu. Była, krótko mówiąc, kobietą interesu. Rozejrzała się po barze, który w oczach chyba każdego gościa stanowił klasyczny przykład bylejakości, miał wypaczoną, wysypaną trocinami podłogę, obracające się pod sufitem wentylatory i niskie stoły. Jednemu brakowało nawet nogi, podtrzymywała go więc laska, którą zostawił tu kiedyś jakiś pijak i nigdy po nią nie wrócił. W roku 1969 Coney Island najlepsze lata miała już za sobą, Rachel wiedziała jednak, gdzie można tanio zrobić zakupy nawet w takim brudnym, bezbarwnym miasteczku. Kilkakrotnie jeździła z Adele do muzeów w Nowym Jorku, choć zawsze miała świadomość, jak wyglądają jej włosy, sukienka i buty, i że mówi z akcentem z Sheepshead Bay. Już po kilku muzealnych minutach miała ochotę wracać do baru i na plażę.

– Tak, córeczko – wyszeptała. – Chyba tak.

ZDECYDOWANA POWAŻNIE TRAKTOWAĆ malarstwo, Adele zapisała się na zajęcia z interpretacji wizualnej dla zawodowych artystów. W pierwszym tygodniu instruktor wziął na warsztat jej akwarelę morską.

– Co istotnego dostrzeżemy w tym obrazie morza?

Popatrzyła na swoją akwarelę. Wyglądała na niewiele więcej niż coś w rodzaju niewyraźnego kolażu Coney Island w pastelowych kolorach. Właściwie mógł to być każdy nadmorski pejzaż. W drugim tygodniu zajęć przemalowała go na spieniony ocean, nad którym unosiły się błyskawica i jakiś cień.

– Obiecujące – stwierdził instruktor, którego brzuszysko stanowiło najcięższy element potężnego ciała. Widziała jego dzieła w galerii w centrum miasta, którą odwiedziła z Yanem, i wydały się jej okropne, lecz nie dysponowała jeszcze odpowiednim słownictwem, by krytykować malarstwo, szczególnie własne. Niewykluczone, rozumowała, że dzieła instruktora są liche, ale ten człowiek może ją uczyć albo motywować, żeby się sama uczyła. Yan zapłacił duże pieniądze za to, by jego żona mogła chodzić na zajęcia grubasa, artysty cieszącego się powszechnym szacunkiem. I jeśli to oznaczało, że będzie musiała co tydzień przemalowywać morze, to niech tak będzie.

– „Obiecujące" stanowi uprzejmy odpowiednik „amatorszczyzny" – stwierdził Yan.

Adele przeszła od pejzaży morskich do abstrakcyjnych rysunków kotów z dziedzińca ich domu, co należało do ćwiczeń obejmujących rysowanie zwierząt w środowisku naturalnym.

Nakapała farby do terpentyny. Lubiła malować w salonie przy szeroko otwartych oknach.

– Co o tym myślisz?

Yan wstał znad gazety, bo miał w zwyczaju czytać prasę rankiem i pod koniec dnia. Przyjrzał się kocurowi syjamskiemu, którego Adele narysowała wyprężonego, gotowego do skoku na gołębia na dziedzińcu.

– Dlaczego nie rysujesz psów? – zapytał.

– Bo lubię koty.

– Z kotami nigdy nic nie wiadomo.

Po ślubie zapuścił brodę. Adele uważała, że jego twarz ma teraz mniej wyraziste rysy i stała się dosyć surowa.

– To zależy od kota.

– Polują na wszystko, co tylko im się nawinie. Znaczy koty. – Yan skrzyżował ręce na piersiach.

– Psy żebrzą o resztki ze stołu.

– Koty miauczą.

– No ale my nie mamy ani psa, ani kota – odpowiedziała, zauważywszy rozdrażnienie w jego głosie. – Więc właściwie o co się sprzeczamy?

– Jeżeli chcesz znać prawdę, uważam, że te rysunki są poniżej twojej godności. Nie można ich traktować poważnie. Wyglądają na dzieło prowincjonalnej artystki.

– Może porozmawiałbyś o tym z moim instruktorem? Bo chyba znasz się na malarstwie lepiej od niego.

– Może i tak.

– Mam prawo do swojej opinii. I sądzę, że nie masz racji.

– Ja płacę za twoje lekcje.

Adele przypomniała sobie słowa Rachel.

– Znajdę pracę jako kelnerka. Wiem, co się robi w barze.

Zacisnął dłonie w pięści, które przypominały piękne kamienie. Nie miała nawet czasu, żeby odłożyć pędzel, bo te kamienie zderzyły się z jej twarzą i złamały jej nos. Usłyszała trzask kości. Zawsze lubiła swój nos, nos Barbry Streisand. W szafie grającej w Dean's Beachside Bar & Grill mieli sześć jej piosenek i Adele znała je wszystkie. Nie mogła się powstrzymać, by nie powtarzać w myślach ich tytułów, gdy krew spływała jej po twarzy na dekolt.

Wieczorem zadzwoniła do Rachel i powiedziała, że w ten piątek nie wpadnie. Nie pracowała już w Dean's, ale jeździła do matki raz w tygodniu i siadała przy barze jak normalna klientka, chociaż czasami nie mogła się powstrzymać, żeby nie przetrzeć blatu sfatygowaną trójkolorową ściereczką.

Yan zawiózł ją do lekarza. Był milutki, przepraszał, próbował zatamować upływ krwi chusteczką. Skomlił, jak gdyby to on miał złamany nos.

– Musimy uważać, żeby nie wpadać na ściany – powiedział.
– Straszna ze mnie gapa! – powiedziała Adele lekarzowi. – Wpadłam na ścianę.
– To więcej się nie powtórzy – powiedział Yan. – Nie ma prawa.

KUPIŁA KILKA PŁYT BARBRY STREISAND w sklepie Colony Records i puszczała je na cały regulator na starym gramofonie Yana, adapter okazał się jednak słabym zamiennikiem szafy grającej.

Tydzień później pokazała się w barze i Rachel zapytała:
– Co ci się stało w nos?

Adele machnęła bagatelizująco ręką, by uniknąć dalszych pytań.

– Teraz przynajmniej mogę go zoperować!

Rachel zawołała Setha, który przed tygodniem wsunął jej na palec pierścionek zaręczynowy. Nie ustalili jeszcze daty ślubu, ale przyrzekli sobie, że się pobiorą. Seth pracował w firmie, która dostarczała alkohol do baru. Wyszedł z kuchni i odstawił trzymane w dłoniach pudło. Właśnie uzupełniali zaopatrzenie na piątkowy wieczór, bo zawsze mieli wtedy hałaśliwy tłum gości.

Przyjrzał się Adele.

– Co to ma znaczyć? – Seth szczycił się tym, że w czasie wojny służył w wojsku i walczył z nazistami. Znalazł się w oddziale, który wyzwolił jego rodaków z Dachau. W wieku chłopięcym wielbił mistrza bokserskiego wagi ciężkiej, Maksa Baera, a potem został zawodowym pięściarzem wagi półśredniej; jego karierę na ringu zakończyła kontuzja. Był świetnym bokserem, zwinnym i eleganckim, nawet gdy zbliżał się już do starości. – Nie pozwolę, żeby Yan traktował cię jak worek treningowy.

– Bóg mi świadkiem, Seth – powiedziała Adele – że to był wypadek.

Seth poczuł odpływ wojowniczych sił. Do sali wkroczył Pan Bóg, a kiedy On wkraczał do sali, wszyscy znajdowali się pod Jego opieką.

NIE ZOPEROWAŁA NOSA. Poczekała, aż rana się zagoi, i całym sercem wróciła do malowania. Malowała koty w różnych kompromitujących pozycjach i rozstawiała obrazy po całym mieszkaniu. Malowała koty z przetrąconymi nosami i złamanymi łapami. Malowała koty po sekcji zwłok i koty o zajęczych uszach. Jej instruktor był zaintrygowany tą tematyką, pozwalał jednak Adele na elastyczność, malowała więc też koty elastyczne, porozciągane na parapetach jej mieszkania, a w końcu namalowała stworzenie będące pół kotem, pół kobietą.

– Ach, jaki cudowny sfinks – stwierdził instruktor. Jego przypominające spodek brzuszysko zatrzęsło się od szczerej wesołości i podziwu dla nowej pewności siebie oraz stylu Adele.

– Adele... – Yan pokręcił głową. – Musisz z tym skończyć. – Nie cierpiał jej obrazów. Wypalały mu oczy. Był człowiekiem hołdującym zdecydowanym opiniom, a te kocury traktował jako afront.

Siedząca na kanapie Adele odpowiedziała:

– Jeżeli wypalają ci oczy, to przecież nic nie widzisz, a skoro nic nie widzisz, to w czym problem?

Usłyszała stukot twardych podeszew Yana i wstała szybko, porzucając kanapową wygodę na rzecz bezpieczeństwa drzwi wejściowych. Złapała pociąg linii Q i pojechała do matki. Musiała trochę uspokoić nerwy przed pokazaniem się tłumowi klientów w barze.

Tym razem nie próbowała okłamywać matki. Kiedy Rachel i Seth wrócili do domu, zastali Adele czekającą na nich w ciemnej kuchni. Usiedli wokół niej przy stole i słuchali.

– A to skurwysyn! – zawołała Rachel.

– Ten facet jest jak dziecko – odezwał się Seth. – A takie dzieci można potraktować tylko w jeden sposób.

Adele wyciągnęła rękę, żeby powstrzymać Setha, który już narzucił na siebie palto.

– Aresztują cię, jeżeli zrobisz mu krzywdę.

Cieszyła się szczęściem matki. Był to dobry znak, zwiastujący szczęście, ponieważ wierzyła, że nadal pozostaje ono w jej zasięgu.

Natomiast Rachel śniły się ryby. Przez pięć dni z rzędu; skakały nad księżycem i pozostawiały za sobą olśniewająco jasne ławice innych ryb. Najpierw pożerały nocne niebo, a potem przeistaczały się w nocne gwiazdy. Rachel zaczekała, aż Adele pójdzie do swojej dawnej sypialni, by wślizgnąć się tam za nią i zapytać:

– No i jak, jesteś w ciąży?

– A ty? – spytała bojaźliwie Adele.

– Złośliwości zostaw dla złych ludzi. – Rachel wzruszyła ramionami. – Ja jestem już na to za stara.

Adele, Rachel i Seth położyli się spać. O drugiej w nocy zadzwonił telefon.

– Wracaj do domu – powiedział Yan.

– Nie – odparła Adele. – Odchodzę od ciebie.

– Odchodzisz?

Rachel weszła do pokoju i odsunęła słuchawkę od ucha córki. Usłyszała, jak Yan powtarza raz za razem „odchodzisz ode mnie".

– Tak. Odchodzę.

Adele odebrała matce telefon. W słuchawce zapadło milczenie. Yan tylko ciężko oddychał.

– Żyły należy przeciąć głęboko – odezwał się w końcu.

ZNALEŹLI GO W COLUMBIA PRESBYTERIAN; półleżał wsparty na pagórku z poduszek i właśnie pracowicie wyrażał pogardę dla worka po kartoflach, który pielęgniarki śmiały nazywać jego koszulą nocną. Prawy nadgarstek miał zabandażowany.

– Następnym razem skończę ze sobą. Przysięgam na Boga, skończę.

– Wyślijcie go do jakiegoś sanatorium. – Rachel tupnęła.

– Zabije się? Zabije? – pienił się Seth. – A tylu ludzi na świecie pragnie żyć! Niech umiera, jeżeli ma ochotę!

– Nie chcę się czuć winna z powodu jego śmierci – powiedziała Adele. Mogła dodać, że go kocha, chociaż w tym względzie targały nią sprzeczne uczucia. Nie było jednak żadnych wątpliwości co do snu jej matki o tych rybach. Opuściła szpital w towarzystwie męża.

Sześć miesięcy później urodziła syna, Maximiliana. Rok później na świat przyszła córka, Freya. Do sypialni Yana i Adele ponownie zawitało pożądanie. Byli dumnymi rodzicami i podobnie jak wszyscy świeżo upieczeni rodzice, czuli się zmęczeni, ale szczęśliwi.

ADELE WCIĄŻ MALOWAŁA. Porzuciła jednak kotki i poszła na intensywny kurs analiz anatomicznych prowadzonych przy użyciu farb akrylowych i olejnych. Na te warsztaty chodziła niewielka grupka wybranych uczniów. Zdumiała się, kiedy przyznano jej niewielkie stypendium. Malowała akty kobiece i linoskoczków na tle nieba rozpalonego jak piec.

– Nasze dzieci będą miały koszmary po tych twoich obrazach – powiedział Yan. – Wyrosną na osoby porąbane i tępe.

Przyjrzała się płótnu. Widziała na nim ludzi, którzy przeczyli prawu grawitacji.

– A może będą miały silną wolę i ciekawość świata?

Czy tylko jej się wydawało, czy Yan zacisnął pięści? Umilkła i w ciszy zauważyła wreszcie cały korowód wynajętych służących i sprzątaczek, które przychodziły do nich i szybko odchodziły bez uprzedzenia. Yan nie musiał mówić ani słowa, by uwijały się szybciej albo całe się spinały w jego obecności. Szanował ich prywatną przestrzeń i dawał im dobre wskazówki, kiedy znajdował się razem z nimi w pokoju, ale Adele chciała je zapytać – chociaż może jednak sprawa dotyczyła wyłącznie jej samej? – dlaczego w obecności Yana świat zdawał się zmieniać.

Namalowała apartamentowiec, do którego wdzierały się olbrzymie poranione dłonie.

– Wspaniałe – ocenił instruktor.

– Chcesz pozabijać nasze dzieci, Adele? – zapytał Yan.

Przestała w ogóle malować.

KIEDY MAX SKOŃCZYŁ TRZY LATKA, a Freya dwa, Rachel wyszła za Setha. Wesele było cudowne. Państwo młodzi poprosili Adele, by w czasie ich podróży poślubnej prowadziła bar i zaopiekowała się domem. Na miejscu znalazła prezenty od nich za tę przysługę: pędzle, sztalugi oraz zestaw farb i płócien. Nie były najwyższej jakości, lecz wystarczyły, by znów zaczęła malować.

Rankiem zabierała Maksa i Freyę na plażę, gdzie pozwalała im robić babki z piasku przy użyciu plastikowych wiaderek. Gdy dzieci zasypiały, zaczynała rysować. Rozkoszowała się fakturą zwyczajnych ołówków i pędzli.

Przez kilka lat dzieci coś tłumiły w Yanie. Poświęcał coraz mniej czasu swoim ciemnym interesom i nadstawiał uszu, słysząc tupot małych nóżek na klepkach parkietu. Śmiech Maksa i Frei napełniał go czarującą nieśmiałością. Dzieci przetrzymywały jego wybuchy dzięki zabawie i przebierały się za czarodziejów. Yan biegał tam i z powrotem po peronie przy 86 Ulicy z Maksem i Freyą w podwójnym wózku spacerowym, czasami hamując tuż przed żółtą linią i białym światłem nadjeżdżającego pociągu metra. Dobry czas, to był dobry czas – aż przyszły czarne nastroje. A kiedy powróciły, Adele, Max i Freya spędzali dnie, wieczory i długie weekendy w domu „baby" i „dziadzia" na Coney Island.

– Czego chcą dzieci? – Yan często pytał o to Adele.

Czy to było podchwytliwe pytanie? Bomba z opóźnionym zapłonem, która miała jej poranić twarz? Adele starannie dobierała słowa.

– Rodziców.

Wzruszał ramionami.

– Wiesz, że nie możemy ich uratować.

– Mieszkamy w Ameryce. Nasze dzieci są najbezpieczniejsze na świecie. Bardzo bezpieczne.

Uważała, że bezwzględnie powinna to powiedzieć, a Yan bezwzględnie powinien ją usłyszeć.

PIĘĆ LAT PRZESZŁO W SIEDEM. Siedem w dziewięć. Dzieci Adele i Yana robiły się coraz starsze. Maximilian i Freya mieli silną wolę i ciekawość świata. Zauważyli, że Yan nigdy nie wspomina o swojej matce, rodzinie ani dzieciństwie. I najeża się, gdy one lub Adele poruszają ten temat albo pytają go o te sprawy. Nie wiedzieli, co było bardziej irytujące: że muszą mieszkać z Yanem czy że Yan nie ma przeszłości.

Maximilian skończył osiemnaście, a Freya siedemnaście lat. Oboje zdali maturę i przenieśli się do San Francisco, na studia do Berkeley. Freya przeskoczyła jedną klasę w liceum i z przyjemnością uciekła na uniwersytet razem z bratem. Adele i Yan zaproponowali, że zawiozą dzieci samochodem na drugi koniec kraju, ale Max i Freya się nie zgodzili.

– Przyjedźcie nas odwiedzić – powiedziała Freya matce.

– Chcemy żyć po swojemu – oznajmił Maximilian Yanowi.

Adele nie pozwoliła im oglądać swoich łez, ale gdy wyjechali, zaczęła lamentować. Yan położył jej rękę na lewym ramieniu.

– Widzisz, co narobiłaś? Przez ciebie nasze dzieci od nas uciekły.

– Przeze mnie? Przeze mnie?

Uderzyła Yana otwartą dłonią w twarz tak mocno, że żyrandole spojrzały w dół i zadrżały.

WIDOK ADELE O KULACH przelał czarę goryczy.

– Wykończ go – Rachel zwróciła się do Setha.

Seth zaczął żałować dnia, w którym poznał Adele z jej przyszłym mężem. Czekał na Yana, aż pojawi się przed swoim apartamentowcem, i dopadł go, zanim ten skręcił za róg 85 Ulicy i West End Avenue. Yan spodziewał się tych odwiedzin i pogroził dawnemu przyjacielowi palcem.

– Jeżeli mnie uderzysz, to powiem Rachel, że sypiasz na boku z innymi kobietami.

Seth mimo to uderzył go i pobiegł do domu, żeby powiedzieć Rachel, że czasami ją zdradzał. Rachel się zaśmiała.

– No to co? Ja ciebie też. Yan to niebezpieczny człowiek. Wykończ go.

Wrócił wykończyć Yana jeszcze tego wieczoru. Tym razem dorwał go przed jaskinią hazardu w Hell's Kitchen, gdzie spotkali się przed laty po raz pierwszy. Spuścił mu gruntowne lanie, obił go jak bokser, zaaplikował mu serię ciosów na korpus i w głowę bardzo zręcznie i szybko, chociaż nie był już przecież taki młody. Naprawdę zamierzał go zabić, lecz przekonał się, że jest nie tylko dobrym bokserem, ale i sędzią ringowym. Zostawił męża Adele krwawiącego na popękanym chodniku.

– Zrobiłeś to? – Rachel zaczęła siwieć z powodu afery z Yanem. Wyglądała teraz na dwa razy starszą.

– Rachel – powiedział Seth. – Zastanów się, o co mnie prosisz.

Adele siedziała na kanapie. Rachel zauważyła już wcześniej w barze, że córka zaczęła pić. Córka, która tańczyła wcześniej wokół pijaków, spijała teraz resztki z ich szklanek. Wysiorbywała z nich cudzą ślinę.

– Potrzeba nam Boga – oświadczyła Rachel.

– Albo dobrego rabina – powiedział Seth.

PRZYGOTOWUJĄC SIĘ DO ROZMOWY z rabinem, Adele przez kilka dni powstrzymywała się od spożywania alkoholu. Lubiła kamikaze – mieszankę soku z limonki, *triple sec* i wódki. Lubiła też martini. Tak, martini najbardziej. Nie w barze. W domu, gdzie czasem szukała pocieszenia w dobrym alkoholu. Oczywiście nie zamierzała mówić o tym rabinowi.

– W każdym małżeństwie obowiązują jakieś zasady – stwierdził rabin. – A jakie wy przyjęliście?

– Kurek od prysznica.

Nie zrozumiał.

– Kurek od prysznica?

– Zmywarka – mruknęła Adele.

– Zmywarka – powtórzył rabin. Był niski i zamyślony, nosił okulary w kształcie sowich oczu i nieustannie poprawiał je na nosie. – Rozumiem, że twój mąż dobrze zarabia. Na pewno kogoś masz... To znaczy wynajętą pomoc domową.

Adele skinęła głową.

– Oczywiście. – Potem kontynuowała swoją listę. – Mata łazienkowa, składanie ubrań. Pralka. Jego kroki w całym domu, w kapciach i bez kapci, w poszukiwaniu czegoś czy kogoś, kto się skrada, chociaż żadnych skradaczy nigdy nikt u nas nie widział. Rozkładanie złożonych wcześniej ubrań. Sondować, żeby zrozumieć, żeby zapytać: Co teraz będzie? Co będzie potem? Wirowanie po wszystkich kątach domu, a potem oznaczający ulgę śmiech albo cisza. Uśmiech, który jest jak maska, kiedy Yan wchodzi przez drzwi, dzień dobry, w którym nie ma nic z dobroci, cześć, które jest jak szpikulec do lodu w pierś, milcząca niechęć w czasie konsumpcji dania, które się przygotowywało cały dzień. Lemoniada nalewana do szklanki. Zanim jego usta dotkną tej szklanki, nim szklanka wróci na stół... „Za dużo cukru", mówią jego usta. Ale ty wiesz, że w ogóle nie dodałaś cukru do lemoniady, bo kiedy zrobiłaś to ostatnim razem, wrzeszczał, że za dużo. Ton głosu, który każe ci dotknąć rąbka sukienki, żeby sprawdzić, czy widać spod niej koszulkę, którą masz pod spodem, albo dezaprobata, z jaką wyciąga rękę, żeby cię dotknąć.

– A kochasz go? – spytał rabin.

Ile razy Adele zadawała sobie to pytanie? Odpowiedź przypominała drinka, na którego właśnie miała ochotę: kamikaze. Piloci kamikaze lecą na spotkanie ze śmiercią. Za każdym razem, kiedy analizowała ten problem, mówiła sobie, że jest współwinna temu, że została z Yanem.

Nagle, ni stąd, ni zowąd, Adele zaczęła krzyczeć na rabina, który pochylił się naprzód, aby tym lepiej ocenić skalę jej gniewu.

– Pojedyncza orchidea pozostawiona w szklanym wazonie! Pudełko trufli z naszego ulubionego sklepu ze słodyczami, Evelyn's! Jakiś drobiazg, który ujawnia cały świat myśli i piękna, zaćmiewającego każdą odrobinę poprzedzającej je brzydoty! Drżenie świeżych, dojrzałych poziomek podanych w zielonym kartoniku, który je osłania!

Może jest jeszcze nadzieja, pomyślał rabin, ale do Adele powiedział tylko tyle:

– Chciałbym się spotkać z twoim mężem. Nie widziałem go od dnia waszego ślubu.

Adele pamiętała dzień ślubu jak przez mgłę. Odwróciła wzrok.

– Nie jesteśmy religijni. Może nie przyjść.

– Musisz go namówić – odparł rabin.

WRÓCIŁA DO DOMU. Po raz pierwszy w czasie trwania ich małżeństwa Yan nie zadzwonił i nie przyjechał po nią do Rachel i Setha. Miał posiniaczoną twarz po solidnych batach, jakie spuścił mu Seth. Wymienił meble w całym mieszkaniu na nowocześniejsze. Wszystkie były białe.

– Oddałbym cały świat za to, żeby być innym człowiekiem – powiedział. Adele prawie mu uwierzyła. Była wdzięczna, że nie zrobił nic, aby znowu przeciąć sobie żyły.

– Wynająłem dom na weekend na Long Island – dodał.

Chciała mu powiedzieć o rabinie. Może wysłucha jej uważniej, jak będzie wypoczęty i zrelaksowany.

PRZEGLĄDAJĄC GAZETĘ „East Hampton Star", zauważyła, że można wreszcie zwiedzać dom Pollocka i Lee Krasner.

Zarówno Jackson Pollock, jak i Lee Krasner już nie żyli. Był rok 1988. Ich dom stał o piętnaście minut jazdy od domu, który Yan wynajął na weekend w Amagansett.

– On – szepnął Yan, kiedy chodzili po domu i zatrzymali się przed obrazem Pollocka *Bez tytułu (Kompozycja z czerwonym łukiem i końmi)*. Geniusz? Nazywają go geniuszem. A cesarz jest w lesie i nagi.

– Ona – powiedziała Adele, która chodząc po skromnych pokojach, westchnęła, natknąwszy się na *Wolną przestrzeń*, sitodruk autorstwa Krasner, jego nasycone, kręte błękity oraz zielenie, buntowniczo abstrakcyjne i sprężyste. Zwalczyła pokusę wejścia na łóżko artystki, by lepiej przyjrzeć się *Różanemu kamieniowi*, litografii aż gorejącej od różu. Yan czekał cierpliwie, kiedy Adele długo oglądała każdą fotografię i skwapliwie robiła niewyraźne zapiski w starym notesie, nie przyszło jej bowiem do głowy, by wziąć ze sobą aparat. Poprosiła, żeby pozwolił jej jeszcze raz obejrzeć pracownię Pollocka, a Yan przyszedł i ukląkł przy niej, gdy dotykała plam farby pozostawionych już na stałe na drewnianej podłodze. Po śmierci męża Krasner przejęła jego pracownię i Adele wszędzie dostrzegała ślady jej obecności. – Podobają mi się pociągnięcia pędzla Lee. Śmiały pokaz barw. Uważam, że oni oboje są genialni, Yan.

Tej nocy spletli się w uścisku, a Adele zasnęła, zanim zdążyła wspomnieć mu o rabinie. Nie spała długo. Kiedy się obudziła, jej mąż siedział na brzegu łóżka.

– Wiesz, że ponieśliśmy porażkę. Nasze dzieci mają wszystko, ale nie są bezpieczne. Dlaczego nie potrafimy zapewnić im bezpieczeństwa?

„Dzieci cię nienawidzą – pomyślała Adele. – A nade mną się litują", przemknęło jej przez głowę. Yanowi odpowiedziała jednak tak:

– Mógłbyś zadać to pytanie rabinowi.

– **NIE – STWIERDZIŁ RABIN.** – Nie potraficie zapewnić bezpieczeństwa swoim dzieciom. Jesteśmy dziećmi Boga, a nawet On nie był w stanie powstrzymać nas przed skosztowaniem zakazanego owocu. Człowiek z natury jest skazany na to, aby poznawać różne poziomy cierpienia, cierpienie nie powinno jednak trwać przez całe życie.

Yan docenił tę odpowiedź, lecz puścił ją mimo uszu.

– Co mógłbym dla ciebie zrobić, rebe?

– Nie chodzi o to, co możesz zrobić dla mnie, Yanie, tylko co możesz zrobić dla siebie. I dla Adele.

– Adele i ja mamy się dobrze, jak sądzę. Lepiej niż większość naszych bliźnich.

Rabin był właścicielem domu na Manhattan Beach, w pobliżu Sheepshead Bay. Pochodził ze starej rodziny producentów zegarów. Słyszał tik, nawet kiedy brakowało tak, i tak, kiedy brakowało tik. Głośny zgiełk czasu ustępował tylko na chwilę, gdy czytał Torę i Talmud. Przyjrzał się Yanowi.

– Wcale nie.

– Ależ tak, rebe – upierał się Yan.

– Bijesz żonę.

– Czasami – przyznał Yan.

– Adele nie zasługuje na takie traktowanie.

Nie odpowiedział.

Potem rabin spytał go, czy uważa się za dobrego Żyda. Yan odparł, że tak.

– To przestań bić Adele. Bo jesteś niedobrym Żydem – powiedział ostrzegawczo.

Yan znowu zamilkł, a na jego wargach igrał grymas przypominający uśmiech. Oczy Yana przyglądały się gabinetowi rabina z więcej niż przelotnym zainteresowaniem. Wszędzie stały książki. Gdyby to były góry, Yan by się na nie wspiął.

– Jeżeli jej nie kochasz – oświadczył rabin – to powinieneś się rozwieść.

– A jaka inna kobieta by ze mną wytrzymała? Adele to grzesznica, a ja jestem jej karą.

Rabin spytał, z jakiej rosyjskiej wioski pochodzi jego rodzina. Wzruszył ramionami. Rabin czekał, ale Yan nie chciał podać nazwy wsi, w której się urodził.

– A co to za różnica? – Znów wzruszył ramionami. – Nosiła nazwę nadaną na cześć Stalina.

Rabin powiedział Yanowi, że jego rodzina pochodzi z Witebska, miasta na Białorusi. Wzywał imiona swojej matki, ojca, dziadków i pradziadków. Ich wymówienie osłabiło odgłosy tik-tak, tik-tak w uszach rabina i uspokoiło go w obecności Yana, który patrzył mu w oczy bez zmrużenia powiek. Rabin był uczonym, ale mocno wierzył w istnienie demonów. Przez czterdzieści lat od końca wojny słyszał o nich wiele opowieści i sam je często widywał, maskujące się pod postacią depresji, smutku oraz tępej złości w ludzkich duszach. Sprowadził rozmowę z powrotem na Adele, wspominając o matkach.

– Pomyśl o swojej matce.

– Nigdy jej nie lubiłem – odparł Yan.

Naprawdę? Żartuje czy mówi poważnie? Wyraz jego twarzy tego nie zdradzał. Rabin zastanawiał się, dlaczego Adele nie poszła po rozum do głowy i wyszła za człowieka niekochającego rodzonej matki. Ale zmiękło mu serce, bo Adele nie znała swojego ojca.

Później tego wieczoru wytłumaczył całą sytuację swojej żonie, Lydii, która stwierdziła, że nigdy nie lubiła matki rabina – bo teściowa była za bardzo wścibska.

Rabin usiadł na łożu małżeńskim z zagłówkiem.

– Wcześniej nic mi o tym nie mówiłaś, Lydio.

– Ja? Miałabym się skarżyć na lubą matkę rabina rabinowi? Daj spokój. Ale ty przecież chyba o tym wiedziałeś, Isaacu? Tylko Bóg mógł kochać twoją matkę.

– Ja też ją kochałem.

Żona odwróciła się do niego plecami.

– Nie codziennie.

– No to tak często, jak mi na to pozwalała. To wojna ją zniszczyła.

– Dlaczego szukasz usprawiedliwień dla ludzi? Wojna zniszczyła nas wszystkich. I niszczy dalej.

Rabin nie spał dobrze tej nocy. Odczekał trzy tygodnie, zanim zadzwonił do Yana.

– UDERZYŁEŚ OSTATNIO ADELE? – zapytał. Znajdowali się w gabinecie rabina. Yan siedział z rękami wciśniętymi między kolana. Jak dzieciak.

– Ostatnio nie – odpowiedział.

– To ma być jakiś postęp?

Yan uśmiechnął się.

– Możesz to nazywać, jak chcesz, rebe.

– Jesteś dobrze prosperującym biznesmenem, tak?

– Jestem właścicielem pewnej firmy, która jest właścicielką innej firmy.

– A twoja specjalność?

– Ściąganie długów.

– Wyobrażam sobie, że to nerwowa praca. My, mężczyźni, mamy swoje problemy, których nasze żony nie rozumieją. – Rabin otworzył Talmud. – Ale Talmud zabrania mężczyźnie niesłusznie bić żonę.

Yan się roześmiał.

– A czy pobicie kogoś w ogóle może być słuszne?

– A więc zgadzamy się, że zgodnie z tym, co napisano w Talmudzie, nie powinieneś podnosić ręki na żonę?

– Talmud poddaje się wielu interpretacjom, czcigodny rebe – rzekł Yan. Od czasu do czasu zapuszczał i golił brodę, niedawno właśnie ją przystrzygł. Nie można było jednak powiedzieć, żeby wyglądał schludnie. – Obaj dobrze to wiemy. Możemy tu sobie siedzieć i argumentować w określony sposób, a potem natrafić na taką interpretację, która każe nam zmienić zapatrywania. Myślisz, rebe, że ja nie znam Talmudu? Znam go lepiej niż ktokolwiek na świecie.

Rabin nie wątpił, że w słowach Yana słyszy rzucone sobie wyzwanie. W szkole rabinackiej był najlepszym uczniem. Duma kusiła, by podjąć rękawicę, lecz skromna posługa boża, jaką wykonywał, skłoniła go do innej odpowiedzi.

– A skąd tak dobrze znasz Talmud? – spytał.

– Mój ojciec był rabinem.

– A jednak ty nie kroczysz ścieżką rabinowego syna.

Yan wstał raptownie – tak raptownie, jak na jego twarz wystąpił rumieniec.

– **BYŁO MI BARDZO MIŁO,** ale chyba właśnie skończyliśmy.

Wcześniej rabin nie dostrzegł u Yana żadnych oznak emocji.

W czasie tej rozmowy do pokoju weszła Lydia; przyniosła im herbatę, nie była bowiem w stanie powściągnąć ciekawości. Na widok Yana, który oddalał się od jej małżonka dumnym krokiem dandysowatego pawia albo alfonsa, zaczęła za nim krzyczeć.

– Jeżeli chcesz zachowywać się jak cham i bić słabszych, to idź do Harlemu i tam się rzuć na kogoś z pięściami!

Rabin zaszedł żonę od tyłu.

– Ćśś.

– Niech się przekona, jak długo by tam wytrzymał z tymi dzikusami!

– Nie poznaję cię, Lydio. Mówisz ostatnio takie rzeczy… – A po chwili dodał: – Myślisz, że jego ojciec naprawdę był rabinem?

HARLEM. POTENCJAŁ TEJ DZIELNICY zaintrygował Yana. Zaintrygowało go gniewne wyzwanie rzucone mu przez Lydię. Na tyle, że w pewne upalne piątkowe popołudnie pojechał metrem na róg 138 Ulicy i Lenox Avenue, żeby sprawdzić, co go tam może spotkać. W przeciwieństwie do rabina, Yan nie potrafił oprzeć się wyzwaniom.

Był rok 1988 i panowała moda na hip-hop. Yan zajął pozycję przed jadłodajnią Pan Pan, śniadaniową knajpą przy 135 Ulicy, gdzie podawano kurczaka z goframi. Stepował, chociaż nie miał na nogach butów do stepowania, i prosił czarnych mieszkańców Harlemu, w tym pijaków i wariatów, by wyszli na ulicę i z nim zatańczyli.

Ale czarnoskórzy mieszkańcy Harlemu nie chcieli nawet o tym słyszeć.

Wtedy odstawił agresywne przedstawienie i zaatakował czarnych przechodniów długim strumieniem rasistowskich obelg i wyzwisk. Ludzie pokazywali go palcami, śmiali się albo odwracali wzrok. Tylko jeden mały chłopiec zostawił swoją mamę i podbiegł popatrzeć na Yana, a przyglądając mu się, oderwał złoty guzik od swojego niebieskiego blezerka. Yan podszedł bliżej, aby podnieść zgubę i podać ją chłopcu, którego matka jednak ostrzegła go:

– Człowieku, są pewne granice. Ani się waż zbliżać do mnie czy mojego synka.

Pewnie myśleli, że to jakaś podpucha. Że Yan jest gliniarzem, działającym pod przykrywką, i że ma gdzieś pod ubraniem pałkę. Albo że to wariat. Nie mogli wiedzieć, że nieżyjący już wujek Yana, Mojsze, był właścicielem kilku hurtowni w Harlemie i Bronksie. Gdy Yan przyjechał do Ameryki, wuj zabierał go do fabryki fortepianów w Mott

Haven, gdzie pozwalał mu krążyć między instrumentami i naciskać klawisze jak popadło.

YAN WRÓCIŁ DO BROOKLYNU, by jeszcze tego wieczoru opowiedzieć rabinowi o swoich przygodach. Nie chciał wyjść z jego domu, chociaż Lydia twierdziła, że mąż udał się już na spoczynek. Rano, gdy ulitowała się nad Yanem i zaprowadziła go do gabinetu, wypił dwa kubki kawy i zjadł pół chałki należącej do gospodarza.

– Przyszedłem ci powiedzieć, rebe, że zachowywałem się jak ostatni cham, ale czarni mieszkańcy Harlemu mają ważniejsze problemy. Widziałem je na własne oczy, czcigodny rebe. Ich ubóstwo. I powiem ci tylko tyle: czarni nigdy nie powinni przestać śpiewać i tańczyć. Ludzie, którzy nie śpiewają i nie tańczą, w końcu kompletnie wariują. Powiedz mi, czcigodny rebe, czy tak nie jest?

Rabin znów spytał Yana, z jakiej rosyjskiej wsi pochodzi jego rodzina. Yan wymienił długą listę wiosek, a potem zaczął się kołysać z boku na bok.

– Gdzieś w Harlemie mieszka mały czarny chłopiec w niebieskim blezerku z oderwanym guzikiem. Noszę ten złoty guzik w kieszeni, bo nasze miasto jest i duże, i małe, dlatego w końcu może się jeszcze spotkamy...

Rabin spytał, czy Yan przypomina sobie, którą szkołę rabinacką kończył jego ojciec.

Yan kopniakiem przewrócił stolik z chałką i kawą. Gorący płyn wylał się z metalowego dzbanuszka i chlusnął na pluszowy turecki dywan, prezent ślubny od ciotecznej babki rabina, Sabiny. Tik. Tak. Tik. Tak. Tik.

– Ktoś tu, kurwa, chce zadzierać z dzieckiem rodziców, którzy należeli do amerykańskiej partii komunistycznej? – spytał Yan. – Ktoś tu, kurwa, chce zadzierać ze mną?

Rabin powiedział Yanowi, że powinien sobie znaleźć dobrego terapeutę. I zaczął go namawiać, żeby czym prędzej wyszedł, zanim Lydia wezwie stróżów prawa.

OD CZASU AMAGANSETT nie było między nimi żadnych spięć. Yan konsekwentnie unikał Adele, która zapisała się na zajęcia plastyczne do Art Students League na 57 Ulicy. Powyciągała z ukrycia płótna, sztalugi, pędzle i farby. Właśnie zaczęła malować ramki nowego obrazu, gdy do mieszkania wszedł Yan. Była jedenasta rano. Po tupocie jego nóg na podłodze poznała, że dojdzie do sprzeczki.

Piła regularnie, a alkohol dodawał jej odwagi. Yan krążył wokół niej w salonie. Okna były otwarte. Adele znowu urządziła sobie tutaj pracownię. Yan patrzył, jak ramki na płótnie zmieniają się w szerokie smugi, a smugi w Kota z Cheshire. Już od dawna nie malowała kotów. Yan również sięgnął po pędzel i zamalował zwierzę.

– Daleko ci do Lee Krasner – powiedział. I zakapał farbą całe płótno.

– Za to ty jesteś... – Adele się uśmiechnęła – ...autokratą.

– Ach, nauczyliśmy się korzystać ze słownika. Nareszcie, choć długo trwało, zanim do tego doszłaś.

– Jesteś tyranem.

– Co ty wiesz o tyranach, Adele? Co ty wiesz o czymkolwiek?

Gdyby tylko chciała, mógłby jej powiedzieć, jacy naprawdę są tyrani i jak postępują. Mógłby opowiedzieć jej o takich zimach, kiedy do głosu dochodziły mrozy, które mówiły „umrzesz dziś w tym pokoju". Mógłby opowiedzieć jej o modłach tamtego rabina, człowieka, który był jego ojcem, i o pokoju, w którym musieli się zebrać na rozkaz Stalina, chociaż przez jakiś czas Stalin wydawał się jeżeli nie ich orędownikiem, to z pewnością przyjacielem. Mógłby opowiedzieć jej o klitkach wielkości szafy i o pozostawaniu jak gdyby w zawieszeniu pomiędzy snem i snami, o czarnych nocach, które robiły się jasne pod wpływem ostrych świateł latarek, i o głośnych krokach, które uczyli się liczyć, o węszących psach, najpierw trzymanych krótko na smyczy, potem luźniej, a potem jeszcze luźniej, o mężczyznach, starych rabinach, takich jak jego ojciec, i o kobietach, tworzących żywy mur, by chronić swoje dzieci. Kto chronił dzieci? „Ja – mógłby jej powiedzieć Yan, gdyby tylko zechciał. – Chroniłem je tak samo, jak chroniono mnie". Ale nigdy jej tego nie powiedział.

– Odchodzę od ciebie, Yanie – powiedziała Adele.

– Dobrze. Odejdź. Myślisz, że coś mnie to obchodzi?

– Odebrałeś mi wszystko, co dla mnie ważne.

– I mówi mi to kobieta, która nigdy nie chodziła głodna. Która zawsze dobrze sypiała.

– Wszystko.

Cofnął się i poinformował Adele, że odbierze jej jeszcze jedną rzecz.

Zdumiała się.

– Co możesz mi jeszcze zabrać, z czego dotąd mnie nie obrabowałeś? – zapytała.

– Twój spokój ducha.

Odłożył pędzel w sraczkowatym kolorze i podbiegł do okna. Wyskoczył, zabierając ze sobą odłamki szkła, ram oraz doniczki z aloesami, które stały na parapecie. Runął dwanaście pięter w dół na spotkanie śmierci.

SZIWA ODBYŁA SIĘ bez łez. Tylko dzieci Adele i Yana, Maximilian i Freya, płakały po człowieku, który je przerażał.

Po śmierci Yana pijaństwo Adele nabrało rozpędu.

– Nie ma nic gorszego niż stara pijaczka – powiedziała Rachel.

– Odszedł, to dar od losu – stwierdził Seth. – Teraz możesz żyć.

Adele beknęła Sethowi i Rachel prosto w twarz.

Maximilian i Freya nie mówili nic. Omijali Adele szerokim łukiem, a ona przeklinała ich za to, że zamieszkali na Zachodnim Wybrzeżu. Posprzątali jej mieszkanie i powiesili obrazy, które trzymała przez całe lata w ukryciu. Przeprowadzili pobieżną inwentaryzację kont bankowych ojca i ze zdumieniem stwierdzili, że wyznaczył ich oboje na wykonawców swojego testamentu i zarządców majątku. Zgromadził niewielką fortunę w nieruchomościach i papierach inwestycyjnych.

Adele aż usiadła, gdy Freya i Max powiedzieli jej, że została właścicielką domu w Amagansett. Wróciła na zajęcia z malarstwa. I mniej piła. Pewnego wieczoru, w czwartą rocznicę śmierci męża, spotkała przypadkiem swojego dawnego instruktora. Jego przypominające spodek brzuszysko wciąż wyglądało śmiesznie, a poza tym miał w oczach katarakty, które bał się usunąć.

– Twój nauczyciel nie widzi! – wykrzyknął. Zaprosił Adele na przyjęcie charytatywne na Upper West Side, na którym goście mieli zbierać fundusze dla jakiejś miejscowej szkoły publicznej. Adele z zasady unikała imprez na Manhattanie, lecz jakiś cichy głos powiedział jej: „Idź, idź".

Poszła, piła jednak ostrożnie. Popijała drinki, zamiast je chłeptać. Zostawiła martini na stoliku i udała się do toalety. Po powrocie spostrzegła, że jakiś przystojny, srebrzystosiwy mężczyzna pije drinka z jej kieliszka.

– Nie, nie, to moje martini – powiedziała, wskazując ślad szminki na brzegu.

– Proszę mi wybaczyć. Wzrok wysiada zawsze jako pierwszy – odpowiedział nieznajomy.

Mimo wszystko dopił jej martini i usiadł na kanapie firmy Shelton. Adele zajęła miejsce obok. Nazywał się James Samuel Vincent i jak jej powiedział, był prawnikiem – rozwiedzionym. Jego syn, Rufus, studiował na Columbia University. Wczoraj wieczorem James poznał jego nową dziewczynę, Claudię. Wydaje mi się, stwierdził, że to dość poważny związek. Mój Ruff nie jest już chłopcem. Opowiadając Adele o tym wszystkim, poprosił jednego z kelnerów, by podał im następną kolejkę martini.

– Tak – powiedziała Adele, myśląc o swoim ukochanym nauczycielu malarstwa i o ślepocie w ogóle. Słuchając jednak, jak James Samuel Vincent opowiada o własnych radościach i absurdach życiowych, odwróciła się do niego i wyłożyła karty na stół.

– To małe okrucieństwa nam doskwierają – powiedziała. – Nie te wielkie krzywdy, które można wskazać palcem i powiedzieć: „Och, widzę ten siniec", ale drobne ranki, których się właściwie nie dostrzega, dopóki pewnego dnia, kiedy jesz akurat miskę zupy z kopru włoskiego albo opalasz się nad basenem, nie poczujesz, że nie jesteś w stanie się poruszyć, nie możesz zrobić nic, bo myślisz: „No tak, coś we mnie umarło, bo ktoś mi zrobił krzywdę, i dlaczego dopuściłam, żeby do tego doszło?". A teraz, teraz, teraz...

NOTATKI HANKA

2010

Piątek, weekend świąteczny Memorial Day

W POSIADŁOŚCI CAMPHORÓW doszło do powtórki z rozrywki, gdy znów zjawiła się tam ich rodzina. Pewnego dnia, powiedział sobie Hank, zawiśnie nad ich głowami miecz, a wtedy nie zawaha się i ciach, ciach – zerwie z nimi kontakty i odetnie się od tych ludzi na zawsze. Tymczasem jednak spędzał kolejny świąteczny weekend Memorial Day na Sunset Beach, na ogrodzonym osiedlu, wśród wyspiarskiej społeczności ze swoich młodych lat. Jak to mieli w zwyczaju Camphorowie, uroczystości rozpoczęły się w piątkowy wieczór, kiedy krewni z tak odległych miejsc jak Spokane w stanie Waszyngton albo tak bliskich jak Duchess w stanie

Georgia wjechali jeden za drugim samochodami i motocyklami na podwójny podjazd Seamusa Camphora III. Przywieźli ze sobą niemowlęta w szpanerskich wózkach i leciwe babcie, które ciągle stosowały talk firmy Avon oraz krem Maybelline, żeby zamaskować plamy wątrobowe. Rozumiało się bez słów, że dalsza rodzina zamieszka w Southside La Quinta albo w Holiday Inn. Hank Camphor spędził spory kawał dzieciństwa w tym właśnie domu – był dla Seamusa Camphora III kuzynem drugiego stopnia – i dlatego musiał nocować w rodzinnej posiadłości w swojej dawnej sypialni, która została przebudowana i przypominała teraz pokój w sieciowym hotelu, miała bidet i pisuar w łazience, kapy na łóżko w geometryczne wzory, trójkątne poduszki oraz duży płaskoekranowy, zamontowany na ścianie telewizor. Można go było włączyć, żeby ci zaśpiewał do snu, jeśli czułeś się chociaż trochę smutny albo samotny.

W OTOCZENIU MROWIA KUZYNÓW Hank pławił się z rozkoszą we własnych uprzedzeniach. Rys próżności dzielił z rodzicami (Barbarą Camphor i już nieżyjącym Charlesem Camphorem). Potrafił tolerować w drugim człowieku właściwie wszystko, z wyjątkiem brudu oraz otyłości, bo wydawało mu się, że każdy człowiek powinien nad tym panować: dbać o swoją tuszę i higienę. Nigdy nie towarzyszył żonie, Susan, podczas dożywiania bezdomnych w miejscowym schronisku i unikał fast foodów tak fanatycznie, że Susan mawiała czasem: „Wyszłam za uroczego, ale próżnego mężczyznę".

„WYSZŁAM ZA UROCZEGO, ale próżnego mężczyznę". Hank powtórzył słowa Susan w swoim pokoju z czasów dzieciństwa. Płaskoekranowy telewizor dotrzymywał mu towarzystwa, mówił do niego, pytał, czy woli Fox, czy raczej CNN. Odmruknął, że pornosy. Był teraz sam, z dala od Susan i Tess, ich trzyletniej córeczki, i pomyślał, że może sobie na to pozwolić. Poczuł się przyjemnie zaskoczony, kiedy telewizor przełączył się automatycznie na zastrzeżony kanał z imponującą liczbą filmów i programów dla dorosłych. Najbardziej lubił porno z czasów Złotego Wieku, z lat siedemdziesiątych, czyli takie ostre i pieprzne oldskulowe klasyki jak *The Devil and Miss Jones*, *Głębokie gardło* albo *Inside Seka*, nabrał bowiem upodobania do nich w wieku chłopięcym, gdy dokonywał najazdów na ojcowską piwnicę. Powiedział: „Porno z lat siedemdziesiątych", i wybałuszył oczy na widok rozświetlającej ekran listy propozycji. Wybrał Johnniego Keyesa i Marilyn Chambers w *Behind the Green Door*.

NIGDY NIE ZDRADZIŁ Susan Camphor, z domu Weatherby, chociaż od czasu do czasu trochę ją oszukiwał. Chodził na przykład po alejkach Rite Aid albo CVS w poszukiwaniu tandetnych, elektryzujących perfum (im więcej nut kwiatowych, tym lepiej), żeby podrażnić orli nos żony i rozbujać jej wyobraźnię. Osobiście najbardziej lubił perfumy Lucky Me.

– Co to za zapach, Hank? – pytała Susan, pociągając nosem.

– Ja tam nic nie czuję – odpowiadał, masując sobie szczękę.

Była wicedyrektorką działu zasobów ludzkich na Duke University. Nie należała do kobiet, które w siebie wątpią, ale on widział plamki niepewności w źrenicach jej brązowych oczu. Niepewność nie skłaniała jej do tego, aby za wszelką cenę trzymać się męża, ale żeby dbać o siebie bardziej niż większość kobiet. Wątpliwości Susan prowadziły do nieprzewidywalnego seksu. Tego, ile warta jest nieprzewidywalność, Hank nauczył się od rodziców. Wstydził się swojego postępowania, chociaż nie na tyle, żeby się poprawić, zwłaszcza kiedy złe zachowanie okazywało się skuteczne.

Sobota, weekend Memorial Day

Rodzinne spędy Camphorów obowiązkowo obejmowały hulaszczy piknik na Sunset Beach. Tego dnia do czerwono-białych lodówek turystycznych wędrowały żeberka wieprzowe z grilla, jajka faszerowane, marynowany w maślance smażony kurczak i płaska fasolka szparagowa. Wycieczka była najjaśniejszym punktem zlotu dla Hanka, który uwielbiał plażę. Przyglądał się, jak dzieci budują zamki z piasku albo surfują na boogie boardach w przerwie między kolejnymi pogoniami za suczką rasy jack russell o imieniu Stella. Należała do Seamusa Camphora III, syna Seamusa II, kuzyna ojca Hanka. Wałęsała się po plaży, obszczekując mewy i rozpruwając worki na śmieci w poszukiwaniu kości. Hankowi przypominała biuściastą czirliderkę, która mogłaby odbić faceta najlepszej przyjaciółce. Sam nie miał psa i nigdy nie chciał go mieć, chociaż kiedy był chłopcem – i to wspomnienie teraz mu dokuczało – przez bardzo krótki czas prosił o basseta.

Z nadejściem wieczoru zaczynało się pieczenie ostryg i gotowanie gulaszu z krabami, krewetkami, ziemniakami oraz kiełbaskami andouille z dodatkiem soli ziołowej. Hank pozwalał innym mężczyznom z rodu Camphorów zajmować nylonowe leżaki, wyposażone w głębokie kieszenie, w których mogli trzymać napoje chłodzące, on jednak czuł się więcej niż szczęśliwy, gdy rozwijał ręcznik plażowy, kładł się na płask na piasku i oglądał wspaniały zachód słońca. Ilekroć w pobliżu przechodził jakiś facet w średnim wieku o zwiotczałym już ciele, które wzięli diabli, Hank upajał się własną prężną piersią i herkulesowo jędrnym tyłkiem. Miał czterdzieści lat, ale wyglądał najwyżej na trzydzieści i ani jeden dzień więcej. Pozostali mężczyźni z rodu Camphorów byli wysocy jak on, stracili jednak dawną młodzieńczość i zwinność.

W NIEDZIELĘ wszyscy wyruszyli w czterogodzinną podróż samochodową na wieś w Georgii, by oddać cześć swoim zmarłym. Ojciec Hanka i Duży Seamus, tata Seamusa III, leżeli na cmentarzu St. Matthew's. Skromny kościół metodystów nie mógł już pomieścić swojego potomstwa. Seamus III ustawił drewniane ławki na trawniku wokół kościoła i zamontował na zewnątrz głośniki, żeby wszyscy słyszeli, jak stary pastor o zaropiałych oczach wygłasza doroczne kazanie na temat syna marnotrawnego. Potrząsał przy tym tamburynem, uderzając nim o biodra, aby dodać kazaniu pikanterii.

Hank nigdy nie stawiał kwiatów na ojcowskim grobie. Zamiast nich przynosił piłkę golfową marki Spalding, chcąc okazać w ten sposób szacunek dla dyscypliny sportu, którą Charles Camphor uwielbiał. Zginął w wypadku żeglarskim, gdy Hank był na ostatnim roku studiów. W czasie posiłku w przybudówce skromnego kościółka matka Hanka chwyciła go za ramię i powiedziała:

– On nie był twoim ojcem.

Hank zawsze widział w oczach Charlesa tyle z samego siebie, iż był przez chwilę pewien, że Barbara okrutnie z niego żartuje albo że na moment, do cholery, postradała zmysły z powodu tragicznej śmierci dobrego męża. Spoglądał ponad burgundowymi krzesłami na tęgie, białe wieśniaczki rozstawiające przygotowane z okazji stypy potrawy, na których skosztowanie zamierzał sobie pozwolić w ramach konsolacji. Miał zostać chirurgiem ortopedą i nauczył się już, że jeśli człowiek będzie czekał dość długo, to w końcu odsłoni się przed nim właściwa ścieżka życiowa, na której zdoła uniknąć nieodwracalnych błędów.

– Jamesa Samuela Vincenta poznałam na jakiejś konferencji, dawno temu. Spędziliśmy razem tylko chwilę – powiedziała Barbara. – Która, jak się okazało, dotyczyła też ciebie. Przepraszam cię, Hank.

„Dziwka". Hank miał ochotę powiedzieć matce: „Bóg mi świadkiem, że nigdy nie ożenię się z dziwką", wydał jednak tylko pełen goryczy okrzyk, a zebrani wokół goście uznali, że powodem łez jest jego zmarły ojciec.

Barbara odeszła i stanęła na początku kolejki po jedzenie. Ruszył za nią i już razem odgrywali role zrozpaczonej żony i syna, pastor pobłogosławił wszystkie potrawy, a przyjaciele i rodzina ustawili się w szeregu, żeby złożyć ostatnie kondolencje. Później, kiedy żałobnicy wyszli i pawilon opustoszał, znalazł matkę przed kościołem, z boku, tam gdzie trawa zdążyła urosnąć wysoko, chociaż ją niedawno przycinano. Barbara odgarnęła na bok jasne jak piasek włosy, zdjęła czarne pumpy i zapaliła marychę z kuzynem swojego ojca, Dużym Seamusem.

– Nie mogłem sobie odmówić świętego zioła w taki smutny dzień, Hank – powiedział Duży Seamus.

Charles Camphor nie przepadał za trawą, koką i w ogóle za dragami, chociaż wysoko cenił dobrą whisky, gin i bourbona. Hank przypatrywał się wymanikiurowanym, pociągniętym czerwonym lakierem paznokciom matki i podziwiał wprawę, z jaką trzymała dżointa.

Wzięła długiego macha i wypuściła dym przez nos i usta, po czym spojrzała na skręta z marihuaną niczym na bliskiego przyjaciela, zanim zaproponowała go Seamusowi. Hank wyrwał dżointa spomiędzy palców matki i sam się zaciągnął. Duży Seamus poklepał go po ramieniu.

– Bardzo ci współczuję z powodu śmierci ojca – powiedział. Ile razy rzucano dziś te słowa w twarz Hankowi? Sto? Dwieście? Na pogrzeb przyjechało dużo ludzi. Z Denver przyleciał Jerome Jenkins, jedyny czarnoskóry kolega, z którym rodzice pozwalali się Hankowi spotykać w dzieciństwie. Przed wyjazdem zapytał Hanka o jego sąsiadów z lat chłopięcych.

– Co się stało z tą rodziną, która mieszkała w domu obok was? I z tym twoim kolegą, Gideonem? Miał taką ładną siostrę, wiecznie siedziała tylko z nosem w książkach... Boże, jaka ona była piękna. Strasznie chciałbym ją teraz zobaczyć!

– Applewoodowie dawno już się stamtąd wyprowadzili – odpowiedział Hank.

SPRAWY SPADKOWE CHARLESA zostały uporządkowane rok po jego pogrzebie. Jeszcze zanim Barbara zdecydowała się wystawić dom na sprzedaż, Duży Seamus próbował ją wybadać.

– To duży dom jak na samotną kobietę – stwierdził. – Masz tam tyle miejsca, że na pewno będziesz po prostu pływać we wspomnieniach.

Hank był wtedy na pierwszym roku medycyny Duke University. Rzadko rozmawiał z matką, zaczęła jednak dręczyć go ciekawość dotycząca jego biologicznego ojca. Barbara przysłała mu polaroidowe zdjęcie przedstawiające Jamesa Samuela Vincenta na meczu bejsbolowym zespołu Yankees w towarzystwie przyrodniego brata Hanka, Rufusa. Hank dokładnie obejrzał fotografię w swoim skąpo umeblowanym mieszkaniu z jedną sypialnią. Zdumiała go siła genów, widok dwóch tak uderzająco podobnych do niego ludzi. Zdjęcie pochodziło co najmniej sprzed dziesięciu lat, a Rufus wyglądał na nim najwyżej na szesnaście albo siedemnaście. Czy to oznacza, że Barbara nie widuje się ostatnio z Jamesem Samuelem Vincentem? Nie miał ochoty ponownie podejmować tego tematu z matką. Kiedy poznał Susan Weatherby na przyjęciu z okazji powrotu do domu, polaroid z Vincentem wyrzucił do kosza. „Mężczyzna sam tworzy swoją rodzinę. Sam zmywa swój talerz".

Hank i jego matka przetrwali trudny okres. Barbara poprosiła go, by sprawę sprzedaży ich dawnego domu wziął we własne ręce.

– Podaj mi swoją najlepszą ofertę – zwrócił się Hank do Dużego Seamusa.

Seamus nigdy nie naciągał Charlesa na pieniądze, jak reszta jego rodziny, a Hank zawsze darzył strażaka pewnym sentymentem, więc nie zdarł z niego skóry. Wydawało mu się nawet w jakimś sensie stosowne, że klucze do dawnego domu ojca przekaże jego bliskiemu kuzynowi.

NIGDY SIĘ NIE DOWIEDZIELI, jak Stelli udało się wyciągnąć rewolwer Smith & Wesson z metalowej skrzynki stojącej pod wielkim łóżkiem Maxine Camphor i Seamusa III. Ważyła co najmniej trzy funty. Mimo to w tym momencie, czyli o wpół do czwartej po południu, gdy wszyscy byli szczęśliwi i nikomu nic nie doskwierało, Stella leżała ze skrzyżowanymi przednimi łapami na rewolwerze, którego lufa skierowana była w stronę rozbawionych gości. Niektórzy zaczęli pić jeszcze przed śniadaniem.

– No tak, prawdziwe przyjęcie zaczyna się dopiero, gdy ktoś wyciąga broń. – Hank usłyszał głos Seamusa III i zdołał pomyśleć tylko: „Dzięki Bogu, że zostawiłem Susan i Tess w Raleigh".

Rodzina wybuchała śmiechem za każdym razem, gdy Stella zaczynała się wiercić. Z każdym jej gwałtowniejszym poruszeniem siedmiostrzałowy srebrzystoczarny rewolwer kalibru dziewięć milimetrów wirował niczym koło rosyjskiej ruletki.

– Są w nim naboje? – spytał Hank, przeciskając się wśród grupki podpitych gapiów w stronę drzwi do sypialni. Na zewnątrz, na ogromnym trawniku, usłyszał bawiące się dzieci. Przynajmniej one nie były narażone na niebezpieczeństwo.

– Tak, cholera, są, ale jest zabezpieczony – odpowiedział Seamus III, podnosząc szklankę szkockiej w swoich grubych, pokrytych bliznami łapach. Był strażakiem i na całym ciele, niczym odznaczenia, nosił pamiątki po walce wręcz z ogniem.

– Stella, złaź z tego rewolweru i idź na bieżnię – odezwała się Maxine, a potem poinformowała gości: – Stella potrafi korzystać z bieżni mechanicznej. Wejdźcie na YouTube'a, to zobaczycie, jak trenuje. Biega.

Hank był pewien, że słyszy na schodach dzieci. Wydawało mu się, że jest też wśród nich Tess, chociaż wciąż sobie powtarzał, że jego trzyletnia córka siedzi teraz bezpiecznie w domu w Raleigh, w Karolinie Północnej.

– Musimy odebrać jej broń – zwrócił się do Seamusa III. Chodź, spróbujemy.

– To jest tylko mały, tłusty piesek – zaśmiał się Seamus, popijając szkocką i mrugając porozumiewawczo do żony, wystrojonej w zwiewną białą suknię, w której, jak sądził Hank, przypominała grecką boginię. Olimpijskie bóstwo, Afrodytę. „Wenus z Milo". Przygnębiało go to, że Maxine wydaje mu się tak diablo pociągająca. Ożenił się z Susan nie tylko dla jej urody – była całkiem, chociaż nie porywająco, ładna – ale i w poszukiwaniu dobroci oraz inteligencji.

– Hank, jeśli skończyłeś już pożerać wzrokiem moją żonę – uśmiechnął się Seamus III – to może zechciałbyś złapać Stellę za przednie łapy, a ja się zajmę tylnymi?

Z respektu dla tych kul, którymi, jak przyznał Seamus, naładowany był rewolwer, Hank i strażak wyprowadzili gości z małżeńskiej sypialni, większej niż niejedna galeria sztuki nowoczesnej. Gdy Hank mieszkał tu jeszcze z rodzicami, ściany miały szarobiały kolor, nie łososiowy, a pokój był o połowę mniejszy. Duży Seamus i Maxine wyburzyli kilka ścian, by zrobić wielki remont i jeszcze bardziej unowocześnić i tak imponujący przecież dom z pięcioma sypialniami i trzema łazienkami. Hank i Seamus ruszyli w stronę Stelli, której ogon poruszył się i zesztywniał. Pies trącił rewolwer mordą, a smith & wesson ponownie zawirował jak koło roweru.

– Jesteś pewien, że ta cholerna broń jest zabezpieczona? – spytał Hank i poczuł, jak południowy akcent, który udało mu się z siebie wycisnąć, marszczy mu kąciki ust.

Rewolwer wypalił dokładnie w chwili, kiedy szeroki w barach, choć zaledwie trzynastoletni syn Seamusa, Gruby Seamus IV, przepchał się po wielkich schodach w hallu na górę, na czworakach, roztrącając gości łokciami na boki, bo postanowił dołączyć do dorosłych, wśród których coś się działo. Kula odbiła się od starej listwy podłogowej przy łososiowej ścianie i drasnęła Seamusa IV w górną część twarzy z prawej strony, na której niemal natychmiast pojawiła się szkarłatna „malina".

– Umieram – powiedział Seamus IV. – Ludzie, pomóżcie mi. Umieram!

– Nic ci nie jest, Seam. – Seamus III podbiegł do IV, podniósł go i otoczył rękami pyzatą twarz syna. – No przecież to najwyżej mały rumieniec.

Huk wystrzału z rewolweru, z tak bliska, spłoszył Stellę. Wypadła pędem z sypialni i puściła się w dół po schodach. Hank, który rozpaczliwie pożądał papierosa i był już zmęczony towarzystwem rodziny, rozpromienił się i ruszył za psem.

Drzwi wejściowe były szeroko otwarte, mniej więcej sześcioro dzieci bawiło się porcelanową zastawą do herbaty albo rzucało piłkami do krokieta. Hank zorientował się, że malców nie pilnuje nikt z dorosłych. Jakaś piegowata dziewczynka ze zdumiewającą wiechą rudych włosów na głowie tarzała się w ataku płaczu na ganku.

– Mój braciszek nie żyje! – łkała. Hank pomyślał, że wygląda jak Tess. Jego zdaniem miała jakieś trzy latka. Pochylił się nad nią, strzepując popiół z chowanego za plecami papierosa w ten sposób, aby wiatr unosił go w stronę ganku. Nie pamiętał, jak mała ma na imię.

– Seam. Seam... – szlochała dziewczynka.

Przypomniał sobie jej imię: Penny. Córka Seamusa III i Maxine. Miał ochotę powiedzieć: „Nie, Penny, w tym debilu, twoim bracie, wciąż tli się jeszcze życie", ale poklepał ją tylko po policzku.

– Tam jest dom wariatów. Zostań lepiej na zewnątrz.

Zgasił papierosa na ganku swojej rodzinnej posiadłości. Od kiedy to jego dom z czasów dzieciństwa stał się posiadłością? Nie przewidywał, że tak będzie, sprzedając go Dużemu Seamusowi. Popiół z papierosa poczernił mu czyste ręce. Można by powiedzieć – ręce chirurga; pewne. Penny z wiechą rudych włosów zaczęła go szarpać za nogawkę spodni.

– Do kibla Stelli nie tędy – powiedziała.

– Co?

Hank myślał czasami, że dobrze by mu zrobiła terapia psychologiczna, nie wierzył jednak w terapię jako w trwałe rozwiązanie jakichkolwiek problemów. W ogóle w nią nie wierzył.

– Stella, wracaj! – zawołała Penny, próbując wyjaśnić głosikiem trzylatki, że Stella zawsze ucieka, choć nie wolno jej biegać przed domem ani na podwórku, chyba że chce zrobić kupę w swoim kiblu. Hank poprosił, żeby mu pokazała, gdzie to jest, i mała zaprowadziła go do ogrodu za domem, blisko bagien. Hank zajrzał do psiego ustępu, czyli dołka w ziemi, pełnego odchodów i podartych gazet. Ponad dwadzieścia pięć lat temu pochował w tym miejscu Tippera. Jego oczy wypełniła sól.

Dziewczynka podniosła wzrok na Hanka.

– Stella lubi swój kibelek. Nie płacz.

– Będę musiał cię przeprosić, Penny – powiedział Hank.

Wycofał się i pobiegł, aby dogonić Stellę, która ze zdenerwowania sadziła gęsto grudki kału na poza tym nieskazitelnym chodniku. Skręciła za róg. Hank też, rozwijając coraz większą prędkość i wyciągając rękę, aby złapać psa za zesztywniały ogon. W końcu chwycił jednak po prostu uciekinierkę wpół, choć wykręcała się i drżała w jego ramionach, ani przez chwilę nie zaprzestając udzielać chodnikowi swojego chrztu z gówna. Jak gdyby łaskawym zrządzeniem losu zaczęło padać. Hank pędem minął w deszczu posiadłość rodziny Camphorów, chcąc znaleźć bezpieczne schronienie w swoim mercedesie. Gwałtownie otworzył drzwiczki i wrzucił psa na podłogę przed fotelem pasażera. Kluczyki trafiły do szczeliny w stacyjce, noga Hanka nacisnęła gaz i jego samochód odjechał, oddalając się od Sunset Beach.

Tydzień później

Hank wysłał Seamusowi Camphorowi III tysiąc dolarów za terierkę jack russell. Seamus wielokrotnie telefonował do niego od czasu Memorial Day. Kiedy Hank wreszcie zdecydował się odebrać telefon, Seamus powiedział z cichą wściekłością:

– Chcę to dobrze zrozumieć. Płacisz mi tysiąc dolarów za to, żebyś mógł zatrzymać pieska moich dzieci?

– Mogę podnieść stawkę jeszcze o pięćset.

– Ich pieska, z którym uciekłeś?

Hank był na polu golfowym, stał przy pierwszym dołku.

– Zawsze możesz tu podjechać i ją zabrać.

– A może raczej odeślesz nam ją tutaj samolotem.

– Wierz mi, jest wrakiem psa. Nie wytrzymałaby takiej podróży.

– Co się z tobą dzieje, chłopie? – Seamus zakaszlał. – Masz szczęście, do cholery, że nasi ojcowie byli spokrewnieni, to wszystko, co mam do powiedzenia na ten temat.

– Nic ze mną nie jest.

Po chwili przerwy Seamus znów się odezwał:

– Chodzi o twoją małą, tak? O Tess?

Hank był zadowolony, że Seamus nie może zobaczyć, jak się teraz wzdrygnął. Była to prawda. Tess i Stella stały się nierozłączne. Terierka spała u stóp łóżka Tess i warowała w wykuszowych oknach drewnianego wiktoriańskiego domu w Oakwood, w centrum Raleigh, niczym wartowniczka, dopóki dziewczynka nie wróciła z przedszkola.

Nie chciał mieć dzieci. To Susan przypomniała mu po pięciu latach małżeństwa, że potomstwo stanowiło część ich umowy. Ale Hank za bardzo lubił nurkować na Turks i Caicos albo jeździć na nartach w Telluride.

– Chociaż jedno.

– Dzieci nas spowolnią.

– Pomogą nam zachować młodość.

– A jeżeli okażę się kiepskim ojcem?

– Jesteś wspaniałym facetem. Poza tym nasze dzieci będą ładne.

Próbowali zajść w ciążę przez dwa lata i odwiedzili z problemem niepłodności kilku specjalistów. Kiedy matka Hanka dowiedziała się, że mają kłopoty, szepnęła Susan do ucha na *Weselu Figara*:

– A nie szykuje się przypadkiem jakaś konferencja na temat zasobów ludzkich, na którą mogłabyś pojechać?

Susan podniosła się z miejsca, mimo że przedstawienie jeszcze trwało.

– Kim jest ta oszustka, która podszywa się pod twoją matkę, Hank? Czy my na pewno znamy tę kobietę?

Tego wieczoru po powrocie do domu Hank zabrał Susan do garażu i położył ją na masce mercedesa. Podciągnął jej rozkloszowaną spódnicę, ściągnął majtki i kochał się z żoną wyjątkowo zawzięcie, chociaż zarazem czule. Kiedy dokładnie dziewięć miesięcy później, co do jednego dnia, Susan urodziła córkę, okazało się, że mała ma jego stalowoniebieskie oczy. Zrozumiał, że Tess to na pewno jego dziecko.

Wkrótce po narodzinach dziewczynki zaczął grać w golfa.

– Coś ci powiem, Hank – odezwał się Seamus. – Nasze społeczeństwo bardziej potrzebuje strażaków niż chirurgów. – I odesłał Hankowi pocztą czek, na którym napisał to samo czerwonym długopisem.

– Do zobaczenia za rok, w maju. – Hank zdumiał się, słysząc swoje słowa i zdając sobie sprawę, że na jakimś najogólniejszym, najbardziej podstawowym poziomie mówi zupełnie poważnie.

KRAINA KOLORÓW

2010

DWA MIESIĄCE PO święcie Memorial Day Hank Camphor dostał pocztą elektroniczną wiadomość od swojego przyrodniego brata, Rufusa Vincenta, że on i jego rodzina wracają właśnie z Georgii do domu, do Nowego Jorku, i chcą zatrzymać się w Raleigh. Może spotkaliby się gdzieś na „neutralnym gruncie", żeby wypić kawę albo zjeść lunch. Hankowi spodobało się, że Rufus ujął „neutralny grunt" w cudzysłów, bo w ten sposób dawał do zrozumienia, że wie, że nie należy przekraczać pewnych granic.

SPOTKALI SIĘ W HOLU gmachu Krainy Kolorów, świeżo wyremontowanego czteropiętrowego centrum sztuk i rzemiosł w śródmieściu Raleigh, gdzie dbano o rodzącego się w każdym dziecku Picassa. Na każdym piętrze co innego: graffiti na ścianach i starych gimbusach, krzykliwie kolorowa moda i sprzęt gospodarstwa domowego, boksy, w których można było projektować, malować albo za pomocą szablonów ozdabiać paski do spodni i portfele, a także klosze do lamp, które jedni zabierali do domu, a drudzy wysyłali znajomym w prezencie na urodziny albo święta Bożego Narodzenia. Największe zainteresowanie gości budziła duża, bulgocąca fontanna – płynne, zmywalne kredki tryskały z niej prosto do foremek, które dzieciaki mogły zanieść do laboratorium Krainy Kolorów i utwardzić ich zawartość. Rodzice i dzieci musieli wkładać płaszcze przeciwdeszczowe, bo Płynna Fontanna, tak jak wodospad Niagara, słynęła z unoszącej się w powietrzu mgiełki. Inną wielką atrakcją była mieszcząca się na trzecim piętrze tak zwana dżunglowa sala gimnastyczna, labirynt składanych ścianek i rur o różnych kształtach i wielkościach, zmieniających kolor, kiedy dzieci przechodziły przez nie na czworakach, koziołkowały, turlały się, szły na huśtawki – służące też jako drabinki lub skrzynie gimnastyczne – albo pograć w kulki, najodważniejsze zjeżdżały zaś w górze tyrolką, śmigając na linie tuż obok sklepu z pamiątkami, gdzie zawodowi wyznawcy Tespisa, przebrani za pędzle malarskie, flamastry i kartki, śpiewali, tańczyli i występowali dla dzieci, które najbardziej lubiły obdarzony soczystym barytonem jasnoczerwony ołówek numer dwa. Ołówek zawsze flirtował z kartką. „Jestem piszącym drewienkiem – powtarzał często. – I na co komu długopis?"

Hank rozejrzał się po wielkim holu. Uznał, że panuje tu nieznośna wrzawa, i dopiero teraz zaczął się domyślać, dlaczego Susan wybrała akurat to miejsce.

RUFUS, JEGO ŻONA I DZIECI przywieźli prezenty dla Tess: całą torbę książek z Books of Wonder, ich ulubionej księgarni na Manhattanie. Oboje pracowali na uniwersytecie, więc można się było spodziewać, że przywiozą książki. Hank ucieszył się, że Susan wpadło do głowy wręczyć im w prezencie dwie zabawki od Jerome'a Jenkinsa, który za ich projekt dostał nawet nagrodę. Hank i Rufus byli tego samego wzrostu, co Hank zauważył natychmiast – ale preferujący swobodną postawę Rufus garbił się trochę, dając Hankowi złudzenie, że jego przyrodni brat jest od niego odrobinę niższy. Luz Rufusa było widać także po niedbałym sposobie ubierania się – nosił czyste, drogie ciuchy, które wyglądały jednak na lekko wymięte.

Hank nie mógł sobie przypomnieć, żeby w zdawkowych mejlach, które wymieniał z Rufusem, jego przyrodni brat wspominał o tym, że jego – ich – ojciec, James Samuel Vincent, przyjedzie razem z nimi. Ale przyjechał. Barbara wybrała dla Charlesa idealnego zastępcę – kochanka, z którym mogła wyprodukować syna, ani przez chwilę niebudzącego ojcowskich podejrzeń co do jego pochodzenia. Zarówno zmarły przybrany ojciec Hanka, jak i ojciec biologiczny byli przystojni i niebieskoocy, tyle tylko że James Vincent miał ciemne włosy, a Charles jasne jak piasek.

– NO, NO! – JAMES SAMUEL VINCENT wysforował się przed Rufusa i podał Hankowi rękę. Najwyraźniej nie zdawał sobie sprawy, że zasłania mu przyrodniego brata i jego żonę, Claudię. Hank przesunął się nieznacznie w bok, ściskając dłoń biologicznemu ojcu, zauważając jednak prostą, koszulową bladozieloną sukienkę i płowe sandały Claudii. Mocno trzymała swoje dzieci za ręce, jak gdyby bała się, że mogłyby się jej wyrwać. Córka Hanka, Tess, jak zawsze najbardziej nieśmiała, chowała się za plecami rodziców. Susan i Hank byli niczym drzewa, które dawały jej cień.

– Nie spodziewałem się, że w Krainie Kolorów będzie taki tłok.

– Wystarczy zmienić końcówkę drugiego rzeczownika i można powiedzieć, że jesteśmy w Krainie Kolorowych – zauważył Rufus Vincent. Odwrócił się do żony i oboje wybuchnęli śmiechem. Hank poczuł, że jego twarz oblewa ciepły rumieniec zakłopotania.

– Winona i Elijah przez cały tydzień nie mogli się doczekać tego wyjazdu – powiedziała Claudia, podając Hankowi rękę.

Hank skinął głową.

– Miło mi, Claudio.

Ucieszył się, że Susan przewidująco zamówiła tak zwane bilety priorytetowe, bo mogli ominąć długą kolejkę oczekujących i wejść od razu do środka. Przy drzwiach rodzice musieli podpisać oświadczenie, że zrzekają się roszczeń wobec firmy, jeśli w Krainie Kolorów ich dzieci zginą lub doznają jakichś obrażeń. Następnie wszyscy dostali firmowe opaski, które należało nosić na przegubie.

– Pomyślałam, że Claudia i ja weźmiemy dzieciaki na górę, do sali gimnastycznej, a wam, panowie, pozwolimy nadrobić stracony czas i pogadać w kawiarni – powiedziała Susan.

Claudia się uśmiechnęła.

– To jest chyba doskonały pomysł.

Hank starał się nie okazać rozczarowania. Patrzył, jak Rufus całuje żonę na pożegnanie.

– Tylko żadnych produktów mlecznych – powiedział na odchodnym.

Susan poprowadziła Claudię i dzieci na górę. To zwykle ona zabierała Tess do Krainy Kolorów. Znała to miejsce na wylot. „Wystarczy zmienić końcówkę drugiego rzeczownika – pomyślał Hank – i można powiedzieć, że jesteśmy w Krainie Kolorowych". Przez cały ten rozgardiasz zapomniał pocałować żonę. A ona zapomniała pocałować jego.

KAWIARNIA W KRAINIE KOLORÓW przypominała jadłodajnię z lat pięćdziesiątych: czarno-białe kafelki, obite czerwonym skajem krzesła i boksy. Zamówiona przez nich kawa okazała się wodnistymi sikami, których smak Hank pamiętał z okresu dojrzewania, z czasów, kiedy jego ciało zmieniało się i rosło, a ciekawość przymuszała go, żeby się dotykał między nogami.

Rufus siedział wpatrzony w kubek z kawą.

– Mogę powiedzieć tylko, że to naprawdę dziwne.

Hank natychmiast wstał.

– No to może znajdziemy inne miejsce? Napiszę esemesa do Susan, a potem możemy pójść do nas albo gdzieś.

– Nie. Chodziło mi o to, że dziwnie jest mieć brata i nic o tym nie wiedzieć – wyjaśnił Rufus. – I to prawie swojego rówieśnika.

– Dla naszych matek to pewnie jeszcze dziwniejsze – odparł Hank.

– Moja do niedawna nic o tym nie wiedziała. – Rufus rzucił spojrzenie Jamesowi Samuelowi. – To znaczy zawsze podejrzewała, że były jakieś kobiety, ale o tej sprawie, dopóki jej nie powiedziałem, nie miała bladego pojęcia.

Hank poruszył nieodpowiedni temat. Zazwyczaj był bardziej taktowny.

– Przepraszam – powiedział.

– Niby za co? – Rufus wzruszył ramionami. – Ty nic nie zrobiłeś.

James wyjrzał przez okno na parking. Był gorący letni dzień. Już jako mały chłopiec nie cierpiał wilgotności na Południu. Przyleciał tutaj natychmiast, gdy Rufus powiedział mu, że spotka się ze swoim przyrodnim bratem. Chciał być przy tym obecny. Ułatwić im kontakt. Działać jako mediator. A świadomość, że spłodził dwóch zdrowych synów, sprawiała mu przyjemność.

– Jaką masz specjalizację lekarską, Hank?

– Jestem chirurgiem. Specjalizuję się w medycynie sportowej.

– Operowałeś kogoś sławnego?

Hank uśmiechnął się.

– Mógłbym się powołać na tajemnicę zawodową, ale ech, co mi tam.

Pochylił się i opowiedział Jamesowi i Rufusowi o dwóch futbolistach, zawodnikach NFL, którzy ciągle łapali kontuzje, bo za dużo chlali, a potem kompromitowali się na boisku i w sypialni. Opowiadając tę historię, zauważył, że on i Rufus mają podobne ręce, smukłe, niemal delikatne palce, lecz dłonie Rufusa były w ciągłym ruchu, krążyły wokół brzegu kubka z kawą, wrzucały do niego cukier i dolewały mleko, podnosiły kubek i odstawiały go, zanim jego przyrodni brat zdążył się napić. Rufus sprawiał wrażenie znudzonego, mimo że Hank próbował go wciągnąć do rozmowy. Ostatecznie matka Hanka była kochanką jego ojca; jeżeli Hank obliczył wszystko dobrze, był o pięć miesięcy starszy od Rufusa. Miał ochotę nazwać go „młodszym braciszkiem", ale ją zwalczył.

– A jaki jest twój ulubiony sport? – zapytał z uśmiechem Hank.

– No, bejsbol – odpowiedział Rufus. – Jak byłem mały, tata często zabierał mnie na mecze Yankees.

– Mój ojciec... – Hank urwał. – To znaczy... Charles Camphor, facet, który zawsze będzie moim ojcem, chodził do Clemson. Był skrzydłowym. Futbol to najpopularniejszy sport na Południu.

– Nigdy nie rozumiałem tej dyscypliny. Wolę europejską piłkę nożną. Tak, ten sport jest interesujący – powiedział Rufus, gryząc mieszadełko do kawy.

– A ty grałeś w futbol na studiach, Hank? – spytał James.

Hank spojrzał na Rufusa.

– Niektórzy za frapujący sport uważają też futbol amerykański, bo to gra strategiczna. I skomplikowana. Dużo się tam dzieje na boisku, chociaż nie wszyscy to widzą. – Hank zwrócił się z kolei do Jamesa Vincenta. – Biegam. Codziennie sześć mil. Nie miałem odpowiednich warunków fizycznych, żeby uprawiać futbol. W Duke byłem w drużynie lekkoatletycznej.

– Ja też biegam – zaśmiał się Rufus. – Z jednej sali wykładowej do drugiej.

James objął Rufusa ramieniem.

– Rufus jest badaczem twórczości Jamesa Joyce'a. Być może najlepszym w Stanach. – Powiedział to z taką pewnością siebie i dumą, że Rufus odstawił kubek i przez chwilę wyglądał na zaskoczonego.

– Dlaczego akurat Joyce? – spytał Hank.

– Nie wiem. Pewnie przeczytałem go w odpowiednim momencie.

– Moja rodzina zbierała kartofle – oświadczył James Samuel.

– Nie wiedziałem. – Smukłe palce Rufusa wciąż okrążały kubek.

– Oczywiście, że wiedziałeś.

– Wciąż nie wiem wielu rzeczy – powiedział Rufus.

James wzruszył ramionami.

– Maine. Dobre łowiska ryb. Marna ziemia uprawna. Jeden z czterech synów. Twój dziadek. Mój stary. W każdym razie tak mówił, jak sobie wypił. W tamtych czasach ludzie musieli niekiedy wybierać, córka czy syn. Ciągnęli słomki, żeby zdecydować, kto pójdzie na studia. Najdłuższą wyciągnął mój ojciec. Wyjechał do Bostonu i nigdy nie patrzył w przeszłość. Został strażakiem.

– Ach tak... W mojej rodzinie też byli strażacy – powiedział Hank.

– No to podtrzymujemy jakąś tradycję – stwierdził James Samuel, patrząc na Hanka, ale trącając Rufusa łokciem. – Jeżeli chodzi o Joyce'a... Joyce jest jak ziemia.

Rufus odchylił się do tyłu.

– Tato, co ty, kurwa... Teraz zostałeś jeszcze znawcą Joyce'a?

James zwrócił się do Rufusa.

– Gorący kartofel wyleczy cię z jęczmyka. Surowy kartofel pod pachami działa lepiej niż dezodorant. Jak włożysz kartofel do buta, nie złapiesz przeziębienia. Oto, proszę ja was, encyklopedia chłopaka ze wsi.

Hank na chwilę przypomniał sobie, w jakiej komitywie pozostawał z człowiekiem, którego nazywał tatą, zwłaszcza w liceum i na studiach. Tęsknił za nim.

– Musicie się jakoś ze sobą dogadać, chłopaki – powiedział James.

Na owalnej ladzie stały babeczki oraz ogromne lizaki w różne esy-floresy i kolorowe smugi. Hank kazał tespijskim ołówkom, długopisom i kartkom trzymać się z daleka i ukradkiem wręczył im suty napiwek, żeby zostawili ich w spokoju. Rufus wstał.

– Chce ktoś lizaka? Bo ja tak.

Hank wybuchnął śmiechem. Myślał, że Rufus stroi sobie żarty.

– Nie – odparł. – Ja dziękuję.

– Co w tym śmiesznego?

– Nie wiem. Nic – odpowiedział przepraszająco Hank.

– To kup sobie lizaka – zwrócił się do Rufusa James. – I weź po jednym dla dzieciaków. Dla Winnie, Elijaha i Bess.

– Tess – poprawił go Hank.

Rufus nachylił się bliżej.

– Córka Hanka ma na imię Tess, tato.

– Tak, Tess – zgodził się James. – Na pewno też by chciała.

Rufus spojrzał na Hanka.

– Ojciec miał wypadek. Uderzył się w głowę i teraz czasami źle słyszy.

Z tymi słowy odszedł od stolika.

– Opowiedz mi o tej kontuzji – poprosił Hank.

James Samuel wysiorbał resztę swojej kawy.

– Jak tam twoja matka? Znaczy Barbara?

– Jest szczęśliwą mężatką i mieszka w Europie.

– Czym się zajmuje jej mąż?

Hankowi wydało się, że w tym pytaniu było słychać niecierpliwość.

– Hoduje angielskie psy myśliwskie.

– Nigdy nie wyobrażałem sobie Barbary na farmie hodowlanej.

– Tylko jak?

– Nie za granicą.

Teraz to Hank się zjeżył. Nie podobało mu się, że James pyta o Barbarę za plecami syna, choć z drugiej strony byłby zawiedziony, gdyby jego biologiczny ojciec w ogóle nie zainteresował się matką.

– No, z tego, co słyszałem, spotykaliście się tylko kilka razy w roku, więc może po prostu niewiele o niej wiesz.

James zmierzył go spojrzeniem.

– Ludzka wiedza jest w ogóle ograniczona.

Hank wyciągnął komórkę i pokazał Jamesowi zdjęcie Barbary. Siedziała przed świąteczną choinką w brzydkim świątecznym swetrze, w towarzystwie męża, Trevora, i nowego psiego miotu.

– Barbara – powiedział James, dotykając telefonu.

– To już przegrana sprawa – odezwał się Hank. – Lepiej nic nie kombinuj.

– Jestem szczęśliwie żonaty – odpowiedział James.

– To dlaczego nie ma tu twojej żony?

– A ty chciałbyś być ze mną na jej miejscu, gdybyś miał poznać syna swojego męża, i to syna z nieprawego łoża, bo poczętego z kochanką w czasie małżeństwa z pierwszą żoną?

– Więc powiedziałeś jej?

– Dopiero kiedy sama się domyśliła – odparł James. – Adele się domyśliła. Inteligentne kobiety potrafią się domyślić takich rzeczy.

Gdy Rufus wrócił do stolika, Hank szepnął mu do ucha:

– Przepraszam cię za to, co nasz ojciec zrobił twojej matce. Ale w gruncie rzeczy gdyby nie on, żadnego z nas nie byłoby na świecie.

WYCIECZKA PO KRAINIE KOLORÓW trwała godzinę i piętnaście minut, a dzieciaki błyskawicznie znalazły wspólny język. Tess, Winona i Elijah biegali po dżunglowej sali gimnastycznej i bawili się pod Płynną Fontanną, dopóki znienacka nie dopadło ich przeciążenie sensoryczne; wtedy zaczęli marudzić, poczuli się zmęczeni i wybuchnęli płaczem, gdy przyszła pora się pożegnać.

– Winnie chce poznać Stellę! – wrzasnęła Tess, kiedy Hank wziął ją na ręce i próbował uciszyć. W duchu był zachwycony. Córeczka podsunęła mu pretekst, którego potrzebował, żeby zmienić to popołudnie w wieczór.

– No tak – zaśmiał się, teraz bardziej swobodny i pewny siebie. – Mam już paru stukniętych krewnych w rodzinie i prawdę mówiąc, Susan to potwierdzi, nie byliśmy pewni, czego się po was spodziewać.

Rufus skinął głową.

– My po was też nie.

Hank zauważył, że dzieci Rufusa kleją się do Jamesa Samuela. Naszło go nieokreślone uczucie, które chciał od siebie odsunąć. Spojrzał na Claudię i pomyślał przelotnie o Lonnie Applewood sprzed wielu lat.

– Jeżeli macie ochotę, to może później, jak dzieci się trochę zdrzemną, zjemy wczesną kolację u nas w domu?

– Byłoby wspaniale – odparł James.

Hank rzucił jednak to pytanie niejako obok niego, Rufusowi i Claudii.

– Claudio? – Rufus zwrócił się do żony.

– To twoja decyzja – odrzekła.

Najwyraźniej oboje bili się z jakimiś myślami. Hank zauważył to na podstawie mowy ich ciał. Pomiar temperatury. Letnia; ani gorąca, ani zimna.

A OTO JAK WYGLĄDA ta kolacja. W pewnym momencie, kiedy dzieci są już po jedzeniu i bawią się w pokoju, Hank zabiera gości na spacer, bo musi wyjść ze Stellą, którą kocha coraz bardziej, ponieważ ona tak dobrze traktuje Winonę i Elijaha, a oni ze swojej strony tarmoszą sunię z czułością. Susan przebrała już Tess w piżamkę w jednorożce, a jej kuzyn Elijah przeczytał opowiadanie *The Funky Snowman* ze swojej ulubionej książeczki, ale Tess i Winona nie zaczęły jeszcze zaplatać i rozplatać włosów lalce American Girl o imieniu Kaya, a kiedy Winona mówi, że nie wolno jej mieć lalki American Girl, Tess pyta dlaczego i Elijah patrzy na Winonę, dając jej do zrozumienia, żeby siedziała cicho. James Samuel Vincent wypił już trzecie martini, Hank zapytał, dokąd jadą później, a Claudia odpowiedziała, że do Nowego Jorku, tylko wpadną jeszcze odwiedzić jej chorą matkę w Georgii. James odparł, że on leci do Nowego Jorku jutro, a przyjechał tutaj tylko po to, żeby spotkać się ze swoim drugim synem. Rufus jeszcze nie zaczął się kołysać w przód i w tył na czubkach palców, podziwiając pięknie oprawione w skórę książki, których Hank nie czyta – nigdy nie był zapalonym czytelnikiem, gromadzi jednak bibliotekę na czas emerytury – chociaż Claudia, fałszując jak jej matka, zaśpiewała już Winonie kołysankę z myślą, że Rufus weźmie potem córkę, a ona będzie mogła spać dalej przez całą drogę w samochodzie. Dziękuje Bogu, że Winona ostatnimi czasy sypia na ogół spokojnie. Hank nie wyszedł jeszcze na papierosa, a James nie zdrzemnął się ze szklanką w ręku, ale Claudia poszła już do łazienki, natomiast Hank, który również wypił dzisiaj więcej, niż powinien, podglądał ją przez przesuwne drzwi na patio, idącą do łazienki, a później zgasił papierosa i wszedł do przedpokoju.

WIDZĄC ROZKOŁYSANĄ ŻÓŁTĄ SUKIENKĘ, w którą Claudia przebrała się na wieczór, chce uciec z czasem pod rękę jak z kochanką, postawić księżyc na głowie, a słońce przewrócić na brzuch i zawrócić bieg zdarzeń, aby znów stać się trzynastoletnim chłopcem, który stoi przed drzwiami domu sąsiadów. To właśnie w tym momencie decyduje, że powinien pójść prosto do biblioteki, usiąść i pogadać z Rufusem, bo ich stary już drzemie, lecz okazuje się, że jakimś cudem nogi niosą go w stronę drzwi łazienki, przy których staje i czeka, aż wyjdzie z nich Claudia. W toalecie spływa woda, szumi niczym morze, płynie, pluszcze jak jezioro, a gdy Claudia otwiera drzwi, wita go coś, co przypomina jak gdyby rzeczny prąd, i wtedy Hank, podpity, nieporadny, nachyla się i próbuje wycisnąć na jej ustach pocałunek, którego żonie Rufusa udaje się uniknąć.

– No tak – mówi Claudia, patrząc, jak Hank opiera się o ścianę. – Ktoś tu za dużo wypił.

– Przypominasz mi kogoś, kogo znam. Znałem.

Claudia przechyla głowę na bok i przez chwilę Hank jest pewien, że wpatruje się w twarz Lonnie Applewood i słyszy jej głos.

– Drogi przyjacielu, czy nie wszystkim nam się tak czasem wydaje?

Nie potrafi odgadnąć, czy Claudia jest rozbawiona, czy zirytowana. Wymija go i wraca do gabinetu. Hank opanowuje się i idzie za nią pogrążonym w półmroku korytarzem. W gabinecie Rufus mówi coś pod nosem do jakiejś książki, Claudia już nalała sobie drinka, Susan nastawiła muzykę klasyczną, James Samuel chrapie, a Rufus po chwili podnosi wzrok i odzywa się do Hanka, coraz wolniej przebiegając nerwowymi palcami po grzbietach pięknych książek:

– Cieszę się, że udało nam się doprowadzić do tego spotkania.

Hank patrzy, jak Rufus ciasno oplata ramionami biodra Claudii. Jego gest skłania Hanka, by zrobić to samo z Susan.

– Tak – mówi cicho Hank. – Mam nadzieję, że zbytnio was nie rozczarowaliśmy.

Bundesarchiv, Bild 183-1983-0121-500
Foto: o.Ang. | 1932

ELOISE ODLATUJE

(CZĘŚĆ DRUGA)

1970 1978 1988 1989 1999 2010

NA ULICY NIEDALEKO FRIEDRICHSHAIN I MIESZKANIA, w którym Eloise Delaney wciągnęła powietrze do płuc po raz ostatni, stoi dziś klub taneczny. Znalazł siedzibę w dawnej hurtowni lodówek, niedaleko muru berlińskiego. W takie wieczory jak dziś przez okna widać tu i ówdzie tańczące, kołyszące się sylwetki; suną niczym mgła i cienie pod światłami, które migają, ciemnieją i wysyłają pulsujące, gorące zaproszenia dla młodych ludzi.

JEST WŚRÓD NICH GRUPA AMERYKAŃSKICH ŻOŁNIERZY, głównie czarnoskórych i latynoskich. Przyjechali z bazy w Londynie, zameldowali się w berlińskim hotelu Marker, po czym wyszli na grudniowy mróz w poszukiwaniu muzyki, nocnego życia i niemieckich kobiet. Wysypują się z zatłoczonej taksówki i dołączają do kolejki klubowiczów. Wszędzie czuć zapach palonej marihuany. Jeden z żołnierzy, drobnej budowy i z urlopowym zarostem, pochodzi z Buckner County w Georgii – z tego samego miasta, w którym urodziła się Eloise. Są dalekimi kuzynami, chociaż on o tym nie wie. Kiedy miał dwa latka, podrzucała go ostrożnie na kolanach, ale Eloise już teraz nie żyje – zmarła kilka lat wcześniej. Z punktu widzenia naszego świata nie jest ani jego częścią, ani wspomnieniem.

W 1972 ROKU POSZŁA na wesele Kinga Tyrone'a o kulach. Jedyny porządny kuzyn w jej rodzinie ożenił się jako pięćdziesięciolatek z wymagającą i kapryśną kobietą, zwaną Sarah Braun, która dziewięć miesięcy później urodziła mu córkę. Wesele odbyło się na molo Tybee Island, państwo młodzi za plecami mieli Atlantyk, a przed sobą nieliczną grupkę gości.

Przyjęcie było dosyć skromne, chociaż na obiad podano duże porcje krewetek, ostryg, małży i strzępieli. Jeżeli nie lubiłeś darów morza, miałeś pecha.

ELOISE WRÓCIŁA DO DOMU z wojny, która wielu Amerykanom zaczynała się nie podobać, mimo że większość z nich do samego końca popierała interwencję w Wietnamie. Miała dwadzieścia pięć lat i po raz pierwszy od skierowania na front czytała amerykańskie gazety i oglądała wiadomości telewizyjne. Twarde fakty wyglądają tak, że na wojnie jedni muszą umrzeć, by drudzy mogli żyć. Wietnam dręczył Eloise w samotne wieczory, czyli bardzo często, ponieważ nie miała wtedy kochanki ani kochanka. Przypomniała sobie, jak Jebediah Applewood mówił, że cały ten syf właściwie nie jest realny. Gdyby mieszkał w Buckner County, z największą przyjemnością poszłaby z nim na piwo albo dwa, albo i trzy, chociażby po to, żeby nabrać innej perspektywy. Zastanawiała się, czy którykolwiek z jej dawnych towarzyszy broni – prawie nikt nie utrzymywał z nią kontaktu – podziela jej głębokie poczucie zdrady i dezorientacji. Od czasu do czasu telefonowała do Agnes, która pozostawała na linii niemal wbrew sobie, czasami odpowiadając na pytania Eloise, a czasem zadowalając się długim milczeniem – chociaż to, że kogoś się nie znosi, wcale nie oznacza, że się go nie kocha.

PRAGNĄC PODNIEŚĆ ELOISE NA DUCHU, na Tybee Island przyjechała któregoś popołudnia Flora Applewood i zabrała ją „w takie jedno nowe miejsce” na peryferiach hrabstwa. Tym nowym miejscem okazała się Magnolia Lake Inn, dawny hotel nad brzegiem sztucznego jeziora. W najlepszym okresie goście przyjeżdżali tu całymi rodzinami na grille, pikniki i przejażdżki konne, spędzali popołudnia na piciu koktajli i słodkiej herbaty mrożonej i zajadali faszerowane jajka oraz delikatne paszteciki krabowe. Nowy właściciel zdarł starą farbę i warstwę ołowiu ze ścian i wyremontował hotel tak, żeby przypominał hollywoodzki plan filmowy. W weekendowe wieczory przyjeżdżał didżej, który puszczał płyty winylowe, a w każdą pierwszą sobotę miesiąca występował jakiś zespół jazzowy. Magnolia Lake Inn była z jednej strony eleganckim, a z drugiej swobodnym przybytkiem, gdzie mężczyzna mógł przywieźć zarówno kochankę, jak i chłopaka, a kobieta kochankę i faceta, i bez najmniejszych problemów wszyscy mogli się rozebrać, by pójść popływać nago w jeziorze o północy. Eloise zdumiała się na widok kobiet pijących alkohol i palących papierosy, i publicznie trzymających się nawzajem pod ręce, ale potem przyjrzała się nieco bliżej ciężkim zasłonom i mrocznej godzinie dnia, i nie chcąc odbierać Florze radości i animuszu, pomyślała tylko: „Na ogół jednak nadal się ukrywamy". Włóczyła się leniwie z Florą tu i tam, kuśtykając na jednej nodze, i pozwalała wszystkim gościom podpisywać się na swoim gipsie. W końcu poinformowała kochaną przyjaciółkę, że wyjeżdża na stałe do Niemiec.

– Kiedy ci mówiłam, że powinnaś opuścić Buckner County, nie chodziło mi o to, że na zawsze.

Ale jak tu powiedzieć Florze, że Buckner masakruje jej serce wspomnieniami. Wspomnienia czekały na nią na każdym rogu: zapijaczona mama, znikający tata, siostra Mary Płacząca, która chyłkiem wymyka się z klasztoru, i oczywiście Agnes: ta, której udało się uciec. I nadal trzymać się z daleka od tego miejsca.

W czasie sześciotygodniowego pobytu w Buckner County Eloise zapisała się na przyspieszony kurs pilotażu, prowadzony przez Southeast Aviation, tę samą firmę, w której pracował kiedyś Claude Johnson. Instruktor, biały facet w średnim wieku, spojrzał na jej podanie i spytał, dlaczego chce się nauczyć pilotować samolot.

Zapaliła papierosa.

– Bo chcę szybować nad tym wszystkim w powietrzu. – Po chwili, w oczekiwaniu na kolejne pytania, którymi mógłby ją zarzucić, dodała: – Na pewno słyszał pan o Bessie Coleman?

Poszukał Bessie w pamięci i podał odpowiedź, wskutek której Eloise zrewidowała swoje pierwsze wrażenie, skłaniające ją do niechęci do tego człowieka.

– To i owo.

Na początku nauczył kursantów rozróżniać typy samolotów i badać ich sprawność. Wkuwała na pamięć rozkład paneli kontrolnych i jakoś wytrzymała monotonię szkoły naziemnej, gdzie codziennie spędzała cztery godziny i musiała prowadzić dziennik lotów. Była jedyną czarną słuchaczką w sali. I pierwszą, którą instruktor nauczył latać nad lotniskiem i bagnem, gdzie widziała aligatory, z zamkniętymi oczami grzejące się w słońcu na brzegu.

– No i jak się pani czuje, panno Delaney? – spytał.

Zaśmiała się w głos.

– O ile nie rozbiję tego samolociku i nie zrobię z nas żeru dla aligatorów, to dobrze.

Krążyła pięćset, siedemset i tysiąc stóp w powietrzu, gdzie otaczały ją tylko poduszki chmur i niebo.

– Lekka jak piórko. Wydaje mi się, że w tej chwili jestem w stanie zrobić właściwie wszystko.

Wyjechała do Niemiec z amatorską licencją pilota.

W LATACH SIEDEMDZIESIĄTYCH sześćdziesiąt procent amerykańskich baz wojskowych w Europie mieściło się w Niemczech Zachodnich. Eloise wiedziała o wyczynach Bessie Coleman we Friedrichshafen i w Berlinie, ale nie o długich i skomplikowanych relacjach historycznych Niemców i Afroamerykanów.

Doktor Martin Luther King odwiedził na przykład NRD i Niemcy Zachodnie w roku 1964 i oczywiście spotkał tam czarnoskórych żołnierzy, którzy wstąpili do wojska w czasie pierwszej i drugiej wojny światowej, by służyć swojemu krajowi i walczyć z Niemcami. We Francji i w Niemczech wielu z nich zasmakowało wolności, której ciągle potem im brakowało po powrocie do domu.

PRZEZ SZESNAŚCIE MIESIĘCY stacjonowała w bazie lotniczej Ramstein, gdzie namówiono ją do przyjęcia posady w wydziale kontaktów międzyrasowych. Opracowywała metody łagodzenia napięć pomiędzy czarnymi i białymi żołnierzami w amerykańskich bazach wojskowych w całych Niemczech.

Kochana Floro,

nie lubię mieszkania w bazie. Siedzę w małym pokoiku i przekładam papiery z miejsca na miejsce. Nie nadaję się na sekretarkę, nawet jeśli wszyscy mnie wynoszą pod niebiosa. Nie po to nadstawiałam dupę w wywiadzie wojskowym w Wietnamie, żeby teraz siedzieć w biurze i prowadzić dziennik czy rekrutację albo rozwiązywać cudze spory. Czy gdybym spróbowała napisać doktorat, byłby to z mojej strony egoizm?

Twoja Eloise

Kochana Eloise,

nigdy nie rozumiałam słowa „egoizm". Czy próba napisania doktoratu uczyni Cię szczęśliwszą? Szczęśliwą?

Twoja Flora

Kochana Floro,

po roku spędzonym w Kwaterze Logistyki wydaje mi się, że nie wrócę już do czynnej służby. Postanowiłam przejść do sektora publicznego i zapisać się na studia podyplomowe na Uniwersytecie Berlińskim. Przyszłość leży w komputerach, satelitach i technologii szpiegowskiej. Może zacznę studiować kryptologię.

kryptologiczna Eloise

Kochana kryptologiczna Eloise,

no tak, to wszystko wspaniale, martwię się tylko tym, że nie piszesz nic o swoim życiu. Jak Ci się wiedzie? Masz jakąś bliską przyjaciółkę? Życie szybko przemija. A samotność to choroba.

ciekawska Flora

PS Musisz mi wyjaśnić, o co chodzi w tej całej kryptologii.

Kochana ciekawska Floro,

pierwszy miesiąc w moim mieszkaniu w Berlinie był parszywy jak diabli. Niemcy są zimni. Wiedziałam o tym, ale wielu z nich jest zimniejszych, niż się spodziewałam.

Raz przechodziłam przez ulicę na czerwonym świetle i o mało nie zabił mnie jakiś kierowca, który na dodatek jeszcze mi nawymyślał. Nie sądzę, że z powodów rasistowskich, bo oni w stosunku do siebie też nie są ciepli ani serdeczni. Mimo to dalej przechodzę na czerwonym. Po prostu nie widzę powodu, żeby stać na chodniku i tracić czas, jeżeli nie nadjeżdża żaden samochód. Jeśli już się więcej do Ciebie nie odezwę, to znaczy, że przejechał mnie jakiś zniecierpliwiony Niemiec.

Eloise, która przechodzi
na czerwonym świetle

Kochana Eloise, która przechodzisz
na czerwonym świetle,

wychodź z domu i poznawaj ludzi. Na pewno nie wszyscy Niemcy są niecierpliwi albo nikczemni. Wychodź z domu, rób więcej różnych rzeczy i więcej zwiedzaj, a kiedy będziesz to robić, pomyśl sobie o mnie. Jestem już stara. Dobry Boże, starsza, niżbym sobie tego życzyła.

zmęczona, stara Flora

Kochana zmęczona, stara Floro,

wysyłam Ci prezent, żebyś go przekazała Kingowi Tyrone'owi dla jego córeczki Deirdre. Przysłali mi jej zdjęcia, jest najsłodszym maleństwem na świecie. W ostatnim liście od Ciebie wyczułam coś jak gdyby żal nad sobą. Jeżeli czujesz się staro, to może nic by Ci nie zaszkodziło, gdybyś wzięła w ramiona coś nowego. Małe dziecko.

Ludzie mówią, że przychodzą na ten świat niewinni, ale ja myślę, że rodzą się, znając wszystkie mądrości, o których my już zdążyliśmy zapomnieć. To tylko zwykła grzechotka. Niemcy umieją produkować proste rzeczy. Jeśli Ty weźmiesz dziecko Tyrone'a na ręce, to ja wyjdę z domu i spotkam się z przyjaciółką. Chociaż muszę przyznać, że jak na mój gust Niemki są trochę zbyt blade, a ja lubię maczać palce w czekoladzie.

Eloise, która lubi maczać
palce w czekoladzie

Kochana Eloise, która lubisz
maczać palce w czekoladzie,

zaniemówiłam po Twoim ostatnim liście. Nie mam zbyt wiele do napisania ani powiedzenia. Noszenie małej Deirdre na rękach bardzo pomogło mi odświeżyć umysł. I dobrze znasz swojego kuzyna Tyrone'a. Ta grzechotka pasuje do wszystkiego. Grzechotka w kształcie ośmiornicy, jak ty coś takiego znalazłaś?

Flora, z powrotem na dobrej drodze

Kochana Floro, z powrotem na dobrej drodze,

od przyjazdu do Berlina przytyłam piętnaście funtów. Po raz pierwszy w życiu zaokrąglił mi się trochę tyłek. Takiego tyłka mogłaby mi pozazdrościć sama Diana Ross – a może nawet Agnes. Wiesz, że o niej myślę? Może dlatego tak dużo ostatnio jem. A może to po prostu ten przeklęty tutejszy chleb i ciastka. Niemcy, jak mi się zdaje, lubią podjeść tłusto. Nóżki wieprzowe, sznycel i bratwurst. To niedaleko od niektórych potraw, którymi przecież i nas karmiono w dzieciństwie. No i ten ich chleb! Mój tyłek to jego robota. Floro moja, potrafię zjeść cały koszyk pieczywa na jedno posiedzenie. A ten chleb każe mi myśleć o piekarni Gottlieb's, ciastkach lady Miller i, tak, o Agnes. Znowu do niej wracam, ale zgodnie ze złożoną Ci obietnicą zaczęłam wychodzić z domu i trochę zwiedzać miasto. Czuję się tutaj jak na Dzikim Zachodzie. Z trudem udaje mi się zorientować, kto przyjeżdża, a kto wyjeżdża. Przez jakiś czas liczba ludności w mieście spadała, ale to już historia. Berlin pozostaje na garnuszku państwa, a po zachodniej stronie przedzielonego murem miasta widać pewną otwartość i energię. Niemcy, którzy w nim zostali, i ci, którzy dopiero teraz się tu osiedlają, sprawiają wrażenie, że chcą mieszkać w Berlinie Zachodnim na stałe. Można tu naprawdę niedrogo żyć, zwłaszcza jeżeli stać cię na pewną dozę codziennego wariactwa. Skłamałabym, gdybym nazwała Berlin pięknym miastem. To nie jest Paryż, skarbie. Są tutaj puste parcele i opuszczone budynki, a ich rozległość i wielkość dla kogoś, kto przyjechał z Buckner County, stają się po prostu przytłaczające. Część tych wrażeń wiąże się z moją nauką niemieckiego, która idzie mi najlepiej, kiedy poznaję otoczenie powoli i po trochu. Na razie najbardziej podoba mi się w Berlinie to, że mogę wyjść za próg swojego domu i być, kim chcę. Nauczę się języka i mogę zacząć tu życie zupełnie od nowa. Powiedzmy tylko, że jestem wolna – w tym sensie, że mogę się oddawać różnym rozrywkom. Udało mi się zaprzyjaźnić z kilkoma ślicznymi i bezczelnymi Niemkami. W Berlinie toczy się intensywne lesbijskie życie nocne, dla każdego coś miłego. I nie trzeba się ciężko napracować, żeby wieczorem pójść z jakąś dziewczyną do łóżka albo obudzić się rano przy jakiejś ładnej buzi. Poznałam między innymi kobietę imieniem Greta – jak Greta Garbo. Studiuje na wydziale historii tutejszego uniwersytetu i jest bardzo radykalna. Ona i jej była dziewczyna mieszkają na squacie z siedmioma innymi studentkami, w Kreuzbergu. Dwa domy dalej znajduje się jedyny gejowski squat w Berlinie. Jak przyjeżdżają gliniarze, to ci faceci wkładają swoje najlepsze stroje i urządzają wspaniałą defiladę, jeśli zostają zmuszeni do opuszczenia domu. Szkoda, że Cię tu nie ma i że nie możesz im kibicować, Floro – że nie możesz ich zobaczyć. Słowa na pewno nie oddadzą tym ludziom sprawiedliwości. Dowiedziałam się, że modny slogan może stać się sposobem na życie, a sposób życia może powołać do istnienia cały ruch społeczny. Wyburza się stare domy, żeby zrobić miejsce na nowsze i bardziej nowoczesne. Postawa squattersów jest taka: dlaczego mielibyśmy pozwolić wam burzyć te domy, skoro możemy je wyremontować i zasiedlić? W Berlinie wszystko wydaje się młodzieńcze i upolitycznione. Kochanie, miejscowi studenci ciągle protestują. Mam wrażenie, że inspirują ich wydarzenia lat sześćdziesiątych w Stanach. Greta pracuje na pół etatu w Café Berio przy Nollendorfplatz. To takie miejsce, gdzie czasem jeżdżę w soboty, by obserwować ludzi i zajadać ciasto marcepanowe. Zaczęłyśmy flirtować, kiedy wylała mi gorącą kawę na kolana. O mało jej za to nie zabiłam, wiesz, ale od tamtej pory chodzimy ze sobą. Chętnie wyciąga mnie na różne wiece, i dobrze, bo w ten sposób uczę się niemieckiego znacznie szybciej niż w bazie. Ostatnio pojechałyśmy zobaczyć wystąpienie Angeli Davis. Słuchałam jej i myślałam, że tyle jest rzeczy na świecie, na których się nie znam. I że nie wystarczyłoby jednego życia, żeby je wszystkie poznać.

Eloise, która ma nową dziewczynę

Kochana Eloise, która masz nową dziewczynę,

jestem zazdrosna.

zazdrosna Flora

Kochana zazdrosna Floro,

nie bądź zazdrosna, moja słodka. Kochałam w swoim życiu tylko dwie kobiety, a jedna z nich to Ty. Greta jest śliczna. I dobra. Znosi moje ciosy, kiedy wyrzucam z siebie cały życiowy syf i walę wszystkich na oślep na prawo i lewo. Przedwczoraj robiłyśmy w jej squacie kiełbaski, a w faszerowaniu flaków surowym mięsem było coś, co przywołało we mnie wspomnienia mamy i taty, którzy przebierali kraby w przetwórni owoców morza. Greta, jej współlokatorki i ja śmiałyśmy się i dobrze bawiłyśmy. Było też sporo piwa, więc gdy już skończyłyśmy napełniać kiełbaski, wybuchnęłam płaczem, wiesz? Kiedy mnie spytały, co się stało, zbluzgałam je jak trzeba. Greta kazała wszystkim się wynosić i zapytała, co ma zrobić, żebym poczuła się lepiej. A potem się pieprzyłyśmy, bo wiesz, że to prawda, Floro, seks jest czasami jedyną rzeczą na świecie, w której można znaleźć jakiś sens. Greta miała czelność zapytać mnie, czy ona, Greta, nie jest moim fetyszem. Nie wiedziałam, co na to odpowiedzieć. To młoda studentka historii, a studenci historii niczego nie lekceważą. Powiedziałam jej prawdę, która wygląda tak, że nie marnuję ani chwili na to, żeby się zastanawiać, czy może to ja jestem jej fetyszem, kiedy przeczesuje mi palcami włosy. To nie jest uczciwa odpowiedź, oświadczyła. Szkoda, że nie możesz jej zobaczyć. Jest cała koloru lnu. Potem poszłyśmy do pubu, a ja opowiedziałam naszym znajomym pewną historię. Jak mnie porządnie podlać, to potrafię dobrze opowiadać. Zyskałam sobie dzięki temu pewien szacunek.

Eloise, która opowiada

Kochana Eloise, która opowiadasz,

takie długie milczenie. Już cztery miesiące. Od dawna nie mam od Ciebie żadnych wieści. Czy w Berlinie wszystko dobrze?

Flora, wciąż tutaj

Najdroższa Floro, która wciąż jesteś tam,

Greta skończyła studia. Zaczęła pracować jako nauczycielka w tureckiej dzielnicy, jeden przystanek od jej dawnego domu. Postanowiłyśmy zamieszkać razem. Wygląda na to, że zostałam oficjalnie udomowiona. Jak to możliwe?

zaszyta w chacie Eloise

Kochana Eloise, która zaszyłaś się w chacie,

gdybym znała odpowiedź na to pytanie, obie byłybyśmy bogate.

nie mam żalu, Flora

Kochana Floro, która nie masz żalu,

życzę Ci miłości – i szczęścia.

Twoja Eloise

W TAMTYM CZASIE Eloise nie mogła tego wiedzieć, ale lata siedemdziesiąte i początek osiemdziesiątych miały okazać się jednym z najszczęśliwszych okresów jej życia. Była to dobra dekada, żeby po zakończeniu ohydnej wojny pracować, podróżować, cieszyć się beztroską i zapomnieć o wszystkim. W Berlinie mieszkał wtedy David Bowie, który tam nagrywał płytę *Heroes*. Iggy Pop zażywał heroinę. Eloise unikała narkotyków i poszła w seks. Jej związek dobiegł końca, kiedy Greta zbudziła się pewnej nocy w mieszkaniu w Kreuzbergu i usłyszała, jak Eloise rozmawia przez telefon z inną kobietą.

– „Miłość…" – powiedziała Eloise do słuchawki.

– Kto to jest? – chciała wiedzieć Greta, gdy Eloise się rozłączyła.

– Po prostu ktoś, z kim kiedyś coś przeżyłam.

– Nie możesz. Nie powinnaś.

Zerwały ze sobą, ale od czasu do czasu uprawiały seks i pozostały bliskimi przyjaciółkami. Eloise wcisnęła gazetowy wycinek z Bessie Coleman do szuflady biurka i zapomniała o niej i o lataniu. Lubiła opowiadać i nadal to robiła, lecz nie licząc tego, o czym opowiadała, wolała nie pamiętać o przeszłości.

– **MOJA RODZINA** ze strony matki to straszni awanturnicy – powtarzała w czasie spotkań w pubach. – Wszyscy zginęli gwałtowną śmiercią: broń palna, maczety i noże. Więcej niż kilkoro moich krewnych zostało powieszonych, chociaż nie wiem, czy w ich przypadku nie należy powiedzieć, że byli raczej ofiarami przemocy. Bunt zaczął się na nizinach, na polach ryżowych, gdzie jakiś mój prapraprzodek harował jako niewolnik, a córka jakiejś mojej praprapraprzodkini, Matilda, dostała szansę pracy w domu właścicieli, bo jej skóra miała jaśniejszy kolor. W ostatniej chwili chimeryczna pani domu powiedziała jednak: „Nie, nie ta, tylko tamta", co rozwścieczyło moją praprzodkinię do tego stopnia, że spoliczkowała swoją panią i tę niewolnicę, którą pani wybrała na miejsce jej córki, a wtedy ich pan z zemsty sprzedał Matildę. Podobno moja praprapraprababcia walczyła o nią jak lwica i tak ją wychłostano, że o mało nie umarła. Kiedy wróciła do zdrowia, nie chciała pracować, tak jak i jej siedmiu zdrowych synów, mimo że i oni byli bici i chłostani. Chwycili więc za broń i zaczęli walczyć, i w końcu pan powiesił wszystkich, i przeżył tylko jeden, bo chociaż zadyndał na sznurze, to nie popękały mu kręgi szyjne. Pan zdał sobie sprawę, że są takie wojny, których nie można wygrać, a w trakcie przeglądania ksiąg rachunkowych zrozumiał, że próbując ujarzmić swoją własność, stracił prawie dziesięć tysięcy dolarów. Tymczasem najmłodszy z braci – który widział, jak bez dobrego powodu zabito jego rodzeństwo – nie dbał już o życie i włóczył się po plantacji, czekając, żeby zabrała go śmierć. No i po tym wszystkim ta dziewczyna o jaśniejszym kolorze skóry, co to pani wprowadziła ją do swojego domu, padła trupem przy podbieraniu jajek kurom, a pani domu cztery razy poroniła, i wtedy w końcu pan, który pochodził z Południa i miał w sercu bojaźń Bożą, uznał, że jego dom został przeklęty, odkupił więc moją praprapraprababcię, Matildę, która zmieniła sobie imię na Daisy*, gdy zobaczyła anemiczne stokrotki rosnące na grobach jej matki i sześciu braci. Straciła całą rodzinę, z wyjątkiem jednego słabego na umyśle brata, i jej dusza zaczęła się skłaniać do złego. Jeżeli na przykład gałąź drzewa otarła się o nią w niemiły dla niej sposób, to brała siekierę i rąbała drzewo. Pan i pani nie uprzykrzali jej życia, chociaż tłukła naczynia, nie opróżniała nocników, z których się przelewało, zostawiała otwarte drzwi do kurnika, żeby mogły do niego wchodzić lisy, i wylewała świeżą wodę na podwórko, jak tylko nosiwoda przynosił wiadra ze studni. A kiedy pluła panu w kuchni do jedzenia, nikt nie

* Daisy (ang.) – stokrotka.

odzywał się słowem, nawet najbardziej służalcze niewolnice i najbardziej oddani właścicielom niewolnicy, bo bali się jej gniewu. Pan doszedł w końcu do wniosku, że każdy kolejny wschód słońca, jaki ogląda, jest znakiem łaski boskiej. Spoglądał na moją prapraprababcię co rano i pytał: „Otrujesz mnie dzisiaj, Daisy?".

„Nie, proszę pana – odpowiadała. – Pewnikiem zrobię to jutro".

– Ale nigdy nie otruła pana ani pani, a kiedy pomarli, ona i jej niespełna rozumu brat zostali wolni... Ale wolni, żeby robić co? I dokąd iść? Podobno pewnego popołudnia na plantację wkroczył generał Sherman ze swoimi żołnierzami z Unii. – Tu Eloise urywała i popijała piwo na oczach swoich niemieckich przyjaciółek, żeby zwiększyć efekt dramatyczny. – W czasie wojny domowej Sherman zawsze maszerował na coś albo na kogoś. Kiedy zobaczył, jak Daisy kładzie muszle, konchy, na siedmiu zadbanych grobach, wysłuchał opowieści mojej prapraprababci i podał jej pochodnię.

„Puść to wszystko z dymem, młoda damo" – krzyknął, bo tak samo pragnął wygrać wojnę i tak samo z wyrachowaniem dążył do tego celu, jak Daisy była trzeźwo myśląca i okrutna.

GDY RUNĄŁ MUR BERLIŃSKI, Eloise bawiła w uroczym średniowiecznym miasteczku Lucca we Włoszech.

Obudziła się z ostrym bólem między nogami, w domu, którego nie znała, w łóżku, w podartej pościeli. Nie mogła sobie przypomnieć, gdzie była ani co robiła poprzedniej nocy, chociaż pamiętała jakiś bar, hulanki i duże ilości czerwonego wina. Wynajęła swoje mieszkanie w Kreuzbergu za cenę trzykrotnie wyższą, niż wynosił czynsz, bo chociaż rozebranie muru miało być pamiętnym wydarzeniem, nie lubiła tłumów. Perspektywa wolności była ekscytująca, lecz stanowiła też źródło podejrzeń i strachu. Niektórzy znajomi zaskoczyli ją – a chyba nikt bardziej niż Greta – nie mogli bowiem uwierzyć, że dojdzie do ponownego zjednoczenia Niemiec. Mur dzielił Berlin Wschodni i Zachodni, a teraz mieszkańcy miasta wracali do przeszłości i używali fragmentów muru jako kamieni milowych symbolizujących ważne wydarzenia – śluby, zgony albo narodziny – w historii ich życia w taki sposób, który uświadomił Eloise, że Berlin nie jest jej domem. Ona była tu tylko amerykańskim uchodźcą, wygnańcem. Nie chciała zmagać się z myślą, że Berlin, jaki znała, za chwilę będzie już inny. Tysiące amerykańskich żołnierzy – w tym wielu czarnoskórych – miało zostać odesłanych do kraju już w kilka tygodni po zburzeniu muru, a niektórzy musieli nawet zostawić w Niemczech swoje dziewczyny, żony i dzieci. Ale Eloise da sobie radę. Pracowała przecież w sektorze publicznym. I przywykła już do tego, że nie codziennie widzi ludzi o takim samym kolorze skóry jak ona. Jednak nie widzieć ich, a wiedzieć, że są gdzieś blisko – no, to jest zupełnie inna sprawa.

KOBIETA O CIEMNYCH WŁOSACH, z wyraźnie rzymskim nosem, w dżinsach i koszuli narzuconej niedbale na smukłe ciało, weszła do sypialni i pocałowała ją na dzień dobry. Łamaną włoszczyzną oznajmiła, że Hans parzy kawę, ale że jej zdaniem będzie lepiej, jeśli wyjdą na śniadanie do miasta. Eloise usiadła na łóżku, zdając sobie sprawę, że materac pod nią bulgocze – było to łóżko wodne – po czym zapatrzyła się na żółte ściany i zieloną niczym liście podłogę, wyłożoną włoskimi kafelkami. Jej ubrania leżały porozrzucane po pokoju. W ostatnich latach coraz częściej budziła się w towarzystwie obcych kobiet – i coraz więcej piła.

– Która godzina? – zwróciła się po włosku do kobiety.

– Po dwunastej – odparła nieznajoma, znów ją pocałowała, po czym powolnym krokiem wycofała się z pokoju. Eloise za żadne skarby świata nie potrafiła przypomnieć sobie jej imienia i odczuła ulgę, kiedy przeglądając swoje rzeczy, znalazła paszport i portfel wraz z całą zawartością.

TO TEN FACET, HANS, kompletnie ją zaskoczył. Weszła do kuchni ubrana, a jego zastała przygotowującego śniadanie w stroju Adama.

– Masz ochotę na bis? – zapytał, mieszając na żeliwnej patelni białka jaj. Dopiero teraz przypomniała sobie wczorajszy wieczór – obłapki z tą kobietą, Victorią, enotekę i Hansa, Hansa z Holandii, który opiekował się domem znajomego pod jego nieobecność. Ujrzała swoje odbicie w oknie wychodzącym na coś, co latem na pewno było wspaniałym ogrodem. W tej chwili wyglądała na uderzająco podobną do swojej matki. Bolały ją głowa i cipa, a jej duma doznała jakby krwotoku, ponieważ utraciła coś cennego. Był rok 1989, 9 listopada, dzień po upadku muru berlińskiego. Przekroczyła czterdziestkę i wciąż wypalała paczkę papierosów bez filtra dziennie, ale postanowiła, że lata picia i podrywania obcych kobiet oficjalnie ma już odtąd za sobą.

W LATACH DZIEWIĘĆDZIESIĄTYCH jeździła do domu raz w roku. Ona, która cieszyła się z gwałtownej śmierci Claude'a

Johnsona, zaczęła teraz szukać jego bliskich. Okazało się, że ledwo sobie radzą, są ubodzy i mają swoje demony – epidemia cracku, powolna jak strużka krwi, dotarła już nawet do nich, na Południe. Nie była bogata, ale potrafiła ciężko pracować, nawet kiedy jeszcze balangowała. Sprzedała mieszkanie z dwiema sypialniami w Kreuzbergu i zamieniła je na mieszkanie z jedną sypialnią na Simon-Dach-Strasse we Friedrichshain. Skonsultowała się z doradcą finansowym i ustanowiła skromny fundusz powierniczy dla ubogich krewnych Claude'a. Bo każda niepijąca i bezdzietna ciotka zrobiłaby coś takiego. Podczas długich spacerów po plaży z Kingiem Tyrone'em, jego żoną i ich córką, Deirdre, zauważyła, że dziewczynka dobrze zna się na ptakach, rybach i skorupiakach. Od tej pory wysyłała jej książki o rafach koralowych i innych morskich stworzeniach, a także mapy i precle w czekoladzie. Kiedy szefowie Eloise w ambasadzie amerykańskiej w Berlinie zaproponowali jej absolutnie zasłużony awans, przyjęła go. „Buckner County zawsze będzie moim domem – powiedziała Florze – ale mieszkam w Niemczech".

W ROKU 2006 położyła kwiaty na grobie Flory i bardzo płakała. W roku 2009 położyła kwiaty na grobie swojej matki i płakała mniej. Grób dla siebie wykupiła obok.

DWA DNI PO POGRZEBIE mamy spotkała przypadkiem na Main Street Agnes Christie. Było to ich pierwsze spotkanie od lat.

– Agnes – powiedziała Eloise.

– Eloise. – Agnes skinęła głową i chciała wyminąć starą przyjaciółkę. Eloise wyciągnęła rękę, żeby ją powstrzymać.

Stanęły na ulicy w chłodny jesienny dzień, a dookoła ciągle krążyli przechodnie. Eloise nagle zdała sobie sprawę, że się postarzała, ale Agnes, hmm, Agnes nadal wygląda jak Agnes, mimo że minęło tyle czasu.

– Co ty tu robisz, Agnes? Znaczy w Buckner?

– Mogłabym cię zapytać o to samo.

– Mama mi umarła.

– No, no, no – powiedziała Agnes. Zalała się łzami, a Eloise pomyślała, że to dziwne, bo jeśli nie liczyć tych dni, kiedy przynosiła Millerom krewetki, Delores Delaney w życiu nie powiedziała do Agnes więcej niż dwa słowa.

– Eddie – wykrztusiła Agnes, wyciągając starą czerwoną chusteczkę do nosa swojego męża. – Zabił go rak.

Eloise złożyła jej kondolencje, tym razem szczere.

– Bardzo ci współczuję.

– Był dobrym człowiekiem.

– Nie znałam go, ale na pewno tak.

– Skąd wiesz? Skąd możesz wiedzieć takie rzeczy, Eloise?

– Bo znam ciebie. Nie wyszłabyś za mąż za złego człowieka.

– Ale dobry człowiek może się ożenić ze złą kobietą.

– No, teraz po prostu popadasz w sprzeczność, Agnes. A ja nie umiem rozmawiać o sprzecznościach na pusty żołądek. Właśnie miałam wstąpić gdzieś na lunch. Masz ochotę pójść ze mną?

Usiadły przy stoliku w jednej z pobliskich kafejek.

– Dlaczego nie jesteś ubrana w swoim stylu? – zapytała Agnes. W jej głosie brzmiała ledwo dosłyszalna nuta dezaprobaty. Eloise miała na sobie sukienkę, a nie spodnie, żeby okazać szacunek zmarłej matce.

Kiedy usłyszała to pytanie, wstąpiła w nią pewna nadzieja.

– A chciałabyś zobaczyć mnie w spodniach?

– Po prostu cieszę się, że cię w ogóle widzę – odparła Agnes, trzepocząc rzęsami. Były równie gęste jak za ich młodych lat.

Eloise poczuła się na tyle ośmielona, żeby przełożyć powrotny lot do Niemiec na późniejszy termin. Zaprosiła Agnes na kolację następnego wieczoru – a wcześniej na drinka do hotelu, w którym zamieszkała, przy Buckner County Riverfront.

– Chyba byłoby miło. – Agnes pokazywała jej zdjęcia swoich dwóch dorosłych córek, Beverly i Claudii, oraz wszystkich wnucząt. Eloise z trudem udawała zainteresowanie.

– Moja młodsza, Claudia, jest badaczką twórczości Shakespeare'a – powiedziała Agnes.

Eloise uśmiechnęła się.

– No to Mary Płacząca byłaby zachwycona!

– Kto? – Agnes zmarszczyła nos, po czym schowała zdjęcia i portfel do skórzanej torebki.

– Siostra Mary Płacząca... Ta młoda zakonnica, która uczyła nas Shakespeare'a w St. Paul's – odpowiedziała Eloise, zapalając papierosa.

– Moja Claudia uczyła się Shakespeare'a od Eddiego, czyli swojego ojca. – Agnes wzruszyła ramionami. – Po co miałabym mówić dziewczynkom o takim miejscu jak St. Paul's? Po co w ogóle ktokolwiek miałby chcieć o tym mówić?

– Nadal popadasz ze skrajności w skrajność.
– Ale jestem raczej gorąca niż zimna.

AGNES NIE PRZYJDZIE jednak na kolację ani na drinka do hotelu Eloise tego wieczoru. A Eloise będzie siedzieć na podwójnym łóżku w pokoju wychodzącym na zanieczyszczoną rzekę, która i tak wydaje się piękna, nie brzydka. Będzie patrzeć, jak nad wodą płynie biały księżyc, i zastanawiać się, czy ten niski, krępy facet, którego widziała w Wietnamie, kiedy występował w sztuce Shakespeare'a, naprawdę dał Agnes szczęście.

I odezwie się:

– Wiedziałam, że nie przyjdzie.

I powie sobie, że w sumie to i dobrze, bo pogaduszki w kawiarni to jedno, a przyznać się do tego, że się starzejemy i siwiejemy, to drugie. „Ja wyglądam młodo, ale Agnes młodziej". Zapali papierosa i na kilka godzin pogrąży się w żalu nad sobą, zastanawiając się nad tym, czego nie pamięta. Czy o czymś zapomniała? Zamknęła serce na miłość. Stała się kimś, kto czeka. Czeka na kogoś, kto nigdy nie będzie czuł tego samego co ona. „Jak mogłaś mnie zostawić, żebym musiała tak się przed sobą obnażyć? Czego ty się tak bardzo boisz, Agnes? Wszystko, co mogło się stać, już chyba się stało, naprawdę...".

W DRODZE DO NIEMIEC przypomni sobie o Bessie Coleman, a po powrocie do domu przetrząśnie szufladę w sypialni w poszukiwaniu tego wycinka, który tak bardzo kochała jako dziecko. Przyblakł, lecz ona wciąż będzie w stanie rozpoznać na nim twarz Bessie i odczytać kilka zdań. Jeszcze w tym samym tygodniu zapisze się do szkoły pilotażu w Berlinie i odzyska miłość do latania, już po sześćdziesiątce. Od czasu do czasu będzie zapraszać swoje co odważniejsze przyjaciółki, żeby jej towarzyszyły na pokładzie. Nadal będzie się zakochiwać albo po prostu będą się jej podobały różne kobiety, które – w różnym stopniu – też ją pokochają. Ale za każdym razem przyjdzie ta nieunikniona chwila, gdy jedna z nich powie: „Nie spodziewałam się…".

A Eloise zacznie przewracać oczami i ułatwi im zadanie. „To nie twoja wina, skarbie. Ja po prostu nie nadaję się do długotrwałych związków".

Kiedy jej kochanki będą się pakować, ona będzie wychodzić do lokalnych pubów we Friedrichshain, zawsze zdąży jednak wrócić na czas, żeby sprawdzić, czy nie pakują niczego, co nie należy do nich.

W CZASIE LOTÓW swoim samolocikiem nie będzie za nimi tęsknić. Ani za nikim. Ani za niczym. Dla czystej frajdy zacznie natomiast studiować budowę silników samolotowych, składać i rozkładać je w myślach i tworzyć jakby ilustracje kobiecej anatomii: wagina, wargi sromowe mniejsze, wargi sromowe większe, szyjka macicy, macica, jajniki… I będzie myśleć: „Eloise, stałaś się żywym przykładem sprośnej staruchy".

Wciąż będzie wypalać półtorej paczki papierosów dziennie; jej jedyna słabość. I nie rzuci palenia, nawet kiedy doradzą jej to lekarze. „A kim wy jesteście, żeby mówić starej kobiecie, że nie może palić? Ja mieszkam w Berlinie".

PRZEZIĘBI SIĘ. W szpitalu przeziębienie zmieni się w zapalenie płuc. Odzyska zdrowie na tyle, by wrócić do swojego mieszkanka we Friedrichshain. Niemieccy przyjaciele zadzwonią do jej rodziny w Buckner County w stanie Georgia, gdy Eloise zachoruje po raz ostatni. Jako sześćdziesięciotrzylatka nie będzie jeszcze stara jak historia – ale nie będzie już młoda.

– **GDZIE MOJA MAMA?** Gdzie tata? Gdzie King Tyrone? Agnes? Agnes? Och, dobry Boże. Gdzie Agnes? – Na łożu śmierci Eloise podniesie wzrok na córkę Tyrone'a, Deirdre, która przyleci do niej zamiast niego, bo jej ojciec będzie zbyt schorowany i za stary, żeby odbyć podróż przez Atlantyk.

ELOISE ZŁAPIE DEIRDRE za ręce i zacznie ją wypytywać o oceany. Ku zachwytowi ciotki Deirdre zostanie biologiem morskim. Będzie wymieniać dla niej nazwy oceanów: Pacyfik, Atlantyk, Ocean Indyjski, Ocean Arktyczny, Ocean Południowy. Eloise będzie kiwać głową i ściskać ręce dziewczyny coraz mocniej, a ponieważ ma w zwyczaju walczyć do upadłego, wypowie wszystkie nienawistne myśli kłębiące się w jej głowie. „Ciociu – szepnie Deirdre – wyrzuć to z siebie". Eloise spojrzy ponad jej ramieniem, gdzie zauważy Florę, swoich rodziców i siostrę Mary Płaczącą. Poszybują w jej stronę, podźwigną ją z łóżka i poniosą w trumnie jak żałobnicy. Będą się śmiać i rozmawiać głucho, a ich słowa zabrzmią szmerem w uszach Eloise, która zacznie wszystkich przeklinać po angielsku i niemiecku.

– Wyciągnijcie mnie z tej jebanej skrzyni. Co jest z wami? Dokąd mnie niesiecie? Gdzie jest Agnes? Wyciągnijcie mnie z tej skrzynki! Chcę zostać skremowana. Zmieniłam zdanie. Nie zakopujcie mnie w ziemi, rozumiecie?

Zmarli będą jednak spacerować z Eloise, leżącą w trumnie niczym dziecko w wózku, a ona – albo to co nazywamy duszą – wyfrunie ze wzburzeniem przez okno sypialni, po czym przeleci koło trzepoczącej na wietrze trójkolorowej flagi i starej hurtowni na tej samej ulicy, zajętej przez nowych squattersów, którzy poruszają się jak cienie pod latarniami, gasnącymi i zapalającymi się na przemian w zależności od tego, jak fachowo okoliczni mieszkańcy kradną prąd elektryczny. Tu dusza Eloise na ułamek sekundy się zatrzyma, żeby zarejestrować cichą muzykę. Ale żadnej muzyki nie słychać.

„Dzień dobry.
Do widzenia.
Pocałujcie mnie w moją czarną dupę".

Jest tylko głos Eloise, płynący ku niebu na spotkanie wiatru, deszczu i słońca.

ILE WAŻY ALIGATOR

2010

CÓRKI AGNES ZDZIWIŁY SIĘ, gdy oświadczyła, że wraca do Georgii, żeby dołączyć do wielkiej fali miastowych emerytów z Północy, którzy posprzedawali swoje domy, musieli je oddać za długi, uciekali przed dysfunkcyjnymi dziećmi i wnukami albo po prostu mieli nadzieję połączyć się ze swoimi bliskimi i umrzeć tam, gdzie kiedyś przyszli na świat. Dla Agnes ta podróż była jednak mniej sentymentalna i bardziej skomplikowana. Dokuczały jej paraliżujące napady reumatyzmu. Czasami, kiedy wychodziła ze swojego mieszkania przy rogu Riverside i 155 Ulicy, wiatr wygrywał dręczące melodie w jej stawach. A teraz, dwa lata po śmierci

Eddiego, nie miała już do dyspozycji żadnych znajomych rąk, które złagodziłyby bóle chińskim balsamem tygrysim. W miesiącach zimowych często czuła się jak więźniarka – za bardzo bała się mrozów, żeby wychodzić z domu. Oddała więc mieszkanie Beverly i jej czworgu dzieciom i wyjechała do Georgii, w poszukiwaniu cieplejszego klimatu, a także tych kilkorga rozproszonych przyjaciół i członków rodziny, którzy tam jeszcze zostali. Szokująco duża liczba jej znajomych przytyła, oślepła, zachorowała na cukrzycę i musiała się poruszać o balkonikach i laskach. Przyglądali się Agnes podejrzliwie.

– Z jakiej krynicy młodości piłaś, co?

– Krynica młodości – odpowiadała, wpatrując się w krzywo starte podeszwy swoich sneakersów Aerosoles. – Przez pół życia mieszkałam w Nowym Jorku i zawsze wszędzie jeździłam, ale dziś sobie myślę, że urodziłam się po to, żeby chodzić pieszo.

W takich chwilach cieszyła się, że wynajęła małe mieszkanie z jedną sypialnią niedaleko miejscowej biblioteki. Cieszyła się, że kupiła używanego saaba w kolorze leśnej zieleni i w razie potrzeby mimo wszystko mogła podjechać do marketu albo na odbywający się raz w tygodniu targ rolny, albo żeby załatwiać różne sprawy. Nie była religijna, ale codziennie rano po wstaniu z łóżka odmawiała bezgłośną modlitwę.

– Boże, błogosław moim rękom i nogom.

PRZEZ TRZY DNI w tygodniu pracowała w bibliotece, a dwa razy na tydzień uczyła angielskiego meksykańskich imigrantów, którzy przyjechali do Buckner pracować w pobliskiej przetwórni kurczaków. To Beverly wpadła na pomysł, żeby Agnes zapisała się na kurs lektorki angielskiego i zdała egzamin przed wyjazdem na Południe.

– Mamo – powiedziała Beverly. – Ja po prostu wiem, że jeżeli czegoś ze sobą nie zrobisz, to wpadniesz w depresję, kiedy tam pojedziesz.

Ale to jej młodsza córka, Claudia, i jej mąż, Rufus, w ramach pożegnalnego prezentu zapisali Agnes na kurs i opłacili go, podobnie jak bilet lotniczy i koszty przeprowadzki.

DO BIBLIOTEKI WSZEDŁ czarnoskóry chłopiec, na oko dziesięcioletni, który zapytał o książkę pod tytułem *The Maganetic Stone**. Agnes najpierw sprawdziła tę pozycję w internetowym katalogu naukowym, sądząc, że może nie zna tego rodzaju kamienia. Dopiero za trzecim razem przejrzała katalog ogólny i wtedy wyświetlił się jej *The Magician's Stone***. Odwróciła monitor w stronę chłopca i wskazała tytuł:

– O to ci chodzi?

Chłopak zamrugał. Miał trójkątną twarz i jak wydało się Agnes, za małe oczy w stosunku do głowy.

– No tak – odpowiedział.

Z czystej ciekawości (nie lubiła myśleć, że jest okrutna) upuściła dwie ćwierćdolarówki, trzy dziesięciocentówki i jednego centa na wyłożoną linoleum podłogę. Obserwowała z zainteresowaniem toczące się monety i chłopca,

---

* Tytuł fikcyjny i zniekształcony – powinien ewentualnie brzmieć *The Magnetic Stone* (magnes, dosłownie „kamień magnetyczny").

** *Kamień czarodzieja.*

pragnąc się przekonać, jak został wychowany w domu i czy je podniesie.

– Ile my tu mamy? – powiedziała wesoło. Ostatnia moneta ocieplała jej dłoń. Chłopiec stał przy stanowisku informacyjnym i odliczał osiemdziesiąt jeden centów, poruszając ustami. Agnes spojrzała na niego, usiłując wzbudzić w sobie litość, tak samo jak próbowała nie przechwalać się swoimi pięknymi wnukami, Elijahem i Winoną, które już w wieku dwóch lat umiały czytać, odejmować i dodawać. Przyglądając się chłopcu, czuła w gardle kwaśny smak, przypominający zgniły owoc kiwi. Głupota chłopaka skierowała myśli Agnes na jej bardziej niepewne wnuczęta: Minervę, Orzeszka, Keishę i Lamara. W złe dni w bibliotece, kiedy dzieci zachowywały się głośno i niegrzecznie, a ona musiała wzywać ochroniarza, żeby wyprowadził je albo uciszył, często wstrzymywała oddech i zastanawiała się, na kogo wyrosną dzieci jej córki Beverly. Nie widziała ich od Bożego Narodzenia.

– Ile masz lat, kochanie? – zapytała.

– Dziesięć – odpowiedział chłopiec.

A zatem trafnie odgadła jego wiek. Powiedziała, żeby zatrzymał drobne, i ukradkiem wsunęła mu jeszcze do ręki nowiutkiego dolara. Po pracy powędrowała pieszo na pocztę aż pięć ulic dalej i w ramach pokuty wrzuciła do skrzynki kopertę z kartką pocztową z napisem „Tęsknię". Dołączyła do niej czterdzieści dolarów, po dziesięć dla każdego dziecka Beverly.

DWA DNI PO TYM, jak chłopak wypożyczył *The Magician's Stone*, wrócił do biblioteki i poprosił Agnes, żeby kupiła od niego baton czekoladowy, bo jego szkoła zbiera pieniądze na cel dobroczynny. Kupiła cztery i powiedziała, żeby więcej nie zawracał jej głowy. Szkoła Purvis Middle stała po drugiej stronie ulicy, dokładnie naprzeciwko biblioteki. Trzy razy w tygodniu, na jakieś czterdzieści minut przed zamknięciem, jej dyrektor przychodził poszperać na półkach z literaturą non-fiction. Wilson Tart niezwykle powoli przeglądał dział sportowy, po czym podchodził do stanowiska dyżurnej bibliotekarki z jedną albo dwiema biografiami jakichś sportowców w ręku, najczęściej dawnych murzyńskich besjbolistów z Negro League, jak na przykład „czarny Babe Ruth", Josh Gibson. Agnes podzielała upodobanie dyrektora Tarta do literatury faktu, ale jej zainteresowania skupiały się głównie na amerykańskiej florze i faunie, nadbrzeżnych bagniskach i zwierzętach, które znajdowały tam schronienie.

NIE SĄDZIŁA, ŻE po Eddiem będzie jeszcze jakiś mężczyzna w jej życiu. Nie chciała żadnego. Myślała, że gdyby Wilson wiedział, ile ona ma lat, z pewnością wycofałby się i poszukał jakiejś młodszej dziewczyny. Odmówiła, kiedy po raz pierwszy zaprosił ją na Buckner County Jazz Festival – festiwale jazzowe przyprawiały ją o ból serca – ale przyjęła zaproszenie na brunch w niedzielnym bufecie w Longhorn, gdzie za jedną opłatą każdy klient mógł najeść się do woli. Te niedzielne brunche wkrótce weszły im w krew. Nad talerzami pełnymi faszerowanej tilapii – ryby, która ich zdaniem właściwie nie miała smaku – Wilson zapytał, czy zdaniem Agnes dzisiejsi młodzi ludzie nie zachowują się bardziej niż swobodnie i czy ich dusze nie zostały być może nieusuwalnie splamione.

– Czasami zaczynają szaleć, Agnes – powiedział, wyskrobując łyżką nadzienie z ryby – a wtedy muszę im przyginać karki aż do samej ziemi.

Był gładko ogolonym, łysym sześćdziesięciolatkiem. Stracił wszystkie włosy w wieku dwudziestu dziewięciu lat. Wcześniej były jego radością i dumą, aureolą naturalnych loków, które nie wymagały używania Dudley's Waving Wax ani Jheri Curl, żeby się kręcić. Czasami wciąż sięgał ręką, żeby się pogładzić po czuprynie, której już nie było.

Wyjaśnił, że przygina dzieciom karki głównie werbalnie, ale jeśli uczeń na to zasługuje, to wciąga go do swojego gabinetu tak, żeby nie widziała tego kamera monitoringu, i daje mu po łbie.

– Do kogo tak mówisz, synu? – odegrał tę scenę i pokazał, jak potrząsa uczniem. – Moja najdroższa babunia obdarłaby mnie ze skóry za mniejsze wykroczenie.

– Jak któryś z nich kiedyś złoży na ciebie skargę, to będzie koniec twojej długiej, wspaniałej kariery – ostrzegła Agnes.

Zmienił pozycję na obitej tapicerką ławie.

– Jak dotąd nikt jeszcze nie złożył. Tym młodym idiotom potrzebna jest dyscyplina.

Agnes sama nigdy nie była zdyscyplinowanym dzieckiem. I nie biła Claudii ani Beverly. Lania pozostawiała Eddiemu, który nie ufał sobie na tyle, żeby wymierzać je zbyt często. Mimo to obie dziewczynki wyrosły na porządne kobiety. Pierwsze dziecko było „potrzebowskie". Beverly przyszła na świat, potrzebując czegoś, czego Agnes nie potrafiła jej dać: solidnej, głębokiej miłości, która byłaby wyczuwalna we wszystkim, na co patrzyła lub czego dotykała. Domagała się miłości z radosnym nastawieniem, odbierającym siły młodej matce, która dopiero co uciekła z Buckner County i odzyskiwała ludzkie uczucia. Drugie dziecko, Claudia, urodziło się, kiedy Agnes znajdowała się w lepszym miejscu w życiu. Gdy powstał odpowiedni dystans pomiędzy tym, do czego doszło na Damascus Road, i osobą, którą, jak sądziła, może być. Jak gdyby zapaliła świeczkę, by uczcić pamięć Claude'a, kochając Claudię tak, jak kochałby ją Claude, gdyby dziewczyna była jego córką.

– Czas – powiedziała Wilsonowi. – Niekiedy młodzi ludzie potrzebują czasu zamiast dyscypliny.

Zmierzył ją spojrzeniem. Ciągle się jej przyglądał.

– W kinie w centrum handlowym jest przedpołudniowy seans. Jeśli zrezygnujemy z deseru, to chyba zdążymy. Albo możemy obejrzeć jakiś film u mnie.

„Niech mu Bóg błogosławi", pomyślała Agnes. Wilson Tart jej pożądał. Zarówno mężczyźni, jak i kobiety zawsze jej pożądali. Widok pełnej nadziei twarzy łysego Tarta dobrze zrobił próżności Agnes. Dobrze jest mieć przy sobie kogoś na starość.

– Pójdziemy w przyszłym tygodniu. – Uśmiechnęła się. – Dzisiaj o ósmej ma do mnie zadzwonić młodsza córka, Claudia. I bardzo nie chciałabym się spieszyć do domu.

PYTANIA, PYTANIA, PYTANIA.

– Mamo, jak dawać człowiekowi wystarczająco dużo miłości? Jak tobie udawało się dać dość miłości tacie? – Claudia ostatnio obudziła Agnes w środku nocy.

Agnes usiadła na łóżku w grubej koszuli nocnej z monogramem i odczuła ulgę, że nocny telefon od córki nie okazał się wiadomością o czyjejś śmierci.

– Moja droga – odpowiedziała, przyzwyczajając oczy do ciemności sypialni i niebieskiego światełka emitowanego przez ekran komórki. – My nie mieliśmy czasu, żeby zastanawiać się nad takimi rzeczami. I ty też nie powinnaś tego robić.

Ale kiedy się rozłączyły, pytania Claudii nie pozwalały Agnes zasnąć. Co to za pomysł, żeby kochać kogoś „wystarczająco", a nie po prostu tu i teraz, w tej chwili, i trzymać się prawdy takiej miłości, bo człowiek nigdy nie wie, który dzień okaże się jego ostatnim. Eddie najważniejsze lata małżeństwa spędził w Wietnamie. Nienawidził tej wojny, ale z powodów w większości nieznanych Agnes wrócił w szeregi armii. Jej Eddie był łazikiem, włóczęgą, nawet gdy stał z żoną twarzą w twarz. Miał po prostu taki temperament.

Kiedy Claudia znowu poruszyła z nią ten temat, matka spytała, co się właściwie stało.

– Kochasz jeszcze Rufusa?

– To ta historia z Winnie... – odparła Claudia. – Czuje się już lepiej. Pracujemy nad nią oboje, mamo, ale czasami wydaje mi się, że nic o sobie nie wiemy.

– To bzdury.

– Nie – odparła. – Nie, mamo. Nie wydawało ci się nigdy, że ty i tata oddaliliście się od siebie?

– A po co chcecie wiedzieć o sobie wszystko?

– Bo w małżeństwie tak powinno być.

„Dzisiaj ludzie myślą, że muszą wiedzieć wszystko o swoich partnerach", pomyślała Agnes, ale Claudii powiedziała tak:

– O pewnych rzeczach nie jest nam dane wiedzieć. Bądź ostrożna. Nie próbuj siłą wydusić tajemnicy z waszej miłości.

GDY EDDIE WALCZYŁ w Wietnamie, Agnes uważała za rzecz całkowicie naturalną, że może pójść wieczorem do baru na drinka, powiedzmy, cosmopolitana. Zabierała dziewczynki na noc do matki Eddiego, by zrobić sobie wolne, siedziała samotnie na krześle z metalowych prętów i upajała się widokiem sali, aż w końcu podchodziła do niej jakaś kobieta. Nigdy nie musiała na to długo czekać. Wtedy wstawała, a zygzaki na jej wzorzystej kopertowej sukni wirowały razem z nią.

– Czekam na przyjaciółkę – kłamała.

Jeżeli nieznajoma próbowała nawiązać z nią rozmowę, usiłowała zgasić jej nagłą chęć ucieczki albo proponowała, że zapłaci za nią rachunek, Agnes wybuchała śmiechem i odrzucała ofertę wzruszeniem ramion.

– Wydaje mi się, że zapraszając mnie tutaj, moja przyjaciółka chciała mi dać coś do zrozumienia. Na pewno starała się dać mi coś do zrozumienia.

Poprawiała pasek sukienki na biodrach, ani na chwilę nie tracąc z oczu kobiet wirujących i gestykulujących gwałtownie w tańcu na parkiecie do *I'll Take You There* zespołu The Staple Singers albo siedzących stadkami wokół obitego czerwonym aksamitem stołu bilardowego.

CZASAMI JEDNAK, ZNACZNIE RZADZIEJ, chociaż o wiele częściej, niż pozwalała Agnes przyznać pamięć, rozsiadała się wygodnie w fotelu przy barze i prosiła barmana o kolejnego drinka.

– Może coś troszkę zmienimy? Tym razem poproszę o sidecar. Eloise powinna przyjść lada chwila.

– Jak ona wygląda? – W ten sposób zwykle zaczynała się rozmowa z kobietą siedzącą po jej lewej albo prawej stronie.

– Och – odpowiadała Agnes, opierając obwieszone bransoletkami ręce na krawędzi baru. – Ma jakieś pięć stóp i sześć cali wzrostu, a cerę koloru jasnego karmelu. Latynosi nazywają to *dulce de leche*. Sądzę, że przyjdzie w pikowanej kamizelce, wąskich spodniach i jakimś kapelusiku.

Popijając mieszankę cointreau, soku cytrynowego i koniaku, składającą się na sidecar, opowiadała, jak się poznały z Eloise. Jak Eloise pomimo wszelkich starań została sierotą, pozostawioną na progu rodzicielskiego domu. Jak będąc nastolatkami, dzieliły ze sobą sypialnię, zanim ich drogi się rozeszły. Dym papierosowy w barze zapewniał odpowiednio gęstą zasłonę dla jej półprawd i improwizowanych kłamstw.

– Ludzie czują się samotni i robią wtedy głupie, bardzo głupie rzeczy – powiedziała. – Na przykład biorą telefon i dzwonią do dawnych kochanków, których lepiej byłoby zostawić w spokoju, albo do przyjaciół, którzy nigdy nie byli prawdziwymi przyjaciółmi.

Czasami w domu Eddiego i Agnes w Bronksie dzwonił telefon – w różne miesiące, dni i o różnych porach. Można by niemal pomyśleć, że urządzenie miało własny rozum. Oczywiście istniały jakieś palce, które wsuwały się w otwory tarczy telefonu stacjonarnego albo wciskały klawisze.

Agnes wiedziała, że dzwoni Eloise, jeszcze zanim jej głos odzywał się w słuchawce.

– Wiem, że ktoś tam jest – mówiła Agnes, przysłaniając mikrofon i zerkając przez ramię, czy nie słyszą jej córki. Wtedy po drugiej stronie rozlegał się znowu czyjś oddech.

– Kto mówi?

– Nikt ważny – odpowiadała Eloise. – Rozłącz się.

– Zrobiłabym to, gdybym rozumiała, dlaczego niektórzy ludzie są tacy uparci.

– „Miłość..." – szeptała Eloise.

– Nie mam o niej pojęcia.

– Tak, przypuszczam, że miłość jest brzemieniem, które muszę dźwigać tylko ja.

– Źle robisz, Eloise, dzwoniąc do mnie do domu.

– A gdzie mam do ciebie dzwonić, Agnes?

– Ni. Gdzie.

– Kiedy się zobaczymy?

– Widzisz mnie codziennie – mówiła Agnes. – Wyciągnij tylko rękę. Jestem wszędzie dokoła.

WIECZOREM ZAWSZE PRZYCHODZIŁA TAKA CHWILA, kiedy nawet najbardziej zdeterminowany podrywacz przyglądał się Agnes zmęczonymi oczami i odchodził, żeby się rozejrzeć za jakąś inną ofiarą. W Hazel's, barze lesbijskim w West Village, gdzie zbierały się kobiety różnych ras, w 1972 roku Sandy Simmens słuchała Agnes przez bite czterdzieści pięć minut, zanim włożyła ręce do kieszeni i wyciągnęła pilnik i obcinacz do paznokci. W ten sposób nauczyła się w dzieciństwie powstrzymywać gniew, kiedy ktoś nazywał ją lesbą albo linijką. Albo trybadą. Po prostu spokojnie obcinała paznokcie, zanim wybuchła bójka. W ten sposób dawała szansę przeciwnikowi, żeby się wycofał, a sama miała chwilę, żeby się zastanowić, czy zwycięży, czy przegra.

– Wiesz co? – powiedziała. – Nikt nie chce słuchać tych pierdół. Możesz tu siedzieć sama albo pójść ze mną do domu i dać mi się wypieprzyć.

Takie praktyczne podejście spodobało się Agnes. Podobnie jak krótko przycięta fryzura afro i wykrochmalona biała koszula, wpuszczona w piżmowego koloru dżinsy od Halstona, zapinane na pasek. O mały włos nie powiedziała Sandy, jak bardzo przypomina jej Eloise.

Z ZASADY NIGDY NIE SYPIAŁA dwa razy z tą samą kobietą. Ale Sandy ją całowała. I ssała. I ujeżdżała. I drażniła się z nią, wygrywała muzykę na jej ciele, podobną do tej, jaką grali jazzmani w restauracji na drugim piętrze Hazel's, restauracji, w której nigdy nie postała noga Agnes, bo od jazzu bolało ją serce i ponieważ aromat kurczaka, krewetek i ryb, obtaczanych w mące, żeby były soczyste, sączył się po schodach i mieszał z dymem mentolowych papierosów w barze, i ta woń wgryzała się w jej ubranie, musiała więc potem je prać raz, dwa, a nawet trzykrotnie, żeby usunąć smród spalonego oleju.

– Kimkolwiek była tamta twoja kochanka, dobrze cię wyszkoliła – powiedziała Sandy, sięgając na drugą stronę wielkiego łóżka po pudełko zapałek z logo firmy Morton Salt. Przez okna wychodzące na balkon jej schludnego mieszkania dochodził uliczny hałas.

– Dlaczego myślisz, że ktoś mnie musiał czegokolwiek uczyć? – Nieoczekiwanie zawstydzona Agnes osłoniła prześcieradłem swoje nagie ramię.

– Luz – odparła Sandy, opierając się łokciem na płaskiej poduszce. – Powinnyśmy to powtórzyć. Zjeść razem kolację. Czy coś.

Znała takich mężczyzn na Południu, którzy porzucali swoje żony i dzieci. Biedna Eloise. Znała też dzieci, które wyglądały zza zasłon w oknach, czekając, aż matka albo ojciec, częściej ojciec, wróci wreszcie do domu. Do takich dzieci należała sama Eloise, chociaż w tamtym czasie ona, Agnes, zbyt była zajęta sobą, żeby to naprawdę zauważyć. Tak, tak, znała mężczyzn, którzy pojawiają się od czasu do czasu, by zobaczyć się ze swoimi pociechami, kupić im torebkę popcornu albo wybierać razem kruche ciasteczka z kosza w sklepie na rogu. Nie była jednak takim dzieckiem, tylko córką diakona, a to zupełnie co innego.

Zaatakowała Sandy pocałunkami, a potem ruszyła do Bronksu okrężną drogą, czyli na południe, w stronę Brooklynu, i dopiero później skręciła na północ, czyli w kierunku domu, i z Arthur Avenue pojechała do siebie już „na łebka". Spotkała się z Sandy jeszcze trzykrotnie, po czym ponownie zamknęła się w czterech ścianach.

EDDIEGO POZNAŁA W 1967 ROKU. Oboje byli gośćmi na spóźnionym przyjęciu weselnym kuzynki Agnes, Charlotte Applewood, a ściśle biorąc, na lunchu wydanym w niedzielne popołudnie przez rodziców Agnes.

– Nad twoją głową wiszą chmury – stwierdził Eddie i zaczął podskakiwać na długim zielonym trawniku, próbując

je rozgonić. Agnes wyciągnęła długą szyję ku niebu, ale nie zauważyła niczego oprócz błękitu.

– Jasne chmury smutku.

– Daj mi spokój. – Prawdę mówiąc, starała się, jak mogła, robić dobrą minę do złej gry. Bo wcale nie była w nastroju na żaden lunch ani przyjęcie.

– Łup, łup – powiedział, krążąc wokół stolików i krzeseł na patio, wściekle waląc w te chmury.

Stłumiła silną chęć, żeby go zepchnąć na bok, w dzień wczorajszy, jutrzejszy albo do połowy przyszłego roku.

Miesiąc wcześniej Edward Christie był drużbą i świadkiem na ślubie Charlotte i Reubena Applewoodów w Las Vegas. Teraz ten niski mężczyzna o brązowej skórze, noszący kurtkę od marynarskiego munduru zapinaną na złote guziki, deptał bujną trawę rodziny Millerów błyszczącymi butami wojskowymi. Pomyślała, że przypomina granatowego pingwina.

– Jesteś nieznośny – rzuciła.

Wyciągnął rękę, by dosięgnąć kolejnej chmury nad jej głową, ale zatrzymał się z na wpół zgiętymi palcami, ujrzawszy kolejkę, która zaczęła się ustawiać do misy z ponczem. Patrzyła, jak Eddie opiera się na piętach i obraca na północny zachód, po czym zostawia ją samą i odchodzi od stołu, by zbierać zamówienia od pań z kościoła. Była wiosna i wszędzie kwitły różowe azalie, najbujniej jednak na ich kwiecistych sukienkach. Pochylił się i uważnie słuchał szepczących mu do ucha staruch. Domyślała się, co mówią. „Mógłbyś powtórzyć, skąd pochodzisz, kochanie? Ach, jaki on milutki. Zechciałbyś zanieść tę kopertę młodej parze? Nie ma w niej za wiele, ale na zestaw naczyń Corningware może wystarczy". Eddie nie sprawiał wrażenia znudzonego ani zniechęconego ich paplaniną, Agnes wiedziała jednak, po prostu wiedziała, że oddech tych starych bab był gorący, wilgotny i zalatywał nieprzyjemną mieszaniną śliny oraz ziołowych tabletek na gardło, które wolały od miętowej gumy do żucia.

Sama ciążyła w stronę stołu z deserami. Na środku stał piękny trzypiętrowy tort weselny. Nie spała przez całą noc, pomagając matce, lady Miller, udekorować go gęstym maślanym lukrem cytrynowym. Lady Miller nieźle zarabiała, piekąc ciasta dla członków kongregacji. Czasami przygotowywała je nawet na kilka tygodni przed ceremonią ślubną i przechowywała w zamrażarce w garażu. Ale tort dla Charlotte, jej jedynej siostrzenicy, był świeży.

– Ostatnio trochę za dużo śpisz – powiedziała lady Miller, spryskując szpatułkę do lukrowania ciepłą wodą, by nie lepiły się do niej okruszki ciasta.

– Czuję się zmęczona.

– Jesteś pewna, że to wszystko?

Trzy tygodnie wcześniej zerwała z Claude'em Johnsonem. Od tamtej pory matka szukała jakiegoś wytłumaczenia dla jej zachowania.

– Nie denerwuj się, mamo – powiedziała Agnes. – Nie jestem w ciąży.

– Chodzi o tamtą dziewczynę?

Agnes wcisnęła palec w lukier. Wiedziała, że matka tego nie pochwala.

– Ona ma imię.

– Eloise – powiedziała lady Miller. To ona ją poprosiła, by opuściła ich dom.

– Eloise Delaney jest najmniejszym z moich zmartwień – stwierdziła Agnes.

Kochała Claude'a bardziej niż kogokolwiek na świecie. Może nawet trochę bardziej niż Eloise, ale jej matka by tego nie zrozumiała. A Agnes brakowało zarówno wytrwałości, jak i wszystkiego innego, co byłoby potrzebne, by jej to wyklarować.

EDDIE SKOŃCZYŁ SERWOWAĆ DRINKI i ruszył w ślad za Agnes do stołu z tortem, pożerając chmury jak połykacz ognia płomienie. Odwróciła się gwałtownie i przyjrzała jego ustom. Przez ułamek sekundy wydawało się jej, że widzi w oddechu Eddiego mgiełkę chmury. Złożył ukłon z galanterią, z trudem przełknął ślinę i zachwiał się na nogach z taką przesadą, że Agnes się uśmiechnęła. Był to jej pierwszy uśmiech po wydarzeniach na Damascus Road. Uśmiechała się, bo Eddie był niskim brzydalem i przypominał jej murzyńskiego pisarza, którego dzieła czytali na zajęciach z literatury angielskiej w Buckner County College: Jamesa Baldwina. Tyle tylko że Baldwin, o ile wiedziała, był szczupły, a Eddie Christie, jeśli nie będzie uważał, może stać się grubasem. Ale co on takiego w sobie miał? Bo było w nim coś urzekającego.

– No, doprawiłem poncz – powiedział. – I jestem gotów na tort.

Ktoś zaczął go wołać w tłumie. „Eddie? Eddie, skarbie?" I tak szybko, jak połykał przedtem skłębione chmury, wycofał się, gdy wezwano go do innego zadania. Agnes czekała, aż Charlotte i Reuben Applewoodowie, trzymając się pod ręce, pokroją tort weselny i poczęstują się nawzajem jego pierwszym kęsem. Uważała całą tę sytuację za równie delikatną jak modna żółta sukienka na fiszbinach, którą nosiła Charlotte. Kobiety od Millerów miały smykałkę krawiecką, może nawet z niej słynęły. I wszystkie dobrze wychodziły za mąż.

– Możesz mi powtórzyć, kto to jest? – szepnęła Agnes do Charlotte, wskazując ruchem głowy Eddiego.

– Kuzyn Reubena, Eddie.

Reuben Applewood był przystojniakiem. Dbał o siebie. Można było popatrzeć na niego pod pięcioma różnymi kątami i z każdej perspektywy wyglądałby atrakcyjnie. Reuben i Agnes chodzili do tej samej katolickiej szkoły, bo ich rodzice wyznawali tego samego Boga. Obserwowała Reubena, jak sunie do stolika, żeby uściskać swoją ciocię, Florę, która była zajęta ściskaniem Eddiego.

– No ale nic a nic nie są do siebie podobni... Znaczy Eddie i Reuben.

Charlotte wygładziła fałdy żółtej sukienki i roześmiała się.

– Przecież wiesz, że mamy kuzynów naszej świeżo wytoczonej krwi i takich przyszywanych, z którymi też pozostajemy blisko.

„To oczywiście prawda", pomyślała Agnes. Ludzie gadali przez całe popołudnie, że ona złapie męża jako następna.

Że Agnes i Charlotte mogłyby uchodzić za bliźniaczki. Starała się o to nie obrażać.

– No tak – odparła w końcu. – Ten Eddie coś nie może usiedzieć na miejscu. A poza tym nie podobają mi się niscy mężczyźni.

– Nie przypominam sobie, żebym cię pytała, co czy kto ci się nie podoba. – Charlotte nie skomentowała też faktu, że Agnes ukroiła sobie aż dwa kawałki tortu. Zawsze dzieliła je przepaść, bo nawet kiedy były jeszcze dziewczynkami, nie umiały się razem ładnie bawić.

– Wyciągnij swoje zabawki – mawiała do niej Charlotte. W dzieciństwie nauczono je chować ulubione rzeczy przed przyjściem koleżanek, więc piękne porcelanowe serwisy do herbaty szybko trafiały na półkę, a zamiast nich rozstawiano plastikowe, na łóżku pojawiała się zeszłoroczna Baby Doll, a lalkę, która umiała robić siusiu i płakać, ukrywano w cedrowej skrzyni. Gdy Agnes nie chciała zdjąć z półki swojego małego porcelanowego serwisu, Charlotte ciągnęła ją za włosy tak długo, aż musiała interweniować jedna z matek.

Coś w rodzaju wzajemnej czułości zapewnił im dystans geograficzny – rodzina Charlotte przeniosła się do Ohio, kiedy dziewczynki miały osiem lat.

POD KONIEC PRZYJĘCIA Eddie i Agnes zaczęli ze sobą rywalizować w kręceniu się dokoła własnej osi i nie przerwali nawet, gdy jedli tort cytrynowy.

– Nie umiesz wytrzymać bez ruchu? – dokuczała mu, chociaż chwiała się na nogach bardziej niż on, bo kręciło się jej w głowie. – Zaczynam myśleć, że naprawdę dolałeś czegoś do ponczu.

Uśmiechnął się.

– Bezczynność to dla mnie problem.

Zauważyła, że ma idealnie białe zęby. Stanowiły jedną z kilku przyjemnych cech jego wyglądu. Powiedział, że za sześć tygodni wyjeżdża do Wietnamu.

– Następnym razem może to ja będę potrzebować, żebyś ty rozganiała chmury nad moją głową.

Nie przychodziło jej do głowy nic pocieszającego, zdjęła więc szpilki. Bez nich była niewiele wyższa od Eddiego. Kręcili się wśród leżaków na trawniku domu jej rodziców. Magia tego, co zaledwie przed kilkoma godzinami było wesołym przyjęciem, gdzieś wyparowała; cykady wyszły z ukrycia, żeby grać swoją muzykę.

Gdy wszystkie leżaki zostały już poskładane, Eddie wyniósł je do małej powozowni, gdzie rodzice Agnes trzymali chłodziarkę i grill, a zimą meble ogrodowe. Matka przyglądała się temu z aprobatą. Oboje jej rodzice z ulgą patrzyli na Agnes zajętą czymś innym niż spanie.

– **JAKIŚ GENIUSZ WPADŁ NA POMYSŁ,** żeby wybrukować nasze podwórko w Bronksie – powiedział Eddie. – Jak wrócę do domu, to zacznę od tego, że rozwalę ten bruk. Do diabła, może posieję tam nawet taką murawę jak ta. Ale zostawię placyk do gry w bocce.

Agnes nigdy nie słyszała o bocce, Eddie wyjaśnił jej więc, że jest to gra należąca do rodziny kręgli, znana już w starożytnym Rzymie. Opowiadał, że Włosi grają w bocce na podwórkach i w parkach, pokazał gestem, jak się rzuca kulą używaną w tej dyscyplinie sportu, i zaczął kląć po włosku, że niby nie trafił. Agnes spodobało się to, że zna włoski, i wtedy wpadli na pomysł, aby pojechać do Searsa i JCPenney i zobaczyć, czy nie mają tam kul do gry w bocce.

– Możesz mnie wspominać, jak będziesz kiedyś w to grać – powiedział Eddie.

Ani w Sears, ani w JCPenney nic nie załatwili, kul do gry w bocce nie było, sprzedawcy jednak twierdzili, że zamówią je z największą przyjemnością. Energia chwili rozproszyła się, głód był jednak prawdziwy. Na przyjęciu sporo zjedli, a mimo to Agnes zaprowadziła Eddiego do niewielkiej grillowej restauracji, gdzie jak przysięgała, podawano najlepsze żeberka w mieście. Dochodziła dziesiąta wieczorem, gdy Eddie wysadził ją przed domem rodziców. Za wykuszowym oknem było widać sylwetki państwa Millerów, którzy oglądali telewizję.

Zostawił samochód na jałowym biegu. Stary buick należał kiedyś do jego ojca. Teraz Eddie przyjechał tym wozem z Bronksu do Georgii.

– Po prostu wyślę ci zestaw do bocce pocztą albo będziesz musiała przyjechać do Nowego Jorku.

Kiwnęła głową i bez słowa pożegnania zaczęła wysiadać z wozu. Zanim postawiła nogi na chodniku, zalała się łzami. Eddie, który nie zdążył wysiąść i otworzyć jej drzwi, nachylił się i położył dłoń na ramieniu Agnes.

– Co się stało? – zapytał.

Otworzyła usta, ale zabrakło jej słów, by mogła opowiedzieć, co przeżyła na Damascus Road. Chciała powiedzieć Eddiemu, jak popatrywała w lewo i w prawo na drzewa, które odchylały się możliwie najdalej od bagniska w poszukiwaniu słońca. Jak się jej wydawało – czy wzrok ją mylił? – że z gałęzi zwieszają się czarne węże. Jak spoglądała w niebo, które sprawiało wrażenie bezkresnego. Jak serce skoczyło jej w piersi, wyrwało się z niej przez usta i wyleciało na spotkanie Claude'a. Zastanawiała się, co robił mu ten policjant. I gdzie był wtedy Pan Bóg. Czy tego wieczoru zachrypł i nie mógł mówić? Albo może, może był zbyt zaspany? Zwierzęta, stworzenia, które wałęsały się po mokradłach, to one zajęły miejsce Pana Boga i były świadkami tego, co się zdarzyło. Tak, tak, chciała opowiedzieć o tym wszystkim Eddiemu, ale zdołała wykrztusić tylko, że lubi się ładnie ubierać: piękny kawałek tkaniny, jedwab gładzący jej ciało, śliczny tiul i koronka, plisowana wełniana spódnica, letnia sukienka, czysta bawełna, która pozwiewa na wietrze, szarpana podmuchami. Jako młoda dziewczyna zbierała wykroje – z „Redbook", „McCormick", „Simplicity", „McCall's" – i rozkładała je na dywanie w sypialni, opadała na kolana, czuła w dłoniach ciężar nożyc krawieckich, podążając wzrokiem za kreską wykroju, a potem zaczynała ciąć, nadając kształt bezkształtowi. Czym jednak jest ubranie, jeśli nie spóźnioną myślą, fałszywym kamuflażem? Taka miękka odzież nie zapewnia ochrony. Policjant odwraca się i mówi: „Panienko, jak sama tego nie zdejmiesz, to ja to zrobię. Lepiej chyba, żebyś ty to zrobiła, a nie ja. Bo ta sukienka kosztowała pewnie małą fortunę". I była to prawda; dosłownie zerwała tę kieckę z wieszaka w Fine's, żeby pójść z Claude'em na festiwal jazzowy.

– Popatrz no, Agnes – powiedziała lady Miller. – Weź tę. Czy nie jest śliczna?

EDDIE PODAŁ JEJ czerwoną chusteczkę do nosa, którą wyjął ze schowka pod deską rozdzielczą. Pozwolił Agnes siedzieć w milczeniu na fotelu pasażera, częściowo w samochodzie, częściowo poza nim; stopami dotykała krawężnika. Nie wiedział, czy powinien może wyciągnąć rękę lub zrobić jakiś gest, by ją pocieszyć. Nie chciał jej do siebie zrazić w żaden sposób. Nie zrozumiał wszystkiego, co mówiła, pojął tylko tyle, że przytrafiło się jej coś okropnego. Zaczął się pocić i chciał wymazać tę informację z pamięci.

– Powinnaś wiedzieć to i owo o Bronksie – powiedział w końcu, jak się wydawało, po dłuższej chwili. – Jest brzydki, ale bywa pięknym miejscem do życia.

Agnes pomyślała, że ten niski człowieczek w pewnym sensie mówi chyba o sobie. Z początku chciała się wymknąć z samochodu, uciec, choć za żadne skarby nie mogła się rozstać z chusteczką Eddiego Christie.

W KAŻDE CZWARTKOWE POPOŁUDNIE w Buckner County w stanie Georgia Agnes i Charlotte Applewood wyrywały chwasty na grobach starszych ludzi, których nie znały za ich życia, ale o których nagle zaczęły dbać, gdy się przenieśli w zaświaty. Obie straciły dobrych mężów i żaden z nich nie spoczywał na cmentarzu St. Andrew's Episcopal. Mąż Agnes odszedł przed dwoma laty na raka wątroby, a ukochany małżonek Charlotte, Reuben, zmarł nagle z powodu tętniaka. W ten sposób dwie kobiety, które z trudem znosiły swoje towarzystwo w dzieciństwie, spotykały się teraz od czasu do czasu i stały się dla siebie drogimi przyjaciółkami. Aby dbać o ciśnienie i bronić się przed cukrzycą, chodziły na spacery – w deszczowe dni po centrum handlowym. Z początku zajęły się opieką nad grobami na cmentarzu St. Andrew's po to, żeby nadać sens własnemu życiu, a później dlatego, że im częściej tam chodziły, tym więcej dowiadywały się o swoich pogrzebanych na nim przodkach.

CMENTARZ ZNAJDOWAŁ SIĘ przy jednym z najstarszych murzyńskich kościołów episkopalnych na Południu. Zbudowali go byli niewolnicy. Agnes i Charlotte nie słyszały o nim w dzieciństwie, ich matki weszły bowiem do domów modlitwy mężów, porzucając oschłość wiary episkopalnej na rzecz nieco żywszych wyznań metodystów i baptystów. Agnes i Charlotte poślubiły wyznawców katolicyzmu, lecz Agnes nie chciała chodzić do żadnego kościoła. Mimo to nigdy nie oponowała, gdy Eddie w niedzielę zabierał dziewczynki na mszę (jeżeli chciały iść). Dzieci, jak sądziła, muszą w coś wierzyć, żeby wypełnić pustkę, która istniała, gdy nie wierzyły w nic.

– Jak tam twoje dziewczyny? – spytała ją Charlotte.

– Dobrze. O ile wiem. – Powstrzymała się, by nie powiedzieć Charlotte, że ma obawy o małżeństwo Claudii. I że nie dostała żadnej wiadomości od Beverly, odkąd posłała jej czterdzieści dolarów w kopercie z kartką pocztową. Uważała, że córka zachowałaby się przyzwoicie, gdyby sięgnęła po telefon i podziękowała jej albo gdyby kazała zadzwonić do niej dzieciom. Agnes była już seniorką o stałych, nierosnących dochodach. Nie miała tak dużo pieniędzy, żeby móc rozdawać je lekką ręką.

– A Gideon i Lonnie? – spytała o dorosłe dzieci kuzynki.

Charlotte na chwilę przerwała wyrywanie chwastów.

– Chciałabym, żeby częściej dzwonili albo odwiedzali mnie chociaż od czasu do czasu.

– Młodzi żyją swoim życiem – odpowiedziała Agnes, lecz jakaś część jej duszy odnotowała z radością, że ukochane dzieci Charlotte też nie zawsze wyciągają do niej rękę na czas.

– Gideon i jego partner adoptują małą dziewczynkę z Nairobi – oświadczyła Charlotte. – Ma jakieś sześć lat, jest mniej więcej w wieku synka Lonnie.

Agnes szukała w twarzy Charlotte wskazówki, która powiedziałaby, jak odnosi się do tego, że Gideon jest gejem. Czy nie była zawiedziona, że nie ma synowej? Jak często ona i Reuben rozmawiali o skłonnościach syna? Ile bezsennych nocy ich to kosztowało? No a poza tym Gideon mieszka chyba w San Francisco, bo gdzieżby indziej?

– A nie mogą adoptować niemowlęcia? Kto wie jakie problemy może już mieć sześcioletnia sierota – powiedziała Agnes.

Okolica wokół St. Andrews była dawniej przystanią dla hippisów, głoszących powrót do ziemi. Na niektórych działkach wciąż hodowali maryśkę, a także cukinię, gorczycę i pomidory, ostatnio jednak w pobliżu zaczęły wyrastać nowe domy dla klasy średniej, wszystkie identyczne i sprawiające wrażenie, że poprzewracają się natychmiast, kiedy tylko uderzy w nie porządny wiatr. Nierzadko można było tu też zobaczyć czarnoskórego mężczyznę w stroju kowbojskim, galopującego na białym koniu, a po południu słychać było gwizd pociągów towarowych.

– Niemowlę też przychodzi na ten świat już z własnymi zmartwieniami – stwierdziła Charlotte, wstając raptownie.

Normalnie pomogłaby Agnes – ze względu na reumatyzm, który czasem unieruchamiał jej stawy – dziś jednak wolała pozwolić, żeby kuzynka sama podźwignęła się na nogi. Ona i Agnes krążyły wokół siebie przez całe życie i Charlotte czuła się z tego powodu smutna i zmęczona. Dała mężowi syna, a Agnes wyczuwała – chociaż nie potrafiła powiedzieć dlaczego – że Eddie też chciał mieć chłopca. Wydawało się jej, że zawiodła go nie tylko pod tym względem.

– A pomyśl o czymś jeszcze! – zawołała Charlotte. – Diakon i lady Millerowie przygarnęli tę twoją przyjaciółkę, Eloise Delaney. Co by się stało, gdyby czekali na dziecko? Przez jakiś czas Eloise zastępowała ci siostrę. A może kogoś więcej? Najlepszą przyjaciółkę?

Agnes mocno stała już na nogach. A Charlotte dawała dziś z siebie wszystko.

– Nie widziałam Eloise od lat – odparła Agnes. Było to kłamstwo, bo spotkała ją rok temu. Niecałe sześć miesięcy po powrocie do Buckner County. Poszły nawet razem na lunch na Main Street. Udał się nadspodziewanie dobrze, ale później Agnes nie dotrzymała słowa i nie wpadła do jej hotelu na drinka. Została w domu i przez całą noc prasowała i układała ubrania. Czuła się za staro, żeby wracać do wspomnień, a Eloise była ich pełna niczym walizka.

Teraz z kolei Charlotte szukała w twarzy Agnes oznak tego, że mówi prawdę albo robi uniki. Włożyła garść chwastów do czarnego worka na śmieci i zmusiła się do złagodzenia głosu. Czy to możliwe, żeby Agnes naprawdę nie wiedziała?

– I chyba nie czytałaś porannej prasy. W gazecie był nekrolog Eloise.

– Dzisiaj rano? – powtórzyła Agnes.

– Obawiam się, że tak, kuzynko. Tak.

Agnes zaczerpnęła powietrza, jakby wsysając je w krtań. Gdy tylko weszła do domu, opadła na łóżko. Skóra na całym ciele piekła ją i szczypała; był to ból całego życia, tak ostry i przenikliwy, że nie mogła rano pójść do pracy, ani nawet sięgnąć po telefon, żeby zawiadomić, że jest chora. W jej ciele krążyło tysiąc igieł, które kłuły ją w stawach i przebijały jej skórę, nie dała jednak cierpieniu tej przyjemności, by zobaczyło, jak płacze. W pewnym momencie udało się jej przewrócić na bok i pomyśleć – „przez sekundę" – że Eloise Delaney leży obok w łóżku i patrzy na nią takim wzrokiem jak wtedy, kiedy były jeszcze tylko głupimi, beztroskimi dziewczynami.

– Strasznie cię przepraszam! – krzyknęła przeraźliwie. – Strasznie cię przepraszam, Eloise.

To Wilson Tart przyszedł zobaczyć, co się dzieje z Agnes, kiedy nie pokazała się w bibliotece. Pukał do drzwi, ale odpowiadała mu cisza. Cisza, od której się oddalił, ponieważ nie chciał patrzeć, jak kobieta, którą z czasem polubił, kona, albo nawet już się może rozkłada. Przypomniał sobie, że Agnes ma w mieście kuzynkę, Charlotte Applewood; dziesięć minut później przyjechała ona do mieszkania Agnes z kluczem, bo kiedyś dostała go od niej na wszelki wypadek.

Charlotte natychmiast zadzwoniła do Beverly i Claudii.

W SZPITALU PODŁĄCZYLI JĄ pod kroplówkę i zwolnili do domu jeszcze tego samego dnia. Wszystkie najważniejsze organy życiowe pracowały normalnie. Cokolwiek jej dolegało, nie było natury fizycznej; tak stwierdzili lekarze jeszcze przed przyjazdem Beverly i Claudii.

– Musisz wstać z tego łóżka – powiedziała Beverly, ściągając kołdrę z matki dwadzieścia cztery godziny później, kiedy przyjechała wraz z siostrą do Buckner County.

– Zdarza się, że gdy seniorzy popadają w depresję – powiedział lekarz – to przestają jeść. I nie mogą spać.

Beverly okazała wobec matki stanowczość.

– Łóżka to wrogowie starszych ludzi. Jak zostaniesz w łóżku jeszcze dzień albo dwa, to sam Mojżesz cię z niego nie wyciągnie.

– Claudio? – powiedziała Agnes, patrząc ponad głową Beverly na córkę, którą zawsze kochała. Na tę córkę, która, jak miała nadzieję, mogła zostać nawet inżynierem. Ale uczona to też chyba dobrze.

Beverly cofnęła się i odezwała do Claudii:

– Teraz twoja kolej.

Claudia nie mogła znieść widoku matki w łóżku – był to dla niej zbyt poważny wstrząs.

– Powinnaś posłuchać Bev – powiedziała.

– Nie musicie tutaj być, dziewczyny – stwierdziła Agnes.

– No a co niby miałybyśmy robić, mamo? – Claudia użyła ostrego tonu, jak siostra. – Pozwolić ci leżeć i umrzeć?

Agnes rozejrzała się po sypialni. Po raz pierwszy zdała sobie sprawę, że nie postarała się za bardzo, żeby w tym pokoju albo w ogóle w mieszkaniu czuć się po domowemu. Będzie musiała powiesić na ścianach obrazki i różne inne rzeczy. Nie może żyć dalej tak prowizorycznie.

– W samotności? Nie, zawsze miałam choć kilkoro znajomych, którzy dotrzymywali mi towarzystwa.

Claudia popatrzyła na Beverly. Siostry toczyły między sobą wojnę w związku z ojcem, ale teraz Beverly położyła rękę na ramieniu Claudii i zapytała:

– Mamo, który mamy rok?

– Dwa tysiące dziesiąty.

– A ile ty masz lat?

– Za dużo jak na mój gust.

– Kto jest prezydentem?

– Jakiś czarny. Mąż Michelle.

– Obama. Nazywa się Obama – dodała Claudia.

– Wiem, jak się nazywa nasz prezydent, Claudio. A jak tam moje wnuki?

– A ile ich masz? – spytała Beverly.

– Mogłabyś poprzestać na pytaniu o rok – odparła Agnes.

– Jadą tu Rufus, Winnie i Elijah. A Chico przywiezie dzieci Beverly.

– Wszystkie?

Beverly skinęła głową.

– Im więcej, tym weselej.

– Wielkie nieba. No to musimy coś zrobić. Wiecie, jaka jestem pedantyczna. Nie mogą mnie zobaczyć w takim stanie.

I TAK BEVERLY, Claudia, Rufus, Winona, Elijah, Minerva, Orzeszek, Keisha, Lamar i Chico zjechali do Buckner County. Agnes upierała się, żeby ze względów oszczędnościowych wszyscy zamieszkali u niej, ale Claudia i Rufus woleli hotel w centrum, z widokiem na rzekę. Wynajęli luksusowy apartament rodzinny, a po spacerze z dziećmi nadrzecznym bulwarem Rufus wyszukał profil Hanka Camphora na LinkedInie i wysłał mu mejl z wiadomością, że on i jego rodzina będą niedługo wracać samochodem do Nowego Jorku, ale po drodze mogliby zatrzymać się w Raleigh – czy to odpowiadałoby Hankowi? „Na jakimś neutralnym i przyjaznym dzieciom gruncie", napisał. Wcześniej tego dnia w mieszkaniu teściowej zobaczył na kominku kilka żelazek. Wziął to za dobry omen i zaczął się zastanawiać, czy badania nad celtyckimi legendami w Bretanii, jakie ostatnimi czasy podjął na nowo, nie sprawiają, że robi się przesądny. Claudia pomiędzy umyciem zębów i włożeniem halki powiedziała, że jej zdaniem nie. Rufus po prostu miał wrodzone skłonności do zabobonów – i był z natury trochę neurotykiem.

Podobnie jak matka, Claudia nigdy nie lubiła szlafroków. Halki podkreślały jej figurę. Były jej ulubionymi koszulkami nocnymi. Zaczęła opowiadać Rufusowi, jak bardzo ją denerwuje, że u mamy nie widać żadnych ich zdjęć. Mieszkanie wydawało się okropnie puste, Agnes właściwie wszystko trzymała w pudłach, potem jednak Claudia przypomniała sobie, co matka powiedziała jej kiedyś na temat wyduszania siłą tajemnicy, która się kryje w miłości. Chyba miała rację, ona i Rufus mogliby spędzić chociaż jeden wieczór bez problemów. I narzekań. „Jeżeli tylko Winnie dobrze prześpi noc – odpowiedział Rufus, podnosząc wzrok znad komputera, żeby podziwiać szarobiałą halkę Claudii. – To jakaś nowa rzecz?"

A BEVERLY... Beverly z dziećmi zamieszkała w Marriotcie. Też w apartamencie rodzinnym, nie zamykała jednak drzwi, bo Minerva zaczęła chodzić z chłopakiem, który mieszkał w ich apartamentowcu w Washington Heights. Miał na imię

Julio i przyjechał z nimi do Georgii. Matka nie zamierzała zostawiać Minervy samej w hotelu, bo nie życzyła sobie, żeby zaszła w ciążę tak jak ona w jej wieku. Podróż wyszła wszystkim na dobre, ponieważ Beverly słyszała teraz, jak Minerva i Orzeszek kłócą się w pokoju obok o to, co oglądać w telewizji, a Julio próbuje ich godzić. Pomyślała, że jeśli chodzi o nastoletnich chłopców, to jej córka mogła trafić gorzej. Odwróciła się, żeby powiedzieć to Chicowi, ale podróż do Buckner County okazała się dla jej faceta za długa. Prowadził przez całą drogę i teraz spał już snem sprawiedliwego. Zasnął nawet wcześniej niż bliźniaki. Normalnie Beverly by się rozgniewała, ale potrzebowała spokoju. Pomyślała, że pewnego dnia zostanie głową tej matriarchalnej rodziny, i to ją otrzeźwiło.

AGNES OPROWADZIŁA SWOJE CÓRKI, ich partnerów i wnuczęta po cmentarzu St. Andrews Episcopal. Obeszli cały teren i w końcu dotarli na schody białego dziewiętnastowiecznego kościoła i domu parafialnego, gdzie kiedyś mieściła się jednoizbowa szkoła dla dzieci wyzwolonych niewolników. Minerva i Orzeszek powtarzali: „Zaraz, czyli to zbudowali nasi przodkowie? Nasi?". Młodsze dzieci, to znaczy Elijah, Winona, Keisha i Lamar, po prostu cieszyły się z tego, że mogą biegać i rozrabiać na trawie przed kościołem, bo miały rzadką okazję, żeby się bawić w komplecie.

KIEDY ZNAJDOWALI SIĘ W DRODZE powrotnej do miasta, malcom zaczęło burczeć w brzuchach, więc rodzice wypatrywali reklam i tablic ogłoszeniowych, wskazujących, gdzie można by szybko zjeść coś lepszego niż fast food. Na dachu restauracji w chacie z drewnianych bali dzieci zauważyły znak z dużym kolorowym ptakiem. Należał do gatunku miejscowych dzięciołów i trzymał w dziobie napis: „The Great Byrd Lodge. Dla samotnych. Dla wszystkich".

Agnes wysiadła z minivana jako pierwsza. Powiedziała sobie, że jeśli będzie się wahać, to za chwilę nie wejdzie do tej knajpy. W środku od razu skierowała się w stronę dębowego kontuaru, za którym urzędował były policjant William Byrd w koszuli w biało-czerwoną szachownicę. Koszulowa czerwień pasowała do płomienia rudych włosów siedemdziesięcioletniego emerytowanego stróża prawa, które połyskiwały jeszcze żywiej, niż kiedy był dwudziestopięciolatkiem. Zastanawiała się, czy zachowały naturalny kolor, czy Byrd je farbuje, bo jej zdaniem kiedyś był blondynem. Miał krzywe, pałąkowate nogi, jedną krótszą, drugą dłuższą – pozostałość po udarze, którego doznał w wieku pięćdziesięciu pięciu lat.

BEVERLY I CLAUDIA WESZŁY do restauracji w ślad za matką. Potem także wnuczęta, które wygłupiały się, majstrując coś przy telefonie Minervy i kłócąc się między sobą. Normalnie Agnes przeszkadzałby hałas, jaki robiły jej wnuki w restauracji. Normalnie zakwestionowałaby ich „dobre wychowanie". Ale – biorąc pod uwagę wszystkie okoliczności – Great Byrd Lodge nie sprawiała wrażenia knajpy, w której dobre wychowanie mogło mieć znaczenie.

– Według mnie jako dorosły samiec osiągnął mniej więcej dziewięćdziesiąt dziewięć funtów – powiedziała Agnes, spoglądając nad głową emerytowanego policjanta na wypchanego aligatora, który wisiał na ścianie. Nie interesowała jej reakcja byłego gliniarza. Usiadła przy jednym z wiejskich stolików i czekała na darmowy poczęstunek – kawałek placka z orzechami pekan.

Byrd spojrzał w stronę stolika, przy którym siedziała Agnes. I coś się rozjaśniło w jego głowie, lecz była to jasność przyćmiona, jak gdyby wbita klinem pomiędzy wszystko to, co w życiu zrobił i kim był, oraz to, kim chciał być lub o czym chciał zapomnieć.

– No proszę – powiedział, kiedy do kontuaru podeszła Beverly. – Ta pani trafiła w dziesiątkę. Pochodzicie z tych stron?

Beverly sięgnęła po menu. Było ciche popołudnie, w restauracji siedziało tu i ówdzie kilka osób. Beverly chciała przede wszystkim zamówić jedzenie dla dzieci, zanim zaczną kaprysić.

– Moja mama tu się urodziła – odpowiedziała.

– No to witajcie w domu – powiedział z uśmiechem Byrd. – A pani mama wygrała właśnie darmowy kawałek placka orzechowego.

– WSZYSTKO W PORZĄDKU, MAMO? – Claudia usiadła przy stole obok Agnes, a Winona i Elijah wpakowali się na ławy przy stoliku bezpośrednio za nimi. Claudia posłała spojrzenie Rufusowi i Chicowi, Rufus natomiast dał gestem znać, że mają oko na dzieci. Beverly, która też zwróciła uwagę na milczenie matki, podeszła i usiadła naprzeciwko niej.

– Mamo? – powiedziała.

Agnes próbowała sobie wyobrazić, jakie życie prowadził ten aligator, zanim wypełzł z bagien. Wiedziała, że to samiec, czytała o nim w gazetach i stąd wiedziała dokładnie, ile ważył. Ale nie wszystko potrafiła odgadnąć z taką łatwością. Na przykład co czuł, kiedy celował do niego mężczyzna o płomiennorudych włosach. Czy instynktownie wiedział, co się z nim stanie? Rzucił się na policjanta z ukrycia czy działał odruchowo?

Emerytowany funkcjonariusz Byrd przyniósł placek orzechowy z pekanami, oszczędzając swoją chorą nogę. Agnes przymknęła oczy i chwyciła Claudię i Beverly za ręce mocniej, niż kiedy były dziećmi i przeprowadzała je przez ulicę. Odczekała chwilę, zanim uniosła powieki, a emerytowany funkcjonariusz Byrd wycofał się do kuchni.

– Cieszę się, że przyjechałyście się ze mną zobaczyć, dziewczyny. I że przywiozłyście dzieci. – Uśmiechnęła się, po czym zatrzepotała długimi rzęsami, patrząc na córki i wnuki. Wyglądała, jakby ubyło jej lat, jak gdyby znowu była w kwiecie wieku; miała tylko jedno ciało, a przecież wiele razy żyło w nim dużo różnych osób i osobowości.

– Dla mnie placek orzechowy jest zdecydowanie za słodki. Ale wy jedzcie wszyscy. Jesteśmy w domu. Bierzcie się do jedzenia.

PODZIĘKOWANIA

Chciałabym podziękować mojej redaktorce z wydawnictwa Hogarth, Alexis Washam, jej asystentce, Jillian Buckley, oraz całemu zespołowi od reklamy i produkcji w Crown, bo wszyscy pracowali tam ze wszystkich sił, aby wreszcie wypchnąć *Podróżnych* w świat. Dziękuję też Molly Stern. Wielki dług wdzięczności mam wobec mojej agentki, Ellen Levine z Trident Media, która od pierwszego dnia stała się orędowniczką tej powieści (wraz z Claire Roberts, Aleksą Stark i Marthą Wydysh). Iowa Writers' Workshop zapewnił mi bezcenny czas na pracę i zajęcia z profesorami, którzy naprawdę cenią słowo pisane, takimi jak: Ethan Canin, Samantha Chang, Charlie D'Ambrosio, Kevin Brockmeier, Allan Gurganus, Paul Harding, Margot Livesey, Ayana Mathis i Marilynne Robinson. Podziękowania za konkretny odzew i wsparcie zechcą przyjąć także moi koledzy i koleżanki z Iowa: Jen Adrian, Mia Bailey, William Basham, Charles Black, Jackson Burgess, Moira Cassidy, Yvonne Cha, Christina Cooke, Tameka Cage Conley, Susannah Davies, Amanda Dennis, Mgbechi Erondu, Jason Hinojosa, Maya Hlavacek, Eskor Johnson, Jade Jones, Aleksandro Khmelnik, Afabwaje Kurian, Maria Kuznetsova, Claire Lombardo, Lee Ye Lim, Paul Maisano, Magogodi Makhene, Daniel Mehrian, Melissa Mogollon, Grayson Morley, Derek Nnuro, Okwiri Oduor, Karen Parkman, Jianan Qian, Sergio Aguilar Rivera, William Shih, Kevin Smith, Lindsay Stern, Keenan Walsh, Dawnie Walton, Monica West, De'Shawn Winslow,

David Ye i Michael Zaken – jak również Joan Silber, Marcus Burke, Garth Greenwall, Van Choojitarom, Connor White oraz poeci: Ryan Tucker, Kelly Smith, Connie Briscoe, Jan Zenisek i Deborah West.

Robin Christianson i jej rodzina zmienili Historic Phillips House w prawdziwy azyl na czas mojego dwuletniego pobytu w Iowa. Pieniądze z Rae Armour West Postgraduate Scholarship umożliwiły mi prowadzenie kwerendy po powrocie do domu. Dzięki stypendium z Tin House Summer Workshop dostałam szansę uczestnictwa w warsztatach z Jimem Shepardem, a Jentel Artist Residency w Wyoming zapewniło mi wspaniałe górskie widoki w czasie prac nad poprawkami w tekście i korektą poredakcyjną.

Danielowi O'Rourke'owi dziękuję za to, że podzielił się ze mną bezcennymi doświadczeniami i wiedzą na temat amerykańskiej marynarki wojennej i Wietnamu; historykowi Allenowi Steinbergowi za to, że pozwolił mi brać udział w swoich zajęciach „Wojna wietnamska w filmie" na University of Iowa; Gregory'emu i Michelle Owensom, dwojgu najinteligentniejszych ludzi, jakich znam, dziękuję za przyjaźń i opinie na temat mojej książki; podziękowania składam też Timowi Cockeyowi (którego opinię również brałam poważnie pod uwagę) i Julii Strohm; Nosquii Callahan dziękuję za wskazówki badawcze oraz prace naukowe na temat losów Afroamerykanów w Niemczech, a doktor Lindzie Brown, Dorothy Roberts-Truell i Xavierowi Gunnowi za to, że znaleźli czas, aby udzielić mi wywiadów na temat ich pobytu na misjach zagranicznych w trakcie służby wojskowej. Dziękuję Brigitte Morel, Anthony'emu Baggettowi i Andreasowi Mertnesowi, którzy przespacerowali się ze mną po ścieżce wspomnień w Berlinie i przedstawili mnie Chuckowi Rootowi. Dziękuję Jake'owi Schneiderowi, Benowi Robbinsowi, Bennettowi Simsowi i Carinie Klugbauer za prywatną wycieczkę po Schwules Museum. Jean Morel był moim kulturowym i estetycznym konsultantem w kwestiach dotyczących rolnictwa i wszystkiego, co bretońskie. Francena i Robert Edwards opowiadali mi, jak wygląda życie codzienne na małej rodzinnej farmie. Vicki Mahaffey dziękuję za to, że podzieliła się ze mną wiedzą na temat Jamesa Joyce'a, Christopherowi Dennisowi za to, że podzielił się ze mną wiedzą na temat Shakespeare'a, a Allie Croker za wspaniałą wycieczkę po Szekspirowskim teatrze Globe. W tym miejscu jeszcze raz dziękuję Margot Livesey, Paulowi Hardingowi i Magogodi Makhene za lekturę kolejnych wersji *Podróżnych*. De'Shawn Winslow, Monica West, Claire Lombardo, Sasha Khmelnik i Mia Bailey (z którą uczestniczyłam we wszystkich zajęciach warsztatowych i podróżowałam z Paryża do Berlina) pozostaną moimi przyjaciółmi na całe życie.

Książki Elizabeth Hadley Freydberg *Bessie Coleman: The Brownskin Ladybird* i Gail Levin *Lee Krasner* przybliżyły mi postacie Bessie Coleman i Lee Krasner, kobiet będących pionierkami w swoich dziedzinach. Dzięki *Black Sailor, White Navy: Racial Unrest in the Fleet During the Vietnam Era* pióra Johna Darrella Sherwooda udało mi się przedstawić Eddiego Christie i Jebediaha Applewooda jako ludzi z krwi i kości. Z kolei artykuł pani generał major Jeanne M. Holm i pani generał brygady Sary P. Wells *Air Force Women in the Vietnam War* oraz materiały z Vietnam Women's Memorial pomogły mi poznać losy amerykańskich żołnierek w czasie wojny wietnamskiej i ocenić ich udział w tym konflikcie.

Na końcu z najgłębszą wdzięcznością pragnę podziękować za wsparcie członkom mojej rodziny – córkom Nuali i Gaby oraz ich ojcu, Brendanowi Merninowi, mojemu nieżyjącemu już wujowi, Robertowi Bookerowi, moim braciom Ronaldowi i Michaelowi, mojej siostrze Jackie, a także siostrzenicy Tamali. Z grona przyjaciół podziękowania zechcą przyjąć Drew Reed, Heather Gillespie, Bridget Battle, Gale Mitchell, Cassandra Medley, Janice Bennett, Steve Garvey, Vernell B. Jenkins, Liz Lazarus, Crystal i Martin Beauchampowie, Tim Sanford, Lynn Connor wraz z całym zespołem Lost Lit, Kareem i Yuka Lawrence'owie, Evan Smith, Tony Scott, Gaby Starr z rodziną, Lynn Nottage, Karen Duda, Julie i Matt Greenbergerowie, Lynn Holst i Lucinda Williams.

SPIS FOTOGRAFII

New York Public Library. *Ira Aldridge w roli Otella*, 1887. Zbiory cyfrowe New York Public Library, http://digitalcollections.nypl.org/items/510d47da-72e5-a3d9-e040-e00a18064a99.

s. 91 Okładka książkowego wydania sztuki Toma Stopparda *Rosenkrantz i Guildenstern nie żyją* (1967), reprodukowana za zgodą wydawnictwa Faber & Faber Ltd.

s. 93 USS Oriskany (CVA-34), *Katapultowy start samolotu szturmowego A-4 Skyhawk w czasie operacji u wybrzeży Wietnamu, 30 sierpnia 1966 roku.* Oficjalna fotografia amerykańskiej marynarki wojennej ze zbiorów National Archives, sygnatura fotografii: USN 1117395.

s. 95 *Robotnicy w fabryce fortepianów*, ok. 1916. Zbiór kart stereograficznych z kolekcji The LaGuardia & Wagner Archives, LaGuardia Community College / University of New York.

s. 108 *Dwaj marynarze prasujący spodnie na drugim rejsie okrętu w czasie wojny wietnamskiej* (USS Intrepid Cruise Book, 1967). Fotografia ze zbiorów Collection of the Intrepid Sea, Air & Space Museum.

s. 111 Program przedstawienia sztuki *Rosenkrantz i Guildenstern nie żyją* w Lyttelton Theatre, 1995. sjtheatre/Alamy Stock Photo.

s. 113 Regina Porter, *Piwnica w Bronksie*, Nowy Jork 2016.

s. 134 George Arents Collection, the New York Public Library. *Most George'a Washingtona.* Fotografia ze zbiorów cyfrowych New York Public Library, http://digitalcollections.nypl.org/items/510d47e2–3624-a3d9-e040-e00a18064a99.

s. 137 *Golferinos*, ok. 1905. Fotografia ze zbiorów Biblioteki Kongresu, https://www.loc.gov/item/2002705510.

s. 179 *Technicy YFU-74, Wietnam 1969*. Oficjalne zdjęcie U.S. Navy ze zbiorów National Archives, sygnatura fotografii: USN 1139720.

s. 187 *Saper oddziałów E.O.D. poszukuje min, Da Nang, Wietnam* 1966. Oficjalne zdjęcie U.S. Navy ze zbiorów National Archives, sygnatura fotografii: 428-K-31466.

s. 189 Schomburg Center for Research in Black Culture, Dział Rękopisów, Archiwów i Druków Rzadkich, New York Public Library, *Green Book, katalog dla kierowców murzyńskich,* 1950. Zbiory cyfrowe New York Public Library, http://digitalcollections.nypl.org/items/283a7180-87c6-0132-13e6-58d385a7b928.

s. 192 Autorka: Marion S. Trikosko, *Memphis, Tennessee. Motel Lorraine*. Fotografia ze zbiorów Biblioteki Kongresu, www.loc.gov/item/2017646278.

s. 196 *Mrożony obiad*, ok. 1955: *martwa natura z trójprzegródkową tacką aluminiową, „TV dinner"*. Fotografia z Hulton Archive / Getty Images.

s. 204 Autor: John Vachon. *Okolice Aberdeen w stanie Maryland. Kierowcy ciężarówek piją kawę w jadłodajni przy U.S. Highway 40*. Luty 1943. Fotografia ze zbiorów Biblioteki Kongresu, www.loc.gov/item/2017846238.

s. 215 *Bessie Coleman, pierwsza licencjonowana pilotka afroamerykańska stoi na kole samolotu Curtiss JN-4 „Jenny" w zaprojektowanym na zamówienie kombinezonie lotniczym*, ok. 1924. Fotografia ze zbiorów Smithsonian National Air and Space Museum, sygnatura fotografii: NASM92–13721.

s. 221 Schomburg Center for Research in Black Culture, Dział Fotografii i Grafiki, New York Public Library, *Murzyńscy uczniowie, Omar, Zachodnia Wirginia*. Fotografia ze zbiorów cyfrowych New York Public Library, http://digitalcollections.nypl.org/items/510d47df-f8f3-a3d9-e040-e00a18064a99.

s. 224 *Fotografia grupowa 16. Kompanii Strażackiej z parowym wozem bojowym*, 1875. Fotografia ze zbiorów Missouri

Historical Society, Saint Louis, https://mohistory.org/collections/item/resource:141351.

s. 235 *Bessie Coleman, pionierka lotnictwa* (domena publiczna). Fotografia ze zbiorów Smithsonian National Air and Space Museum, sygnatura fotografii: SI-980-12873.

s. 246 *Lyndon Johnson podpisuje rozkaz numer 5894 o zasobach ludzkich*. Fotografia ze zbiorów U.S. Army Women's Museum.

s. 250 *Żołnierz U.S. Army szkoli wietnamskich partyzantów z ludu Degar*, ok. 1966 (domena publiczna). Fotografia U.S. Army.

s. 255 USS Oklahoma City (CLG-5), *Sajgon, Republika Wietnamu*, 1964. Oficjalna fotografia U.S. Army, ze zbiorów National Archives, sygnatura fotografii: CC-26860.

s. 267 Basil Lanneau Gildersleeve, *Athena Parthenos*, ilustracja, kwiecień 1882, „Harper's Magazine".

s. 279 Reklama żelazek Asbestos, ok. 1906 (domena publiczna).

s. 307 *Wesołe miasteczko*, Keystone / Getty Images.

s. 312 *Fotografia Jolly Mazie, otyłej artystki cyrkowej. Oficjalnie odnotowana waga ciała: 450 funtów*. Fotografia ze zbiorów Circus World Museum, Baraboo w stanie Wisconsin.

s. 315 *Kładki dla pieszych na nowym Manhattan Bridge* (między 1907 i 1915 r.). Fotografia ze zbiorów Biblioteki Kongresu, www.loc.gov/item/97517149.

s. 319 *Luna Park, 1904*. 1904, v1974.022.5.023. Zdjęcia i albumy Eugene'a L. Armbrustera, ARC.308, Brooklyn Historical Society.

s. 330 *Lawrence Larkin, Jackson Pollock i Lee Krasner w pracowni Pollocka*, 1949. Fotografia autorstwa Lawrence'a Larkina ze zbiorów Pollock-Krasner House and Study Center, East Hampton, New York.

s. 343 *Chłopiec i pies, grający w golfa*. Fotografia ze zbiorów Hulton Deutsch / Getty Images.

s. 359 Patrick Brien, 2019. Olej i akryl na płótnie.

s. 373 *El Dorado*, Bundesarchiv, Bild 183–1983–0121–500 / License CC-BY-SA 3.0.

s. 374 *Portret stojącej pary, atelier*. Fotografia ze zbiorów Smithsonian National Museum, dział historii i kultury afroamerykańskiej.

s. 378 *Martin Luther King jr w Berlinie*. Photoquest Photography / Getty Images.

s. 379 *Żołnierze amerykańscy, w tym Afroamerykanie z kompanii dowództwa i obsługi technicznej 183. inżynierskiego batalionu bojowego 8. Korpusu 3. Armii Stanów Zjednoczonych, oglądają zwłoki więźniów w obozie koncentracyjnym w Buchenwaldzie*, 17 kwietnia 1945. Buchenwald, Niemcy; United States Holocaust Memorial Museum, zdjęcie opublikowane dzięki uprzejmości Williama Alexandra Scotta III.

s. 388 Schomburg Center for Research in Black Culture, Jean Blackwell Hutson Research and Reference Division, New York Public Library, *Bessie Coleman sfotografowana w Berlinie*, 1925. Fotografia ze zbiorów cyfrowych New York Public Library, http://digitalcollections.nypl.org/items/510d47de-5184-a3d9-e040-e00a18064a99.

s. 401 *Aligator schwytany w bagnisku namorzynowym*, 1882. Czarno-biała odbitka fotograficzna, ze zbiorów State Archives of Florida, Florida Memory, https://www.floridamemory.com/items/show/31258.

s. 414 *Francuski manekin*, domena publiczna, ok. 1800.

Spis treści

TYTUŁ ORYGINAŁU
The Travelers

WYDANIE PIERWSZE

OPIEKA REDAKCYJNA
Anita Kasperek

REDAKCJA
Kamil Bogusiewicz

KOREKTA
Ewa Polańska, Jacek Błach, Henryka Salawa

PROJEKT OKŁADKI
Michael Morris

ILUSTRACJE
Liz Lazarus

OPRACOWANIE OKŁADKI NA PODSTAWIE ORYGINAŁU
Marek Pawłowski

REDAKCJA TECHNICZNA
Robert Gębuś

Książkę wydrukowano na papierze Ecco Book Cream 80 g vol. 1,6

PRINTED IN POLAND
Wydawnictwo Literackie Sp. z o.o., 2021
ul. Długa 1, 31-147 Kraków
bezpłatna linia telefoniczna: 800 42 10 40
księgarnia internetowa: www.wydawnictwoliterackie.pl
e-mail: ksiegarnia@wydawnictwoliterackie.pl
fax: (+48-12) 430 00 96
tel.: (+48-12) 619 27 70
Skład i łamanie: Nordic Style
Druk i oprawa: Drukarnia Pozkal

ISBN 978-83-08-07422-0